GAME OF THRONES
5: A DANCE WITH DRAGONS
Part 2: After the Feast

George R.R. Martin is the author of fifteen novels and novellas, including five volumes of A SONG OF ICE AND FIRE, several collections of short stories, as well as numerous screenplays for television drama and feature films. Dubbed 'the American Tolkien', he has won numerous awards including the Hugo and the World Fantasy Lifetime Achievement Award. He is an Executive Producer on HBO's Emmy Award-winning GAME OF THRONES, which is based on his A SONG OF ICE AND FIRE series. He lives in Santa Fe, New Mexico.

Praise for *A Song of Ice and Fire*:

'When times are tough, there is no better distraction than these magical tales'   *Guardian*

'Martin has not only raised the bar for writers of epic fantasy but pushed and stretched the boundaries of the novel itself'   *The Times*

'Fantasy fiction's equivalent to *The Wire*'   *Telegraph*

'Complex storylines, fascinating characters, great dialogue, perfect pacing, and the willingness to kill off even his major characters'
LA Times

'Mr Martin is a literary dervish, bursting with the wild vision of the very best tale tellers'   *New York Times*

By George R.R. Martin

A SONG OF ICE AND FIRE
Book One: *A Game of Thrones*
Book Two: *A Clash of Kings*
Book Three, part one: *A Storm of Swords: Steel and Snow*
Book Three, part two: *A Storm of Swords: Blood and Gold*
Book Four: *A Feast for Crows*
Book Five, part one: *A Dance with Dragons: Dreams and Dust*
Book Five, part two: *A Dance with Dragons: After the Feast*

The Lands of Ice and Fire (with Jonathan Roberts)
The Wit & Wisdom of Tyrion Lannister
*The World of Ice & Fire: The Untold History of Westeros and the
Game of Thrones* (with Elio M. Garcia Jr. and Linda Antonsson)
A Knight of the Seven Kingdoms (with Gary Gianni)
The Ice Dragon (with Luis Royo)
The Official A Game of Thrones Colouring Book
(with Yvonne Gilbert, John Howe, Tomislav Tomic,
Adam Stower and Levi Pinfold)

Hunter's Run (with Gardner Dozois and Daniel Abraham)
Songs of the Dying Earth (co-edited with Gardner Dozois)
Dangerous Women (co-edited with Gardner Dozois)

GEORGE R.R. MARTIN

GAME OF THRONES

5: A DANCE WITH DRAGONS
PART 2: AFTER THE FEAST

BOOK FIVE, PART TWO OF
A SONG OF ICE AND FIRE

HARPER
Voyager

Harper*Voyager*
An imprint of HarperCollins*Publishers* Ltd
1 London Bridge Street
London SE1 9GF

www.harpervoyagerbooks.co.uk

This paperback edition 2016
1

Previously published in paperback by Harper*Voyager* in 2012, 2014

First published in Great Britain by Harper*Voyager* in 2011

A catalogue record for this book is
available from the British Library

ISBN: 978-0-00-812234-8

Printed and bound in Great Britain by
Clays Ltd, St Ives plc

A CAVIL ON CHRONOLOGY

It has been a while between books, I know. So a reminder may be in order.

The book you hold in your hands is the fifth volume of *A Song of Ice and Fire*. The fourth volume was *A Feast for Crows*. However, this volume does not follow that one in the traditional sense, so much as run in tandem with it.

Both *Dance* and *Feast* take up the story immediately after the events of the third volume in the series, *A Storm of Swords*. Whereas *Feast* focused on events in and around King's Landing, on the Iron Islands, and down in Dorne, *Dance* takes us north to Castle Black and the Wall (and beyond), and across the narrow sea to Pentos and Slaver's Bay, to pick up the tales of Tyrion Lannister, Jon Snow, Daenerys Targaryen, and all the other characters you did not see in the preceding volume. Rather than being sequential, the two books are parallel . . . divided geographically, rather than chronologically.

But only up to a point.

A Dance with Dragons is a longer book than *A Feast for Crows*, and covers a longer time period. In the latter half of this volume, you will notice certain of the viewpoint characters from *A Feast for Crows* popping up again. And that means just what you think it means: the narrative has moved past the time frame of *Feast,* and the two streams have once again rejoined each other.

Next up, *The Winds of Winter.* Wherein, I hope, everybody will be shivering together once again . . .

—George R. R. Martin
April 2011

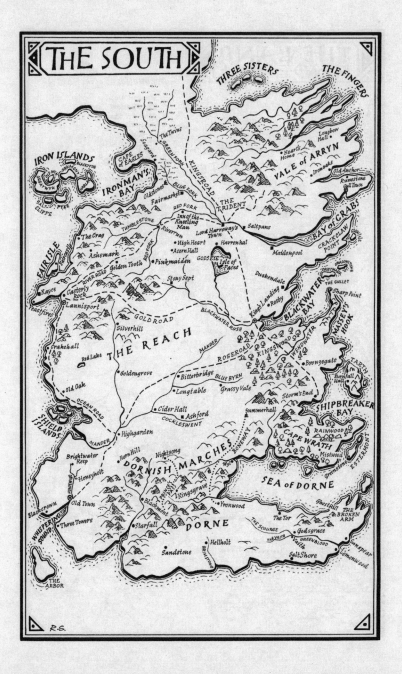

THE LAND
BEYOND THE WALL

STRONGHOLDS of the NORTH

1 Westwatch-by-the-Bridge
2 **The Shadow Tower**
3 Sentinel Stand
4 Greyguard
5 Stonedoor
6 Hoarfrost Hill
7 Icemark
8 The Nightfort
9 Deep Lake
10 Queensgate
11 **Castle Black**
12 Oakenshield
13 Woodswatch-by-the-Pool
14 Sable Hall
15 Rimegate
16 The Long Barrow
17 The Torches
18 Greenguard
19 **Eastwatch-by-the-Sea**

THE LAND OF
ALWAYS WINTER
(UNMAPPED)

THENN

THE SHIVERING
SEA

Hardhome

MILKWATER

THE SKIRLING PASS

Fist of the
First Men

ANTLER RIVER

STORRALDS POINT

THE
FROSTFANGS

THE
HAUNTED
FOREST

Craster's
Keep

Whitetree

THE GORGE

THE WALL
2 3 4 5 6 7 8 9 10 11 12 13 14 15 16 17 18

BAY of
SEALS

SKAGOS

BRANDON'S GIFT

Queenscrown

BAY of ICE

THE NEW GIFT

KINGSROAD

R.O.

THE LANDS OF THE SUMMER SEA

Meereen
Skahazadhan
Mantarys
THE BLACK CLIFF
Tolos
SLAVER'S BAY
Yunkai
THE SEA OF SIGHS
Elyria
Astapor
Isle of Cedars
WORM RIVER
THE LANDS OF THE LONG SUMMER
GHISCAR
Oros
THE SMOKING SEA
Old Ghiscar
Tyria
THE GULF OF GRIEF
GHISCARI STRAIT
Valyria
GHAEN
New Ghis
WESTEROS and the SUMMER ISLES
QARTH and the JADE SEA
THE SUMMER SEA
Zamettar
AX ISLE
BASILISK ISLES
NAATH
Isle of TEARS
Yeen
BASILISK POINT
SOTHORYOS

R·G·

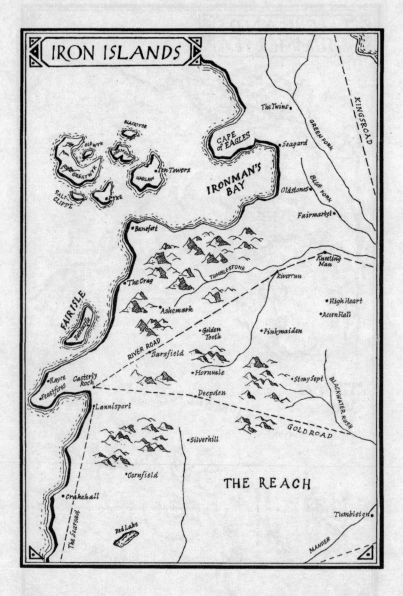

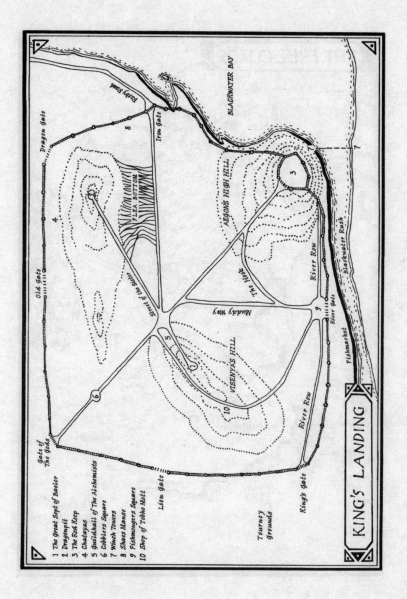

KING'S LANDING

1 The Great Sept of Baelor
2 Dragonpit
3 The Red Keep
4 Chataya's
5 Guildhall of The Alchemists
6 Cobblers Square
7 Winch Towers
8 Shae's Manse
9 Fishmongers Square
10 Shop of Tobho Mott

THE TURNCLOAK

The first flakes came drifting down as the sun was setting in the west. By nightfall snow was coming down so heavily that the moon rose behind a white curtain, unseen.

"The gods of the north have unleashed their wroth on Lord Stannis," Roose Bolton announced come morning as men gathered in Winterfell's Great Hall to break their fast. "He is a stranger here, and the old gods will not suffer him to live."

His men roared their approval, banging their fists on the long plank tables. Winterfell might be ruined, but its granite walls would still keep the worst of the wind and weather at bay. They were well stocked with food and drink; they had fires to warm them when off duty, a place to dry their clothes, snug corners to lie down and sleep. Lord Bolton had laid by enough wood to keep the fires fed for half a year, so the Great Hall was always warm and cozy. Stannis had none of that.

Theon Greyjoy did not join the uproar. Neither did the men of House Frey, he did not fail to note. *They are strangers here as well,* he thought, watching Ser Aenys Frey and his half-brother Ser Hosteen. Born and bred in the riverlands, the Freys had never seen a snow like this. *The north has already claimed three of their blood,* Theon thought, recalling the men that Ramsay had searched for fruitlessly, lost between White Harbor and Barrowton.

On the dais, Lord Wyman Manderly sat between a pair of his White Harbor knights, spooning porridge into his fat face. He did not seem to be enjoying it near as much as he had the pork pies at the wedding. Elsewhere one-armed Harwood Stout talked quietly with the cadaverous Whoresbane Umber.

Theon queued up with the other men for porridge, ladled into wooden bowls from a row of copper kettles. The lords and knights had milk and honey and even a bit of butter to sweeten their portions, he saw, but none of that would be offered him. His reign as prince of Winterfell had been a brief one. He had played his part in the mummer's show, giving the feigned Arya to be wed, and now he was of no further use to Roose Bolton.

"First winter I remember, the snows came over my head," said a Hornwood man in the queue ahead of him.

"Aye, but you were only three foot tall at the time," a rider from the Rills replied.

Last night, unable to sleep, Theon had found himself brooding on escape, of slipping away unseen whilst Ramsay and his lord father had their attention elsewhere. Every gate was closed and barred and heavily guarded, though; no one was allowed to enter or depart the castle without Lord Bolton's leave. Even if he found some secret way out, Theon would not have trusted it. He had not forgotten Kyra and her keys. And if he did get out, where would he go? His father was dead, and his uncles had no use for him. Pyke was lost to him. The nearest thing to a home that remained to him was here, amongst the bones of Winterfell.

A ruined man, a ruined castle. This is my place.

He was still waiting for his porridge when Ramsay swept into the hall with his Bastard's Boys, shouting for music. Abel rubbed the sleep from his eyes, took up his lute, and launched into "The Dornishman's Wife," whilst one of his washerwomen beat time on her drum. The singer changed the words, though. Instead of tasting a Dornishman's wife, he sang of tasting a northman's daughter.

He could lose his tongue for that, Theon thought, as his bowl was being filled. *He is only a singer. Lord Ramsay could flay the skin off both his hands, and no one would say a word.* But Lord Bolton smiled at the lyric and Ramsay laughed aloud. Then others knew that it was safe to laugh as well. Yellow Dick found the song so funny that wine snorted out his nose.

Lady Arya was not there to share the merriment. She had not been seen outside her chambers since her wedding night. Sour Alyn had been saying that Ramsay kept his bride naked and chained to a bedpost, but Theon knew that was only talk. There were no chains, at least none that men could see. Just a pair of guards outside the bedchamber, to keep the girl from wandering. *And she is only naked when she bathes.*

That she did most every night, though. Lord Ramsay wanted his wife clean. "She has no handmaids, poor thing," he had said to Theon. "That leaves you, Reek. Should I put you in a dress?" He laughed. "Perhaps if you beg it of me. Just now, it will suffice for you to be her bath maid. I won't have her smelling like you." So whenever Ramsay had an itch to bed his wife, it fell to Theon to borrow some servingwomen from Lady Walda or Lady Dustin and fetch hot water from the kitchens. Though Arya never spoke to any of them, they could not fail to see her bruises. *It is her own fault. She has not pleased him.* "Just be *Arya,*" he told the girl once, as he helped her into the water. "Lord Ramsay does not want to hurt you. He only hurts us when we . . . when we forget. He never cut me without cause."

"Theon . . ." she whispered, weeping.

"*Reek.*" He grabbed her arm and shook her. "In here I'm Reek. You have to *remember,* Arya." But the girl was no true Stark, only a steward's whelp. *Jeyne, her name is Jeyne. She should not look to me for rescue.* Theon Greyjoy might have tried to help her, once. But Theon had been ironborn, and a braver man than Reek. *Reek, Reek, it rhymes with weak.*

Ramsay had a new plaything to amuse him, one with teats and a cunny . . . but soon Jeyne's tears would lose their savor, and Ramsay would want his Reek again. *He will flay me inch by inch. When my fingers are gone he will take my hands. After my toes, my feet. But only when I beg for it, when the pain grows so bad that I plead for him to give me some relief.* There would be no hot baths for Reek. He would roll in shit again, forbidden to wash. The clothes he wore would turn to rags, foul and stinking, and he would be made to wear them till they rotted. The best he could hope for was to be returned to the kennels with Ramsay's girls for company. *Kyra,* he remembered. *The new bitch he calls Kyra.*

He took his bowl to the back of the hall and found a place on an empty bench, yards away from the nearest torch. Day or night, the benches below the salt were never less than half-full with men drinking, dicing, talking, or sleeping in their clothes in quiet corners. Their serjeants would kick them awake when it came their turn to shrug back into their cloaks and walk the walls. But no man of them would welcome the company of Theon Turncloak, nor did he have much taste for theirs.

The gruel was grey and watery, and he pushed it away after his third spoonful and let it congeal in the bowl. At the next table, men were arguing about the storm and wondering aloud how long the snow would fall. "All day and all night, might be even longer," insisted one big, black-bearded archer with a Cerwyn axe sewn on his breast. A few of the older men spoke of other snowstorms and insisted this was no more than a light dusting compared to what they'd seen in the winters of their youth. The riverlanders were aghast. *They have no love of snow and cold, these southron swords.* Men entering the hall huddled by the fires or clapped their hands together over glowing braziers as their cloaks hung dripping from pegs inside the door.

The air was thick and smoky and a crust had formed atop his porridge when a woman's voice behind him said, "Theon Greyjoy."

My name is Reek, he almost said. "What do you want?"

She sat down next to him, straddling the bench, and pushed a wild mop of red-brown hair out of her eyes. "Why do you eat alone, m'lord? Come, rise, join the dance."

He went back to his porridge. "I don't dance." The Prince of Winterfell had been a graceful dancer, but Reek with his missing toes would be grotesque. "Leave me be. I have no coin."

The woman smiled crookedly. "Do you take me for a whore?" She was one of the singer's washerwomen, the tall skinny one, too lean and leathery to be called pretty ... though there was a time when Theon would have tumbled her all the same, to see how it felt to have those long legs wrapped around me. "What good would coin do me here? What would I buy with it, some snow?" She laughed. "You could pay me with a smile. I've never seen you smile, not even during your sister's wedding feast."

"Lady Arya is not my sister." *I do not smile either,* he might have told her. *Ramsay hated my smiles, so he took a hammer to my teeth. I can hardly eat.* "She never was my sister."

"A pretty maid, though."

I was never beautiful like Sansa, but they all said I was pretty. Jeyne's words seemed to echo in his head, to the beat of the drums two of Abel's other girls were pounding. Another one had pulled Little Walder Frey up onto the table to teach him how to dance. All the men were laughing. "Leave me be," said Theon.

"Am I not to m'lord's taste? I could send Myrtle to you if you want. Or Holly, might be you'd like her better. All the men like Holly. They're not my sisters neither, but they're sweet." The woman leaned close. Her breath smelled of wine. "If you have no smile for me, tell me how you captured Winterfell. Abel will put it in a song, and you will live forever."

"As a betrayer. As Theon Turncloak."

"Why not Theon the Clever? It was a daring feat, the way we heard it. How many men did you have? A hundred? Fifty?"

Fewer. "It was madness."

"Glorious madness. Stannis has five thousand, they say, but Abel claims ten times as many still could not breach these walls. So how did *you* get in, m'lord? Did you have some secret way?"

I had ropes, Theon thought. *I had grapnels. I had darkness on my side, and surprise. The castle was but lightly held, and I took them unawares.* But he said none of that. If Abel made a song about him, like as not Ramsay would prick his eardrums to make certain that he never heard it.

"You can trust me, m'lord. Abel does." The washerwoman put her hand upon his own. His hands were gloved in wool and leather. Hers were bare, long-fingered, rough, with nails chewed to the quick. "You never asked my name. It's Rowan."

Theon wrenched away. This was a ploy, he knew it. *Ramsay sent her. She's another of his japes, like Kyra with the keys. A jolly jape, that's all. He wants me to run, so he can punish me.*

He wanted to hit her, to smash that mocking smile off her face. He wanted to kiss her, to fuck her right there on the table and make her cry his name. But he knew he dare not touch her, in anger or in lust. *Reek, Reek, my name is Reek. I must not forget my name.* He jerked to his feet and made his way wordlessly to the doors, limping on his maimed feet.

Outside the snow was falling still. Wet, heavy, silent, it had already begun to cover the footsteps left by the men coming and going from the hall. The drifts came almost to the top of his boots. *It will be deeper in the wolfswood . . . and out on the kingsroad, where the wind is blowing, there will be no escape from it.* A battle was being fought in the yard; Ryswells pelting Barrowton boys with snowballs. Above, he could see some squires building snowmen along the battlements. They were arming them with spears and shields, putting iron half-helms on their heads, and arraying them along the inner wall, a rank of snowy sentinels. "Lord Winter has joined us with his levies," one of the sentries outside the Great Hall japed . . . until he saw Theon's face and realized who he was talking to. Then he turned his head and spat.

Beyond the tents the big destriers of the knights from White Harbor and the Twins were shivering in their horse lines. Ramsay had burned the stables when he sacked Winterfell, so his father had thrown up new ones twice as large as the old, to accommodate the warhorses and palfreys of his lords' bannermen and knights. The rest of the horses were tethered in the wards. Hooded grooms moved amongst them, covering them with blankets to keep them warm.

Theon made his way deeper into the ruined parts of the castle. As he picked through the shattered stone that had once been Maester Luwin's turret, ravens looked down from the gash in the wall above, muttering to one another. From time to time one would let out a raucous scream. He stood in the doorway of a bedchamber that had once been his own (ankle deep in snow that had blown in through a shattered window), visited the ruins of Mikken's forge and Lady Catelyn's sept. Beneath the Burned Tower, he passed Rickard Ryswell nuzzling at the neck of another one of Abel's washerwomen, the plump one with the apple cheeks and pug nose. The girl was barefoot in the snow, bundled up in a fur cloak. He thought she might be naked underneath. When she saw him, she said something to Ryswell that made him laugh aloud.

Theon trudged away from them. There was a stair beyond the mews, seldom used; it was there his feet took him. The steps were steep and treacherous. He climbed carefully and found himself alone on the battlements of the inner wall, well away from the squires and their snowmen. No one had given him freedom of the castle, but no one had denied it to him either. He could go where he would within the walls.

Winterfell's inner wall was the older and taller of the two, its ancient grey crenellations rising one hundred feet high, with square towers at every corner. The outer wall, raised many centuries later, was twenty feet lower, but thicker and in better repair, boasting octagonal towers in place of square ones. Between the two walls was the moat, deep and wide . . . and frozen. Drifts of snow had begun to creep across its icy surface. Snow was building up along the battlements too, filling the gaps between the merlons and putting pale, soft caps on every tower top.

Beyond the walls, as far as he could see, the world was turning white. The woods, the fields, the kingsroad—the snows were covering all of them beneath a pale soft mantle, burying the remnants of the winter town, hiding the blackened walls Ramsay's men had left behind when they put the houses to the torch. *The wounds Snow made, snow conceals,* but that was wrong. Ramsay was a Bolton now, not a Snow, never a Snow.

Farther off, the rutted kingsroad had vanished, lost amidst the fields and rolling hills, all one vast expanse of white. And still the snow was falling, drifting down in silence from a windless sky. *Stannis Baratheon is out there somewhere, freezing.* Would Lord Stannis try to take Winterfell by storm? *If he does, his cause is doomed.* The castle was too strong. Even with the moat frozen over, Winterfell's defenses remained formidable. Theon had captured the castle by stealth, sending his best men to scale the walls and swim the moat under the cover of darkness. The defenders had not even known they were under attack until it was too late. No such subterfuge was possible for Stannis.

He might prefer to cut the castle off from the outside world and starve out its defenders. Winterfell's storerooms and cellar vaults were empty. A long supply train had come with Bolton and his friends of Frey up through the Neck, Lady Dustin had brought food and fodder from Barrowton, and Lord Manderly had arrived well provisioned from White Harbor . . . but the host was large. With so many mouths to feed, their stores could not last for long. *Lord Stannis and his men will be just as hungry, though. And cold and footsore as well, in no condition for a fight . . . but the storm will make them desperate to get inside the castle.*

Snow was falling on the godswood too, melting when it touched the ground. Beneath the white-cloaked trees the earth had turned to mud. Tendrils of mist hung in the air like ghostly ribbons. *Why did I come here? These are not my gods. This is not my place.* The heart tree stood before him, a pale giant with a carved face and leaves like bloody hands.

A thin film of ice covered the surface of the pool beneath the weirwood. Theon sank to his knees beside it. "Please," he murmured through his broken teeth, "I never meant . . ." The words caught in his throat. "Save me," he finally managed. "Give me . . ." *What? Strength? Courage? Mercy?* Snow fell around him, pale and silent, keeping its own counsel. The only sound was a faint soft sobbing. *Jeyne,* he thought. *It is her, sobbing in her bridal bed. Who else could it be? Gods do not weep. Or do they?*

The sound was too painful to endure. Theon grabbed hold of a branch and pulled himself back to his feet, knocked the snow off his legs, and limped back toward the lights. *There are ghosts in Winterfell,* he thought, *and I am one of them.*

More snowmen had risen in the yard by the time Theon Greyjoy made his way back. To command the snowy sentinels on the walls, the squires had erected a dozen snowy lords. One was plainly meant to be Lord Manderly; it was the fattest snowman that Theon had ever seen. The one-armed lord could only be Harwood Stout, the snow lady Barbrey Dustin. And the one closest to the door with the beard made of icicles had to be old Whoresbane Umber.

Inside, the cooks were ladling out beef-and-barley stew, thick with carrots and onions, served in trenchers hollowed from loaves of yesterday's bread. Scraps were thrown onto the floor to be gobbled up by Ramsay's girls and the other dogs.

The girls were glad to see him. They knew him by his smell. Red Jeyne loped over to lick at his hand, and Helicent slipped under the table and curled up by his feet, gnawing at a bone. They were good dogs. It was easy to forget that every one was named for a girl that Ramsay had hunted and killed.

Weary as he was, Theon had appetite enough to eat a little stew, washed down with ale. By then the hall had grown raucous. Two of Roose Bolton's scouts had come straggling back through the Hunter's Gate to report that Lord Stannis's advance had slowed to a crawl. His knights rode destriers, and the big warhorses were foundering in the snow. The small, sure-footed garrons of the hill clans were faring better, the scouts said, but the clansmen dared not press too far ahead or the whole host would come apart. Lord Ramsay commanded Abel to give them a marching song in honor of Stannis trudging through the snows, so the bard took up his lute again, whilst one of his washerwomen coaxed a sword from Sour Alyn and mimed Stannis slashing at the snowflakes.

Theon was staring down into the last dregs of his third tankard when Lady Barbrey Dustin swept into the hall and sent two of her sworn swords to bring him to her. When he stood below the dais, she looked him up and down, and sniffed. "Those are the same clothes you wore for the wedding."

"Yes, my lady. They are the clothes I was given." That was one of the lessons he had learned at the Dreadfort: to take what he was given and never ask for more.

Lady Dustin wore black, as ever, though her sleeves were lined with vair. Her gown had a high stiff collar that framed her face. "You know this castle."

"Once."

"Somewhere beneath us are the crypts where the old Stark kings sit in darkness. My men have not been able to find the way down into them. They have been through all the undercrofts and cellars, even the dungeons, but . . ."

"The crypts cannot be accessed from the dungeons, my lady."

"Can you show me the way down?"

"There's nothing down there but—"

"—dead Starks? Aye. And all my favorite Starks are dead, as it happens. Do you know the way or not?"

"I do." He did not like the crypts, had never liked the crypts, but he was no stranger to them.

"Show me. Serjeant, fetch a lantern."

"My lady will want a warm cloak," cautioned Theon. "We will need to go outside."

The snow was coming down heavier than ever when they left the hall, with Lady Dustin wrapped in sable. Huddled in their hooded cloaks, the guards outside were almost indistinguishable from the snowmen. Only their breath fogging the air gave proof that they still lived. Fires burned along the battlements, a vain attempt to drive the gloom away. Their small party found themselves slogging through a smooth, unbroken expanse of white that came halfway up their calves. The tents in the yard were half-buried, sagging under the weight of the accumulation.

The entrance to the crypts was in the oldest section of the castle, near the foot of the First Keep, which had sat unused for hundreds of years. Ramsay had put it to the torch when he sacked Winterfell, and much of what had not burned had collapsed. Only a shell remained, one side open to the elements and filling up with snow. Rubble was strewn all about it: great chunks of shattered masonry, burned beams, broken gargoyles. The falling snow had covered almost all of it, but part of one gargoyle still poked above the drift, its grotesque face snarling sightless at the sky.

This is where they found Bran when he fell. Theon had been out hunting that day, riding with Lord Eddard and King Robert, with no hint of the dire news that awaited them back at the castle. He remembered Robb's face when they told him. No one had expected the broken boy to live. *The gods could not kill Bran, no more than I could.*

It was a strange thought, and stranger still to remember that Bran might still be alive.

"There." Theon pointed to where a snowbank had crept up the wall of the keep. "Under there. Watch for broken stones."

It took Lady Dustin's men the better part of half an hour to uncover the entrance, shoveling through the snow and shifting rubble. When they did, the door was frozen shut. Her serjeant had to go find an axe before he could pull it open, hinges screaming, to reveal stone steps spiraling down into darkness.

"It is a long way down, my lady," Theon cautioned.

Lady Dustin was undeterred. "Beron, the light."

The way was narrow and steep, the steps worn in the center by centuries of feet. They went single file—the serjeant with the lantern, then Theon and Lady Dustin, her other man behind them. He had always thought of the crypts as cold, and so they seemed in summer, but now as they descended the air grew warmer. Not *warm*, never warm, but warmer than above. Down there below the earth, it would seem, the chill was constant, unchanging.

"The bride weeps," Lady Dustin said, as they made their way down, step by careful step. "Our little Lady Arya."

Take care now. Take care, take care. He put one hand on the wall. The shifting torchlight made the steps seem to move beneath his feet. "As . . . as you say, m'lady."

"Roose is not pleased. Tell your bastard that."

He is not my bastard, he wanted to say, but another voice inside him said, *He is, he is. Reek belongs to Ramsay, and Ramsay belongs to Reek. You must not forget your name.*

"Dressing her in grey and white serves no good if the girl is left to sob. The Freys may not care, but the northmen . . . they fear the Dreadfort, but they love the Starks."

"Not you," said Theon.

"Not me," the Lady of Barrowton confessed, "but the rest, yes. Old Whoresbane is only here because the Freys hold the Greatjon captive. And do you imagine the Hornwood men have forgotten the Bastard's last marriage, and how his lady wife was left to starve, chewing her own fingers? What do you think passes through their heads when they hear the new bride weeping? Valiant Ned's precious little girl."

No, he thought. *She is not of Lord Eddard's blood, her name is Jeyne, she is only a steward's daughter.* He did not doubt that Lady Dustin suspected, but even so . . .

"Lady Arya's sobs do us more harm than all of Lord Stannis's swords and spears. If the Bastard means to remain Lord of Winterfell, he had best teach his wife to laugh."

"My lady," Theon broke in. "Here we are."

"The steps go farther down," observed Lady Dustin.

"There are lower levels. Older. The lowest level is partly collapsed, I hear. I have never been down there." He pushed the door open and led them out into a long vaulted tunnel, where mighty granite pillars marched two by two into blackness.

Lady Dustin's serjeant raised the lantern. Shadows slid and shifted. *A small light in a great darkness.* Theon had never felt comfortable in the crypts. He could feel the stone kings staring down at him with their stone eyes, stone fingers curled around the hilts of rusted long-swords. None had any love for ironborn. A familiar sense of dread filled him.

"So many," Lady Dustin said. "Do you know their names?"

"Once . . . but that was a long time ago." Theon pointed. "The ones on this side were Kings in the North. Torrhen was the last."

"The King Who Knelt."

"Aye, my lady. After him they were only lords."

"Until the Young Wolf. Where is Ned Stark's tomb?"

"At the end. This way, my lady."

Their footsteps echoed through the vault as they made their way between the rows of pillars. The stone eyes of the dead men seemed to follow them, and the eyes of their stone direwolves as well. The faces stirred faint memories. A few names came back to him, unbidden, whispered in the ghostly voice of Maester Luwin. King Edrick Snowbeard, who had ruled the north for a hundred years. Brandon the Shipwright, who had sailed beyond the sunset. Theon Stark, the Hungry Wolf. *My namesake.* Lord Beron Stark, who made common cause with Casterly Rock to war against Dagon Greyjoy, Lord of Pyke, in the days when the Seven Kingdoms were ruled in all but name by the bastard sorcerer men called Bloodraven.

"That king is missing his sword," Lady Dustin observed.

It was true. Theon did not recall which king it was, but the longsword he should have held was gone. Streaks of rust remained to show where it had been. The sight disquieted him. He had always heard that the iron in the sword kept the spirits of the dead locked within their tombs. If a sword was missing . . .

There are ghosts in Winterfell. And I am one of them.

They walked on. Barbrey Dustin's face seemed to harden with every step. *She likes this place no more than I do.* Theon heard himself say, "My lady, why do you hate the Starks?"

She studied him. "For the same reason you love them."

Theon stumbled. "Love them? I never . . . I took this castle from them, my lady. I had . . . had Bran and Rickon put to death, mounted their heads on spikes, I . . ."

". . . rode south with Robb Stark, fought beside him at the Whispering Wood and Riverrun, returned to the Iron Islands as his envoy to treat with your own father. Barrowton sent men with the Young Wolf as well. I gave him as few men as I dared, but I knew that I must needs give him some or risk the wroth of Winterfell. So I had my own eyes and ears in that host. They kept me well informed. I know who you are. I know what you are. Now answer my question. Why do you love the Starks?"

"I . . ." Theon put a gloved hand against a pillar. ". . . I wanted to be one of them . . ."

"And never could. We have more in common than you know, my lord. But come."

Only a little farther on, three tombs were closely grouped together. That was where they halted. "Lord Rickard," Lady Dustin observed, studying the central figure. The statue loomed above them—long-faced, bearded, solemn. He had the same stone eyes as the rest, but his looked sad. "He lacks a sword as well."

It was true. "Someone has been down here stealing swords. Brandon's is gone as well."

"He would hate that." She pulled off her glove and touched his knee, pale flesh against dark stone. "Brandon loved his sword. He loved to hone it. 'I want it sharp enough to shave the hair from a woman's cunt,' he used to say. And how he loved to use it. 'A bloody sword is a beautiful thing,' he told me once."

"You knew him," Theon said.

The lantern light in her eyes made them seem as if they were afire. "Brandon was fostered at Barrowton with old Lord Dustin, the father of the one I'd later wed, but he spent most of his time riding the Rills. He loved to ride. His little sister took after him in that. A pair of centaurs, those two. And my lord father was always pleased to play host to the heir to Winterfell. My father had great ambitions for House Ryswell. He would have served up my maidenhead to any Stark who happened by, but there was no need. Brandon was never shy about taking what he wanted. I am old now, a dried-up thing, too long a widow, but I still remember the look of my maiden's blood on his cock the night he claimed me. I think Brandon liked the sight as well. A bloody sword is a beautiful thing, yes. It hurt, but it was a sweet pain.

"The day I learned that Brandon was to marry Catelyn Tully, though . . . there was nothing sweet about *that* pain. He never wanted her, I promise you that. He told me so, on our last night together . . . but Rickard Stark had great ambitions too. *Southron* ambitions that would not be served by having his heir marry the daughter of one of his own vassals. Afterward my father nursed some hope of wedding me to Brandon's brother Eddard, but Catelyn Tully got that one as well. I was left with young Lord Dustin, until Ned Stark took him from me."

"Robert's Rebellion . . ."

"Lord Dustin and I had not been married half a year when Robert rose and Ned Stark called his banners. I begged my husband not to go. He had kin he might have sent in his stead. An uncle famed for his prowess with an axe, a great-uncle who had fought in the War of the Ninepenny Kings. But he was a man and full of pride, nothing would serve but that he lead the Barrowton levies himself. I gave him a horse the day he set out, a red stallion with a fiery mane, the pride of my lord father's herds. My lord swore that he would ride him home when the war was done.

"Ned Stark returned the horse to me on his way back home to Winterfell. He told me that my lord had died an honorable death, that his body had been laid to rest beneath the red mountains of Dorne. He brought his sister's bones back north, though, and there she rests . . . but I promise you, Lord Eddard's bones will never rest beside hers. I mean to feed them to my dogs."

Theon did not understand. "His . . . his bones . . . ?"

Her lips twisted. It was an ugly smile, a smile that reminded him of Ramsay's. "Catelyn Tully dispatched Lord Eddard's bones north before the Red Wedding, but your iron uncle seized Moat Cailin and closed the way. I have been watching ever since. Should those bones ever emerge from the swamps, they will get no farther than Barrowton." She threw one last lingering look at the likeness of Eddard Stark. "We are done here."

The snowstorm was still raging when they emerged from the crypts. Lady Dustin was silent during their ascent, but when they stood beneath the ruins of the First Keep again she shivered and said, "You would do well not to repeat anything I might have said down there. Is that understood?"

It was. "Hold my tongue or lose it."

"Roose has trained you well." She left him there.

THE KING'S PRIZE

The king's host departed Deepwood Motte by the light of a golden dawn, uncoiling from behind the log palisades like a long, steel serpent emerging from its nest.

The southron knights rode out in plate and mail, dinted and scarred by the battles they had fought, but still bright enough to glitter when they caught the rising sun. Faded and stained, torn and mended, their banners and surcoats still made a riot of colors amidst the winter wood—azure and orange, red and green, purple and blue and gold, glimmering amongst bare brown trunks, grey-green pines and sentinels, drifts of dirty snow.

Each knight had his squires, servants, and men-at-arms. Behind them came armorers, cooks, grooms; ranks of spearmen, axemen, archers; grizzled veterans of a hundred battles and green boys off to fight their first. Before them marched the clansmen from the hills; chiefs and champions astride shaggy garrons, their hirsute fighters trotting beside them, clad in furs and boiled leather and old mail. Some painted their faces brown and green and tied bundles of brush about them, to hide amongst the trees.

Back of the main column the baggage train followed: mules, horses, oxen, a mile of wayns and carts laden with food, fodder, tents, and other provisions. Last the rear guard—more knights in plate and mail, with a screening of outriders following half-hidden to make certain no foe could steal up on them unawares.

Asha Greyjoy rode in the baggage train, in a covered wayn with two huge iron-rimmed wheels, fettered at wrist and ankle and watched over day and night by a She-Bear who snored worse than any man. His Grace King Stannis was taking no chances on his prize escaping captivity. He meant to carry her to Winterfell, to display her there in chains for the lords of the north to see, the kraken's daughter bound and broken, proof of his power.

Trumpets saw the column on its way. Spearpoints shone in the light of the rising sun, and all along the verges the grass glistened with the morning frost. Between Deepwood Motte and Winterfell lay one hundred leagues of forest. Three hundred miles as the raven flies. "Fifteen days," the knights told each other.

"Robert would have done it in ten," Asha heard Lord Fell boasting. His grandsire had been slain by Robert at Summerhall; somehow this had elevated his slayer to godlike prowess in the grandson's eyes. "Robert would have been inside Winterfell a fortnight ago, thumbing his nose at Bolton from the battlements."

"Best not mention that to Stannis," suggested Justin Massey, "or he'll have us marching nights as well as days."

This king lives in his brother's shadow, Asha thought.

Her ankle still gave a stab of pain whenever she tried to put her weight on it. Something was broken down inside, Asha did not doubt. The swelling had gone down at Deepwood, but the pain remained. A sprain would surely have healed by now. Her irons *clack*ed every time she moved. The fetters chafed at her wrists and at her pride. But that was the cost of submission.

"No man has ever died from bending his knee," her father had once told her. "He who kneels may rise again, blade in hand. He who will not kneel stays dead, stiff legs and all." Balon Greyjoy had proved the truth of his own words when his first rebellion failed; the kraken bent the knee to stag and direwolf, only to rise again when Robert Baratheon and Eddard Stark were dead.

And so at Deepwood the kraken's daughter had done the same when she was dumped before the king, bound and limping (though blessedly unraped), her ankle a blaze of pain. "I yield, Your Grace.

Do as you wish with me. I ask only that you spare my men." Qarl and Tris and the rest who had survived the wolfswood were all she had to care about. Only nine remained. *We ragged nine,* Cromm named them. He was the worst wounded.

Stannis had given her their lives. Yet she sensed no true mercy in the man. He was determined, beyond a doubt. Nor did he lack for courage. Men said he was just . . . and if his was a harsh, hard-handed sort of justice, well, life on the Iron Islands had accustomed Asha Greyjoy to that. All the same, she could not like this king. Those deep-set blue eyes of his seemed always slitted in suspicion, cold fury boiling just below their surface. Her life meant little and less to him. She was only his hostage, a prize to show the north that he could vanquish the ironborn.

More fool him. Bringing down a woman was not like to awe any northmen, if she knew the breed, and her worth as a hostage was less than naught. Her uncle ruled the Iron Islands now, and the Crow's Eye would not care if she lived or died. It might matter some to the wretched ruin of a husband that Euron had inflicted upon her, but Eric Ironmaker did not have coin enough to ransom her. But there was no explaining such things to Stannis Baratheon. Her very woman-hood seemed to offend him. Men from the green lands liked their women soft and sweet in silk, she knew, not clad in mail and leather with a throwing axe in each hand. But her short acquaintance with the king at Deepwood Motte convinced her that he would have been no more fond of her in a gown. Even with Galbart Glover's wife, the pious Lady Sybelle, he had been correct and courteous but plainly uncomfortable. This southron king seemed to be one of those men to whom women are another race, as strange and unfathomable as giants and grumkins and the children of the forest. The She-Bear made him grind his teeth as well.

There was only one woman that Stannis listened to, and he had left her on the Wall. "Though I would sooner she was with us," confessed Ser Justin Massey, the fair-haired knight who commanded the baggage train. "The last time we went into battle without Lady Melisandre was the Blackwater, when Lord Renly's shade came down upon us and drove half our host into the bay."

"The last time?" Asha said. "Was this sorceress at Deepwood Motte? I did not see her."

"Hardly a battle," Ser Justin said, smiling. "Your ironmen fought bravely, my lady, but we had many times your numbers, and we took you unawares. Winterfell will know that we are coming. And Roose Bolton has as many men as we do."

Or more, thought Asha.

Even prisoners have ears, and she had heard all the talk at Deepwood Motte, when King Stannis and his captains were debating this march. Ser Justin had opposed it from the start, along with many of the knights and lords who had come with Stannis from the south. But the wolves insisted; Roose Bolton could not be suffered to hold Winterfell, and the Ned's girl must be rescued from the clutches of his bastard. So said Morgan Liddle, Brandon Norrey, Big Bucket Wull, the Flints, even the She-Bear. "One hundred leagues from Deepwood Motte to Winterfell," said Artos Flint, the night the argument boiled to a head in Galbart Glover's longhall. "Three hundred miles as the raven flies."

"A long march," a knight named Corliss Penny said.

"Not so long as that," insisted Ser Godry, the big knight the others called the Giantslayer. "We have come as far already. The Lord of Light will blaze a path for us."

"And when we arrive before Winterfell?" said Justin Massey. "Two walls with a moat between them, and the inner wall a hundred feet high. Bolton will never march out to face us in the field, and we do not have the provisions to mount a siege."

"Arnolf Karstark will join his strength to ours, never forget," said Harwood Fell. "Mors Umber as well. We will have as many northmen as Lord Bolton. And the woods are thick north of the castle. We will raise siege towers, build rams . . ."

And die by the thousands, Asha thought.

"We might do best to winter here," suggested Lord Peasebury.

"*Winter* here?" Big Bucket roared. "How much food and fodder do you think Galbart Glover has laid by?"

Then Ser Richard Horpe, the knight with the ravaged face and the death's-head moths on his surcoat, turned to Stannis and said, "Your Grace, your brother—"

The king cut him off. "We all know what my brother would do. Robert would gallop up to the gates of Winterfell alone, break them with his warhammer, and ride through the rubble to slay Roose Bolton with his left hand and the Bastard with his right." Stannis rose to his feet. "I am not Robert. But we will march, and we will free Winterfell . . . or die in the attempt."

Whatever doubts his lords might nurse, the common men seemed to have faith in their king. Stannis had smashed Mance Rayder's wildlings at the Wall and cleaned Asha and her ironborn out of Deepwood Motte; he was Robert's brother, victor in a famous sea battle off Fair Isle, the man who had held Storm's End all through Robert's Rebellion. And he bore a hero's sword, the enchanted blade Lightbringer, whose glow lit up the night.

"Our foes are not as formidable as they appear," Ser Justin assured Asha on the first day of the march. "Roose Bolton is feared, but little loved. And his friends the Freys . . . the north has not forgotten the Red Wedding. Every lord at Winterfell lost kinsmen there. Stannis need only bloody Bolton, and the northmen will abandon him."

So you hope, thought Asha, *but first the king must bloody him. Only a fool deserts the winning side.*

Ser Justin called upon her cart half a dozen times that first day, to bring her food and drink and tidings of the march. A man of easy smiles and endless japes, large and well fleshed, with pink cheeks, blue eyes, and a wind-tossed tangle of white-blond hair as pale as flax, he was a considerate gaoler, ever solicitous of his captive's comfort.

"He wants you," said the She-Bear, after his third visit.

Her proper name was Alysane of House Mormont, but she wore the other name as easily as she wore her mail. Short, chunky, muscular, the heir to Bear Island had big thighs, big breasts, and big hands ridged with callus. Even in sleep she wore ringmail under her furs, boiled leather under that, and an old sheepskin under the leather, turned inside out for warmth. All those layers made her look almost as wide as she was tall. *And ferocious.* Sometimes it was hard for Asha Greyjoy to remember that she and the She-Bear were almost of an age.

"He wants my lands," Asha replied. "He wants the Iron Islands."

She knew the signs. She had seen the same before in other suitors. Massey's own ancestral holdings, far to the south, were lost to him, so he must needs make an advantageous marriage or resign himself to being no more than a knight of the king's household. Stannis had frustrated Ser Justin's hopes of marrying the wildling princess that Asha had heard so much of, so now he had set his sights on her. No doubt he dreamed of putting her in the Seastone Chair on Pyke and ruling through her, as her lord and master. That would require ridding her of her present lord and master, to be sure . . . not to mention the uncle who had married her to him. *Not likely,* Asha judged. *The Crow's Eye could eat Ser Justin to break his fast and never even belch.*

It made no matter. Her father's lands would never be hers, no matter whom she married. The ironborn were not a forgiving people, and Asha had been defeated twice. Once at the kingsmoot by her uncle Euron, and again at Deepwood Motte by Stannis. More than enough to stamp her as unfit to rule. Wedding Justin Massey, or any of Stannis Baratheon's lordlings, would hurt more than it helped. *The kraken's daughter turned out to be just a woman after all,* the captains and the kings would say. *See how she spreads her legs for this soft green land lord.*

Still, if Ser Justin wished to court her favor with food and wine and words, Asha was not like to discourage him. He made for better company than the taciturn She-Bear, and she was elsewise alone amongst five thousand foes. Tris Botley, Qarl the Maid, Cromm, Roggon, and the rest of her bloodied band had been left behind at Deepwood Motte, in Galbart Glover's dungeons.

The army covered twenty-two miles the first day, by the reckoning of the guides Lady Sybelle had given them, trackers and hunters sworn to Deepwood with clan names like Forrester and Woods, Branch and Bole. The second day the host made twenty-four, as their vanguard passed beyond the Glover lands into the thick of the wolfswood. "*R'hllor, send your light to lead us through this gloom,*" the faithful prayed that night as they gathered about a roaring blaze outside the king's pavilion. Southron knights and men-at-arms, the lot of them. Asha would have called them king's men, but the other stormlanders and crownlands men named them queen's men . . . though the queen they followed was the red one at Castle Black, not the wife that Stannis Baratheon had left behind at Eastwatch-by-the-Sea. "*Oh, Lord of Light, we beseech you, cast your fiery eye upon us and keep us safe and warm,*" they sang to the flames, "*for the night is dark and full of terrors.*"

A big knight named Ser Godry Farring led them. *Godry the Giantslayer. A big name for a small man.* Farring was broad-chested and well muscled under his plate and mail. He was also arrogant and vain, it seemed to Asha, hungry for glory, deaf to caution, a glutton for praise, and contemptuous of smallfolk, wolves, and women. In the last, he was not unlike his king.

"Let me have a horse," Asha asked Ser Justin, when he rode up to the wayn with half a ham. "I am going mad in these chains. I will not attempt escape. You have my word on that."

"Would that I could, my lady. You are the king's captive, not mine own."

"Your king will not take a woman's word."

The She-Bear growled. "Why should we trust the word of any ironman after what your brother did at Winterfell?"

"I am not Theon," Asha insisted . . . but the chains remained.

As Ser Justin galloped down the column, she found herself remembering the last time she had seen her mother. It had been on Harlaw, at Ten Towers. A candle had been flickering in her mother's chamber, but her great carved bed was empty beneath its dusty canopy. Lady Alannys sat beside a window, staring out across the sea. "Did you bring my baby boy?" she'd asked, mouth trembling. "Theon could not come," Asha had told her, looking down upon the ruin of the woman who had given her birth, a mother who had lost two of her sons. And the third . . .

I send you each a piece of prince.

Whatever befell when battle was joined at Winterfell, Asha Greyjoy did not think her brother likely to survive it. *Theon Turncloak. Even the She-Bear wants his head on a spike.*

"Do you have brothers?" Asha asked her keeper.

"Sisters," Alysane Mormont replied, gruff as ever. "Five, we were. All girls. Lyanna is back on Bear Island. Lyra and Jory are with our mother. Dacey was murdered."

"The Red Wedding."

"Aye." Alysane stared at Asha for a moment. "I have a son. He's only two. My daughter's nine."

"You started young."

"Too young. But better that than wait too late."

A stab at me, Asha thought, *but let it be.* "You are wed."

"No. My children were fathered by a bear." Alysane smiled. Her teeth were crooked, but there was something ingratiating about that smile. "Mormont women are skinchangers. We turn into bears and find mates in the woods. Everyone knows."

Asha smiled back. "Mormont women are all fighters too."

The other woman's smile faded. "What we are is what you made us. On Bear Island every child learns to fear krakens rising from the sea."

The Old Way. Asha turned away, chains *clink*ing faintly. On the third day the forest pressed close around them, and the rutted roads dwindled down to game trails that soon proved to be too narrow for their larger wagons. Here and there they wound their way past familiar landmarks: a stony hill that looked a bit like a wolf's head when seen from a certain angle, a half-frozen waterfall, a natural stone arch bearded with grey-green moss. Asha knew them all. She had come this way before, riding to Winterfell to persuade her brother Theon to abandon his conquest and return with her to the safety of Deepwood Motte. *I failed in that as well.*

That day they made fourteen miles, and were glad of it.

When dusk fell, the driver pulled the wayn off under the tree. As he was loosing the horses from the traces, Ser Justin trotted up and undid the fetters around Asha's ankles. He and the She-Bear escorted her through the camp to the king's tent. A captive she might be, but she was still a Greyjoy of Pyke, and it pleased Stannis Baratheon to feed her scraps from his own table, where he supped with his captains and commanders.

The king's pavilion was near as large as the longhall back at Deepwood Motte, but there was little grand about it beyond its size. Its stiff walls of heavy yellow canvas were badly faded, stained by mud and water, with spots of mildew showing. Atop its center pole flew the royal standard, golden, with a stag's head within a burning heart.

On three sides the pavilions of the southron lordlings who had come north with Stannis surrounded it. On the fourth side the nightfire roared, lashing at the darkening sky with swirls of flame.

A dozen men were splitting logs to feed the blaze when Asha came limping up with her keepers. *Queen's men.* Their god was Red R'hllor, and a jealous god he was. Her own god, the Drowned God of the Iron Isles, was a demon to their eyes, and if she did not embrace this Lord of Light, she would be damned and doomed. *They would as gladly burn me as those logs and broken branches.* Some had urged that very thing within her hearing after the battle in the woods. Stannis had refused.

The king stood outside his tent, staring into the nightfire. *What does he see there? Victory? Doom? The face of his red and hungry god?* His eyes were sunk in deep pits, his close-cropped beard no more than a shadow across his hollow cheeks and bony jawbone. Yet there was power in his stare, an iron ferocity that told Asha this man would never, ever turn back from his course.

She went to one knee before him. "Sire." *Am I humbled enough for you, Your Grace? Am I beaten, bowed, and broken sufficiently for your liking?* "Strike these chains from my wrists, I beg you. Let me ride. I will attempt no escape."

Stannis looked at her as he might look at a dog who presumed to hump against his leg. "You earned those irons."

"I did. Now I offer you my men, my ships, my wits."

"Your ships are mine, or burnt. Your men . . . how many are left? Ten? Twelve?"

Nine. Six, if you count only those strong enough to fight. "Dagmer Cleftjaw holds Torrhen's Square. A fierce fighter, and a leal servant of House Greyjoy. I can deliver that castle to you, and its garrison as well." *Perhaps,* she might have added, but it would not serve her cause to show doubt before this king.

"Torrhen's Square is not worth the mud beneath my heels. It is Winterfell that matters."

"Strike off these irons and let me help you take it, Sire. Your Grace's royal brother was renowned for turning fallen foes into friends. Make me your man."

"The gods did not make you a man. How can I?" Stannis turned back to the nightfire and whatever he saw dancing there amongst the orange flames.

Ser Justin Massey grasped Asha by the arm and pulled her inside the royal tent. "That was ill judged, my lady," he told her. "Never speak to him of Robert."

I should have known better. Asha knew how it went with little brothers. She remembered Theon as a boy, a shy child who lived in awe, and fear, of Rodrik and Maron. *They never grow out of it,* she decided. *A little brother may live to be a hundred, but he will always be a little brother.* She rattled her iron jewelry and imagined how pleasant it would be to step up behind Stannis and throttle him with the chain that bound her wrists.

They supped that night on a venison stew made from a scrawny hart that a scout called Benjicot Branch had brought down. But only in the royal tent. Beyond those canvas walls, each man got a heel of bread and a chunk of black sausage no longer than a finger, washed down with the last of Galbart Glover's ale.

One hundred leagues from Deepwood Motte to Winterfell. Three hundred miles as the raven flies. "Would that we were ravens," Justin Massey said on the fourth day of the march, the day the snow began to fall. Only a few small flurries at first. Cold and wet, but nothing they could not push through easily.

But it snowed again the next day, and the day after, and the day after that. The thick beards of the wolves were soon caked with ice where their breath had frozen, and every clean-shaved southron boy was letting his whiskers grow out to keep his face warm. Before long the ground ahead of the column was blanketed in white, concealing stones and twisted roots and deadfalls, turning every step into an adventure. The wind picked up as well, driving the snow before it. The king's host became a column of snowmen, staggering through knee-high drifts.

On the third day of snow, the king's host began to come apart. Whilst the southron knights and lordlings struggled, the men of the northern hills fared better. Their garrons were sure-footed beasts that ate less than palfreys, and much less than the big destriers, and the men who rode them were at home in the snow. Many of the wolves donned curious footwear. Bear-paws, they called them, queer elongated things made with bent wood and leather strips. Lashed onto the bottoms of their boots, the things somehow allowed them to walk on top of the snow without breaking through the crust and sinking down to their thighs.

Some had bear-paws for their horses too, and the shaggy little garrons wore them as easily as other mounts wore iron horseshoes ... but the palfreys and destriers wanted no part of them. When a few of the king's knights strapped them onto their feet nonetheless, the big southern horses balked and refused to move, or tried to shake the things off their feet. One destrier broke an ankle trying to walk in them.

The northmen on their bear-paws soon began to outdistance the rest of the host. They overtook the knights in the main column, then Ser Godry Farring and his vanguard. And meanwhile, the wayns and wagons of the baggage train were falling farther and farther behind, so much so that the men of the rear guard were constantly chivvying them to keep up a faster pace.

On the fifth day of the storm, the baggage train crossed a rippling expanse of waist-high snowdrifts that concealed a frozen pond. When the hidden ice cracked beneath the weight of the wagons, three teamsters and four horses were swallowed up by the freezing water, along with two of the men who tried to rescue them. One was Harwood Fell. His knights pulled him out before he drowned, but not before his lips turned blue and his skin as pale as milk. Nothing they did could seem to warm him afterward. He shivered violently for hours, even when they cut him out of his sodden clothes, wrapped him in warm furs, and sat him by the fire. That same night he slipped into a feverish sleep. He never woke.

That was the night that Asha first heard the queen's men muttering about a sacrifice—an offering to their red god, so he might end the storm. "The gods of the north have unleashed this storm on us," Ser Corliss Penny said.

"False gods," insisted Ser Godry, the Giantslayer.

"R'hllor is with us," said Ser Clayton Suggs.

"Melisandre is not," said Justin Massey.

The king said nothing. But he heard. Asha was certain of that. He sat at the high table as a dish of onion soup cooled before him, hardly tasted, staring at the flame of the nearest candle with those hooded eyes, ignoring the talk around him. The second-in-command, the lean tall knight named Richard Horpe, spoke for him. "The storm must break soon," he declared.

But the storm only worsened. The wind became a lash as cruel as any slaver's whip. Asha thought she had known cold on Pyke, when the wind came howling off the sea, but that was nothing compared to this. *This is a cold that drives men mad.*

Even when the shout came down the line to make camp for the night, it was no easy thing to warm yourself. The tents were damp and heavy, hard to raise, harder to take down, and prone to sudden collapse if too much snow accumulated on top of them. The king's host was creeping through the heart of the largest forest in the Seven Kingdoms, yet dry wood became difficult to find. Every camp saw fewer fires burning, and those that were lit threw off more smoke than heat. Oft as not food was eaten cold, even raw.

Even the nightfire shrank and grew feeble, to the dismay of the queen's men. "*Lord of Light, preserve us from this evil,*" they prayed, led by the deep voice of Ser Godry the Giantslayer. "*Show us your bright sun again, still these winds, and melt these snows, that we may reach your foes and smite them. The night is dark and cold and full of terrors, but yours is the power and glory and the light. R'hllor, fill us with your fire.*"

Later, when Ser Corliss Penny wondered aloud whether an entire army had ever frozen to death in a winter storm, the wolves laughed. "This is no winter," declared Big Bucket Wull. "Up in the hills we say that autumn kisses you, but winter fucks you hard. This is only autumn's kiss."

God grant that I never know true winter, then. Asha herself was spared the worst of it; she was the king's prize, after all. Whilst others hungered, she was fed. Whilst others shivered, she was warm. Whilst others struggled through the snows atop weary horses, she rode upon a bed of furs inside a wayn, with a stiff canvas roof to keep the snow off, comfortable in her chains.

The horses and the common men had it hardest. Two squires from the stormlands stabbed a man-at-arms to death in a quarrel over who would sit closest to the fire. The next night some archers desperate for warmth somehow managed to set their tent afire, which had at least the virtue of heating the adjacent tents. Destriers began to perish of exhaustion and exposure. "What is a knight without a horse?" men riddled. "A snowman with a sword." Any horse that went down was butchered on the spot for meat. Their provisions had begun to run low as well.

Peasebury, Cobb, Foxglove, and other southron lords urged the king to make camp until the storm had passed. Stannis would have none of that. Nor would he heed the queen's men when they came to urge him to make an offering to their hungry red god.

That tale she had from Justin Massey, who was less devout than most. "A sacrifice will prove our faith still burns true, Sire," Clayton Suggs had told the king. And Godry the Giantslayer said, "The old gods of the north have sent this storm upon us. Only R'hllor can end it. We must give him an unbeliever."

"Half my army is made up of unbelievers," Stannis had replied. "I will have no burnings. Pray harder."

No burnings today, and none tomorrow . . . but if the snows continue, how long before the king's resolve begins to weaken? Asha had never shared her uncle Aeron's faith in the Drowned God, but that night she prayed as fervently to He Who Dwells Beneath the Waves as ever the Damphair had. The storm did not abate. The march continued, slowing to a stagger, then a crawl. Five miles was a good day. Then three. Then two.

By the ninth day of the storm, every camp saw the captains and commanders entering the king's tent wet and weary, to sink to one knee and report their losses for the day.

"One man dead, three missing."

"Six horses lost, one of them mine own."

"Two dead men, one a knight. Four horses down. We got one up again. The others are lost. Destriers, and one palfrey."

The cold count, Asha heard it named. The baggage train suffered the worst: dead horses, lost men, wayns overturned and broken. "The horses founder in the snow," Justin Massey told the king. "Men wander off or just sit down to die."

"Let them," King Stannis snapped. "We press on."

The northmen fared much better, with their garrons and their bear-paws. Black Donnel Flint and his half-brother Artos only lost one man between them. The Liddles, the Wulls, and the Norreys lost none at all. One of Morgan Liddle's mules had gone astray, but he seemed to think the Flints had stolen him.

One hundred leagues from Deepwood Motte to Winterfell. Three hundred miles as the raven flies. Fifteen days. The fifteenth day of the march came and went, and they had crossed less than half the distance. A trail of broken wayns and frozen corpses stretched back behind them, buried beneath the blowing snow. The sun and moon and stars had been gone so long that Asha was starting to wonder whether she had dreamed them.

It was the twentieth day of the advance when she finally won free of her ankle chains. Late that afternoon, one of the horses drawing her wayn died in the traces. No replacement could be found; what draft horses remained were needed to pull the wagons that held their food and fodder. When Ser Justin Massey rode up, he told them to butcher the dead horse for meat and break up the wagon for firewood. Then he removed the fetters around Asha's ankles, rubbing the stiffness from her calves. "I have no mount to give you, my lady," he said, "and if we tried to ride double, it would be the end of my horse as well. You must walk."

Asha's ankle throbbed beneath her weight with every step. *The cold will numb it soon enough,* she told herself. *In an hour I won't feel my feet at all.* She was only part wrong; it took less time than that. By the time darkness halted the column, she was stumbling and yearning for the comforts of her rolling prison. *The irons made me weak.* Supper found her so exhausted that she fell asleep at the table.

On the twenty-sixth day of the fifteen-day march, the last of the vegetables was consumed. On the thirty-second day, the last of the grain and fodder. Asha wondered how long a man could live on raw, half-frozen horse meat.

"Branch swears we are only three days from Winterfell," Ser Richard Horpe told the king that night after the cold count.

"*If* we leave the weakest men behind," said Corliss Penny.

"The weakest men are beyond saving," insisted Horpe. "Those still strong enough must reach Winterfell or die as well."

"The Lord of Light will deliver us the castle," said Ser Godry Farring. "If Lady Melisandre were with us—"

Finally, after a nightmarish day when the column advanced a bare mile and lost a dozen horses and four men, Lord Peasebury turned against the northmen. "This march was madness. More dying every day, and for what? Some girl?"

"Ned's girl," said Morgan Liddle. He was the second of three sons, so the other wolves called him Middle Liddle, though not often in his hearing. It was Morgan who had almost slain Asha in the fight by Deepwood Motte. He had come to her later, on the march, to beg her pardon . . . for calling her *cunt* in his battle lust, not for trying to split her head open with an axe.

"Ned's girl," echoed Big Bucket Wull. "And we should have had her and the castle both if you prancing southron jackanapes didn't piss your satin breeches at a little snow."

"A *little* snow?" Peasebury's soft girlish mouth twisted in fury. "Your ill counsel forced this march upon us, Wull. I am starting to suspect you have been Bolton's creature all along. Is that the way of it? Did he send you to us to whisper poison in the king's ear?"

Big Bucket laughed in his face. "Lord Pea Pod. If you were a man, I would kill you for that, but my sword is made of too fine a steel to besmirch with craven's blood." He took a drink of ale and wiped his mouth. "Aye, men are dying. More will die before we see Winterfell. What of it? This is war. Men die in war. That is as it should be. As it has always been."

Ser Corliss Penny gave the clan chief an incredulous look. "Do you *want* to die, Wull?"

That seemed to amuse the northman. "I want to live forever in a land where summer lasts a thousand years. I want a castle in the clouds where I can look down over the world. I want to be six-and-twenty again. When I was six-and-twenty I could fight all day and fuck all night. What men want does not matter.

"Winter is almost upon us, boy. And winter is death. I would sooner my men die fighting for the Ned's little girl than alone and hungry in the snow, weeping tears that freeze upon their cheeks. No one sings songs of men who die like that. As for me, I am old. This will be my last winter. Let me bathe in Bolton blood before I die. I want to feel it spatter across my face when my axe bites deep into a Bolton skull. I want to lick it off my lips and die with the taste of it on my tongue."

"*Aye!*" shouted Morgan Liddle. "*Blood and battle!*" Then all the hillmen were shouting, banging their cups and drinking horns on the table, filling the king's tent with the clangor.

Asha Greyjoy would have welcomed a fight herself. *One battle, to put an end to this misery. Steel on steel, pink snow, broken shields and severed limbs, and it would all be done.*

The next day the king's scouts chanced upon an abandoned crofters' village between two lakes—a mean and meagre place, no more than a few huts, a longhall, and a watchtower. Richard Horpe commanded a halt, though the army had advanced no more than a half-mile that day and they were hours shy of dark. It was well past moonrise before the baggage train and rear guard straggled in. Asha was amongst them.

"There are fish in those lakes," Horpe told the king. "We'll cut holes in the ice. The northmen know how it's done."

Even in his bulky fur cloak and heavy armor, Stannis looked like a man with one foot in the grave. What little flesh he'd carried on his tall, spare frame at Deepwood Motte had melted away during the march. The shape of his skull could be seen under his skin, and his jaw was clenched so hard Asha feared his teeth might shatter. "Fish, then," he said, biting off each word with a snap. "But we march at first light."

Yet when light came, the camp woke to snow and silence. The sky turned from black to white, and seemed no brighter. Asha Greyjoy awoke cramped and cold beneath the pile of sleeping furs, listening to the She-Bear's snores. She had never known a woman to snore so loudly, but she had grown used to it whilst on the march, and even took some comfort in it now. It was the silence that troubled her. No trumpets blew to rouse the men to mount up, form column, prepare to march. No warhorns summoned forth the northmen. *Something is wrong.*

Asha crawled out from under her sleeping furs and pushed her way out of the tent, knocking aside the wall of snow that had sealed them in during the night. Her irons *clank*ed as she climbed to her feet and took a breath of the icy morning air. The snow was still falling, even more heavily than when she'd crawled inside the tent. The lakes had vanished, and the woods as well. She could see the shapes of other tents and lean-tos and the fuzzy orange glow of the beacon fire burning atop the watchtower, but not the tower itself. The storm had swallowed the rest.

Somewhere ahead Roose Bolton awaited them behind the walls of Winterfell, but Stannis Baratheon's host sat snowbound and unmoving, walled in by ice and snow, starving.

DAENERYS

The candle was almost gone. Less than an inch remained, jutting from a pool of warm melted wax to cast its light over the queen's bed. The flame had begun to gutter.

It will go out before much longer, Dany realized, *and when it does another night will be at its end.*

Dawn always came too soon.

She had not slept, could not sleep, would not sleep. She had not even dared to close her eyes, for fear it would be morning when she opened them again. If only she had the power, she would have made their nights go on forever, but the best that she could do was stay awake to try and savor every last sweet moment before daybreak turned them into no more than fading memories.

Beside her, Daario Naharis was sleeping as peacefully as a newborn babe. He had a gift for sleeping, he'd boasted, smiling in that cocksure way of his. In the field, he would sleep in the saddle oft as not, he claimed, so as to be well rested should he come upon a battle. Sun or storm, it made no matter. "A warrior who cannot sleep soon has no strength to fight," he said. He was never vexed by nightmares either. When Dany told him how Serwyn of the Mirror Shield was haunted by the ghosts of all the knights he'd killed, Daario only laughed. "If the ones I killed come bother me, I will kill them all again." *He has a sellsword's conscience,* she realized then. *That is to say, none at all.*

Daario lay upon his stomach, the light linen coverlets tangled about his long legs, his face half-buried in the pillows.

Dany ran her hand down his back, tracing the line of his spine. His skin was smooth beneath her touch, almost hairless. *His skin is silk and satin.* She loved the feel of him beneath her fingers. She loved to run her fingers through his hair, to knead the ache from his calves after a long day in the saddle, to cup his cock and feel it harden against her palm.

If she had been some ordinary woman, she would gladly have spent her whole life touching Daario, tracing his scars and making him tell her how he'd come by every one. *I would give up my crown if he asked it of me,* Dany thought . . . but he had not asked it, and never would. Daario might whisper words of love when the two of them were as one, but she knew it was the dragon queen he loved. *If I gave up my crown, he would not want me.* Besides, kings who lost their crowns oft lost their heads as well, and she could see no reason why it would be any different for a queen.

The candle flickered one last time and died, drowned in its own wax. Darkness swallowed the feather bed and its two occupants, and filled every corner of the chamber. Dany wrapped her arms around her captain and pressed herself against his back. She drank in the scent of him, savoring the warmth of his flesh, the feel of his skin against her own. *Remember,* she told herself. *Remember how he felt.* She kissed him on his shoulder.

Daario rolled toward her, his eyes open. "Daenerys." He smiled a lazy smile. That was another of his talents; he woke all at once, like a cat. "Is it dawn?"

"Not yet. We have a while still."

"Liar. I can see your eyes. Could I do that if it were the black of night?" Daario kicked loose of the coverlets and sat up. "The half-light. Day will be here soon."

"I do not want this night to end."

"No? And why is that, my queen?"

"You know."

"The wedding?" He laughed. "Marry me instead."

"You know I cannot do that."

"You are a queen. You can do what you like." He slid a hand along her leg. "How many nights remain to us?"

Two. Only two. "You know as well as I. This night and the next, and we must end this."

"Marry me, and we can have all the nights forever."

If I could, I would. Khal Drogo had been her sun-and-stars, but he had been dead so long that Daenerys had almost forgotten how it felt to love and be loved. Daario had helped her to remember. *I was dead and he brought me back to life. I was asleep and he woke me. My brave captain.* Even so, of late he grew too bold. On the day that he returned from his latest sortie, he had tossed the head of a Yunkish lord at her feet and kissed her in the hall for all the world to see, until Barristan Selmy pulled the two of them apart. Ser Grandfather had been so wroth that Dany feared blood might be shed. "We cannot wed, my love. You know why."

He climbed from her bed. "Marry Hizdahr, then. I will give him a nice set of horns for his wedding gift. Ghiscari men like to prance about in horns. They make them from their own hair, with combs and wax and irons." Daario found his breeches and pulled them on. He did not trouble himself with smallclothes.

"Once I am wed it will be high treason to desire me." Dany pulled the coverlet up over her breasts.

"Then I must be a traitor." He slipped a blue silk tunic over his head and straightened the prongs of his beard with his fingers. He had dyed it afresh for her, taking it from purple back to blue, as it had been when first she met him. "I smell of you," he said, sniffing at his fingers and grinning.

Dany loved the way his gold tooth gleamed when he grinned. She loved the fine hairs on his chest. She loved the strength in his arms, the sound of his laughter, the way he would always look into her eyes and say her name as he slid his cock inside her. "You are beautiful," she blurted as she watched him don his riding boots and lace them up. Some days he let her do that for him, but not today, it seemed. *That's done with too.*

"Not beautiful enough to marry." Daario took his sword belt off the peg where he had hung it.

"Where are you going?"

"Out into your city," he said, "to drink a keg or two and pick a quarrel. It has been too long since I've killed a man. Might be I should seek out your betrothed."

Dany threw a pillow at him. "You will leave Hizdahr be!"

"As my queen commands. Will you hold court today?"

"No. On the morrow I will be a woman wed, and Hizdahr will be king. Let *him* hold court. These are his people."

"Some are his, some are yours. The ones you freed."

"Are you chiding me?"

"The ones you call your children. They want their mother."

"You are. You are *chiding* me."

"Only a little, bright heart. Will you come hold court?"

"After my wedding, perhaps. After the peace."

"This *after* that you speak of never comes. You should hold court. My new men do not believe that you are real. The ones who came over from the Windblown. Bred and born in Westeros, most of them, full of tales about Targaryens. They want to see one with their own eyes. The Frog has a gift for you."

"The Frog?" she said, giggling. "And who is he?"

He shrugged. "Some Dornish boy. He squires for the big knight they call Greenguts. I told him he could give his gift to me and I'd deliver it, but he wouldn't have it."

"Oh, a clever frog. '*Give the gift to me.*'" She threw the other pillow at him. "Would I have ever seen it?"

Daario stroked his gilded mustachio. "Would I steal from my sweet queen? If it were a gift worthy of you, I would have put it into your soft hands myself."

"As a token of your love?"

"As to that I will not say, but I told him that he could give it to you. You would not make a liar of Daario Naharis?"

Dany was helpless to refuse. "As you wish. Bring your frog to court tomorrow. The others too. The Westerosi." It would be nice to hear the Common Tongue from someone besides Ser Barristan.

"As my queen commands." Daario bowed deeply, grinned, and took his leave, his cloak swirling behind him.

Dany sat amongst the rumpled bedclothes with her arms about her knees, so forlorn that she did not hear when Missandei came creeping in with bread and milk and figs. "Your Grace? Are you unwell? In the black of night this one heard you scream."

Dany took a fig. It was black and plump, still moist with dew. *Will Hizdahr ever make me scream?* "It was the wind that you heard screaming." She took a bite, but the fruit had lost its savor now that Daario was gone. Sighing, she rose and called to Irri for a robe, then wandered out onto her terrace.

Her foes were all about her. There were never less than a dozen ships drawn up on the shore. Some days there were as many as a hundred, when the soldiers were disembarking. The Yunkai'i were even bringing in wood by sea. Behind their ditches, they were building catapults, scorpions, tall trebuchets. On still nights she could hear the hammers ringing through the warm, dry air. *No siege towers, though. No battering rams.* They would not try to take Meereen by storm. They would wait behind their siege lines, flinging stones at her until famine and disease had brought her people to their knees.

Hizdahr will bring me peace. He must.

That night her cooks roasted her a kid with dates and carrots, but Dany could only eat a bite of it. The prospect of wrestling with Meereen once more left her feeling weary. Sleep came hard, even when Daario came back, so drunk that he could hardly stand. Beneath her coverlets she tossed and turned, dreaming that Hizdahr was kissing her . . . but his lips were blue and bruised, and when he thrust himself inside her, his manhood was cold as ice. She sat up with her hair disheveled and the bedclothes atangle. Her captain slept beside her, yet she was alone. She wanted to shake him, wake him, make him hold her, fuck her, help her forget, but she knew that if she did, he would only smile and yawn and say, "It was just a dream, my queen. Go back to sleep."

Instead she slipped into a hooded robe and stepped out onto her terrace. She went to the parapet and stood there gazing down upon the city as she had done a hundred times before. *It will never be my city. It will never be my home.*

The pale pink light of dawn found her still out on her terrace, asleep upon the grass beneath a blanket of fine dew. "I promised Daario that I would hold court today," Daenerys told her handmaids when they woke her. "Help me find my crown. Oh, and some clothes to wear, something light and cool."

She made her descent an hour later. "*All kneel for Daenerys Stormborn, the Unburnt, Queen of Meereen, Queen of the Andals and the Rhoynar and the First Men, Khaleesi of Great Grass Sea, Breaker of Shackles and Mother of Dragons,*" Missandei called.

Reznak mo Reznak bowed and beamed. "Magnificence, every day you grow more beautiful. I think the prospect of your wedding has given you a glow. Oh, my shining queen!"

Dany sighed. "Summon the first petitioner."

It had been so long since she last held court that the crush of cases was almost overwhelming. The back of the hall was a solid press of people, and scuffles broke out over precedence. Inevitably it was Galazza Galare who stepped forward, her head held high, her face hidden behind a shimmering green veil. "Your Radiance, it might be best were we to speak in private."

"Would that I had the time," said Dany sweetly. "I am to be wed upon the morrow." Her last meeting with the Green Grace had not gone well. "What would you have of me?"

"I would speak to you about the presumption of a certain sellsword captain."

She dares say that in open court? Dany felt a blaze of anger. *She has courage, I grant that, but if she thinks I am about to suffer another scolding, she could not be more wrong.* "The treachery of Brown Ben Plumm has shocked us all," she said, "but your warning comes too late. And now I know you will want to return to your temple to pray for peace."

The Green Grace bowed. "I shall pray for you as well."

Another slap, thought Dany, color rising to her face.

The rest was a tedium the queen knew well. She sat upon her cushions, listening, one foot jiggling with impatience. Jhiqui brought a platter of figs and ham at midday. There seemed to be no end to the petitioners. For every two she sent off smiling, one left red-eyed or muttering.

It was close to sunset before Daario Naharis appeared with his new Stormcrows, the Westerosi who had come over to him from the Windblown. Dany found herself glancing at them as yet another petitioner droned on and on. *These are my people. I am their rightful queen.* They seemed a scruffy bunch, but that was only to be expected of sellswords. The youngest could not have been more than a year older than her; the oldest must have seen sixty namedays. A few sported signs of wealth: gold arm rings, silken tunics, silver-studded sword belts. *Plunder.* For the most part, their clothes were plainly made and showed signs of hard wear.

When Daario brought them forward, she saw that one of them was a woman, big and blonde and all in mail. "Pretty Meris," her captain named her, though *pretty* was the last thing Dany would have called her. She was six feet tall and earless, with a slit nose, deep scars in both cheeks, and the coldest eyes the queen had ever seen. As for the rest . . .

Hugh Hungerford was slim and saturnine, long-legged, long-faced, clad in faded finery. Webber was short and muscular, with spiders tattooed across his head and chest and arms. Red-faced Orson Stone claimed to be a knight, as did lanky Lucifer Long. Will of the Woods leered at her even as he took a knee. Dick Straw had cornflower-blue eyes, hair as white as flax, and an unsettling smile. Ginger Jack's face was hidden behind a bristly orange beard, and his speech was unintelligible. "He bit off half his tongue in his first battle," Hungerford explained to her.

The Dornishmen seemed different. "If it please Your Grace," said Daario, "these three are Greenguts, Gerrold, and Frog."

Greenguts was huge and bald as a stone, with arms thick enough to rival even Strong Belwas. Gerrold was a lean, tall youth with sun streaks in his hair and laughing blue-green eyes. *That smile has won many a maiden's heart, I'll wager.* His cloak was made of soft brown wool lined with sandsilk, a goodly garment.

Frog, the squire, was the youngest of the three, and the least impressive, a solemn, stocky lad, brown of hair and eye. His face was squarish, with a high forehead, heavy jaw, and broad nose. The stubble on his cheeks and chin made him look like a boy trying to grow his first beard. Dany had no inkling why anyone would call him Frog. *Perhaps he can jump farther than the others.*

"You may rise," she said. "Daario tells me you come to us from Dorne. Dornishmen will always have a welcome at my court. Sunspear stayed loyal to my father when the Usurper stole his throne. You must have faced many perils to reach me."

"Too many," said Gerrold, the handsome one with the sun-streaked hair. "We were six when we left Dorne, Your Grace."

"I am sorry for your losses." The queen turned to his large companion. "Greenguts is a queer sort of name."

"A jape, Your Grace. From the ships. I was greensick the whole way from Volantis. Heaving and . . . well, I shouldn't say."

Dany giggled. "I think that I can guess, ser. It is *ser,* is it not? Daario tells me that you are a knight."

"If it please Your Grace, we are all three knights."

Dany glanced at Daario and saw anger flash across his face. *He did not know.* "I have need of knights," she said.

Ser Barristan's suspicions had awakened. "Knighthood is easily claimed this far from Westeros. Are you prepared to defend that boast with sword or lance?"

"If need be," said Gerrold, "though I will not claim that any of us is the equal of Barristan the Bold. Your Grace, I beg your pardon, but we have come before you under false names."

"I knew someone else who did that once," said Dany, "a man called Arstan Whitebeard. Tell me your true names, then."

"Gladly . . . but if we may beg the queen's indulgence, is there some place with fewer eyes and ears?"

Games within games. "As you wish. Skahaz, clear my court."

The Shavepate roared out orders. His Brazen Beasts did the rest, herding the other Westerosi and the rest of the day's petitioners from the hall. Her counselors remained.

"Now," Dany said, "your names."

Handsome young Gerrold bowed. "Ser Gerris Drinkwater, Your Grace. My sword is yours."

Greenguts crossed his arms against his chest. "And my warhammer. I'm Ser Archibald Yronwood."

"And you, ser?" the queen asked the boy called Frog.

"If it please Your Grace, may I first present my gift?"

"If you wish," Daenerys said, curious, but as Frog started forward Daario Naharis stepped in front of him and held out a gloved hand. "Give this gift to me."

Stone-faced, the stocky lad bent, unlaced his boot, and drew a yellowed parchment from a hidden flap within.

"This is your gift? A scrap of writing?" Daario snatched the parchment out of the Dornishman's hands and unrolled it, squinting at the seals and signatures. "Very pretty, all the gold and ribbons, but I do not read your Westerosi scratchings."

"Bring it to the queen," Ser Barristan commanded. "Now."

Dany could feel the anger in the hall. "I am only a young girl, and young girls must have their gifts," she said lightly. "Daario, please, you must not tease me. Give it here."

The parchment was written in the Common Tongue. The queen unrolled it slowly, studying the seals and signatures. When she saw the name Ser Willem Darry, her heart beat a little faster. She read it over once, and then again.

"May we know what it says, Your Grace?" asked Ser Barristan.

"It is a secret pact," Dany said, "made in Braavos when I was just a little girl. Ser Willem Darry signed for us, the man who spirited my brother and myself away from Dragonstone before the Usurper's men could take us. Prince Oberyn Martell signed for Dorne, with the Sealord of Braavos as witness." She handed the parchment to Ser Barristan, so he might read it for himself. "The alliance is to be sealed by a marriage, it says. In return for Dorne's help overthrowing the Usurper, my brother Viserys is to take Prince Doran's daughter Arianne for his queen."

The old knight read the pact slowly. "If Robert had known of this, he would have smashed Sunspear as he once smashed Pyke, and claimed the heads of Prince Doran and the Red Viper . . . and like as not, the head of this Dornish princess too."

"No doubt that was why Prince Doran chose to keep the pact a secret," suggested Daenerys. "If my brother Viserys had known that he had a Dornish princess waiting for him, he would have crossed to Sunspear as soon as he was old enough to wed."

"And thereby brought Robert's warhammer down upon himself, and Dorne as well," said Frog. "My father was content to wait for the day that Prince Viserys found his army."

"Your father?"

"Prince Doran." He sank back onto one knee. "Your Grace, I have the honor to be Quentyn Martell, a prince of Dorne and your most leal subject."

Dany laughed.

The Dornish prince flushed red, whilst her own court and counselors gave her puzzled looks. "Radiance?" said Skahaz Shavepate, in the Ghiscari tongue. "Why do you laugh?"

"They call him *frog*," she said, "and we have just learned why. In the Seven Kingdoms there are children's tales of frogs who turn into enchanted princes when kissed by their true love." Smiling at the Dornish knights, she switched back to the Common Tongue. "Tell me, Prince Quentyn, are you enchanted?"

"No, Your Grace."

"I feared as much." *Neither enchanted nor enchanting, alas. A pity he's the prince, and not the one with the wide shoulders and the sandy hair.* "You have come for a kiss, however. You mean to marry me. Is that the way of it? The gift you bring me is your own sweet self. Instead of Viserys and your sister, you and I must seal this pact if I want Dorne."

"My father hoped that you might find me acceptable."

Daario Naharis gave a scornful laugh. "I say you are a pup. The queen needs a man beside her, not a mewling boy. You are no fit husband for a woman such as her. When you lick your lips, do you still taste your mother's milk?"

Ser Gerris Drinkwater darkened at his words. "Mind your tongue, sellsword. You are speaking to a prince of Dorne."

"And to his wet nurse, I am thinking." Daario brushed his thumbs across his sword hilts and smiled dangerously.

Skahaz scowled, as only he could scowl. "This boy might serve for Dorne, but Meereen needs a king of Ghiscari blood."

"I know of this Dorne," said Reznak mo Reznak. "Dorne is sand and scorpions, and bleak red mountains baking in the sun."

Prince Quentyn answered him. "Dorne is fifty thousand spears and swords, pledged to our queen's service."

"Fifty thousand?" mocked Daario. "I count three."

"*Enough,*" Daenerys said. "Prince Quentyn has crossed half the world to offer me his gift, I will not have him treated with discourtesy." She turned to the Dornishmen. "Would that you had come a year ago. I am pledged to wed the noble Hizdahr zo Loraq."

Ser Gerris said, "It is not too late—"

"I will be the judge of that," Daenerys said. "Reznak, see that the prince and his companions are given quarters suitable to their high birth, and that their wants are attended to."

"As you wish, Your Radiance."

The queen rose. "Then we are done for now."

Daario and Ser Barristan followed her up the steps to her apartments. "This changes everything," the old knight said.

"This changes nothing," Dany said, as Irri removed her crown. "What good are three men?"

"Three knights," said Selmy.

"Three liars," Daario said darkly. "They deceived me."

"And bought you too, I do not doubt." He did not trouble to deny it. Dany unrolled the parchment and examined it again. *Braavos. This was done in Braavos, while we were living in the house with the red door.* Why did that make her feel so strange?

She found herself remembering her nightmare. *Sometimes there is truth in dreams.* Could Hizdahr zo Loraq be working for the warlocks, was that what the dream had meant? Could the dream have been a sending? Were the gods telling her to put Hizdahr aside and wed this Dornish prince instead? Something tickled at her memory. "Ser Barristan, what are the arms of House Martell?"

"A sun in splendor, transfixed by a spear."

The sun's son. A shiver went through her. "Shadows and whispers." What else had Quaithe said? *The pale mare and the sun's son. There was a lion in it too, and a dragon. Or am I the dragon?* "Beware the perfumed seneschal." That she remembered. "Dreams and prophecies. Why must they always be in riddles? I hate this. Oh, leave me, ser. Tomorrow is my wedding day."

That night Daario had her every way a man can have a woman, and she gave herself to him willingly. The last time, as the sun was coming up, she used her mouth to make him hard again, as Doreah had taught her long ago, then rode him so wildly that his wound began to bleed again, and for one sweet heartbeat she could not tell whether he was inside of her, or her inside of him.

But when the sun rose upon her wedding day so did Daario Naharis, donning his clothes and buckling on his sword belt with its gleaming golden wantons. "Where are you going?" Dany asked him. "I forbid you to make a sortie today."

"My queen is cruel," her captain said. "If I cannot slay your foes, how shall I amuse myself whilst you are being wed?"

"By nightfall I shall have no foes."

"It is only dawn, sweet queen. The day is long. Time enough for one last sortie. I will bring you back the head of Brown Ben Plumm for a wedding gift."

"No heads," Dany insisted. "Once you brought me flowers."

"Let Hizdahr bring you flowers. He is not one to stoop and pluck a dandelion, true, but he has servants who will be pleased to do it for him. Do I have your leave to go?"

"No." She wanted him to stay and hold her. *One day he will go and not return,* she thought. *One day some archer will put an arrow through his chest, or ten men will fall on him with spears and swords and axes, ten would-be heroes.* Five of them would die, but that would not make her grief easier to bear. *One day I will lose him, as I lost my sun-and-stars. But please gods, not today.* "Come back to bed and kiss me." No one had ever kissed her like Daario Naharis. "I am your queen, and I command you to fuck me."

She had meant it playfully, but Daario's eyes hardened at her words. "Fucking queens is king's work. Your noble Hizdahr can attend to that, once you're wed. And if he proves to be too highborn for such sweaty work, he has servants who will be pleased to do that for him as well. Or perhaps you can call the Dornish boy into your bed, and his pretty friend as well, why not?" He strode from the bedchamber.

He is going to make a sortie, Dany realized, *and if he takes Ben*

Plumm's head, he'll walk into the wedding feast and throw it at my feet. Seven save me. Why couldn't he be better born?

When he was gone, Missandei brought the queen a simple meal of goat cheese and olives, with raisins for a sweet. "Your Grace needs more than wine to break her fast. You are such a tiny thing, and you will surely need your strength today."

That made Daenerys laugh, coming from a girl so small. She relied so much on the little scribe that she oft forgot that Missandei had only turned eleven. They shared the food together on her terrace. As Dany nibbled on an olive, the Naathi girl gazed at her with eyes like molten gold and said, "It is not too late to tell them that you have decided not to wed."

It is, though, the queen thought, sadly. "Hizdahr's blood is ancient and noble. Our joining will join my freedmen to his people. When we become as one, so will our city."

"Your Grace does not love the noble Hizdahr. This one thinks you would sooner have another for your husband."

I must not think of Daario today. "A queen loves where she must, not where she will." Her appetite had left her. "Take this food away," she told Missandei. "It is time I bathed."

Afterward, as Jhiqui was patting Daenerys dry, Irri approached with her *tokar.* Dany envied the Dothraki maids their loose sandsilk trousers and painted vests. They would be much cooler than her in her *tokar,* with its heavy fringe of baby pearls. "Help me wind this round myself, please. I cannot manage all these pearls by myself."

She should be eager with anticipation for her wedding and the night that would follow, she knew. She remembered the night of her first wedding, when Khal Drogo had claimed her maidenhead beneath the stranger stars. She remembered how frightened she had been, and how excited. Would it be the same with Hizdahr? *No. I am not the girl I was, and he is not my sun-and-stars.*

Missandei reemerged from inside the pyramid. "Reznak and Skahaz beg the honor of escorting Your Grace to the Temple of the Graces. Reznak has ordered your palanquin made ready."

Meereenese seldom rode within their city walls. They preferred palanquins, litters, and sedan chairs, borne upon the shoulders of their slaves. "Horses befoul the streets," one man of Zakh had told her, "slaves do not." Dany had freed the slaves, yet palanquins, litters, and sedan chairs still choked the streets as before, and none of them floated magically through the air.

"The day is too hot to be shut up in a palanquin," said Dany. "Have my silver saddled. I would not go to my lord husband upon the backs of bearers."

"Your Grace," said Missandei, "this one is so sorry, but you cannot ride in a *tokar.*"

The little scribe was right, as she so often was. The *tokar* was not a garment meant for horseback. Dany made a face. "As you say. Not the palanquin, though. I would suffocate behind those drapes. Have them ready a sedan chair." If she must wear her floppy ears, let all the rabbits see her.

When Dany made her descent, Reznak and Skahaz dropped to their knees. "Your Worship shines so brightly, you will blind every man who dares to look upon you," said Reznak. The seneschal wore a *tokar* of maroon samite with golden fringes. "Hizdahr zo Loraq is most fortunate in you . . . and you in him, if I may be so bold as to say. This match will save our city, you will see."

"So we pray. I want to plant my olive trees and see them fruit." *Does it matter that Hizdahr's kisses do not please me? Peace will please me. Am I a queen or just a woman?*

"The crowds will be thick as flies today." The Shavepate was clad in a pleated black skirt and a muscled breastplate, with a brazen helm shaped like a serpent's head beneath one arm.

"Should I be afraid of flies? Your Brazen Beasts will keep me safe from any harm."

It was always dusk inside the base of the Great Pyramid. Walls thirty feet thick muffled the tumult of the streets and kept the heat outside, so it was cool and dim within. Her escort was forming up inside the gates. Horses, mules, and donkeys were stabled in the western walls, elephants in the eastern. Dany had acquired three of those huge, queer beasts with her pyramid. They reminded her of hairless grey mammoths, though their tusks had been bobbed and gilded, and their eyes were sad.

She found Strong Belwas eating grapes, as Barristan Selmy watched a stableboy cinch the girth on his dapple grey. The three Dornishmen were with him, talking, but they broke off when the queen appeared. Their prince went to one knee. "Your Grace, I must entreat you. My father's strength is failing, but his devotion to your cause is as strong as ever. If my manner or my person have displeased you, that is my sorrow, but—"

"If you would please me, ser, be happy for me," Daenerys said. "This is my wedding day. They will be dancing in the Yellow City, I do not doubt." She sighed. "Rise, my prince, and smile. One day I shall return to Westeros to claim my father's throne, and look to Dorne for help. But on this day the Yunkai'i have my city ringed in steel. I may die before I see my Seven Kingdoms. Hizdahr may die. Westeros may be swallowed by the waves." Dany kissed his cheek. "Come. It's time I wed."

Ser Barristan helped her up onto her sedan chair. Quentyn rejoined his fellow Dornishmen. Strong Belwas bellowed for the gates to be opened, and Daenerys Targaryen was carried forth into the sun. Selmy fell in beside her on his dapple grey.

"Tell me," Dany said, as the procession turned toward the Temple of the Graces, "if my father and my mother had been free to follow their own hearts, whom would they have wed?"

"It was long ago. Your Grace would not know them."

"You know, though. Tell me."

The old knight inclined his head. "The queen your mother was always mindful of her duty." He was handsome in his gold-and-silver armor, his white cloak streaming from his shoulders, but he sounded like a man in pain, as if every word were a stone he had to pass. "As a girl, though . . . she was once smitten with a young knight from the stormlands who wore her favor at a tourney and named her queen of love and beauty. A brief thing."

"What happened to this knight?"

"He put away his lance the day your lady mother wed your father. Afterward he became most pious, and was heard to say that only the Maiden could replace Queen Rhaella in his heart. His passion was impossible, of course. A landed knight is no fit consort for a princess of royal blood."

And Daario Naharis is only a sellsword, not fit to buckle on the golden spurs of even a landed knight. "And my father? Was there some woman he loved better than his queen?"

Ser Barristan shifted in the saddle. "Not . . . not loved. Mayhaps *wanted* is a better word, but . . . it was only kitchen gossip, the whispers of washerwomen and stableboys . . ."

"I want to know. I never knew my father. I want to know everything about him. The good and . . . the rest."

"As you command." The white knight chose his words with care. "Prince Aerys . . . as a youth, he was taken with a certain lady of Casterly Rock, a cousin of Tywin Lannister. When she and Tywin wed, your father drank too much wine at the wedding feast and was heard to say that it was a great pity that the lord's right to the first night had been abolished. A drunken jape, no more, but Tywin Lannister was not a man to forget such words, or the . . . the liberties your father took during the bedding." His face reddened. "I have said too much, Your Grace. I—"

"Gracious queen, well met!" Another procession had come up beside her own, and Hizdahr zo Loraq was smiling at her from his own sedan chair. *My king.* Dany wondered where Daario Naharis was, what he was doing. *If this were a story, he would gallop up just as we reached the temple, to challenge Hizdahr for my hand.*

Side by side the queen's procession and Hizdahr zo Loraq's made their slow way across Meereen, until finally the Temple of the Graces loomed up before them, its golden domes flashing in the sun. *How beautiful,* the queen tried to tell herself, but inside her was some foolish little girl who could not help but look about for Daario. *If he loved you, he would come and carry you off at swordpoint, as Rhaegar carried off his northern girl,* the girl in her insisted, but the queen knew that was folly. Even if her captain was mad enough to attempt it, the Brazen Beasts would cut him down before he got within a hundred yards of her.

Galazza Galare awaited them outside the temple doors, surrounded by her sisters in white and pink and red, blue and gold and purple. *There are fewer than there were.* Dany looked for Ezzara and did not see her. *Has the bloody flux taken even her?* Though the queen had let the Astapori starve outside her walls to keep the bloody flux from spreading, it was spreading nonetheless. Many had been stricken: freedmen, sellswords, Brazen Beasts, even Dothraki, though as yet none of the Unsullied had been touched. She prayed the worst was past.

The Graces brought forth an ivory chair and a golden bowl. Holding her *tokar* daintily so as not to tread upon its fringes, Daenerys Targaryen eased herself onto the chair's plush velvet seat, and Hizdahr zo Loraq went to his knees, unlaced her sandals, and washed her feet whilst fifty eunuchs sang and ten thousand eyes looked on. *He has gentle hands,* she mused, as warm fragrant oils ran between her toes. *If he has a gentle heart as well, I may grow fond of him in time.*

When her feet were clean, Hizdahr dried them with a soft towel, laced her sandals on again, and helped her stand. Hand in hand, they followed the Green Grace inside the temple, where the air was thick with incense and the gods of Ghis stood cloaked in shadows in their alcoves.

Four hours later, they emerged again as man and wife, bound together wrist and ankle with chains of yellow gold.

JON

Queen Selyse descended upon Castle Black with her daughter and her daughter's fool, her serving girls and lady companions, and a retinue of knights, sworn swords, and men-at-arms fifty strong. *Queen's men all,* Jon Snow knew. *They may attend Selyse, but it is Melisandre they serve.* The red priestess had warned him of their coming almost a day before the raven arrived from Eastwatch with the same message.

He met the queen's party by the stables, accompanied by Satin, Bowen Marsh, and half a dozen guards in long black cloaks. It would never do to come before this queen without a retinue of his own, if half of what they said of her was true. She might mistake him for a stableboy and hand him the reins of her horse.

The snows had finally moved off to the south and given them a respite. There was even a hint of warmth in the air as Jon Snow took a knee before this southron queen. "Your Grace. Castle Black welcomes you and yours."

Queen Selyse looked down at him. "My thanks. Please escort me to your lord commander."

"My brothers chose me for that honor. I am Jon Snow."

"You? They said you were young, but . . ." Queen Selyse's face was pinched and pale. She wore a crown of red gold with points in the shape of flames, a twin to that worn by Stannis. "... you may rise, Lord Snow. This is my daughter, Shireen."

"Princess." Jon inclined his head. Shireen was a homely child, made even uglier by the greyscale that had left her neck and part of her cheek stiff and grey and cracked. "My brothers and I are at your service," he told the girl.

Shireen reddened. "Thank you, my lord."

"I believe you are acquainted with my kinsman, Ser Axell Florent?" the queen went on.

"Only by raven." *And report.* The letters he'd received from Eastwatch-by-the-Sea had a deal to say of Axell Florent, very little of it good. "Ser Axell."

"Lord Snow." A stout man, Florent had short legs and a thick chest. Coarse hair covered his cheeks and jowls and poked from his ears and nostrils.

"My loyal knights," Queen Selyse went on. "Ser Narbert, Ser Benethon, Ser Brus, Ser Patrek, Ser Dorden, Ser Malegorn, Ser Lambert, Ser Perkin." Each worthy bowed in turn. She did not trouble to name her fool, but the cowbells on his antlered hat and the motley tattooed across his puffy cheeks made him hard to overlook. *Patchface.* Cotter Pyke's letters had made mention of him as well. Pyke claimed he was a simpleton.

Then the queen beckoned to another curious member of her entourage: a tall gaunt stick of a man, his height accentuated by an outlandish three-tiered hat of purple felt. "And here we have the honorable Tycho Nestoris, an emissary of the Iron Bank of Braavos, come to treat with His Grace King Stannis."

The banker doffed his hat and made a sweeping bow. "Lord Commander. I thank you and your brothers for your hospitality." He spoke the Common Tongue flawlessly, with only the slightest hint of accent. Half a foot taller than Jon, the Braavosi sported a beard as thin as a rope sprouting from his chin and reaching almost to his waist. His robes were a somber purple, trimmed with ermine. A high stiff collar framed his narrow face. "I hope we shall not inconvenience you too greatly."

"Not at all, my lord. You are most welcome." *More welcome than this queen, if truth be told.* Cotter Pyke had sent a raven ahead to advise them of the banker's coming. Jon Snow had thought of little since.

Jon turned back to the queen. "The royal chambers in the King's Tower have been prepared for Your Grace for so long as you wish to remain with us. This is our Lord Steward, Bowen Marsh. He will find quarters for your men."

"How kind of you to make room for us." The queen's words were courteous enough, though her tone said, *It is no more than your duty, and you had best hope these quarters please me.* "We will not be with you long. A few days at the most. It is our intent to press on to our new seat at the Nightfort as soon as we are rested. The journey from Eastwatch was wearisome."

"As you say, Your Grace," said Jon. "You will be cold and hungry, I am sure. A hot meal awaits you in our common room."

"Very good." The queen glanced about the yard. "First, though, we wish to consult with the Lady Melisandre."

"Of course, Your Grace. Her apartments are in the King's Tower as well. This way, if you will?" Queen Selyse nodded, took her daughter by the hand, and permitted him to lead them from the stables. Ser Axell, the Braavosi banker, and the rest of her party followed, like so many ducklings done up in wool and fur.

"Your Grace," said Jon Snow, "my builders have done all they can to make the Nightfort ready to receive you . . . yet much of it remains in ruins. It is a large castle, the largest on the Wall, and we have only been able to restore a part of it. You might be more comfortable back at Eastwatch-by-the-Sea."

Queen Selyse sniffed. "We are done with Eastwatch. We did not like it there. A queen should be mistress beneath her own roof. We found your Cotter Pyke to be an uncouth and unpleasant man, quarrelsome and niggardly."

You should hear what Cotter says of you. "I am sorry for that, but I fear Your Grace will find conditions at the Nightfort even less to your liking. We speak of a fortress, not a palace. A grim place, and cold. Whereas Eastwatch—"

"Eastwatch *is not safe.*" The queen put a hand on her daughter's shoulder. "This is the king's true heir. Shireen will one day sit the Iron Throne and rule the Seven Kingdoms. She must be kept from harm, and Eastwatch is where the attack will come. This Nightfort is the place my husband has chosen for our seat, and there we shall abide. We—oh!"

An enormous shadow emerged from behind the shell of the Lord Commander's Tower. Princess Shireen gave a shriek, and three of the queen's knights gasped in harmony. Another swore. "*Seven save us,*" he said, quite forgetting his new red god in his shock.

"Don't be afraid," Jon told them. "There's no harm in him, Your Grace. This is Wun Wun."

"Wun Weg Wun Dar Wun." The giant's voice rumbled like a boulder crashing down a mountainside. He sank to his knees before them. Even kneeling, he loomed over them. "Kneel queen. Little queen." Words that Leathers had taught him, no doubt.

Princess Shireen's eyes went wide as dinner plates. "He's a *giant*! A real true giant, like from the stories. But why does he talk so funny?"

"He only knows a few words of the Common Tongue as yet," said Jon. "In their own land, giants speak the Old Tongue."

"Can I touch him?"

"Best not," her mother warned. "Look at him. A filthy creature." The queen turned her frown on Jon. "Lord Snow, what is this bestial creature doing on our side of the Wall?"

"Wun Wun is a guest of the Night's Watch, as you are."

The queen did not like that answer. Nor did her knights. Ser Axell grimaced in disgust, Ser Brus gave a nervous titter, Ser Narbert said, "I had been told all the giants were dead."

"Almost all." *Ygritte wept for them.*

"In the dark the dead are dancing." Patchface shuffled his feet in a grotesque dance step. "I know, I know, oh oh oh." At Eastwatch someone had sewn him a motley cloak of beaver pelts, sheepskins, and rabbit fur. His hat sported antlers hung with bells and long brown flaps of squirrel fur that hung down over his ears. Every step he took set him to ringing.

Wun Wun gaped at him with fascination, but when the giant reached for him the fool hopped back away, jingling. "Oh no, oh no, oh no." That brought Wun Wun lurching to his feet. The queen grabbed hold of Princess Shireen and pulled her back, her knights reached for their swords, and Patchface reeled away in alarm, lost his footing, and plopped down on his arse in a snowdrift.

Wun Wun began to laugh. A giant's laughter could put to shame a dragon's roar. Patchface covered his ears, Princess Shireen pressed her face into her mother's furs, and the boldest of the queen's knights moved forward, steel in hand. Jon raised an arm to block his path. "You do *not* want to anger him. Sheathe your steel, ser. Leathers, take Wun Wun back to Hardin's."

"Eat now, Wun Wun?" asked the giant.

"Eat now," Jon agreed. To Leathers he said, "I'll send out a bushel of vegetables for him and meat for you. Start a fire."

Leathers grinned. "I will, m'lord, but Hardin's is bone cold. Perhaps m'lord could send out some wine to warm us?"

"For you. Not him." Wun Wun had never tasted wine until he came to Castle Black, but once he had, he had taken a gigantic liking to it. *Too much a liking.* Jon had enough to contend with just now without adding a drunken giant to the mix. He turned back to the queen's knights. "My lord father used to say a man should never draw his sword unless he means to use it."

"Using it was my intent." The knight was clean-shaved and wind-burnt; beneath a cloak of white fur he wore a cloth-of-silver surcoat emblazoned with a blue five-pointed star. "I had been given to understand that the Night's Watch defended the realm against such monsters. No one mentioned keeping them as pets."

Another bloody southron fool. "You are . . . ?"

"Ser Patrek of King's Mountain, if it please my lord."

"I do not know how you observe guest right on your mountain, ser. In the north we hold it sacred. Wun Wun is a guest here."

Ser Patrek smiled. "Tell me, Lord Commander, should the Others turn up, do you plan to offer hospitality to them as well?" The knight turned to his queen. "Your Grace, that is the King's Tower there, if I am not mistaken. If I may have the honor?"

"As you wish." The queen took his arm and swept past the men of the Night's Watch with never a second glance.

Those flames on her crown are the warmest thing about her. "Lord Tycho," Jon called. "A moment, please."

The Braavosi halted. "No lord I. Only a simple servant of the Iron Bank of Braavos."

"Cotter Pyke informs me that you came to Eastwatch with three ships. A galleas, a galley, and a cog."

"Just so, my lord. The crossing can be perilous in this season. One ship alone may founder, where three together may aid one another. The Iron Bank is always prudent in such matters."

"Perhaps before you leave we might have a quiet word?"

"I am at your service, Lord Commander. And in Braavos we say there is no time like the present. Will that suit?"

"As good as any. Shall we repair to my solar, or would you like to see the top of the Wall?"

The banker glanced up, to where the ice loomed vast and pale against the sky. "I fear it will be bitter cold up top."

"That, and windy. You learn to walk well away from the edge. Men have been blown off. Still. The Wall is like nothing else on earth. You may never have another chance to see it."

"No doubt I shall rue my caution upon my deathbed, but after a long day in the saddle, a warm room sounds preferable to me."

"My solar, then. Satin, some mulled wine, if you would."

Jon's rooms behind the armory were quiet enough, if not especially warm. His fire had gone out some time ago; Satin was not as diligent in feeding it as Dolorous Edd had been. Mormont's raven greeted them with a shriek of "*Corn!*" Jon hung up his cloak. "You come seeking Stannis, is that correct?"

"It is, my lord. Queen Selyse has suggested that we might send word to Deepwood Motte by raven, to inform His Grace that I await his pleasure at the Nightfort. The matter that I mean to put to him is too delicate to entrust to letters."

"A debt." *What else could it be?* "His own debt? Or his brother's?"

The banker pressed his fingers together. "It would not be proper for me to discuss Lord Stannis's indebtedness or lack of same. As to King Robert . . . it was indeed our pleasure to assist His Grace in his need. For so long as Robert lived, all was well. Now, however, the Iron Throne has ceased all repayment."

Could the Lannisters truly be so foolish? "You cannot mean to hold Stannis responsible for his brother's debts."

"The debts belong to the Iron Throne," Tycho declared, "and whosoever sits on that chair must pay them. Since young King Tommen and his counsellors have become so obdurate, we mean to broach the subject with King Stannis. Should he prove himself more worthy of our trust, it would of course be our great pleasure to lend him whatever help he needs."

"*Help,*" the raven screamed. "*Help, help, help.*"

Much of this Jon had surmised the moment he learned that the Iron Bank had sent an envoy to the Wall. "When last we heard, His Grace was marching on Winterfell to confront Lord Bolton and his allies. You may seek him there if you wish, though that carries a risk. You could find yourself caught up in his war."

Tycho bowed his head. "We who serve the Iron Bank face death full as often as you who serve the Iron Throne."

Is that whom I serve? Jon Snow was no longer certain. "I can provide you with horses, provisions, guides, whatever is required to get you as far as Deepwood Motte. From there you will need to make your own way to Stannis." *And you may well find his head upon a spike.* "There will be a price."

"*Price,*" screamed Mormont's raven. "*Price, price.*"

"There is always a price, is there not?" The Braavosi smiled. "What does the Watch require?"

"Your ships, for a start. With their crews."

"All three? How will I return to Braavos?"

"I only need them for a single voyage."

"A hazardous voyage, I assume. *For a start,* you said?"

"We need a loan as well. Gold enough to keep us fed till spring. To buy food and hire ships to bring it to us."

"Spring?" Tycho sighed. "It is not possible, my lord."

What was it Stannis had said to him? *You haggle like a crone with a codfish, Lord Snow. Did Lord Eddard father you on a fishwife?* Perhaps he had at that.

It took the better part of an hour before the impossible became possible, and another hour before they could agree on terms. The flagon of mulled wine that Satin delivered helped them settle the more nettlesome points. By the time Jon Snow signed the parchment the Braavosi drew up, both of them were half-drunk and quite unhappy. Jon thought that a good sign.

The three Braavosi ships would bring the fleet at Eastwatch up to eleven, including the Ibbenese whaler that Cotter Pyke had commandeered on Jon's order, a trading galley out of Pentos similarly impressed, and three battered Lysene warships, remnants of Salladhor Saan's former fleet driven back north by the autumn storms. All three of Saan's ships had been in dire need of refitting, but by now the work should be complete.

Eleven ships was not wise enough, but if he waited any longer, the free folk at Hardhome would be dead by the time the rescue fleet arrived. *Sail now or not at all.* Whether Mother Mole and her people would be desperate enough to entrust their lives to the Night's Watch, though . . .

The day had darkened by the time he and Tycho Nestoris left the solar. Snow had begun to fall. "Our respite was a brief one, it would seem." Jon drew his cloak about himself more tightly.

"Winter is nigh upon us. The day I left Braavos, there was ice on the canals."

"Three of my men passed through Braavos not long ago," Jon told him. "An old maester, a singer, and a young steward. They were escorting a wildling girl and her child to Oldtown. I do not suppose you chanced to encounter them?"

"I fear not, my lord. Westerosi pass through Braavos every day, but most come and go from the Ragman's Harbor. The ships of the Iron Bank moor at the Purple Harbor. If you wish, I can make inquiries after them when I return home."

"No need. By now they should be safe in Oldtown."

"Let us hope so. The narrow sea is perilous this time of year, and of late there have been troubling reports of strange ships seen amongst the Stepstones."

"Salladhor Saan?"

"The Lysene pirate? Some say he has returned to his old haunts, this is so. And Lord Redwyne's war fleet creeps through the Broken Arm as well. On its way home, no doubt. But these men and their ships are well-known to us. No, these other sails . . . from farther east, perhaps . . . one hears queer talk of dragons."

"Would that we had one here. A dragon might warm things up a bit."

"My lord jests. You will forgive me if I do not laugh. We Braavosi are descended from those who fled Valyria and the wroth of its dragonlords. We do not jape of dragons."

No, I suppose not. "My apologies, Lord Tycho."

"None is required, Lord Commander. Now I find that I am hungry. Lending such large sums of gold will give a man an appetite. Will you be so good as to point me to your feast hall?"

"I will take you there myself." Jon gestured. "This way."

Once there, it would have been discourteous not to break bread with the banker, so Jon sent Satin off to fetch them food. The novelty of newcomers had brought out almost all the men who were not on duty or asleep, so the cellar was crowded and warm.

The queen herself was absent, as was her daughter. By now presumably they were settling into the King's Tower. But Ser Brus and Ser Malegorn were on hand, entertaining such brothers as had gathered with the latest tidings from Eastwatch and beyond the sea. Three of the queen's ladies sat together, attended by their serving maids and a dozen admiring men of the Night's Watch.

Nearer the door, the Queen's Hand was attacking a brace of capons, sucking the meat off the bones and washing down each bite with ale. When he espied Jon Snow, Axell Florent tossed a bone aside, wiped his mouth with the back of his hand, and sauntered over. With his bowed legs, barrel chest, and prominent ears, he presented a comical appearance, but Jon knew better than to laugh at him. He was an uncle to Queen Selyse and had been among the first to follow her in accepting Melisandre's red god. *If he is not a kinslayer, he is the next best thing.* Axell Florent's brother had been burned by Melisandre, Maester Aemon had informed him, yet Ser Axell had done little and less to stop it. *What sort of man can stand by idly and watch his own brother being burned alive?*

"Nestoris," said Ser Axell, "and the lord commander. Might I join you?" He lowered himself to the bench before they could reply. "Lord Snow, if I may ask . . . this wildling princess His Grace King Stannis wrote of . . . where might she be, my lord?"

Long leagues from here, Jon thought. *If the gods are good, by now she has found Tormund Giantsbane.* "Val is the younger sister of Dalla, who was Mance Rayder's wife and mother to his son. King Stannis took Val and the child captive after Dalla died in childbed, but she is no princess, not as you mean it."

Ser Axell shrugged. "Whatever she may be, at Eastwatch men claimed the wench was fair. I'd like to see with mine own eyes. Some of these wildling women, well, a man would need to turn them over to do his duty as a husband. If it please the lord commander, bring her out, let us have a look."

"She is not a horse to be paraded for inspection, ser."

"I promise not to count her teeth." Florent grinned. "Oh, never fear, I'll treat her with all the courtesy she is due."

He knows I do not have her. A village has no secrets, and no more did Castle Black. Val's absence was not spoken of openly, but some men knew, and in the common hall at night the brothers talked. *What has he heard?* Jon wondered. *How much does he believe?* "Forgive me, ser, but Val will not be joining us."

"I'll go to her. Where do you keep the wench?"

Away from you. "Somewhere safe. Enough, ser."

The knight's face grew flushed. "My lord, have you forgotten who I am?" His breath smelled of ale and onions. "Must I speak to the queen? A word from Her Grace and I can have this wildling girl delivered naked to the hall for our inspection."

That would be a pretty trick, even for a queen. "The queen would never presume upon our hospitality," Jon said, hoping that was true. "Now I fear I must take my leave, before I forget the duties of a host. Lord Tycho, pray excuse me."

"Yes, of course," the banker said. "A pleasure."

Outside, the snow was coming down more heavily. Across the yard the King's Tower had turned into a hulking shadow, the lights in its windows obscured by falling snow.

Back in his solar, Jon found the Old Bear's raven perched on the back of the oak-and-leather chair behind the trestle table. The bird began to scream for food the moment he entered. Jon took a fistful of dried kernels from the sack by the door and scattered them on the floor, then claimed the chair.

Tycho Nestoris had left behind a copy of their agreement. Jon read it over thrice. *That was simple,* he reflected. *Simpler than I dared hope. Simpler than it should have been.*

It gave him an uneasy feeling. Braavosi coin would allow the Night's Watch to buy food from the south when their own stores ran short, food enough to see them through the winter, however long it might prove to be. *A long hard winter will leave the Watch so deep in debt that we will never climb out,* Jon reminded himself, *but when the choice is debt or death, best borrow.*

He did not have to like it, though. And come spring, when the time came to repay all that gold, he would like it even less. Tycho Nestoris had impressed him as cultured and courteous, but the Iron Bank of Braavos had a fearsome reputation when collecting debts. Each of the Nine Free Cities had its bank, and some had more than one, fighting over every coin like dogs over a bone, but the Iron Bank was richer and more powerful than all the rest combined. When princes defaulted on their debts to lesser banks, ruined bankers sold their wives and children into slavery and opened their own veins. When princes failed to repay the Iron Bank, new princes sprang up from nowhere and took their thrones.

As poor plump Tommen may be about to learn. No doubt the Lannisters had good reason for refusing to honor King Robert's debts, but it was folly all the same. If Stannis was not too stiff-necked to accept their terms, the Braavosi would give him all the gold and silver he required, coin enough to buy a dozen sellsword companies, to bribe a hundred lords, to keep his men paid, fed, clothed, and armed. *Unless Stannis is lying dead beneath the walls of Winterfell, he may just have won the Iron Throne.* He wondered if Melisandre had seen *that* in her fires.

Jon sat back, yawned, stretched. On the morrow he would draft orders for Cotter Pyke. *Eleven ships to Hardhome. Bring back as many as you can, women and children first.* It was time they set sail. *Should I go myself, though, or leave it to Cotter?* The Old Bear had led a ranging. *Aye. And never returned.*

Jon closed his eyes. Just for a moment . . .

. . . and woke, stiff as a board, with the Old Bear's raven muttering, "*Snow, Snow,*" and Mully shaking him. "M'lord, you're wanted. Beg pardon, m'lord. A girl's been found."

"A girl?" Jon sat, rubbing the sleep from his eyes with the back of his hands. "Val? Has Val returned?"

"Not Val, m'lord. This side of the Wall, it were."

Arya. Jon straightened. It had to be her.

"*Girl,*" screamed the raven. "*Girl, girl.*"

"Ty and Dannel came on her two leagues south of Mole's Town. They were chasing down some wildlings who scampered off down the kingsroad. Brought them back as well, but then they come on the girl. She's highborn, m'lord, and she's been asking for you."

"How many with her?" He moved to his basin, splashed water on his face. Gods, but he was tired.

"None, m'lord. She come alone. Her horse was dying under her. All skin and ribs it was, lame and lathered. They cut it loose and took the girl for questioning."

A grey girl on a dying horse. Melisandre's fires had not lied, it would seem. But what had become of Mance Rayder and his spearwives? "Where is the girl now?"

"Maester Aemon's chambers, m'lord." The men of Castle Black still called it that, though by now the old maester should be warm and safe in Oldtown. "Girl was blue from the cold, shivering like all get out, so Ty wanted Clydas to have a look at her."

"That's good." Jon felt fifteen years old again. *Little sister.* He rose and donned his cloak.

The snow was still falling as he crossed the yard with Mully. A golden dawn was breaking in the east, but behind Lady Melisandre's window in the King's Tower a reddish light still flickered. *Does she never sleep? What game are you playing, priestess? Did you have some other task for Mance?*

He wanted to believe it would be Arya. He wanted to see her face again, to smile at her and muss her hair, to tell her she was safe. *She won't be safe, though. Winterfell is burned and broken and there are no more safe places.*

He could not keep her here with him, no matter how much he might want to. The Wall was no place for a woman, much less a girl of noble birth. Nor was he about to turn her over to Stannis or Melisandre. The king would only want to marry her to one of his own men, Horpe or Massey or Godry Giantslayer, and the gods alone knew what use the red woman might want to make of her.

The best solution he could see would mean dispatching her to Eastwatch and asking Cotter Pyke to put her on a ship to someplace across the sea, beyond the reach of all these quarrelsome kings. It would need to wait until the ships returned from Hardhome, to be sure. *She could return to Braavos with Tycho Nestoris. Perhaps the Iron Bank could help find some noble family to foster her.* Braavos was the nearest of the Free Cities, though . . . which made it both the best and the worst choice. *Lorath or the Port of Ibben might be safer.* Wherever he might send her, though, Arya would need silver to support her, a roof above her head, someone to protect her. She was only a child.

Maester Aemon's old chambers were so warm that the sudden cloud of steam when Mully pulled the door open was enough to blind the both of them. Within, a fresh fire was burning in the hearth, the logs crackling and spitting. Jon stepped over a puddle of damp clothing. "*Snow, Snow, Snow,*" the ravens called down from above. The girl was curled up near the fire, wrapped in a black woolen cloak three times her size and fast asleep.

She looked enough like Arya to give him pause, but only for a moment. A tall, skinny, coltish girl, all legs and elbows, her brown hair was woven in a thick braid and bound about with strips of leather. She had a long face, a pointy chin, small ears.

But she was too old, far too old. *This girl is almost of an age with me.* "Has she eaten?" Jon asked Mully.

"Only bread and broth, my lord." Clydas rose from a chair. "It is best to go slow, Maester Aemon always said. Any more and she might not have been able to digest it."

Mully nodded. "Dannel had one o' Hobb's sausages and offered her a bite, but she wouldn't touch it."

Jon could not blame her for that. Hobb's sausages were made of grease and salt and things that did not bear thinking about. "Perhaps we should just let her rest."

That was when the girl sat up, clutching the cloak to her small, pale breasts. She looked confused. "Where . . . ?"

"Castle Black, my lady."

"The Wall." Her eyes filled up with tears. "I'm here."

Clydas moved closer. "Poor child. How old are you?"

"Sixteen on my next nameday. And no child, but a woman grown and flowered." She yawned, covered her mouth with the cloak. One bare knee peeked through its folds. "You do not wear a chain. Are you a maester?"

"No," said Clydas, "but I have served one."

She does look a bit like Arya, Jon thought. *Starved and skinny, but her hair's the same color, and her eyes.* "I am told you have been asking after me. I am—"

"—Jon Snow." The girl tossed her braid back. "My house and yours are bound in blood and honor. Hear me, kinsman. My uncle Cregan is hard upon my trail. You must not let him take me back to Karhold."

Jon was staring. *I know this girl.* There was something about her eyes, the way she held herself, the way she talked. For a moment the memory eluded him. Then it came. "Alys Karstark."

That brought the ghost of a smile to her lips. "I was not sure you would remember. I was six the last time you saw me."

"You came to Winterfell with your father." *The father Robb beheaded.* "I don't recall what for."

She blushed. "So I could meet your brother. Oh, there was some other pretext, but that was the real reason. I was almost of an age with Robb, and my father thought we might make a match. There was a feast. I danced with you and your brother both. *He* was very courteous and said that I danced beautifully. You were sullen. My father said that was to be expected in a bastard."

"I remember." It was only half a lie.

"You're still a little sullen," the girl said, "but I will forgive you that if you will save me from my uncle."

"Your uncle . . . would that be Lord Arnolf?"

"He is no lord," Alys said scornfully. "My brother Harry is the rightful lord, and by law I am his heir. A daughter comes before an uncle. Uncle Arnolf is only castellan. He's my great-uncle, actually, my *father's* uncle. Cregan is his son. I suppose that makes him a cousin, but we always called him uncle. Now they mean to make me call him husband." She made a fist. "Before the war I was betrothed to Daryn Hornwood. We were only waiting till I flowered to be wed, but the Kingslayer killed Daryn in the Whispering Wood. My father wrote that he would find some southron lord to wed me, but he never did. Your brother Robb cut off his head for killing Lannisters." Her mouth twisted. "I thought the whole reason they marched south was to kill some Lannisters."

"It was . . . not so simple as that. Lord Karstark slew two prisoners, my lady. Unarmed boys, squires in a cell."

The girl did not seem surprised. "My father never bellowed like the Greatjon, but he was no less dangerous in his wroth. He is dead now too, though. So is your brother. But you and I are here, still living. Is there blood feud between us, Lord Snow?"

"When a man takes the black he puts his feuds behind him. The Night's Watch has no quarrel with Karhold, nor with you."

"Good. I was afraid . . . I begged my father to leave one of my brothers as castellan, but none of them wished to miss the glory and ransoms to be won in the south. Now Torr and Edd are dead. Harry was a prisoner at Maidenpool when last we heard, but that was almost a year ago. He may be dead as well. I did not know where else to turn but to the last son of Eddard Stark."

"Why not the king? Karhold declared for Stannis."

"My *uncle* declared for Stannis, in hopes it might provoke the Lannisters to take poor Harry's head. Should my brother die, Karhold should pass to me, but my uncles want my birthright for their own. Once Cregan gets a child by me they won't need me anymore. He's buried two wives already." She rubbed away a tear angrily, the way Arya might have done it. "Will you help me?"

"Marriages and inheritance are matters for the king, my lady. I will write to Stannis on your behalf, but—"

Alys Karstark laughed, but it was the laughter of despair. "Write, but do not look for a reply. Stannis will be dead before he gets your message. My uncle will see to that."

"What do you mean?"

"Arnolf is rushing to Winterfell, 'tis true, but only so he might put his dagger in your king's back. He cast his lot with Roose Bolton long ago . . . for gold, the promise of a pardon, and poor Harry's head. Lord Stannis is marching to a slaughter. So he cannot help me, and would not even if he could." Alys knelt before him, clutching the black cloak. "You are my only hope, Lord Snow. In your father's name, I beg you. Protect me."

THE BLIND GIRL

er nights were lit by distant stars and the shimmer of moonlight on snow, but every dawn she woke to darkness.

She opened her eyes and stared up blind at the black that
shrouded her, her dream already fading. *So beautiful.* She licked her
lips, remembering. The bleating of the sheep, the terror in the shepherd's eyes, the sound the dogs had made as she killed them one by
one, the snarling of her pack. Game had become scarcer since the
snows began to fall, but last night they had feasted. Lamb and dog
and mutton and the flesh of man. Some of her little grey cousins
were afraid of men, even dead men, but not her. Meat was meat, and
men were prey. She was the night wolf.

But only when she dreamed.

The blind girl rolled onto her side, sat up, sprang to her feet,
stretched. Her bed was a rag-stuffed mattress on a shelf of cold stone,
and she was always stiff and tight when she awakened. She padded
to her basin on small, bare, callused feet, silent as a shadow, splashed
cool water on her face, patted herself dry. *Ser Gregor,* she thought.
Dunsen, Raff the Sweetling. Ser Ilyn, Ser Meryn, Queen Cersei. Her
morning prayer. Or was it? *No,* she thought, *not mine. I am no one.
That is the night wolf's prayer. Someday she will find them, hunt them,
smell their fear, taste their blood. Someday.*

She found her smallclothes in a pile, sniffed at them to make sure they were fresh enough to wear, donned them in her darkness. Her servant's garb was where she'd hung it—a long tunic of undyed wool, roughspun and scratchy. She snapped it out and pulled it down over her head with one smooth practiced motion. Socks came last. One black, one white. The black one had stitching round the top, the white none; she could feel which was which, make sure she got each sock on the right leg. Skinny as they were, her legs were strong and springy and growing longer every day. She was glad of that. A water dancer needs good legs. Blind Beth was no water dancer, but she would not be Beth forever.

She knew the way to the kitchens, but her nose would have led her there even if she hadn't. *Hot peppers and fried fish,* she decided, sniffing down the hall, *and bread fresh from Umma's oven.* The smells made her belly rumble. The night wolf had feasted, but that would not fill the blind girl's belly. Dream meat could not nourish her, she had learned that early on.

She broke her fast on sardines, fried crisp in pepper oil and served so hot they burned her fingers. She mopped up the leftover oil with a chunk of bread torn off the end of Umma's morning loaf and washed it all down with a cup of watered wine, savoring the tastes and the smells, the rough feel of the crust beneath her fingers, the slickness of the oil, the sting of the hot pepper when it got into the half-healed scrape on the back of the hand. *Hear, smell, taste, feel,* she reminded herself. *There are many ways to know the world for those who cannot see.*

Someone had entered the room behind her, moving on soft padded slippers quiet as a mouse. Her nostrils flared. *The kindly man.* Men had a different smell than women, and there was a hint of orange in the air as well. The priest was fond of chewing orange rinds to sweeten his breath, whenever he could get them.

"And who are you this morning?" she heard him ask, as he took his seat at the head of the table. *Tap, tap,* she heard, then a tiny crackling sound. *Breaking his first egg.*

"No one," she replied.

"A lie. I know you. You are that blind beggar girl."

"Beth." She had known a Beth once, back at Winterfell when she was Arya Stark. Maybe that was why she'd picked the name. Or maybe it was just because it went so well with *blind*.

"Poor child," said the kindly man. "Would you like to have your eyes back? Ask, and you shall see."

He asked the same question every morning. "I may want them on the morrow. Not today." Her face was still water, hiding all, revealing nothing.

"As you will." She could hear him peeling the egg, then a faint silvery *clink* as he picked up the salt spoon. He liked his eggs well salted. "Where did my poor blind girl go begging last night?"

"The Inn of the Green Eel."

"And what three new things do you know that you did not know when last you left us?"

"The Sealord is still sick."

"This is no new thing. The Sealord was sick yesterday, and he will still be sick upon the morrow."

"Or dead."

"When he is dead, that will be a new thing."

When he is dead, there will be a choosing, and the knives will come out. That was the way of it in Braavos. In Westeros, a dead king was followed by his eldest son, but the Braavosi had no kings. "Tormo Fregar will be the new sealord."

"Is that what they are saying at the Inn of the Green Eel?"

"Yes."

The kindly man took a bite of his egg. The girl heard him chewing. He never spoke with his mouth full. He swallowed, and said, "Some men say there is wisdom in wine. Such men are fools. At other inns other names are being bruited about, never doubt." He took another bite of egg, chewed, swallowed. "What three new things do you *know,* that you did not know before?"

"I *know* that some men are *saying* that Tormo Fregar will surely be the new sealord," she answered. "Some drunken men."

"Better. And what else do you know?"

It is snowing in the riverlands, in Westeros, she almost said. But he would have asked her how she knew that, and she did not think that he would like her answer. She chewed her lip, thinking back to last night. "The whore S'vrone is with child. She is not certain of the father, but thinks it might have been that Tyroshi sellsword that she killed."

"This is good to know. What else?"

"The Merling Queen has chosen a new Mermaid to take the place of the one that drowned. She is the daughter of a Prestayn serving maid, thirteen and penniless, but lovely."

"So are they all, at the beginning," said the priest, "but you cannot know that she is lovely unless you have seen her with your own eyes, and you have none. Who are you, child?"

"No one."

"Blind Beth the beggar girl is who I see. She is a wretched liar, that one. See to your duties. *Valar morghulis.*"

"*Valar dohaeris.*" She gathered up her bowl and cup, knife and spoon, and pushed to her feet. Last of all she grasped her stick. It was five feet long, slender and supple, thick as her thumb, with leather wrapped around the shaft a foot from the top. *Better than eyes, once you learn how to use it,* the waif had told her.

That was a lie. They often lied to her, to test her. No stick was better than a pair of eyes. It was good to have, though, so she always kept it close. Umma had taken to calling her Stick, but names did not matter. She was her. *No one. I am no one. Just a blind girl, just a servant of Him of Many Faces.*

Each night at supper the waif brought her a cup of milk and told her to drink it down. The drink had a queer, bitter taste that the blind girl soon learned to loathe. Even the faint smell that warned her what it was before it touched her tongue soon made her feel like retching, but she drained the cup all the same.

"How long must I be blind?" she would ask.

"Until darkness is as sweet to you as light," the waif would say, "or until you ask us for your eyes. Ask and you shall see."

And then you will send me away. Better blind than that. They would not make her yield.

On the day she had woken blind, the waif took her by the hand and led her through the vaults and tunnels of the rock on which the House of Black and White was built, up the steep stone steps into the temple proper. "Count the steps as you climb," she had said. "Let your fingers brush the wall. There are markings there, invisible to the eye, plain to the touch."

That was her first lesson. There had been many more.

Poisons and potions were for the afternoons. She had smell and touch and taste to help her, but touch and taste could be perilous when grinding poisons, and with some of the waif's more toxic concoctions even smell was less than safe. Burned pinky tips and blistered lips became familiar to her, and once she made herself so sick she could not keep down any food for days.

Supper was for language lessons. The blind girl understood Braavosi and could speak it passably, she had even lost most of her barbaric accent, but the kindly man was not content. He was insisting that she improve her High Valyrian and learn the tongues of Lys and Pentos too.

In the evening she played the lying game with the waif, but without eyes to see the game was very different. Sometimes all she had to go on was tone and choice of words; other times the waif allowed her to lay hands upon her face. At first the game was much, much harder, the next thing to impossible . . . but just when she was near the point of screaming with frustration, it all became much easier. She learned to *hear* the lies, to feel them in the play of the muscles around the mouth and eyes.

Many of her other duties had remained the same, but as she went about them she stumbled over furnishings, walked into walls, dropped trays, got hopelessly helplessly lost inside the temple. Once she almost fell headlong down the steps, but Syrio Forel had taught her balance in another lifetime, when she was the girl called Arya, and somehow she recovered and caught herself in time.

Some nights she might have cried herself to sleep if she had still been Arry or Weasel or Cat, or even Arya of House Stark . . . but no one had no tears. Without eyes, even the simplest task was perilous. She burned herself a dozen times as she worked with Umma in the kitchens. Once, chopping onions, she cut her finger down to the bone. Twice she could not even find her own room in the cellar and had to sleep on the floor at the base of the steps. All the nooks and alcoves made the temple treacherous, even after the blind girl had learned to use her ears; the way her footsteps bounced off the ceiling and echoed round the legs of the thirty tall stone gods made the walls themselves seem to move, and the pool of still black water did strange things to sound as well.

"You have five senses," the kindly man said. "Learn to use the other four, you will have fewer cuts and scrapes and scabs."

She could feel air currents on her skin now. She could find the kitchens by their smell, tell men from women by their scents. She knew Umma and the servants and the acolytes by the pattern of their footfalls, could tell one from the other before they got close enough to smell (but not the waif or the kindly man, who hardly made a sound at all unless they wanted to). The candles burning in the temple had scents as well; even the unscented ones gave off faint wisps of smoke from their wicks. They had as well been shouting, once she had learned to use her nose.

The dead men had their own smell too. One of her duties was to find them in the temple every morning, wherever they had chosen to lie down and close their eyes after drinking from the pool.

This morning she found two.

One man had died at the feet of the Stranger, a single candle flickering above him. She could feel its heat, and the scent that it gave off tickled her nose. The candle burned with a dark red flame, she knew; for those with eyes, the corpse would have seemed awash in a ruddy glow. Before summoning the serving men to carry him away, she knelt and felt his face, tracing the line of his jaw, brushing her fingers across his cheeks and nose, touching his hair. *Curly hair, and thick. A handsome face, unlined. He was young.* She wondered what had brought him here to seek the gift of death. Dying bravos oft found their way to the House of Black and White, to hasten their ends, but this man had no wounds that she could find.

The second body was that of an old woman. She had gone to sleep upon a dreaming couch, in one of the hidden alcoves where special candles conjured visions of things loved and lost. A sweet death and a gentle one, the kindly man was fond of saying. Her fingers told her that the old woman had died with a smile on her face. She had not been dead long. Her body was still warm to the touch. *Her skin is so soft, like old thin leather that's been folded and wrinkled a thousand times.*

When the serving men arrived to bear the corpse away, the blind girl followed them. She let their footsteps be her guide, but when they made their descent she counted. She knew the counts of all the steps by heart. Under the temple was a maze of vaults and tunnels where even men with two good eyes were often lost, but the blind girl had learned every inch of it, and she had her stick to help her find her way should her memory falter.

The corpses were laid out in the vault. The blind girl went to work in the dark, stripping the dead of boots and clothes and other possessions, emptying their purses and counting out their coins. Telling one coin from another by touch alone was one of the first things the waif had taught her, after they took away her eyes. The Braavosi coins were old friends; she need only brush her fingertips across their faces to recognize them. Coins from other lands and cities were harder, especially those from far away. Volantene honors were most common, little coins no bigger than a penny with a crown on one side and a skull on the other. Lysene coins were oval and showed a naked woman. Other coins had ships stamped onto them, or elephants, or goats. The Westerosi coins showed a king's head on the front and a dragon on the back.

The old woman had no purse, no wealth at all but for a ring on one thin finger. On the handsome man she found four golden dragons out of Westeros. She was running the ball of her thumb across the most worn of them, trying to decide which king it showed, when she heard the door opening softly behind her.

"Who is there?" she asked.

"No one." The voice was deep, harsh, cold.

And moving. She stepped to one side, grabbed for her stick, snapped it up to protect her face. Wood *clacked* against wood. The force of the blow almost knocked the stick from her hand. She held on, slashed back . . . and found only empty air where he should have been. "Not there," the voice said. "Are you blind?"

She did not answer. Talking would only muddle any sounds he

might be making. He would be moving, she knew. *Left or right?* She jumped left, swung right, hit nothing. A stinging cut from behind her caught her in the back of the legs. "Are you deaf?" She spun, the stick in her left hand, whirling, missing. From the left she heard the sound of laughter. She slashed right.

This time she connected. Her stick smacked off his own. The impact sent a jolt up her arm. "Good," the voice said.

The blind girl did not know whom the voice belonged to. One of the acolytes, she supposed. She did not remember ever hearing his voice before, but what was there to say that the servants of the Many-Faced God could not change their voices as easily as they did their faces? Besides her, the House of Black and White was home to two serving men, three acolytes, Umma the cook, and the two priests that she called the waif and the kindly man. Others came and went, sometimes by secret ways, but those were the only ones who lived here. Her nemesis could be any of them.

The girl darted sideways, her stick spinning, heard a sound behind her, whirled in that direction, struck at air. And all at once his own stick was between her legs, tangling them as she tried to turn again, scraping down her shin. She stumbled and went down to one knee, so hard she bit her tongue.

There she stopped. *Still as stone. Where is he?*

Behind her, he laughed. He rapped her smartly on one ear, then cracked her knuckles as she was scrambling to her feet. Her stick fell clattering to the stone. She hissed in fury.

"Go on. Pick it up. I am done beating you for today."

"No one beat me." The girl crawled on all fours until she found her stick, then sprang back to her feet, bruised and dirty. The vault was still and silent. He was gone. Or was he? He could be standing right beside her, she would never know. *Listen for his breathing,* she told herself, but there was nothing. She gave it another moment, then put her stick aside and resumed her work. *If I had my eyes, I could beat him bloody.* One day the kindly man would give them back, and she would show them all.

The old woman's corpse was cool by now, the bravo's body stiffening. The girl was used to that. Most days, she spent more time with the dead than with the living. She missed the friends she'd had when she was Cat of the Canals; Old Brusco with his bad back, his daughters Talea and Brea, the mummers from the Ship, Merry and her whores at the Happy Port, all the other rogues and wharfside scum. She missed Cat herself the most of all, even more than she missed her eyes. She had liked being Cat, more than she had ever liked being Salty or Squab or Weasel or Arry. *I killed Cat when I killed that singer.* The kindly man had told her that they would have taken her eyes from her anyway, to help her to learn to use her other senses, but not for half a year. Blind acolytes were common in the House of Black and White, but few as young as she. The girl was not sorry, though. Dareon had been a deserter from the Night's Watch; he had deserved to die.

She had said as much to the kindly man. "And are you a god, to decide who should live and who should die?" he asked her. "We give the gift to those marked by Him of Many Faces, after prayers and sacrifice. So has it always been, from the beginning. I have told you of the founding of our order, of how the first of us answered the prayers of slaves who wished for death. The gift was given only to those who yearned for it, in the beginning . . . but one day, the first of us heard a slave praying not for his own death but for his master's. So fervently did he desire this that he offered all he had, that his prayer might be answered. And it seemed to our first brother that this sacrifice would be pleasing to Him of Many Faces, so that night he granted the prayer. Then he went to the slave and said, 'You offered all you had for this man's death, but slaves have nothing but their lives. That is what the god desires of you. For the rest of your days on earth, you will serve him.' And from that moment, we were two." His hand closed around her arm, gently but firmly. "All men must die. We are but death's instruments, not death himself. When you slew the singer, you took god's powers on yourself. We kill men, but we do not presume to judge them. Do you understand?"

No, she thought. "Yes," she said.

"You lie. And that is why you must now walk in darkness until you see the way. Unless you wish to leave us. You need only ask, and you may have your eyes back."

No, she thought. "No," she said.

That evening, after supper and a short session of the lying game, the blind girl tied a strip of rag around her head to hide her useless eyes, found her begging bowl, and asked the waif to help her don Beth's face. The waif had shaved her head for her when they took her eyes; a mummer's cut, she called it, since many mummers did the same so their wigs might fit them better. But it worked for beggars too and helped to keep their heads free from fleas and lice. More than a wig was needed, though. "I could cover you with weeping sores," the waif said, "but then innkeeps and taverners would chase you from their doors." Instead she gave her pox scars and a mummer's mole on one cheek with a dark hair growing from it. "Is it ugly?" the blind girl asked.

"It is not pretty."

"Good." She had never cared if she was pretty, even when she was stupid Arya Stark. Only her father had ever called her that. *Him, and Jon Snow, sometimes.* Her mother used to say she *could* be pretty if she would just wash and brush her hair and take more care with her dress, the way her sister did. To her sister and sister's friends and all the rest, she had just been Arya Horseface. But they were all dead now, even Arya, everyone but her half-brother, Jon. Some nights she heard talk of him, in the taverns and brothels of the Ragman's Harbor. The Black Bastard of the Wall, one man had called him. *Even Jon would never know Blind Beth, I bet.* That made her sad.

The clothes she wore were rags, faded and fraying, but warm clean rags for all that. Under them she hid three knives—one in a boot, one up a sleeve, one sheathed at the small of her back. Braavosi were a kindly folk, by and large, more like to help the poor blind beggar girl than try to do her harm, but there were always a few bad ones who might see her as someone they could safely rob or rape. The blades were for them, though so far the blind girl had not been forced to use them. A cracked wooden begging bowl and belt of hempen rope completed her garb.

She set out as the Titan roared the sunset, counting her way down the steps from the temple door, then tapping to the bridge that took her over the canal to the Isle of the Gods. She could tell that the fog was thick from the clammy way her clothes clung to her and the damp feeling of the air on her bare hands. The mists of Braavos did queer things to sounds as well, she had found. *Half the city will be half-blind tonight.*

As she made her way past the temples, she could hear the acolytes of the Cult of Starry Wisdom atop their scrying tower, singing to the evening stars. A wisp of scented smoke hung in the air, drawing her down the winding path to where the red priests had fired the great iron braziers outside the house of the Lord of Light. Soon she could even feel the heat in the air, as red R'hllor's worshipers lifted their voices in prayer. "*For the night is dark and full of terrors,*" they prayed.

Not for me. Her nights were bathed in moonlight and filled with the songs of her pack, with the taste of red meat torn off the bone, with the warm familiar smells of her grey cousins. Only during the days was she alone and blind.

She was no stranger to the waterfront. Cat used to prowl the wharves and alleys of the Ragman's Harbor selling mussels and oysters and clams for Brusco. With her rag and her shaved head and her mummer's mole, she did not look the same as she had then, but just to be safe she stayed away from the Ship and the Happy Port and the other places where Cat had been best known.

She knew each inn and tavern by its scent. The Black Bargeman had a briny smell. Pynto's stank of sour wine, stinky cheese, and Pynto himself, who never changed his clothes or washed his hair. At the Sailmender's the smoky air was always spiced with the scent of roasting meat. The House of Seven Lamps was fragrant with incense, the Satin Palace with the perfumes of pretty young girls who dreamed of being courtesans.

Each place had its own sounds too. Moroggo's and the Inn of the Green Eel had singers performing most nights. At the Outcast Inn the patrons themselves did the singing, in drunken voices and half a hundred tongues. The Foghouse was always crowded with polemen off the serpent boats, arguing about gods and courtesans and whether or not the Sealord was a fool. The Satin Palace was much quieter, a place of whispered endearments, the soft rustle of silk gowns, and the giggling of girls.

Beth did her begging at a different place every night. She had learned early on that innkeeps and taverners were more apt to tolerate her presence if it was not a frequent occurrence. Last night she had spent outside the Inn of the Green Eel, so tonight she turned right instead of left after the Bloody Bridge and made her way to Pynto's at the other end of Ragman's Harbor, right on the edge of the Drowned Town. Loud and smelly he might be, but Pynto had a soft heart under all his unwashed clothes and bluster. Oft as not, he would let her come inside where it was warm if the place was not too crowded, and now and again he might even let her have a mug of ale and a crust of food whilst regaling her with his stories. In his younger days Pynto had been the most notorious pirate in the Stepstones, to hear him tell it; he loved nothing better than to speak at great length about his exploits.

She was in luck tonight. The tavern was near empty, and she was able to claim a quiet corner not far from the fire. No sooner had she settled there and crossed her legs than something brushed up against her thigh. "You again?" said the blind girl. She scratched his head behind one ear, and the cat jumped up into her lap and began to purr. Braavos was full of cats, and no place more than Pynto's. The old pirate believed they brought good luck and kept his tavern free of vermin. "You know me, don't you?" she whispered. Cats were not fooled by a mummer's moles. They remembered Cat of the Canals.

It was a good night for the blind girl. Pynto was in a jolly mood and gave her a cup of watered wine, a chunk of stinky cheese, and half of an eel pie. "Pynto is a very good man," he announced, then settled down to tell her of the time he seized the spice ship, a tale she had heard a dozen times before.

As the hours passed the tavern filled. Pynto was soon too busy to pay her any mind, but several of his regulars dropped coins into her begging bowl. Other tables were occupied by strangers: Ibbenese whalers who reeked of blood and blubber, a pair of bravos with scented oil in their hair, a fat man out of Lorath who complained that Pynto's booths were too small for his belly. And later three Lyseni, sailors off the *Goodheart*, a storm-wracked galley that had limped into Braavos last night and been seized this morning by the Sealord's guards.

The Lyseni took the table nearest to the fire and spoke quietly over cups of black tar rum, keeping their voices low so no one could overhear. But she was no one and she heard most every word. And for a time it seemed that she could see them too, through the slitted yellow eyes of the tomcat purring in her lap. One was old and one was young and one had lost an ear, but all three had the white-blond hair and smooth fair skin of Lys, where the blood of the old Freehold still ran strong.

The next morning, when the kindly man asked her what three things she knew that she had not known before, she was ready.

"I know why the Sealord seized the *Goodheart*. She was carrying slaves. Hundreds of slaves, women and children, roped together in her hold." Braavos had been founded by escaped slaves, and the slave trade was forbidden here.

"I know where the slaves came from. They were wildlings from Westeros, from a place called Hardhome. An old ruined place, accursed." Old Nan had told her tales of Hardhome, back at Winterfell when she had still been Arya Stark. "After the big battle where the King-Beyond-the-Wall was killed, the wildlings ran away, and this woods witch said that if they went to Hardhome, ships would come and carry them away to someplace warm. But no ships came, except these two Lyseni pirates, *Goodheart* and *Elephant*, that had been driven north by a storm. They dropped anchor off Hardhome to make repairs, and saw the wildlings, but there were thousands and they didn't have room for all of them, so they said they'd just take the women and the children. The wildlings had nothing to eat, so the men sent out their wives and daughters, but as soon as the ships were out to sea, the Lyseni drove them below and roped them up. They meant to sell them all in Lys. Only then they ran into another storm and the ships were parted. The *Goodheart* was so damaged her captain had no choice but to put in here, but the *Elephant* may have made it back to Lys. The Lyseni at Pynto's think that she'll return with more ships. The price of slaves is rising, they said, and there are thousands more women and children at Hardhome."

"It is good to know. This is two. Is there a third?"

"Yes. I know that you're the one who has been hitting me." Her stick flashed out, and cracked against his fingers, sending his own stick clattering to the floor.

The priest winced and snatched his hand back. "And how could a blind girl know that?"

I saw you. "I gave you three. I don't need to give you four." Maybe on the morrow she would tell him about the cat that had followed her home last night from Pynto's, the cat that was hiding in the rafters, looking down on them. *Or maybe not.* If he could have secrets, so could she.

That evening Umma served salt-crusted crabs for supper. When her cup was presented to her, the blind girl wrinkled her nose and drank it down in three long gulps. Then she gasped and dropped the cup. Her tongue was on fire, and when she gulped a cup of wine the flames spread down her throat and up her nose.

"Wine will not help, and water will just fan the flames," the waif told her. "Eat this." A heel of bread was pressed into her hand. The girl stuffed it in her mouth, chewed, swallowed. It helped. A second chunk helped more.

And come the morning, when the night wolf left her and she opened her eyes, she saw a tallow candle burning where no candle had been the night before, its uncertain flame swaying back and forth like a whore at the Happy Port. She had never seen anything so beautiful.

A GHOST IN WINTERFELL

The dead man was found at the base of the inner wall, with his neck broken and only his left leg showing above the snow that had buried him during the night.

If Ramsay's bitches had not dug him up, he might have stayed buried till spring. By the time Ben Bones pulled them off, Grey Jeyne had eaten so much of the dead man's face that half the day was gone before they knew for certain who he'd been: a man-at-arms of four-and-forty years who had marched north with Roger Ryswell. "A drunk," Ryswell declared. "Pissing off the wall, I'll wager. He slipped and fell." No one disagreed. But Theon Greyjoy found himself wondering why any man would climb the snow-slick steps to the battlements in the black of night just to take a piss.

As the garrison broke its fast that morning on stale bread fried in bacon grease (the lords and knights ate the bacon), the talk along the benches was of little but the corpse.

"Stannis has friends inside the castle," Theon heard one serjeant mutter. He was an old Tallhart man, three trees sewn on his ragged surcoat. The watch had just changed. Men were coming in from the cold, stomping their feet to knock the snow off their boots and breeches as the midday meal was served—blood sausage, leeks, and brown bread still warm from the ovens.

"Stannis?" laughed one of Roose Ryswell's riders. "Stannis is snowed to death by now. Else he's run back to the Wall with his tail froze between his legs."

"He could be camped five feet from our walls with a hundred thousand men," said an archer wearing Cerwyn colors. "We'd never see a one o' them through this storm."

Endless, ceaseless, merciless, the snow had fallen day and night. Drifts climbed the walls and filled the crenels along the battlements, white blankets covered every roof, tents sagged beneath the weight. Ropes were strung from hall to hall to help men keep from getting lost as they crossed the yards. Sentries crowded into the guard turrets to warm half-frozen hands over glowing braziers, leaving the wallwalks to the snowy sentinels the squires had thrown up, who grew larger and stranger every night as wind and weather worked their will upon them. Ragged beards of ice grew down the spears clasped in their snowy fists. No less a man than Hosteen Frey, who had been heard growling that he did not fear a little snow, lost an ear to frostbite.

The horses in the yards suffered most. The blankets thrown over them to keep them warm soaked through and froze if not changed regularly. When fires were lit to keep the cold at bay, they did more harm than good. The warhorses feared the flames and fought to get away, injuring themselves and other horses as they twisted at their lines. Only the horses in the stables were safe and warm, but the stables were already overcrowded.

"The gods have turned against us," old Lord Locke was heard to say in the Great Hall. "This is their wroth. A wind as cold as hell itself and snows that never end. We are cursed."

"*Stannis* is cursed," a Dreadfort man insisted. "He is the one out there in the storm."

"Lord Stannis might be warmer than we know," one foolish freerider argued. "His sorceress can summon fire. Might be her red god can melt these snows."

That was unwise, Theon knew at once. The man spoke too loudly, and in the hearing of Yellow Dick and Sour Alyn and Ben Bones. When the tale reached Lord Ramsay, he sent his Bastard's Boys to seize the man and drag him out into the snow. "As you seem so fond of Stannis, we will send you to him," he said. Damon Dance-for-Me gave the freerider a few lashes with his long greased whip. Then, whilst Skinner and Yellow Dick made wagers on how fast his blood would freeze, Ramsay had the man dragged up to the Battlements Gate.

Winterfell's great main gates were closed and barred, and so choked with ice and snow that the portcullis would need to be chipped free before it could be raised. Much the same was true of the Hunter's Gate, though there at least ice was not a problem, since the gate had seen recent use. The Kingsroad Gate had not, and ice had frozen those drawbridge chains rock hard. Which left the Battlements Gate, a small arched postern in the inner wall. Only half a gate, in truth, it had a drawbridge that spanned the frozen moat but no corresponding gateway through the outer wall, offering access to the outer ramparts but not the world beyond.

The bleeding freerider was carried across the bridge and up the steps, still protesting. Then Skinner and Sour Alyn seized his arms and legs and tossed him from the wall to the ground eighty feet below. The drifts had climbed so high that they swallowed the man bodily . . . but bowmen on the battlements claimed they glimpsed him sometime later, dragging a broken leg through the snow. One feathered his rump with an arrow as he wriggled away. "He will be dead within the hour," Lord Ramsay promised.

"Or he'll be sucking Lord Stannis's cock before the sun goes down," Whoresbane Umber threw back.

"He best take care it don't break off," laughed Rickard Ryswell. "Any man out there in this, his cock is frozen hard."

"Lord Stannis is lost in the storm," said Lady Dustin. "He's leagues away, dead or dying. Let winter do its worst. A few more days and the snows will bury him and his army both."

And us as well, thought Theon, marveling at her folly. Lady Barbrey was of the north and should have known better. The old gods might be listening.

Supper was pease porridge and yesterday's bread, and that caused muttering amongst the common men as well; above the salt, the lords and knights were seen to be eating ham.

Theon was bent over a wooden bowl finishing the last of his own portion of pease porridge when a light touch on his shoulder made him drop his spoon. "Never touch me," he said, twisting down to snatch the fallen utensil off the floor before one of Ramsay's girls could get hold of it. "*Never* touch me."

She sat down next to him, too close, another of Abel's washerwomen. This one was young, fifteen or maybe sixteen, with shaggy blonde hair in need of a good wash and a pair of pouty lips in need of a good kiss. "Some girls like to touch," she said, with a little half-smile. "If it please m'lord, I'm Holly."

Holly the whore, he thought, but she was pretty enough. Once he might have laughed and pulled her into his lap, but that day was done. "What do you want?"

"To see these crypts. Where are they, m'lord? Would you show me?" Holly toyed with a strand of her hair, coiling it around her little finger. "Deep and dark, they say. A good place for touching. All the dead kings watching."

"Did Abel send you to me?"

"Might be. Might be I sent myself. But if it's Abel you're wanting, I could bring him. He'll sing m'lord a sweet song."

Every word she said persuaded Theon that this was all some ploy. *But whose, and to what end?* What could Abel want of him? The man was just a singer, a pander with a lute and a false smile. *He wants to know how I took the castle, but not to make a song of it.* The answer came to him. *He wants to know how we got in so he can get out.* Lord Bolton had Winterfell sewn up tight as a babe's swaddling clothes. No one could come or go without his leave. *He wants to flee, him and his washerwoman.* Theon could not blame him, but even so he said, "I want no part of Abel, or you, or any of your sisters. Just leave me be."

Outside the snow was swirling, dancing. Theon groped his way to the wall, then followed it to the Battlements Gate. He might have taken the guards for a pair of Little Walder's snowmen if he had not seen the white plumes of their breath. "I want to walk the walls," he told them, his own breath frosting in the air.

"Bloody cold up there," one warned.

"Bloody cold down here," the other said, "but you do as you like, turncloak." He waved Theon through the gate.

The steps were snow-packed and slippery, treacherous in the dark.

Once he reached the wallwalk, it did not take him long to find the place where they'd thrown down the freerider. He knocked aside the wall of fresh-fallen snow filling up the crenel and leaned out between the merlons. *I could jump,* he thought. *He lived, why shouldn't I?* He could jump, and . . . *And what? Break a leg and die beneath the snow? Creep away to freeze to death?*

It was madness. Ramsay would hunt him down, with the girls. Red Jeyne and Jez and Helicent would tear him to pieces if the gods were good. Or worse, he might be taken back alive. "I have to remember my *name,*" he whispered.

The next morning Ser Aenys Frey's grizzled squire was found naked and dead of exposure in the old castle lichyard, his face so obscured by hoarfrost that he appeared to be wearing a mask. Ser Aenys put it forth that the man had drunk too much and gotten lost in the storm, though no one could explain why he had taken off his clothes to go outside. *Another drunkard,* Theon thought. Wine could drown a host of suspicions.

Then, before the day was done, a crossbowman sworn to the Flints turned up in the stables with a broken skull. Kicked by a horse, Lord Ramsay declared. *A club, more like,* Theon decided.

It all seemed so familiar, like a mummer show that he had seen before. Only the mummers had changed. Roose Bolton was playing the part that Theon had played the last time round, and the dead men were playing the parts of Aggar, Gynir Rednose, and Gelmarr the Grim. *Reek was there too,* he remembered, *but he was a different Reek, a Reek with bloody hands and lies dripping from his lips, sweet as honey. Reek, Reek, it rhymes with sneak.*

The deaths set Roose Bolton's lords to quarreling openly in the Great Hall. Some were running short of patience. "How long must we sit here waiting for this king who never comes?" Ser Hosteen Frey demanded. "We should take the fight to Stannis and make an end to him."

"Leave the castle?" croaked one-armed Harwood Stout. His tone suggested he would sooner have his remaining arm hacked off. "Would you have us charge blindly into the snow?"

"To fight Lord Stannis we would first need to find him," Roose

Ryswell pointed out. "Our scouts go out the Hunter's Gate, but of late, none of them return."

Lord Wyman Manderly slapped his massive belly. "White Harbor does not fear to ride with you, Ser Hosteen. Lead us out, and my knights will ride behind you."

Ser Hosteen turned on the fat man. "Close enough to drive a lance through my back, aye. Where are my kin, Manderly? Tell me that. Your guests, who brought your son back to you."

"His bones, you mean." Manderly speared a chunk of ham with his dagger. "I recall them well. Rhaegar of the round shoulders, with his glib tongue. Bold Ser Jared, so swift to draw his steel. Symond the spymaster, always clinking coins. They brought home Wendel's bones. It was Tywin Lannister who returned Wylis to me, safe and whole, as he had promised. A man of his word, Lord Tywin, Seven save his soul." Lord Wyman popped the meat into his mouth, chewed it noisily, smacked his lips, and said, "The road has many dangers, ser. I gave your brothers guest gifts when we took our leave of White Harbor. We swore we would meet again at the wedding. Many and more bore witness to our parting."

"Many and more?" mocked Aenys Frey. "Or you and yours?"

"What are you suggesting, Frey?" The Lord of White Harbor wiped his mouth with his sleeve. "I do not like your tone, ser. No, not one bloody bit."

"Step out into the yard, you sack of suet, and I'll serve you all the bloody bits that you can stomach," Ser Hosteen said.

Wyman Manderly laughed, but half a dozen of his knights were on their feet at once. It fell to Roger Ryswell and Barbrey Dustin to calm them with quiet words. Roose Bolton said nothing at all. But Theon Greyjoy saw a look in his pale eyes that he had never seen before—an uneasiness, even a hint of fear.

That night the new stable collapsed beneath the weight of the snow that had buried it. Twenty-six horses and two grooms died, crushed beneath the falling roof or smothered under the snows. It took the best part of the morning to dig out the bodies. Lord Bolton appeared briefly in the outer ward to inspect the scene, then ordered the remaining horses brought inside, along with the mounts still tethered

in the outer ward. And no sooner had the men finished digging out
the dead men and butchering the horses than another corpse was
found.

This one could not be waved away as some drunken tumble or
the kick of a horse. The dead man was one of Ramsay's favorites, the
squat, scrofulous, ill-favored man-at-arms called Yellow Dick. Whether
his dick had actually been yellow was hard to determine, as someone
had sliced it off and stuffed it into his mouth so forcefully they had
broken three of his teeth. When the cooks found him outside the
kitchens, buried up to his neck in a snowdrift, both dick and man
were blue from cold. "Burn the body," Roose Bolton ordered, "and
see that you do not speak of this. I'll not have this tale spread."

The tale spread nonetheless. By midday most of Winterfell had
heard, many from the lips of Ramsay Bolton, whose "boy" Yellow
Dick had been. "When we find the man who did this," Lord Ramsay
promised, "I will flay the skin off him, cook it crisp as crackling, and
make him eat it, every bite." Word went out that the killer's name
would be worth a golden dragon.

The reek within the Great Hall was palpable by eventide. With
hundreds of horses, dogs, and men squeezed underneath one roof,
the floors slimy with mud and melting snow, horseshit, dog turds,
and even human feces, the air redolent with the smells of wet dog,
wet wool, and sodden horse blankets, there was no comfort to be
found amongst the crowded benches, but there was food. The cooks
served up great slabs of fresh horsemeat, charred outside and bloody
red within, with roast onions and neeps . . . and for once, the common
soldiers ate as well as the lords and knights.

The horsemeat was too tough for the ruins of Theon's teeth. His
attempts to chew gave him excruciating pain. So he mashed the neeps
and onions up together with the flat of his dagger and made a meal
of that, then cut the horse up very small, sucked on each piece, and
spat it out. That way at least he had the taste, and some nourishment
from the grease and blood. The bone was beyond him, though, so he
tossed it to the dogs and watched Grey Jeyne make off with it whilst
Sara and Willow snapped at her heels.

Lord Bolton commanded Abel to play for them as they ate. The

bard sang "Iron Lances," then "The Winter Maid." When Barbrey
Dustin asked for something more cheerful, he gave them "The Queen
Took Off Her Sandal, the King Took Off His Crown," and "The Bear
and the Maiden Fair." The Freys joined the singing, and even a few
northmen slammed their fists on the table to the chorus, bellowing,
"*A bear! A bear!*" But the noise frightened the horses, so the singers
soon let off and the music died away.

The Bastard's Boys gathered beneath a wall sconce where a torch
was flaming smokily. Luton and Skinner were throwing dice. Grunt
had a woman in his lap, a breast in his hand. Damon Dance-for-Me
sat greasing up his whip. "*Reek,*" he called. He tapped the whip against
his calf as a man might do to summon his dog. "You are starting to
stink again, Reek."

Theon had no reply for that beyond a soft "Yes."

"Lord Ramsay means to cut your lips off when all this is done,"
said Damon, stroking his whip with a greasy rag.

*My lips have been between his lady's legs. That insolence cannot go
unpunished.* "As you say."

Luton guffawed. "I think he wants it."

"Go away, Reek," Skinner said. "The smell of you turns my
stomach." The others laughed.

He fled quickly, before they changed their minds. His tormentors
would not follow him outside. Not so long as there was food and
drink within, willing women and warm fires. As he left the hall, Abel
was singing "The Maids That Bloom in Spring."

Outside the snow was coming down so heavily that Theon could
not see more than three feet ahead of him. He found himself alone
in a white wilderness, walls of snow looming up to either side of him
chest high. When he raised his head, the snowflakes brushed his cheeks
like cold soft kisses. He could hear the sound of music from the hall
behind him. A soft song now, and sad. For a moment he felt almost
at peace.

Farther on, he came upon a man striding in the opposite direction,
a hooded cloak flapping behind him. When they found themselves
face-to-face their eyes met briefly. The man put a hand on his dagger.
"Theon Turncloak. Theon Kinslayer."

"I'm not. I never . . . I was ironborn."

"False is all you were. How is it you still breathe?"

"The gods are not done with me," Theon answered, wondering if this could be the killer, the night walker who had stuffed Yellow Dick's cock into his mouth and pushed Roger Ryswell's groom off the battlements. Oddly, he was not afraid. He pulled the glove from his left hand. "Lord Ramsay is not done with me."

The man looked, and laughed. "I leave you to him, then."

Theon trudged through the storm until his arms and legs were caked with snow and his hands and feet had gone numb from cold, then climbed to the battlements of the inner wall again. Up here, a hundred feet high, a little wind was blowing, stirring the snow. All the crenels had filled up. Theon had to punch through a wall of snow to make a hole . . . only to find that he could not see beyond the moat. Of the outer wall, nothing remained but a vague shadow and a few dim lights floating in the dark.

The world is gone. King's Landing, Riverrun, Pyke, and the Iron Islands, all the Seven Kingdoms, every place that he had ever known, every place that he had ever read about or dreamed of, all gone. Only Winterfell remained.

He was trapped here, with the ghosts. The old ghosts from the crypts and the younger ones that he had made himself, Mikken and Farlen, Gynir Rednose, Aggar, Gelmarr the Grim, the miller's wife from Acorn Water and her two young sons, and all the rest. *My work. My ghosts. They are all here, and they are angry.* He thought of the crypts and those missing swords.

Theon returned to his own chambers. He was stripping off his wet clothes when Steelshanks Walton found him. "Come with me, turn-cloak. His lordship wants words with you."

He had no clean dry clothes, so he wriggled back into the same damp rags and followed. Steelshanks led him back to the Great Keep and the solar that had once been Eddard Stark's. Lord Bolton was not alone. Lady Dustin sat with him, pale-faced and severe; an iron horsehead brooch clasped Roger Ryswell's cloak; Aenys Frey stood near the fire, pinched cheeks flushed with cold.

"I am told you have been wandering the castle," Lord Bolton began.

"Men have reported seeing you in the stables, in the kitchens, in the barracks, on the battlements. You have been observed near the ruins of collapsed keeps, outside Lady Catelyn's old sept, coming and going from the godswood. Do you deny it?"

"No, m'lord." Theon made sure to muddy up the word. He knew that pleased Lord Bolton. "I cannot sleep, m'lord. I walk." He kept his head down, fixed upon the old stale rushes scattered on the floor. It was not wise to look his lordship in the face.

"I was a boy here before the war. A ward of Eddard Stark."

"You were a hostage," Bolton said.

"Yes, m'lord. A hostage." *It was my home, though. Not a true home, but the best I ever knew.*

"Someone has been killing my men."

"Yes, m'lord."

"Not you, I trust?" Bolton's voice grew even softer. "You would not repay all my kindnesses with such treachery."

"No, m'lord, not me. I wouldn't. I . . . only walk, is all."

Lady Dustin spoke up. "Take off your gloves."

Theon glanced up sharply. "Please, no. I . . . I . . ."

"Do as she says," Ser Aenys said. "Show us your hands."

Theon peeled his gloves off and held his hands up for them to see. *It is not as if I stand before them naked. It is not so bad as that.* His left hand had three fingers, his right four. Ramsay had taken only the pinky off the one, the ring finger and forefinger from the other.

"The Bastard did this to you," Lady Dustin said.

"If it please m'lady, I . . . I asked it of him." Ramsay always made him ask. *Ramsay always makes me beg.*

"Why would you do that?"

"I . . . I did not need so many fingers."

"Four is enough." Ser Aenys Frey fingered the wispy brown beard that sprouted from his weak chin like a rat's tail. "Four on his right hand. He could still hold a sword. A dagger."

Lady Dustin laughed. "Are all Freys such fools? Look at him. Hold a dagger? He hardly has the strength to hold a spoon. Do you truly think he could have overcome the Bastard's disgusting creature and shoved his manhood down his throat?"

"These dead were all strong men," said Roger Ryswell, "and none of them were stabbed. The turncloak's not our killer."

Roose Bolton's pale eyes were fixed on Theon, as sharp as Skinner's flaying knife. "I am inclined to agree. Strength aside, he does not have it in him to betray my son."

Roger Ryswell grunted. "If not him, who? Stannis has some man inside the castle, that's plain."

Reek is no man. Not Reek. Not me. He wondered if Lady Dustin had told them about the crypts, the missing swords.

"We must look at Manderly," muttered Ser Aenys Frey. "Lord Wyman loves us not."

Ryswell was not convinced. "He loves his steaks and chops and meat pies, though. Prowling the castle by dark would require him to leave the table. The only time he does that is when he seeks the privy for one of his hour-long squats."

"I do not claim Lord Wyman does the deeds himself. He brought three hundred men with him. A hundred knights. Any of them might have—"

"Night work is not knight's work," Lady Dustin said. "And Lord Wyman is not the only man who lost kin at your Red Wedding, Frey. Do you imagine Whoresbane loves you any better? If you did not hold the Greatjon, he would pull out your entrails and make you eat them, as Lady Hornwood ate her fingers. Flints, Cerwyns, Tallharts, Slates . . . they all had men with the Young Wolf."

"House Ryswell too," said Roger Ryswell.

"Even Dustins out of Barrowton." Lady Dustin parted her lips in a thin, feral smile. "The north remembers, Frey."

Aenys Frey's mouth quivered with outrage. "Stark dishonored us. That is what you northmen had best remember."

Roose Bolton rubbed at his chapped lips. "This squabbling will not serve." He flicked his fingers at Theon. "You are free to go. Take care where you wander. Else it might be you we find upon the morrow, smiling a red smile."

"As you say, m'lord." Theon drew his gloves on over his maimed hands and took his leave, limping on his maimed foot.

The hour of the wolf found him still awake, wrapped in layers of heavy wool and greasy fur, walking yet another circuit of the inner walls, hoping to exhaust himself enough to sleep. His legs were caked with snow to the knee, his head and shoulders shrouded in white. On this stretch of the wall the wind was in his face, and melting snow ran down his cheeks like icy tears.

Then he heard the horn.

A long low moan, it seemed to hang above the battlements, lingering in the black air, soaking deep into the bones of every man who heard it. All along the castle walls, sentries turned toward the sound, their hands tightening around the shafts of their spears. In the ruined halls and keeps of Winterfell, lords hushed other lords, horses nickered, and sleepers stirred in their dark corners. No sooner had the sound of the warhorn died away than a drum began to beat: *BOOM doom BOOM doom BOOM doom.* And a name passed from the lips of each man to the next, written in small white puffs of breath. *Stannis,* they whispered, *Stannis is here, Stannis is come, Stannis, Stannis, Stannis.*

Theon shivered. Baratheon or Bolton, it made no matter to him. Stannis had made common cause with Jon Snow at the Wall, and Jon would take his head off in a heartbeat. *Plucked from the clutches of one bastard to die at the hands of another, what a jape.* Theon would have laughed aloud if he'd remembered how.

The drumming seemed to be coming from the wolfswood beyond the Hunter's Gate. *They are just outside the walls.* Theon made his way along the wallwalk, one more man amongst a score doing the same. But even when they reached the towers that flanked the gate itself, there was nothing to be seen beyond the veil of white.

"Do they mean to try and *blow* our walls down?" japed a Flint when the warhorn sounded once again. "Mayhaps he thinks he's found the Horn of Joramun."

"Is Stannis fool enough to storm the castle?" a sentry asked.

"He's not Robert," declared a Barrowton man. "He'll sit, see if he don't. Try and starve us out."

"He'll freeze his balls off first," another sentry said.

"We should take the fight to him," declared a Frey.

Do that, Theon thought. *Ride out into the snow and die. Leave*

Winterfell to me and the ghosts. Roose Bolton would welcome such a fight, he sensed. *He needs an end to this.* The castle was too crowded to withstand a long siege, and too many of the lords here were of uncertain loyalty. Fat Wyman Manderly, Whoresbane Umber, the men of House Hornwood and House Tallhart, the Lockes and Flints and Ryswells, all of them were *northmen,* sworn to House Stark for generations beyond count. It was the girl who held them here, Lord Eddard's blood, but the girl was just a mummer's ploy, a lamb in a direwolf's skin. So why not send the northmen forth to battle Stannis before the farce unraveled? *Slaughter in the snow. And every man who falls is one less foe for the Dreadfort.*

Theon wondered if he might be allowed to fight. Then at least he might die a man's death, sword in hand. That was a gift Ramsay would never give him, but Lord Roose might. *If I beg him. I did all he asked of me, I played my part, I gave the girl away.*

Death was the sweetest deliverance he could hope for.

In the godswood the snow was still dissolving as it touched the earth. Steam rose off the hot pools, fragrant with the smell of moss and mud and decay. A warm fog hung in the air, turning the trees into sentinels, tall soldiers shrouded in cloaks of gloom. During daylight hours, the steamy wood was often full of northmen come to pray to the old gods, but at this hour Theon Greyjoy found he had it all to himself.

And in the heart of the wood the weirwood waited with its knowing red eyes. Theon stopped by the edge of the pool and bowed his head before its carved red face. Even here he could hear the drumming, *boom DOOM boom DOOM boom DOOM boom DOOM.* Like distant thunder, the sound seemed to come from everywhere at once.

The night was windless, the snow drifting straight down out of a cold black sky, yet the leaves of the heart tree were rustling his name. "Theon," they seemed to whisper, "Theon."

The old gods, he thought. *They know me. They know my name. I was Theon of House Greyjoy. I was a ward of Eddard Stark, a friend and brother to his children.* "Please." He fell to his knees. "A sword, that's all I ask. Let me die as Theon, not as Reek." Tears trickled down his cheeks, impossibly warm. "I was ironborn. A son ... a son of Pyke, of the islands."

A leaf drifted down from above, brushed his brow, and landed in the pool. It floated on the water, red, five-fingered, like a bloody hand. "... Bran," the tree murmured.

They know. The gods know. They saw what I did. And for one strange moment it seemed as if it were Bran's face carved into the pale trunk of the weirwood, staring down at him with eyes red and wise and sad. *Bran's ghost,* he thought, but that was madness. Why should Bran want to haunt him? He had been fond of the boy, had never done him any harm. *It was not Bran we killed. It was not Rickon. They were only miller's sons, from the mill by the Acorn Water.* "I had to have two heads, else they would have mocked me ... laughed at me ... they ..."

A voice said, "Who are you talking to?"

Theon spun, terrified that Ramsay had found him, but it was just the washerwomen—Holly, Rowan, and one whose name he did not know. "The ghosts," he blurted. "They whisper to me. They ... they know my name."

"Theon Turncloak." Rowan grabbed his ear, twisting. "You had to have two heads, did you?"

"Elsewise men would have *laughed* at him," said Holly.

They do not understand. Theon wrenched free. "What do you want?" he asked.

"You," said the third washerwoman, an older woman, deep-voiced, with grey streaks in her hair.

"I told you. I want to touch you, turncloak." Holly smiled. In her hand a blade appeared.

I could scream, Theon thought. *Someone will hear. The castle is full of armed men.* He would be dead before help reached him, to be sure, his blood soaking into the ground to feed the heart tree. *And what would be so wrong with that?* "Touch me," he said. "Kill me." There was more despair than defiance in his voice. "Go on. Do me, the way you did the others. Yellow Dick and the rest. It was you."

Holly laughed. "How could it be us? We're women. Teats and cunnies. Here to be fucked, not feared."

"Did the Bastard hurt you?" Rowan asked. "Chopped off your

fingers, did he? Skinned your widdle toes? Knocked your teeth out? Poor lad." She patted his cheek. "There will be no more o' that, I promise. You prayed, and the gods sent us. You want to die as Theon? We'll give you that. A nice quick death, 'twill hardly hurt at all." She smiled. "But not till you've sung for Abel. He's waiting for you."

TYRION

"Lot ninety-seven." The auctioneer snapped his whip. "A pair of dwarfs, well trained for your amusement."

The auction block had been thrown up where the broad brown Skahazadhan flowed into Slaver's Bay. Tyrion Lannister could smell the salt in the air, mingled with the stink from the latrine ditches behind the slave pens. He did not mind the heat so much as he did the damp. The very air seemed to weigh him down, like a warm wet blanket across his head and shoulders.

"Dog and pig included in lot," the auctioneer announced. "The dwarfs ride them. Delight the guests at your next feast or use them for a folly."

The bidders sat on wooden benches sipping fruit drinks. A few were being fanned by slaves. Many wore *tokar*s, that peculiar garment beloved by the old blood of Slaver's Bay, as elegant as it was impractical. Others dressed more plainly—men in tunics and hooded cloaks, women in colored silks. Whores or priestesses, most like; this far east it was hard to tell the two apart.

Back behind the benches, trading japes and making mock of the proceedings, stood a clot of westerners. *Sellswords*, Tyrion knew. He spied longswords, dirks and daggers, a brace of throwing axes, mail beneath their cloaks. Their hair and beards and faces marked most for men of the Free Cities, but here and there were a few who might have been Westerosi. *Are they buying? Or did they just turn up for the show?*

"Who will open for this pair?"

"Three hundred," bid a matron on an antique palanquin.

"Four," called a monstrously fat Yunkishman from the litter where he sprawled like a leviathan. Covered all in yellow silk fringed with gold, he looked as large as four Illyrios. Tyrion pitied the slaves who had to carry him. *At least we will be spared that duty. What joy to be a dwarf.*

"And one," said a crone in a violet *tokar*. The auctioneer gave her a sour look but did not disallow the bid.

The slave sailors off the *Selaesori Qhoran,* sold singly, had gone for prices ranging from five hundred to nine hundred pieces of silver. Seasoned seamen were a valuable commodity. None had put up any sort of fight when the slavers boarded their crippled cog. For them this was just a change of owner. The ship's mates had been free men, but the widow of the waterfront had written them a binder, promising to stand their ransom in such a case as this. The three surviving fiery fingers had not been sold yet, but they were chattels of the Lord of Light and could count on being bought back by some red temple. The flames tattooed upon their faces were their binders.

Tyrion and Penny had no such reassurance.

"Four-fifty," came the bid.

"Four-eighty."

"Five hundred."

Some bids were called out in High Valyrian, some in the mongrel tongue of Ghis. A few buyers signaled with a finger, the twist of a wrist, or the wave of a painted fan.

"I'm glad they are keeping us together," Penny whispered.

The slave trader shot them a look. "No talk."

Tyrion gave Penny's shoulder a squeeze. Strands of hair, pale blond and black, clung to his brow, the rags of his tunic to his back. Some of that was sweat, some dried blood. He had not been so foolish as to fight the slavers, as Jorah Mormont had, but that did not mean he had escaped punishment. In his case it was his mouth that earned him lashes.

"Eight hundred."

"And fifty."

"And one."

We're worth as much as a sailor, Tyrion mused. *Though perhaps it was Pretty Pig the buyers wanted. A well-trained pig is hard to find.* They certainly were not bidding by the pound.

At nine hundred pieces of silver, the bidding began to slow. At nine hundred fifty-one (from the crone), it stopped. The auctioneer had the scent, though, and nothing would do but that the dwarfs give the crowd a taste of their show. Crunch and Pretty Pig were led up onto the platform. Without saddles or bridles, mounting them proved tricky. The moment the sow began to move Tyrion slid off her rump and landed on his own, provoking gales of laughter from the bidders.

"One thousand," bid the grotesque fat man.

"And one." The crone again.

Penny's mouth was frozen in a rictus of a smile. *Well trained for your amusement.* Her father had a deal to answer for, in whatever small hell was reserved for dwarfs.

"Twelve hundred." The leviathan in yellow. A slave beside him handed him a drink. *Lemon, no doubt.* The way those yellow eyes were fixed upon the block made Tyrion uncomfortable.

"Thirteen hundred."

"And one." The crone.

My father always said a Lannister was worth ten times as much as any common man.

At sixteen hundred the pace began to flag again, so the slave trader invited some of the buyers to come up for a closer look at the dwarfs. "The female's young," he promised. "You could breed the two of them, get good coin for the whelps."

"Half his nose is gone," complained the crone once she'd had a good close look. Her wrinkled face puckered with displeasure. Her flesh was maggot white; wrapped in the violet *tokar,* she looked like a prune gone to mold. "His eyes don't match neither. An ill-favored thing."

"My lady hasn't seen my best part yet." Tyrion grabbed his crotch, in case she missed his meaning.

The hag hissed in outrage, and Tyrion got a lick of the whip across his back, a stinging cut that drove him to his knees. The taste of blood filled his mouth. He grinned and spat.

"Two thousand," called a new voice, back of the benches.

And what would a sellsword want with a dwarf? Tyrion pushed himself back to his feet to get a better look. The new bidder was an older man, white-haired yet tall and fit, with leathery brown skin and a close-cropped salt-and-pepper beard. Half-hidden under a faded purple cloak were a longsword and a brace of daggers.

"Twenty-five hundred." A female voice this time; a girl, short, with a thick waist and heavy bosom, clad in ornate armor. Her sculpted black steel breastplate was inlaid in gold and showed a harpy rising with chains dangling from her claws. A pair of slave soldiers lifted her to shoulder height on a shield.

"Three thousand." The brown-skinned man pushed through the crowd, his fellow sellswords shoving buyers aside to clear a path. *Yes. Come closer.* Tyrion knew how to deal with sellswords. He did not think for a moment that this man wanted him to frolic at feasts. *He knows me. He means to take me back to Westeros and sell me to my sister.* The dwarf rubbed his mouth to hide his smile. Cersei and the Seven Kingdoms were half a world away. Much and more could happen before he got there. *I turned Bronn. Give me half a chance, might be I could turn this one too.*

The crone and the girl on the shield gave up the chase at three thousand, but not the fat man in yellow. He weighed the sellswords with his yellow eyes, flicked his tongue across his yellow teeth, and said, "Five thousand silvers for the lot."

The sellsword frowned, shrugged, turned away.

Seven hells. Tyrion was quite certain that he did not want to become the property of the immense Lord Yellowbelly. Just the sight of him sagging across his litter, a mountain of sallow flesh with piggy yellow eyes and breasts big as Pretty Pig pushing at the silk of his *tokar* was enough to make the dwarf's skin crawl. And the smell wafting off him was palpable even on the block.

"If there are no further bids—"

"Seven thousand," shouted Tyrion.

Laughter rippled across the benches. "The dwarf wants to buy himself," the girl on the shield observed.

Tyrion gave her a lascivious grin. "A clever slave deserves a clever master, and you lot all look like fools."

That provoked more laughter from the bidders, and a scowl from the auctioneer, who was fingering his whip indecisively as he tried to puzzle out whether this would work to his benefit.

"Five thousand is an insult!" Tyrion called out. "I joust, I sing, I say amusing things. I'll fuck your wife and make her scream. Or your enemy's wife if you prefer, what better way to shame him? I'm murder with a crossbow, and men three times my size quail and tremble when we meet across a *cyvasse* table. I have even been known to cook from time to time. I bid *ten* thousand silvers for myself! I'm good for it, I am, I am. My father told me I must always pay my debts."

The sellsword in the purple cloak turned back. His eyes met Tyrion's across the rows of other bidders, and he smiled. *A warm smile, that,* the dwarf reflected. *Friendly. But my, those eyes are cold. Might be I don't want him to buy us after all.*

The yellow enormity was squirming in his litter, a look of annoyance on his huge pie face. He muttered something sour in Ghiscari that Tyrion did not understand, but the tone of it was plain enough. "Was that another bid?" The dwarf cocked his head. "I offer all the gold of Casterly Rock."

He heard the whip before he felt it, a whistle in the air, thin and sharp. Tyrion grunted under the blow, but this time he managed to stay on his feet. His thoughts flashed back to the beginnings of his journey, when his most pressing problem had been deciding which wine to drink with his midmorning snails. *See what comes of chasing dragons.* A laugh burst from his lips, spattering the first row of buyers with blood and spit.

"You are sold," the auctioneer announced. Then he hit him again, just because he could. This time Tyrion went down.

One of the guards yanked him back to his feet. Another prodded Penny down off the platform with the butt of his spear. The next piece of chattel was already being led up to take their place. A girl, fifteen or sixteen, not off the *Selaesori Qhoran* this time. Tyrion did not know her. *The same age as Daenerys Targaryen, or near enough.* The slaver soon had her naked. *At least we were spared that humiliation.*

Tyrion gazed across the Yunkish camp to the walls of Meereen. Those gates looked so close . . . and if the talk in the slave pens could be believed, Meereen remained a free city for the nonce. Within those crumbling walls, slavery and the slave trade were still forbidden. All he had to do was reach those gates and pass beyond, and he would be a free man again.

But that was hardly possible unless he abandoned Penny. *She'd want to take the dog and the pig along.*

"It won't be so terrible, will it?" Penny whispered. "He paid so much for us. He'll be kind, won't he?"

So long as we amuse him. "We're too valuable to mistreat," he reassured her, with blood still trickling down his back from those last two lashes. *When our show grows stale, however . . . and it does, it does grow stale . . .*

Their master's overseer was waiting to take charge of them, with a mule cart and two soldiers. He had a long narrow face and a chin beard bound about with golden wire, and his stiff red-black hair swept out from his temples to form a pair of taloned hands. "What darling little creatures you are," he said. "You remind me of my own children . . . or would, if my little ones were not dead. I shall take good care of you. Tell me your names."

"Penny." Her voice was a whisper, small and scared.

Tyrion, of House Lannister, rightful lord of Casterly Rock, you sniveling worm. "Yollo."

"Bold Yollo. Bright Penny. You are the property of the noble and valorous Yezzan zo Qaggaz, scholar and warrior, revered amongst the Wise Masters of Yunkai. Count yourselves fortunate, for Yezzan is a kindly and benevolent master. Think of him as you would your father."

Gladly, thought Tyrion, but this time he held his tongue. They would have to perform for their new master soon enough, he did not doubt, and he could not take another lash.

"Your father loves his special treasures best of all, and he will cherish you," the overseer was saying. "And me, think of me as you would the nurse who cared for you when you were small. Nurse is what all my children call me."

"Lot ninety-nine," the auctioneer called. "A warrior."

The girl had sold quickly and was being bundled off to her new owner, clutching her clothing to small, pink-tipped breasts. Two slavers dragged Jorah Mormont onto the block to take her place. The knight was naked but for a breechclout, his back raw from the whip, his face so swollen as to be almost unrecognizable. Chains bound his wrists and ankles. *A little taste of the meal he cooked for me,* Tyrion thought, yet he found that he could take no pleasure from the big knight's miseries.

Even in chains, Mormont looked dangerous, a hulking brute with big, thick arms and sloped shoulders. All that coarse dark hair on his chest made him look more beast than man. Both his eyes were blackened, two dark pits in that grotesquely swollen face. Upon one cheek he bore a brand: a demon's mask.

When the slavers had swarmed aboard the *Selaesori Qhoran,* Ser Jorah had met them with longsword in hand, slaying three before they overwhelmed him. Their shipmates would gladly have killed him, but the captain forbade it; a fighter was always worth good silver. So Mormont had been chained to an oar, beaten within an inch of his life, starved, and branded.

"Big and strong, this one," the auctioneer declared. "Plenty of piss in him. He'll give a good show in the fighting pits. Who will start me out at three hundred?"

No one would.

Mormont paid no mind to the mongrel crowd; his eyes were fixed beyond the siege lines, on the distant city with its ancient walls of many-colored brick. Tyrion could read that look as easy as a book: *so near and yet so distant.* The poor wretch had returned too late. Daenerys Targaryen was wed, the guards on the pens had told them, laughing. She had taken a Meereenese slaver as her king, as wealthy as he was noble, and when the peace was signed and sealed the fighting pits of Meereen would open once again. Other slaves insisted that the guards were lying, that Daenerys Targaryen would never make peace with slavers. *Mhysa,* they called her. Someone told him that meant *Mother*. Soon the silver queen would come forth from her city, smash the Yunkai'i, and break their chains, they whispered to one another.

And then she'll bake us all a lemon pie and kiss our widdle wounds and make them better, the dwarf thought. He had no faith in royal rescues. If need be, he would see to their deliverance himself. The mushrooms jammed into the toe of his boot should be sufficient for both him and Penny. Crunch and Pretty Pig would need to fend for themselves.

Nurse was still lecturing his master's new prizes. "Do all you are told and nothing more, and you shall live like little lords, pampered and adored," he promised. "Disobey . . . but you would never do that, would you? Not my sweetlings." He reached down and pinched Penny on her cheek.

"Two hundred, then," the auctioneer said. "A big brute like this, he's worth three times as much. What a bodyguard he will make! No enemy will dare molest you!"

"Come, my little friends," Nurse said, "I will show you to your new home. In Yunkai you will dwell in the golden pyramid of Qaggaz and dine off silver plates, but here we live simply, in the humble tents of soldiers."

"Who will give me one hundred?" cried the auctioneer.

That drew a bid at last, though it was only fifty silvers. The bidder was a thin man in a leather apron.

"And one," said the crone in the violet *tokar*.

One of the soldiers lifted Penny onto the back of the mule cart. "Who is the old woman?" the dwarf asked him.

"Zahrina," the man said. "Cheap fighters, hers. Meat for heroes. Your friend dead soon."

He was no friend to me. Yet Tyrion Lannister found himself turning to Nurse and saying, "You cannot let her have him."

Nurse squinted at him. "What is this noise you make?"

Tyrion pointed. "That one is part of our show. The bear and the maiden fair. Jorah is the bear, Penny is the maiden, I am the brave knight who rescues her. I dance about and hit him in the balls. Very funny."

The overseer squinted at the auction block. "Him?" The bidding for Jorah Mormont had reached two hundred silvers.

"And one," said the crone in the violet *tokar*.

"Your bear. I see." Nurse went scuttling off through the crowd, bent over the huge yellow Yunkishman in his litter, whispered in his ear. His master nodded, chins wobbling, then raised his fan. "Three hundred," he called out in a wheezy voice.

The crone sniffed and turned away.

"Why did you do that?" Penny asked, in the Common Tongue.

A fair question, thought Tyrion. *Why did I?* "Your show was growing dull. Every mummer needs a dancing bear."

She gave him a reproachful look, then retreated to the back of the cart and sat with her arms around Crunch, as if the dog was her last true friend in the world. *Perhaps he is.*

Nurse returned with Jorah Mormont. Two of their master's slave soldiers flung him into the back of the mule cart between the dwarfs. The knight did not struggle. *All the fight went out of him when he heard that his queen had wed,* Tyrion realized. One whispered word had done what fists and whips and clubs could not; it had broken him. *I should have let the crone have him. He's going to be as useful as nipples on a breastplate.*

Nurse climbed onto the front of the mule cart and took up the reins, and they set off through the siege camp to the compound of their new master, the noble Yezzan zo Qaggaz. Four slave soldiers marched beside them, two on either side of the cart.

Penny did not weep, but her eyes were red and miserable, and she never lifted them from Crunch. *Does she think all this might fade away if she does not look at it?* Ser Jorah Mormont looked at no one and nothing. He sat huddled, brooding in his chains.

Tyrion looked at everything and everyone.

The Yunkish encampment was not one camp but a hundred camps raised up cheek by jowl in a crescent around the walls of Meereen, a city of silk and canvas with its own avenues and alleys, taverns and trollops, good districts and bad. Between the siege lines and the bay, tents had sprouted up like yellow mushrooms. Some were small and mean, no more than a flap of old stained canvas to keep off the rain and sun, but beside them stood barracks tents large enough to sleep a hundred men and silken pavilions as big as palaces with harpies gleaming atop their roof poles. Some camps were orderly, with the tents arrayed around a fire pit in concentric circles, weapons and armor stacked around the inner ring, horse lines outside. Elsewhere, pure chaos seemed to reign.

The dry, scorched plains around Meereen were flat and bare and treeless for long leagues, but the Yunkish ships had brought lumber and hides up from the south, enough to raise six huge trebuchets. They were arrayed on three sides of the city, all but the river side, surrounded by piles of broken stone and casks of pitch and resin just waiting for a torch. One of the soldiers walking along beside the cart saw where Tyrion was looking and proudly told him that each of the trebuchets had been given a name: Dragonbreaker, Harridan, Harpy's Daughter, Wicked Sister, Ghost of Astapor, Mazdhan's Fist. Towering above the tents to a height of forty feet, the trebuchets were the siege camp's chief landmarks. "Just the sight of them drove the dragon queen to her knees," he boasted. "And there she will stay, sucking Hizdahr's noble cock, else we smash her walls to rubble."

Tyrion saw a slave being whipped, blow after blow, until his back was nothing but blood and raw meat. A file of men marched past in irons, clanking with every step; they carried spears and wore short swords, but chains linked them wrist to wrist and ankle to ankle. The air smelled of roasting meat, and he saw one man skinning a dog for his stewpot.

He saw the dead as well, and heard the dying. Under the drifting smoke, the smell of horses, and the sharp salt tang of the bay was a stink of blood and shit. *Some flux,* he realized, as he watched two sellswords carry the corpse of a third from one of the tents. That made his fingers twitch. Disease could wipe out an army quicker than any battle, he had heard his father say once.

All the more reason to escape, and soon.

A quarter mile on, he found good reason to reconsider. A crowd had formed around three slaves taken whilst trying to escape. "I know my little treasures will be sweet and obedient," Nurse said. "See what befalls ones who try to run."

The captives had been tied to a row of crossbeams, and a pair of slingers were using them to test their skills. "Tolosi," one of the guards told them. "The best slingers in the world. They throw soft lead balls in place of stones."

Tyrion had never seen the point of slings, when bows had so much better range . . . but he had never seen Tolosi at work before. Their lead balls did vastly more damage then the smooth stones other slingers used, and more than any bow as well. One struck the knee of one of the captives, and it burst apart in a gout of blood and bone that left the man's lower leg dangling by a rope of dark red tendon. *Well, he won't run again,* Tyrion allowed, as the man began to scream. His shrieks mingled in the morning air with the laughter of camp followers and the curses of those who'd wagered good coin that the slinger would miss. Penny looked away, but Nurse grasped her under the chin and twisted her head back around. "Watch," he commanded. "You too, bear."

Jorah Mormont raised his head and stared at Nurse. Tyrion could see the tightness in his arms. *He's going to throttle him, and that will be the end for all of us.* But the knight only grimaced, then turned to watch the bloody show.

To the east the massive brick walls of Meereen shimmered through the morning heat. That was the refuge these poor fools had hoped to reach. *How long will it remain a refuge, though?*

All three of the would-be escapees were dead before Nurse gathered up the reins again. The mule cart rumbled on.

Their master's camp was south and east of the Harridan, almost in its shadow, and spread over several acres. The humble tent of Yezzan zo Qaggaz proved to be a palace of lemon-colored silk. Gilded harpies stood atop the center poles of each of its nine peaked roofs, shining in the sun. Lesser tents ringed it on all sides. "Those are the dwellings of our noble master's cooks, concubines, and warriors, and a few less-favored kinsmen," Nurse told them, "but you little darlings shall have the rare privilege of sleeping within Yezzan's own pavilion. It pleases him to keep his treasures close." He frowned at Mormont. "Not you, bear. You are big and ugly, you will be chained outside." The knight did not respond. "First, all of you must be fitted for collars."

The collars were made of iron, lightly gilded to make them glitter in the light. Yezzan's name was incised into the metal in Valyrian glyphs, and a pair of tiny bells were affixed below the ears, so the wearer's every step produced a merry little tinkling sound. Jorah Mormont accepted his collar in a sullen silence, but Penny began to cry as the armorer was fastening her own into place. "It's so heavy," she complained.

Tyrion squeezed her hand. "It's solid gold," he lied. "In Westeros, highborn ladies dream of such a necklace." *Better a collar than a brand. A collar can be removed.* He remembered Shae, and the way the golden chain had glimmered as he twisted it tighter and tighter about her throat.

Afterward, Nurse had Ser Jorah's chains fastened to a stake near the cookfire whilst he escorted the two dwarfs inside the master's pavilion and showed them where they would sleep, in a carpeted alcove separated from the main tent by walls of yellow silk. They would share this space with Yezzan's other treasures: a boy with twisted, hairy "goat legs," a two-headed girl out of Mantarys, a bearded woman, and a willowy creature called Sweets who dressed in moonstones and Myrish lace. "You are trying to decide if I'm a man or woman," Sweets said, when she was brought before the dwarfs. Then she lifted her skirts and showed them what was underneath. "I'm both, and master loves me best."

A grotesquerie, Tyrion realized. *Somewhere some god is laughing.* "Lovely," he said to Sweets, who had purple hair and violet eyes, "but we were hoping to be the pretty ones for once."

Sweets sniggered, but Nurse was not amused. "Save your japes for this evening, when you perform for our noble master. If you please him, you will be well rewarded. If not . . ." He slapped Tyrion across the face.

"You will want to be careful with Nurse," said Sweets when the overseer had departed. "He is the only true monster here." The bearded woman spoke an incomprehensible variety of Ghiscari, the goat boy some guttural sailor's pidgin called the trade talk. The two-headed girl was feeble-minded; one head was no bigger than an orange and did not speak at all, the other had filed teeth and was like to growl at anyone who came too close to her cage. But Sweets was fluent in four tongues, one of them High Valyrian.

"What is the master like?" Penny asked, anxiously.

"His eyes are yellow, and he stinks," said Sweets. "Ten years ago he went to Sothoros, and he has been rotting from the inside out ever since. Make him forget that he is dying, even for a little while, and he can be most generous. Deny him nothing."

They had only the afternoon to learn the ways of chattel. Yezzan's body slaves filled a tub with hot water, and the dwarfs were allowed to bathe—Penny first, then Tyrion. Afterward another slave spread a stinging ointment across the cuts on his back to keep them from mortifying, then covered them with a cool poultice. Penny's hair was cut, and Tyrion's beard got a trim. They were given soft slippers and fresh clothing, plain but clean.

As evening fell, Nurse returned to tell them that it was time to don their mummer's plate. Yezzan would be hosting the Yunkish supreme commander, the noble Yurkhaz zo Yunzak, and they would be expected to perform. "Shall we unchain your bear?"

"Not this night," Tyrion said. "Let us joust for our master first and save the bear for some other time."

"Just so. After your capers are concluded, you will help serve and pour. See that you do not spill on the guests, or it will go ill for you."

A juggler began the evening's frolics. Then came a trio of energetic tumblers. After them the goat-legged boy came out and did a grotesque jig whilst one of Yurkhaz's slaves played on a bone flute. Tyrion had half a mind to ask him if he knew "The Rains of Castamere." As they waited their own turn to perform, he watched Yezzan and his guests. The human prune in the place of honor was evidently the Yunkish supreme commander, who looked about as formidable as a loose stool. A dozen other Yunkish lords attended him. Two sellsword captains were on hand as well, each accompanied by a dozen men of his company. One was an elegant Pentoshi, grey-haired and clad in silk but for his cloak, a ragged thing sewn from dozens of strips of torn, bloodstained cloth. The other captain was the man who'd tried to buy them that morning, the brown-skinned bidder with the salt-and-pepper beard. "Brown Ben Plumm," Sweets named him. "Captain of the Second Sons."

A Westerosi, and a Plumm. Better and better.

"You are next," Nurse informed them. "Be amusing, my little darlings, or you will wish you had."

Tyrion had not mastered half of Groat's old tricks, but he could ride the sow, fall off when he was meant to, roll, and pop back onto his feet. All of that proved well received. The sight of little people running about drunkenly and whacking at one another with wooden weapons appeared to be just as hilarious in a siege camp by Slaver's Bay as at Joffrey's wedding feast in King's Landing. *Contempt,* thought Tyrion, *the universal tongue.*

Their master Yezzan laughed loudest and longest whenever one of his dwarfs suffered a fall or took a blow, his whole vast body shaking like suet in an earthquake; his guests waited to see how Yurkhaz zo Yunzak responded before joining in. The supreme commander appeared so frail that Tyrion was afraid laughing might kill him. When Penny's helm was struck off and flew into the lap of a sour-faced Yunkishman in a striped green-and-gold *tokar,* Yurkhaz cackled like a chicken. When said lord reached inside the helm and drew out a large purple melon dribbling pulp, he wheezed until his face turned the same color as the fruit. He turned to his host and whispered something that made their master chortle and lick his lips . . . though there was a hint of anger in those slitted yellow eyes, it seemed to Tyrion.

Afterward the dwarfs stripped off their wooden armor and the sweat-soaked clothing beneath and changed into the fresh yellow tunics that had been provided them for serving. Tyrion was given a flagon of purple wine, Penny a flagon of water. They moved about the tent filling cups, their slippered feet whispering over thick carpets. It was harder work than it appeared. Before long his legs were cramping badly, and one of the cuts on his back had begun to bleed again, the red seeping through the yellow linen of his tunic. Tyrion bit his tongue and kept on pouring.

Most of the guests paid them no more mind than they did the other slaves . . . but one Yunkishman declared drunkenly that Yezzan should make the two dwarfs fuck, and another demanded to know how Tyrion had lost his nose. *I shoved it up your wife's cunt and she bit it off,* he almost replied . . . but the storm had persuaded him that he did not want to die as yet, so instead he said, "It was cut off to punish me for insolence, lord."

Then a lord in a blue *tokar* fringed with tiger's eyes recalled that Tyrion had boasted of his skill at *cyvasse* on the auction block. "Let us put him to the test," he said. A table and set of pieces was duly produced. A scant few moments later, the red-faced lord shoved the table over in fury, scattering the pieces across the carpets to the sound of Yunkish laughter.

"You should have let him win," Penny whispered.

Brown Ben Plumm lifted the fallen table, smiling. "Try me next, dwarf. When I was younger, the Second Sons took contract with Volantis. I learned the game there."

"I am only a slave. My noble master decides when and who I play." Tyrion turned to Yezzan. "Master?"

The yellow lord seemed amused by the notion. "What stakes do you propose, Captain?"

"If I win, give this slave to me," said Plumm.

"No," Yezzan zo Qaggaz said. "But if you can defeat my dwarf, you may have the price I paid for him, in gold."

"Done," the sellsword said. The scattered pieces were picked up off the carpet, and they sat down to play.

Tyrion won the first game. Plumm took the second, for double the stakes. As they set up for their third contest, the dwarf studied his opponent. Brown-skinned, his cheeks and jaw covered by a close-cropped bristly beard of grey and white, his face creased by a thousand wrinkles and a few old scars, Plumm had an amiable look to him, especially when he smiled. *The faithful retainer,* Tyrion decided. *Every man's favorite nuncle, full of chuckles and old sayings and roughspun wisdom.* It was all sham. Those smiles never touched Plumm's eyes, where greed hid behind a veil of caution. *Hungry, but wary, this one.*

The sellsword was nearly as bad a player as the Yunkish lord had been, but his play was stolid and tenacious rather than bold. His opening arrays were different every time, yet all the same—conservative, defensive, passive. *He does not play to win,* Tyrion realized. *He plays so as not to lose.* It worked in their second game, when the little man overreached himself with an unsound assault. It did not work in the third game, nor the fourth, nor the fifth, which proved to be their last.

Near the end of that final contest, with his fortress in ruins, his dragon dead, elephants before him and heavy horse circling round his rear, Plumm looked up smiling and said, "Yollo wins again. Death in four."

"Three." Tyrion tapped his dragon. "I was lucky. Perhaps you should give my head a good rub before our next game, Captain. Some of that luck might rub off on your fingers." *You will still lose, but you might give me a better game.* Grinning, he pushed back from the *cyvasse* table, picked up his wine flagon, and returned to pouring with Yezzan zo Qaggaz considerably richer and Brown Ben Plumm considerably impoverished. His gargantuan master had fallen off into drunken sleep during the third game, his goblet slipping from his yellowed fingers to spill its contents on the carpet, but perhaps he would be pleased when he awakened.

When the supreme commander Yurkhaz zo Yunzak departed, supported by a pair of burly slaves, that seemed to be a general signal for the other guests to take their leaves as well. After the tent had emptied out, Nurse reappeared to tell the servers that they might make their own feast from the leavings. "Eat quickly. All this must be clean again before you sleep."

Tyrion was on his knees, his legs aching and his bloody back screaming with pain, trying to scrub out the stain that the noble Yezzan's spilled wine had left upon the noble Yezzan's carpet, when the overseer tapped his cheek gently with the end of his whip. "Yollo. You have done well. You and your wife."

"She is not my wife."

"Your whore, then. On your feet, both of you."

Tyrion rose unsteadily, one leg trembling beneath him. His thighs were knots, so cramped that Penny had to lend him a hand to pull him to his feet. "What have we done?"

"Much and more," said the overseer. "Nurse said you would be rewarded if you pleased your father, did he not? Though the noble Yezzan is loath to lose his little treasures, as you have seen, Yurkhaz zo Yunzak persuaded him that it would be selfish to keep such droll antics to himself. Rejoice! To celebrate the signing of the peace, you shall have the honor of jousting in the Great Pit of Daznak. Thousands will come see you! Tens of thousands! And, oh, how we shall laugh!"

JAIME

Raventree Hall was old. Moss grew thick between its ancient stones, spiderwebbing up its walls like the veins in a crone's legs. Two huge towers flanked the castle's main gate, and smaller ones defended every angle of its walls. All were square. Drum towers and half-moons held up better against catapults, since thrown stones were more apt to deflect off a curved wall, but Raventree predated that particular bit of builder's wisdom.

The castle dominated the broad fertile valley that maps and men alike called Blackwood Vale. A vale it was, beyond a doubt, but no wood had grown here for several thousand years, be it black or brown or green. Once, yes, but axes had long since cleared the trees away. Homes and mills and holdfasts had risen where once the oaks stood tall. The ground was bare and muddy, and dotted here and there with drifts of melting snow.

Inside the castle walls, however, a bit of the forest still remained. House Blackwood kept the old gods, and worshiped as the First Men had in the days before the Andals came to Westeros. Some of the trees in their godswood were said to be as old as Raventree's square towers, especially the heart tree, a weirwood of colossal size whose upper branches could be seen from leagues away, like bony fingers scratching at the sky.

As Jaime Lannister and his escort wound through the rolling hills into the vale, little remained of the fields and farms and orchards that had once surrounded Raventree—only mud and ashes, and here and there the blackened shells of homes and mills. Weeds and thorns and nettles grew in that wasteland, but nothing that could be called a crop. Everywhere Jaime looked he saw his father's hand, even in the bones they sometimes glimpsed beside the road. Most were sheep bones, but there were horses too, and cattle, and now and again a human skull, or a headless skeleton with weeds poking up through its rib cage.

No great hosts encircled Raventree, as Riverrun had been encircled. This siege was a more intimate affair, the latest step in a dance that went back many centuries. At best Jonos Bracken had five hundred men about the castle. Jaime saw no siege towers, no battering rams, no catapults. Bracken did not mean to break the gates of Raventree nor storm its high, thick walls. With no prospect of relief in sight, he was content to starve his rival out. No doubt there had been sorties and skirmishes at the start of the siege, and arrows flying back and forth; half a year into it, everyone was too tired for such nonsense. Boredom and routine had taken over, the enemies of discipline.

Past time this was ended, thought Jaime Lannister. With Riverrun now safely in Lannister hands, Raventree was the remnant of the Young Wolf's short-lived kingdom. Once it yielded, his work along the Trident would be done, and he would be free to return to King's Landing. *To the king,* he told himself, but another part of him whispered, *to Cersei.*

He would have to face her, he supposed. Assuming the High Septon had not put her to death by the time he got back to the city. "*Come at once,*" she had written, in the letter he'd had Peck burn at Riverrun. "*Help me. Save me. I need you now as I have never needed you before. I love you. I love you. I love you. Come at once.*" Her need was real enough, Jaime did not doubt. As for the rest . . . *she's been fucking Lancel and Osmund Kettleblack and Moon Boy for all I know . . .* Even if he had gone back, he could not hope to save her. She was guilty of every treason laid against her, and he was short a sword hand.

When the column came trotting from the fields, the sentries stared at them with more curiosity than fear. No one sounded the alarm, which suited Jaime well enough. Lord Bracken's pavilion did not prove difficult to find. It was the largest in the camp, and the best sited; sitting atop a low rise beside a stream, it commanded a clear view of two of Raventree's gates.

The tent was brown, like the standard flapping from its center pole, where the red stallion of House Bracken reared upon its gold escutcheon. Jaime gave the order to dismount and told his men that they might mingle if they liked. "Not you two," he said to his banner-bearers. "Stay close. This will not keep me long." Jaime vaulted down off Honor and strode to Bracken's tent, his sword rattling in its scabbard.

The guards outside the tent flap exchanged an anxious look at his approach. "My lord," said one. "Shall we announce you?"

"I'll announce myself." Jaime pushed aside the flap with his golden hand and ducked inside.

They were well and truly at it when he entered, so intent on their rutting that neither took any note of his arrival. The woman had her eyes closed. Her hands clutched the coarse brown hair on Bracken's back. She gasped every time he drove into her. His lordship's head was buried in her breasts, his hands locked around her hips. Jaime cleared his throat. "Lord Jonos."

The woman's eyes flew open, and she gave a startled shriek. Jonos Bracken rolled off her, grabbed for his scabbard, and came up with naked steel in hand, cursing. "*Seven bloody hells,*" he started, "*who dares—*" Then he saw Jaime's white cloak and golden breastplate. His swordpoint dropped. "Lannister?"

"I am sorry to disturb you at your pleasure, my lord," said Jaime, with a half-smile, "but I am in some haste. May we talk?"

"Talk. Aye." Lord Jonos sheathed his sword. He was not quite so tall as Jaime, but he was heavier, with thick shoulders and arms that would have made a blacksmith envious. Brown stubble covered his cheeks and chin. His eyes were brown as well, the anger in them poorly hidden. "You took me unawares, my lord. I was not told of your coming."

"And I seem to have prevented yours." Jaime smiled at the woman in the bed. She had one hand over her left breast and the other between her legs, which left her right breast exposed. Her nipples were darker than Cersei's and thrice the size. When she felt Jaime's gaze she covered her right nipple, but that revealed her mound. "Are all camp followers so modest?" he wondered. "If a man wants to sell his turnips, he needs to set them out."

"You been looking at my turnips since you came in, ser." The woman found the blanket and pulled it up high enough to cover herself to the waist, then raised one hand to push her hair back from her eyes. "And they're not for sale, neither."

Jaime gave a shrug. "My apologies if I mistook you for something you're not. My little brother has known a hundred whores, I'm sure, but I've only ever bedded one."

"She's a prize of war." Bracken retrieved his breeches from the floor and shook them out. "She belonged to one of Blackwood's sworn swords till I split his head in two. Put your hands down, woman. My lord of Lannister wants a proper look at those teats."

Jaime ignored that. "You are putting those breeches on backwards, my lord," he told Bracken. As Jonos cursed, the woman slipped off the bed to snatch up her scattered clothing, her fingers fluttering nervously between her breasts and cleft as she bent and turned and reached. Her efforts to conceal herself were oddly provocative, far more so than if she'd simply gone about the business naked. "Do you have a name, woman?" he asked her.

"My mother named me Hildy, ser." She pulled a soiled shift down over her head and shook her hair out. Her face was almost as dirty as her feet and she had enough hair between her legs to pass for Bracken's sister, but there was something appealing about her all the same. That pug nose, her shaggy mane of hair . . . or the way she did a little curtsy after she had stepped into her skirt. "Have you seen my other shoe, m'lord?"

The question seemed to vex Lord Bracken. "Am I a bloody hand-maid, to fetch you shoes? Go barefoot if you must. Just go."

"Does that mean m'lord won't be taking me home with him, to pray with his little wife?" Laughing, Hildy gave Jaime a brazen look. "Do you have a little wife, ser?"

No, I have a sister. "What color is my cloak?"

"White," she said, "but your hand is solid gold. I like that in a man. And what is it you like in a woman, m'lord?"

"Innocence."

"In a woman, I said. Not a daughter."

He thought of Myrcella. *I will need to tell her too.* The Dornishmen might not like that. Doran Martell had betrothed her to his son in the belief that she was Robert's blood. *Knots and tangles,* Jaime thought, wishing he could cut through all of it with one swift stroke of his sword. "I have sworn a vow," he told Hildy wearily.

"No turnips for you, then," the girl said, saucily.

"*Get out,*" Lord Jonos roared at her.

She did. But as she slipped past Jaime, clutching one shoe and a pile of her clothes, she reached down and gave his cock a squeeze through his breeches. "*Hildy,*" she reminded him, before she darted half-clothed from the tent.

Hildy, Jaime mused. "And how fares your lady wife?" he asked Lord Jonos when the girl was gone.

"How would I know? Ask her septon. When your father burned our castle, she decided the gods were punishing us. Now all she does is pray." Jonos had finally gotten his breeches turned the right way round and was lacing them up the front. "What brings you here, my lord? The Blackfish? We heard how he escaped."

"Did you?" Jaime settled on a camp stool. "From the man himself, perchance?"

"Ser Brynden knows better than to come running to me. I am fond of the man, I won't deny that. That won't stop me clapping him in chains if he shows his face near me or mine. He knows I've bent the knee. He should have done the same, but he always was a stubborn one. His brother could have told you that."

"Tytos Blackwood has not bent the knee," Jaime pointed out. "Might the Blackfish seek refuge at Raventree?"

"He might seek it, but to find it he'd need to get past my siege lines, and last I heard he hadn't grown wings. Tytos will be needing refuge himself before much longer. They're down to rats and roots in there. He'll yield before the next full moon."

"He'll yield before the sun goes down. I mean to offer him terms and accept him back into the king's peace."

"I see." Lord Jonos shrugged into a brown woolen tunic with the red stallion of Bracken embroidered on the front. "Will my lord take a horn of ale?"

"No, but don't go dry on my account."

Bracken filled a horn for himself, drank half of it, and wiped his mouth. "You spoke of terms. What sort of terms?"

"The usual sort. Lord Blackwood shall be required to confess his treason and abjure his allegiance to the Starks and Tullys. He will swear solemnly before gods and men to henceforth remain a leal vassal of Harrenhal and the Iron Throne, and I will give him pardon in the king's name. We will take a pot or two of gold, of course. The price of rebellion. I'll claim a hostage as well, to ensure that Raventree does not rise again."

"His daughter," suggested Bracken. "Blackwood has six sons, but only the one daughter. He dotes on her. A snot-nosed little creature, couldn't be more than seven."

"Young, but she might serve."

Lord Jonos drained the last of his ale and tossed the horn aside. "What of the lands and castles we were promised?"

"What lands were these?"

"The east bank of the Widow's Wash, from Crossbow Ridge to Rutting Meadow, and all the islands in the stream. Grindcorn Mill and Lord's Mill, the ruins of Muddy Hall, the Ravishment, Battle Valley, Oldforge, the villages of Buckle, Blackbuckle, Cairns, and Claypool, and the market town at Mudgrave. Waspwood, Lorgen's Wood, Greenhill, and Barba's Teats. Missy's Teats, the Blackwoods call them, but they were Barba's first. Honeytree and all the hives. Here, I've marked them out if my lord would like a look." He rooted about on a table and produced a parchment map.

Jaime took it with his good hand, but he had to use the gold to open it and hold it flat. "This is a deal of land," he observed. "You will be increasing your domains by a quarter."

Bracken's mouth set stubbornly. "All these lands belonged to Stone Hedge once. The Blackwoods stole them from us."

"What about this village here, between the Teats?" Jaime tapped the map with a gilded knuckle.

"Pennytree. That was ours once too, but it's been a royal fief for a hundred years. Leave that out. We ask only for the lands stolen by the Blackwoods. Your lord father promised to restore them to us if we would subdue Lord Tytos for him."

"Yet as I was riding up, I saw Tully banners flying from the castle walls, and the direwolf of Stark as well. That would seem to suggest that Lord Tytos has not been subdued."

"We've driven him and his from the field and penned them up inside Raventree. Give me sufficient men to storm his walls, my lord, and I will subdue the whole lot of them to their graves."

"If I gave you sufficient men, they would be doing the subduing, not you. In which case I should reward myself." Jaime let the map roll up again. "I'll keep this if I might."

"The map is yours. The lands are ours. It's said that a Lannister always pays his debts. We fought for you."

"Not half as long as you fought against us."

"The king has pardoned us for that. I lost my nephew to your swords, and my natural son. Your Mountain stole my harvest and burned everything he could not carry off. He put my castle to the torch and raped one of my daughters. I will have recompense."

"The Mountain's dead, as is my father," Jaime told him, "and some might say your head was recompense enough. You *did* declare for Stark, and kept faith with him until Lord Walder killed him."

"Murdered him, and a dozen good men of my own blood." Lord Jonos turned his head and spat. "Aye, I kept faith with the Young Wolf. As I'll keep faith with you, so long as you treat me fair. I bent the knee because I saw no sense in dying for the dead nor shedding Bracken blood in a lost cause."

"A prudent man." *Though some might say that Lord Blackwood has been more honorable.* "You'll get your lands. Some of them, at least. Since you partly subdued the Blackwoods."

That seemed to satisfy Lord Jonos. "We will be content with whatever portion my lord thinks fair. If I may offer you some counsel, though, it does not serve to be too gentle with these Blackwoods.

Treachery runs in their blood. Before the Andals came to Westeros, House Bracken ruled this river. We were kings and the Blackwoods were our vassals, but they betrayed us and usurped the crown. Every Blackwood is born a turncloak. You would do well to remember that when you are making terms."

"Oh, I shall," Jaime promised.

When he rode from Bracken's siege camp to the gates of Raventree, Peck went before him with a peace banner. Before they reached the castle, twenty pairs of eyes were watching them from the gatehouse ramparts. He drew Honor to a halt at the edge of the moat, a deep trench lined with stone, its green waters choked by scum. Jaime was about to command Ser Kennos to sound the Horn of Herrock when the drawbridge began to descend.

Lord Tytos Blackwood met him in the outer ward, mounted on a destrier as gaunt as himself. Very tall and very thin, the Lord of Raventree had a hook nose, long hair, and a ragged salt-and-pepper beard that showed more salt than pepper. In silver inlay on the breastplate of his burnished scarlet armor was a white tree bare and dead, surrounded by a flock of onyx ravens taking flight. A cloak of raven feathers fluttered from his shoulders.

"Lord Tytos," Jaime said.

"Ser."

"Thank you for allowing me to enter."

"I will not say that you are welcome. Nor will I deny that I have hoped that you might come. You are here for my sword."

"I am here to make an end of this. Your men have fought valiantly, but your war is lost. Are you prepared to yield?"

"To the king. Not to Jonos Bracken."

"I understand."

Blackwood hesitated a moment. "Is it your wish that I dismount and kneel before you here and now?"

A hundred eyes were looking on. "The wind is cold and the yard is muddy," said Jaime. "You can do your kneeling on the carpet in your solar once we've agreed on terms."

"That is chivalrous of you," said Lord Tytos. "Come, ser. My hall might lack for food, but never for courtesy."

Blackwood's solar was on the second floor of a cavernous timber keep. There was a fire burning in the hearth when they entered. The room was large and airy, with great beams of dark oak supporting the high ceiling. Woolen tapestries covered the walls, and a pair of wide latticework doors looked out upon the godswood. Through their thick, diamond-shaped panes of yellow glass Jaime glimpsed the gnarled limbs of the tree from which the castle took its name. It was a weirwood ancient and colossal, ten times the size of the one in the Stone Garden at Casterly Rock. This tree was bare and dead, though.

"The Brackens poisoned it," said his host. "For a thousand years it has not shown a leaf. In another thousand it will have turned to stone, the maesters say. Weirwoods never rot."

"And the ravens?" asked Jaime. "Where are they?"

"They come at dusk and roost all night. Hundreds of them. They cover the tree like black leaves, every limb and every branch. They have been coming for thousands of years. How or why, no man can say, yet the tree draws them every night." Blackwood settled in a high-backed chair. "For honor's sake I must ask about my liege lord."

"Ser Edmure is on his way to Casterly Rock as my captive. His wife will remain at the Twins until their child is born. Then she and the babe will join him. So long as he does not attempt escape or plot rebellion, Edmure will live a long life."

"Long and bitter. A life without honor. Until his dying day, men will say he was afraid to fight."

Unjustly, Jaime thought. *It was his child he feared for. He knew whose son I am, better than mine own aunt.* "The choice was his. His uncle would have made us bleed."

"We agree on that much." Blackwood's voice gave nothing away. "What have you done with Ser Brynden, if I may ask?"

"I offered to let him take the black. Instead he fled." Jaime smiled. "Do you have him here, perchance?"

"No."

"Would you tell me if you did?"

It was Tytos Blackwood's turn to smile.

Jaime brought his hands together, the gold fingers inside the fleshy ones. "Perhaps it is time we talked of terms."

"Is this where I get down on my knees?"

"If it please you. Or we can say you did."

Lord Blackwood remained seated. They soon reached agreement on the major points: confession, fealty, pardon, a certain sum of gold and silver to be paid. "What lands will you require?" Lord Tytos asked. When Jaime handed him the map, he took one look and chuckled. "To be sure. The turncloak must be given his reward."

"Yes, but a smaller one than he imagines, for a smaller service. Which of these lands will you consent to part with?"

Lord Tytos considered for a moment. "Woodhedge, Crossbow Ridge, and Buckle."

"A ruin, a ridge, and a few hovels? Come, my lord. You must suffer for your treason. He will want one of the mills, at least." Mills were a valuable source of tax. The lord received a tenth of all the grain they ground.

"Lord's Mill, then. Grindcorn is ours."

"And another village. Cairns?"

"I have forebears buried beneath the rocks of Cairns." He looked at the map again. "Give him Honeytree and its hives. All that sweet will make him fat and rot his teeth."

"Done, then. But for one last thing."

"A hostage."

"Yes, my lord. You have a daughter, I believe."

"Bethany." Lord Tytos looked stricken. "I also have two brothers and a sister. A pair of widowed aunts. Nieces, nephews, cousins. I had thought you might consent . . ."

"It must be a child of your blood."

"Bethany is only eight. A gentle girl, full of laughter. She has never been more than a day's ride from my hall."

"Why not let her see King's Landing? His Grace is almost of an age with her. He would be pleased to have another friend."

"One he can hang if the friend's father should displease him?" asked Lord Tytos. "I have four sons. Would you consider one of them instead? Ben is twelve and thirsty for adventure. He could squire for you if it please my lord."

"I have more squires than I know what to do with. Every time I take a piss, they fight for the right to hold my cock. And you have six sons, my lord, not four."

"Once. Robert was my youngest and never strong. He died nine days ago, of a looseness of the bowels. Lucas was murdered at the Red Wedding. Walder Frey's fourth wife was a Blackwood, but kinship counts for no more than guest right at the Twins. I should like to bury Lucas beneath the tree, but the Freys have not yet seen fit to return his bones to me."

"I'll see that they do. Was Lucas your eldest son?"

"My second. Brynden is my eldest, and my heir. Next comes Hoster. A bookish boy, I fear."

"They have books in King's Landing too. I recall my little brother reading them from time to time. Perhaps your son would like a look at them. I will accept Hoster as our hostage."

Blackwood's relief was palpable. "Thank you, my lord." He hesitated a moment. "If I may be so bold, you would do well to require a hostage from Lord Jonos too. One of his daughters. For all his rutting, he has not proved man enough to father sons."

"He had a bastard son killed in the war."

"Did he? Harry was a bastard, true enough, but whether Jonos sired him is a thornier question. A fair-haired boy, he was, and comely. Jonos is neither." Lord Tytos got to his feet. "Will you do me the honor of taking supper with me?"

"Some other time, my lord." The castle was starving; no good would be served by Jaime stealing food from their mouths. "I cannot linger. Riverrun awaits."

"Riverrun? Or King's Landing?"

"Both."

Lord Tytos did not attempt to dissuade him. "Hoster can be ready to depart within the hour."

He was. The boy met Jaime by the stables, with a bedroll slung over one shoulder and a bundle of scrolls beneath his arm. He could not have been any older than sixteen, yet he was even taller than his father, almost seven feet of legs and shins and elbows, a gangling, gawky boy with a cowlick. "Lord Commander. I'm your hostage, Hoster. Hos, they call me." He grinned.

Does he think this is a lark? "Pray, who are *they*?"

"My friends. My brothers."

"I am not your friend and I am not your brother." That cleaned the grin off the boy's face. Jaime turned to Lord Tytos. "My lord, let there be no misunderstanding here. Lord Beric Dondarrion, Thoros of Myr, Sandor Clegane, Brynden Tully, this woman Stoneheart . . . all these are outlaws and rebels, enemies to the king and all his leal subjects. If I should learn that you or yours are hiding them, protecting them, or assisting them in any way, I will not hesitate to send you your son's head. I hope you understand that. Understand this as well: I am not Ryman Frey."

"No." All trace of warmth had left Lord Blackwood's mouth. "I know who I am dealing with. Kingslayer."

"Good." Jaime mounted and wheeled Honor toward the gate. "I wish you a good harvest and the joy of the king's peace."

He did not ride far. Lord Jonos Bracken was waiting for him outside Raventree, just beyond the range of a good crossbow. He was mounted on an armored destrier and had donned his plate and mail, and a grey steel greathelm with a horsehair crest. "I saw them pull the direwolf banner down," he said when Jaime reached him. "Is it done?"

"Done and done. Go home and plant your fields."

Lord Bracken raised his visor. "I trust I have more fields to plant than when you went into that castle."

"Buckle, Woodhedge, Honeytree and all its hives." He was forgetting one. "Oh, and Crossbow Ridge."

"A mill," said Bracken. "I must have a mill."

"Lord's Mill."

Lord Jonos snorted. "Aye, that will serve. For now." He pointed at Hoster Blackwood, riding back with Peck. "Is this what he gave you for a hostage? You were cozened, ser. A weakling, this one. Water for blood. Never mind how tall he is, any one of my girls could snap him like a rotten twig."

"How many daughters do you have, my lord?" Jaime asked him.

"Five. Two by my first wife and three by my third." Too late, he seemed to realize that he might have said too much.

"Send one of them to court. She will have the privilege of attending the Queen Regent."

Bracken's face grew dark as he realized the import of those words. "Is this how you repay the friendship of Stone Hedge?"

"It is a great honor to wait upon the queen," Jaime reminded his lordship. "You might want to impress that on her. We'll look for the girl before the year is out." He did not wait for Lord Bracken to reply but touched Honor lightly with his golden spurs and trotted off. His men formed up and followed, banners streaming. Castle and camp were soon lost behind them, obscured by the dust of their hooves.

Neither outlaws nor wolves had troubled them on their way to Raventree, so Jaime decided to return by a different route. If the gods were good, he might stumble on the Blackfish, or lure Beric Dondarrion into an unwise attack.

They were following the Widow's Wash when they ran out of day. Jaime called his hostage forward and asked him where to find the nearest ford, and the boy led them there. As the column splashed across the shallow waters, the sun was setting behind a pair of grassy hills. "The Teats," said Hoster Blackwood.

Jaime recalled Lord Bracken's map. "There's a village between those hills."

"Pennytree," the lad confirmed.

"We'll camp there for the night." If there were villagers about, they might have knowledge of Ser Brynden or the outlaws. "Lord Jonos made some remark about whose teats they were," he recalled to the Blackwood boy as they rode toward the darkening hills and the last light of the day. "The Brackens call them by one name and the Blackwoods by another."

"Aye, my lord. For a hundred years or so. Before that, they were the Mother's Teats, or just the Teats. There are two of them, and it was thought that they resembled . . ."

"I can see what they resemble." Jaime found himself thinking back on the woman in the tent and the way she'd tried to hide her large, dark nipples. "What changed a hundred years ago?"

"Aegon the Unworthy took Barba Bracken as his mistress," the bookish boy replied. "She was a very buxom wench, they say, and one day when the king was visiting at the Stone Hedge he went out hunting and saw the Teats and . . ."

". . . named them for his mistress." Aegon the Fourth had died long before Jaime had been born, but he recalled enough of the history of his reign to guess what must have happened next. "Only later he put the Bracken girl aside and took up with a Blackwood, was that the way of it?"

"Lady Melissa," Hoster confirmed. "Missy, they called her. There's a statue of her in our godswood. She was *much* more beautiful than Barba Bracken, but slender, and Barba was heard to say that Missy was flat as a boy. When King Aegon heard, he . . ."

". . . gave her Barba's teats." Jaime laughed. "How did all this begin, between Blackwood and Bracken? Is it written down?"

"It is, my lord," the boy said, "but some of the histories were penned by their maesters and some by ours, centuries after the events that they purport to chronicle. It goes back to the Age of Heroes. The Blackwoods were kings in those days. The Brackens were petty lords, renowned for breeding horses. Rather than pay their king his just due, they used the gold their horses brought them to hire swords and cast him down."

"When did all this happen?"

"Five hundred years before the Andals. A thousand, if the *True History* is to be believed. Only no one knows when the Andals crossed the narrow sea. The *True History* says four thousand years have passed since then, but some maesters claim that it was only two. Past a certain point, all the dates grow hazy and confused, and the clarity of history becomes the fog of legend."

Tyrion would like this one. They could talk from dusk to dawn, arguing about books. For a moment his bitterness toward his brother was forgotten, until he remembered what the Imp had done. "So you are fighting over a crown that one of you took from the other back when the Casterlys still held Casterly Rock, is that the root of it? The crown of a kingdom that has not existed for thousands of years?" He chuckled. "So many years, so many wars, so many kings . . . you'd think someone would have made a peace."

"Someone did, my lord. Many someones. We've had a hundred

peaces with the Brackens, many sealed with marriages. There's Blackwood blood in every Bracken, and Bracken blood in every Blackwood. The Old King's Peace lasted half a century. But then some fresh quarrel broke out, and the old wounds opened and began to bleed again. That's how it always happens, my father says. So long as men remember the wrongs done to their forebears, no peace will ever last. So we go on century after century, with us hating the Brackens and them hating us. My father says there will never be an end to it."

"There could be."

"How, my lord? The old wounds never heal, my father says."

"My father had a saying too. Never wound a foe when you can kill him. Dead men don't claim vengeance."

"Their sons do," said Hoster, apologetically.

"Not if you kill the sons as well. Ask the Casterlys about that if you doubt me. Ask Lord and Lady Tarbeck, or the Reynes of Castamere. Ask the Prince of Dragonstone." For an instant, the deep red clouds that crowned the western hills reminded him of Rhaegar's children, all wrapped up in crimson cloaks.

"Is that why you killed all the Starks?"

"Not all," said Jaime. "Lord Eddard's daughters live. One has just been wed. The other . . ." *Brienne, where are you? Have you found her?* ". . . if the gods are good, she'll forget she was a Stark. She'll wed some burly blacksmith or fat-faced innkeep, fill his house with children, and never need to fear that some knight might come along to smash their heads against a wall."

"The gods are good," his hostage said, uncertainly.

You go on believing that. Jaime let Honor feel his spurs.

Pennytree proved to be a much larger village than he had anticipated. The war had been here too; blackened orchards and the scorched shells of broken houses testified to that. But for every home in ruins three more had been rebuilt. Through the gathering blue dusk Jaime glimpsed fresh thatch upon a score of roofs, and doors made of raw green wood. Between a duck pond and a blacksmith's forge, he came upon the tree that gave the place its name, an oak ancient and tall. Its gnarled roots twisted in and out of the earth like a nest of slow brown serpents, and hundreds of old copper pennies had been nailed to its huge trunk.

Peck stared at the tree, then at the empty houses. "Where are the people?"

"Hiding," Jaime told him.

Inside the homes all the fires had been put out, but some still smoked, and none of them were cold. The nanny goat that Hot Harry Merrell found rooting through a vegetable garden was the only living creature to be seen . . . but the village had a holdfast as strong as any in the riverlands, with thick stone walls twelve feet high, and Jaime knew that was where he'd find the villagers. *They hid behind those walls when raiders came, that's why there's still a village here. And they are hiding there again, from me.*

He rode Honor up to the holdfast gates. "You in the holdfast. We mean you no harm. We're king's men."

Faces appeared on the wall above the gate. "They was king's men burned our village," one man called down. "Before that, some other king's men took our sheep. They were for a different king, but that didn't matter none to our sheep. King's men killed Harsley and Ser Ormond, and raped Lacey till she died."

"Not my men," Jaime said. "Will you open your gates?"

"When you're gone we will."

Ser Kennos rode close to him. "We could break that gate down easy enough, or put it to the torch."

"While they drop stones on us and feather us with arrows." Jaime shook his head. "It would be a bloody business, and for what? These people have done us no harm. We'll shelter in the houses, but I'll have no stealing. We have our own provisions."

As a half-moon crept up the sky, they staked their horses out in the village commons and supped on salted mutton, dried apples, and hard cheese. Jaime ate sparingly and shared a skin of wine with Peck and Hos the hostage. He tried to count the pennies nailed to the old oak, but there were too many of them and he kept losing count. *What's that all about?* The Blackwood boy would tell him if he asked, but that would spoil the mystery.

He posted sentries to see that no one left the confines of the village.

He sent out scouts as well, to make certain no enemy took them unawares. It was near midnight when two came riding back with a woman they had taken captive. "She rode up bold as you please, m'lord, demanding words with you."

Jaime scrambled to his feet. "My lady. I had not thought to see you again so soon." *Gods be good, she looks ten years older than when I saw her last. And what's happened to her face?* "That bandage . . . you've been wounded . . ."

"A bite." She touched the hilt of her sword, the sword that he had given her. *Oathkeeper.* "My lord, you gave me a quest."

"The girl. Have you found her?"

"I have," said Brienne, Maid of Tarth.

"Where is she?"

"A day's ride. I can take you to her, ser . . . but you will need to come alone. Elsewise, the Hound will kill her."

JON

"R'hllor," sang Melisandre, her arms upraised against the falling snow, "you are the light in our eyes, the fire in our hearts, the heat in our loins. Yours is the sun that warms our days, yours the stars that guard us in the dark of night."

"*All praise R'hllor, the Lord of Light,*" the wedding guests answered in ragged chorus before a gust of ice-cold wind blew their words away. Jon Snow raised the hood of his cloak.

The snowfall was light today, a thin scattering of flakes dancing in the air, but the wind was blowing from the east along the Wall, cold as the breath of the ice dragon in the tales Old Nan used to tell. Even Melisandre's fire was shivering; the flames huddled down in the ditch, crackling softly as the red priestess sang. Only Ghost seemed not to feel the chill.

Alys Karstark leaned close to Jon. "Snow during a wedding means a cold marriage. My lady mother always said so."

He glanced at Queen Selyse. *There must have been a blizzard the day she and Stannis wed.* Huddled beneath her ermine mantle and surrounded by her ladies, serving girls, and knights, the southron queen seemed a frail, pale, shrunken thing. A strained smile was frozen into place on her thin lips, but her eyes brimmed with reverence. *She hates the cold but loves the flames.* He had only to look at her to see that. *A word from Melisandre, and she would walk into the fire willingly, embrace it like a lover.*

Not all her queen's men seemed to share her fervor. Ser Brus appeared half-drunk, Ser Malegorn's gloved hand was cupped round the arse of the lady beside him, Ser Narbert was yawning, and Ser Patrek of King's Mountain looked angry. Jon Snow had begun to understand why Stannis had left them with his queen.

"The night is dark and filled with terrors," Melisandre sang. "Alone we are born and alone we die, but as we walk through this black vale we draw strength from one another, and from you, our lord." Her scarlet silks and satins swirled with every gust of wind. "Two come forth today to join their lives, so they may face this world's darkness together. Fill their hearts with fire, my lord, so they may walk your shining path hand in hand forever."

"*Lord of Light, protect us,*" cried Queen Selyse. Other voices echoed the response. Melisandre's faithful: pallid ladies, shivering serving girls, Ser Axell and Ser Narbert and Ser Lambert, men-at-arms in iron mail and Thenns in bronze, even a few of Jon's black brothers. "*Lord of Light, bless your children.*"

Melisandre's back was to the Wall, on one side of the deep ditch where her fire burned. The couple to be joined faced her across the ditch. Behind them stood the queen, with her daughter and her tattooed fool. Princess Shireen was wrapped in so many furs that she looked round, breathing in white puffs through the scarf that covered most of her face. Ser Axell Florent and his queen's men surrounded the royal party.

Though only a few men of the Night's Watch had gathered about the ditchfire, more looked down from rooftops and windows and the steps of the great switchback stair. Jon took careful note of who was there and who was not. Some men had the duty; many just off watch were fast asleep. But others had chosen to absent themselves to show their disapproval. Othell Yarwyck and Bowen Marsh were amongst the missing. Septon Chayle had emerged briefly from the sept, fingering the seven-sided crystal on the thong about his neck, only to retreat inside again once the prayers began.

Melisandre raised her hands, and the ditchfire leapt upward toward her fingers, like a great red dog springing for a treat. A swirl of sparks rose to meet the snowflakes coming down. "Oh, Lord of Light, we thank you," she sang to the hungry flames. "We thank you for brave Stannis, by your grace our king. Guide him and defend him, R'hllor. Protect him from the treacheries of evil men and grant him strength to smite the servants of the dark."

"*Grant him strength*," answered Queen Selyse and her knights and ladies. "*Grant him courage. Grant him wisdom.*"

Alys Karstark slipped her arm through Jon's. "How much longer, Lord Snow? If I'm to be buried beneath this snow, I'd like to die a woman wed."

"Soon, my lady," Jon assured her. "Soon."

"*We thank you for the sun that warms us*," chanted the queen. "*We thank you for the stars that watch over us in the black of night. We thank you for our hearths and for our torches that keep the savage dark at bay. We thank you for our bright spirits, the fires in our loins and in our hearts.*"

And Melisandre said, "Let them come forth, who would be joined." The flames cast her shadow on the Wall behind her, and her ruby gleamed against the paleness of her throat.

Jon turned to Alys Karstark. "My lady. Are you ready?"

"Yes. Oh, yes."

"You're not scared?"

The girl smiled in a way that reminded Jon so much of his little sister that it almost broke his heart. "Let him be scared of me." The snowflakes were melting on her cheeks, but her hair was wrapped in a swirl of lace that Satin had found somewhere, and the snow had begun to collect there, giving her a frosty crown. Her cheeks were flushed and red, and her eyes sparkled.

"Winter's lady." Jon squeezed her hand.

The Magnar of Thenn stood waiting by the fire, clad as if for battle, in fur and leather and bronze scales, a bronze sword at his hip. His receding hair made him look older than his years, but as he turned to watch his bride approach, Jon could see the boy in him. His eyes were big as walnuts, though whether it was the fire, the priestess, or the woman that had put the fear in him Jon could not say. *Alys was more right than she knew.*

"Who brings this woman to be wed?" asked Melisandre.

"I do," said Jon. "Now comes Alys of House Karstark, a woman grown and flowered, of noble blood and birth." He gave her hand one last squeeze and stepped back to join the others.

"Who comes forth to claim this woman?" asked Melisandre.

"Me." Sigorn slapped his chest. "Magnar of Thenn."

"Sigorn," asked Melisandre, "will you share your fire with Alys, and warm her when the night is dark and full of terrors?"

"I swear me." The Magnar's promise was a white cloud in the air. Snow dappled his shoulders. His ears were red. "By the red god's flames, I warm her all her days."

"Alys, do you swear to share your fire with Sigorn, and warm him when the night is dark and full of terrors?"

"Till his blood is boiling." Her maiden's cloak was the black wool of the Night's Watch. The Karstark sunburst sewn on its back was made of the same white fur that lined it.

Melisandre's eyes shone as bright as the ruby at her throat. "Then come to me and be as one." As she beckoned, a wall of flames roared upward, licking at the snowflakes with hot orange tongues. Alys Karstark took her Magnar by the hand.

Side by side they leapt the ditch.

"Two went into the flames." A gust of wind lifted the red woman's scarlet skirts till she pressed them down again. "One emerges." Her coppery hair danced about her head. "What fire joins, none may put asunder."

"*What fire joins, none may put asunder,*" came the echo, from queen's men and Thenns and even a few of the black brothers.

Except for kings and uncles, thought Jon Snow.

Cregan Karstark had turned up a day behind his niece. With him came four mounted men-at-arms, a huntsman, and a pack of dogs, sniffing after Lady Alys as if she were a deer. Jon Snow met them on the kingsroad half a league south of Mole's Town, before they could turn up at Castle Black, claim guest right, or call for parley. One of Karstark's men had loosed a crossbow quarrel at Ty and died for it. That left four, and Cregan himself.

Fortunately they had a dozen ice cells. *Room for all.*

Like so much else, heraldry ended at the Wall. The Thenns had no family arms as was customary amongst the nobles of the Seven Kingdoms, so Jon told the stewards to improvise. He thought they had done well. The bride's cloak Sigorn fastened about Lady Alys's shoulders showed a bronze disk on a field of white wool, surrounded by flames made with wisps of crimson silk. The echo of the Karstark sunburst was there for those who cared to look, but differenced to make the arms appropriate for House Thenn.

The Magnar all but ripped the maiden's cloak from Alys's shoulders, but when he fastened her bride's cloak about her he was almost tender. As he leaned down to kiss her cheek, their breath mingled. The flames roared once again. The queen's men began to sing a song of praise.

"Is it done?" Jon heard Satin whisper.

"Done and done," muttered Mully, "and a good thing. They're wed and I'm half-froze." He was muffled up in his best blacks, woolens so new that they had hardly had a chance to fade yet, but the wind had turned his cheeks as red as his hair. "Hobb's mulled some wine with cinnamon and cloves. That'll warm us some."

"What's cloves?" asked Owen the Oaf.

The snow had started to descend more heavily and the fire in the ditch was guttering out. The crowd began to break apart and stream from the yard, queen's men, king's men, and free folk alike, all anxious to get out of the wind and the cold. "Will my lord be feasting with us?" Mully asked Jon Snow.

"Shortly." Sigorn might take it as a slight if he did not appear. *And this marriage is mine own work, after all.* "I have other matters to attend to first, however."

Jon crossed to Queen Selyse, with Ghost beside him. His boots crunched through piles of old snow. It was growing ever more time-consuming to shovel out the paths from one building to another; more and more, the men were resorting to the underground passages they called wormways.

". . . such a beautiful rite," the queen was saying. "I could feel our lord's fiery gaze upon us. Oh, you cannot know how many times I have begged Stannis to let us be wed again, a true joining of body and spirit blessed by the Lord of Light. I know that I could give His Grace more children if we were bound in fire."

To give him more children you would first need to get him into your bed. Even at the Wall, it was common knowledge that Stannis Baratheon had shunned his wife for years. One could only imagine how His Grace had responded to the notion of a second wedding in the midst of his war.

Jon bowed. "If it please Your Grace, the feast awaits."

The queen glanced at Ghost suspiciously, then raised her head to Jon. "To be sure. Lady Melisandre knows the way."

The red priestess spoke up. "I must attend my fires, Your Grace. Perhaps R'hllor will vouchsafe me a glimpse of His Grace. A glimpse of some great victory, mayhaps."

"Oh." Queen Selyse looked stricken. "To be sure . . . let us pray for a vision from our lord . . ."

"Satin, show Her Grace to her place," said Jon.

Ser Malegorn stepped forward. "I will escort Her Grace to the feast. We shall not require your . . . steward." The way the man drew out the last word told Jon that he had been considering saying something else. *Boy? Pet? Whore?*

Jon bowed again. "As you wish. I shall join you shortly."

Ser Malegorn offered his arm, and Queen Selyse took it stiffly. Her other hand settled on her daughter's shoulder. The royal ducklings fell in behind them as they made their way across the yard, marching to the music of the bells on the fool's hat. "Under the sea the mermen feast on starfish soup, and all the serving men are crabs," Patchface proclaimed as they went. "I know, I know, oh, oh, oh."

Melisandre's face darkened. "That creature is dangerous. Many a time I have glimpsed him in my flames. Sometimes there are skulls about him, and his lips are red with blood."

A wonder you haven't had the poor man burned. All it would take was a word in the queen's ear, and Patchface would feed her fires. "You see fools in your fire, but no hint of Stannis?"

"When I search for him all I see is snow."

The same useless answer. Clydas had dispatched a raven to Deepwood Motte to warn the king of Arnolf Karstark's treachery, but whether the bird had reached His Grace in time Jon did not know. The Braavosi banker was off in search of Stannis as well, accompanied by the guides that Jon had given him, but between the war and weather, it would be a wonder if he found him. "Would you know if the king was dead?" Jon asked the red priestess.

"He is not dead. Stannis is the Lord's chosen, destined to lead the fight against the dark. I have seen it in the flames, read of it in ancient prophecy. When the red star bleeds and the darkness gathers, Azor Ahai shall be born again amidst smoke and salt to wake dragons out of stone. Dragonstone is the place of smoke and salt."

Jon had heard all this before. "Stannis Baratheon was the Lord of Dragonstone, but he was not born there. He was born at Storm's End, like his brothers." He frowned. "And what of Mance? Is he lost as well? What do your fires show?"

"The same, I fear. Only snow."

Snow. It was snowing heavily to the south, Jon knew. Only two days' ride from here, the kingsroad was said to be impassable. *Melisandre knows that too.* And to the east, a savage storm was raging on the Bay of Seals. At last report, the ragtag fleet they had assembled to rescue the free folk from Hardhome still huddled at Eastwatch-by-the-Sea, confined to port by the rough seas. "You are seeing cinders dancing in the updraft."

"I am seeing skulls. And you. I see your face every time I look into the flames. The danger that I warned you of grows very close now."

"Daggers in the dark. I know. You will forgive my doubts, my lady. *A grey girl on a dying horse, fleeing from a marriage,* that was what you said."

"I was not wrong."

"You were not right. Alys is not Arya."

"The vision was a true one. It was my reading that was false. I am as mortal as you, Jon Snow. All mortals err."

"Even lord commanders." Mance Rayder and his spearwives had not returned, and Jon could not help but wonder whether the red woman had lied of a purpose. *Is she playing her own game?*

"You would do well to keep your wolf beside you, my lord."

"Ghost is seldom far." The direwolf raised his head at the sound of his name. Jon scratched him behind the ears. "But now you must excuse me. Ghost, with me."

Carved from the base of the Wall and closed with heavy wooden doors, the ice cells ranged from small to smaller. Some were big enough to allow a man to pace, others so small that prisoners were forced to sit; the smallest were too cramped to allow even that.

Jon had given his chief captive the largest cell, a pail to shit in, enough furs to keep him from freezing, and a skin of wine. It took the guards some time to open his cell, as ice had formed inside the lock. Rusted hinges screamed like damned souls when Wick Whittlestick yanked the door wide enough for Jon to slip through. A faint fecal odor greeted him, though less overpowering than he'd expected. Even shit froze solid in such bitter cold. Jon Snow could see his own reflection dimly inside the icy walls.

In one corner of the cell a heap of furs was piled up almost to the height of a man. "Karstark," said Jon Snow. "Wake up."

The furs stirred. Some had frozen together, and the frost that covered them glittered when they moved. An arm emerged, then a face—brown hair, tangled and matted and streaked with grey, two fierce eyes, a nose, a mouth, a beard. Ice caked the prisoner's mustache, clumps of frozen snot. "Snow." His breath steamed in the air, fogging the ice behind his head. "You have no right to hold me. The laws of hospitality—"

"You are no guest of mine. You came to the Wall without my leave, armed, to carry off your niece against her will. Lady Alys was given bread and salt. She is a guest. You are a prisoner." Jon let that hang for a moment, then said, "Your niece is wed."

Cregan Karstark's lips skinned back from his teeth. "Alys was promised to me." Though past fifty, he had been a strong man when he went into the cell. The cold had robbed him of that strength and left him stiff and weak. "My lord father—"

"Your father is a castellan, not a lord. And a castellan has no right to make marriage pacts."

"My father, Arnolf, is Lord of Karhold."

"A son comes before an uncle by all the laws I know."

Cregan pushed himself to his feet and kicked aside the furs clinging to his ankles. "Harrion is dead."

Or will be soon. "A daughter comes before an uncle too. If her brother is dead, Karhold belongs to Lady Alys. And she has given her hand in marriage to Sigorn, Magnar of Thenn."

"A wildling. A filthy, murdering wildling." Cregan's hands closed into fists. The gloves that covered them were leather, lined with fur to match the cloak that hung matted and stiff from his broad shoulders. His black wool surcoat was emblazoned with the white sunburst of his house. "I see what you are, Snow. Half a wolf and half a wildling, baseborn get of a traitor and a whore. You would deliver a highborn maid to the bed of some stinking savage. Did you sample her yourself first?" He laughed. "If you mean to kill me, do it and be damned for a kinslayer. Stark and Karstark are one blood."

"My name is Snow."

"*Bastard.*"

"Guilty. Of that, at least."

"Let this Magnar come to Karhold. We'll hack off his head and stuff it in a privy, so we can piss into his mouth."

"Sigorn leads two hundred Thenns," Jon pointed out, "and Lady Alys believes Karhold will open its gates to her. Two of your men have already sworn her their service and confirmed all she had to say concerning the plans your father made with Ramsay Snow. You have close kin at Karhold, I am told. A word from you could save their lives. Yield the castle. Lady Alys will pardon the women who betrayed her and allow the men to take the black."

Cregan shook his head. Chunks of ice had formed about the tangles in his hair, and *click*ed together softly when he moved. "Never," he said. "Never, never, never."

I should make his head a wedding gift for Lady Alys and her Magnar, Jon thought, but dare not take the risk. The Night's Watch took no part in the quarrels of the realm; some would say he had already given Stannis too much help. *Behead this fool, and they will claim I am killing northmen to give their lands to wildlings. Release him, and he will do his best to rip apart all I've done with Lady Alys and the Magnar.* Jon wondered what his father would do, how his uncle might deal with this. But Eddard Stark was dead, Benjen Stark lost in the frozen wilds beyond the Wall. *You know nothing, Jon Snow.*

"Never is a long time," Jon said. "You may feel differently on the morrow, or a year from now. Soon or late King Stannis will return to the Wall, however. When he does he will have you put to death . . . unless it happens that you are wearing a black cloak. When a man takes the black, his crimes are wiped away." *Even such a man as you.* "Now pray excuse me. I have a feast to attend."

After the biting cold of the ice cells, the crowded cellar was so hot that Jon felt suffocated from the moment he came down the steps. The air smelled of smoke and roasting meat and mulled wine. Axell Florent was making a toast as Jon took his place upon the dais. "To King Stannis and his wife, Queen Selyse, Light of the North!" Ser Axell bellowed. "To R'hllor, the Lord of Light, may he defend us all! One land, one god, one king!"

"*One land, one god, one king!*" the queen's men echoed.

Jon drank with the rest. Whether Alys Karstark would find any joy in her marriage he could not say, but this one night at least should be one of celebration.

The stewards began to bring out the first dish, an onion broth flavored with bits of goat and carrot. Not precisely royal fare, but nourishing; it tasted good enough and warmed the belly. Owen the Oaf took up his fiddle, and several of the free folk joined in with pipes and drums. *The same pipes and drums they played to sound Mance Rayder's attack upon the Wall.* Jon thought they sounded sweeter now. With the broth came loaves of coarse brown bread, warm from the oven. Salt and butter sat upon the tables. The sight made Jon gloomy. They were well provided with salt, Bowen Marsh had told him, but the last of the butter would be gone within a moon's turn.

Old Flint and The Norrey had been given places of high honor just below the dais. Both men had been too old to march with Stannis; they had sent their sons and grandsons in their stead. But they had been quick enough to descend on Castle Black for the wedding. Each had brought a wet nurse to the Wall as well. The Norrey woman was forty, with the biggest breasts Jon Snow had ever seen. The Flint girl was fourteen and flat-chested as a boy, though she did not lack for milk. Between the two of them, the child Val called Monster seemed to be thriving.

For that much Jon was grateful . . . but he did not believe for a moment that two such hoary old warriors would have hied down from their hills for that alone. Each had brought a tail of fighting men—five for Old Flint, twelve for The Norrey, all clad in ragged skins and studded leathers, fearsome as the face of winter. Some had long beards, some had scars, some had both; all worshiped the old gods of the north, those same gods worshiped by the free folk beyond the Wall. Yet here they sat, drinking to a marriage hallowed by some queer red god from beyond the seas.

Better that than refuse to drink. Neither Flint nor Norrey had turned their cups over to spill their wine upon the floor. That might betoken a certain acceptance. *Or perhaps they just hate to waste good southron wine. They will not have tasted much of it up in those stony hills of theirs.*

Between courses, Ser Axell Florent led Queen Selyse out onto the floor to dance. Others followed—the queen's knights first, partnered with her ladies. Ser Brus gave Princess Shireen her first dance, then took a turn with her mother. Ser Narbert danced with each of Selyse's lady companions in turn.

The queen's men outnumbered the queen's ladies three to one, so even the humblest serving girls were pressed into the dance. After a few songs some black brothers remembered skills learned at the courts and castles of their youth, before their sins had sent them to the Wall, and took the floor as well. That old rogue Ulmer of the Kingswood proved as adept at dancing as he was at archery, no doubt regaling his partners with his tales of the Kingswood Brotherhood, when he rode with Simon Toyne and Big Belly Ben and helped Wenda the White Fawn burn her mark in the buttocks of her highborn captives. Satin was all grace, dancing with three serving girls in turn but never presuming to approach a highborn lady. Jon judged that wise. He did not like the way some of the queen's knights were looking at the steward, particularly Ser Patrek of King's Mountain. *That one wants to shed a bit of blood,* he thought. *He is looking for some provocation.*

When Owen the Oaf began to dance with Patchface the fool, laughter echoed off the vaulted ceiling. The sight made Lady Alys smile. "Do you dance often, here at Castle Black?"

"Every time we have a wedding, my lady."

"You could dance with me, you know. It would be only courteous. You danced with me anon."

"Anon?" teased Jon.

"When we were children." She tore off a bit of bread and threw it at him. "As you know well."

"My lady should dance with her husband."

"My Magnar is not one for dancing, I fear. If you will not dance with me, at least pour me some of the mulled wine."

"As you command." He signaled for a flagon.

"So," said Alys, as Jon poured, "I am now a woman wed. A wildling husband with his own little wildling army."

"Free folk is what they call themselves. Most, at least. The Thenns are a people apart, though. Very old." Ygritte had told him that. *You know nothing, Jon Snow.* "They come from a hidden vale at the north end of the Frostfangs, surrounded by high peaks, and for thousands of years they've had more truck with the giants than with other men. It made them different."

"Different," she said, "but more like us."

"Aye, my lady. The Thenns have lords and laws." *They know how to kneel.* "They mine tin and copper for bronze, forge their own arms and armor instead of stealing it. A proud folk, and brave. Mance Rayder had to best the old Magnar thrice before Styr would accept him as King-Beyond-the-Wall."

"And now they are here, on our side of the Wall. Driven from their mountain fastness and into my bedchamber." She smiled a wry smile. "It is my own fault. My lord father told me I must charm your brother Robb, but I was only six and didn't know how."

Aye, but now you're almost six-and-ten, and we must pray you will know how to charm your new husband. "My lady, how do things stand at Karhold with your food stores?"

"Not well." Alys sighed. "My father took so many of our men south with him that only the women and young boys were left to bring the harvest in. Them, and the men too old or crippled to go off to war. Crops withered in the fields or were pounded into the mud by autumn rains. And now the snows are come. This winter will be hard. Few of the old people will survive it, and many children will perish as well."

It was a tale that any northmen knew well. "My father's grandmother was a Flint of the mountains, on his mother's side," Jon told her. "The First Flints, they call themselves. They say the other Flints are the blood of younger sons, who had to leave the mountains to find food and land and wives. It has always been a harsh life up there. When the snows fall and food grows scarce, their young must travel to the winter town or take service at one castle or the other. The old men gather up what strength remains in them and announce that they are going hunting. Some are found come spring. More are never seen again."

"It is much the same at Karhold."

That did not surprise him. "When your stores begin to dwindle, my lady, remember us. Send your old men to the Wall, let them say our words. Here at least they will not die alone in the snow, with only memories to warm them. Send us boys as well, if you have boys to spare."

"As you say." She touched his hand. "Karhold remembers."

The elk was being carved. It smelled better than Jon had any reason to expect. He dispatched a portion to Leathers out at Hardin's Tower, along with three big platters of roast vegetables for Wun Wun, then ate a healthy slice himself. *Three-Finger Hobb's acquitted himself well.* That had been a concern. Hobb had come to him two nights ago complaining that he'd joined the Night's Watch to kill wildlings, not to cook for them. "Besides, I never done no wedding feast, m'lord. Black brothers don't never take no wifes. It's in the bloody vows, I swear 'tis."

Jon was washing the roast down with a sip of mulled wine when Clydas appeared at his elbow. "A bird," he announced, and slipped a parchment into Jon's hand. The note was sealed with a dot of hard black wax. *Eastwatch,* Jon knew, even before he broke the seal. The letter had been written by Maester Harmune; Cotter Pyke could neither read nor write. But the words were Pyke's, set down as he had spoken them, blunt and to the point.

Calm seas today. Eleven ships set sail for Hardhome on the morning tide. Three Braavosi, four Lyseni, four of ours. Two of the Lyseni barely seaworthy. We may drown more wildlings than we save. Your command. Twenty ravens aboard, and Maester Harmune. Will send reports. I command from Talon, *Tattersalt second on* Blackbird, *Ser Glendon holds Eastwatch.*

"Dark wings, dark words?" asked Alys Karstark.

"No, my lady. This news was long awaited." *Though the last part troubles me.* Glendon Hewett was a seasoned man and a strong one, a sensible choice to command in Cotter Pyke's absence. But he was also as much a friend as Alliser Thorne could boast, and a crony of sorts with Janos Slynt, however briefly. Jon could still recall how Hewett had dragged him from his bed, and the feel of his boot slamming into his ribs. *Not the man I would have chosen.* He rolled the parchment up and slipped it into his belt.

The fish course was next, but as the pike was being boned Lady Alys dragged the Magnar up onto the floor. From the way he moved it was plain that Sigorn had never danced before, but he had drunk enough mulled wine so that it did not seem to matter.

"A northern maid and a wildling warrior, bound together by the Lord of Light." Ser Axell Florent slipped into Lady Alys's vacant seat. "Her Grace approves. I am close to her, my lord, so I know her mind. King Stannis will approve as well."

Unless Roose Bolton has stuck his head on a spear.

"Not all agree, alas." Ser Axell's beard was a ragged brush beneath his sagging chin; coarse hair sprouted from his ears and nostrils. "Ser Patrek feels he would have made a better match for Lady Alys. His lands were lost to him when he came north."

"There are many in this hall who have lost far more than that," said Jon, "and more who have given up their lives in service to the realm. Ser Patrek should count himself fortunate."

Axell Florent smiled. "The king might say the same if he were here. Yet some provision must be made for His Grace's leal knights, surely? They have followed him so far and at such cost. And we must needs bind these wildlings to king and realm. This marriage is a good first step, but I know that it would please the queen to see the wildling princess wed as well."

Jon sighed. He was weary of explaining that Val was no true princess. No matter how often he told them, they never seemed to hear. "You are persistent, Ser Axell, I grant you that."

"Do you blame me, my lord? Such a prize is not easily won. A nubile girl, I hear, and not hard to look upon. Good hips, good breasts, well made for whelping children."

"Who would father these children? Ser Patrek? You?"

"Who better? We Florents have the blood of the old Gardener kings in our veins. Lady Melisandre could perform the rites, as she did for Lady Alys and the Magnar."

"All you are lacking is a bride."

"Easily remedied." Florent's smile was so false that it looked painful. "Where is she, Lord Snow? Have you moved her to one of your other castles? Greyguard or the Shadow Tower? Whore's Burrow, with t'other wenches?" He leaned close. "Some say you have her tucked away for your own pleasure. It makes no matter to me, so long as she is not with child. I'll get my own sons on her. If you've broken her to saddle, well . . . we are both men of the world, are we not?"

Jon had heard enough. "Ser Axell, if you are truly the Queen's Hand, I pity Her Grace."

Florent's face grew flushed with anger. "So it *is* true. You mean to keep her for yourself, I see it now. The bastard wants his father's seat."

The bastard refused his father's seat. If the bastard had wanted Val, all he had to do was ask for her. "You must excuse me, ser," he said. "I need a breath of fresh air." *It stinks in here.* His head turned. "That was a horn."

Others had heard it too. The music and the laughter died at once. Dancers froze in place, listening. Even Ghost pricked up his ears. "Did you hear that?" Queen Selyse asked her knights.

"A warhorn, Your Grace," said Ser Narbert.

The queen's hand went fluttering to her throat. "Are we under attack?"

"No, Your Grace," said Ulmer of the Kingswood. "It's the watchers on the Wall, is all."

One blast, thought Jon Snow. *Rangers returning.*

Then it came again. The sound seemed to fill the cellar.

"Two blasts," said Mully.

Black brothers, northmen, free folk, Thenns, queen's men, all of them fell quiet, listening. Five heartbeats passed. Ten. Twenty. Then Owen the Oaf tittered, and Jon Snow could breathe again. "Two blasts," he announced. "Wildlings." *Val.*

Tormund Giantsbane had come at last.

DAENERYS

T he hall rang to Yunkish laughter, Yunkish songs, Yunkish prayers. Dancers danced; musicians played queer tunes with bells and squeaks and bladders; singers sang ancient love songs in the incomprehensible tongue of Old Ghis. Wine flowed—not the thin pale stuff of Slaver's Bay but rich sweet vintages from the Arbor and dreamwine from Qarth, flavored with strange spices. The Yunkai'i had come at King Hizdahr's invitation, to sign the peace and witness the rebirth of Meereen's far-famed fighting pits. Her noble husband had opened the Great Pyramid to fete them.

I hate this, thought Daenerys Targaryen. *How did this happen, that I am drinking and smiling with men I'd sooner flay?*

A dozen different sorts of meat and fish were served: camel, crocodile, singing squid, lacquered ducks and spiny grubs, with goat and ham and horse for those whose tastes were less exotic. Plus dog. No Ghiscari feast was complete without a course of dog. Hizdahr's cooks prepared dog four different ways. "Ghiscari will eat anything that swims or flies or crawls, but for man and dragon," Daario had warned her, "and I'd wager they'd eat dragon too if given half a chance." Meat alone does not make a meal, though, so there were fruits and grains and vegetables as well. The air was redolent with the scents of saffron, cinnamon, cloves, pepper, and other costly spices.

Dany scarce touched a bite. *This is peace,* she told herself. *This is what I wanted, what I worked for, this is why I married Hizdahr. So why does it taste so much like defeat?*

"It is only for a little while more, my love," Hizdahr had assured her. "The Yunkai'i will soon be gone, and their allies and hirelings with them. We shall have all we desired. Peace, food, trade. Our port is open once again, and ships are being permitted to come and go."

"They are *permitting* that, yes," she had replied, "but their warships remain. They can close their fingers around our throat again whenever they wish. *They have opened a slave market within sight of my walls!*"

"*Outside* our walls, sweet queen. That was a condition of the peace, that Yunkai would be free to trade in slaves as before, unmolested."

"In their own city. Not where I have to see it." The Wise Masters had established their slave pens and auction block just south of the Skahazadhan, where the wide brown river flowed into Slaver's Bay. "They are mocking me to my face, making a show of how powerless I am to stop them."

"Posing and posturing," said her noble husband. "A show, as you have said. Let them have their mummery. When they are gone, we will make a fruit market of what they leave behind."

"When they are gone," Dany repeated. "And when will they be gone? Riders have been seen beyond the Skahazadhan. Dothraki scouts, Rakharo says, with a *khalasar* behind them. They will have captives. Men, women, and children, gifts for the slavers." Dothraki did not buy or sell, but they gave gifts and received them. "That is why the Yunkai'i have thrown up this market. They will leave here with thousands of new slaves."

Hizdahr zo Loraq shrugged. "But they will leave. That is the important part, my love. Yunkai will trade in slaves, Meereen will not, this is what we have agreed. Endure this for a little while longer, and it shall pass."

So Daenerys sat silent through the meal, wrapped in a vermilion *tokar* and black thoughts, speaking only when spoken to, brooding on the men and women being bought and sold outside her walls, even as they feasted here within the city. Let her noble husband make the speeches and laugh at the feeble Yunkish japes. That was a king's right and a king's duty.

Much of the talk about the table was of the matches to be fought upon the morrow. Barsena Blackhair was going to face a boar, his tusks against her dagger. Khrazz was fighting, as was the Spotted Cat. And in the day's final pairing, Goghor the Giant would go against Belaquo Bonebreaker. One would be dead before the sun went down. *No queen has clean hands,* Dany told herself. She thought of Doreah, of Quaro, of Eroeh ... of a little girl she had never met, whose name had been Hazzea. *Better a few should die in the pit than thousands at the gates. This is the price of peace, I pay it willingly. If I look back, I am lost.*

The Yunkish Supreme Commander, Yurkhaz zo Yunzak, might have been alive during Aegon's Conquest, to judge by his appearance. Bent-backed, wrinkled, and toothless, he was carried to the table by two strapping slaves. The other Yunkish lords were hardly more impressive. One was small and stunted, though the slave soldiers who attended him were grotesquely tall and thin. The third was young, fit, and dashing, but so drunk that Dany could scarce understand a word he said. *How could I have been brought to this pass by creatures such as these?*

The sellswords were a different matter. Each of the four free companies serving Yunkai had sent its commander. The Windblown were represented by the Pentoshi nobleman known as the Tattered Prince, the Long Lances by Gylo Rhegan, who looked more shoemaker than soldier and spoke in murmurs. Bloodbeard, from the Company of the Cat, made enough noise for him and a dozen more. A huge man with a great bush of beard and a prodigious appetite for wine and women, he bellowed, belched, farted like a thunderclap, and pinched every serving girl who came within his reach. From time to time he would pull one down into his lap to squeeze her breasts and fondle her between the legs.

The Second Sons were represented too. *If Daario were here, this meal would end in blood.* No promised peace could ever have persuaded her captain to permit Brown Ben Plumm to stroll back into Meereen and leave alive. Dany had sworn that no harm would come to the seven envoys and commanders, though that had not been enough for the Yunkai'i. They had required hostages of her as well. To balance the three Yunkish nobles and four sellsword captains, Meereen sent seven of its own out to the siege camp: Hizdahr's sister, two of his cousins, Dany's bloodrider Jhogo, her admiral Groleo, the Unsullied captain Hero, and Daario Naharis.

"I will leave my girls with you," her captain had said, handing her his sword belt and its gilded wantons. "Keep them safe for me, beloved. We would not want them making bloody mischief amongst the Yunkai'i."

The Shavepate was absent as well. The first thing Hizdahr had done upon being crowned was to remove him from command of the Brazen Beasts, replacing him with his own cousin, the plump and pasty Marghaz zo Loraq. *It is for the best. The Green Grace says there is blood between Loraq and Kandaq, and the Shavepate never made a secret of his disdain for my lord husband. And Daario . . .*

Daario had only grown wilder since her wedding. Her peace did not please him, her marriage pleased him less, and he had been furious at being deceived by the Dornishmen. When Prince Quentyn told them that the other Westerosi had come over to the Stormcrows at the command of the Tattered Prince, only the intercession of Grey Worm and his Unsullied prevented Daario from killing them all. The false deserters had been imprisoned safely in the bowels of the pyramid . . . but Daario's rage continued to fester.

He will be safer as a hostage. My captain was not made for peace. Dany could not risk his cutting down Brown Ben Plumm, making mock of Hizdahr before the court, provoking the Yunkai'i, or otherwise upsetting the agreement that she had given up so much to win. Daario was war and woe. Henceforth, she must keep him out of her bed, out of her heart, and out of her. If he did not betray her, he would master her. She did not know which of those she feared the most.

When the gluttony was done and all the half-eaten food had been cleared away—to be given to the poor who gathered below, at the queen's insistence—tall glass flutes were filled with a spiced liqueur from Qarth as dark as amber. Then began the entertainments.

A troupe of Yunkish castrati owned by Yurkhaz zo Yunzak sang them songs in the ancient tongue of the Old Empire, their voices high and sweet and impossibly pure. "Have you ever heard such singing, my love?" Hizdahr asked her. "They have the voices of gods, do they not?"

"Yes," she said, "though I wonder if they might not have preferred to have the fruits of men."

All of the entertainers were slaves. That had been part of the peace, that slaveowners be allowed the right to bring their chattels into Meereen without fear of having them freed. In return the Yunkai'i had promised to respect the rights and liberties of the former slaves that Dany had freed. A fair bargain, Hizdahr said, but the taste it left in the queen's mouth was foul. She drank another cup of wine to wash it out.

"If it please you, Yurkhaz will be pleased to give us the singers, I do not doubt," her noble husband said. "A gift to seal our peace, an ornament to our court."

He will give us these castrati, Dany thought, *and then he will march home and make some more. The world is full of boys.*

The tumblers who came next failed to move her either, even when they formed a human pyramid nine levels high, with a naked little girl on top. *Is that meant to represent my pyramid?* the queen wondered. *Is the girl on top meant to be me?*

Afterward her lord husband led his guests onto the lower terrace, so the visitors from the Yellow City might behold Meereen by night. Wine cups in hand, the Yunkai'i wandered the garden in small groups, beneath lemon trees and night-blooming flowers, and Dany found herself face-to-face with Brown Ben Plumm.

He bowed low. "Worship. You look lovely. Well, you always did. None of them Yunkishmen are half so pretty. I thought I might bring a wedding gift for you, but the bidding went too high for old Brown Ben."

"I want no gifts from you."

"This one you might. The head of an old foe."

"Your own?" she said sweetly. "You betrayed me."

"Now that's a harsh way o' putting it, if you don't mind me saying." Brown Ben scratched at his speckled grey-and-white whiskers. "We went over to the winning side, is all. Same as we done before. It weren't all me, neither. I put it to my men."

"So *they* betrayed me, is that what you are saying? Why? Did I mistreat the Second Sons? Did I cheat you on your pay?"

"Never that," said Brown Ben, "but it's not all about the coin, Your High-and-Mightiness. I learned that a long time back, at my first battle. Morning after the fight, I was rooting through the dead, looking for the odd bit o' plunder, as it were. Came upon this one corpse, some axeman had taken his whole arm off at the shoulder. He was covered with flies, all crusty with dried blood, might be why no one else had touched him, but under them he wore this studded jerkin, looked to be good leather. I figured it might fit me well enough, so I chased away the flies and cut it off him. The damn thing was heavier than it had any right to be, though. Under the lining, he'd sewn a fortune in coin. *Gold*, Your Worship, sweet yellow gold. Enough for any man to live like a lord for the rest o' his days. But what good did it do him? There he was with all his coin, lying in the blood and mud with his fucking arm cut off. And that's the lesson, see? Silver's sweet and gold's our mother, but once you're dead they're worth less than that last shit you take as you lie dying. I told you once, there are old sellswords and there are bold sellswords, but there are no old bold sellswords. My boys didn't care to die, that's all, and when I told them that you couldn't unleash them dragons against the Yunkishmen, well . . ."

You saw me as defeated, Dany thought, *and who am I to say that you were wrong?* "I understand." She might have ended it there, but she was curious. "Enough gold to live like a lord, you said. What did you do with all that wealth?"

Brown Ben laughed. "Fool boy that I was, I told a man I took to be my friend, and he told our serjeant, and my brothers-in-arms come and relieved me o' that burden. Serjeant said I was too young, that I'd only waste it all on whores and such. He let me keep the jerkin, though." He spat. "You don't never want to trust a sellsword, m'lady."

"I have learned that much. One day I must be sure to thank you for the lesson."

Brown Ben's eyes crinkled up. "No need. I know the sort o' thanks you have in mind." He bowed again and moved away.

Dany turned to gaze out over her city. Beyond her walls the yellow tents of the Yunkai'i stood in orderly rows beside the sea, protected by the ditches their slaves had dug for them. Two iron legions out of New Ghis, trained and armed in the same fashion as Unsullied, were encamped across the river to the north. Two more Ghiscari legions had made camp to the east, choking off the road to the Khyzai Pass. The horse lines and cookfires of the free companies lay to the south. By day thin plumes of smoke hung against the sky like ragged grey ribbons. By night distant fires could be seen. Hard by the bay was the abomination, the slave market at her door. She could not see it now, with the sun set, but she knew that it was there. That just made her angrier.

"Ser Barristan?" she said softly.

The white knight appeared at once. "Your Grace."

"How much did you hear?"

"Enough. He was not wrong. Never trust a sellsword."

Or a queen, thought Dany. "Is there some man in the Second Sons who might be persuaded to . . . remove . . . Brown Ben?"

"As Daario Naharis once removed the other captains of the Stormcrows?" The old knight looked uncomfortable. "Perhaps. I would not know, Your Grace."

No, she thought, *you are too honest and too honorable.* "If not, the Yunkai'i employ three other companies."

"Rogues and cutthroats, scum of a hundred battlefields," Ser Barristan warned, "with captains full as treacherous as Plumm."

"I am only a young girl and know little of such things, but it seems to me that we *want* them to be treacherous. Once, you'll recall, I convinced the Second Sons and Stormcrows to join us."

"If Your Grace wishes a privy word with Gylo Rhegan or the Tattered Prince, I could bring them up to your apartments."

"This is not the time. Too many eyes, too many ears. Their absence would be noted even if you could separate them discreetly from the Yunkai'i. We must find some quieter way of reaching out to them . . . not tonight, but soon."

"As you command. Though I fear this is not a task for which I am well suited. In King's Landing work of this sort was left to Lord

Littlefinger or the Spider. We old knights are simple men, only good for fighting." He patted his sword hilt.

"Our prisoners," suggested Dany. "The Westerosi who came over from the Windblown with the three Dornishmen. We still have them in cells, do we not? Use them."

"Free them, you mean? Is that wise? They were sent here to worm their way into your trust, so they might betray Your Grace at the first chance."

"Then they failed. I do not trust them. I will never trust them." If truth be told, Dany was forgetting how to trust. "We can still use them. One was a woman. Meris. Send her back, as a . . . a gesture of my regard. If their captain is a clever man, he will understand."

"The woman is the worst of all."

"All the better." Dany considered a moment. "We should sound out the Long Lances too. And the Company of the Cat."

"Bloodbeard." Ser Barristan's frown deepened. "If it please Your Grace, we want no part of him. Your Grace is too young to remember the Ninepenny Kings, but this Bloodbeard is cut from the same savage cloth. There is no honor in him, only hunger . . . for gold, for glory, for blood."

"You know more of such men than me, ser." If Bloodbeard might be truly the most dishonorable and greedy of the sellswords, he might be the easiest to sway, but she was loath to go against Ser Barristan's counsel in such matters. "Do as you think best. But do it soon. If Hizdahr's peace should break, I want to be ready. I do not trust the slavers." *I do not trust my husband.* "They will turn on us at the first sign of weakness."

"The Yunkai'i grow weaker as well. The bloody flux has taken hold amongst the Tolosi, it is said, and spread across the river to the third Ghiscari legion."

The pale mare. Daenerys sighed. *Quaithe warned me of the pale mare's coming. She told me of the Dornish prince as well, the sun's son. She told me much and more, but all in riddles.* "I cannot rely on plague to save me from my enemies. Set Pretty Meris free. At once."

"As you command. Though . . . Your Grace, if I may be so bold, there is another road . . ."

"The Dornish road?" Dany sighed. The three Dornishmen had been at the feast, as befit Prince Quentyn's rank, though Reznak had taken care to seat them as far as possible from her husband. Hizdahr did not seem to be of a jealous nature, but no man would be pleased by the presence of a rival suitor near his new bride. "The boy seems pleasant and well spoken, but . . ."

"House Martell is ancient and noble, and has been a leal friend to House Targaryen for more than a century, Your Grace. I had the honor of serving with Prince Quentyn's great-uncle in your father's seven. Prince Lewyn was as valiant a brother-in-arms as any man could wish for. Quentyn Martell is of the same blood, if it please Your Grace."

"It would please me if he had turned up with these fifty thousand swords he speaks of. Instead he brings two knights and a parchment. Will a parchment shield my people from the Yunkai'i? If he had come with a fleet . . ."

"Sunspear has never been a sea power, Your Grace."

"No." Dany knew enough of Westerosi history to know that. Nymeria had landed ten thousand ships upon Dorne's sandy shores, but when she wed her Dornish prince she had burned them all and turned her back upon the sea forever. "Dorne is too far away. To please this prince, I would need to abandon all my people. You should send him home."

"Dornishmen are notoriously stubborn, Your Grace. Prince Quentyn's forebears fought your own for the better part of two hundred years. He will not go without you."

Then he will die here, Daenerys thought, *unless there is more to him than I can see.* "Is he still within?"

"Drinking with his knights."

"Bring him to me. It is time he met my children."

A flicker of doubt passed across the long, solemn face of Barristan Selmy. "As you command."

Her king was laughing with Yurkhaz zo Yunzak and the other Yunkish lords. Dany did not think that he would miss her, but just in case she instructed her handmaids to tell him that she was answering a call of nature, should he inquire after her.

Ser Barristan was waiting by the steps with the Dornish prince.

Martell's square face was flushed and ruddy. *Too much wine,* the queen concluded, though he was doing his best to conceal that. Apart from the line of copper suns that ornamented his belt, the Dornishman was plainly dressed. *They call him Frog,* Dany recalled. She could see why. He was not a handsome man.

She smiled. "My prince. It is a long way down. Are you certain that you wish to do this?"

"If it would please Your Grace."

"Then come."

A pair of Unsullied went down the steps before them, bearing torches; behind came two Brazen Beasts, one masked as a fish, the other as a hawk. Even here in her own pyramid, on this happy night of peace and celebration, Ser Barristan insisted on keeping guards about her everywhere she went. The small company made the long descent in silence, stopping thrice to refresh themselves along the way. "The dragon has three heads," Dany said when they were on the final flight. "My marriage need not be the end of all your hopes. I know why you are here."

"For you," said Quentyn, all awkward gallantry.

"No," said Dany. "For fire and blood."

One of the elephants trumpeted at them from his stall. An answering roar from below made her flush with sudden heat. Prince Quentyn looked up in alarm. "The dragons know when she is near," Ser Barristan told him.

Every child knows its mother, Dany thought. *When the seas go dry and mountains blow in the wind like leaves* . . . "They call to me. Come." She took Prince Quentyn by the hand and led him to the pit where two of her dragons were confined. "Remain outside," Dany told Ser Barristan, as the Unsullied were opening the huge iron doors. "Prince Quentyn will protect me." She drew the Dornish prince inside with her, to stand above the pit.

The dragons craned their necks around, gazing at them with burning eyes. Viserion had shattered one chain and melted the others. He clung to the roof of the pit like some huge white bat, his claws dug deep into the burnt and crumbling bricks. Rhaegal, still chained, was gnawing on the carcass of a bull. The bones on the floor of the pit were deeper than the last time she had been down here, and the walls and floors were black and grey, more ash than brick. They would not hold much longer . . . but behind them was only earth and stone. *Can dragons tunnel through rock, like the firewyrms of old Valyria?* She hoped not.

The Dornish prince had gone as white as milk. "I . . . I had heard that there were three."

"Drogon is hunting." He did not need to hear the rest. "The white one is Viserion, the green is Rhaegal. I named them for my brothers." Her voice echoed off the scorched stone walls. It sounded small—a girl's voice, not the voice of a queen and conqueror, nor the glad voice of a new-made bride.

Rhaegal roared in answer, and fire filled the pit, a spear of red and yellow. Viserion replied, his own flames gold and orange. When he flapped his wings, a cloud of grey ash filled the air. Broken chains clanked and clattered about his legs. Quentyn Martell jumped back a foot.

A crueler woman might have laughed at him, but Dany squeezed his hand and said, "They frighten me as well. There is no shame in that. My children have grown wild and angry in the dark."

"You . . . you mean to ride them?"

"One of them. All I know of dragons is what my brother told me when I was a girl, and some I read in books, but it is said that even Aegon the Conqueror never dared mount Vhagar or Meraxes, nor did his sisters ride Balerion the Black Dread. Dragons live longer than men, some for hundreds of years, so Balerion had other riders after Aegon died . . . but no rider ever flew two dragons."

Viserion hissed again. Smoke rose between his teeth, and deep down in his throat they could see gold fire churning.

"They are . . . they are fearsome creatures."

"They are *dragons*, Quentyn." Dany stood on her toes and kissed him lightly, once on each cheek. "And so am I."

The young prince swallowed. "I . . . I have the blood of the dragon in me as well, Your Grace. I can trace my lineage back to the first Daenerys, the Targaryen princess who was sister to King Daeron the Good and wife to the Prince of Dorne. He built the Water Gardens for her."

"The Water Gardens?" She knew little and less of Dorne or its history, if truth be told.

"My father's favorite palace. It would please me to show them to you one day. They are all of pink marble, with pools and fountains, overlooking the sea."

"They sound lovely." She drew him away from the pit. *He does not belong here. He should never have come.* "You ought to return there. My court is no safe place for you, I fear. You have more enemies than you know. You made Daario look a fool, and he is not a man to forget such a slight."

"I have my knights. My sworn shields."

"Two knights. Daario has five hundred Stormcrows. And you would do well to beware of my lord husband too. He seems a mild and pleasant man, I know, but do not be deceived. Hizdahr's crown derives from mine, and he commands the allegiance of some of the most fearsome fighters in the world. If one of them should think to win his favor by disposing of a rival . . ."

"I am a prince of Dorne, Your Grace. I will not run from slaves and sellswords."

Then you truly are a fool, Prince Frog. Dany gave her wild children one last lingering look. She could hear the dragons screaming as she led the boy back to the door, and see the play of light against the bricks, reflections of their fires. *If I look back, I am lost.* "Ser Barristan will have summoned a pair of sedan chairs to carry us back up to the banquet, but the climb can still be wearisome." Behind them, the great iron doors closed with a resounding *clang.* "Tell me of this other Daenerys. I know less than I should of the history of my father's kingdom. I never had a maester growing up." *Only a brother.*

"It would be my pleasure, Your Grace," said Quentyn.

It was well past midnight before the last of their guests took their leave and Dany retired to her own apartments to join her lord and king. Hizdahr at least was happy, if somewhat drunk. "I keep my promises," he told her, as Irri and Jhiqui were robing them for bed. "You wished for peace, and it is yours."

And you wished for blood, and soon enough I must give it to you, Dany thought, but what she said was, "I am grateful."

The excitement of the day had inflamed her husband's passions. No sooner had her handmaids retired for the night than he tore the robe from her and tumbled her backwards into bed. Dany slid her arms around him and let him have his way. Drunk as he was, she knew he would not be inside her long.

Nor was he. Afterward he nuzzled at her ear and whispered, "Gods grant that we have made a son tonight."

The words of Mirri Maz Duur rang in her head. *When the sun rises in the west and sets in the east. When the seas go dry and mountains blow in the wind like leaves. When your womb quickens again, and you bear a living child. Then he will return, and not before.* The meaning was plain enough; Khal Drogo was as like to return from the dead as she was to bear a living child. But there are some secrets she could not bring herself to share, even with a husband, so she let Hizdahr zo Loraq keep his hopes.

Her noble husband was soon fast asleep. Daenerys could only twist and turn beside him. She wanted to shake him, wake him, make him hold her, kiss her, fuck her again, but even if he did, he would fall back to sleep again afterward, leaving her alone in the darkness. She wondered what Daario was doing. Was he restless as well? Was he thinking about her? Did he love her, truly? Did he hate her for marrying Hizdahr? *I should never have taken him into my bed.* He was only a sellsword, no fit consort for a queen, and yet . . .

I knew that all along, but I did it anyway.

"My queen?" said a soft voice in the darkness.

Dany flinched. "Who is there?"

"Only Missandei." The Naathi scribe moved closer to the bed. "This one heard you crying."

"Crying? I was not crying. Why would I cry? I have my peace, I have my king, I have everything a queen might wish for. You had a bad dream, that was all."

"As you say, Your Grace." She bowed and made to go.

"Stay," said Dany. "I do not wish to be alone."

"His Grace is with you," Missandei pointed out.

"His Grace is dreaming, but I cannot sleep. On the morrow I must bathe in blood. The price of peace." She smiled wanly and patted the bed. "Come. Sit. Talk with me."

"If it please you." Missandei sat down beside her. "What shall we talk of?"

"Home," said Dany. "Naath. Butterflies and brothers. Tell me of the things that make you happy, the things that make you giggle, all your sweetest memories. Remind me that there is still good in the world."

Missandei did her best. She was still talking when Dany finally fell to sleep, to dream queer, half-formed dreams of smoke and fire.

The morning came too soon.

THEON

Day stole upon them just as Stannis had: unseen.

Winterfell had been awake for hours, its battlements and towers crammed with men in wool and mail and leather awaiting an attack that never came. By the time the sky began to lighten the sound of drums had faded away, though warhorns were heard thrice more, each time a little closer. And still the snow fell.

"The storm will end today," one of the surviving stableboys was insisting loudly. "Why, it isn't even winter." Theon would have laughed if he had dared. He remembered tales Old Nan had told them of storms that raged for forty days and forty nights, for a year, for ten years . . . storms that buried castles and cities and whole kingdoms under a hundred feet of snow.

He sat in the back of the Great Hall, not far from the horses, watching Abel, Rowan, and a mousy brown-haired washerwoman called Squirrel attack slabs of stale brown bread fried in bacon grease. Theon broke his own fast with a tankard of dark ale, cloudy with yeast and thick enough to chew on. A few more tankards, and perhaps Abel's plan might not seem quite so mad.

Roose Bolton entered, pale-eyed and yawning, accompanied by his plump and pregnant wife, Fat Walda. Several lords and captains had preceded him, amongst them Whoresbane Umber, Aenys Frey, and Roger Ryswell. Farther down the table Wyman Manderly sat wolfing down sausages and boiled eggs, whilst old Lord Locke beside him spooned gruel into his toothless mouth.

Lord Ramsay soon appeared as well, buckling on his sword belt as he made his way to the front of the hall. *His mood is foul this morning.* Theon could tell. *The drums kept him awake all night,* he guessed, *or someone has displeased him.* One wrong word, an ill-considered look, an ill-timed laugh, any of them could provoke his lordship's wroth and cost a man a strip of skin. *Please, m'lord, don't look this way.* One glance would be all it would take for Ramsay to know everything. *He'll see it written on my face. He'll know. He always knows.*

Theon turned to Abel. "This will not work." His voice was pitched so low that even the horses could not have overheard. "We will be caught before we leave the castle. Even if we do escape, Lord Ramsay will hunt us down, him and Ben Bones and the girls."

"Lord Stannis is outside the walls, and not far by the sound of it. All we need do is reach him." Abel's fingers danced across the strings of his lute. The singer's beard was brown, though his long hair had largely gone to grey. "If the Bastard does come after us, he might live long enough to rue it."

Think that, Theon thought. *Believe that. Tell yourself it's true.* "Ramsay will use your women as his prey," he told the singer. "He'll hunt them down, rape them, and feed their corpses to his dogs. If they lead him a good chase, he may name his next litter of bitches after them. You he'll flay. Him and Skinner and Damon Dance-for-Me, they will make a game of it. You'll be begging them to kill you." He clutched the singer's arm with a maimed hand. "You swore you would not let me fall into his hands again. I have your word on that." He needed to hear it again.

"Abel's word," said Squirrel. "Strong as oak." Abel himself only shrugged. "No matter what, my prince."

Up on the dais, Ramsay was arguing with his father. They were too far away for Theon to make out any of the words, but the fear on Fat Walda's round pink face spoke volumes. He did hear Wyman Manderly calling for more sausages and Roger Ryswell's laughter at some jape from one-armed Harwood Stout.

Theon wondered if he would ever see the Drowned God's watery halls, or if his ghost would linger here at Winterfell. *Dead is dead. Better dead than Reek.* If Abel's scheme went awry, Ramsay would make their dying long and hard. *He will flay me from head to heel this time, and no amount of begging will end the anguish.* No pain Theon had ever known came close to the agony that Skinner could evoke with a little flensing blade. Abel would learn that lesson soon enough. And for what? *Jeyne, her name is Jeyne, and her eyes are the wrong color.* A mummer playing a part. *Lord Bolton knows, and Ramsay, but the rest are blind, even this bloody bard with his sly smiles. The jape is on you, Abel, you and your murdering whores. You'll die for the wrong girl.*

He had come this close to telling them the truth when Rowan had delivered him to Abel in the ruins of the Burned Tower, but at the last instant he had held his tongue. The singer seemed intent on making off with the daughter of Eddard Stark. If he knew that Lord Ramsay's bride was but a steward's whelp, well . . .

The doors of the Great Hall opened with a crash.

A cold wind came swirling through, and a cloud of ice crystals sparkled blue-white in the air. Through it strode Ser Hosteen Frey, caked with snow to the waist, a body in his arms. All along the benches men put down their cups and spoons to turn and gape at the grisly spectacle. The hall grew quiet.

Another murder.

Snow slid from Ser Hosteen's cloaks as he stalked toward the high table, his steps ringing against the floor. A dozen Frey knights and men-at-arms entered behind him. One was a boy Theon knew—Big Walder, the little one, fox-faced and skinny as a stick. His chest and arms and cloak were spattered with blood.

The scent of it set the horses to screaming. Dogs slid out from under the tables, sniffing. Men rose from the benches. The body in Ser Hosteen's arms sparkled in the torchlight, armored in pink frost. The cold outside had frozen his blood.

"My brother Merrett's son." Hosteen Frey lowered the body to the floor before the dais. "Butchered like a hog and shoved beneath a snowbank. A *boy*."

Little Walder, thought Theon. *The big one.* He glanced at Rowan.

There are six of them, he remembered. *Any of them could have done this.* But the washerwoman felt his eyes. "This was no work of ours," she said.

"Be quiet," Abel warned her.

Lord Ramsay descended from the dais to the dead boy. His father rose more slowly, pale-eyed, still-faced, solemn. "This was foul work." For once Roose Bolton's voice was loud enough to carry. "Where was the body found?"

"Under that ruined keep, my lord," replied Big Walder. "The one with the old gargoyles." The boy's gloves were caked with his cousin's blood. "I told him not to go out alone, but he said he had to find a man who owed him silver."

"What man?" Ramsay demanded. "Give me his name. Point him out to me, boy, and I will make you a cloak of his skin."

"He never said, my lord. Only that he won the coin at dice." The Frey boy hesitated. "It was some White Harbor men who taught dice. I couldn't say which ones, but it was them."

"My lord," boomed Hosteen Frey. "We know the man who did this. Killed this boy and all the rest. Not by his own hand, no. He is too fat and craven to do his own killing. But by his word." He turned to Wyman Manderly. "Do you deny it?"

The Lord of White Harbor bit a sausage in half. "I confess . . ." He wiped the grease from his lips with his sleeve. ". . . I confess that I know little of this poor boy. Lord Ramsay's squire, was he not? How old was the lad?"

"Nine, on his last nameday."

"So young," said Wyman Manderly. "Though mayhaps this was a blessing. Had he lived, he would have grown up to be a Frey."

Ser Hosteen slammed his foot into the tabletop, knocking it off its trestles, back into Lord Wyman's swollen belly. Cups and platters flew, sausages scattered everywhere, and a dozen Manderly men came cursing to their feet. Some grabbed up knives, platters, flagons, anything that might serve as a weapon.

Ser Hosteen Frey ripped his longsword from its scabbard and leapt toward Wyman Manderly. The Lord of White Harbor tried to jerk away, but the tabletop pinned him to his chair. The blade slashed through three of his four chins in a spray of bright red blood. Lady Walda gave a shriek and clutched at her lord husband's arm. "Stop," Roose Bolton shouted. "*Stop this madness.*" His own men rushed forward as the Manderlys vaulted over the benches to get at the Freys. One lunged at Ser Hosteen with a dagger, but the big knight pivoted and took his arm off at the shoulder. Lord Wyman pushed to his feet, only to collapse. Old Lord Locke was shouting for a maester as Manderly flopped on the floor like a clubbed walrus in a spreading pool of blood. Around him dogs fought over sausages.

It took two score Dreadfort spearmen to part the combatants and put an end to the carnage. By that time six White Harbor men and two Freys lay dead upon the floor. A dozen more were wounded and one of the Bastard's Boys, Luton, was dying noisily, crying for his mother as he tried to shove a fistful of slimy entrails back through a gaping belly wound. Lord Ramsay silenced him, yanking a spear from one of Steelshanks's men and driving it down through Luton's chest. Even then the rafters still rang with shouts and prayers and curses, the shrieks of terrified horses and the growls of Ramsay's bitches. Steelshanks Walton had to slam the butt of his spear against the floor a dozen times before the hall quieted enough for Roose Bolton to be heard.

"I see you all want blood," the Lord of the Dreadfort said. Maester Rhodry stood beside him, a raven on his arm. The bird's black plumage shone like coal oil in the torchlight. *Wet,* Theon realized. *And in his lordship's hand, a parchment. That will be wet as well. Dark wings, dark words.* "Rather than use our swords upon each other, you might try them on Lord Stannis." Lord Bolton unrolled the parchment. "His host lies not three days' ride from here, snowbound and starving, and I for one am tired of waiting on his pleasure. Ser Hosteen, assemble your knights and men-at-arms by the main gates. As you are so eager for battle, you shall strike our first blow. Lord Wyman, gather your White Harbor men by the east gate. They shall go forth as well."

Hosteen Frey's sword was red almost to the hilt. Blood spatters speckled his cheeks like freckles. He lowered his blade and said, "As my lord commands. But after I deliver you the head of Stannis Baratheon, I mean to finish hacking off Lord Lard's."

Four White Harbor knights had formed a ring around Lord Wyman, as Maester Medrick labored over him to staunch his bleeding. "First you must needs come through us, ser," said the eldest of them, a hard-faced greybeard whose bloodstained surcoat showed three silvery mermaids upon a violet field.

"Gladly. One at a time or all at once, it makes no matter."

"*Enough,*" roared Lord Ramsay, brandishing his bloody spear. "Another threat, and I'll gut you all myself. My lord father has spoken! Save your wroth for the pretender Stannis."

Roose Bolton gave an approving nod. "As he says. There will be time enough to fight each other once we are done with Stannis." He turned his head, his pale cold eyes searching the hall until they found the bard Abel beside Theon. "Singer," he called, "come sing us something soothing."

Abel bowed. "If it please your lordship." Lute in hand, he sauntered to the dais, hopping nimbly over a corpse or two, and seated himself cross-legged on the high table. As he began to play—a sad, soft song that Theon Greyjoy did not recognize—Ser Hosteen, Ser Aenys, and their fellow Freys turned away to lead their horses from the hall.

Rowan grasped Theon's arm. "The bath. It must be now."

He wrenched free of her touch. "By day? We will be seen."

"The snow will hide us. Are you deaf? Bolton is sending forth his swords. We have to reach King Stannis before they do."

"But . . . Abel . . ."

"Abel can fend for himself," murmured Squirrel.

This is madness. Hopeless, foolish, doomed. Theon drained the last dregs of his ale and rose reluctantly to his feet. "Find your sisters. It takes a deal of water to fill my lady's tub."

Squirrel slipped away, soft-footed as she always was. Rowan walked Theon from the hall. Since she and her sisters had found him in the godswood, one of them had dogged his every step, never letting him out of sight. They did not trust him. *Why should they? I was Reek before and might be Reek again. Reek, Reek, it rhymes with sneak.*

Outside the snow still fell. The snowmen the squires had built had grown into monstrous giants, ten feet tall and hideously misshapen.

White walls rose to either side as he and Rowan made their way to the godswood; the paths between keep and tower and hall had turned into a maze of icy trenches, shoveled out hourly to keep them clear. It was easy to get lost in that frozen labyrinth, but Theon Greyjoy knew every twist and turning.

Even the godswood was turning white. A film of ice had formed upon the pool beneath the heart tree, and the face carved into its pale trunk had grown a mustache of little icicles. At this hour they could not hope to have the old gods to themselves. Rowan pulled Theon away from the northmen praying before the tree, to a secluded spot back by the barracks wall, beside a pool of warm mud that stank of rotten eggs. Even the mud was icing up about the edges, Theon saw. "Winter is coming . . ."

Rowan gave him a hard look. "You have no right to mouth Lord Eddard's words. Not you. Not ever. After what you did—"

"You killed a boy as well."

"That was not us. I told you."

"Words are wind." *They are no better than me. We're just the same.* "You killed the others, why not him? Yellow Dick—"

"—stank as bad as you. A pig of a man."

"And Little Walder was a piglet. Killing him brought the Freys and Manderlys to dagger points, that was cunning, you—"

"*Not us.*" Rowan grabbed him by the throat and shoved him back against the barracks wall, her face an inch from his. "Say it again and I will rip your lying tongue out, kinslayer."

He smiled through his broken teeth. "You won't. You need my tongue to get you past the guards. You need my lies."

Rowan spat in his face. Then she let him go and wiped her gloved hands on her legs, as if just touching him had soiled her.

Theon knew he should not goad her. In her own way, this one was as dangerous as Skinner or Damon Dance-for-Me. But he was cold and tired, his head was pounding, he had not slept in days. "I have done terrible things . . . betrayed my own, turned my cloak, ordered the death of men who trusted me . . . but I am no kinslayer."

"Stark's boys were never brothers to you, aye. We know."

That was true, but it was not what Theon had meant. *They were not my blood, but even so, I never harmed them. The two we killed were just some miller's sons.* Theon did not want to think about their mother. He had known the miller's wife for years, had even bedded her. *Big heavy breasts with wide dark nipples, a sweet mouth, a merry laugh. Joys that I will never taste again.*

But there was no use telling Rowan any of that. She would never believe his denials, any more than he believed hers. "There is blood on my hands, but not the blood of brothers," he said wearily. "And I've been punished."

"Not enough." Rowan turned her back on him.

Foolish woman. He might well be a broken thing, but Theon still wore a dagger. It would have been a simple thing to slide it out and drive it down between her shoulder blades. That much he was still capable of, missing teeth and broken teeth and all. It might even be a kindness—a quicker, cleaner end than the one she and her sisters would face when Ramsay caught them.

Reek might have done it. *Would* have done it, in hopes it might please Lord Ramsay. These whores meant to steal Ramsay's bride; Reek could not allow that. But the old gods had known him, had called him Theon. *Ironborn, I was ironborn, Balon Greyjoy's son and rightful heir to Pyke.* The stumps of his fingers itched and twitched, but he kept his dagger in its sheath.

When Squirrel returned, the other four were with her: gaunt grey-haired Myrtle, Willow Witch-Eye with her long black braid, Frenya of the thick waist and enormous breasts, Holly with her knife. Clad as serving girls in layers of drab grey roughspun, they wore brown woolen cloaks lined with white rabbit fur. *No swords,* Theon saw. *No axes, no hammers, no weapons but knives.* Holly's cloak was fastened with a silver clasp, and Frenya had a girdle of hempen rope wound about her middle from her hips to breasts. It made her look even more massive than she was.

Myrtle had servant's garb for Rowan. "The yards are crawling with fools," she warned them. "They mean to ride out."

"Kneelers," said Willow, with a snort of contempt. "Their lordly lord spoke, they must obey."

"They're going to die," chirped Holly, happily.

"Them and us," said Theon. "Even if we do get past the guards, how do you mean to get Lady Arya out?"

Holly smiled. "Six women go in, six come out. Who looks at serving girls? We'll dress the Stark girl up as Squirrel."

Theon glanced at Squirrel. *They are almost of a size. It might work.* "And how does Squirrel get out?"

Squirrel answered for herself. "Out a window, and straight down to the godswood. I was twelve the first time my brother took me raiding south o' your Wall. That's where I got my name. My brother said I looked like a squirrel running up a tree. I've done that Wall six times since, over and back again. I think I can climb down some stone tower."

"Happy, turncloak?" Rowan asked. "Let's be about it."

Winterfell's cavernous kitchen occupied a building all its own, set well apart from the castle's main halls and keeps in case of fire. Inside, the smells changed hour by hour—an ever-changing perfume of roast meats, leeks and onions, fresh-baked bread. Roose Bolton had posted guards at the kitchen door. With so many mouths to feed, every scrap of food was precious. Even the cooks and potboys were watched constantly. But the guards knew Reek. They liked to taunt him when he came to fetch hot water for Lady Arya's bath. None of them dared go further than that, though. Reek was known to be Lord Ramsay's pet.

"The Prince of Stink is come for some hot water," one guard announced when Theon and his serving girls appeared before him. He pushed the door open for them. "Quick now, before all that sweet warm air escapes."

Within, Theon grabbed a passing potboy by the arm. "Hot water for m'lady, boy," he commanded. "Six pails full, and see that it's good and hot. Lord Ramsay wants her pink and clean."

"Aye, m'lord," the boy said. "At once, m'lord."

"At once" took longer than Theon would have liked. None of the big kettles was clean, so the potboy had to scrub one out before filling it with water. Then it seemed to take forever to come to a rolling boil and twice forever to fill six wooden pails. All the while Abel's women waited, their faces shadowed by their cowls. *They are doing it all wrong.* Real serving girls were always teasing the potboys, flirting with the cooks, wheedling a taste of this, a bite of that. Rowan and her scheming sisters did not want to attract notice, but their sullen silence soon had the guards giving them queer looks. "Where's Maisie and Jez and t'other girls?" one asked Theon. "The usual ones."

"Lady Arya was displeased with them," he lied. "Her water was cold before it reached the tub last time."

The hot water filled the air with clouds of steam, melting the snowflakes as they came drifting down. Back through the maze of ice-walled trenches went the procession. With every sloshing step the water cooled. The passages were clogged with troops: armored knights in woolen surcoats and fur cloaks, men-at-arms with spears across their shoulders, archers carrying unstrung bows and sheaves of arrows, freeriders, grooms leading warhorses. The Frey men wore the badge of the two towers, those from White Harbor displayed merman and trident. They shouldered through the storm in opposite directions and eyed each other warily as they passed, but no swords were drawn. Not here. *It may be different out there in the woods.*

Half a dozen seasoned Dreadfort men guarded the doors of the Great Keep. "Another bloody bath?" said their serjeant when he saw the pails of steaming water. He had his hands tucked up into his armpits against the cold. "She had a bath last night. How dirty can one woman get in her own bed?"

Dirtier than you know, when you share that bed with Ramsay, Theon thought, remembering the wedding night and the things that he and Jeyne had been made to do. "Lord Ramsay's command."

"Get in there, then, before the water freezes," the serjeant said. Two of the guards pushed open the double doors.

The entryway was nigh as cold as the air outside. Holly kicked snow from her boots and lowered the hood of her cloak. "I thought that would be harder." Her breath frosted the air.

"There are more guards upstairs at m'lord's bedchamber," Theon warned her. "Ramsay's men." He dare not call them the Bastard's Boys, not here. You never knew who might be listening. "Keep your heads down and your hoods up."

"Do as he says, Holly," Rowan said. "There's some will know your face. We don't need that trouble."

Theon led the way up the stairs. *I have climbed these steps a thousand times before.* As a boy he would run up; descending, he would take the steps three at a time, leaping. Once he leapt right into Old Nan and knocked her to the floor. That earned him the worst thrashing he ever had at Winterfell, though it was almost tender compared to the beatings his brothers used to give him back on Pyke. He and Robb had fought many a heroic battle on these steps, slashing at one another with wooden swords. Good training, that; it brought home how hard it was to fight your way up a spiral stair against determined opposition. Ser Rodrik liked to say that one good man could hold a hundred, fighting down.

That was long ago, though. They were all dead now. Jory, old Ser Rodrik, Lord Eddard, Harwin and Hullen, Cayn and Desmond and Fat Tom, Alyn with his dreams of knighthood, Mikken who had given him his first real sword. Even Old Nan, like as not.

And Robb. Robb who had been more a brother to Theon than any son born of Balon Greyjoy's loins. *Murdered at the Red Wedding, butchered by the Freys. I should have been with him. Where was I? I should have died with him.*

Theon stopped so suddenly that Willow almost plowed into his back. The door to Ramsay's bedchamber was before him. And guarding it were two of the Bastard's Boys, Sour Alyn and Grunt.

The old gods must wish us well. Grunt had no tongue and Sour Alyn had no wits, Lord Ramsay liked to say. One was brutal, the other mean, but both had spent most of their lives in service at the Dreadfort. They did as they were told.

"I have hot water for the Lady Arya," Theon told them.

"Try a wash yourself, Reek," said Sour Alyn. "You smell like horse piss." Grunt grunted in agreement. Or perhaps that noise was meant to be a laugh. But Alyn unlocked the door to the bedchamber, and Theon waved the women through.

No day had dawned inside this room. Shadows covered all. One last log crackled feebly amongst the dying embers in the hearth, and a candle flickered on the table beside a rumpled, empty bed. *The girl is gone,* Theon thought. *She has thrown herself out a window in despair.* But the windows here were shuttered against the storm, sealed up by crusts of blown snow and frost. "Where is she?" Holly asked. Her sisters emptied their pails into the big round wooden tub. Frenya shut the chamber door and put her back against it. "*Where is she?*" Holly said again. Outside a horn was blowing. *A trumpet. The Freys, assembling for battle.* Theon could feel an itching in his missing fingers.

Then he saw her. She was huddled in the darkest corner of the bedchamber, on the floor, curled up in a ball beneath a pile of wolf-skins. Theon might never have spotted her but for the way she trembled. Jeyne had pulled the furs up over herself to hide. *From us? Or was she expecting her lord husband?* The thought that Ramsay might be coming made him want to scream. "My lady." Theon could not bring himself to call her Arya and dare not call her Jeyne. "No need to hide. These are friends."

The furs stirred. An eye peered out, shining with tears. *Dark, too dark. A brown eye.* "Theon?"

"Lady Arya." Rowan moved closer. "You must come with us, and quickly. We've come to take you to your brother."

"Brother?" The girl's face emerged from underneath the wolfskins. "I . . . I have no brothers."

She has forgotten who she is. She has forgotten her name. "That's so," said Theon, "but you had brothers once. Three of them. Robb and Bran and Rickon."

"They're dead. I have no brothers now."

"You have a half-brother," Rowan said. "Lord Crow, he is."

"Jon Snow?"

"We'll take you to him, but you must come at once."

Jeyne pulled her wolfskins up to her chin. "No. This is some trick. It's him, it's my . . . my lord, my sweet lord, he sent you, this is just some test to make sure that I love him. I do, I do, I love him more than anything." A tear ran down her cheek. "Tell him, you tell him. I'll do what he wants . . . whatever he wants . . . with him or . . . or with the dog or . . . please . . . he doesn't need to cut my feet off, I won't try to run away, not ever, I'll give him sons, I swear it, I swear it . . ."

Rowan whistled softly. "Gods curse the man."

"I'm a *good* girl," Jeyne whimpered. "They *trained* me."

Willow scowled. "Someone stop her crying. That guard was mute, not deaf. They're going to hear."

"Get her *up*, turncloak." Holly had her knife in hand. "Get her up or I will. *We have to go.* Get the little cunt up on her feet and shake some courage into her."

"And if she screams?" said Rowan.

We are all dead, Theon thought. *I told them this was folly, but none of them would listen.* Abel had doomed them. All singers were half-mad. In songs, the hero always saved the maiden from the monster's castle, but life was not a song, no more than Jeyne was Arya Stark. *Her eyes are the wrong color. And there are no heroes here, only whores.* Even so, he knelt beside her, pulled down the furs, touched her cheek. "You know me. I'm Theon, you remember. I know you too. I know your name."

"My name?" She shook her head. "My name . . . it's . . ."

He put a finger to her lips. "We can talk about that later. You need to be quiet now. Come with us. With me. We will take you away from here. Away from him."

Her eyes widened. "Please," she whispered. "Oh, please."

Theon slipped his hand through hers. The stumps of his lost fingers tingled as he drew the girl to her feet. The wolfskins fell away from her. Underneath them she was naked, her small pale breasts covered with teeth marks. He heard one of the women suck in her breath. Rowan thrust a bundle of clothes into his hands. "Get her dressed. It's cold outside." Squirrel had stripped down to her smallclothes, and was rooting through a carved cedar chest in search of something warmer. In the end she settled for one of Lord Ramsay's quilted doublets and a well-worn pair of breeches that flapped about her legs like a ship's sails in a storm.

With Rowan's help, Theon got Jeyne Poole into Squirrel's clothes. *If the gods are good and the guards are blind, she may pass.* "Now we are going out and down the steps," Theon told the girl. "Keep your head down and your hood up. Follow Holly. Don't run, don't cry, don't speak, don't look anyone in the eye."

"Stay close to me," Jeyne said. "Don't leave me."

"I will be right beside you," Theon promised as Squirrel slipped into Lady Arya's bed and pulled the blanket up.

Frenya opened the bedchamber door.

"You give her a good wash, Reek?" asked Sour Alyn as they emerged. Grunt gave Willow's breast a squeeze as she went by. They were fortunate in his choice. If the man had touched Jeyne, she might have screamed. Then Holly would have opened his throat for him with the knife hidden up her sleeve. Willow simply twisted away and past him.

For a moment Theon felt almost giddy. *They never looked. They never saw. We walked the girl right by them!*

But on the steps the fear returned. What if they met Skinner or Damon Dance-for-Me or Steelshanks Walton? Or Ramsay himself? *Gods save me, not Ramsay, anyone but him.* What use was it to smuggle the girl out of her bedchamber? They were still inside the castle, with every gate closed and barred and the battlements thick with sentries. Like as not, the guards outside the keep would stop them. Holly and her knife would be of small use against six men in mail with swords and spears.

But the guards outside were huddled by the doors, backs turned against the icy wind and blown snow. Even the serjeant did not spare them more than a quick glance. Theon felt a stab of pity for him and his men. Ramsay would flay them all when he learned his bride was gone, and what he would do to Grunt and Sour Alyn did not bear thinking about.

Not ten yards from the door, Rowan dropped her empty pail, and her sisters did likewise. The Great Keep was already lost to sight behind them. The yard was a white wilderness, full of half-heard sounds that echoed strangely amidst the storm. The icy trenches rose around them, knee high, then waist high, then higher than their heads. They were in the heart of Winterfell with the castle all around them, but no sign of it could be seen. They might have easily been lost amidst the Land of Always Winter, a thousand leagues beyond the Wall. "It's cold," Jeyne Poole whimpered as she stumbled along at Theon's side.

And soon to be colder. Beyond the castle walls, winter was waiting with its icy teeth. *If we get that far.* "This way," he said when they came to a junction where three trenches crossed.

"Frenya, Holly, go with them," Rowan said. "We will be along with Abel. Do not wait for us." And with that, she whirled and plunged into the snow, toward the Great Hall. Willow and Myrtle hurried after her, cloaks snapping in the wind.

Madder and madder, thought Theon Greyjoy. Escape had seemed unlikely with all six of Abel's women; with only two, it seemed impossible. But they had gone too far to return the girl to her bedchamber and pretend none of this had ever happened. Instead he took Jeyne by the arm and drew her down the pathway to the Battlements Gate. *Only a half-gate,* he reminded himself. *Even if the guards let us pass, there is no way through the outer wall.* On other nights, the guards had allowed Theon through, but all those times he'd come alone. He would not pass so easily with three serving girls in tow, and if the guards looked beneath Jeyne's hood and recognized Lord Ramsay's bride . . .

The passage twisted to the left. There before them, behind a veil of falling snow, yawned the Battlements Gate, flanked by a pair of guards. In their wool and fur and leather, they looked as big as bears. The spears they held were eight feet tall. "Who goes there?" one called out. Theon did not recognize the voice. Most of the man's features were covered by the scarf about his face. Only his eyes could be seen. "Reek, is that you?"

Yes, he meant to say. Instead he heard himself reply, "Theon Greyjoy. I . . . I have brought some women for you."

"You poor boys must be freezing," said Holly. "Here, let me warm you up." She slipped past the guard's spearpoint and reached up to his face, pulling loose the half-frozen scarf to plant a kiss upon his mouth. And as their lips touched, her blade slid through the meat of his neck, just below the ear. Theon saw the man's eyes widen. There was blood on Holly's lips as she stepped back, and blood dribbling from his mouth as he fell.

The second guard was still gaping in confusion when Frenya grabbed the shaft of his spear. They struggled for a moment, tugging, till the woman wrenched the weapon from his fingers and clouted him across the temple with its butt. As he stumbled backwards, she spun the spear around and drove its point through his belly with a grunt.

Jeyne Poole let out a shrill, high scream.

"Oh, bloody shit," said Holly. "That will bring the kneelers down on us, and no mistake. *Run!*"

Theon clapped one hand around Jeyne's mouth, grabbed her about the waist with the other, and pulled her past the dead and dying guards, through the gate, and over the frozen moat. And perhaps the old gods were still watching over them; the drawbridge had been left down, to allow Winterfell's defenders to cross to and from the outer battlements more quickly. From behind them came alarums and the sounds of running feet, then the blast of a trumpet from the ramparts of the inner wall.

On the drawbridge, Frenya stopped and turned. "Go on. I will hold the kneelers here." The bloody spear was still clutched in her big hands.

Theon was staggering by the time he reached the foot of the stair. He slung the girl over his shoulder and began to climb. Jeyne had ceased to struggle by then, and she was such a little thing besides . . . but the steps were slick with ice beneath soft powdery snow, and halfway up he lost his footing and went down hard on one knee. The pain was so bad he almost lost the girl, and for half a heartbeat he feared this was as far as he would go. But Holly pulled him back onto his feet, and between the two of them they finally got Jeyne up to the battlements.

As he leaned up against a merlon, breathing hard, Theon could hear the shouting from below, where Frenya was fighting half a dozen guardsmen in the snow. "Which way?" he shouted at Holly. "Where do we go now? *How do we get out?*"

The fury on Holly's face turned to horror. "Oh, fuck me bloody. The rope." She gave a hysterical laugh. *"Frenya has the rope."* Then she grunted and grabbed her stomach. A quarrel had sprouted from her gut. When she wrapped a hand around it, blood leaked through her fingers. "Kneelers on the inner wall . . ." she gasped, before a second shaft appeared between her breasts. Holly grabbed for the nearest merlon and fell. The snow that she'd knocked loose buried her with a soft *thump.*

Shouts rang out from their left. Jeyne Poole was staring down at Holly as the snowy blanket over her turned from white to red. On the inner wall the crossbowman would be reloading, Theon knew. He started right, but there were men coming from that direction too, racing toward them with swords in hand. Far off to the north he heard a warhorn sound. *Stannis,* he thought wildly. *Stannis is our only hope, if we can reach him.* The wind was howling, and he and the girl were trapped.

The crossbow snapped. A bolt passed within a foot of him, shattering the crust of frozen snow that had plugged the closest crenel. Of Abel, Rowan, Squirrel, and the others there was no sign. He and the girl were alone. *If they take us alive, they will deliver us to Ramsay.*

Theon grabbed Jeyne about the waist and jumped.

DAENERYS

The sky was a merciless blue, without a wisp of cloud in sight. *The bricks will soon be baking in the sun,* thought Dany. *Down on the sands, the fighters will feel the heat through the soles of their sandals.*

Jhiqui slipped Dany's silk robe from her shoulders and Irri helped her into her bathing pool. The light of the rising sun shimmered on the water, broken by the shadow of the persimmon tree. "Even if the pits must open, must Your Grace go yourself?" asked Missandei as she was washing the queen's hair.

"Half of Meereen will be there to see me, gentle heart."

"Your Grace," said Missandei, "this one begs leave to say that half of Meereen will be there to watch men bleed and die."

She is not wrong, the queen knew, *but it makes no matter.*

Soon Dany was as clean as she was ever going to be. She pushed herself to her feet, splashing softly. Water ran down her legs and beaded on her breasts. The sun was climbing up the sky, and her people would soon be gathering. She would rather have drifted in the fragrant pool all day, eating iced fruit off silver trays and dreaming of a house with a red door, but a queen belongs to her people, not to herself.

Jhiqui brought a soft towel to pat her dry. "*Khaleesi,* which *tokar* will you want today?" asked Irri.

"The yellow silk." The queen of the rabbits could not be seen without her floppy ears. The yellow silk was light and cool, and it would be blistering down in the pit. *The red sands will burn the soles of those about to die.* "And over it, the long red veils." The veils would keep the wind from blowing sand into her mouth. *And the red will hide any blood spatters.*

As Jhiqui brushed Dany's hair and Irri painted the queen's nails, they chattered happily about the day's matches. Missandei reemerged. "Your Grace. The king bids you join him when you are dressed. And Prince Quentyn has come with his Dornish Men. They beg a word, if that should please you."

Little about this day shall please me. "Some other day."

At the base of the Great Pyramid, Ser Barristan awaited them beside an ornate open palanquin, surrounded by Brazen Beasts. *Ser Grandfather,* Dany thought. Despite his age, he looked tall and handsome in the armor that she'd given him. "I would be happier if you had Unsullied guards about you today, Your Grace," the old knight said, as Hizdahr went to greet his cousin. "Half of these Brazen Beasts are untried freedmen." *And the other half are Meereenese of doubtful loyalty,* he left unsaid. Selmy mistrusted all the Meereenese, even shavepates.

"And untried they shall remain unless we try them."

"A mask can hide many things, Your Grace. Is the man behind the owl mask the same owl who guarded you yesterday and the day before? How can we know?"

"How should Meereen ever come to trust the Brazen Beasts if I do not? There are good brave men beneath those masks. I put my life into their hands." Dany smiled for him. "You fret too much, ser. I will have you beside me, what other protection do I need?"

"I am one old man, Your Grace."

"Strong Belwas will be with me as well."

"As you say." Ser Barristan lowered his voice. "Your Grace. We set the woman Meris free, as you commanded. Before she went, she asked to speak with you. I met with her instead. She claims this Tattered Prince meant to bring the Windblown over to your cause from the beginning. That he sent her here to treat with you secretly, but the Dornishmen unmasked them and betrayed them before she could make her own approach."

Treachery on treachery, the queen thought wearily. *Is there no end to it?* "How much of this do you believe, ser?"

"Little and less, Your Grace, but those were her words."

"Will they come over to us, if need be?"

"She says they will. But for a price."

"Pay it." Meereen needed iron, not gold.

"The Tattered Prince will want more than coin, Your Grace. Meris says that he wants Pentos."

"Pentos?" Her eyes narrowed. "How can I give him Pentos? It is half a world away."

"He would be willing to wait, the woman Meris suggested. Until we march for Westeros."

And if I never march for Westeros? "Pentos belongs to the Pentoshi. And Magister Illyrio is in Pentos. He who arranged my marriage to Khal Drogo and gave me my dragon eggs. Who sent me you, and Belwas, and Groleo. I owe him much and more. I will *not* repay that debt by giving his city to some sellsword. No."

Ser Barristan inclined his head. "Your Grace is wise."

"Have you ever seen such an auspicious day, my love?" Hizdahr zo Loraq commented when she rejoined him. He helped Dany up onto the palanquin, where two tall thrones stood side by side.

"Auspicious for you, perhaps. Less so for those who must die before the sun goes down."

"All men must die," said Hizdahr, "but not all can die in glory, with the cheers of the city ringing in their ears." He lifted a hand to the soldiers on the doors. "Open."

The plaza that fronted on her pyramid was paved with bricks of many colors, and the heat rose from them in shimmering waves. People swarmed everywhere. Some rode litters or sedan chairs, some forked donkeys, many were afoot. Nine of every ten were moving westward, down the broad brick thoroughfare to Daznak's Pit. When they caught sight of the palanquin emerging from the pyramid, a cheer went up from those nearest and spread across the plaza. *How queer,* the queen thought. *They cheer me on the same plaza where I once impaled one hundred sixty-three Great Masters.*

A great drum led the royal procession to clear their way through the streets. Between each beat, a shavepate herald in a shirt of polished copper disks cried for the crowd to part. *BOMM.* "They come!" *BOMM.* "Make way!" *BOMM.* "The queen!" *BOMM.* "The king!" *BOMM.* Behind the drum marched Brazen Beasts four abreast. Some carried cudgels, others staves; all wore pleated skirts, leathern sandals, and patchwork cloaks sewn from squares of many colors to echo the many-colored bricks of Meereen. Their masks gleamed in the sun: boars and bulls, hawks and herons, lions and tigers and bears, fork-tongued serpents and hideous basilisks.

Strong Belwas, who had no love for horses, walked in front of them in his studded vest, his scarred brown belly jiggling with every step. Irri and Jhiqui followed ahorse, with Aggo and Rakharo, then Reznak in an ornate sedan chair with an awning to keep the sun off his head. Ser Barristan Selmy rode at Dany's side, his armor flashing in the sun. A long cloak flowed from his shoulders, bleached as white as bone. On his left arm was a large white shield. A little farther back was Quentyn Martell, the Dornish prince, with his two companions.

The column crept slowly down the long brick street. *BOMM.* "They come!" *BOMM.* "Our queen. Our king." *BOMM.* "Make way."

Dany could hear her handmaids arguing behind her, debating who was going to win the day's final match. Jhiqui favored the gigantic Goghor, who looked more bull than man, even to the bronze ring in his nose. Irri insisted that Belaquo Bonebreaker's flail would prove the giant's undoing. *My handmaids are Dothraki,* she told herself. *Death rides with every* khalasar. The day she wed Khal Drogo, the *arakh*s had flashed at her wedding feast, and men had died whilst others drank and mated. Life and death went hand in hand amongst the horselords, and a sprinkling of blood was thought to bless a marriage. Her new marriage would soon be drenched in blood. How blessed it would be.

BOMM, BOMM, BOMM, BOMM, BOMM, BOMM, came the drumbeats, faster than before, suddenly angry and impatient. Ser Barristan drew his sword as the column ground to an abrupt halt between the pink-and-white pyramid of Pahl and the green-and-black of Naqqan.

Dany turned. "Why are we stopped?"

Hizdahr stood. "The way is blocked."

A palanquin lay overturned athwart their way. One of its bearers had collapsed to the bricks, overcome by heat. "Help that man," Dany commanded. "Get him off the street before he's stepped on and give him food and water. He looks as though he has not eaten in a fortnight."

Ser Barristan glanced uneasily to left and right. Ghiscari faces were visible on the terraces, looking down with cool and unsympathetic eyes. "Your Grace, I do not like this halt. This may be some trap. The Sons of the Harpy—"

"—have been tamed," declared Hizdahr zo Loraq. "Why should they seek to harm my queen when she has taken me for her king and consort? Now help that man, as my sweet queen has commanded." He took Dany by the hand and smiled.

The Brazen Beasts did as they were bid. Dany watched them at their work. "Those bearers were slaves before I came. I made them free. Yet that palanquin is no lighter."

"True," said Hizdahr, "but those men are paid to bear its weight now. Before you came, that man who fell would have an overseer standing over him, stripping the skin off his back with a whip. Instead he is being given aid."

It was true. A Brazen Beast in a boar mask had offered the litter bearer a skin of water. "I suppose I must be thankful for small victories," the queen said.

"One step, then the next, and soon we shall be running. Together we shall make a new Meereen." The street ahead had finally cleared. "Shall we continue on?"

What could she do but nod? *One step, then the next, but where is it I'm going?*

At the gates of Daznak's Pit two towering bronze warriors stood locked in mortal combat. One wielded a sword, the other an axe; the sculptor had depicted them in the act of killing one another, their blades and bodies forming an archway overhead.

The mortal art, thought Dany.

She had seen the fighting pits many times from her terrace. The small ones dotted the face of Meereen like pockmarks; the larger were weeping sores, red and raw. None compared to this one, though. Strong Belwas and Ser Barristan fell in to either side as she and her lord husband passed beneath the bronzes, to emerge at the top of a great brick bowl ringed by descending tiers of benches, each a different color.

Hizdahr zo Loraq led her down, through black, purple, blue, green, white, yellow, and orange to the red, where the scarlet bricks took the color of the sands below. Around them peddlers were selling dog sausages, roast onions, and unborn puppies on a stick, but Dany had no need of such. Hizdahr had stocked their box with flagons of chilled wine and sweetwater, with figs, dates, melons, and pomegranates, with pecans and peppers and a big bowl of honeyed locusts. Strong Belwas bellowed, "*Locusts!*" as he seized the bowl and began to crunch them by the handful.

"Those are very tasty," advised Hizdahr. "You ought to try a few yourself, my love. They are rolled in spice before the honey, so they are sweet and hot at once."

"That explains the way Belwas is sweating," Dany said. "I believe I will content myself with figs and dates."

Across the pit the Graces sat in flowing robes of many colors, clustered around the austere figure of Galazza Galare, who alone amongst them wore the green. The Great Masters of Meereen occupied the red and orange benches. The women were veiled, and the men had brushed and lacquered their hair into horns and hands and spikes. Hizdahr's kin of the ancient line of Loraq seemed to favor *tokar*s of purple and indigo and lilac, whilst those of Pahl were striped in pink and white. The envoys from Yunkai were all in yellow and filled the box beside the king's, each of them with his slaves and servants. Meereenese of lesser birth crowded the upper tiers, more distant from the carnage. The black and purple benches, highest and most distant from the sand, were crowded with freedmen and other common folk. The sellswords had been placed up there as well, Daenerys saw, their captains seated right amongst the common soldiers. She spied Brown Ben's weathered face and Bloodbeard's fiery red whiskers and long braids.

Her lord husband stood and raised his hands. "*Great Masters!* My queen has come this day, to show her love for you, her people. By her grace and with her leave, I give you now your mortal art. *Meereen!* Let Queen Daenerys hear your love!"

Ten thousand throats roared out their thanks; then twenty thousand; then all. They did not call her name, which few of them could pronounce. "*Mother!*" they cried instead; in the old dead tongue of Ghis, the word was *Mhysa!* They stamped their feet and slapped their bellies and shouted, "*Mhysa, Mhysa, Mhysa,*" until the whole pit seemed to tremble. Dany let the sound wash over her. *I am not your mother,* she might have shouted back, *I am the mother of your slaves, of every boy who ever died upon these sands whilst you gorged on honeyed locusts.* Behind her, Reznak leaned in to whisper in her ear, "Magnificence, hear how they love you!"

No, she knew, *they love their mortal art.* When the cheers began to ebb, she allowed to herself to sit. Their box was in the shade, but her head was pounding. "Jhiqui," she called, "sweet water, if you would. My throat is very dry."

"Khrazz will have the honor of the day's first kill," Hizdahr told her. "There has never been a better fighter."

"Strong Belwas was better," insisted Strong Belwas.

Khrazz was Meereenese, of humble birth—a tall man with a brush of stiff red-black hair running down the center of his head. His foe was an ebon-skinned spearman from the Summer Isles whose thrusts kept Khrazz at bay for a time, but once he slipped inside the spear with his shortsword, only butchery remained. After it was done, Khrazz cut the heart from the black man, raised it above his head red and dripping, and took a bite from it.

"Khrazz believes the hearts of brave men make him stronger," said Hizdahr. Jhiqui murmured her approval. Dany had once eaten a stallion's heart to give strength to her unborn son . . . but that had not saved Rhaego when the *maegi* murdered him in her womb. *Three treasons shall you know. She was the first, Jorah was the second, Brown Ben Plumm the third.* Was she done with betrayals?

"Ah," said Hizdahr, pleased. "Now comes the Spotted Cat. See how he moves, my queen. A poem on two feet."

The foe Hizdahr had found for the walking poem was as tall as Goghor and as broad as Belwas, but slow. They were fighting six feet from Dany's box when the Spotted Cat hamstrung him. As the man stumbled to his knees, the Cat put a foot on his back and a hand around his head and opened his throat from ear to ear. The red sands drank his blood, the wind his final words. The crowd screamed its approval.

"Bad fighting, good dying," said Strong Belwas. "Strong Belwas hates it when they scream." He had finished all the honeyed locusts. He gave a belch and took a swig of wine.

Pale Qartheen, black Summer Islanders, copper-skinned Dothraki, Tyroshi with blue beards, Lamb Men, Jogos Nhai, sullen Braavosi, brindle-skinned half-men from the jungles of Sothoros—from the ends of the world they came to die in Daznak's Pit. "This one shows much promise, my sweet," Hizdahr said of a Lysene youth with long blond hair that fluttered in the wind . . . but his foe grabbed a handful of that hair, pulled the boy off-balance, and gutted him. In death he looked even younger than he had with blade in hand.

"A boy," said Dany. "He was only a boy."

"Six-and-ten," Hizdahr insisted. "A man grown, who freely chose to risk his life for gold and glory. No children die today in Daznak's, as my gentle queen in her wisdom has decreed."

Another small victory. Perhaps I cannot make my people good, she told herself, *but I should at least try to make them a little less bad.* Daenerys would have prohibited contests between women as well, but Barsena Blackhair protested that she had as much right to risk her life as any man. The queen had also wished to forbid the follies, comic combats where cripples, dwarfs, and crones had at one another with cleavers, torches, and hammers (the more inept the fighters, the funnier the folly, it was thought), but Hizdahr said his people would love her more if she laughed with them, and argued that without such frolics, the cripples, dwarfs, and crones would starve. So Dany had relented.

It had been the custom to sentence criminals to the pits; that practice she agreed might resume, but only for certain crimes. "Murderers and rapers may be forced to fight, and all those who persist in slaving, but not thieves or debtors."

Beasts were still allowed, though. Dany watched an elephant make short work of a pack of six red wolves. Next a bull was set against a bear in a bloody battle that left both animals torn and dying. "The flesh is not wasted," said Hizdahr. "The butchers use the carcasses to make a healthful stew for the hungry. Any man who presents himself at the Gates of Fate may have a bowl."

"A good law," Dany said. *You have so few of them.* "We must make certain that this tradition is continued."

After the beast fights came a mock battle, pitting six men on foot against six horsemen, the former armed with shields and longswords, the latter with Dothraki *arakh*s. The mock knights were clad in mail hauberks, whilst the mock Dothraki wore no armor. At first the riders seemed to have the advantage, riding down two of their foes and slashing the ear from a third, but then the surviving knights began to attack the horses, and one by one the riders were unmounted and slain, to Jhiqui's great disgust. "That was no true *khalasar*," she said.

"These carcasses are not destined for your healthful stew, I would hope," Dany said, as the slain were being removed.

"The horses, yes," said Hizdahr. "The men, no."

"Horsemeat and onions makes you strong," said Belwas.

The battle was followed by the day's first folly, a tilt between a pair of jousting dwarfs, presented by one of the Yunkish lords that Hizdahr had invited to the games. One rode a hound, the other a sow. Their wooden armor had been freshly painted, so one bore the stag of the usurper Robert Baratheon, the other the golden lion of House Lannister. That was for her sake, plainly. Their antics soon had Belwas snorting laughter, though Dany's smile was faint and forced. When the dwarf in red tumbled from the saddle and began to chase his sow across the sands, whilst the dwarf on the dog galloped after him, whapping at his buttocks with a wooden sword, she said, "This is sweet and silly, but . . ."

"Be patient, my sweet," said Hizdahr. "They are about to loose the lions."

Daenerys gave him a quizzical look. "Lions?"

"Three of them. The dwarfs will not expect them."

She frowned. "The dwarfs have wooden swords. Wooden armor. How do you expect them to fight lions?"

"Badly," said Hizdahr, "though perhaps they will surprise us. More like they will shriek and run about and try to climb out of the pit. That is what makes this a folly."

Dany was not pleased. "I forbid it."

"Gentle queen. You do not want to disappoint your people."

"You swore to me that the fighters would be grown men who had freely consented to risk their lives for gold and honor. These dwarfs did not consent to battle lions with wooden swords. You will stop it. Now."

The king's mouth tightened. For a heartbeat Dany thought she saw a flash of anger in those placid eyes. "As you command." Hizdahr beckoned to his pitmaster. "No lions," he said when the man trotted over, whip in hand.

"Not one, Magnificence? Where is the fun in that?"

"My queen has spoken. The dwarfs will not be harmed."

"The crowd will not like it."

"Then bring on Barsena. That should appease them."

"Your Worship knows best." The pitmaster snapped his whip and shouted out commands. The dwarfs were herded off, pig and dog and all, as the spectators hissed their disapproval and pelted them with stones and rotten fruit.

A roar went up as Barsena Blackhair strode onto the sands, naked save for breechclout and sandals. A tall, dark woman of some thirty years, she moved with the feral grace of a panther. "Barsena is much loved," Hizdahr said, as the sound swelled to fill the pit. "The bravest woman I have ever seen."

Strong Belwas said, "Fighting girls is not so brave. Fighting Strong Belwas would be brave."

"Today she fights a boar," said Hizdahr.

Aye, thought Dany, *because you could not find a woman to face her, no matter how plump the purse.* "And not with a wooden sword, it would seem."

The boar was a huge beast, with tusks as long as a man's forearm and small eyes that swam with rage. She wondered whether the boar that had killed Robert Baratheon had looked as fierce. *A terrible creature and a terrible death.* For a heartbeat she felt almost sorry for the Usurper.

"Barsena is very quick," Reznak said. "She will dance with the boar,

Magnificence, and slice him when he passes near her. He will be awash in blood before he falls, you shall see."

It began just as he said. The boar charged, Barsena spun aside, her blade flashed silver in the sun. "She needs a spear," Ser Barristan said, as Barsena vaulted over the beast's second charge. "That is no way to fight a boar." He sounded like someone's fussy old grandsire, just as Daario was always saying.

Barsena's blade was running red, but the boar soon stopped. *He is smarter than a bull,* Dany realized. *He will not charge again.* Barsena came to the same realization. Shouting, she edged closer to the boar, tossing her knife from hand to hand. When the beast backed away, she cursed and slashed at his snout, trying to provoke him . . . and succeeding. This time her leap came an instant too late, and a tusk ripped her left leg open from knee to crotch.

A moan went up from thirty thousand throats. Clutching at her torn leg, Barsena dropped her knife and tried to hobble off, but before she had gone two feet the boar was on her once again. Dany turned her face away. "Was that brave enough?" she asked Strong Belwas, as a scream rang out across the sand.

"Fighting pigs is brave, but it is not brave to scream so loud. It hurts Strong Belwas in the ears." The eunuch rubbed his swollen stomach, crisscrossed with old white scars. "It makes Strong Belwas sick in his belly too."

The boar buried his snout in Barsena's belly and began rooting out her entrails. The smell was more than the queen could stand. The heat, the flies, the shouts from the crowd . . . *I cannot breathe.* She lifted her veil and let it flutter away. She took her *tokar* off as well. The pearls rattled softly against one another as she unwound the silk.

"*Khaleesi?*" Irri asked. "What are you doing?"

"Taking off my floppy ears." A dozen men with boar spears came trotting out onto the sand to drive the boar away from the corpse and back to his pen. The pitmaster was with them, a long barbed whip in his hand. As he snapped it at the boar, the queen rose. "Ser Barristan, will you see me safely back to my garden?"

Hizdahr looked confused. "There is more to come. A folly, six old women, and three more matches. Belaquo and Goghor!"

"Belaquo will win," Irri declared. "It is known."

"It is *not* known," Jhiqui said. "Belaquo will die."

"One will die, or the other will," said Dany. "And the one who lives will die some other day. This was a mistake."

"Strong Belwas ate too many locusts." There was a queasy look on Belwas's broad brown face. "Strong Belwas needs milk."

Hizdahr ignored the eunuch. "Magnificence, the people of Meereen have come to celebrate our union. You heard them cheering you. Do not cast away their love."

"It was my floppy ears they cheered, not me. Take me from this abbatoir, husband." She could hear the boar snorting, the shouts of the spearmen, the *crack* of the pitmaster's whip.

"Sweet lady, no. Stay only a while longer. For the folly, and one last match. Close your eyes, no one will see. They will be watching Belaquo and Ghogor. This is no time for—"

A shadow rippled across his face.

The tumult and the shouting died. Ten thousand voices stilled. Every eye turned skyward. A warm wind brushed Dany's cheeks, and above the beating of her heart she heard the sound of wings. Two spearmen dashed for shelter. The pitmaster froze where he stood. The boar went snuffling back to Barsena. Strong Belwas gave a moan, stumbled from his seat, and fell to his knees.

Above them all the dragon turned, dark against the sun. His scales were black, his eyes and horns and spinal plates blood red. Ever the largest of her three, in the wild Drogon had grown larger still. His wings stretched twenty feet from tip to tip, black as jet. He flapped them once as he swept back above the sands, and the sound was like a clap of thunder. The boar raised his head, snorting . . . and flame engulfed him, black fire shot with red. Dany felt the wash of heat thirty feet away. The beast's dying scream sounded almost human. Drogon landed on the carcass and sank his claws into the smoking flesh. As he began to feed, he made no distinction between Barsena and the boar.

"Oh, gods," moaned Reznak, "he's *eating her!*" The seneschal covered his mouth. Strong Belwas was retching noisily. A queer look passed across Hizdahr zo Loraq's long, pale face—part fear, part lust, part rapture. He licked his lips. Dany could see the Pahls streaming up the steps, clutching their *tokars* and tripping over the fringes in their haste to be away. Others followed. Some ran, shoving at one another. More stayed in their seats.

One man took it on himself to be a hero.

He was one of the spearmen sent out to drive the boar back to his pen. Perhaps he was drunk, or mad. Perhaps he had loved Barsena Blackhair from afar or had heard some whisper of the girl Hazzea. Perhaps he was just some common man who wanted bards to sing of him. He darted forward, his boar spear in his hands. Red sand kicked up beneath his heels, and shouts rang out from the seats. Drogon raised his head, blood dripping from his teeth. The hero leapt onto his back and drove the iron spearpoint down at the base of the dragon's long scaled neck.

Dany and Drogon screamed as one.

The hero leaned into his spear, using his weight to twist the point in deeper. Drogon arched upward with a hiss of pain. His tail lashed sideways. She watched his head crane around at the end of that long serpentine neck, saw his black wings unfold. The dragonslayer lost his footing and went tumbling to the sand. He was trying to struggle back to his feet when the dragon's teeth closed hard around his forearm. "No" was all the man had time to shout. Drogon wrenched his arm from his shoulder and tossed it aside as a dog might toss a rodent in a rat pit.

"Kill it," Hizdahr zo Loraq shouted to the other spearmen. "*Kill the beast!*"

Ser Barristan held her tightly. "Look away, Your Grace."

"Let me *go!*" Dany twisted from his grasp. The world seemed to slow as she cleared the parapet. When she landed in the pit she lost a sandal. Running, she could feel the sand between her toes, hot and rough. Ser Barristan was calling after her. Strong Belwas was still vomiting. She ran faster.

The spearmen were running too. Some were rushing toward the dragon, spears in hand. Others were rushing away, throwing down their weapons as they fled. The hero was jerking on the sand, the bright blood pouring from the ragged stump of his shoulder. His spear remained in Drogon's back, wobbling as the dragon beat his wings. Smoke rose from the wound. As the other spears closed in, the dragon spat fire, bathing two men in black flame. His tail lashed sideways and caught the pitmaster creeping up behind him, breaking him in two. Another attacker stabbed at his eyes until the dragon caught him in his jaws and tore his belly out. The Meereenese were screaming, cursing, howling. Dany could hear someone pounding after her. "Drogon," she screamed. "*Drogon.*"

His head turned. Smoke rose between his teeth. His blood was smoking too, where it dripped upon the ground. He beat his wings again, sending up a choking storm of scarlet sand. Dany stumbled into the hot red cloud, coughing. He snapped.

"No" was all that she had time to say. *No, not me, don't you know me?* The black teeth closed inches from her face. *He meant to tear my head off.* The sand was in her eyes. She stumbled over the pitmaster's corpse and fell on her backside.

Drogon roared. The sound filled the pit. A furnace wind engulfed her. The dragon's long scaled neck stretched toward her. When his mouth opened, she could see bits of broken bone and charred flesh between his black teeth. His eyes were molten. *I am looking into hell, but I dare not look away.* She had never been so certain of anything. *If I run from him, he will burn me and devour me.* In Westeros the septons spoke of seven hells and seven heavens, but the Seven Kingdoms and their gods were far away. If she died here, Dany wondered, would the horse god of the Dothraki part the grass and claim her for his starry *khalasar,* so she might ride the nightlands beside her sun-and-stars? Or would the angry gods of Ghis send their harpies to seize her soul and drag her down to torment? Drogon roared full in her face, his breath hot enough to blister skin. Off to her right Dany heard Barristan Selmy shouting, "*Me!* Try me. Over here. *Me!*"

In the smoldering red pits of Drogon's eyes, Dany saw her own reflection. How small she looked, how weak and frail and scared. *I cannot let him see my fear.* She scrabbled in the sand, pushing against the pitmaster's corpse, and her fingers brushed against the handle of his whip. Touching it made her feel braver. The leather was warm, alive. Drogon roared again, the sound so loud that she almost dropped the whip. His teeth snapped at her.

Dany hit him. "*No*," she screamed, swinging the lash with all the strength that she had in her. The dragon jerked his head back. "*No*," she screamed again. "*NO!*" The barbs raked along his snout. Drogon rose, his wings covering her in shadow. Dany swung the lash at his scaled belly, back and forth until her arm began to ache. His long serpentine neck bent like an archer's bow. With a *hisssssss,* he spat black fire down at her. Dany darted underneath the flames, swinging the whip and shouting, "*No, no, no. Get DOWN!*" His answering roar was full of fear and fury, full of pain. His wings beat once, twice . . .

. . . and folded. The dragon gave one last *hiss* and stretched out flat upon his belly. Black blood was flowing from the wound where the spear had pierced him, smoking where it dripped onto the scorched sands. *He is fire made flesh,* she thought, *and so am I.*

Daenerys Targaryen vaulted onto the dragon's back, seized the spear, and ripped it out. The point was half-melted, the iron red-hot, glowing. She flung it aside. Drogon twisted under her, his muscles rippling as he gathered his strength. The air was thick with sand. Dany could not see, she could not breathe, she could not think. The black wings cracked like thunder, and suddenly the scarlet sands were falling away beneath her.

Dizzy, Dany closed her eyes. When she opened them again, she glimpsed the Meereenese beneath her through a haze of tears and dust, pouring up the steps and out into the streets.

The lash was still in her hand. She flicked it against Drogon's neck and cried, "*Higher!*" Her other hand clutched at his scales, her fingers scrabbling for purchase. Drogon's wide black wings beat the air. Dany could feel the heat of him between her thighs. Her heart felt as if it were about to burst. *Yes,* she thought, *yes, now, now, do it, do it, take me, take me, FLY!*

JON

He was not a tall man, Tormund Giantsbane, but the gods had given him a broad chest and massive belly. Mance Rayder had named him Tormund Horn-Blower for the power of his lungs, and was wont to say that Tormund could laugh the snow off mountaintops. In his wroth, his bellows reminded Jon of a mammoth trumpeting.

That day Tormund bellowed often and loudly. He roared, he shouted, he slammed his fist against the table so hard that a flagon of water overturned and spilled. A horn of mead was never far from his hand, so the spittle he sprayed when making threats was sweet with honey. He called Jon Snow a craven, a liar, and a turncloak, cursed him for a black-hearted buggering kneeler, a robber, and a carrion crow, accused him of wanting to fuck the free folk up the arse. Twice he flung his drinking horn at Jon's head, though only after he had emptied it. Tormund was not the sort of man to waste good mead. Jon let it all wash over him. He never raised his own voice nor answered threat with threat, but neither did he give more ground than he had come prepared to give.

Finally, as the shadows of the afternoon grew long outside the tent, Tormund Giantsbane—Tall-Talker, Horn-Blower, and Breaker of Ice, Tormund Thunderfist, Husband to Bears, Mead-King of Ruddy Hall, Speaker to Gods and Father of Hosts—thrust out his hand.

"Done then, and may the gods forgive me. There's a hundred mothers never will, I know."

Jon clasped the offered hand. The words of his oath rang through his head. *I am the sword in the darkness. I am the watcher on the walls. I am the fire that burns against the cold, the light that brings the dawn, the horn that wakes the sleepers, the shield that guards the realms of men.* And for him a new refrain: *I am the guard who opened the gates and let the foe march through.* He would have given much and more to know that he was doing the right thing. But he had gone too far to turn back. "Done and done," he said.

Tormund's grip was bone-crushing. That much had not changed about him. The beard was the same as well, though the face under that thicket of white hair had thinned considerably, and there were deep lines graven in those ruddy cheeks. "Mance should have killed you when he had the chance," he said as he did his best to turn Jon's hand to pulp and bone. "Gold for gruel, and boys . . . a cruel price. Whatever happened to that sweet lad I knew?"

They made him lord commander. "A fair bargain leaves both sides unhappy, I've heard it said. Three days?"

"If I live that long. Some o' my own will spit on me when they hear these terms." Tormund released Jon's hand. "Your crows will grumble too, if I know them. And I ought to. I have killed more o' you black buggers than I can count."

"It might be best if you did not mention that so loudly when you come south of the Wall."

"Har!" Tormund laughed. That had not changed either; he still laughed easily and often. "Wise words. I'd not want you crows to peck me to death." He slapped Jon's back. "When all my folk are safe behind your Wall, we'll share a bit o' meat and mead. Till then . . ." The wildling pulled off the band from his left arm and tossed it at Jon, then did the same with its twin upon his right. "Your first payment. Had those from my father and him from his. Now they're yours, you thieving black bastard."

The armbands were old gold, solid and heavy, engraved with the ancient runes of the First Men. Tormund Giantsbane had worn them as long as Jon had known him; they had seemed as much a part of him as his beard. "The Braavosi will melt these down for the gold. That seems a shame. Perhaps you ought to keep them."

"No. I'll not have it said that Tormund Thunderfist made the free folk give up their treasures whilst he kept his own." He grinned. "But I'll keep the ring I wear about me member. Much bigger than those little things. On you it'd be a torque."

Jon had to laugh. "You never change."

"Oh, I do." The grin melted away like snow in summer. "I am not the man I was at Ruddy Hall. Seen too much death, and worse things too. My sons . . ." Grief twisted Tormund's face. "Dormund was cut down in the battle for the Wall, and him still half a boy. One o' your king's knights did for him, some bastard all in grey steel with moths upon his shield. I saw the cut, but my boy was dead before I reached him. And Torwynd . . . it was the cold claimed him. Always sickly, that one. He just up and died one night. The worst o' it, before we ever knew he'd died he rose pale with them blue eyes. Had to see to him m'self. That was hard, Jon." Tears shone in his eyes. "He wasn't much of a man, truth be told, but he'd been me little boy once, and I loved him."

Jon put a hand on his shoulder. "I am so sorry."

"Why? Weren't your doing. There's blood on your hands, aye, same as mine. But not his." Tormund shook his head. "I still have two strong sons."

"Your daughter . . . ?"

"Munda." That brought Tormund's smile back. "Took that Longspear Ryk to husband, if you believe it. Boy's got more cock than sense, you ask me, but he treats her well enough. I told him if he ever hurt her, I'd yank his member off and beat him bloody with it." He gave Jon another hearty slap. "Time you were going back. Keep you any longer, they're like to think we ate you."

"Dawn, then. Three days from now. The boys first."

"I heard you the first ten times, crow. A man'd think there was no trust between us." He spat. "Boys first, aye. Mammoths go the long way round. You make sure Eastwatch expects them. I'll make sure there's no fighting, nor rushing at your bloody gate. Nice and orderly we'll be, ducklings in a row. And me the mother duck. Har!" Tormund led Jon from his tent.

Outside the day was bright and cloudless. The sun had returned to the sky after a fortnight's absence, and to the south the Wall rose blue-white and glittering. There was a saying Jon had heard from the older men at Castle Black: *the Wall has more moods than Mad King Aerys,* they'd say, or sometimes, *the Wall has more moods than a woman.* On cloudy days it looked to be white rock. On moonless nights it was as black as coal. In snowstorms it seemed carved of snow. But on days like this, there was no mistaking it for anything but ice. On days like this the Wall shimmered bright as a septon's crystal, every crack and crevasse limned by sunlight, as frozen rainbows danced and died behind translucent ripples. On days like this the Wall was beautiful.

Tormund's eldest son stood near the horses, talking with Leathers. Tall Toregg, he was called amongst the free folk. Though he barely had an inch on Leathers, he overtopped his father by a foot. Hareth, the strapping Mole's Town boy called Horse, huddled near the fire, his back to the other two. He and Leathers were the only men Jon had brought with him to the parley; any more might have been seen as a sign of fear, and twenty men would have been of no more use than two if Tormund had been intent on blood. Ghost was the only protection Jon needed; the direwolf could sniff out foes, even those who hid their enmity behind smiles.

Ghost was gone, though. Jon peeled off one black glove, put two fingers in his mouth, and whistled. "*Ghost!* To me."

From above came the sudden sound of wings. Mormont's raven flapped from a limb of an old oak to perch upon Jon's saddle. "*Corn,*" it cried. "*Corn, corn, corn.*"

"Did you follow me as well?" Jon reached to shoo the bird away but ended up stroking its feathers. The raven cocked its eye at him. "*Snow,*" it muttered, bobbing its head knowingly. Then Ghost emerged from between two trees, with Val beside him.

They look as though they belong together. Val was clad all in white; white woolen breeches tucked into high boots of bleached white leather, white bearskin cloak pinned at the shoulder with a carved weirwood face, white tunic with bone fastenings. Her breath was white as well . . . but her eyes were blue, her long braid the color of dark honey, her cheeks flushed red from the cold. It had been a long while since Jon Snow had seen a sight so lovely.

"Have you been trying to steal my wolf?" he asked her.

"Why not? If every woman had a direwolf, men would be much sweeter. Even crows."

"Har!" laughed Tormund Giantsbane. "Don't bandy words with this one, Lord Snow, she's too clever for the likes o' you and me. Best steal her quick, before Toregg wakes up and takes her first."

What had that oaf Axell Florent said of Val? *"A nubile girl, not hard to look upon. Good hips, good breasts, well made for whelping children."* All true enough, but the wildling woman was so much more. She had proved that by finding Tormund where seasoned rangers of the Watch had failed. *She may not be a princess, but she would make a worthy wife for any lord.*

But that bridge had been burned a long time ago, and Jon himself had thrown the torch. "Toregg is welcome to her," he announced. "I took a vow."

"She won't mind. Will you, girl?"

Val patted the long bone knife on her hip. "Lord Crow is welcome to steal into my bed any night he dares. Once he's been gelded, keeping those vows will come much easier for him."

"*Har!*" Tormund snorted again. "You hear that, Toregg? Stay away from this one. I have one daughter, don't need another." Shaking his head, the wildling chief ducked back inside his tent.

As Jon scratched Ghost behind the ear, Toregg brought up Val's horse for her. She still rode the grey garron that Mully had given her the day she left the Wall, a shaggy, stunted thing blind in one eye. As she turned it toward the Wall, she asked, "How fares the little monster?"

"Twice as big as when you left us, and thrice as loud. When he wants the teat, you can hear him wail in Eastwatch." Jon mounted his own horse.

Val fell in beside him. "So . . . I brought you Tormund, as I said I would. What now? Am I to be returned to my old cell?"

"Your old cell is occupied. Queen Selyse has claimed the King's Tower, for her own. Do you remember Hardin's Tower?"

"The one that looks about to collapse?"

"It's looked that way for a hundred years. I've had the top floor made ready for you, my lady. You will have more room than in the King's Tower, though you may not be as comfortable. No one has ever called it Hardin's Palace."

"I would choose freedom over comfort every time."

"Freedom of the castle you shall have, but I regret to say you must remain a captive. I can promise that you will not be troubled by unwanted visitors, however. My own men guard Hardin's Tower, not the queen's. And Wun Wun sleeps in the entry hall."

"A giant as protector? Even Dalla could not boast of that."

Tormund's wildlings watched them pass, peering out from tents and lean-tos beneath leafless trees. For every man of fighting age, Jon saw three women and as many children, gaunt-faced things with hollow cheeks and staring eyes. When Mance Rayder had led the free folk down upon the Wall, his followers drove large herds of sheep and goats and swine before them, but now the only animals to be seen were the mammoths. If not for the ferocity of the giants, those would have been slaughtered too, he did not doubt. There was a lot of meat on a mammoth's bones.

Jon saw signs of sickness too. That disquieted him more than he could say. If Tormund's band were starved and sick, what of the thousands who had followed Mother Mole to Hardhome? *Cotter Pyke should reach them soon. If the winds were kind, his fleet might well be on its way back to Eastwatch even now, with as many of the free folk as he could cram aboard.*

"How did you fare with Tormund?" asked Val.

"Ask me a year from now. The hard part still awaits me. The part where I convince mine own to eat this meal I've cooked for them. None of them are going to like the taste, I fear."

"Let me help."

"You have. You brought me Tormund."

"I can do more."

Why not? thought Jon. *They are all convinced she is a princess.* Val looked the part and rode as if she had been born on horseback. *A warrior princess,* he decided, *not some willowy creature who sits up in a tower, brushing her hair and waiting for some knight to rescue her.* "I must inform the queen of this agreement," he said. "You are welcome to come meet her, if you can find it in yourself to bend a knee." It would never do to offend Her Grace before he even opened his mouth.

"May I laugh when I kneel?"

"You may not. This is no game. A river of blood runs between our peoples, old and deep and red. Stannis Baratheon is one of the few who favors admitting wildlings to the realm. I need his queen's support for what I've done."

Val's playful smile died. "You have my word, Lord Snow. I will be a proper wildling princess for your queen."

She is not my queen, he might have said. *If truth be told, the day of her departure cannot come too fast for me. And if the gods are good, she will take Melisandre with her.*

They rode the rest of the way in silence, Ghost loping at their heels. Mormont's raven followed them as far as the gate, then flapped upward as the rest of them dismounted. Horse went ahead with a brand to light the way through the icy tunnel.

A small crowd of black brothers was waiting by the gate when Jon and his companions emerged south of the Wall. Ulmer of the Kingswood was amongst them, and it was the old archer who came forward to speak for the rest. "If it please m'lord, the lads were wondering. Will it be peace, m'lord? Or blood and iron?"

"Peace," Jon Snow replied. "Three days hence, Tormund Giantsbane will lead his people through the Wall. As friends, not foes. Some may even swell our ranks, as brothers. It will be for us to make them welcome. Now back to your duties." Jon handed the reins of his horse to Satin. "I must see Queen Selyse." Her Grace would take it as a slight if he did not come to her at once. "Afterward I will have letters to write. Bring parchment, quills, and a pot of maester's black to my chambers. Then summon Marsh, Yarwyck, Septon Cellador, Clydas." Cellador would be half-drunk, and Clydas was a poor substitute for a real maester, but they were what he had. *Till Sam returns.* "The northmen too. Flint and Norrey. Leathers, you should be there as well."

"Hobb is baking onion pies," said Satin. "Shall I request that they all join you for supper?"

Jon considered. "No. Ask them to join me atop the Wall at sunset." He turned to Val. "My lady. With me, if you please."

"The crow commands, the captive must obey." Her tone was playful. "This queen of yours must be fierce if the legs of grown men give out beneath them when they meet her. Should I have dressed in mail instead of wool and fur? These clothes were given to me by Dalla, I would sooner not get bloodstains all over them."

"If words drew blood, you might have cause to fear. I think your clothes are safe enough, my lady."

They made their way toward the King's Tower, along fresh-shoveled pathways between mounds of dirty snow. "I have heard it said that your queen has a great dark beard."

Jon knew he should not smile, but he did. "Only a mustache. Very wispy. You can count the hairs."

"How disappointing."

For all her talk about wanting to be mistress of her seat, Selyse Baratheon seemed in no great haste to abandon the comforts of Castle Black for the shadows of the Nightfort. She kept guards, of course—four men posted at the door, two outside on the steps, two inside by the brazier. Commanding them was Ser Patrek of King's Mountain, clad in his knightly raiment of white and blue and silver, his cloak a spatter of five-pointed stars. When presented to Val, the knight sank to one knee to kiss her glove. "You are even lovelier than I was told, princess," he declared. "The queen has told me much and more of your beauty."

"How odd, when she has never seen me." Val patted Ser Patrek on the head. "Up with you now, ser kneeler. Up, up." She sounded as if she were talking to a dog.

It was all that Jon could do not to laugh. Stone-faced, he told the knight that they required audience with the queen. Ser Patrek sent one of the men-at-arms scrambling up the steps to inquire as to whether Her Grace would receive them. "The wolf stays here, though," Ser Patrek insisted.

Jon had expected that. The direwolf made Queen Selyse anxious, almost as much as Wun Weg Wun Dar Wun. "Ghost, stay."

They found Her Grace sewing by the fire, whilst her fool danced about to music only he could hear, the cowbells on his antlers *clang*ing. "The crow, the crow," Patchface cried when he saw Jon. "Under the sea the crows are white as snow, I know, I know, oh, oh, oh." Princess Shireen was curled up in a window seat, her hood drawn up to hide the worst of the greyscale that had disfigured her face.

There was no sign of Lady Melisandre. For that much Jon was grateful. Soon or late he would need to face the red priestess, but he would sooner it was not in the queen's presence. "Your Grace." He took a knee. Val did likewise.

Queen Selyse set aside her sewing. "You may rise."

"If it please Your Grace, may I present the Lady Val? Her sister Dalla was—"

"—mother to that squalling babe who keeps us awake at night. I know who she is, Lord Snow." The queen sniffed. "You are fortunate that she returned to us before the king my husband, else it might have gone badly for you. Very badly indeed."

"Are you the wildling princess?" Shireen asked Val.

"Some call me that," said Val. "My sister was wife to Mance Rayder, the King-Beyond-the-Wall. She died giving him a son."

"I'm a princess too," Shireen announced, "but I never had a sister. I used to have a cousin once, before he sailed away. He was just a bastard, but I liked him."

"Honestly, Shireen," her mother said. "I am sure the lord commander did not come to hear about Robert's by-blows. Patchface, be a good fool and take the princess to her room."

The bells on his hat rang. "Away, away," the fool sang. "Come with me beneath the sea, away, away, away." He took the little princess by one hand and drew her from the room, skipping.

Jon said, "Your Grace, the leader of the free folk has agreed to my terms."

Queen Selyse gave the tiniest of nods. "It was ever my lord husband's wish to grant sanctuary to these savage peoples. So long as they keep the king's peace and the king's laws, they are welcome in our realm." She pursed her lips. "I am told they have more giants with them."

Val answered. "Almost two hundred of them, Your Grace. And more than eighty mammoths."

The queen shuddered. "Dreadful creatures." Jon could not tell if she was speaking of the mammoths or the giants. "Though such beasts might be useful to my lord husband in his battles."

"That may be, Your Grace," Jon said, "but the mammoths are too big to pass through our gate."

"Cannot the gate be widened?"

"That . . . that would be unwise, I think."

Selyse sniffed. "If you say so. No doubt you know about such things. Where do you mean to settle these wildlings? Surely Mole's Town is not large enough to contain . . . how many are they?"

"Four thousand, Your Grace. They will help us garrison our abandoned castles, the better to defend the Wall."

"I had been given to understand that those castles were ruins. Dismal places, bleak and cold, hardly more than heaps of rubble. At Eastwatch we heard talk of rats and spiders."

The cold will have killed the spiders by now, thought Jon, *and the rats may be a useful source of meat come winter.* "All true, Your Grace . . . but even ruins offer some shelter. And the Wall will stand between them and the Others."

"I see you have considered all this carefully, Lord Snow. I am sure King Stannis will be pleased when he returns triumphant from his battle."

Assuming he returns at all.

"Of course," the queen went on, "the wildlings must first acknowledge Stannis as their king and R'hllor as their god."

And here we are, face-to-face in the narrow passage. "Your Grace, forgive me. Those were not the terms that we agreed to."

The queen's face hardened. "A grievous oversight." What faint traces of warmth her voice had held vanished all at once.

"Free folk do not kneel," Val told her.

"Then they must be knelt," the queen declared.

"Do that, Your Grace, and we will rise again at the first chance," Val promised. "Rise with blades in hand."

The queen's lips tightened, and her chin gave a small quiver. "You are insolent. I suppose that is only to be expected of a wildling. We must find you a husband who can teach you courtesy." The queen turned her glare on Jon. "I do not approve, Lord Commander. Nor will my lord husband. I cannot prevent you from opening your gate, as we both know full well, but I promise you that you shall answer for it when the king returns from battle. Mayhaps you might want to reconsider."

"Your Grace." Jon knelt again. This time Val did not join him. "I am sorry my actions have displeased you. I did as I thought best. Do I have your leave to go?"

"You do. At once."

Once outside and well away from the queen's men, Val gave vent to her wroth. "You lied about her beard. That one has more hair on her chin than I have between my legs. And the daughter . . . her face . . ."

"Greyscale."

"The grey death is what we call it."

"It is not always mortal in children."

"North of the Wall it is. Hemlock is a sure cure, but a pillow or a blade will work as well. If I had given birth to that poor child, I would have given her the gift of mercy long ago."

This was a Val that Jon had never seen before. "Princess Shireen is the queen's only child."

"I pity both of them. The child is not clean."

"If Stannis wins his war, Shireen will stand as heir to the Iron Throne."

"Then I pity your Seven Kingdoms."

"The maesters say greyscale is not—"

"The maesters may believe what they wish. Ask a woods witch if you would know the truth. The grey death sleeps, only to wake again. *The child is not clean!*"

"She seems a sweet girl. You cannot know—"

"I can. You know nothing, Jon Snow." Val seized his arm. "I want the monster out of there. Him and his wet nurses. You cannot leave them in that same tower as the dead girl."

Jon shook her hand away. *"She is not dead."*

"She is. Her mother cannot see it. Nor you, it seems. Yet death is there." She walked away from him, stopped, turned back. "I brought you Tormund Giantsbane. Bring me my monster."

"If I can, I will."

"Do. You owe me a debt, Jon Snow."

Jon watched her stride away. *She is wrong. She must be wrong. Greyscale is not so deadly as she claims, not in children.*

Ghost was gone again. The sun was low in the west. *A cup of hot spiced wine would serve me well just now. Two cups would serve me even better.* But that would have to wait. He had foes to face. Foes of the worst sort: brothers.

He found Leathers waiting for him by the winch cage. The two of them rode up together. The higher they went, the stronger the wind. Fifty feet up, the heavy cage began to sway with every gust. From time to time it scraped against the Wall, starting small crystalline showers of ice that sparkled in the sunlight as they fell. They rose above the tallest towers of the castle. At four hundred feet the wind had teeth, and tore at his black cloak so it slapped noisily at the iron bars. At seven hundred it cut right through him. *The Wall is mine,* Jon reminded himself as the winchmen were swinging in the cage, *for two more days, at least.*

Jon hopped down onto the ice, thanked the men on the winch, and nodded to the spearmen standing sentry. Both wore woolen hoods pulled down over their heads, so nothing could be seen of their faces but their eyes, but he knew Ty by the tangled rope of greasy black hair falling down his back and Owen by the sausage stuffed into the scabbard at his hip. He might have known them anyway, just by the way they stood. *A good lord must know his men,* his father had once told him and Robb, back at Winterfell.

Jon walked to the edge of the Wall and gazed down upon the killing ground where Mance Rayder's host had died. He wondered where Mance was now. *Did he ever find you, little sister? Or were you just a ploy he used so I would set him free?*

It had been so long since he had last seen Arya. What would she look like now? Would he even know her? *Arya Underfoot. Her face was always dirty.* Would she still have that little sword he'd had Mikken forge for her? *Stick them with the pointy end,* he'd told her. Wisdom for her wedding night if half of what he heard of Ramsay Snow was true. *Bring her home, Mance. I saved your son from Melisandre, and now I am about to save four thousand of your free folk. You owe me this one little girl.*

In the haunted forest to the north, the shadows of the afternoon crept through the trees. The western sky was a blaze of red, but to the east the first stars were peeking out. Jon Snow flexed the fingers of his sword hand, remembering all he'd lost. *Sam, you sweet fat fool, you played me a cruel jape when you made me lord commander. A lord commander has no friends.*

"Lord Snow?" said Leathers. "The cage is coming up."

"I hear it." Jon moved back from the edge.

First to make the ascent were the clan chiefs Flint and Norrey, clad in fur and iron. The Norrey looked like some old fox—wrinkled and slight of build, but sly-eyed and spry. Torghen Flint was half a head shorter but must weigh twice as much—a stout gruff man with gnarled, red-knuckled hands as big as hams, leaning heavily on a blackthorn cane as he limped across the ice. Bowen Marsh came next, bundled up in a bearskin. After him Othell Yarwyck. Then Septon Cellador, half in his cups.

"Walk with me," Jon told them. They walked west along the Wall, down gravel-strewn paths toward the setting sun. When they had come fifty yards from the warming shed, he said, "You know why I've summoned you. Three days hence at dawn the gate will open, to allow Tormund and his people through the Wall. There is much we need to do in preparation."

Silence greeted his pronouncement. Then Othell Yarwyck said, "Lord Commander, there are *thousands* of—"

"—scrawny wildlings, bone weary, hungry, far from home." Jon pointed at the lights of their campfires. "There they are. Four thousand, Tormund claims."

"Three thousand, I make them, by the fires." Bowen Marsh lived for counts and measures. "More than twice that number at Hardhome with the woods witch, we are told. And Ser Denys writes of great camps in the mountains beyond the Shadow Tower . . ."

Jon did not deny it. "Tormund says the Weeper means to try the Bridge of Skulls again."

The Old Pomegranate touched his scar. He had gotten it defending the Bridge of Skulls the last time the Weeping Man had tried to cut his way across the Gorge. "Surely the lord commander cannot mean to allow that . . . that demon through as well?"

"Not gladly." Jon had not forgotten the heads the Weeping Man had left him, with bloody holes where their eyes had been. *Black Jack Bulwer, Hairy Hal, Garth Greyfeather. I cannot avenge them, but I will not forget their names.* "But yes, my lord, him as well. We cannot pick and choose amongst the free folk, saying this one may pass, this one may not. Peace means peace for all."

The Norrey hawked and spat. "As well make peace with wolves and carrion crows."

"It's peaceful in my dungeons," grumbled Old Flint. "Give the Weeping Man to me."

"How many rangers has the Weeper killed?" asked Othell Yarwyck. "How many women has he raped or killed or stolen?"

"Three of mine own ilk," said Old Flint. "And he blinds the girls he does not take."

"When a man takes the black, his crimes are forgiven," Jon reminded them. "If we want the free folk to fight beside us, we must pardon their past crimes as we would for our own."

"The Weeper will not say the words," insisted Yarwyck. "He will not wear the cloak. Even other raiders do not trust him."

"You need not trust a man to use him." *Else how could I make use of all of you?* "We need the Weeper, and others like him. Who knows the wild better than a wildling? Who knows our foes better than a man who has fought them?"

"All the Weeper knows is rape and murder," said Yarwyck.

"Once past the Wall, the wildlings will have thrice our numbers," said Bowen Marsh. "And that is only Tormund's band. Add the Weeper's men and those at Hardhome, and they will have the strength to end the Night's Watch in a single night."

"Numbers alone do not win a war. You have not seen them. Half of them are dead on their feet."

"I would sooner have them dead in the ground," said Yarwyck. "If it please my lord."

"It does *not* please me." Jon's voice was as cold as the wind snapping at their cloaks. "There are children in that camp, hundreds of them, thousands. Women as well."

"Spearwives."

"Some. Along with mothers and grandmothers, widows and maids . . . would you condemn them all to die, my lord?"

"Brothers should not squabble," Septon Cellador said. "Let us kneel and pray to the Crone to light our way to wisdom."

"Lord Snow," said The Norrey, "where do you mean to put these wildlings o' yours? Not on *my* lands, I hope."

"Aye," declared Old Flint. "You want them in the Gift, that's your folly, but see they don't wander off or I'll send you back their heads. Winter is nigh, I want no more mouths to feed."

"The wildlings will remain upon the Wall," Jon assured them. "Most will be housed in one of our abandoned castles." The Watch now had garrisons at Icemark, Long Barrow, Sable Hall, Greyguard, and Deep Lake, all badly undermanned, but ten castles still stood empty and abandoned. "Men with wives and children, all orphan girls and any orphan boys below the age of ten, old women, widowed mothers, any woman who does not care to fight. The spearwives we'll send to Long Barrow to join their sisters, single men to the other forts we've reopened. Those who take the black will remain here, or be posted to Eastwatch or the Shadow Tower. Tormund will take Oakenshield as his seat, to keep him close at hand."

Bowen Marsh sighed. "If they do not slay us with their swords, they will do so with their mouths. Pray, how does the lord commander propose to feed Tormund and his thousands?"

Jon had anticipated that question. "Through Eastwatch. We will bring in food by ship, as much as might be required. From the riverlands and the stormlands and the Vale of Arryn, from Dorne and the Reach, across the narrow sea from the Free Cities."

"And this food will be paid for . . . how, if I may ask?"

With gold, from the Iron Bank of Braavos, Jon might have replied. Instead he said, "I have agreed that the free folk may keep their furs and pelts. They will need those for warmth when winter comes. All other wealth they must surrender. Gold and silver, amber, gemstones, carvings, anything of value. We will ship it all across the narrow sea to be sold in the Free Cities."

"All the wealth o' the wildlings," said The Norrey. "That should buy you a bushel o' barleycorn. Two bushels, might be."

"Lord Commander, why not demand that the wildlings give up their arms as well?" asked Clydas.

Leathers laughed at that. "You want the free folk to fight beside you against the common foe. How are we to do that without arms? Would you have us throw snowballs at the wights? Or will you give us sticks to hit them with?"

The arms most wildlings carry are little more than sticks, thought Jon. Wooden clubs, stone axes, mauls, spears with fire-hardened points, knives of bone and stone and dragonglass, wicker shields, bone armor, boiled leather. The Thenns worked bronze, and raiders like the Weeper carried stolen steel and iron swords looted off some corpse . . . but even those were oft of ancient vintage, dinted from years of hard use and spotted with rust.

"Tormund Giantsbane will never willingly disarm his people," Jon said. "He is not the Weeping Man, but he is no craven either. If I had asked that of him, it would have come to blood."

The Norrey fingered his beard. "You may put your wildlings in these ruined forts, Lord Snow, but how will you make them stay? What is there to stop them moving south to fairer, warmer lands?"

"*Our* lands," said Old Flint.

"Tormund has given me his oath. He will serve with us until the spring. The Weeper and their other captains will swear the same or we will not let them pass."

Old Flint shook his head. "They will betray us."

"The Weeper's word is worthless," said Othell Yarwyck.

"These are godless savages," said Septon Cellador. "Even in the south the treachery of wildlings is renowned."

Leathers crossed his arms. "That battle down below? I was on t'other side, remember? Now I wear your blacks and train your boys to kill. Some might call me turncloak. Might be so . . . but I am no more savage than you crows. We have gods too. The same gods they keep in Winterfell."

"The gods of the North, since before this Wall was raised," said Jon. "Those are the gods that Tormund swore by. He will keep his word. I know him, as I knew Mance Rayder. I marched with them for a time, you may recall."

"I had not forgotten," said the Lord Steward.

No, thought Jon, *I did not think you had.*

"Mance Rayder swore an oath as well," Marsh went on. "He vowed to wear no crowns, take no wife, father no sons. Then he turned his cloak, did all those things, and led a fearsome host against the realm. It is the remnants of that host that waits beyond the Wall."

"Broken remnants."

"A broken sword can be reforged. A broken sword can kill."

"The free folk have neither laws nor lords," Jon said, "but they love their children. Will you admit that much?"

"It is not their children who concern us. We fear the fathers, not the sons."

"As do I. So I insisted upon hostages." *I am not the trusting fool you take me for . . . nor am I half wildling, no matter what you believe.* "One hundred boys between the ages of eight and sixteen. A son from each of their chiefs and captains, the rest chosen by lot. The boys will serve as pages and squires, freeing our own men for other duties. Some may choose to take the black one day. Queerer things have happened. The rest will stand hostage for the loyalty of their sires."

The northmen glanced at one another. "Hostages," mused The Norrey. "Tormund has agreed to this?"

It was that, or watch his people die. "My blood price, he called it," said Jon Snow, "but he will pay."

"Aye, and why not?" Old Flint stomped his cane against the ice. "Wards, we always called them, when Winterfell demanded boys of us, but they were hostages, and none the worse for it."

"None but them whose sires displeased the Kings o' Winter," said The Norrey. "Those came home shorter by a head. So you tell me, boy . . . if these wildling friends o' yours prove false, do you have the belly to do what needs be done?"

Ask Janos Slynt. "Tormund Giantsbane knows better than to try me. I may seem a green boy in your eyes, Lord Norrey, but I am still a son of Eddard Stark."

Yet even that did not appease his Lord Steward. "You say these boys will serve as squires. Surely the lord commander does not mean they will be trained *at arms*?"

Jon's anger flared. "No, my lord, I mean to set them to sewing lacy smallclothes. Of course they shall be trained at arms. They shall also churn butter, hew firewood, muck stables, empty chamber pots, and run messages . . . and in between they will be drilled with spear and sword and longbow."

Marsh flushed a deeper shade of red. "The lord commander must pardon my bluntness, but I have no softer way to say this. What you propose is nothing less than treason. For eight thousand years the men of the Night's Watch have stood upon the Wall and fought these wildlings. Now you mean to let them pass, to shelter them in our castles, to feed them and clothe them and teach them how to fight. Lord Snow, must I remind you? *You swore an oath.*"

"I know what I swore." Jon said the words. "*I am the sword in the darkness. I am the watcher on the walls. I am the fire that burns against the cold, the light that brings the dawn, the horn that wakes the sleepers, the shield that guards the realms of men.* Were those the same words you said when you took your vows?"

"They were. As the lord commander knows."

"Are you certain that I have not forgotten some? The ones about the king and his laws, and how we must defend every foot of his land and cling to each ruined castle? How does that part go?" Jon waited for an answer. None came. "*I am the shield that guards the realms of men.* Those are the words. So tell me, my lord—what are these wildlings, if not men?"

Bowen Marsh opened his mouth. No words came out. A flush crept up his neck.

Jon Snow turned away. The last light of the sun had begun to fade. He watched the cracks along the Wall go from red to grey to black, from streaks of fire to rivers of black ice. Down below, Lady Melisandre would be lighting her nightfire and chanting, *Lord of Light, defend us, for the night is dark and full of terrors.*

"Winter is coming," Jon said at last, breaking the awkward silence, "and with it the white walkers. The Wall is where we stop them. The Wall was *made* to stop them . . . but the Wall must be manned. This discussion is at an end. We have much to do before the gate is opened. Tormund and his people will need to be fed and clothed and housed. Some are sick and will need nursing. Those will fall to you, Clydas. Save as many as you can."

Clydas blinked his dim pink eyes. "I will do my best, Jon. My lord, I mean."

"We will need every cart and wagon made ready to transport the free folk to their new homes. Othell, you shall see to that."

Yarwyck grimaced. "Aye, Lord Commander."

"Lord Bowen, you shall collect the tolls. The gold and silver, the amber, the torques and armbands and necklaces. Sort it all, count it, see that it reaches Eastwatch safely."

"Yes, Lord Snow," said Bowen Marsh.

And Jon thought, "*Ice,*" she said, "*and daggers in the dark. Blood frozen red and hard, and naked steel.*" His sword hand flexed. The wind was rising.

CERSEI

Each night seemed colder than the last.

The cell had neither fireplace nor brazier. The only window was too high to allow her a view and too small to squeeze through, but more than large enough to let in the chill. Cersei had torn up the first shift they gave her, demanding the return of her own clothes, but that only left her naked and shivering. When they brought her another shift, she pulled it down over her head and thanked them, choking upon the words.

The window let in sounds as well. That was the only way the queen had to know what might be happening in the city. The septas who brought her food would tell her nothing.

She hated that. Jaime would be coming for her, but how would she know when he arrived? Cersei only hoped he was not so foolish as to go racing ahead of his army. He would need every sword to deal with the ragged horde of Poor Fellows surrounding the Great Sept. She asked about her twin often, but her gaolers gave no answer. She asked about Ser Loras too. At last report the Knight of Flowers had been dying on Dragonstone of wounds received whilst taking the castle. *Let him die,* Cersei thought, *and let him be quick about it.* The boy's death would mean an empty place on the Kingsguard, and that might be her salvation. But the septas were as close-mouthed about Loras Tyrell as they were about Jaime.

Lord Qyburn had been her last and only visitor. Her world had a population of four: herself and her three gaolers, pious and unyielding. Septa Unella was big-boned and mannish, with callused hands and homely, scowling features. Septa Moelle had stiff white hair and small mean eyes perpetually crinkled in suspicion, peering out of a wrinkled face as sharp as the blade of an axe. Septa Scolera was thick-waisted and short, with heavy breasts, olive skin, and a sour smell to her, like milk on the verge of going bad. They brought her food and water, emptied her chamber pot, and took away her shift for washing every few days, leaving her to huddle naked under her blanket until it was returned to her. Sometimes Scolera would read to her from *The Seven-Pointed Star* or *The Book of Holy Prayer,* but elsewise none of them would speak with her or answer any of her questions.

She hated and despised all three of them, almost as much as she hated and despised the men who had betrayed her.

False friends, treacherous servants, men who had professed undying love, even her own blood ... all of them had deserted her in her hour of need. Osney Kettleblack, that weakling, had broken beneath the lash, filling the High Sparrow's ears with secrets he should have taken to his grave. His brothers, scum of the streets whom she had raised high, did no more than sit upon their hands. Aurane Waters, her admiral, had fled to sea with the dromonds she had built for him. Orton Merryweather had gone running back to Longtable, taking his wife, Taena, who had been the queen's one true friend in these terrible times. Harys Swyft and Grand Maester Pycelle had abandoned her to captivity and offered the realm to the very men who had conspired against her. Meryn Trant and Boros Blount, the king's sworn protectors, were nowhere to be found. Even her cousin Lancel, who once had claimed to love her, was one of her accusers. Her uncle had refused to help her rule when she would have made him the King's Hand.

And Jaime ...

No, that she could not believe, would not believe. Jaime would be here once he knew of her plight. "*Come at once,*" she had written to him. "*Help me. Save me. I need you now as I have never needed you before. I love you. I love you. I love you. Come at once.*" Qyburn had sworn that he would see that her letter reached her twin, off in the riverlands with his army. Qyburn had never returned, however. For all she knew, he might be dead, his head impaled upon a spike above the city Keep's gates. Or perhaps he was languishing in one of the black cells beneath the Red Keep, her letter still unsent. The queen had asked after him a hundred times, but her captors would not speak of him. All she knew for certain was that Jaime had not come.

Not yet, she told herself. *But soon. And once he comes the High Sparrow and his bitches will sing a different song.*

She hated feeling helpless.

She had threatened, but her threats had been received with stony faces and deaf ears. She had commanded, but her commands had been ignored. She had invoked the Mother's mercy, appealing to the natural sympathy of one woman for another, but the three shriveled septas must have put their womanhood aside when they spoke their vows. She had tried charm, speaking to them gently, accepting each new outrage meekly. They were not swayed. She had offered them rewards, promised leniency, honors, gold, positions at court. They treated her promises as they did her threats.

And she had prayed. Oh, how she had prayed. Prayer was what they wanted, so she served it to them, served it on her knees as if she were some common trollop of the streets and not a daughter of the Rock. She had prayed for relief, for deliverance, for Jaime. Loudly she asked the gods to defend her in her innocence; silently she prayed for her accusers to suffer sudden, painful deaths. She prayed until her knees were raw and bloody, until her tongue felt so thick and heavy that she was like to choke on it. All the prayers they had taught her as a girl came back to Cersei in her cell, and she made up new ones as needed, calling on the Mother and the Maiden, on the Father and the Warrior, on the Crone and the Smith. She had even prayed to the Stranger. *Any god in a storm.* The Seven proved as deaf as their earthly servants. Cersei gave them all the words that she had in her, gave them everything but tears. *That they will never have,* she told herself.

She hated feeling weak.

If the gods had given her the strength they gave Jaime and that swaggering oaf Robert, she could have made her own escape. *Oh, for a sword and the skill to wield it.* She had a warrior's heart, but the gods in their blind malice had given her the feeble body of a woman. The queen had tried to fight them early on, but the septas had overwhelmed her. There were too many of them, and they were stronger than they looked. Ugly old women, every one of them, but all that praying and scrubbing and beating novices with sticks had left them tough as roots.

And they would not let her rest. Night or day, whenever the queen closed her eyes to sleep, one of her captors would appear to wake her and demand that she confess her sins. She stood accused of adultery, fornication, high treason, even murder, for Osney Kettleblack had confessed to smothering the last High Septon at her command. "I am come to hear you tell of all your murders and fornications," Septa Unella would growl when she shook the queen awake. Septa Moelle would tell her that it was her sins that kept her sleepless. "Only the innocent know the peace of untroubled sleep. Confess your sins, and you will sleep like a newborn babe."

Wake and sleep and wake again, every night was broken into pieces by the rough hands of her tormentors, and every night was colder and crueler than the night before. The hour of the owl, the hour of the wolf, the hour of the nightingale, moonrise and moonset, dusk and dawn, they staggered past like drunkards. What hour was it? What day was it? Where was she? Was this a dream, or had she woken? The little shards of sleep that they allowed her turned into razors, slicing at her wits. Each day found her duller than the day before, exhausted and feverish. She had lost all sense of how long she had been imprisoned in this cell, high up in one of the seven towers of the Great Sept of Baelor. *I will grow old and die here,* she thought, despairing.

Cersei could not allow that to happen. Her son had need of her. The realm had need of her. She had to free herself, no matter what the risk. Her world had shrunk to a cell six feet square, a chamber pot, a lumpy pallet, and a brown wool blanket thin as hope that made her skin itch, but she was still Lord Tywin's heir, a daughter of the Rock.

Exhausted by her lack of sleep, shivering from the cold that stole into the tower cell each night, feverish and famished by turns, Cersei came at last to know she must confess.

That night, when Septa Unella came to wrench her out of sleep, she found the queen waiting on her knees. "I have sinned," said Cersei. Her tongue was thick in her mouth, her lips raw and chapped. "I have sinned most grievously. I see that now. How could I have been so blind for so long? The Crone came to me with her lamp raised high, and by its holy light I saw the road that I must walk. I want to be clean again. I want only absolution. Please, good septa, I beg of you, take me to the High Septon so that I might confess my crimes and fornications."

"I will tell him, Your Grace," said Septa Unella. "His High Holiness will be most pleased. Only through confession and true repentance may our immortal souls be saved."

And for the rest of that long night they let her sleep. Hours and hours of blessed sleep. The owl and the wolf and the nightingale slipped by for once with their passage unseen and unremarked, whilst Cersei dreamed a long sweet dream where Jaime was her husband and their son was still alive.

Come morning, the queen felt almost like herself again. When her captors came for her, she made pious noises at them again and told them how determined she was to confess her sins and be forgiven for all that she had done.

"We rejoice to hear it," said Septa Moelle.

"It will be a great weight off your soul," said Septa Scolera. "You will feel much better afterward, Your Grace."

Your Grace. Those two simple words thrilled her. During her long captivity, her gaolers had not oft bothered with even that simple courtesy.

"His High Holiness awaits," said Septa Unella.

Cersei lowered her head, humble and obedient. "Might I be allowed to bathe first? I am in no fit state to attend him."

"You may wash later if His High Holiness allows," said Septa Unella. "It is the cleanliness of your immortal soul that should concern you now, not such vanities of the flesh."

The three septas led her down the tower stairs, with Septa Unella going before her and Septa Moelle and Septa Scolera at her heels, as if they were afraid that she might try to flee. "It has been so long since I have had a visitor," Cersei murmured in a quiet voice as they made their descent. "Is the king well? I ask only as a mother, fearful for her child."

"His Grace is in good health," said Septa Scolera, "and well protected, day and night. The queen is with him, always."

I am the queen! She swallowed, smiled, and said, "That is good to know. Tommen loves her so. I never believed those terrible things that were being said of her." Had Margaery Tyrell somehow wriggled free of the accusations of fornication, adultery, and high treason? "Was there a trial?"

"Soon," said Septa Scolera, "but her brother—"

"*Hush.*" Septa Unella turned to glare back over her shoulder at Scolera. "You chatter too much, you foolish old woman. It is not for us to speak of such things."

Scolera lowered her head. "Pray forgive me."

They made the rest of the descent in silence.

The High Sparrow received her in his sanctum, an austere seven-sided chamber where crudely carved faces of the Seven stared out from the stone walls with expressions almost as sour and disapproving as His High Holiness himself. When she entered, he was seated behind a rough-hewn table, writing. The High Septon had not changed since the last time she had been in his presence, the day he had her seized and imprisoned. He was still a scrawny grey-haired man with a lean, hard, half-starved look, his face sharp-featured, lined, his eyes suspicious. In place of the rich robes of his predecessors, he wore a shapeless tunic of undyed wool that fell down to his ankles. "Your Grace," he said, by way of greeting. "I understand that you wish to make confession."

Cersei dropped to her knees. "I do, High Holiness. The Crone came to me as I slept with her lamp held high—"

"To be sure. Unella, you will stay and make a record of Her Grace's words. Scolera, Moelle, you have my leave to go." He pressed the fingers of his hands together, the same gesture she had seen her father use a thousand times.

Septa Unella took a seat behind her, spread out a parchment, dipped a quill in maester's ink. Cersei felt a stab of fright. "Once I have confessed, will I be permitted to—"

"Your Grace shall be dealt with according to your sins."

This man is implacable, she realized once again. She gathered herself for a moment. "Mother have mercy on me, then. I have lain with men outside the bonds of marriage. I confess it."

"Who?" The High Septon's eyes were fixed on hers.

Cersei could hear Unella writing behind her. Her quill made a faint, soft scratching sound. "Lancel Lannister, my cousin. And Osney Kettleblack." Both men had confessed to bedding her, it would do her no good to deny it. "His brothers too. Both of them." She had no way of knowing what Osfryd and Osmund might say. Safer to confess too much than too little. "It does not excuse my sin, High Holiness, but I was lonely and afraid. The gods took King Robert from me, my love and my protector. I was alone, surrounded by schemers, false friends, and traitors who were conspiring at the death of my children. I did not know who to trust, so I . . . I used the only means that I had to bind the Kettleblacks to me."

"By which you mean your female parts?"

"My flesh." She pressed a hand to her face, shuddering. When she lowered it again, her eyes were wet with tears. "Yes. May the Maid forgive me. It was for my children, though, for the realm. I took no pleasure in it. The Kettleblacks . . . they are hard men, and cruel, and they used me roughly, but what else was I to do? Tommen needed men around him I could trust."

"His Grace was protected by the Kingsguard."

"The Kingsguard stood by useless as his brother Joffrey died, murdered at his own wedding feast. I watched one son die, I could not bear to lose another. I have sinned, I have committed wanton fornication, but I did it for Tommen. Forgive me, High Holiness, but I would open my legs for every man in King's Landing if that was what I had to do to keep my children safe."

"Forgiveness comes only from the gods. What of Ser Lancel, who was your cousin and your lord husband's squire? Did you take him into your bed to win his loyalty as well?"

"Lancel." Cersei hesitated. *Careful,* she told herself, *Lancel will have told him everything.* "Lancel loved me. He was half a boy, but I never doubted his devotion to me or my son."

"And yet you still corrupted him."

"I was lonely." She choked back a sob. "I had lost my husband, my son, my lord father. I was regent, but a queen is still a woman, and women are weak vessels, easily tempted . . . Your High Holiness knows the truth of that. Even holy septas have been known to sin. I took comfort with Lancel. He was kind and gentle and I needed someone. It was wrong, I know, but I had no one else . . . a woman *needs* to be loved, she needs a man beside her, she . . . she . . ." She began to sob uncontrollably.

The High Septon made no move to comfort her. He sat there with his hard eyes fixed on her, watching her weep, as stony as the statues of the Seven in the sept above. Long moments passed, but finally her tears were all dried up. By then her eyes were red and raw from crying, and she felt as if she might faint.

The High Sparrow was not done with her, however. "These are common sins," he said. "The wickedness of widows is well-known, and all women are wantons at heart, given to using their wiles and their beauty to work their wills on men. There is no treason here, so long as you did not stray from your marriage bed whilst His Grace King Robert was still alive."

"Never," she whispered, shivering. "*Never,* I swear it."

He paid that no mind. "There are other charges laid against Your Grace, crimes far more grievous than simple fornications. You admit Ser Osney Kettleblack was your lover, and Ser Osney insists that he smothered my predecessor at your behest. He further insists that he bore false witness against Queen Margaery and her cousins, telling tales of fornications, adultery, and high treason, again at your behest."

"No," said Cersei. "It is not true. I love Margaery as I would a daughter. And the other . . . I complained of the High Septon, I admit it. He was Tyrion's creature, weak and corrupt, a stain upon our Holy Faith. Your High Holiness knows that as well as I. It may be that Osney thought that his death would please me. If so, I bear some part of the blame . . . but murder? No. Of that I am innocent. Take me to the sept and I will stand before the Father's judgment seat and swear the truth of that."

"In time," said the High Septon. "You also stand accused of conspiring at the murder of your own lord husband, our late beloved King Robert, First of His Name."

Lancel, Cersei thought. "Robert was killed by a boar. Do they say I am a skinchanger now? A warg? Am I accused of killing Joffrey too, my own sweet son, my firstborn?"

"No. Just your husband. Do you deny it?"

"I deny it. I do. Before gods and men, I deny it."

He nodded. "Last of all, and worst of all, there are some who say your children were not fathered by King Robert, that they are bastards born of incest and adultery."

"Stannis says that," Cersei said at once. "A lie, a lie, a palpable lie. Stannis wants the Iron Throne for himself, but his brother's children stand in his way, so he must needs claim that they are not his brother's. That filthy letter . . . there is no shred of truth to it. I deny it."

The High Septon placed both hands flat upon the table and pushed himself to his feet. "Good. Lord Stannis has turned from the truth of the Seven to worship a red demon, and his false faith has no place in these Seven Kingdoms."

That was almost reassuring. Cersei nodded.

"Even so," His High Holiness went on, "these are terrible charges, and the realm must know the truth of them. If Your Grace has told it true, no doubt a trial will prove your innocence."

A trial, still. "I have confessed—"

"—to certain sins, aye. Others you deny. Your trial will separate the truths from the falsehoods. I shall ask the Seven to forgive the sins you have confessed and pray that you be found innocent of these other accusations."

Cersei rose slowly from her knees. "I bow to the wisdom of Your High Holiness," she said, "but if I might beg for just one drop of the Mother's mercy, I . . . it has been so long since I last saw my son, please . . ."

The old man's eyes were chips of flint. "It would not be fitting to allow you near the king until you have been cleansed of all your wickedness. You have taken the first step on your path back to righteous-ness, however, and in light of that I shall permit you other visitors. One each day."

The queen began to weep again. This time the tears were true. "You are too kind. Thank you."

"The Mother is merciful. It is her that you should thank."

Moelle and Scolera were waiting to lead her back up to her tower cell. Unella followed close behind them. "We have all been praying for Your Grace," Septa Moelle said as they were climbing.

"Yes," Septa Scolera echoed, "and you must feel so much lighter now, clean and innocent as a maid on the morning of her wedding."

I fucked Jaime on the morning of my wedding, the queen recalled. "I do," she said, "I feel reborn, as if a festering boil has been lanced and now at last I can begin to heal. I could almost fly." She imagined how sweet it would be to slam an elbow into Septa Scolera's face and send her careening down the spiral steps. If the gods were good, the wrinkled old cunt might crash into Septa Unella and take her down with her.

"It is good to see you smiling again," Scolera said.

"His High Holiness said I might have visitors?"

"He did," said Septa Unella. "If Your Grace will tell us whom you wish to see, we will send word to them."

Jaime, I need Jaime. But if her twin was in the city, why had he not come to her? It might be wiser to wait on Jaime until she had a better notion of what was happening beyond the walls of the Great Sept of Baelor. "My uncle," she said. "Ser Kevan Lannister, my father's brother. Is he in the city?"

"He is," said Septa Unella. "The Lord Regent has taken up residence in the Red Keep. We will send for him at once."

"Thank you," said Cersei, thinking, *Lord Regent, is it?* She could not pretend to be surprised.

A humble and a contrite heart proved to have benefits over and beyond cleansing the soul of sin. That night the queen was moved to a larger cell two floors down, with a window she could actually look out of and warm, soft blankets for her bed. And when time came for supper, instead of stale bread and oaten porridge, she was served a roast capon, a bowl of crisp greens sprinkled with crushed walnuts, and a mound of mashed neeps aswim in butter. That night she crawled into her bed with a full stomach for the first time since she was taken, and slept through the black watches of the night undisturbed.

The next morning, with the dawn, there came her uncle.

Cersei was still at her breakfast when the door swung open and Ser Kevan Lannister stepped through. "Leave us," he told her gaolers. Septa Unella ushered Scolera and Moelle away and closed the door behind them. The queen rose to her feet.

Ser Kevan looked older than when she'd seen him last. He was a big man, broad in the shoulder and thick about the waist, with a close-cropped blond beard that followed the line of his heavy jaw and short blond hair in full retreat from his brow. A heavy woolen cloak, dyed crimson, was clasped at one shoulder with a golden brooch in the shape of a lion's head.

"Thank you for coming," the queen said.

Her uncle frowned. "You should sit. There are things that I must needs tell you—"

She did not want to sit. "You are still angry with me. I hear it in your voice. Forgive me, Uncle. It was wrong of me to throw my wine at you, but—"

"You think I care about a cup of wine? Lancel is my *son*, Cersei. Your own cousin. If I am angry with you, that is the cause. You should have looked after him, guided him, found him a likely girl of good family. Instead you—"

"I know. I know." *Lancel wanted me more than I ever wanted him. He still does, I will wager.* "I was alone, weak. Please. Uncle. Oh, Uncle. It is so good to see your face, your sweet sweet face. I have done wicked things, I know, but I could not bear for you to hate me." She threw her arms around him, kissed his cheek. "Forgive me. Forgive me."

Ser Kevan suffered the embrace for a few heartbeats before he finally raised his own arms to return it. His hug was short and awkward. "Enough," he said, his voice still flat and cold. "You are forgiven. Now sit. I bring some hard tidings, Cersei."

His words frightened her. "Has something happened to Tommen?

Please, no. I have been so afraid for my son. No one will tell me anything. Please tell me that Tommen is well."

"His Grace is well. He asks about you often." Ser Kevan laid his hands on her shoulders, held her at arm's length.

"Jaime, then? Is it Jaime?"

"No. Jaime is still in the riverlands, somewhere."

"Somewhere?" She did not like the sound of that.

"He took Raventree and accepted Lord Blackwood's surrender," said her uncle, "but on his way back to Riverrun he left his tail and went off with a woman."

"A woman?" Cersei stared at him, uncomprehending. "What woman? Why? Where did they go?"

"No one knows. We've had no further word of him. The woman may have been the Evenstar's daughter, Lady Brienne."

Her. The queen remembered the Maid of Tarth, a huge, ugly, shambling thing who dressed in man's mail. *Jaime would never abandon me for such a creature. My raven never reached him, elsewise he would have come.*

"We have had reports of sellswords landing all over the south," Ser Kevan was saying. "Tarth, the Stepstones, Cape Wrath . . . where Stannis found the coin to hire a free company I would dearly love to know. I do not have the strength to deal with them, not here. Mace Tyrell does, but he refuses to bestir himself until this matter with his daughter has been settled."

A headsman would settle Margaery quick enough. Cersei did not care a fig for Stannis or his sellswords. *The Others take him and the Tyrells both. Let them slaughter each other, the realm will be the better for it.* "Please, Uncle, take me out of here."

"How? By force of arms?" Ser Kevan walked to the window and gazed out, frowning. "I would need to make an abbatoir of this holy place. And I do not have the men. The best part of our forces were at Riverrun with your brother. I had no time to raise up a new host." He turned back to face her. "I have spoken with His High Holiness. He will not release you until you have atoned for your sins."

"I have confessed."

"*Atoned,* I said. Before the city. A walk—"

"No." She knew what her uncle was about to say, and she did not want to hear it. "Never. Tell him that, if you speak again. I am a queen, not some dockside whore."

"No harm would come to you. No one will touch—"

"*No,*" she said, more sharply. "I would sooner die."

Ser Kevan was unmoved. "If that is your wish, you may soon have it granted. His High Holiness is resolved that you be tried for regicide, deicide, incest, and high treason."

"Deicide?" She almost laughed. "When did I kill a god?"

"The High Septon speaks for the Seven here on earth. Strike at him, and you are striking at the gods themselves." Her uncle raised a hand before she could protest. "It does no good to speak of such things. Not here. The time for all that is at trial." He gazed about her cell. The look on his face spoke volumes.

Someone is listening. Even here, even now, she dare not speak freely. She took a breath. "Who will try me?"

"The Faith," her uncle said, "unless you insist on a trial by battle. In which case you must be championed by a knight of the Kingsguard. Whatever the outcome, your rule is at an end. I will serve as Tommen's regent until he comes of age. Mace Tyrell has been named King's Hand. Grand Maester Pycelle and Ser Harys Swyft will continue as before, but Paxter Redwyne is now lord admiral and Randyll Tarly has assumed the duties of justiciar."

Tyrell bannermen, the both of them. The whole governance of the realm was being handed to her enemies, Queen Margaery's kith and kin. "Margaery stands accused as well. Her and those cousins of hers. How is it that the sparrows freed her and not me?"

"Randyll Tarly insisted. He was the first to reach King's Landing when this storm broke, and he brought his army with him. The Tyrell girls will still be tried, but the case against them is weak, His High Holiness admits. All of the men named as the queen's lovers have denied the accusation or recanted, save for your maimed singer, who appears to be half-mad. So the High Septon handed the girls over to Tarly's custody and Lord Randyll swore a holy oath to deliver them for trial when the time comes."

"And her accusers?" the queen demanded. "Who holds them?"

"Osney Kettleblack and the Blue Bard are here, beneath the sept. The Redwyne twins have been declared innocent, and Hamish the Harper has died. The rest are in the dungeons under the Red Keep, in the charge of your man Qyburn."

Qyburn, thought Cersei. That was good, one straw at least that she could clutch. Lord Qyburn had them, and Lord Qyburn could do wonders. *And horrors. He can do horrors as well.*

"There is more, worse. *Will* you sit down?"

"Sit down?" Cersei shook her head. What could be worse? She was to be tried for high treason whilst the little queen and her cousins flew off as free as birds. "Tell me. What is it?"

"Myrcella. We have had grave news from Dorne."

"*Tyrion,*" she said at once. Tyrion had sent her little girl to Dorne, and Cersei had dispatched Ser Balon Swann to bring her home. All Dornishmen were snakes, and the Martells were the worst of them. The Red Viper had even tried to defend the Imp, had come within a hairbreadth of a victory that would have allowed the dwarf to escape the blame for Joffrey's murder. "It's him, he's been in Dorne all this time, and now he's seized my daughter."

Ser Kevan gave her another scowl. "Myrcella was attacked by a Dornish knight named Gerold Dayne. She's alive, but hurt. He slashed her face open, she . . . I'm sorry . . . she lost an ear."

"An ear." Cersei stared at him, aghast. *She was just a child, my precious princess. She was so pretty, too.* "He cut off her ear. And Prince Doran and his Dornish knights, where were they? They could not defend one little girl? Where was Arys Oakheart?"

"Slain, defending her. Dayne cut him down, it's said."

The Sword of the Morning had been a Dayne, the queen recalled, but he was long dead. Who was this Ser Gerold and why would he wish to harm her daughter? She could not make any sense of this, unless . . . "Tyrion lost half his nose in the Battle of the Blackwater. Slashing her face, cutting off an ear . . . the Imp's grubby little fingers are all over this."

"Prince Doran says nothing of your brother. And Balon Swann writes that Myrcella puts it all on this Gerold Dayne. Darkstar, they call him."

She gave a bitter laugh. "Whatever they call him, he is my brother's catspaw. Tyrion has friends amongst the Dornish. The Imp planned this all along. It was Tyrion who betrothed Myrcella to Prince Trystane. Now I see why."

"You see Tyrion in every shadow."

"He is a creature of the shadows. He killed Joffrey. He killed Father. Did you think he would stop there? I feared that the Imp was still in King's Landing plotting harm to Tommen, but he must have gone to Dorne instead to kill Myrcella first." Cersei paced the width of the cell. "I need to be with Tommen. These Kingsguard knights are as useless as nipples on a breastplate." She rounded on her uncle. "Ser Arys was killed, you said."

"At the hands of this man Darkstar, yes."

"Dead, he's *dead*, you are certain of that?"

"That is what we have been told."

"Then there is an empty place amongst the Kingsguard. It must be filled at once. Tommen must be protected."

"Lord Tarly is drawing up a list of worthy knights for your brother to consider, but until Jaime reappears . . ."

"The king can give a man a white cloak. Tommen's a good boy. Tell him who to name and he will name him."

"And who would you have him name?"

She did not have a ready answer. *My champion will need a new name as well as a new face.* "Qyburn will know. Trust him in this. You and I have had our differences, Uncle, but for the blood we share and the love you bore my father, for Tommen's sake and the sake of his poor maimed sister, do as I ask you. Go to Lord Qyburn on my behalf, bring him a white cloak, and tell him that the time has come."

THE QUEENSGUARD

"Y ou were the queen's man," said Reznak mo Reznak. "The king desires his own men about him when he holds court."

I am the queen's man still. Today, tomorrow, always, until my last breath, or hers. Barristan Selmy refused to believe that Daenerys Targaryen was dead.

Perhaps that was why he was being put aside. *One by one, Hizdahr removes us all.* Strong Belwas lingered at the door of death in the temple, under the care of the Blue Graces ... though Selmy half suspected they were finishing the job those honeyed locusts had begun. Skahaz Shavepate had been stripped of his command. The Unsullied had withdrawn to their barracks. Jhogo, Daario Naharis, Admiral Groleo, and Hero of the Unsullied remained hostages of the Yunkai'i. Aggo and Rakharo and the rest of the queen's *khalasar* had been dispatched across the river to search for their lost queen. Even Missandei had been replaced; the king did not think it fit to use a child as his herald, and a one-time Naathi slave at that. *And now me.*

There was a time when he might have taken this dismissal as a blot upon his honor. But that was in Westeros. In the viper's pit that was Meereen, honor seemed as silly as a fool's motley. And this mistrust was mutual. Hizdahr zo Loraq might be his queen's consort, but he would never be his king. "If His Grace wishes for me to remove myself from court ..."

"His Radiance," the seneschal corrected. "No, no, no, you misunderstand me. His Worship is to receive a delegation from the Yunkai'i, to discuss the withdrawal of their armies. They may ask for ... ah ... recompense for those who lost their lives to the dragon's wroth. A delicate situation. The king feels it will be better if they see a Meereenese king upon the throne, protected by Meereenese warriors. Surely you can understand that, ser."

I understand more than you know. "Might I know which men His Grace has chosen to protect him?"

Reznak mo Reznak smiled his slimy smile. "Fearsome fighters, who love His Worship well. Goghor the Giant. Khrazz. The Spotted Cat. Belaquo Bonebreaker. Heroes all."

Pit fighters all. Ser Barristan was unsurprised. Hizdahr zo Loraq sat uneasily on his new throne. It had been a thousand years since Meereen last had a king, and there were some even amongst the old blood who thought they might have made a better choice than him. Outside the city sat the Yunkai'i with their sellswords and their allies; inside were the Sons of the Harpy.

And the king's protectors grew fewer every day. Hizdahr's blunder with Grey Worm had cost him the Unsullied. When His Grace had tried to put them under the command of a cousin, as he had the Brazen Beasts, Grey Worm had informed the king that they were free men who took commands only from their mother. As for the Brazen Beasts, half were freedmen and the rest shavepates, whose true loyalty might still be to Skahaz mo Kandaq. The pit fighters were King Hizdahr's only reliable support, against a sea of enemies.

"May they defend His Grace against all threats." Ser Barristan's tone gave no hint of his true feelings; he had learned to hide such back in King's Landing years ago.

"His *Magnificence*," Reznak mo Reznak stressed. "Your other duties shall remain unchanged, ser. Should this peace fail, His Radiance would still wish for you to command his forces against the enemies of our city."

He has that much sense, at least. Belaquo Bonebreaker and Goghor the Giant might serve as Hizdahr's shields, but the notion of either leading an army into battle was so ludicrous that the old knight almost smiled. "I am His Grace's to command."

"Not *Grace*," the seneschal complained. "That style is Westerosi. His Magnificence, His Radiance, His Worship."

His Vanity would fit better. "As you say."

Reznak licked his lips. "Then we are done." This time his oily smile betokened dismissal. Ser Barristan took his leave, grateful to leave the stench of the seneschal's perfume behind him. *A man should smell of sweat, not flowers.*

The Great Pyramid of Meereen was eight hundred feet high from base to point. The seneschal's chambers were on the second level. The queen's apartments, and his own, occupied the highest step. *A long climb for a man my age,* Ser Barristan thought, as he started up. He had been known to make that climb five or six times a day on the queen's business, as the aches in his knees and the small of his back could attest. *There will come a day when I can no longer face these steps,* he thought, *and that day will be here sooner than I would like.* Before it came, he must make certain that at least a few of his lads were ready to take his place at the queen's side. *I will knight them myself when they are worthy, and give them each a horse and golden spurs.*

The royal apartments were still and silent. Hizdahr had not taken up residence there, preferring to establish his own suite of rooms deep in the heart of the Great Pyramid, where massive brick walls surrounded him on all sides. Mezzara, Miklaz, Qezza, and the rest of the queen's young cupbearers—hostages in truth, but both Selmy and the queen had become so fond of them that it was hard for him to think of them that way—had gone with the king, whilst Irri and Jhiqui departed with the other Dothraki. Only Missandei remained, a forlorn little ghost haunting the queen's chambers at the apex of the pyramid.

Ser Barristan walked out onto the terrace. The sky above Meereen was the color of corpse flesh, dull and white and heavy, a mass of unbroken cloud from horizon to horizon. The sun was hidden behind a wall of cloud. It would set unseen, as it had risen unseen that morning. The night would be hot, a sweaty, suffocating, sticky sort of night without a breath of air. For three days rain had threatened, but not a drop had fallen. *Rain would come as a relief. It might help wash the city clean.*

From here he could see four lesser pyramids, the city's western walls, and the camps of the Yunkishmen by the shores of Slaver's Bay, where a thick column of greasy smoke twisted upward like some monstrous serpent. *The Yunkishmen burning their dead,* he realized. *The pale mare is galloping through their siege camps.* Despite all the queen had done, the sickness had spread, both within the city walls and without. Meereen's markets were closed, its streets empty. King Hizdahr had allowed the fighting pits to remain open, but the crowds were sparse. The Meereenese had even begun to shun the Temple of the Graces, reportedly.

The slavers will find some way to blame Daenerys for that as well, Ser Barristan thought bitterly. He could almost hear them whispering—Great Masters, Sons of the Harpy, Yunkai'i, all telling one another that his queen was dead. Half of the city believed it, though as yet they did not have the courage to say such words aloud. *But soon, I think.*

Ser Barristan felt very tired, very old. *Where have all the years gone?* Of late, whenever he knelt to drink from a still pool, he saw a stranger's face gazing up from the water's depths. When had those crow's-feet first appeared around his pale blue eyes? How long ago had his hair turned from sunlight into snow? *Years ago, old man. Decades.*

Yet it seemed like only yesterday that he had been raised to knighthood, after the tourney at King's Landing. He could still recall the touch of King Aegon's sword upon his shoulder, light as a maiden's kiss. His words had caught in his throat when he spoke his vows. At the feast that night he had eaten ribs of wild boar, prepared the Dornish way with dragon peppers, so hot they burned his mouth. Forty-seven years, and the taste still lingered in his memory, yet he could not have said what he had supped on ten days ago if all seven kingdoms had depended on it. *Boiled dog, most like. Or some other foul dish that tasted no better.*

Not for the first time, Selmy wondered at the strange fates that had brought him here. He was a knight of Westeros, a man of the ˙rmlands and the Dornish marches; his place was in the Seven

Kingdoms, not here upon the sweltering shores of Slaver's Bay. *I came to bring Daenerys home.* Yet he had lost her, just as he had lost her father and her brother. *Even Robert. I failed him too.*

Perhaps Hizdahr was wiser than he knew. *Ten years ago I would have sensed what Daenerys meant to do. Ten years ago I would have been quick enough to stop her.* Instead he had stood befuddled as she leapt into the pit, shouting her name, then running uselessly after her across the scarlet sands. *I am become old and slow.* Small wonder Naharis mocked him as Ser Grandfather. *Would Daario have moved more quickly if he had been beside the queen that day?* Selmy thought he knew the answer to that, though it was not one he liked.

He had dreamed of it again last night: Belwas on his knees retching up bile and blood, Hizdahr urging on the dragonslayers, men and women fleeing in terror, fighting on the steps, climbing over one another, screaming and shouting. And Daenerys . . .

Her hair was aflame. She had the whip in her hand and she was shouting, then she was on the dragon's back, flying. The sand that Drogon stirred as he took wing had stung Ser Barristan's eyes, but through a veil of tears he had watched the beast fly from the pit, his great black wings slapping at the shoulders of the bronze warriors at the gates.

The rest he learned later. Beyond the gates had been a solid press of people. Maddened by the smell of dragon, horses below reared in terror, lashing out with iron-shod hooves. Food stalls and palanquins alike were overturned, men knocked down and trampled. Spears were thrown, crossbows were fired. Some struck home. The dragon twisted violently in the air, wounds smoking, the girl clinging to his back. Then he loosed the fire.

It had taken the rest of the day and most of the night for the Brazen Beasts to gather up the corpses. The final count was two hundred fourteen slain, three times as many burned or wounded. Drogon was gone from the city by then, last seen high over the Skahazadhan, flying north. Of Daenerys Targaryen, no trace had been found. Some swore they saw her fall. Others insisted that the dragon had carried her off to devour her. *They are wrong.*

Ser Barristan knew no more of dragons than the tales every child hears, but he knew Targaryens. Daenerys had been *riding* that dragon, as Aegon had once ridden Balerion of old.

"She might be flying home," he told himself, aloud.

"No," murmured a soft voice behind him. "She would not do that, ser. She would not go home without us."

Ser Barristan turned. "Missandei. Child. How long have you been standing there?"

"Not long. This one is sorry if she has disturbed you." She hesitated. "Skahaz mo Kandaq wishes words with you."

"The Shavepate? You spoke with him?" That was rash, rash. The enmity ran deep between Shakaz and the king, and the girl was clever enough to know that. Skahaz had been outspoken in his opposition to the queen's marriage, a fact Hizdahr had not forgotten. "Is he here? In the pyramid?"

"When he wishes. He comes and goes, ser."

Yes. He would. "Who told you he wants words with me?"

"A Brazen Beast. He wore an owl mask."

He wore an owl mask when he spoke to you. By now he could be a jackal, a tiger, a sloth. Ser Barristan had hated the masks from the start and never more than now. Honest men should never need to hide their faces. And the Shavepate . . .

What could he be thinking? After Hizdahr had given command of the Brazen Beasts to his cousin Marghaz zo Loraq, Skahaz had been named Warden of the River, with charge of all the ferries, dredges, and irrigation ditches along the Skahazadhan for fifty leagues, but the Shavepate had refused that ancient and honorable office, as Hizdahr called it, preferring to retire to the modest pyramid of Kandaq. *Without the queen to protect him, he takes a great risk coming here.* And if Ser Barristan were seen speaking with him, suspicion might fall on the knight as well.

He did not like the taste of this. It smelled of deceit, of whispers and lies and plots hatched in the dark, all the things he'd hoped to leave behind with the Spider and Lord Littlefinger and their ilk. Barristan Selmy was not a bookish man, but he had often glanced through the pages of the White Book, where the deeds of his predecessors had been recorded. Some had been heroes, some weaklings, knaves, or cravens. Most were only men—quicker and stronger than most, more skilled with sword and shield, but still prey to pride, ambition, lust, love, anger, jealousy, greed for gold, hunger for power, and all the other failings that afflicted lesser mortals. The best of them overcame their flaws, did their duty, and died with their swords in their hands. The worst . . .

The worst were those who played the game of thrones. "Can you find this owl again?" he asked Missandei.

"This one can try, ser."

"Tell him I will speak with . . . with our friend . . . after dark, by the stables." The pyramid's main doors were closed and barred at sunset. The stables would be quiet at that hour. "Make certain it is the same owl." It would not serve to have the wrong Brazen Beast hear of this.

"This one understands." Missandei turned as if to go, then paused a moment and said, "It is said that the Yunkai'i have ringed the city all about with scorpions, to loose iron bolts into the sky should Drogon return."

Ser Barristan had heard that too. "It is no simple thing to slay a dragon in the sky. In Westeros, many tried to bring down Aegon and his sisters. None succeeded."

Missandei nodded. It was hard to tell if she was reassured. "Do you think that they will find her, ser? The grasslands are so vast, and dragons leave no tracks across the sky."

"Aggo and Rakharo are blood of her blood . . . and who knows the Dothraki sea better than Dothraki?" He squeezed her shoulder. "They will find her if she can be found." *If she still lives.* There were other khals who prowled the grass, horselords with *khalasar*s whose riders numbered in the tens of thousands. But the girl did not need to hear that. "You love her well, I know. I swear, I shall keep her safe."

The words seemed to give the girl some comfort. *Words are wind, though,* Ser Barristan thought. *How can I protect the queen when I am not with her?*

Barristan Selmy had known many kings. He had been born during the troubled reign of Aegon the Unlikely, beloved by the common folk, had received his knighthood at his hands. Aegon's son Jaehaerys had bestowed the white cloak on him when he was three-and-twenty, after he slew Maelys the Monstrous during the War of the Ninepenny Kings. In that same cloak he had stood beside the Iron Throne as madness consumed Jaehaerys's son Aerys. *Stood, and saw, and heard, and yet did nothing.*

But no. That was not fair. He did his duty. Some nights, Ser Barristan wondered if he had not done that duty too well. He had sworn his vows before the eyes of gods and men, he could not in honor go against them ... but the keeping of those vows had grown hard in the last years of King Aerys's reign. He had seen things that it pained him to recall, and more than once he wondered how much of the blood was on his own hands. If he had not gone into Duskendale to rescue Aerys from Lord Darklyn's dungeons, the king might well have died there as Tywin Lannister sacked the town. Then Prince Rhaegar would have ascended the Iron Throne, mayhaps to heal the realm. Duskendale had been his finest hour, yet the memory tasted bitter on his tongue.

It was his failures that haunted him at night, though. *Jaehaerys, Aerys, Robert. Three dead kings. Rhaegar, who would have been a finer king than any of them. Princess Elia and the children. Aegon just a babe, Rhaenys with her kitten.* Dead, every one, yet he still lived, who had sworn to protect them. And now Daenerys, his bright shining child queen. *She is not dead. I will not believe it.*

Afternoon brought Ser Barristan a brief respite from his doubts. He spent it in the training hall on the pyramid's third level, working with his boys, teaching them the art of sword and shield, horse and lance ... and chivalry, the code that made a knight more than any pit fighter. Daenerys would need protectors her own age about her after he was gone, and Ser Barristan was determined to give her such.

The lads he was instructing ranged in age from eight to twenty. He had started with more than sixty of them, but the training had proved too rigorous for many. Less than half that number now remained, but some showed great promise. *With no king to guard, I will have more time to train them now,* he realized as he walked from pair to pair, watching them go at one another with blunted swords and spears with rounded heads. *Brave boys. Baseborn, aye, but some* will make good knights, and they love the queen. If not for her, all of them would have ended in the pits. King Hizdahr has his pit fighters, but Daenerys will have knights.

"Keep your shield up," he called. "Show me your strokes. Together now. Low, high, low, low, high, low . . ."

Selmy took his simple supper out onto the queen's terrace that night and ate it as the sun went down. Through the purple twilight he watched fires waken one by one in the great stepped pyramids, as the many-colored bricks of Meereen faded to grey and then to black. Shadows gathered in the streets and alleys below, making pools and rivers. In the dusk, the city seemed a tranquil place, even beautiful. *That is pestilence, not peace,* the old knight told himself with his last sip of wine.

He did not wish to be conspicuous, so when he was finished with his supper he changed out of his court clothes, trading the white cloak of the Queensguard for a hooded brown traveler's cloak such as any common man might wear. He kept his sword and dagger. *This could still be some trap.* He had little trust in Hizdahr and less in Reznak mo Reznak. The perfumed seneschal could well be part of this, trying to lure him into a secret meeting so he could sweep up him and Skahaz both and charge them with conspiring against the king. *If the Shavepate speaks treason, he will leave me no choice but to arrest him. Hizdahr is my queen's consort, however little I may like it. My duty is to him, not Skahaz.*

Or was it?

The first duty of the Kingsguard was to defend the king from harm or threat. The white knights were sworn to obey the king's commands as well, to keep his secrets, counsel him when counsel was requested and keep silent when it was not, serve his pleasure and defend his name and honor. Strictly speaking, it was purely the king's choice whether or not to extend Kingsguard protection to others, even those of royal blood. Some kings thought it right and proper to dispatch Kingsguard to serve and defend their wives and children, siblings, aunts, uncles, and cousins of greater and lesser degree, and occasionally even their lovers, mistresses, and bastards. But others preferred to use household knights and men-at-arms for those purposes, whilst keeping their seven as their own personal guard, never far from their sides.

If the queen had commanded me to protect Hizdahr, I would have had no choice but to obey. But Daenerys Targaryen had never established a proper Queensguard even for herself nor issued any commands in respect to her consort. *The world was simpler when I had a lord commander to decide such matters,* Selmy reflected. *Now I am the lord commander, and it is hard to know which path is right.*

When at last he came to the bottom of the last flight of steps, he found himself all but alone amongst the torchlit corridors inside the pyramid's massive brick walls. The great gates were closed and barred, as he had anticipated. Four Brazen Beasts stood guard outside those doors, four more within. It was those that the old knight encountered—big men, masked as boar, bear, vole, and manticore.

"All quiet, ser," the bear told him.

"Keep it so." It was not unknown for Ser Barristan to walk around at night, to make certain the pyramid was secure.

Deeper inside the pyramid, another four Brazen Beasts had been set to guard the iron doors outside the pit where Viserion and Rhaegal were chained. The light of the torches shimmered off their masks— ape, ram, wolf, crocodile.

"Have they been fed?" Ser Barristan asked.

"Aye, ser," replied the ape. "A sheep apiece."

And how long will that suffice, I wonder? As the dragons grew, so did their appetites.

It was time to find the Shavepate. Ser Barristan made his way past the elephants and the queen's silver mare, to the back of the stables. An ass nickered as he went by, and a few of the horses stirred at the light of his lantern. Elsewise all was dark and silent.

Then a shadow detached itself from inside an empty stall and became another Brazen Beast, clad in pleated black skirt, greaves, and muscled breastplate. "A cat?" said Barristan Selmy when he saw the brass beneath the hood. When the Shavepate had commanded the Brazen Beasts, he had favored a serpent's-head mask, imperious and frightening.

"Cats go everywhere," replied the familiar voice of Skahaz mo Kandaq. "No one ever looks at them."

"If Hizdahr should learn that you are here . . ."

"Who will tell him? Marghaz? Marghaz knows what I want him to know. The Beasts are still mine. Do not forget it." The Shavepate's voice was muffled by his mask, but Selmy could hear the anger in it. "I have the poisoner."

"Who?"

"Hizdahr's confectioner. His name would mean nothing to you. The man was just a catspaw. The Sons of the Harpy took his daughter and swore she would be returned unharmed once the queen was dead. Belwas and the dragon saved Daenerys. No one saved the girl. She was returned to her father in the black of night, in nine pieces. One for every year she lived."

"Why?" Doubts gnawed at him. "The Sons had stopped their killing. Hizdahr's peace—"

"—is a sham. Not at first, no. The Yunkai'i were afraid of our queen, of her Unsullied, of her dragons. This land has known dragons before. Yurkhaz zo Yunzak had read his histories, he knew. Hizdahr as well. Why not a peace? Daenerys wanted it, they could see that. Wanted it too much. She should have marched to Astapor." Skahaz moved closer. "That was before. The pit changed all. Daenerys gone, Yurkhaz dead. In place of one old lion, a pack of jackals. Bloodbeard . . . that one has no taste for peace. And there is more. Worse. Volantis has launched its fleet against us."

"Volantis." Selmy's sword hand tingled. *We made a peace with Yunkai. Not with Volantis.* "You are certain?"

"Certain. The Wise Masters know. So do their friends. The Harpy, Reznak, Hizdahr. This king will open the city gates to the Volantenes when they arrive. All those Daenerys freed will be enslaved again. Even some who were never slaves will be fitted for chains. You may end your days in a fighting pit, old man. Khrazz will eat your heart."

His head was pounding. "Daenerys must be told."

"Find her first." Skahaz grasped his forearm. His fingers felt like iron. "We cannot wait for her. I have spoken with the Free Brothers, the Mother's Men, the Stalwart Shields. They have no trust in Loraq.

We must break the Yunkai'i. But we need the Unsullied. Grey Worm will listen to you. Speak to him."

"To what end?" *He is speaking treason. Conspiracy.*

"Life." The Shavepate's eyes were black pools behind the brazen cat mask. "We must strike before the Volantenes arrive. Break the siege, kill the slaver lords, turn their sellswords. The Yunkai'i do not expect an attack. I have spies in their camps. There's sickness, they say, worse every day. Discipline has gone to rot. The lords are drunk more oft than not, gorging themselves at feasts, telling each other of the riches they'll divide when Meereen falls, squabbling over primacy. Bloodbeard and the Tattered Prince despise each other. No one expects a fight. Not now. Hizdahr's peace has lulled us to sleep, they believe."

"Daenerys signed that peace," Ser Barristan said. "It is not for us to break it without her leave."

"And if she is dead?" demanded Skahaz. "What then, ser? I say she would want us to protect her city. Her children."

Her children were the freedmen. *Mhysa, they called her, all those whose chains she broke. "Mother."* The Shavepate was not wrong. Daenerys would want her children protected. "What of Hizdahr? He is still her consort. Her king. Her husband."

"Her poisoner."

Is he? "Where is your proof?"

"The crown he wears is proof enough. The throne he sits. Open your eyes, old man. That is all he needed from Daenerys, all he ever wanted. Once he had it, why share the rule?"

Why indeed? It had been so hot down in the pit. He could still see the air shimmering above the scarlet sands, smell the blood spilling from the men who'd died for their amusement. And he could still hear Hizdahr, urging his queen to try the honeyed locusts. *Those are very tasty . . . sweet and hot . . . yet he never touched so much as one himself . . .* Selmy rubbed his temple. *I swore no vows to Hizdahr zo Loraq. And if I had, he has cast me aside, just as Joffrey did.* "This . . . this confectioner, I want to question him myself. Alone."

"Is it that way?" The Shavepate crossed his arms against his chest. "Done, then. Question him as you like."

"If . . . if what he has to say convinces me . . . if I join with you in this, this . . . I would require your word that no harm would come to Hizdahr zo Loraq until . . . unless . . . it can be proved that he had some part in this."

"Why do you care so much for Hizdahr, old man? If he is not the Harpy, he is the Harpy's firstborn son."

"All I know for certain is that he is the queen's consort. I want your word on this, or I swear, I shall oppose you."

Skahaz's smile was savage. "My word, then. No harm to Hizdahr till his guilt is proved. But when we have the proof, I mean to kill him with my own hands. I want to pull his entrails out and show them to him before I let him die."

No, the old knight thought. *If Hizdahr conspired at my queen's death, I will see to him myself, but his death will be swift and clean.* The gods of Westeros were far away, yet Ser Barristan Selmy paused for a moment to say a silent prayer, asking the Crone to light his way to wisdom. *For the children,* he told himself. *For the city. For my queen.*

"I will talk to Grey Worm," he said.

THE IRON SUITOR

G rief appeared alone at daybreak, her black sails stark against the pale pink skies of morning.

Fifty-four, Victarion thought sourly when they woke him, *and she sails alone.* Silently he cursed the Storm God for his malice, his rage a black stone in his belly. *Where are my ships?*

He had set sail from the Shields with ninety-three of the hundred that had once made up the Iron Fleet, a fleet belonging not to a single lord but to the Seastone Chair itself, captained and crewed by men from all the islands. Ships smaller than the great war dromonds of the green lands, aye, but thrice the size of any common longship, with deep hulls and savage rams, fit to meet the king's own fleets in battle.

In the Stepstones they had taken on grain and game and fresh water, after the long voyage along the bleak and barren coast of Dorne with its shoals and whirlpools. There, the *Iron Victory* had captured a fat merchant ship, the great cog *Noble Lady,* on her way to Oldtown by way of Gulltown, Duskendale, and King's Landing, with a cargo of salt cod, whale oil, and pickled herring. The food was a welcome addition to their stores. Five other prizes taken in the Redwyne Straights and along the Dornish coast—three cogs, a galleas, and a galley—had brought their numbers to ninety-nine.

Nine-and-ninety ships had left the Stepstones in three proud fleets, with orders to join up again off the southern tip of the Isle of Cedars.

Forty-five had now arrived on the far side of the world. Twenty-two of Victarion's own had straggled in, by threes and fours, sometimes alone; fourteen of Ralf the Limper's; only nine of those that had sailed with Red Ralf Stonehouse. Red Ralf himself was amongst the missing. To their number the fleet had added nine new prizes taken on the seas, so the sum was fifty-four . . . but the captured ships were cogs and fishing boats, merchantmen and slavers, not warships. In battle, they would be poor substitutes for the lost ships of the Iron Fleet.

The last ship to appear had been the *Maiden's Bane,* three days previous. The day before that, three ships had come out of the south together—his captive *Noble Lady,* lumbering along between *Ravenfeeder* and *Iron Kiss.* But the day before and the day before there had been nothing, and only *Headless Jeyne* and *Fear* before that, then two more days of empty seas and cloudless skies after Ralf the Limper appeared with the remnants of his squadron. *Lord Quellon, White Widow, Lamentation, Woe, Leviathan, Iron Lady, Reaper's Wind,* and *Warhammer,* with six more ships behind, two of them storm-wracked and under tow.

"Storms," Ralf the Limper had muttered when he came crawling to Victarion. "Three big storms, and foul winds between. Red winds out of Valyria that smelled of ash and brimstone, and black winds that drove us toward that blighted shore. This voyage was cursed from the first. The Crow's Eye fears you, my lord, why else send you so far away? He does not mean for us to return."

Victarion had thought the same when he met the first storm a day out of Old Volantis. *The gods hate kinslayers,* he brooded, *elsewise Euron Crow's Eye would have died a dozen deaths by my hand.* As the sea crashed around him and the deck rose and fell beneath his feet, he had seen *Dagon's Feast* and *Red Tide* slammed together so violently that both exploded into splinters. *My brother's work,* he'd thought. Those were the first two ships he'd lost from his own third of the fleet. But not the last.

So he had slapped the Limper twice across the face and said, "The first is for the ships you lost, the second for your talk of curses. Speak of that again and I will nail your tongue to the mast. If the Crow's Eye can make mutes, so can I." The throb of pain in his left hand made the words harsher than they might have been elsewise, but he meant what he said. "More ships will come. The storms are done for now. I will have my fleet."

A monkey on the mast above howled derision, almost as if it could taste his frustration. *Filthy, noisy beast.* He could send a man up after it, but the monkeys seemed to like that game and had proved themselves more agile than his crew. The howls rang in his ears, though, and made the throbbing in his hand seem worse.

"Fifty-four," he grumbled. It would have been too much to hope for the full strength of the Iron Fleet after a voyage of such length . . . but seventy ships, even eighty, the Drowned God might have granted him that much. *Would that we had the Damphair with us, or some other priest.* Victarion had made sacrifice before setting sail, and again in the Stepstones when he split the fleet in three, but perhaps he had said the wrong prayers. *That, or the Drowned God has no power here.* More and more, he had come to fear that they had sailed too far, into strange seas where even the gods were queer . . . but such doubts he confided only to his dusky woman, who had no tongue to repeat them.

When *Grief* appeared, Victarion summoned Wulfe One-Ear. "I will want words with the Vole. Send word to Ralf the Limper, Bloodless Tom, and the Black Shepherd. All hunting parties are to be recalled, the shore camps broken up by first light. Load as much fruit as can be gathered and drive the pigs aboard the ships. We can slaughter them at need. *Shark* is to remain here to tell any stragglers where we've gone." She would need that long to make repairs; the storms had left her little more than a hulk. That would bring them down to fifty-three, but there was no help for it. "The fleet departs upon the morrow, on the evening tide."

"As you command," said Wulfe, "but another day might mean another ship, lord Captain."

"Aye. And ten days might mean ten ships, or none at all. We have squandered too many days waiting on the sight of sails. Our victory will be that much the sweeter if we win it with a smaller fleet." *And I must needs reach the dragon queen before the Volantenes.*

In Volantis he had seen the galleys taking on provisions. The whole city had seemed drunk. Sailors and soldiers and tinkers had been observed dancing in the streets with nobles and fat merchants, and in every inn and winesink cups were being raised to the new triarchs. All the talk had been of the gold and gems and slaves that would flood into Volantis once the dragon queen was dead. One day of such reports was all that Victarion Greyjoy could stomach; he paid the gold price for food and water, though it shamed him, and took his ships back out to sea.

The storms would have scattered and delayed the Volantenes, even as they had his own ships. If fortune smiled, many of their warships might have sunk or run aground. But not all. No god was that good, and those green galleys that survived by now could well have sailed around Valyria. *They will be sweeping north toward Meereen and Yunkai, great dromonds of war teeming with slave soldiers. If the Storm God spared them, by now they could be in the Gulf of Grief. Three hundred ships, perhaps as many as five hundred.* Their allies were already off Meereen: Yunkishmen and Astapors, men from New Ghis and Qarth and Tolos and the Storm God knew where else, even Meereen's own warships, the ones that fled the city before its fall. Against all that, Victarion had four-and-fifty. Three-and-fifty, less the *Shark.*

The Crow's Eye had sailed halfway across the world, reaving and plundering from Qarth to Tall Trees Town, calling at unholy ports beyond where only madmen went. Euron had even braved the Smoking Sea and lived to tell of it. *And that with only one ship. If he can mock the gods, so can I.*

"Aye, Captain," said Wulfe One-Ear. He was not half the man that Nute the Barber was, but the Crow's Eye had stolen Nute. By raising him to Lord of Oakenshield, his brother made Victarion's best man his own. "Is it still to be Meereen?"

"Where else? The dragon queen awaits me in Meereen." *The fairest woman in the world if my brother could be believed. Her hair is silver-gold, her eyes are amethysts.*

Was it too much to hope that for once Euron had told it true? *Perhaps.* Like as not, the girl would prove to be some pock-faced slattern with teats slapping against her knees, her "dragons" no more than tattooed lizards from the swamps of Sothoryos. *If she is all that Euron claims, though . . .* They had heard talk of the beauty of Daenerys Targaryen from the lips of pirates in the Stepstones and fat merchants in Old Volantis. It might be true. And Euron had not made Victarion a gift of her; the Crow's Eye meant to take her for himself. *He sends me like a serving man to fetch her. How he will howl when I claim her for myself.* Let the men mutter. They had sailed too far and lost too much for Victarion to turn west without his prize.

The iron captain closed his good hand into a fist. "Go see that my commands are carried out. And find the maester wherever he is hiding and send him to my cabin."

"Aye." Wulfe hobbled off.

Victarion Greyjoy turned back toward the prow, his gaze sweeping across his fleet. Longships filled the sea, sails furled and oars shipped, floating at anchor or run up on the pale sand shore. *The Isle of Cedars.* Where were these cedars? Drowned four hundred years ago, it seemed. Victarion had gone ashore a dozen times, hunting fresh meat, and had yet to see a cedar.

The girlish maester Euron had inflicted upon him back in Westeros claimed this place had once been called 'the Isle of a Hundred Battles,' but the men who had fought those battles had all gone to dust centuries ago. *The Isle of Monkeys, that's what they should call it.* There were pigs as well: the biggest, blackest boars that any of the ironborn had ever seen and plenty of squealing piglets in the brush, bold creatures that had no fear of man. *They were learning, though.* The larders of the Iron Fleet were filling up with smoked hams, salted pork, and bacon.

The monkeys, though . . . the monkeys were a plague. Victarion had forbidden his men to bring any of the demonic creatures aboard ship, yet somehow half his fleet was now infested with them, even his own *Iron Victory.* He could see some now, swinging from spar to spar and ship to ship. *Would that I had a crossbow.*

Victarion did not like this sea, nor these endless cloudless skies, nor the blazing sun that beat down on their heads and baked the decks until the boards were hot enough to scorch bare feet. He did not like these storms, which seemed to come up out of nowhere. The seas around Pyke were often stormy, but there at least a man could smell them coming. These southron storms were as treacherous as women. Even the water was the wrong color—a shimmering turquoise close to shore, and farther out a blue so deep that it was almost black. Victarion missed the grey-green waters of home, with their whitecaps and surges.

He did not like this Isle of Cedars either. The hunting might be good, but the forests were too green and still, full of twisted trees and queer bright flowers like none his men had ever seen before, and there were horrors lurking amongst the broken palaces and shattered statues of drowned Velos, half a league north of the point where the fleet lay at anchor. The last time Victarion had spent a night ashore, his dreams had been dark and disturbing and when he woke his mouth was full of blood. The maester said he had bitten his own tongue in his sleep, but he took it for a sign from the Drowned God, a warning that if he lingered here too long, he would choke on his own blood.

On the day the Doom came to Valyria, it was said, a wall of water three hundred feet high had descended on the island, drowning hundreds of thousands of men, women, and children, leaving none to tell the tale but some fisherfolk who had been at sea and a handful of Velosi spearmen posted in a stout stone tower on the island's highest hill, who had seen the hills and valleys beneath them turn into a raging sea. Fair Velos with its palaces of cedar and pink marble had vanished in a heartbeat. On the north end of the island, the ancient brick walls and stepped pyramids of the slaver port Ghozai had suffered the same fate.

So many drowned men, the Drowned God will be strong there, Victarion had thought when he chose the island for the three parts of his fleet to join up again. He was no priest, though. What if he had gotten it backwards? Perhaps the Drowned God had destroyed the island in his wroth. His brother Aeron might have known, but the Damphair was back on the Iron Islands, preaching against the Crow's Eye and his rule. *No godless man may sit the Seastone Chair.* Yet the captains and kings had cried for Euron at the kingsmoot, choosing him above Victarion and other godly men.

The morning sun was shining off the water in ripples of light too bright to look upon. Victarion's head had begun to pound, though whether from the sun, his hand, or the doubts that troubled him, he could not say. He made his way below to his cabin, where the air was cool and dim. The dusky woman knew what he wanted without his even asking. As he eased himself into his chair, she took a soft damp cloth from the basin and laid it across his brow. "Good," he said. "Good. And now the hand."

The dusky woman made no reply. Euron had sliced her tongue out before giving her to him. Victarion did not doubt that the Crow's Eye had bedded her as well. That was his brother's way. *Euron's gifts are poisoned,* the captain had reminded himself the day the dusky woman came aboard. *I want none of his leavings.* He had decided then that he would slit her throat and toss her in the sea, a blood sacrifice to the Drowned God. Somehow, though, he had never quite gotten around to it.

They had come a long way since. Victarion could talk to the dusky woman. She never attempted to talk back. "*Grief* is the last," he told her, as she eased his glove off. "The rest are lost or late or sunk." He grimaced as the woman slid the point of her knife beneath the soiled linen wound about his shield hand. "Some will say I should not have split the fleet. Fools. Nine-and-ninety ships we had . . . a cumbersome beast to shepherd across the seas to the far end of the world. If I'd kept them together, the faster ships would have been held hostage to the slowest. And where to find provisions for so many mouths? No port wants so many warships in their waters. The storms would have scattered us, in any case. Like leaves strewn across the Summer Sea."

Instead he had broken the great fleet into squadrons, and sent each by a different route to Slaver's Bay. The swiftest ships he gave to Red Ralf Stonehouse to sail the corsair's road along the northern coast of Sothoryos. The dead cities rotting on that fervid, sweltering shore were best avoided, every seaman knew, but in the mud-and-blood towns of the Basilisks Isles, teeming with escaped slaves, slavers, skinners, whores, hunters, brindled men, and worse, there were always provisions to be had for men who were not afraid to pay the iron price.

The larger, heavier, slower ships made for Lys, to sell the captives taken on the Shields, the women and children of Lord Hewett's Town and other islands, along with such men who decided they would sooner yield than die. Victarion had only contempt for such weaklings. Even so, the selling left a foul taste in his mouth. Taking a man as thrall or a woman as a salt wife, that was right and proper, but men were not goats or fowl to be bought and sold for gold. He was glad to leave the selling to Ralf the Limper, who would use the coin to load his big ships with provisions for the long slow middle passage east.

His own ships crept along the shores of the Disputed Lands to take on food and wine and fresh water at Volantis before swinging south around Valyria. That was the most common way east, and the one most heavily trafficked, with prizes for the taking and small islands where they could shelter during storms, make repairs, and renew their stores if need be.

"Four-and-fifty ships is too few," he told the dusky woman, "but I can wait no longer. The only way"—He grunted as she peeled the bandage off, tearing a crust of scab as well. The flesh beneath was green and black where the sword had sliced him. "—the only way to do this is to take the slavers unawares, as once I did at Lannisport. Sweep in from the sea and smash them, then take the girl and race for home before the Volantenes descend upon us." Victarion was no craven, but no more was he a fool; he could not defeat three hundred ships with fifty-four. "She'll be my wife, and you will be her maid." A maid without a tongue could never let slip any secrets.

He might have said more, but that was when the maester came, rapping at the cabin door as timid as a mouse. "Enter," Victarion called out, "and bar the door. You know why you are here."

"Lord Captain." The maester looked like a mouse as well, with his grey robes and little brown mustachio. *Does he think that makes him look more manly?* Kerwin was his name. He was very young, two-and-twenty maybe. "May I see your hand?" he asked.

A fool's question. Maesters had their uses, but Victarion had nothing but contempt for this Kerwin. With his smooth pink cheeks, soft hands, and brown curls, he looked more girlish than most girls. When first he came aboard the *Iron Victory,* he had a smirky little smile too, but one night off the Stepstones he had smiled at the wrong man, and Burton Humble had knocked out four of his teeth. Not long after that Kerwin had come creeping to the captain to complain that four of the crew had dragged him belowdecks and used him as a woman. "Here is how you put an end to that," Victarion had told him, slamming a dagger down on the table between them. Kerwin took the blade—too afraid to refuse it, the captain judged—but he had never used it.

"My hand is here," Victarion said. "Look all you like."

Maester Kerwin went down to one knee, the better to inspect the wound. He even sniffed at it, like a dog. "I will need to let the pus again. The color . . . lord Captain, the cut is not healing. It may be that I will need to take your hand."

They had talked of this before. "If you take my hand, I will kill you. But first I will tie you over the rail and make the crew a gift of your arse. Get on with it."

"There will be pain."

"Always." *Life is pain, you fool. There is no joy but in the Drowned God's watery halls.* "Do it."

The boy—it was hard to think of one so soft and pink as a man— laid the edge of the dagger across the captain's palm and slashed. The pus that burst forth was thick and yellow as sour milk. The dusky woman wrinkled her nose at the smell, the maester gagged, and even Victarion himself felt his stomach churn. "Cut deeper. Get it all. Show me the blood."

Maester Kerwin pressed the dagger deep. This time it hurt, but blood welled up as well as pus, blood so dark that it looked black in the lantern light.

Blood was good. Victarion grunted in approval. He sat there unflinching as the maester dabbed and squeezed and cleaned the pus away with squares of soft cloth boiled in vinegar. By the time he finished, the clean water in his basin had become a scummy soup. The sight alone would sicken any man. "Take that filth and go." Victarion nodded at the dusky woman. "She can bind me up."

Even after the boy had fled, the stink remained. Of late, there was no escaping it. The maester had suggested that the wound might best be drained up on deck, amidst fresh air and sunlight, but Victarion forbade it. This was not something that his crew could see. They were half a world away from home, too far to let them see that their iron captain had begun to rust.

His left hand still throbbed—a dull pain, but persistent. When he closed his hand into a fist it sharpened, as if a knife were stabbing up his arm. *Not a knife, a longsword. A longsword in the hand of a ghost.* Serry, that had been his name. A knight, and heir to Southshield. *I killed him, but he stabs at me from beyond the grave. From the hot heart of whatever hell I sent him to, he thrusts his steel into my hand and twists.*

Victarion remembered the fight as if it had been yesterday. His shield had been in shards, hanging useless from his arm, so when Serry's longsword came flashing down he had reached up and caught it. The stripling had been stronger than he looked; his blade bit through the lobstered steel of the captain's gauntlet and the padded glove beneath into the meat of his palm. *A scratch from a little kitten,* Victarion told himself afterward. He had washed the cut, poured some boiled vinegar over it, bound it up, and thought little more of it, trusting that the pain would fade and the hand heal itself in time.

Instead the wound had festered, until Victarion began to wonder whether Serry's blade had been poisoned. Why else would the cut refuse to heal? The thought made him rage. No true man killed with poison. At Moat Cailin the bog devils had loosed poisoned arrows at his men, but that was to be expected from such degraded creatures. Serry had been a knight, highborn. Poison was for cravens, women, and Dornishmen.

"If not Serry, who?" he asked the dusky woman. "Could that mouse of a maester be doing this? Maesters know spells and other tricks. He might be using one to poison me, hoping I will let him cut my hand off." The more he thought on it, the more likely it seemed. "The Crow's Eye gave him to me, wretched creature that he is." Euron had taken Kerwin off Greenshield, where he had been in service to Lord Chester, tending his ravens and teaching his children, or perhaps the other away around. And how the mouse had squealed when one of Euron's mutes delivered him aboard the *Iron Victory,* dragging him along by the convenient chain about his neck. "If this is his revenge, he wrongs me. It was Euron who insisted he be taken, to keep him from making mischief with his birds." His brother had given him three cages of ravens too, so Kerwin could send back word of their voyaging, but Victarion had forbidden him to loose them. *Let the Crow's Eye stew and wonder.*

The dusky woman was binding his hand with fresh linen, wrapping it six times around his palm, when Longwater Pyke came pounding at the cabin door to tell him that the captain of *Grief* had come aboard with a prisoner. "Says he's brought us a wizard, Captain. Says he fished him from the sea."

"A wizard?" Could the Drowned God have sent a gift to him, here on the far side of the world? His brother Aeron would have known, but Aeron had seen the majesty of the Drowned God's watery halls below the sea before being returned to life. Victarion had a healthy fear of his god, as all men should, but put his faith in steel. He flexed his wounded hand, grimacing, then pulled his glove on and rose. "Show me this wizard."

Grief's master awaited them on deck. A small man, as hairy as he was homely, he was a Sparr by birth. His men called him the Vole. "Lord Captain," he said when Victarion appeared, "this is Moqorro. A gift to us from the Drowned God."

The wizard was a monster of a man, as tall as Victarion himself and twice as wide, with a belly like a boulder and a tangle of bone-white hair that grew about his face like a lion's mane. His skin was black. Not the nut brown of the Summer Islanders on their swan ships, nor the red-brown of the Dothraki horselords, nor the charcoal-and-earth color of the dusky woman's skin, but *black.* Blacker than coal, blacker than jet, blacker than a raven's wing. *Burned,* Victarion thought, *like a man who has been roasted in the flames until his flesh chars and crisps and falls smoking from his bones.* The fires that had charred him still danced across his cheeks and forehead, where his eyes peered out from amongst a mask of frozen flames. *Slave tattoos,* the captain knew. *Marks of evil.*

"We found him clinging to a broken spar," said the Vole. "He was ten days in the water after his ship went down."

"If he were ten days in the water, he'd be dead, or mad from drinking seawater." Salt water was holy; Aeron Damphair and other priests might bless men with it and swallow a mouthful or two from time to time to strengthen their faith, but no mortal man could drink of the deep sea for days at a time and hope to live. "You claim to be a sorcerer?" Victarion asked the prisoner.

"No, Captain," the black man answered in the Common Tongue. His voice was so deep it seemed to come from the bottom of the sea. "I am but a humble slave of R'hllor, the Lord of Light."

R'hllor. A red priest, then. Victarion had seen such men in foreign cities, tending their sacred fires. Those had worn rich red robes of silk and velvet and lambswool. This one was dressed in faded, salt-stained rags that clung to his thick legs and hung about his torso in tatters ... but when the captain peered at the rags more closely, it did appear as if they might once have been red. "A pink priest," Victarion announced.

"A demon priest," said Wulfe One-Ear. He spat.

"Might be his robes caught fire, so he jumped overboard to put them out," suggested Longwater Pyke, to general laughter. Even the monkeys were amused. They chattered overhead, and one flung down a handful of his own shit to spatter on the boards.

Victarion Greyjoy mistrusted laughter. The sound of it always left him with the uneasy feeling that he was the butt of some jape he did not understand. Euron Crow's Eye had oft made mock of him when they were boys. So had Aeron, before he had become the Damphair. Their mockery oft came disguised as praise, and sometimes Victarion had not even realized he was being mocked. Not until he heard the laughter. Then came the anger, boiling up in the back of his throat until he was like to choke upon the taste. That was how he felt about the monkeys. Their antics never brought so much as a smile to the captain's face, though his crew would roar and hoot and whistle.

"Send him down to the Drowned God before he brings a curse upon us," urged Burton Humble.

"A ship gone down, and only him clinging to the wreckage," said Wulfe One-Ear. "Where's the crew? Did he call down demons to devour them? What happened to this ship?"

"A storm." Moqorro crossed his arms against his chest. He did not appear frightened, though all around him men were calling for his death. Even the monkeys did not seem to like this wizard. They leapt from line to line overhead, screaming.

Victarion was uncertain. *He came out of the sea. Why would the Drowned God cast him up unless he meant for us to find him?* His brother Euron had his pet wizards. Perhaps the Drowned God meant for Victarion to have one too. "Why do you say this man is a wizard?" he asked the Vole. "I see only a ragged red priest."

"I thought the same, lord Captain . . . but he *knows* things. He knew that we made for Slaver's Bay before any man could tell him, and he knew you would be here, off this island." The small man hesitated. "Lord Captain, he told me . . . he told me you would surely die unless we brought him to you."

"That *I* would die?" Victarion snorted. *Cut his throat and throw him in the sea,* he was about to say, until a throb of pain in his bad hand went stabbing up his arm almost to the elbow, the agony so intense that his words turned to bile in his throat. He stumbled and seized the rail to keep from falling.

"The sorcerer's cursed the captain," a voice said.

Other men took up the cry. "*Cut his throat! Kill him before he calls his demons down on us!*" Longwater Pyke was the first to draw his dirk.

"*NO!*" Victarion bellowed. "Stand back! All of you. Pyke, put up your steel. Vole, back to your ship. Humble, take the wizard to my cabin. The rest of you, about your duties." For half a heartbeat he was not certain they would obey. They stood about muttering, half with blades to hand, each looking to the others for resolve. Monkey shit rained down around them all, *splat splat splat.* No one moved until Victarion seized the sorcerer by the arm and pulled him to the hatchway.

As he opened the door to the captain's cabin, the dusky woman turned toward him, silent and smiling . . . but when she saw the red priest at his side her lips drew back from her teeth, and she *hisssss*ed in sudden fury, like a snake. Victarion gave her the back of his good hand and knocked her to the deck. "Be quiet, woman. Wine for both of us." He turned to the black man. "Did the Vole speak true? You saw my death?"

"That, and more."

"Where? When? Will I die in battle?" His good hand opened and closed. "If you lie to me, I will split your head open like a melon and let the monkeys eat your brains."

"Your death is with us now, my lord. Give me your hand."

"My hand. What do you know of my hand?"

"I have seen you in the nightfires, Victarion Greyjoy. You come striding through the flames stern and fierce, your great axe dripping blood, blind to the tentacles that grasp you at wrist and neck and ankle, the black strings that make you dance."

"*Dance?*" Victarion bristled. "Your nightfires lie. I was not made for dancing, and I am no man's puppet." He yanked off his glove and shoved his bad hand at the priest's face. "Here. Is this what you wanted?" The new linen was already discolored by blood and pus. "He had a rose on his shield, the man who gave this to me. I scratched my hand on a thorn."

"Even the smallest scratch can prove mortal, lord Captain, but if you will allow me, I will heal this. I will need a blade. Silver would be best, but iron will serve. A brazier as well. I must needs light a fire. There will be pain. Terrible pain, such as you have never known. But when we are done, your hand will be returned to you."

They are all the same, these magic men. The mouse warned me of pain as well. "I am ironborn, priest. I laugh at pain. You will have what you require . . . but if you fail, and my hand is not healed, I will cut your throat myself and give you to the sea."

Moqorro bowed, his dark eyes shining. "So be it."

The iron captain was not seen again that day, but as the hours passed the crew of his *Iron Victory* reported hearing the sound of wild laughter coming from the captain's cabin, laughter deep and dark and mad, and when Longwater Pyke and Wulfe One-Eye tried the cabin door they found it barred. Later singing was heard, a strange high wailing song in a tongue the maester said was High Valyrian. That was when the monkeys left the ship, screeching as they leapt into the water.

Come sunset, as the sea turned black as ink and the swollen sun tinted the sky a deep and bloody red, Victarion came back on deck.

He was naked from the waist up, his left arm blood to the elbow. As his crew gathered, whispering and trading glances, he raised a charred and blackened hand. Wisps of dark smoke rose from his fingers as he pointed at the maester. "That one. Cut his throat and throw him in the sea, and the winds will favor us all the way to Meereen." Moqorro had seen that in his fires. He had seen the wench wed too, but what of it? She would not be the first woman Victarion Greyjoy had made a widow.

TYRION

The healer entered the tent murmuring pleasantries, but one sniff of the foul air and a glance at Yezzan zo Qaggaz put an end to that. "The pale mare," the man told Sweets.

What a surprise, Tyrion thought. *Who could have guessed? Aside from any man with a nose and me with half of one.* Yezzan was burning with fever, squirming fitfully in a pool of his own excrement. His shit had turned to brown slime streaked with blood ... and it fell to Yollo and Penny to wipe his yellow bottom clean. Even with assistance, their master could not lift his own weight; it took all his failing strength to roll onto one side.

"My arts will not avail here," the healer announced. "The noble Yezzan's life is in the hands of the gods. Keep him cool if you can. Some say that helps. Bring him water." Those afflicted by the pale mare were always thirsty, drinking gallons between their shits. "Clean fresh water, as much as he will drink."

"Not river water," said Sweets.

"By no means." And with that, the healer fled.

We need to flee as well, thought Tyrion. He was a slave in a golden collar, with little bells that tinkled cheerfully with every step he took. *One of Yezzan's special treasures. An honor indistinguishable from a death warrant.* Yezzan zo Qaggaz liked to keep his darlings close, so it had fallen to Yollo and Penny and Sweets and his other treasures to attend him when he grew sick.

Poor old Yezzan. The lord of suet was not so bad as masters went. Sweets had been right about that. Serving at his nightly banquets, Tyrion had soon learned that Yezzan stood foremost amongst those Yunkish lords who favored honoring the peace with Meereen. Most of the others were only biding their time, waiting for the armies of Volantis to arrive. A few wanted to assault the city immediately, lest the Volantenes rob them of their glory and the best part of the plunder. Yezzan would have no part of that. Nor would he consent to returning Meereen's hostages by way of trebuchet, as the sellsword Bloodbeard had proposed.

But much and more can change in two days. Two days ago Nurse had been hale and healthy. Two days ago Yezzan had not heard the pale mare's ghostly hoofbeats. Two days ago the fleets of Old Volantis had been two days farther off. And now . . .

"Is Yezzan going to die?" Penny asked, in that please-say-it-is-not-so voice of hers.

"We are all going to die."

"Of the flux, I meant."

Sweets gave them both a desperate look. "Yezzan *must not* die." The hermaphrodite stroked the brow of their gargantuan master, pushing back his sweat-damp hair. The Yunkishman moaned, and another flood of brown water gushed down his legs. His bedding was stained and stinking, but they had no way to move him.

"Some masters free their slaves when they die," said Penny.

Sweets tittered. It was a ghastly sound. "Only favorites. They free them from the woes of the world, to accompany their beloved master to the grave and serve him in the afterlife."

Sweets should know. His will be the first throat slit.

The goat boy spoke up. "The silver queen—"

"—is dead," insisted Sweets. "Forget her! The dragon took her across the river. She's drowned in that Dothraki sea."

"You can't drown in *grass*," the goat boy said.

"If we were free," said Penny, "we could find the queen. Or go search for her, at least."

You on your dog and me on my sow, chasing a dragon across the Dothraki sea. Tyrion scratched his scar to keep from laughing. "This particular dragon has already evinced a fondness for roast pork. And roast dwarf is twice as tasty."

"It was just a wish," said Penny wistfully. "We could sail away. There are ships again, now that the war is over."

Is it? Tyrion was inclined to doubt that. Parchments had been signed, but wars were not fought on parchments.

"We could sail to Qarth," Penny went on. "The streets are paved with jade there, my brother always said. The city walls are one of the wonders of the world. When we perform in Qarth, gold and silver will rain down on us, you'll see."

"Some of those ships out on the bay are Qartheen," Tyrion reminded her. "Lomas Longstrider saw the walls of Qarth. His books suffice for me. I have gone as far east as I intend to go."

Sweets dabbed at Yezzan's fevered face with a damp cloth. "Yezzan must live. Or we all die with him. The pale mare does not carry off every rider. The master will recover."

That was a bald-faced lie. It would be a wonder if Yezzan lived another day. The lord of suet was already dying from whatever hideous disease he had brought back from Sothoryos, it seemed to Tyrion. This would just hasten his end. *A mercy, really.* But not the sort the dwarf craved for himself. "The healer said he needs fresh water. We will see to that."

"That is good of you." Sweets sounded numb. It was more than just fear of having her throat cut; alone amongst Yezzan's treasures, she actually seemed fond of their immense master.

"Penny, come with me." Tyrion opened the tent flap and ushered her out into the heat of a Meereenese morning. The air was muggy and oppressive, yet still a welcome relief from the miasma of sweat, shit, and sickness that filled the inside of Yezzan's palatial pavilion.

"Water will help the master," Penny said. "That's what the healer said, it must be so. Sweet fresh water."

"Sweet fresh water didn't help Nurse." *Poor old Nurse.* Yezzan's soldiers had tossed him onto the corpse wagon last night at dusk, another victim of the pale mare. When men are dying every hour, no one looks too hard at one more dead man, especially one as well despised as Nurse. Yezzan's other slaves had refused to go near the overseer once the cramps began, so it was left to Tyrion to keep him warm and bring him drinks. *Watered wine and lemonsweet and some nice hot dogtail soup, with slivers of mushroom in the broth. Drink it down, Nursey, that shitwater squirting from your arse needs to be replaced.* The last word Nurse ever said was, "No." The last words he ever heard were, "A Lannister always pays his debts."

Tyrion had kept the truth of that from Penny, but she needed to understand how things stood with their master. "If Yezzan lives to see the sunrise, I'll be stunned."

She clutched his arm. "What will happen to us?"

"He has heirs. Nephews." Four such had come with Yezzan from Yunkai to command his slave soldiers. One was dead, slain by Targaryen sellswords during a sortie. The other three would divide the yellow enormity's slaves amongst them, like as not. Whether any of the nephews shared Yezzan's fondness for cripples, freaks, and grotesques was far less certain. "One of them may inherit us. Or we could end up back on the auction block."

"No." Her eyes got big. "Not that. Please."

"It is not a prospect I relish either."

A few yards away, six of Yezzan's slave soldiers were squatting in the dust, throwing the bones and passing a wineskin from hand to hand. One was the serjeant called Scar, a black-tempered brute with a head as smooth as stone and the shoulders of an ox. *Clever as an ox too,* Tyrion recalled.

He waddled toward them. "Scar," he barked out, "the noble Yezzan has need of fresh, clean water. Take two men and bring back as many pails as you can carry. And be quick about it."

The soldiers broke off their game. Scar rose to his feet, brow beetling. "What did you say, dwarf? Who do you think you are?"

"You know who I am. Yollo. One of our lord's treasures. Now do as I told you."

The soldiers laughed. "Go on, Scar," one mocked, "and be quick about it. Yezzan's monkey gave you a command."

"You do *not* tell soldiers what to do," Scar said.

"Soldiers?" Tyrion affected puzzlement. "Slaves, is what I see. You wear a collar round your neck the same as me."

The savage backhand blow Scar dealt him knocked him to the ground and broke his lip. "Yezzan's collar. Not yours."

Tyrion wiped the blood from his split lip with the back of his hand. When he tried to rise, one leg went out from under him, and he stumbled back onto his knees. He needed Penny's help to regain his feet. "Sweets said the master must have water," he said in his best whine.

"Sweets can go fuck himself. He's made for it. We don't take commands from that freak neither."

No, thought Tyrion. Even amongst slaves there were lords and peasants, as he had been quick to learn. The hermaphrodite had long been their master's special pet, indulged and favored, and the noble Yezzan's other slaves hated him for it.

The soldiers were accustomed to taking their commands from their masters and their overseer. But Nurse was dead and Yezzan too sick to name a successor. As for the three nephews, those brave free men had remembered urgent business elsewhere at the first sound of the pale mare's hooves.

"The w-water," said Tyrion, cringing. "Not river water, the healer said. Clean, fresh well water."

Scar grunted. "*You* go for it. And be quick about it."

"Us?" Tyrion exchanged a hopeless glance with Penny. "Water's heavy. We're not so strong as you. Can we ... can we take the mule cart?"

"Take your legs."

"We'll need to make a dozen trips."

"Make a hundred trips. It's no shit to me."

"Just the two of us ... we won't be able to carry all the water that the master needs."

"Take your bear," suggested Scar. "Fetching water is about all that one is good for."

Tyrion backed away. "As you say, master."

Scar grinned. *Master. Oh, he liked that.* "Morgo, bring the keys. You fill the pails and come right back, dwarf. You know what happens to slaves who try to escape."

"Bring the pails," Tyrion told Penny. He went off with the man Morgo to fetch Ser Jorah Mormont from his cage.

The knight had not adapted well to bondage. When called upon to play the bear and carry off the maiden fair, he had been sullen and uncooperative, shuffling lifelessly through his paces when he deigned to take part in their mummery at all. Though he had not attempted escape, nor offered violence to his captors, he would ignore their commands oft as not or reply with muttered curses. None of this had amused Nurse, who made his displeasure clear by confining Mormont in an iron cage and having him beaten every evening as the sun sank into Slaver's Bay. The knight absorbed the beatings silently; the only sounds were the muttered curses of the slaves who beat him and the dull *thuds* of their clubs pounding against Ser Jorah's bruised and battered flesh.

The man is a shell, Tyrion thought, the first time he saw the big knight beaten. *I should have held my tongue and let Zahrina have him. It might have been a kinder fate than this.*

Mormont emerged from the cramped confines of the cage bent and squinting, with both eyes blackened and his back crusty with dried blood. His face was so bruised and swollen that he hardly looked human. He was naked except for a breechclout, a filthy bit of yellow rag. "You're to help them carry water," Morgo told him.

Ser Jorah's only reply was a sullen stare. *Some men would sooner die free than live a slave, I suppose.* Tyrion was not stricken with that affliction himself, thankfully, but if Mormont murdered Morgo, the other slaves might not draw that distinction. "Come," he said, before the knight did something brave and stupid. He waddled off and hoped Mormont would follow.

The gods were good for once. Mormont followed.

Two pails for Penny, two for Tyrion, and four for Ser Jorah, two in either hand. The nearest well was south and west of the Harridan, so they set off in that direction, the bells on their collars ringing merrily with every step. No one paid them any mind. They were just slaves fetching water for their master. Wearing a collar conferred certain advantages, particularly a gilded collar inscribed with the name of Yezzan zo Qaggaz. The chime of those little bells proclaimed their value to anyone with ears. A slave was only as important as his master; Yezzan was the richest man in the Yellow City and had brought six hundred slave soldiers to the war, even if he did look like a monstrous yellow slug and smell of piss. Their collars gave them leave to go anywhere they might wish within the camp.

Until Yezzan dies.

The Clanker Lords had their slave soldiers drilling in the nearest field. The clatter of the chains that bound them made a harsh metallic music as they marched across the sand in lockstep and formed up with their long spears. Elsewhere teams of slaves were raising ramps of stone and sand beneath their mangonels and scorpions, angling them upward at the sky, the better to defend the camp should the black dragon return. It made the dwarf smile to see them sweating and cursing as they wrestled the heavy machines onto the inclines. Crossbows were much in evidence as well. Every other man seemed to be clutching one, with a quiver full of bolts hanging from his hip.

If anyone had thought to ask him, Tyrion could have told them not to bother. Unless one of those long iron scorpion bolts chanced to find an eye, the queen's pet monster was not like to be brought down by such toys. *Dragons are not so easy to kill as that. Tickle him with these and you'll only make him angry.*

The eyes were where a dragon was most vulnerable. The eyes, and the brain behind them. Not the underbelly, as certain old tales would have it. The scales there were just as tough as those along a dragon's back and flanks. And not down the gullet either. That was madness. These would-be dragonslayers might as well try to quench a fire with a spear thrust. "Death comes out of the dragon's mouth," Septon Barth had written in his *Unnatural History,* "but death does not go in that way."

Farther on, two legions from New Ghis were facing off shield wall to shield wall whilst serjeants in iron halfhelms with horsehair crests screamed commands in their own incomprehensible dialect. To the naked eye the Ghiscari looked more formidable than the Yunkish slave soldiers, but Tyrion nursed doubts. The legionaries might be armed and organized in the same manner as Unsullied . . . but the eunuchs knew no other life, whereas the Ghiscari were free citizens who served for three-year terms.

The line at the well stretched back a quarter mile.

There were only a handful of wells within a day's march of Meereen, so the wait was always long. Most of the Yunkish host drew their drinking water from the Skahazadhan, which Tyrion had known was a very bad idea even before the healer's warning. The clever ones took care to stay upstream of the latrines, but they were still downstream of the city.

The fact that there were any good wells at all within a day's march of the city only went to prove that Daenerys Targaryen was still an innocent where siegecraft was concerned. *She should have poisoned every well. Then all the Yunkishmen would be drinking from the river. See how long their siege lasts then.* That was what his lord father would have done, Tyrion did not doubt.

Every time they shuffled forward another place, the bells on their collars tinkled brightly. *Such a happy sound, it makes me want to scoop out someone's eyeballs with a spoon.* By now Griff and Duck and Haldon Halfmaester should be in Westeros with their young prince. *I should be with them . . . but no, I had to have a whore. Kinslaying was not enough, I needed cunt and wine to seal my ruin, and here I am on the wrong side of the world, wearing a slave collar with little golden bells to announce my coming. If I dance just right, maybe I can ring "The Rains of Castamere."*

There was no better place to hear the latest news and rumors than around the well. "I know what I saw," an old slave in a rusted iron collar was saying, as Tyrion and Penny shuffled along in the queue, "and I saw that dragon ripping off arms and legs, tearing men in half, burning them down to ash and bones. People started running, trying to get out of that pit, but I come to see a show, and by all the gods of Ghis, I saw one. I was up in the purple, so I didn't think the dragon was like to trouble me."

"The queen climbed onto the dragon's back and flew away," insisted a tall brown woman.

"She tried," said the old man, "but she couldn't hold on. The crossbows wounded the dragon, and the queen was struck right between her sweet pink teats, I hear. That was when she fell. She died in the gutter, crushed beneath a wagon's wheels. I know a girl who knows a man who saw her die."

In this company, silence was the better part of wisdom, but Tyrion could not help himself. "No corpse was found," he said.

The old man frowned. "What would you know about it?"

"They were there," said the brown woman. "It's them, the jousting dwarfs, the ones who tilted for the queen."

The old man squinted down as if seeing him and Penny for the first time. "You're the ones who rode the pigs."

Our notoriety precedes us. Tyrion sketched a courtly bow, and refrained from pointing out that one of the pigs was really a dog. "The sow I ride is actually my sister. We have the same nose, could you tell? A wizard cast a spell on her, but if you give her a big wet kiss, she will turn into a beautiful woman. The pity is, once you get to know her, you'll want to kiss her again to turn her back."

Laughter erupted all around them. Even the old man joined in. "You saw her, then," said the redheaded boy behind them. "You saw the queen. Is she as beautiful as they say?"

I saw a slender girl with silvery hair wrapped in a tokar, he might have told them. *Her face was veiled, and I never got close enough for a good look. I was riding on a pig.* Daenerys Targaryen had been seated in the owner's box beside her Ghiscari king, but Tyrion's eyes had been drawn to the knight in the white-and-gold armor behind her. Though his features were concealed, the dwarf would have known Barristan Selmy anywhere. *Illyrio was right about that much, at least,* he remembered thinking. *Will Selmy know me, though? And what will he do if he does?*

He had almost revealed himself then and there, but something stopped him—caution, cowardice, instinct, call it what you will. He could not imagine Barristan the Bold greeting him with anything but hostility. Selmy had never approved of Jaime's presence in his precious Kingsguard. Before the rebellion, the old knight thought him too young and untried; afterward, he had been known to say that the Kingslayer should exchange that white cloak for a black one. And his own crimes were worse. Jaime had killed a madman. Tyrion had put a quarrel through the groin of his own sire, a man Ser Barristan had known and served for years. He might have chanced it all the same, but then Penny had landed a blow on his shield and the moment was gone, never to return.

"The queen watched us tilt," Penny was telling the other slaves in line, "but that was the only time we saw her."

"You must have seen the dragon," said the old man.

Would that we had. The gods had not even vouchsafed him that much. As Daenerys Targaryen was taking wing, Nurse had been clapping irons round their ankles to make certain they would not attempt escape on their way back to their master. If the overseer had only taken his leave after delivering them to the abbatoir, or fled with the rest of the slavers when the dragon descended from the sky, the two dwarfs might have strolled away free. *Or run away, more like, our little bells a-jingle.*

"Was there a dragon?" Tyrion said with a shrug. "All I know is that no dead queens were found."

The old man was not convinced. "Ah, they found corpses by the hundred. They dragged them inside the pit and burned them, though half was crisp already. Might be they didn't know her, burned and bloody and crushed. Might be they did but decided to say elsewise, to keep you slaves quiet."

"*Us* slaves?" said the brown woman. "You wear a collar too."

"*Ghazdor's* collar," the old man boasted. "Known him since we was born. I'm almost like a brother to him. Slaves like you, sweepings out of Astapor and Yunkai, you whine about being free, but I wouldn't give the dragon queen my collar if she offered to suck my cock for it. Man has the right master, that's better."

Tyrion did not dispute him. The most insidious thing about bondage was how easy it was to grow accustomed to it. The life of most slaves was not all that different from the life of a serving man at Casterly Rock, it seemed to him. True, some slaveowners and their overseers were brutal and cruel, but the same was true of some Westerosi lords and their stewards and bailiffs. Most of the Yunkai'i treated their chattels decently enough, so long as they did their jobs and caused no trouble . . . and this old man in his rusted collar, with his fierce loyalty to Lord Wobblecheeks, his owner, was not at all atypical.

"Ghazdor the Great-hearted?" Tyrion said, sweetly. "Our master Yezzan has often spoken of his wits." What Yezzan had actually said was on the order of, *I have more wits in the left cheek of my arse than Ghazdor and his brothers have between them.* He thought it prudent to omit the actual words.

Midday had come and gone before he and Penny reached the well, where a scrawny one-legged slave was drawing water. He squinted at them suspiciously. "Nurse always comes for Yezzan's water, with four men and a mule cart." He dropped the bucket down the well once more. There was a soft *splash.* The one-legged man let the bucket fill, then began to draw it upward. His arms were sunburnt and peeling, scrawny to look at but all muscle.

"The mule died," said Tyrion. "So did Nurse, poor man. And now Yezzan himself has mounted the pale mare, and six of his soldiers have the shits. May I have two pails full?"

"As you like." That was the end of idle talk. *Is that hoofbeats you hear?* The lie about the soldiers got old one-leg moving much more quickly.

They started back, each of the dwarfs carrying two brim-full pails of sweet water and Ser Jorah with two pails in each hand. The day was growing hotter, the air as thick and wet as damp wool, and the pails seemed to grow heavier with every step. *A long walk on short legs.* Water sloshed from his pails with every stride, splashing round his legs, whilst his bells played a marching song. *Had I known it would come to this, Father, I might have let you live.* Half a mile east, a dark plume of smoke was rising where a tent had been set afire. *Burning last night's dead.* "This way," Tyrion said, jerking his head to the right.

Penny gave him a puzzled look. "That's not how we came."

"We don't want to breathe that smoke. It's full of malign humors." It was not a lie. *Not entirely.*

Penny was soon puffing, struggling with the weight of her pails. "I need to rest."

"As you wish." Tyrion set the pails of water on the ground, grateful for the halt. His legs were cramping badly, so he found himself a likely rock and sat on it to rub his thighs.

"I could do that for you," offered Penny.

"I know where the knots are." As fond as he had grown of the girl, it still made him uncomfortable when she touched him. He turned to Ser Jorah. "A few more beatings and you'll be uglier than I am, Mormont. Tell me, is there any fight left in you?"

The big knight raised two blackened eyes and looked at him as he might look at a bug. "Enough to crack your neck, Imp."

"Good." Tyrion picked up his pails. "This way, then."

Penny wrinkled her brow. "No. It's to the left." She pointed. "That's the Harridan there."

"And that's the Wicked Sister." Tyrion nodded in the other direction. "Trust me," he said. "My way is quicker." He set off, his bells jingling. Penny would follow, he knew.

Sometimes he envied the girl all her pretty little dreams. She reminded him of Sansa Stark, the child bride he had wed and lost. Despite the horrors Penny had suffered, she remained somehow trusting. *She should know better. She is older than Sansa. And she's a dwarf. She acts as if she has forgotten that, as if she were highborn and fair to look upon, instead of a slave in a grotesquerie.* At night Tyrion would oft hear her praying. *A waste of words. If there are gods to listen, they are monstrous gods who torment us for their sport. Who else would make a world like this, so full of bondage, blood, and pain? Who else would shape us as they have?* Sometimes he wanted to slap her, shake her, scream at her, anything to wake her from her dreams. *No one is going to save us,* he wanted to scream at her. *The worst is yet to come.* Yet somehow he could never say the words. Instead of giving her a good hard crack across that ugly face of hers to knock the blinders from her eyes, he would find himself squeezing her shoulder or giving her a hug. *Every touch a lie. I have paid her so much false coin that she half thinks she's rich.*

He had even kept the truth of Daznak's Pit from her.

Lions. They were going to set lions on us. It would have been exquisitely ironic, that. Perhaps he would have had time for a short, bitter chortle before being torn apart.

No one ever told him the end that had been planned for them, not in so many words, but it had not been hard to puzzle out, down beneath the bricks of Daznak's Pit, in the hidden world below the seats, the dark domain of the pit fighters and the serving men who tended to them, quick and dead—the cooks who fed them, the iron-mongers who armed them, the barber-surgeons who bled them and shaved them and bound up their wounds, the whores who serviced them before and after fights, the corpse handlers who dragged the losers off the sands with chains and iron hooks.

Nurse's face had given Tyrion his first inkling. After their show, he and Penny had returned to the torchlit vault where the fighters gathered before and after their matches. Some sat sharpening their weapons; others sacrificed to queer gods, or dulled their nerves with milk of the poppy before going out to die. Those who'd fought and won were dicing in a corner, laughing as only men who have just faced death and lived can laugh.

Nurse was paying out some silver to a pit man on a lost wager when he spied Penny leading Crunch. The confusion in his eyes was gone in half a heartbeat, but not before Tyrion grasped what it meant. *Nurse did not expect us back.* He had looked around at other faces. *None of them expected us back. We were meant to die out there.* The final piece fell into place when he overheard an animal trainer complaining loudly to the pitmaster. "The lions are hungry. Two days since they ate. I was told not to feed them, and I haven't. The queen should pay for meat."

"You take that up with her the next time she holds court," the pitmaster threw back at him.

Even now, Penny did not suspect. When she spoke about the pit, her chief worry was that more people had not laughed. *They would have pissed themselves laughing if the lions had been loosed,* Tyrion almost told her. Instead he'd squeezed her shoulder.

Penny came to a sudden halt. "We're going the wrong way."

"We're not." Tyrion lowered his pails to the ground. The handles had gouged deep grooves in his fingers. "Those are the tents we want, there."

"The Second Sons?" A queer smile split Ser Jorah's face. "If you think to find help there, you don't know Brown Ben Plumm."

"Oh, I do. Plumm and I have played five games of *cyvasse*. Brown Ben is shrewd, tenacious, not unintelligent . . . but wary. He likes to let his opponent take the risks whilst he sits back and keeps his options open, reacting to the battle as it takes shape."

"Battle? What battle?" Penny backed away from him. "We have to get *back*. The master needs clean water. If we take too long, we'll be whipped. And Pretty Pig and Crunch are there."

"Sweets will see that they are taken care of," Tyrion lied. More like, Scar and his friends would soon be feasting on ham and bacon and a savory dog stew, but Penny did not need to hear that. "Nurse is dead and Yezzan's dying. It could be dark before anyone thinks to miss us. We will never have a better chance than now."

"*No.* You know what they do when they catch slaves trying to escape. You *know*. Please. They'll never let us leave the camp."

"We haven't left the camp." Tyrion picked up his pails. He set off at a brisk waddle, never looking back. Mormont fell in beside him. After a moment he heard the sounds of Penny hurrying after him, down a sandy slope to a circle of ragged tents.

The first guard appeared as they neared the horse lines, a lean spearman whose maroon beard marked him as Tyroshi. "What do we have here? And what have you got in those pails?"

"Water," said Tyrion, "if it please you."

"Beer would please me better." A spearpoint pricked him in the back—a second guard, come up behind them. Tyrion could hear King's Landing in his voice. *Scum from Flea Bottom.* "You lost, dwarf?" the guard demanded.

"We're here to join your company."

A pail slipped from Penny's grasp and overturned. Half the water had spilled before she could right it once again.

"We got fools enough in this company. Why would we want three more?" The Tyroshi flicked at Tyrion's collar with his spearpoint, ringing the little golden bell. "A runaway slave is what I see. Three runaway slaves. Whose collar?"

"The Yellow Whale's." That from a third man, drawn by their voices—a skinny stubble-jawed piece of work with teeth stained red from sourleaf. *A serjeant,* Tyrion knew, from the way the other two deferred to him. He had a hook where his right hand should have been. *Bronn's meaner bastard shadow, or I'm Baelor the Beloved.* "These are the dwarfs Ben tried to buy," the serjeant told the spearmen, squinting, "but the big one . . . best bring him too. All three."

The Tyroshi gestured with his spear. Tyrion moved along. The other sellsword—a stripling, hardly more than a boy, with fuzz on his cheeks and hair the color of dirty straw—scooped up Penny under one arm. "Ooh, mine has teats," he said, laughing. He slipped a hand under Penny's tunic, just to be sure.

"Just bring her," snapped the serjeant.

The stripling slung Penny over one shoulder. Tyrion went ahead as quick as his stunted legs would allow. He knew where they were going: the big tent on the far side of the fire pit, its painted canvas walls cracked and faded by years of sun and rain. A few sellswords turned to watch them pass, and a camp follower sniggered, but no one moved to interfere.

Within the tent, they found camp stools and a trestle table, a rack of spears and halberds, a floor covered with threadbare carpets in half a dozen clashing colors, and three officers. One was slim and elegant, with a pointed beard, a bravo's blade, and a slashed pink doublet. One was plump and balding, with ink stains on his fingers and a quill clutched in one hand.

The third was the man he sought. Tyrion bowed. "Captain."

"We caught them creeping into camp." The stripling dumped Penny onto the carpet.

"Runaways," the Tyroshi declared. "With pails."

"Pails?" said Brown Ben Plumm. When no one ventured to explain, he said, "Back to your posts, boys. And not a word o' this, to anyone." When they were gone, he smiled at Tyrion. "Come for another game of *cyvasse*, Yollo?"

"If you wish. I do enjoy defeating you. I hear you're twice a turn-cloak, Plumm. A man after mine own heart."

Brown Ben's smile never reached his eyes. He studied Tyrion as a man might study a talking snake. "Why are you here?"

"To make your dreams come true. You tried to buy us at auction.

Then you tried to win us at *cyvasse*. Even when I had my nose, I was not so handsome as to provoke such passion . . . save in one who happened to know my true worth. Well, here I am, free for the taking. Now be a friend, send for your smith, and get these collars off us. I'm sick of tinkling when I tinkle."

"I want no trouble with your noble master."

"Yezzan has more urgent matters to concern him than three missing slaves. He's riding the pale mare. And why should they think to look for us here? You have swords enough to discourage anyone who comes nosing round. A small risk for a great gain."

The jackanapes in the slashed pink doublet hissed. "They've brought the sickness amongst us. Into our very tents." He turned to Ben Plumm. "Shall I cut his head off, Captain? We can toss the rest in a latrine pit." He drew a sword, a slender bravo's blade with a jeweled hilt.

"Do be careful with my head," said Tyrion. "You don't want to get any of my blood on you. Blood carries the disease. And you'll want to boil our clothes, or burn them."

"I've a mind to burn them with you still in them, Yollo."

"That is not my name. But you know that. You have known that since you first set eyes on me."

"Might be."

"I know you as well, my lord," said Tyrion. "You're less purple and more brown than the Plumms at home, but unless your name's a lie, you're a westerman, by blood if not by birth. House Plumm is sworn to Casterly Rock, and as it happens I know a bit of its history. Your branch sprouted from a stone spit across the narrow sea, no doubt. A younger son of Viserys Plumm, I'd wager. The queen's dragons were fond of you, were they not?"

That seemed to amuse the sellsword. "Who told you that?"

"No one. Most of the stories you hear about dragons are fodder for fools. Talking dragons, dragons hoarding gold and gems, dragons with four legs and bellies big as elephants, dragons riddling with sphinxes . . . nonsense, all of it. But there are truths in the old books as well. Not only do I know that the queen's dragons took to you, but I know why."

"My mother said my father had a drop of dragon blood."

"Two drops. That, or a cock six feet long. You know that tale? I do. Now, you're a clever Plumm, so you know this head of mine is worth a lordship . . . back in Westeros, half a world away. By the time you get it there, only bone and maggots will remain. My sweet sister will deny the head is mine and cheat you of the promised reward. You know how it is with queens. Fickle cunts, the lot of them, and Cersei is the worst."

Brown Ben scratched at his beard. "Could deliver you alive and wriggling, then. Or pop your head into a jar and pickle it."

"Or throw in with me. That's the wisest move." He grinned. "I was born a second son. This company is my destiny. "

"The Second Sons have no place for mummers," the bravo in pink said scornfully. "It's fighters we need."

"I've brought you one." Tyrion jerked a thumb at Mormont.

"That creature?" The bravo laughed. "An ugly brute, but scars alone don't make a Second Son."

Tyrion rolled his mismatched eyes. "Lord Plumm, who are these two friends of yours? The pink one is annoying."

The bravo curled a lip, whilst the fellow with the quill chuckled at his insolence. But it was Jorah Mormont who supplied their names. "Inkpots is the company paymaster. The peacock calls himself Kasporio the Cunning, though Kasporio the Cunt would be more apt. A nasty piece of work."

Mormont's face might have been unrecognizable in its battered state, but his voice was unchanged. Kasporio gave him a startled look, whilst the wrinkles around Plumm's eyes crinkled in amusement. "Jorah *Mormont*? Is that you? Less proud than when you scampered off, though. Must we still call you *ser*?"

Ser Jorah's swollen lips twisted into a grotesque grin. "Give me a sword and you can call me what you like, Ben."

Kasporio edged backward. "You . . . she sent you away . . ."

"I came back. Call me a fool."

A fool in love. Tyrion cleared his throat. "You can talk of old times later . . . after I am done explaining why my head would be of more use to you upon my shoulders. You will find, Lord Plumm, that I can be very generous to my friends. If you doubt me, ask Bronn. Ask Shagga, son of Dolf. Ask Timett, son of Timett."

"And who would they be?" asked the man called Inkpots.

"Good men who pledged me their swords and prospered greatly by that service." He shrugged. "Oh, very well, I lied about the 'good' part. They're bloodthirsty bastards, like you lot."

"Might be," said Brown Ben. "Or might be you just made up some names. *Shagga,* did you say? Is that a woman's name?"

"His teats are big enough. Next time we meet I'll peek beneath his breeches to be sure. Is that a *cyvasse* set over there? Bring it out and we'll have that game. But first, I think, a cup of wine. My throat is dry as an old bone, and I can see that I have a deal of talking to do."

JON

That night he dreamt of wildlings howling from the woods, advancing to the moan of warhorns and the roll of drums. *Boom DOOM boom DOOM boom DOOM* came the sound, a thousand hearts with a single beat. Some had spears and some had bows and some had axes. Others rode on chariots made of bones, drawn by teams of dogs as big as ponies. Giants lumbered amongst them, forty feet tall, with mauls the size of oak trees.

"Stand fast," Jon Snow called. "Throw them back." He stood atop the Wall, alone. "Flame," he cried, "feed them flame," but there was no one to pay heed.

They are all gone. They have abandoned me.

Burning shafts hissed upward, trailing tongues of fire. Scarecrow brothers tumbled down, black cloaks ablaze. "*Snow,*" an eagle cried, as foemen scuttled up the ice like spiders. Jon was armored in black ice, but his blade burned red in his fist. As the dead men reached the top of the Wall he sent them down to die again. He slew a greybeard and a beardless boy, a giant, a gaunt man with filed teeth, a girl with thick red hair. Too late he recognized Ygritte. She was gone as quick as she'd appeared.

The world dissolved into a red mist. Jon stabbed and slashed and cut. He hacked down Donal Noye and gutted Deaf Dick Follard. Qhorin Halfhand stumbled to his knees, trying in vain to staunch the flow of blood from his neck. "I *am* the Lord of Winterfell," Jon screamed. It was Robb before him now, his hair wet with melting snow. Longclaw took his head off. Then a gnarled hand seized Jon roughly by the shoulder. He whirled . . .

. . . and woke with a raven pecking at his chest. "*Snow,*" the bird cried. Jon swatted at it. The raven shrieked its displeasure and flapped up to a bedpost to glare down balefully at him through the predawn gloom.

The day had come. It was the hour of the wolf. Soon enough the sun would rise, and four thousand wildlings would come pouring through the Wall. *Madness.* Jon Snow ran his burned hand through his hair and wondered once again what he was doing. Once the gate was opened there would be no turning back. *It should have been the Old Bear to treat with Tormund. It should have been Jaremy Rykker or Qhorin Halfhand or Denys Mallister or some other seasoned man. It should have been my uncle.* It was too late for such misgivings, though. Every choice had its risks, every choice its consequences. He would play the game to its conclusion.

He rose and dressed in darkness, as Mormont's raven muttered across the room. "*Corn,*" the bird said, and, "*King,*" and, "*Snow, Jon Snow, Jon Snow.*" That was queer. The bird had never said his full name before, as best Jon could recall.

He broke his fast in the cellar with his officers. Fried bread, fried eggs, blood sausages, and barley porridge made up the meal, washed down with thin yellow beer. As they ate they went over the preparations yet again. "All is in readiness," Bowen Marsh assured him. "If the wildlings uphold the terms of the bargain, all will go as you've commanded."

And if not, it may turn to blood and carnage. "Remember," Jon said, "Tormund's people are hungry, cold, and fearful. Some of them hate us as much as some of you hate them. We are dancing on rotten ice here, them and us. One crack, and we all drown. If blood should be shed today, it had best not be one of us who strikes the first blow, or I swear by the old gods and the new that I will have the head of the man who strikes it."

They answered him with ayes and nods and muttered words, with

"As you command," and "It will be done," and "Yes, my lord." And one by one they rose and buckled on their swords and donned their warm black cloaks and strode out into the cold.

Last to leave the table was Dolorous Edd Tollett, who had come in during the night with six wagons from the Long Barrow. Whore's Barrow, the black brothers called the fortress now. Edd had been sent to gather up as many spearwives as his wagons would hold and bring them back to join their sisters.

Jon watched him mop up a runny yolk with a chunk of bread. It was strangely comforting to see Edd's dour face again. "How goes the restoration work?" he asked his old steward.

"Ten more years should do it," Tollett replied in his usual gloomy tone. "Place was overrun with rats when we moved in. The spearwives killed the nasty buggers. Now the place is overrun with spearwives. There's days I want the rats back."

"How do you find serving under Iron Emmett?" Jon asked.

"Mostly it's Black Maris serving under him, m'lord. Me, I have the mules. Nettles claims we're kin. It's true we have the same long face, but I'm not near as stubborn. Anyway I never knew their mothers, on my honor." He finished the last of his eggs and sighed. "I do like me a nice runny egg. If it please m'lord, don't let the wildlings eat all our chickens."

Out in the yard, the eastern sky had just begun to lighten. There was not a wisp of cloud in sight. "We have a good day for this, it would seem," Jon said. "A bright day, warm and sunny."

"The Wall will weep. And winter almost on us. It's unnatural, m'lord. A bad sign, you ask me."

Jon smiled. "And if it were to snow?"

"A worse sign."

"What sort of weather would you prefer?"

"The sort they keep indoors," said Dolorous Edd. "If it please m'lord, I should get back to my mules. They miss me when I'm gone. More than I can say for them spearwives."

They parted there, Tollett for the east road, where his wagons waited, Jon Snow for the stables. Satin had his horse saddled and bridled and waiting for him, a fiery grey courser with a mane as black and shiny as maester's ink. He was not the sort of mount that Jon would have chosen for a ranging, but on this morning all that mattered was that he look impressive, and for that the stallion was a perfect choice.

His tail was waiting too. Jon had never liked surrounding himself with guards, but today it seemed prudent to keep a few good men beside him. They made a grim display in their ringmail, iron halfhelms, and black cloaks, with tall spears in their hands and swords and daggers on their belts. For this Jon had passed over all the green boys and greybeards in his command, choosing eight men in their prime: Ty and Mully, Left Hand Lew, Big Liddle, Rory, Fulk the Flea, Garrett Greenspear. And Leathers, Castle Black's new master-at-arms, to show the free folk that even a man who had fought for Mance in the battle beneath the Wall could find a place of honor in the Night's Watch.

A deep red blush had appeared in the east by the time they all assembled at the gate. *The stars are going out,* Jon thought. When next they reappeared, they would be shining down upon a world forever changed. A few queen's men stood watching from beside the embers of Lady Melisandre's nightfire. When Jon glanced at the King's Tower, he glimpsed a flash of red behind a window. Of Queen Selyse he saw no sign.

It was time. "Open the gate," Jon Snow said softly.

"*OPEN THE GATE!*" Big Liddle roared. His voice was thunder.

Seven hundred feet above, the sentries heard and raised their warhorns to their lips. The sound rang out, echoing off the Wall and out across the world. *Ahoooooooooooooooooooooooooooo000.* One long blast. For a thousand years or more, that sound had meant rangers coming home. Today it meant something else. Today it called the free folk to their new homes.

On either end of the long tunnel, gates swung open and iron bars unlocked. Dawn light shimmered on the ice above, pink and gold and purple. Dolorous Edd had not been wrong. The Wall would soon be weeping. *Gods grant it weeps alone.*

Satin led them underneath the ice, lighting the way through the gloom of the tunnel with an iron lantern. Jon followed, leading his horse. Then his guardsmen. After them came Bowen Marsh and his stewards, a score of them, every man assigned a task. Above, Ulmer of the Kingswood had the Wall. Two score of Castle Black's best bowmen stood with him, ready to respond to any trouble down below with a rain of arrows.

North of the Wall, Tormund Giantsbane was waiting, mounted on a runty little garron that looked far too weedy to support his weight. His two remaining sons were with him, tall Toregg and young Dryn, along with three score warriors.

"*Har!*" Tormund called. "Guards, is it? Now where's the trust in that, crow?"

"You brought more men than I did."

"So I did. Come here by me, lad. I want my folk to see you. I got thousands ne'er saw a lord commander, grown men who were told as boys that your rangers would eat them if they didn't behave. They need to see you plain, a long-faced lad in an old black cloak. They need to learn that the Night's Watch is naught t'be feared."

That is a lesson I would sooner they never learned. Jon peeled the glove off his burned hand, put two fingers in his mouth, and whistled. Ghost came racing from the gate. Tormund's horse shied so hard that the wildling almost lost his saddle. "Naught to be feared?" Jon said. "Ghost, stay."

"You are a black-hearted bastard, Lord Crow." Tormund Horn-Blower lifted his own warhorn to his lips. The sound of it echoed off the ice like rolling thunder, and the first of the free folk began to stream toward the gate.

From dawn till dusk Jon watched the wildlings pass.

The hostages went first—one hundred boys between the ages of eight and sixteen. "Your blood price, Lord Crow," Tormund declared. "I hope the wailing o' their poor mothers don't haunt your dreams at night." Some of the boys were led to the gate by a mother or a father, others by older siblings. More came alone. Fourteen- and fifteen-year-old boys were almost men, and did not want to be seen clinging to a woman's skirts.

Two stewards counted the boys as they went by, noting each name on long sheepskin scrolls. A third collected their valuables for the toll and wrote that down as well. The boys were going to a place that none had ever been before, to serve an order that had been the enemy of their kith and kin for thousands of years, yet Jon saw no tears, heard no wailing mothers. *These are winter's people,* he reminded himself. *Tears freeze upon your cheeks where they come from.* Not a single hostage balked or tried to slink away when his turn came to enter that gloomy tunnel.

Almost all the boys were thin, some past the point of gauntness, with spindly shanks and arms like twigs. That was no more than Jon expected. Elsewise they came in every shape and size and color. He saw tall boys and short boys, brown-haired boys and black-haired boys, honey blonds and strawberry blonds and redheads kissed by fire, like Ygritte. He saw boys with scars, boys with limps, boys with pockmarked faces. Many of the older boys had downy cheeks or wispy little mustachios, but there was one fellow with a beard as thick as Tormund's. Some dressed in fine soft furs, some in boiled leather and oddments of armor, more in wool and sealskins, a few in rags. One was naked. Many had weapons: sharpened spears, stone-headed mauls, knives made of bone or stone or dragonglass, spiked clubs, tanglenets, even here and there a rust-eaten old sword. The Hornfoot boys walked blithe and barefoot through the snowdrifts. Other lads had bear-paws on their boots and walked on top of the same drifts, never sinking through the crust. Six boys arrived on horses, two on mules. A pair of brothers turned up with a goat. The biggest hostage was six-and-a-half feet tall but had a baby's face; the smallest was a runty boy who claimed nine years but looked no more than six.

Of special note were the sons of men of renown. Tormund took care to point them out as they went by. "The boy there is the son of Soren Shieldbreaker," he said of one tall lad. "Him with the red hair, he's Gerrick Kingsblood's get. Comes o' the line o' Raymun Redbeard, to hear him tell it. The line o' Redbeard's little brother, you want it true." Two boys looked enough alike to be twins, but Tormund insisted they were cousins, born a year apart. "One was sired by Harle the Huntsman, t'other by Harle the Handsome, both on the same woman. Fathers hate each other. I was you, I'd send one to Eastwatch and t'other to your Shadow Tower."

Other hostages were named as sons of Howd Wanderer, of Brogg, of Devyn Sealskinner, Kyleg of the Wooden Ear, Morna White Mask, the Great Walrus . . .

"The Great Walrus? Truly?"

"They have queer names along the Frozen Shore."

Three hostages were sons of Alfyn Crowkiller, an infamous raider slain by Qhorin Halfhand. Or so Tormund insisted. "They do not look like brothers," Jon observed.

"Half-brothers, born o' different mothers. Alfyn's member was a wee thing, even smaller than yours, but he was never shy with where he stuck it. Had a son in every village, that one."

Of a certain runty rat-faced boy, Tormund said, "That one's a whelp of Varamyr Sixskins. You remember Varamyr, Lord Crow?"

He did. "The skinchanger."

"Aye, he was that. A vicious little runt besides. Dead now, like as not. No one's seen him since the battle."

Two of the boys were girls in disguise. When Jon saw them, he dispatched Rory and Big Liddle to bring them to him. One came meekly enough, the other kicking and biting. *This could end badly.* "Do these two have famous fathers?"

"Har! Them skinny things? Not likely. Picked by lot."

"They're girls."

"Are they?" Tormund squinted at the pair of them from his saddle. "Me and Lord Crow made a wager on which o' you has the biggest member. Pull them breeches down, give us a look."

One of the girls turned red. The other glared defiantly. "You leave us alone, Tormund Giantstink. You let us go."

"*Har!* You win, crow. Not a cock between 'em. The little one's got her a set o' balls, though. A spearwife in the making, her." He called to his own men. "Go find them something girly to put on before Lord Snow wets his smallclothes."

"I'll need two boys to take their places."

"How's that?" Tormund scratched his beard. "A hostage is a hostage, seems to me. That big sharp sword o' yours can snick a girl's head off as easy as a boy's. A father loves his daughters too. Well, most fathers."

It is not their fathers who concern me. "Did Mance ever sing of Brave Danny Flint?"

"Not as I recall. Who was he?"

"A girl who dressed up like a boy to take the black. Her song is sad and pretty. What happened to her wasn't." In some versions of the song, her ghost still walked the Nightfort. "I'll send the girls to Long Barrow." The only men there were Iron Emmett and Dolorous Edd, both of whom he trusted. That was not something he could say of all his brothers.

The wildling understood. "Nasty birds, you crows." He spat. "Two more boys, then. You'll have them."

When nine-and-ninety hostages had shuffled by them to pass beneath the Wall, Tormund Giantsbane produced the last one. "My son Dryn. You'll see he's well taken care of, crow, or I'll cook your black liver up and eat it."

Jon gave the boy a close inspection. *Bran's age, or the age he would have been if Theon had not killed him.* Dryn had none of Bran's sweetness, though. He was a chunky boy, with short legs, thick arms, and a wide red face—a miniature version of his father, with a shock of dark brown hair. "He'll serve as my own page," Jon promised Tormund.

"Hear that, Dryn? See that you don't get above yourself." To Jon he said, "He'll need a good beating from time to time. Be careful o' his teeth, though. He bites." He reached down for his horn again, raised it, and blew another blast.

This time it was warriors who came forward. And not just one hundred of them. *Five hundred,* Jon Snow judged, as they moved out from beneath the trees, *perhaps as many as a thousand.* One in every ten of them came mounted but all of them came armed. Across their backs they bore round wicker shields covered with hides and boiled leather, displaying painted images of snakes and spiders, severed heads, bloody hammers, broken skulls, and demons. A few were clad in stolen steel, dinted oddments of armor looted from the corpses of fallen rangers. Others had armored themselves in bones, like Rattleshirt. All wore fur and leather.

There were spearwives with them, long hair streaming. Jon could not look at them without remembering Ygritte: the gleam of fire in her hair, the look on her face when she'd disrobed for him in the grotto, the sound of her voice. "You know nothing, Jon Snow," she'd told him a hundred times.

It is as true now as it was then. "You might have sent the women first," he said to Tormund. "The mothers and the maids."

The wildling gave him a shrewd look. "Aye, I might have. And you crows might decide to close that gate. A few fighters on t'other side, well, that way the gate stays open, don't it?" He grinned. "I bought your bloody horse, Jon Snow. Don't mean that we can't count his teeth. Now don't you go thinking me and mine don't trust you. We trust you just as much as you trust us." He snorted. "You wanted warriors, didn't you? Well, there they are. Every one worth six o' your black crows."

Jon had to smile. "So long as they save those weapons for our common foe, I am content."

"Gave you my word on it, didn't I? The word of Tormund Giantsbane. Strong as iron, 'tis." He turned and spat.

Amongst the stream of warriors were the fathers of many of Jon's hostages. Some stared with cold dead eyes as they went by, fingering their sword hilts. Others smiled at him like long-lost kin, though a few of those smiles discomfited Jon Snow more than any glare. None knelt, but many gave him their oaths. "What Tormund swore, I swear," declared black-haired Brogg, a man of few words. Soren Shieldbreaker bowed his head an inch and growled, "Soren's axe is yours, Jon Snow, if ever you have need of such." Red-bearded Gerrick Kingsblood brought three daughters. "They will make fine wives, and give their husbands strong sons of royal blood," he boasted. "Like their father, they are descended from Raymun Redbeard, who was King-Beyond-the-Wall."

Blood meant little and less amongst the free folk, Jon knew. Ygritte had taught him that. Gerrick's daughters shared her same flame-red hair, though hers had been a tangle of curls and theirs hung long and straight. *Kissed by fire.* "Three princesses, each lovelier than the last," he told their father. "I will see that they are presented to the queen." Selyse Baratheon would take to these three better than she had to Val, he suspected; they were younger and considerably more cowed. *Sweet enough to look at them, though their father seems a fool.*

Howd Wanderer swore his oath upon his sword, as nicked and pitted a piece of iron as Jon had ever seen. Devyn Sealskinner presented him with a sealskin hat, Harle the Huntsman with a bear-claw necklace. The warrior witch Morna removed her weirwood mask just long enough to kiss his gloved hand and swear to be his man or his woman, whichever he preferred. And on and on and on.

As they passed, each warrior stripped off his treasures and tossed them into one of the carts that the stewards had placed before the gate. Amber pendants, golden torques, jeweled daggers, silver brooches set with gemstones, bracelets, rings, niello cups and golden goblets, warhorns and drinking horns, a green jade comb, a necklace of freshwater pearls . . . all yielded up and noted down by Bowen Marsh. One man surrendered a shirt of silver scales that had surely been made for some great lord. Another produced a broken sword with three sapphires in the hilt.

And there were queerer things: a toy mammoth made of actual mammoth hair, an ivory phallus, a helm made from a unicorn's head, complete with horn. How much food such things would buy in the Free Cities, Jon Snow could not begin to say.

After the riders came the men of the Frozen Shore. Jon watched a dozen of their big bone chariots roll past him one by one, clattering like Rattleshirt. Half still rolled as before; others had replaced their wheels with runners. They slid across the snowdrifts smoothly, where the wheeled chariots were foundering and sinking.

The dogs that drew the chariots were fearsome beasts, as big as direwolves. Their women were clad in sealskins, some with infants at their breasts. Older children shuffled along behind their mothers and looked up at Jon with eyes as dark and hard as the stones they clutched. Some of the men wore antlers on their hats, and some wore walrus tusks. The two sorts did not love each other, he soon gathered. A few thin reindeer brought up the rear, with the great dogs snapping at the heels of stragglers.

"Be wary o' that lot, Jon Snow," Tormund warned him. "A savage folk. The men are bad, the women worse." He took a skin off his saddle and offered it up to Jon. "Here. This will make them seem less fearsome, might be. And warm you for the night. No, go on, it's yours to keep. Drink deep."

Within was a mead so potent it made Jon's eyes water and sent tendrils of fire snaking through his chest. He drank deep. "You're a good man, Tormund Giantsbane. For a wildling."

"Better than most, might be. Not so good as some."

On and on the wildlings came, as the sun crept across the bright blue sky. Just before midday, the movement stopped when an oxcart became jammed at a turn inside the tunnel. Jon Snow went to have a look for himself. The cart was now wedged solid. The men behind were threatening to hack it apart and butcher the ox where he stood, whilst the driver and his kin swore to kill them if they tried. With the help of Tormund and his son Toregg, Jon managed to keep the wildlings from coming to blood, but it took the best part of an hour before the way was opened again.

"You need a bigger gate," Tormund complained to Jon with a sour look up at the sky, where a few clouds had blown in. "Too bloody slow this way. Like sucking the Milkwater through a reed. *Har.* Would that I had the Horn of Joramun. I'd give it a nice toot and we'd climb through the rubble."

"Melisandre burned the Horn of Joramun."

"Did she?" Tormund slapped his thigh and hooted. "She burned that fine big horn, aye. A bloody sin, I call it. A thousand years old, that was. We found it in a giant's grave, and no man o' us had ever seen a horn so big. That must have been why Mance got the notion to tell you it were Joramun's. He wanted you crows to think he had it in his power to blow your bloody Wall down about your knees. But we never found the true horn, not for all our digging. If we had, every kneeler in your Seven Kingdoms would have chunks o' ice to cool his wine all summer."

Jon turned in his saddle, frowning. *And Joramun blew the Horn of Winter and woke giants from the earth.* That huge horn with its bands of old gold, incised with ancient runes . . . had Mance Rayder lied to him, or was Tormund lying now? *If Mance's horn was just a feint, where is the true horn?*

By afternoon the sun had gone, and the day turned grey and gusty. "A snow sky," Tormund announced grimly.

Others had seen the same omen in those flat white clouds. It seemed to spur them on to haste. Tempers began to fray. One man was stabbed when he tried to slip in ahead of others who had been hours in the column. Toregg wrenched the knife away from his attacker, dragged both men from the press, and sent them back to the wildling camp to start again.

"Tormund," Jon said, as they watched four old women pull a cartful of children toward the gate, "tell me of our foe. I would know all there is to know of the Others."

The wildling rubbed his mouth. "Not here," he mumbled, "not this side o' your Wall." The old man glanced uneasily toward the trees in their white mantles. "They're never far, you know. They won't come out by day, not when that old sun's shining, but don't think that means they went away. Shadows never go away. Might be you don't see them, but they're always clinging to your heels."

"Did they trouble you on your way south?"

"They never came in force, if that's your meaning, but they were with us all the same, nibbling at our edges. We lost more outriders than I care to think about, and it was worth your life to fall behind or wander off. Every nightfall we'd ring our camps with fire. They don't like fire much, and no mistake. When the snows came, though . . . snow and sleet and freezing rain, it's bloody hard to find dry wood or get your kindling lit, and the *cold* . . . some nights our fires just seemed to shrivel up and die. Nights like that, you always find some dead come the morning. 'Less they find you first. The night that Torwynd . . . my boy, he . . ." Tormund turned his face away.

"I know," said Jon Snow.

Tormund turned back. "You know nothing. You killed a dead man, aye, I heard. Mance killed a hundred. A man can fight the dead, but when their masters come, when the white mists rise up . . . how do you fight a *mist*, crow? Shadows with teeth . . . air so cold it hurts to breathe, like a knife inside your chest . . . you do not know, you cannot know . . . can your sword cut *cold*?"

We will see, Jon thought, remembering the things that Sam had told him, the things he'd found in his old books. Longclaw had been forged in the fires of old Valyria, forged in dragonflame and set with spells. *Dragonsteel, Sam called it. Stronger than any common steel, lighter, harder, sharper . . .* But words in a book were one thing. The true test came in battle.

"You are not wrong," Jon said. "I do not know. And if the gods are good, I never will."

"The gods are seldom good, Jon Snow." Tormund nodded toward the sky. "The clouds roll in. Already it grows darker, colder. Your Wall no longer weeps. Look." He turned and called out to his son Toregg. "Ride back to the camp and get them moving. The sick ones and the weak ones, the slugabeds and cravens, get them on their bloody feet. Set their bloody tents afire if you must. The gate must close at night-fall. Any man not through the Wall by then had best pray the Others get to him afore I do. You hear?"

"I hear." Toregg put his heels into his horse and galloped back down the column.

On and on the wildlings came. The day grew darker, just as Tormund said. Clouds covered the sky from horizon to horizon, and warmth fled. There was more shoving at the gate, as men and goats and bullocks jostled each other out of the way. *It is more than impatience,* Jon realized. *They are afraid. Warriors, spearwives, raiders, they are frightened of those woods, of shadows moving through the trees. They want to put the Wall between them before the night descends.*

A snowflake danced upon the air. Then another. *Dance with me, Jon Snow,* he thought. *You'll dance with me anon.*

On and on and on the wildlings came. Some were moving faster now, hastening across the battleground. Others—the old, the young, the feeble—could scarce move at all. This morning the field had been covered with a thick blanket of old snow, its white crust shining in the sun. Now the field was brown and black and slimy. The passage of the free folk had turned the ground to mud and muck: wooden wheels and horses' hooves, runners of bone and horn and iron, pig trotters, heavy boots, the cloven feet of cows and bullocks, the bare black feet of the Hornfoot folk, all had left their marks. The soft footing slowed the column even more. "You need a bigger gate," Tormund complained again.

By late afternoon the snow was falling steadily, but the river of wildlings had dwindled to a stream. Columns of smoke rose from the trees where their camp had been. "Toregg," Tormund explained. "Burning the dead. Always some who go to sleep and don't wake up. You find them in their tents, them as have tents, curled up and froze. Toregg knows what to do."

The stream was no more than a trickle by the time Toregg emerged from the wood. With him rode a dozen mounted warriors armed with spears and swords. "My rear guard," Tormund said, with a gap-toothed smile. "You crows have rangers. So do we. Them I left in camp in case we were attacked before we all got out."

"Your best men."

"Or my worst. Every man o' them has killed a crow."

Amongst the riders came one man afoot, with some big beast trotting at his heels. *A boar,* Jon saw. *A monstrous boar.* Twice the size of Ghost, the creature was covered with coarse black hair, with tusks as long as a man's arm. Jon had never seen a boar so huge or ugly. The man beside him was no beauty either; hulking, black-browed, he had a flat nose, heavy jowls dark with stubble, small black close-set eyes.

"Borroq." Tormund turned his head and spat.

"A skinchanger." It was not a question. Somehow he knew.

Ghost turned his head. The falling snow had masked the boar's scent, but now the white wolf had the smell. He padded out in front of Jon, his teeth bared in a silent snarl.

"*No!*" Jon snapped. "Ghost, down. Stay. *Stay!*"

"Boars and wolves," said Tormund. "Best keep that beast o' yours locked up tonight. I'll see that Borroq does the same with his pig." He glanced up at the darkening sky. "Them's the last, and none too soon. It's going to snow all night, I feel it. Time I had a look at what's on t'other side of all that ice."

"You go ahead," Jon told him. "I mean to be the last one through the ice. I will join you at the feast."

"Feast? *Har!* Now that's a word I like to hear." The wildling turned his garron toward the Wall and slapped her on the rump. Toregg and the riders followed, dismounting by the gate to lead their horses through. Bowen Marsh stayed long enough to supervise as his stewards pulled the last carts into the tunnel. Only Jon Snow and his guards were left.

The skinchanger stopped ten yards away. His monster pawed at the mud, snuffling. A light powdering of snow covered the boar's humped black back. He gave a snort and lowered his head, and for half a heartbeat Jon thought he was about to charge. To either side of him, his men lowered their spears.

"Brother," Borroq said.

"You'd best go on. We are about to close the gate."

"You do that," Borroq said. "You close it good and tight. They're coming, crow." He smiled as ugly a smile as Jon had ever seen and made his way to the gate. The boar stalked after him. The falling snow covered up their tracks behind them.

"That's done, then," Rory said when they were gone.

No, thought Jon Snow, *it has only just begun.*

Bowen Marsh was waiting for him south of the Wall, with a tablet full of numbers. "Three thousand one hundred and nineteen wildlings passed through the gate today," the Lord Steward told him. "Sixty of your hostages were sent off to Eastwatch and the Shadow Tower after they'd been fed. Edd Tollett took six wagons of women back to Long Barrow. The rest remain with us."

"Not for long," Jon promised him. "Tormund means to lead his own folk to Oakenshield within a day or two. The rest will follow, as soon as we sort where to put them."

"As you say, Lord Snow." The words were stiff. The tone suggested that Bowen Marsh knew where *he* would put them.

The castle Jon returned to was far different from the one he'd left that morning. For as long as he had known it, Castle Black had been a place of silence and shadows, where a meagre company of men in black moved like ghosts amongst the ruins of a fortress that had once housed ten times their numbers. All that had changed. Lights now shone through windows where Jon Snow had never seen lights shine before. Strange voices echoed down the yards, and free folk were coming and going along icy paths that had only known the black boots of crows for years. Outside the old Flint Barracks, he came across a dozen men pelting one another with snow. *Playing,* Jon thought in astonishment, *grown men playing like children, throwing snowballs the way Bran and Arya once did, and Robb and me before them.*

Donal Noye's old armory was still dark and silent, however, and Jon's rooms back of the cold forge were darker still. But he had no sooner taken off his cloak than Dannel poked his head through the door to announce that Clydas had brought a message.

"Send him in." Jon lit a taper from an ember in his brazier and three candles from the taper.

Clydas entered pink and blinking, the parchment clutched in one soft hand. "Beg pardon, Lord Commander. I know you must be weary, but I thought you would want to see this at once."

"You did well." Jon read:

At Hardhome, with six ships. Wild seas. Blackbird *lost with all hands, two Lyseni ships driven aground on Skane,* Talon *taking water. Very bad here. Wildlings eating their own dead. Dead things in the woods. Braavosi captains will only take women, children on their ships. Witch women call us slavers. Attempt to take Storm Crow defeated, six crew dead, many wildlings. Eight ravens left. Dead things in the water. Send help by land, seas wracked by storms. From* Talon, *by hand of Maester Harmune.*

Cotter Pyke had made his angry mark below.

"Is it grievous, my lord?" asked Clydas.

"Grievous enough." *Dead things in the wood. Dead things in the water. Six ships left, of the eleven that set sail.* Jon Snow rolled up the parchment, frowning. *Night falls,* he thought, *and now my war begins.*

THE DISCARDED KNIGHT

"*A*ll kneel for His Magnificence Hizdahr zo Loraq, Fourteenth of That Noble Name, King of Meereen, Scion of Ghis, Octarch of the Old Empire, Master of the Skahazadhan, Consort to Dragons and Blood of the Harpy," roared the herald. His voice echoed off the marble floor and rang amongst the pillars.

Ser Barristan Selmy slipped a hand beneath the fold of his cloak and loosened his sword in its scabbard. No blades were allowed in the presence of the king save those of his protectors. It seemed as though he still counted amongst that number despite his dismissal. No one had tried to take his sword, at least.

Daenerys Targaryen had preferred to hold court from a bench of polished ebony, smooth and simple, covered with the cushions that Ser Barristan had found to make her more comfortable. King Hizdahr had replaced the bench with two imposing thrones of gilded wood, their tall backs carved into the shape of dragons. The king seated himself in the right-hand throne with a golden crown upon his head and a jeweled sceptre in one pale hand. The second throne remained vacant.

The important throne, thought Ser Barristan. *No dragon chair can replace a dragon no matter how elaborately it's carved.*

To the right of the twin thrones stood Goghor the Giant, a huge hulk of a man with a brutal, scarred face. To the left was the Spotted

Cat, a leopard skin flung over one shoulder. Back of them were Belaquo Bonebreaker and the cold-eyed Khrazz. *Seasoned killers all,* thought Selmy, *but it is one thing to face a foe in the pit when his coming is heralded by horns and drums and another to find a hidden killer before he can strike.*

The day was young and fresh, and yet he felt bone-tired, as if he'd fought all night. The older he got, the less sleep Ser Barristan seemed to need. As a squire he could sleep ten hours a night and still be yawning when he stumbled out onto the practice yard. At three-and-sixty he found that five hours a night was more than enough. Last night, he had scarce slept at all. His bedchamber was a small cell off the queen's apartments, originally slave quarters; his furnishings consisted of a bed, a chamber pot, a wardrobe for his clothing, even a chair should he want to sit. On a bedside table he kept a beeswax candle and a small carving of the Warrior. Though he was not a pious man, the carving made him feel less alone here in this queer alien city, and it was to that he had turned in the black watches of night. *Shield me from these doubts that gnaw at me,* he had prayed, *and give me the strength to do what is right.* But neither prayer nor dawn had brought him certainty.

The hall was as crowded as the old knight had ever seen it, but it was the missing faces that Barristan Selmy noted most: Missandei, Belwas, Grey Worm, Aggo and Jhogo and Rakharo, Irri and Jhiqui, Daario Naharis. In the Shavepate's place stood a fat man in a muscled breastplate and lion's mask, his heavy legs poking out beneath a skirt of leather straps: Marghaz zo Loraq, the king's cousin, new commander of the Brazen Beasts. Selmy had already formed a healthy contempt for the man. He had known his sort in King's Landing—fawning to his superiors, harsh to his inferiors, as blind as he was boastful and too proud by half.

Skahaz could be in the hall as well, Selmy realized, *that ugly face of his concealed behind a mask.* Two score Brazen Beasts stood between the pillars, torchlight shining off the polished brass of their masks. The Shavepate could be any one of them.

The hall thrummed to the sound of a hundred low voices, echoing off the pillars and the marble floor. It made an ominous sound, angry.

It reminded Selmy of the sound a hornets' nest might make an instant before hornets all came boiling out. And on the faces in the crowd he saw anger, grief, suspicion, fear.

Hardly had the king's new herald called the court to order than the ugliness began. One woman began to wail about a brother who had died at Daznak's Pit, another of the damage to her palanquin. A fat man tore off his bandages to show the court his burned arm, where the flesh was still raw and oozing. And when a man in a blue-and-gold *tokar* began to speak of Harghaz the Hero, a freedman behind him shoved him to the floor. It took six Brazen Beasts to pull them apart and drag them from the hall. *Fox, hawk, seal, locust, lion, toad.* Selmy wondered if the masks had meaning to the men who wore them. Did the same men wear the same masks every day, or did they choose new faces every morning?

"Quiet!" Reznak mo Reznak was pleading. "Please! I will answer if you will only . . ."

"Is it true?" a freedwoman shouted. "Is our mother dead?"

"No, no, no," Reznak screeched. "Queen Daenerys will return to Meereen in her own time in all her might and majesty. Until such time, His Worship King Hizdahr shall—"

"He is no king of mine," a freedman yelled.

Men began to shove at one another. "*The queen is not dead,*" the seneschal proclaimed. "Her bloodriders have been dispatched across the Skahazadhan to find Her Grace and return her to her loving lord and loyal subjects. Each has ten picked riders, and each man has three swift horses, so they may travel fast and far. Queen Daenerys shall be found."

A tall Ghiscari in a brocade robe spoke next, in a voice as sonorous as it was cold. King Hizdahr shifted on his dragon throne, his face stony as he did his best to appear concerned but unperturbed. Once again his seneschal gave answer.

Ser Barristan let Reznak's oily words wash over him. His years in the Kingsguard had taught him the trick of listening without hearing, especially useful when the speaker was intent on proving that words were truly wind. Back at the rear of the hall, he spied the Dornish princeling and his two companions. *They should not have come. Martell does not realize his danger. Daenerys was his only friend at this court, and she is gone.* He wondered how much they understood of what was being said. Even he could not always make sense of the mongrel Ghiscari tongue the slavers spoke, especially when they were speaking fast.

Prince Quentyn was listening intently, at least. *That one is his father's son.* Short and stocky, plain-faced, he seemed a decent lad, sober, sensible, dutiful ... but not the sort to make a young girl's heart beat faster. And Daenerys Targaryen, whatever else she might be, was still a young girl, as she herself would claim when it pleased her to play the innocent. Like all good queens she put her people first—else she would never have wed Hizdahr zo Loraq—but the girl in her still yearned for poetry, passion, and laughter. *She wants fire, and Dorne sent her mud.*

You could make a poultice out of mud to cool a fever. You could plant seeds in mud and grow a crop to feed your children. Mud would nourish you, where fire would only consume you, but fools and children and young girls would choose fire every time.

Behind the prince, Ser Gerris Drinkwater was whispering something to Yronwood. Ser Gerris was all his prince was not: tall and lean and comely, with a swordsman's grace and a courtier's wit. Selmy did not doubt that many a Dornish maiden had run her fingers through that sun-streaked hair and kissed that teasing smile off his lips. *If this one had been the prince, things might have gone elsewise,* he could not help but think ... but there was something a bit too pleasant about Drinkwater for his taste. *False coin,* the old knight thought. He had known such men before.

Whatever he was whispering must have been amusing, for his big bald friend gave a sudden snort of laughter, loud enough so that the king himself turned his head toward the Dornishmen. When he saw the prince, Hizdahr zo Loraq frowned.

Ser Barristan did not like that frown. And when the king beckoned his cousin Marghaz closer, leaned down, and whispered in his ear, he liked that even less.

I swore no oath to Dorne, Ser Barristan told himself. But Lewyn Martell had been his Sworn Brother, back in the days when the bonds between the Kingsguard still went deep. *I could not help Prince Lewyn on the Trident, but I can help his nephew now.* Martell was dancing in a vipers' nest, and he did not even see the snakes. His continued presence, even after Daenerys had given herself to another before the eyes of gods and men, would provoke any husband, and Quentyn no longer had the queen to shield him from Hizdahr's wroth. *Although . . .*

The thought hit him like a slap across the face. Quentyn had grown up amongst the courts of Dorne. Plots and poisons were no strangers to him. Nor was Prince Lewyn his only uncle. *He is kin to the Red Viper.* Daenerys had taken another for her consort, but if Hizdahr died, she would be free to wed again. *Could the Shavepate have been wrong? Who can say that the locusts were meant for Daenerys? It was the king's own box. What if he was meant to be the victim all along?* Hizdahr's death would have smashed the fragile peace. The Sons of the Harpy would have resumed their murders, the Yunkishmen their war. Daenerys might have had no better choice than Quentyn and his marriage pact.

Ser Barristan was still wrestling with that suspicion when he heard the sound of heavy boots ascending the steep stone steps at the back of the hall. The Yunkishmen had come. Three Wise Masters led the procession from the Yellow City, each with his own armed retinue. One slaver wore a *tokar* of maroon silk fringed with gold, one a striped *tokar* of teal and orange, the third an ornate breastplate inlaid with erotic scenes done in jet and jade and mother-of-pearl. The sellsword captain Bloodbeard accompanied them with a leathern sack slung across one massive shoulder and a look of mirth and murder on his face.

No Tattered Prince, Selmy noted. *No Brown Ben Plumm.* Ser Barristan eyed Bloodbeard coolly. *Give me half a reason to dance with you, and we will see who is laughing at the end.*

Reznak mo Reznak wormed his way forward. "Wise Masters, you honor us. His Radiance King Hizdahr bids welcome to his friends from Yunkai. We understand—"

"Understand this." Bloodbeard pulled a severed head from his sack and flung it at the seneschal.

Reznak gave a squeak of fright and leapt aside. The head bounced past him, leaving spots of blood on the purple marble floor as it rolled until it fetched up against the foot of King Hizdahr's dragon throne. Up and down the length of the hall, Brazen Beasts lowered their spears. Goghor the Giant lumbered forward to place himself before the king's throne, and the Spotted Cat and Khrazz moved to either side of him to form a wall.

Bloodbeard laughed. "He's dead. He won't bite."

Gingerly, so gingerly, the seneschal approached the head, lifted it delicately by the hair. "Admiral Groleo."

Ser Barristan glanced toward the throne. He had served so many kings, he could not help but imagine how they might have reacted to this provocation. Aerys would have flinched away in horror, likely cutting himself on the barbs of the Iron Throne, then shrieked at his swordsmen to cut the Yunkishmen to pieces. Robert would have shouted for his hammer to repay Bloodbeard in kind. Even Jaehaerys, reckoned weak by many, would have ordered the arrest of Bloodbeard and the Yunkish slavers.

Hizdahr sat frozen, a man transfixed. Reznak set the head on a satin pillow at the king's feet, then scampered away, his mouth twisted up in a moue of distaste. Ser Barristan could smell the seneschal's heavy floral perfume from several yards away.

The dead man stared up reproachfully. His beard was brown with caked blood, but a trickle of red still leaked from his neck. From the look of him, it had taken more than one blow to part his head from his body. In the back of the hall, petitioners began to slip away. One of the Brazen Beasts ripped off his brass hawk's mask and began to spew up his breakfast.

Barristan Selmy was no stranger to severed heads. This one, though . . . he had crossed half the world with the old seafarer, from Pentos to Qarth and back again to Astapor. *Groleo was a good man. He did not deserve this end. All he ever wanted was to go home.* The knight tensed, waiting.

"This," King Hizdahr said at last, "this is not . . . we are not pleased, this . . . what is the meaning of this . . . this . . ."

The slaver in the maroon *tokar* produced a parchment. "I have the honor to bear this message from the council of masters." He unrolled the scroll. "It is here written, '*Seven entered Meereen to sign the peace accords and witness the celebratory games at the Pit of Daznak. As surety for their safety, seven hostages were tendered us. The Yellow City mourns its noble son Yurkhaz zo Yunzak, who perished cruelly whilst a guest of Meereen. Blood must pay for blood.*'"

Groleo had a wife back in Pentos. Children, grandchildren. *Why him, of all the hostages?* Jhogo, Hero, and Daario Naharis all commanded fighting men, but Groleo had been an admiral without a fleet. *Did they draw straws, or did they think Groleo the least valuable to us, the least likely to provoke reprisal?* the knight asked himself . . . but it was easier to pose that question than to answer it. *I have no skill at unraveling such knots.*

"Your Grace," Ser Barristan called out. "If it please you to recall, the noble Yurkhaz died by happenstance. He stumbled on the steps as he tried to flee the dragon and was crushed beneath the feet of his own slaves and companions. That, or his heart burst in terror. He was old."

"Who is this who speaks without the king's leave?" asked the Yunkish lord in the striped *tokar,* a small man with a receding chin and teeth too big for his mouth. He reminded Selmy of a rabbit. "Must the lords of Yunkai attend to the natterings of guards?" He shook the pearls that fringed his *tokar.*

Hizdahr zo Loraq could not seem to look away from the head. Only when Reznak whispered something in his ear did he finally bestir himself. "Yurkhaz zo Yunzak was your supreme commander," he said. "Which of you speaks for Yunkai now?"

"All of us," said the rabbit. "The council of masters."

King Hizdahr found some steel. "Then all of you bear the responsibility for this breach of our peace."

The Yunkishman in the breastplate gave answer. "Our peace has not been breached. Blood pays for blood, a life for a life. To show our good faith, we return three of your hostages." The iron ranks behind him parted. Three Meereenese were ushered forward, clutching at their *tokars*—two women and a man.

"Sister," said Hizdahr zo Loraq, stiffly. "Cousins." He gestured at the bleeding head. "Remove that from our sight."

"The admiral was a man of the sea," Ser Barristan reminded him. "Mayhaps Your Magnificence might ask the Yunkai'i to return his body to us, so we may bury him beneath the waves?"

The rabbit-toothed lord waved a hand. "If it please Your Radiance, this shall be done. A sign of our respect."

Reznak mo Reznak cleared his throat noisily. "Meaning no offense, yet it seems to me that Her Worship Queen Daenerys gave you . . . ah . . . seven hostages. The other three . . ."

"The others shall remain our guests," announced the Yunkish lord in the breastplate, "until the dragons have been destroyed."

A hush fell across the hall. Then came the murmurs and the mutters, whispered curses, whispered prayers, the hornets stirring in their hive.

"The dragons . . ." said King Hizdahr.

". . . are monsters, as all men saw in Daznak's Pit. No true peace is possible whilst they live."

Reznak replied. "Her Magnificence Queen Daenerys is Mother of Dragons. Only she can—"

Bloodbeard's scorn cut him off. "She is gone. Burned and devoured. Weeds grow through her broken skull."

A roar greeted those words. Some began to shout and curse. Others stamped their feet and whistled their approval. It took the Brazen Beasts pounding the butts of their spears against the floor before the hall quieted again.

Ser Barristan never once took his eyes off Bloodbeard. *He came to sack a city, and Hizdahr's peace has cheated him of his plunder. He will do whatever he must to start the bloodshed.*

Hizdahr zo Loraq rose slowly from his dragon throne. "I must consult my council. This court is done."

"*All kneel for His Magnificence Hizdahr zo Loraq, Fourteenth of That Ancient Name, King of Meereen, Scion of Ghis, Octarch of the Old Empire, Master of the Skahazadhan, Consort to Dragons and Blood of the Harpy,*" the herald shouted. Brazen Beasts swung out amongst the pillars to form a line, then began a slow advance in lockstep, ushering the petitioners from the hall.

The Dornishmen did not have as far to go as most. As befit his rank and station, Quentyn Martell had been given quarters within the Great Pyramid, two levels down—a handsome suite of rooms with its own privy and walled terrace. Perhaps that was why he and his companions lingered, waiting until the press had lessened before beginning to make their way toward the steps.

Ser Barristan watched them, thoughtful. *What would Daenerys want?* he asked himself. He thought he knew. The old knight strode across the hall, his long white cloak rippling behind him. He caught the Dornishmen at the top of the steps. "Your father's court was never half so lively," he heard Drinkwater japing.

"Prince Quentyn," Selmy called. "Might I beg a word?"

Quentyn Martell turned. "Ser Barristan. Of course. My chambers are one level down."

No. "It is not my place to counsel you, Prince Quentyn . . . but if I were you, I would not return to my chambers. You and your friends should go down the steps and leave."

Prince Quentyn stared. "Leave the pyramid?"

"Leave the city. Return to Dorne."

The Dornishmen exchanged a look. "Our arms and armor are back in our apartments," said Gerris Drinkwater. "Not to mention most of the coin that we have left."

"Swords can be replaced," said Ser Barristan. "I can provide you with coin enough for passage back to Dorne. Prince Quentyn, the king made note of you today. He frowned."

Gerris Drinkwater laughed. "Should we be frightened of Hizdahr zo Loraq? You saw him just now. He quailed before the Yunkishmen. They sent him a *head,* and he did nothing."

Quentyn Martell nodded in agreement. "A prince does well to think before he acts. This king . . . I do not know what to think of him. The queen warned me against him as well, true, but . . ."

"She warned you?" Selmy frowned. "Why are you still here?"

Prince Quentyn flushed. "The marriage pact—"

"—was made by two dead men and contained not a word about the queen or you. It promised your sister's hand to the queen's brother, another dead man. It has no force. Until you turned up here, Her Grace was ignorant of its existence. Your father keeps his secrets well, Prince Quentyn. Too well, I fear. If the queen had known of this pact in Qarth, she might never have turned aside for Slaver's Bay, but you came too late. I have no wish to salt your wounds, but Her Grace has a new husband and an old paramour, and seems to prefer the both of them to you."

Anger flashed in the prince's dark eyes. "This Ghiscari lordling is no fit consort for the queen of the Seven Kingdoms."

"That is not for you to judge." Ser Barristan paused, wondering if he had said too much already. *No. Tell him the rest of it.* "That day at Daznak's Pit, some of the food in the royal box was poisoned. It was only chance that Strong Belwas ate it all. The Blue Graces say that only his size and freakish strength have saved him, but it was a near thing. He may yet die."

The shock was plain on Prince Quentyn's face. "Poison . . . meant for Daenerys?"

"Her or Hizdahr. Perhaps both. The box was his, though. His Grace made all the arrangements. If the poison was his doing . . . well, he will need a scapegoat. Who better than a rival from a distant land who has no friends at this court? Who better than a suitor the queen spurned?"

Quentyn Martell went pale. "*Me?* I would never . . . you cannot think I had any part in any . . ."

That was the truth, or he is a master mummer. "Others might," said Ser Barristan. "The Red Viper was your uncle. And you have good reason to want King Hizdahr dead."

"So do others," suggested Gerris Drinkwater. "Naharis, for one. The queen's . . ."

". . . paramour," Ser Barristan finished, before the Dornish knight could say anything that might besmirch the queen's honor. "That is what you call them down in Dorne, is it not?" He did not wait for a reply. "Prince Lewyn was my Sworn Brother. In those days there were few secrets amongst the Kingsguard. I know he kept a paramour. He did not feel there was any shame in that."

"No," said Quentyn, red-faced, "but . . ."

"Daario would kill Hizdahr in a heartbeat if he dared," Ser Barristan went on. "But not with poison. Never. And Daario was not there in any case. Hizdahr would be pleased to blame him for the locusts, all the same . . . but the king may yet have need of the Stormcrows, and he will lose them if he appears complicit in the death of their captain. No, my prince. If His Grace needs a poisoner, he will look to you." He had said all that he could safely say. In a few more days, if the gods smiled on them, Hizdahr zo Loraq would no longer rule Meereen . . . but no good would be served by having Prince Quentyn caught up in the bloodbath that was coming. "If you must remain in Meereen, you would do well to stay away from court and hope Hizdahr forgets you," Ser Barristan finished, "but a ship for Volantis would be wiser, my prince. Whatever course you choose, I wish you well."

Before he had gone three steps, Quentyn Martell called out to him. "Barristan the Bold, they call you."

"Some do." Selmy had won that name when he was ten years old, a new-made squire, yet so vain and proud and foolish that he got it in his head that he could joust with tried and proven knights. So he'd borrowed a warhorse and some plate from Lord Dondarrion's armory and entered the lists at Blackhaven as a mystery knight. *Even the herald laughed. My arms were so thin that when I lowered my lance it was all I could do to keep the point from furrowing the ground.* Lord Dondarrion would have been within his rights to pull him off the horse and spank him, but the Prince of Dragonflies had taken pity on the addlepated boy in the ill-fitting armor and accorded him the respect of taking up his challenge. One course was all that it required. Afterward Prince Duncan helped him to his feet and removed his helm. "A boy," he had proclaimed to the crowd. "A bold boy." *Fifty-three years ago. How many men are still alive who were there at Blackhaven?*

"What name do you think they will give me, should I return to Dorne without Daenerys?" Prince Quentyn asked. "Quentyn the Cautious? Quentyn the Craven? Quentyn the Quail?"

The Prince Who Came Too Late, the old knight thought . . . but if a knight of the Kingsguard learns nothing else, he learns to guard his tongue. "Quentyn the Wise," he suggested. And hoped that it was true.

THE SPURNED SUITOR

The hour of ghosts was almost upon them when Ser Gerris Drinkwater returned to the pyramid to report that he had found Beans, Books, and Old Bill Bone in one of Meereen's less savory cellars, drinking yellow wine and watching naked slaves kill one another with bare hands and filed teeth.

"Beans pulled a blade and proposed a wager to determine if deserters had bellies full of yellow slime," Ser Gerris reported, "so I tossed him a dragon and asked if yellow gold would do. He bit the coin and asked what I meant to buy. When I told him he slipped the knife away and asked if I was drunk or mad."

"Let him think what he wants, so long as he delivers the message," said Quentyn.

"He'll do that much. I'll wager you get your meeting too, if only so Rags can have Pretty Meris cut your liver out and fry it up with onions. We should be heeding Selmy. When Barristan the Bold tells you to run, a wise man laces up his boots. We should find a ship for Volantis whilst the port is still open."

Just the mention turned Ser Archibald's cheeks green. "No more ships. I'd sooner hop back to Volantis on one foot."

Volantis, Quentyn thought. *Then Lys, then home. Back the way I came, empty-handed. Three brave men dead, for what?*

It would be sweet to see the Greenblood again, to visit Sunspear and the Water Gardens and breathe the clean sweet mountain air of Yronwood in place of the hot, wet, filthy humors of Slaver's Bay. His father would speak no word of rebuke, Quentyn knew, but the disappointment would be there in his eyes. His sister would be scornful, the Sand Snakes would mock him with smiles sharp as swords, and Lord Yronwood, his second father, who had sent his own son along to keep him safe . . .

"I will not keep you here," Quentyn told his friends. "My father laid this task on me, not you. Go home, if that is what you want. By whatever means you like. I am staying."

The big man shrugged. "Then Drink and me are staying too."

The next night, Denzo D'han turned up at Prince Quentyn's door to talk terms. "He will meet with you on the morrow, by the spice market. Look for a door marked with a purple lotus. Knock twice and call for freedom."

"Agreed," said Quentyn. "Arch and Gerris will be with me. He can bring two men as well. No more."

"If it please my prince." The words were polite enough, but Denzo's tone was edged with malice, and the eyes of the warrior poet gleamed bright with mockery. "Come at sunset. And see that you are not followed."

The Dornishmen left the Great Pyramid an hour shy of sunset in case they took a wrong turn or had difficulty finding the purple lotus. Quentyn and Gerris wore their sword belts. The big man had his warhammer slung across his broad back.

"It is still not too late to abandon this folly," Gerris said, as they made their way down a foetid alley toward the old spice market. The smell of piss was in the air, and they could hear the rumble of a corpse cart's iron-rimmed wheels off ahead. "Old Bill Bone used to say that Pretty Maris could stretch out a man's dying for a moon's turn. We *lied* to them, Quent. Used them to get us here, then went over to the Stormcrows."

"As we were commanded."

"Tatters never meant for us to do it for real, though," put in the big man. "His other boys, Ser Orson and Dick Straw, Hungerford, Will of the Woods, that lot, they're still down in some dungeon thanks to us. Old Rags can't have liked that much."

"No," Prince Quentyn said, "but he likes gold."

Gerris laughed. "A pity we have none. Do you trust this peace, Quent? I don't. Half the city is calling the dragonslayer a hero, and the other half spits blood at the mention of his name."

"Harzoo," the big man said.

Quentyn frowned. "His name was Harghaz."

"Hizdahr, Humzum, Hagnag, what does it matter? I call them all Harzoo. He was no dragonslayer. All he did was get his arse roasted black and crispy."

"He was brave." *Would I have the courage to face that monster with nothing but a spear?*

"He died bravely, is what you mean."

"He died screaming," said Arch.

Gerris put a hand on Quentyn's shoulder. "Even if the queen returns, she'll still be married."

"Not if I give King Harzoo a little smack with my hammer," suggested the big man.

"Hizdahr," said Quentyn. "His name is Hizdahr."

"One kiss from my hammer and no one will care what his name was," said Arch.

They do not see. His friends had lost sight of his true purpose here. *The road leads through her, not to her. Daenerys is the means to the prize, not the prize itself.* " 'The dragon has three heads,' she said to me. 'My marriage need not be the end of all your hopes,' she said. 'I know why you are here. For fire and blood.' I have Targaryen blood in me, you know that. I can trace my lineage back—"

"Fuck your lineage," said Gerris. "The dragons won't care about your blood, except maybe how it tastes. You cannot tame a dragon with a history lesson. They're monsters, not maesters. Quent, is this truly what you want to do?"

"This is what I have to do. For Dorne. For my father. For Cletus and Will and Maester Kedry."

"They're dead," said Gerris. "They won't care."

"All dead," Quentyn agreed. "For what? To bring me here, so I might wed the dragon queen. A grand adventure, Cletus called it. Demon roads and stormy seas, and at the end of it the most beautiful woman in the world. A tale to tell our grandchildren. But Cletus will never father a child, unless he left a bastard in the belly of that tavern wench he liked. Will will never have his wedding. Their deaths should have some meaning."

Gerris pointed to where a corpse slumped against a brick wall, attended by a cloud of glistening green flies. "Did his death have meaning?"

Quentyn looked at the body with distaste. "He died of the flux. Stay well away from him." The pale mare was inside the city walls. Small wonder that the streets seemed so empty. "The Unsullied will send a corpse cart for him."

"No doubt. But that was not my question. Men's lives have meaning, not their deaths. I loved Will and Cletus too, but this will not bring them back to us. This is a mistake, Quent. You cannot trust in sellswords."

"They are men like any other men. They want gold, glory, power. That's all I am trusting in." *That, and my own destiny. I am a prince of Dorne, and the blood of dragons is in my veins.*

The sun had sunk below the city wall by the time they found the purple lotus, painted on the weathered wooden door of a low brick hovel squatting amidst a row of similar hovels in the shadow of the great yellow-and-green pyramid of Rhazdar. Quentyn knocked twice, as instructed. A gruff voice answered through the door, growling something unintelligible in the mongrel tongue of Slaver's Bay, an ugly blend of Old Ghiscari and High Valyrian. The prince answered in the same tongue. "Freedom."

The door opened. Gerris entered first, for caution's sake, with Quentyn close behind him and the big man bringing up the rear. Within, the air was hazy with bluish smoke, whose sweet smell could not quite cover up the deeper stinks of piss and sour wine and rotting meat. The space was much larger than it had seemed from without, stretching off to right and left into the adjoining hovels. What had appeared to be a dozen structures from the street turned into one long hall inside.

At this hour the house was less than half full. A few of the patrons favored the Dornishmen with looks bored or hostile or curious. The rest were crowded around the pit at the far end of the room, where a pair of naked men were slashing at each other with knives whilst the watchers cheered them on.

Quentyn saw no sign of the men they had come to meet. Then a door he had not seen before swung open, and an old woman emerged, a shriveled thing in a dark red *tokar* fringed with tiny golden skulls. Her skin was white as mare's milk, her hair so thin that he could see the scalp beneath. "Dorne," she said, "I be Zahrina. Purple Lotus. Go down here, you find them." She held the door and gestured them through.

Beyond was a flight of wooden steps, steep and twisting. This time the big man led the way and Gerris was the rear guard, with the prince between them. *An undercellar.* It was a long way down, and so dark that Quentyn had to feel his way to keep from slipping. Near the bottom Ser Archibald pulled his dagger.

They emerged in a brick vault thrice the size of the winesink above. Huge wooden vats lined the walls as far as the prince could see. A red lantern hung on a hook just inside the door, and a greasy black candle flickered on an overturned barrel serving as a table. That was the only light.

Caggo Corpsekiller was pacing by the wine vats, his black *arakh* hanging at his hip. Pretty Meris stood cradling a crossbow, her eyes as cold and dead as two grey stones. Denzo D'han barred the door once the Dornishmen were inside, then took up a position in front of it, arms crossed against his chest.

One too many, Quentyn thought.

The Tattered Prince himself was seated at the table, nursing a cup of wine. In the yellow candlelight his silver-grey hair seemed almost golden, though the pouches underneath his eyes were etched as large as saddlebags. He wore a brown wool traveler's cloak, with silvery chain mail glimmering underneath. Did that betoken treachery or simple prudence? *An old sellsword is a cautious sellsword.* Quentyn approached his table. "My lord. You look different without your cloak."

"My ragged raiment?" The Pentoshi gave a shrug. "A poor thing . . . yet those tatters fill my foes with fear, and on the battlefield the sight of my rags blowing in the wind emboldens my men more than any banner. And if I want to move unseen, I need only slip it off to become plain and unremarkable." He gestured at the bench across from him. "Sit. I understand you are a prince. Would that I had known. Will you drink? Zahrina offers food as well. Her bread is stale and her stew is unspeakable. Grease and salt, with a morsel or two of meat. Dog, she says, but I think rat is more likely. It will not kill you, though. I have found that it is only when the food is tempting that one must beware. Poisoners invariably choose the choicest dishes."

"You brought three men," Ser Gerris pointed out, with an edge in his voice. "We agreed on two apiece."

"Meris is no man. Meris, sweet, undo your shirt, show him."

"That will not be necessary," said Quentyn. If the talk he had heard was true, beneath that shirt Pretty Meris had only the scars left by the men who'd cut her breasts off. "Meris is a woman, I agree. You've still twisted the terms."

"Tattered and twisty, what a rogue I am. Three to two is not much of an advantage, it must be admitted, but it counts for something. In this world, a man must learn to seize whatever gifts the gods chose to send him. That was a lesson I learned at some cost. I offer it to you as a sign of my good faith." He gestured at the chair again. "Sit, and say what you came to say. I promise not to have you killed until I have heard you out. That is the least I can do for a fellow prince. Quentyn, is it?"

"Quentyn of House Martell."

"Frog suits you better. It is not my custom to drink with liars and deserters, but you've made me curious."

Quentyn sat. *One wrong word, and this could turn to blood in half a heartbeat.* "I ask your pardon for our deception. The only ships sailing for Slaver's Bay were those that had been hired to bring you to the wars."

The Tattered Prince gave a shrug. "Every turncloak has his tale. You are not the first to swear me your swords, take my coin, and run. All of them have *reasons.* 'My little son is sick,' or 'My wife is putting horns on me,' or 'The other men all make me suck their cocks.' Such a charming boy, the last, but I did not excuse his desertion. Another fellow told me our food was so wretched that he had to flee before it made him sick, so I had his foot cut off, roasted it up, and fed it to him. Then I made him our camp cook. Our meals improved markedly, and when his contract was fulfilled he signed another. You, though . . . several of my best are locked up in the queen's dungeons thanks to that lying tongue of yours, and I doubt that you can even cook."

"I am a prince of Dorne," said Quentyn. "I had a duty to my father and my people. There was a secret marriage pact."

"So I heard. And when the silver queen saw your scrap of parchment she fell into your arms, yes?"

"No," said Pretty Meris.

"No? Oh, I recall. Your bride flew off on a dragon. Well, when she returns, do be sure to invite us to your nuptials. The men of the company would love to drink to your happiness, and I do love a Westerosi wedding. The bedding part especially, only . . . oh, wait . . ." He turned to Denzo D'han. "Denzo, I thought you told me that the dragon queen had married some Ghiscari."

"A Meereenese nobleman. Rich."

The Tattered Prince turned back to Quentyn. "Could that be true? Surely not. What of your marriage pact?"

"She laughed at him," said Pretty Meris.

Daenerys never laughed. The rest of Meereen might see him as an amusing curiosity, like the exiled Summer Islander King Robert used to keep at King's Landing, but the queen had always spoken to him gently. "We came too late," said Quentyn.

"A pity you did not desert me sooner." The Tattered Prince sipped at his wine. "So . . . no wedding for Prince Frog. Is that why you've come hopping back to me? Have my three brave Dornish lads decided to honor their contracts?"

"No."

"How vexing."

"Yurkhaz zo Yunzak is dead."

"Ancient tidings. I saw him die. The poor man saw a dragon and stumbled as he tried to flee. Then a thousand of his closest friends stepped on him. No doubt the Yellow City is awash in tears. Did you ask me here to toast his memory?"

"No. Have the Yunkishmen chosen a new commander?"

"The council of masters has been unable to agree. Yezzan zo Qaggaz had the most support, but now he's died as well. The Wise Masters are rotating the supreme command amongst themselves. Today our leader is the one your friends in the ranks dubbed the Drunken Conqueror. On the morrow, it will be Lord Wobblecheeks."

"The Rabbit," said Meris. "Wobblecheeks was yesterday."

"I stand corrected, my sweetling. Our Yunkish friends were kind enough to provide us with a chart. I must strive to be more assiduous about consulting it."

"Yurkhaz zo Yunzak was the man who hired you."

"He signed our contract on behalf of his city. Just so."

"Meereen and Yunkai have made peace. The siege is to be lifted, the armies disbanded. There will be no battle, no slaughter, no city to sack and plunder."

"Life is full of disappointments."

"How long do you think the Yunkishmen will want to continue paying wages to four free companies?"

The Tattered Prince took a sip of wine and said, "A vexing question. But this is the way of life for we men of the free companies. One war ends, another begins. Fortunately there is always someone fighting someone somewhere. Perhaps here. Even as we sit here drinking, Bloodbeard is urging our Yunkish friends to present King Hizdahr with another head. Freedmen and slavers eye each other's necks and sharpen their knives, the Sons of the Harpy plot in their pyramids, the pale mare rides down slave and lord alike, our friends from the Yellow City gaze out to sea, and somewhere in the grasslands a dragon nibbles the tender flesh of Daenerys Targaryen. Who rules Meereen tonight? Who will rule it on the morrow?" The Pentoshi gave a shrug. "One thing I am certain of. Someone will have need of our swords."

"I have need of those swords. Dorne will hire you."

The Tattered Prince glanced at Pretty Meris. "He does not lack for gall, this Frog. Must I remind him? My dear prince, the last contract we signed you used to wipe your pretty pink bottom."

"I will double whatever the Yunkishmen are paying you."

"And pay in gold upon the signing of our contract, yes?"

"I will pay you part when we reach Volantis, the rest when I am back in Sunspear. We brought gold with us when we set sail, but it would have been hard to conceal once we joined the company, so we gave it over to the banks. I can show you papers."

"Ah. Papers. But we will be paid *double.*"

"Twice as many papers," said Pretty Meris.

"The rest you'll have in Dorne," Quentyn insisted. "My father is a man of honor. If I put my seal to an agreement, he will fulfill its terms. You have my word on that."

The Tattered Prince finished his wine, turned the cup over, and set it down between them. "So. Let me see if I understand. A proven liar and oathbreaker wishes to contract with us and pay in promises. And for what services? I wonder. Are my Windblown to smash the Yunkai'i and sack the Yellow City? Defeat a Dothraki *khalasar* in the field? Escort you home to your father? Or will you be content if we deliver Queen Daenerys to your bed wet and willing? Tell me true, Prince Frog. What would you have of me and mine?"

"I need you to help me steal a dragon."

Caggo Corpsekiller chuckled. Pretty Meris curled her lip in a half-smile. Denzo D'han whistled.

The Tattered Prince only leaned back on his stool and said, "Double does not pay for dragons, princeling. Even a frog should know that much. Dragons come dear. And men who pay in promises should have at least the sense to promise *more.*"

"If you want me to triple—"

"What I want," said the Tattered Prince, "is Pentos."

THE GRIFFIN REBORN

He sent the archers in first.

Black Balaq commanded one thousand bows. In his youth, Jon Connington had shared the disdain most knights had for bowmen, but he had grown wiser in exile. In its own way, the arrow was as deadly as the sword, so for the long voyage he had insisted that Homeless Harry Strickland break Balaq's command into ten companies of one hundred men and place each company upon a different ship.

Six of those ships had stayed together well enough to deliver their passengers to the shores of Cape Wrath (the other four were lagging but would turn up eventually, the Volantenes assured them, but Griff thought it just as likely they were lost or had landed elsewhere), which left the company with six hundred bows. For this, two hundred proved sufficient. "They will try to send out ravens," he told Black Balaq. "Watch the maester's tower. Here." He pointed to the map he had drawn in the mud of their campsite. "Bring down every bird that leaves the castle."

"This we do," replied the Summer Islander.

A third of Balaq's men used crossbows, another third the double-curved horn-and-sinew bows of the east. Better than these were the big yew longbows borne by the archers of Westerosi blood, and best of all were the great bows of goldenheart treasured by Black

Balaq himself and his fifty Summer Islanders. Only a dragonbone bow could outrange one made of goldenheart. Whatever bow they carried, all of Balaq's men were sharp-eyed, seasoned veterans who had proved their worth in a hundred battles, raids, and skirmishes. They proved it again at Griffin's Roost.

The castle rose from the shores of Cape Wrath, on a lofty crag of dark red stone surrounded on three sides by the surging waters of Shipbreaker Bay. Its only approach was defended by a gatehouse, behind which lay the long bare ridge the Conningtons called the griffin's throat. To force the throat could be a bloody business, since the ridge exposed the attackers to the spears, stones, and arrows of defenders in the two round towers that flanked the castle's main gates. And once they reached those gates, the men inside could pour down boiling oil on their heads. Griff expected to lose a hundred men, perhaps more.

They lost four.

The woods had been allowed to encroach on the field beyond the gatehouse, so Franklyn Flowers was able to use the brush for concealment and lead his men within twenty yards of the gates before emerging from the trees with the ram they'd fashioned back at camp. The crash of wood on wood brought two men to the battlements; Black Balaq's archers took down both of them before they could rub the sleep out of their eyes. The gate turned out to be closed but not barred; it gave way at the second blow, and Ser Franklyn's men were halfway up the throat before a warhorn sounded the alarum from the castle proper.

The first raven took flight as their grapnels were arcing above the curtain wall, the second a few moments later. Neither bird had flown a hundred yards before an arrow took it down. A guard inside dumped down a bucket of oil on the first men to reach the gates, but as he'd had no time to heat it, the bucket caused more damage than its contents. Swords were soon ringing in half a dozen places along the battlements. The men of the Golden Company clambered through the merlons and raced along the wallwalks, shouting "*A griffin! A griffin!*," the ancient battle cry of House Connington, which must have left the defenders even more confused.

It was over within minutes. Griff rode up the throat on a white courser beside Homeless Harry Strickland. As they neared the castle, he saw a third raven flap from the maester's tower, only to be feathered by Black Balaq himself. "No more messages," he told Ser Franklyn Flowers in the yard. The next thing to come flying from the maester's tower was the maester. The way his arms were flapping, he might have been mistaken for another bird.

That was the end of all resistance. What guards remained had thrown down their weapons. And quick as that, Griffin's Roost was his again, and Jon Connington was once more a lord.

"Ser Franklyn," he said, "go through the keep and kitchens and roust out everyone you find. Malo, do the same with the maester's tower and the armory. Ser Brendel, the stables, sept, and barracks. Bring them out into the yard, and try not to kill anyone who does not insist on dying. We want to win the stormlands, and we won't do that with slaughter. Be sure you look under the altar of the Mother, there's a hidden stair there that leads down to a secret bolt-hole. And another under the northwest tower that goes straight down to the sea. No one is to escape."

"They won't, m'lord," promised Franklyn Flowers.

Connington watched them dash off, then beckoned to the Halfmaester. "Haldon, take charge of the rookery. I'll have messages to send out tonight."

"Let us hope they left some ravens for us."

Even Homeless Harry was impressed by the swiftness of their victory. "I never thought that it would be so easy," the captain-general said, as they walked into the great hall to have a look at the carved and gilded Griffin Seat where fifty generations of Conningtons had sat and ruled.

"It will get harder. So far we have taken them unawares. That cannot last forever, even if Black Balaq brings down every raven in the realm."

Strickland studied the faded tapestries on the walls, the arched windows with their myriad diamond-shaped panes of red and white glass, the racks of spears and swords and warhammers. "Let them come. This place can stand against twenty times our number, so long as we are well provisioned. And you say there is a way in and out by sea?"

"Below. A hidden cove beneath the crag, which appears only when the tide is out." But Connington had no intention of "letting them come." Griffin's Roost was strong but small, and so long as they sat here they would seem small as well. But there was another castle nearby, vastly larger and impregnable. *Take that, and the realm will shake.* "You must excuse me, Captain-General. My lord father is buried beneath the sept, and it has been too many years since last I prayed for him."

"Of course, my lord."

Yet when they parted, Jon Connington did not go to the sept. Instead his steps led him up to the roof of the east tower, the tallest at Griffin's Roost. As he climbed he remembered past ascents—a hundred with his lord father, who liked to stand and look out over woods and crags and sea and know that all he saw belonged to House Connington, and one (only one!) with Rhaegar Targaryen. Prince Rhaegar was returning from Dorne, and he and his escort had lingered here a fortnight. *He was so young then, and I was younger. Boys, the both of us.* At the welcoming feast, the prince had taken up his silver-stringed harp and played for them. *A song of love and doom,* Jon Connington recalled, *and every woman in the hall was weeping when he put down the harp.* Not the men, of course. Particularly not his own father, whose only love was land. Lord Armond Connington spent the entire evening trying to win the prince to his side in his dispute with Lord Morrigen.

The door to the roof of the tower was stuck so fast that it was plain no one had opened it in years. He had to put his shoulder to it to force it open. But when Jon Connington stepped out onto the high battlements, the view was just as intoxicating as he remembered: the crag with its wind-carved rocks and jagged spires, the sea below growling and worrying at the foot of the castle like some restless beast, endless leagues of sky and cloud, the wood with its autumnal colors. "Your father's lands are beautiful," Prince Rhaegar had said, standing right where Jon was standing now. And the boy he'd been had replied, "One day they will all be mine." *As if that could impress a prince who was heir to the entire realm, from the Arbor to the Wall.*

Griffin's Roost *had* been his, eventually, if only for a few short years. From here, Jon Connington had ruled broad lands extending many leagues to the west, north, and south, just as his father and his father's father had before him. But his father and his father's father had never lost their lands. He had. *I rose too high, loved too hard, dared too much. I tried to grasp a star, overreached, and fell.*

After the Battle of the Bells, when Aerys Targaryen had stripped him of his titles and sent him into exile in a mad fit of ingratitude and suspicion, the lands and lordship had remained within House Connington, passing to his cousin Ser Ronald, the man whom Jon had made his castellan when he went to King's Landing to attend Prince Rhaegar. Robert Baratheon had completed the destruction of the griffins after the war. Cousin Ronald was permitted to retain his castle and his head, but he lost his lordship, thereafter being merely the Knight of Griffin's Roost, and nine-tenths of his lands were taken from him and parceled out to neighbor lords who had supported Robert's claim.

Ronald Connington had died years before. The present Knight of Griffin's Roost, his son Ronnet, was said to be off at war in the riverlands. That was for the best. In Jon Connington's experience, men would fight for things they felt were theirs, even things they'd gained by theft. He did not relish the notion of celebrating his return by killing one of his own kin. Red Ronnet's sire had been quick to take advantage of his lord cousin's downfall, true, but his son had been a child at the time. Jon Connington did not even hate the late Ser Ronald as much as he might have. The fault was his.

He had lost it all at Stoney Sept, in his arrogance.

Robert Baratheon had been hiding somewhere in the town, wounded and alone. Jon Connington had known that, and he had also known that Robert's head upon a spear would have put an end to the rebellion, then and there. He was young and full of pride. How not? King Aerys had named him Hand and given him an army, and he meant to prove himself worthy of that trust, of Rhaegar's love. He would slay the rebel lord himself and carve a place out for himself in all the histories of the Seven Kingdoms.

And so he swept down on Stoney Sept, closed off the town, and began a search. His knights went house to house, smashed in every door, peered into every cellar. He had even sent men crawling through the sewers, yet somehow Robert still eluded him. The townsfolk were *hiding* him. They moved him from one secret bolt-hole to the next, always one step ahead of the king's men. The whole town was a nest of traitors. At the end they had the usurper hidden in a brothel. What sort of king was that, who would hide behind the skirts of women? Yet whilst the search dragged on, Eddard Stark and Hoster Tully came down upon the town with a rebel army. Bells and battle followed, and Robert emerged from his brothel with a blade in hand, and almost slew Jon on the steps of the old sept that gave the town its name.

For years afterward, Jon Connington told himself that he was not to blame, that he had done all that any man could do. His soldiers searched every hole and hovel, he offered pardons and rewards, he took hostages and hung them in crow cages and swore that they would have neither food nor drink until Robert was delivered to him. All to no avail. "Tywin Lannister himself could have done no more," he had insisted one night to Blackheart, during his first year of exile.

"There is where you're wrong," Myles Toyne had replied. "Lord Tywin would not have bothered with a search. He would have burned that town and every living creature in it. Men and boys, babes at the breast, noble knights and holy septons, pigs and whores, rats and rebels, he would have burned them all. When the fires guttered out and only ash and cinders remained, he would have sent his men in to find the bones of Robert Baratheon. Later, when Stark and Tully turned up with their host, he would have offered pardons to the both of them, and they would have accepted and turned for home with their tails between their legs."

He was not wrong, Jon Connington reflected, leaning on the battlements of his forebears. *I wanted the glory of slaying Robert in single combat, and I did not want the name of butcher. So Robert escaped me and cut down Rhaegar on the Trident.* "I failed the father," he said, "but I will not fail the son."

By the time Connington made his descent, his men had gathered the castle garrison and surviving smallfolk together in the yard.

Though Ser Ronnet was indeed off north somewhere with Jaime Lannister, Griffin's Roost was not quite bereft of griffins. Amongst the prisoners were Ronnet's younger brother Raymund, his sister Alynne, and his natural son, a fierce red-haired boy they called Ronald Storm. All would make for useful hostages if and when Red Ronnet should return to try and take back the castle that his father had stolen. Connington ordered them confined to the west tower, under guard. The girl began to cry at that, and the bastard boy tried to bite the spearman closest to him. "Stop it, the both of you," he snapped at them. "No harm will come to any of you unless Red Ronnet proves an utter fool."

Only a few of the captives had been in service here when Jon Connington had last been lord: a grizzled serjeant, blind in one eye; a couple of the washerwomen; a groom who had been a stableboy during Robert's Rebellion; the cook, who had grown enormously fat; the castle armorer. Griff had let his beard grow out during the voyage, for the first time in many years, and to his surprise it had come in mostly red, though here and there ash showed amidst the fire. Clad in a long red-and-white tunic embroidered with the twin griffins of his House, counterchanged and combatant, he looked an older, sterner version of the young lord who had been Prince Rhaegar's friend and companion . . . but the men and women of Griffin's Roost still looked at him with strangers' eyes.

"Some of you will know me," he told them. "The rest will learn. I am your rightful lord, returned from exile. My enemies have told you I am dead. Those tales are false, as you can see. Serve me as faithfully as you have served my cousin, and no harm need come to any of you."

He brought them forward one by one, asked each man his name, then bid them kneel and swear him their allegiance. It all went swiftly. The soldiers of the garrison—only four had survived the attack, the old serjeant and three boys—laid their swords at his feet. No one balked. No one died.

That night in the great hall the victors feasted on roast meats and fresh-caught fish, washed down with rich red wines from the castle cellars. Jon Connington presided from the Griffin's Seat, sharing the high table with Homeless Harry Strickland, Black Balaq, Franklyn Flowers, and the three young griffins they had taken captive. The children were of his blood and he felt that he should know them, but when the bastard boy announced, "My father's going to kill you," he decided that his knowledge was sufficient, ordered them back to their cells, and excused himself.

Haldon Halfmaester had been absent from the feast. Lord Jon found him in the maester's tower, bent over a pile of parchments, with maps spread out all around him. "Hoping to determine where the rest of the company might be?" Connington asked him.

"Would that I could, my lord."

Ten thousand men had sailed from Volon Therys, with all their weapons, horses, elephants. Not quite half that number had turned up thus far on Westeros, at or near their intended landing site, a deserted stretch of coast on the edge of the rainwood . . . lands that Jon Connington knew well, as they had once been his.

Only a few years ago, he would never have dared attempt a landing on Cape Wrath; the storm lords were too fiercely loyal to House Baratheon and to King Robert. But with both Robert and his brother Renly slain, everything was changed. Stannis was too harsh and cold a man to inspire much in the way of loyalty, even if he had not been half a world away, and the stormlands had little reason to love House Lannister. And Jon Connington was not without his own friends here. *Some of the older lords will still remember me, and their sons will have heard the stories. And every man of them will know of Rhaegar, and his young son whose head was smashed against a cold stone wall.*

Fortunately his own ship had been one of the first to reach their destination. Then it had only been a matter of establishing a campsite, assembling his men as they came ashore and moving quickly, before the local lordlings had any inkling of their peril. And there the Golden Company had proved its mettle. The chaos that would inevitably have delayed such a march with a hastily assembled host of household knights and local levies had been nowhere in evidence. These were the heirs of Bittersteel, and discipline was mother's milk to them.

"By this time on the morrow we ought to hold three castles," he said. The force that had taken Griffin's Roost represented a quarter of their available strength; Ser Tristan Rivers had set off simultaneously for the seat of House Morrigen at Crow's Nest, and Laswell Peake for Rain House, the stronghold of the Wyldes, each with a force of comparable size. The rest of their men had remained in camp to guard their landing site and prince, under the command of the company's Volantene paymaster, Gorys Edoryen. Their numbers would continue to swell, one hoped; more ships were straggling in every day. "We still have too few horses."

"And no elephants," the Halfmaester reminded him. Not one of the great cogs carrying the elephants had turned up yet. They had last seen them at Lys, before the storm that had scattered half the fleet. "Horses can be found in Westeros. Elephants—"

"—do not matter." The great beasts would be useful in a pitched battle, no doubt, but it would be some time before they had the strength to face their foes in the field. "Have those parchments told you anything of use?"

"Oh, much and more, my lord." Haldon gave him a thin smile. "The Lannisters make enemies easily but seem to have a harder time keeping friends. Their alliance with the Tyrells is fraying, to judge from what I read here. Queen Cersei and Queen Margaery are fighting over the little king like two bitches with a chicken bone, and both have been accused of treason and debauchery. Mace Tyrell has abandoned his siege of Storm's End to march back to King's Landing and save his daughter, leaving only a token force behind to keep Stannis's men penned up inside the castle."

Connington sat. "Tell me more."

"In the north the Lannisters are relying on the Boltons and in the riverlands upon the Freys, both houses long renowned for treachery and cruelty. Lord Stannis Baratheon remains in open rebellion and the ironborn of the islands have raised up a king as well. No one ever seems to mention the Vale, which suggests to me that the Arryns have taken no part in any of this."

"And Dorne?" The Vale was far away; Dorne was close.

"Prince Doran's younger son has been betrothed to Myrcella Baratheon, which would suggest that the Dornishmen have thrown in with House Lannister, but they have an army in the Boneway and another in the Prince's Pass, just waiting . . ."

"Waiting." He frowned. "For what?" Without Daenerys and her dragons, Dorne was central to their hopes. "Write Sunspear. Doran Martell must know that his sister's son is still alive and has come home to claim his father's throne."

"As you say, my lord." The Halfmaester glanced at another parchment. "We could scarcely have timed our landing better. We have potential friends and allies at every hand."

"But no dragons," said Jon Connington, "so to win these allies to our cause, we must needs have something to offer them."

"Gold and land are the traditional incentives."

"Would that we had either. Promises of land and promises of gold may suffice for some, but Strickland and his men will expect first claim on the choicest fields and castles, those that were taken from their forebears when they fled into exile. No."

"My lord does have one prize to offer," Haldon Halfmaester pointed out. "Prince Aegon's hand. A marriage alliance, to bring some great House to our banners."

A bride for our bright prince. Jon Connington remembered Prince Rhaegar's wedding all too well. *Elia was never worthy of him. She was frail and sickly from the first, and childbirth only left her weaker.* After the birth of Princess Rhaenys, her mother had been bedridden for half a year, and Prince Aegon's birth had almost been the death of her. She would bear no more children, the maesters told Prince Rhaegar afterward.

"Daenerys Targaryen may yet come home one day," Connington told the Halfmaester. "Aegon must be free to marry her."

"My lord knows best," said Haldon. "In that case, we might consider offering potential friends a lesser prize."

"What would you suggest?"

"You. You are unwed. A great lord, still virile, with no heirs except these cousins we have just now dispossessed, the scion of an ancient House with a fine stout castle and wide, rich lands that will no doubt be restored and perhaps expanded by a grateful king, once we have triumphed. You have a name as a warrior, and as King Aegon's Hand you will speak with his voice and rule this realm in all but name. I would think that many an ambitious lord might be eager to wed his daughter to such a man. Even, perhaps, the prince of Dorne."

Jon Connington's answer was a long cold stare. There were times when the Halfmaester vexed him almost as much as that dwarf had. "I think not." *Death is creeping up my arm. No man must ever know, nor any wife.* He got back to his feet. "Prepare the letter to Prince Doran."

"As my lord commands."

Jon Connington slept that night in the lord's chambers, in the bed that had once been his father's, beneath a dusty canopy of red-and-white velvet. He woke at dawn to the sound of falling rain and the timid knock of a serving man anxious to learn how his new lord would break his fast. "Boiled eggs, fried bread, and beans. And a jug of wine. The worst wine in the cellar."

"The . . . the *worst*, m'lord?"

"You heard me."

When the food and wine had been brought up, he barred the door, emptied the jug into a bowl, and soaked his hand in it. Vinegar soaks and vinegar baths were the treatment Lady Lemore had prescribed for the dwarf, when she feared he might have greyscale, but asking for a jug of vinegar each morning would give the game away. Wine would need to serve, though he saw no sense in wasting a good vintage. The nails on all four fingers were black now, though not yet on his thumb. On the middle finger, the grey had crept up past the second knuckle. *I should hack them off,* he thought, *but how would I explain two missing fingers?* He dare not let the greyscale become known. Queer as it seemed, men who would cheerfully face battle and risk death to rescue a companion would abandon that same companion in a heartbeat if he were known to have greyscale. *I should have let the damned dwarf drown.*

Later that day, garbed and gloved once more, Connington made an inspection of the castle and sent word to Homeless Harry Strickland and his captains to join him for a war council. Nine of them assembled in the solar: Connington and Strickland, Haldon Halfmaester, Black Balaq, Ser Franklyn Flowers, Malo Jayn, Ser Brendel Byrne, Dick Cole and Lymond Pease. The Halfmaester had good tidings. "Word's reached the camp from Marq Mandrake. The Volantenes put him ashore on what turned out to be Estermont, with close to five hundred men. He's taken Greenstone."

Estermont was an island off Cape Wrath, never one of their objectives. "The damned Volantenes are so eager to be rid of us they are dumping us ashore on any bit of land they see," said Franklyn Flowers. "I'll wager you that we've got lads scattered all over half the bloody Stepstones too."

"With my elephants," Harry Strickland said, in a mournful tone. He missed his elephants, did Homeless Harry.

"Mandrake had no archers with him," said Lymond Pease. "Do we know if Greenstone got off any ravens before it fell?"

"I expect they did," said Jon Connington, "but what messages would they have carried? At best, some garbled account of raiders from the sea." Even before they had sailed from Volon Therys, he had instructed his captains to show no banners during these first attacks—not Prince Aegon's three-headed dragon, nor his own griffins, nor the skulls and golden battle standards of the company. "Let the Lannisters suspect Stannis Baratheon, pirates from the Stepstones, outlaws out of the woods, or whoever else they cared to blame. If the reports that reached King's Landing were confused and contradictory, so much the better. The slower the Iron Throne was to react, the longer they would have to gather their strength and bring allies to the cause. There should be ships on Estermont. It *is* an island. Haldon, send word to Mandrake to leave a garrison behind and bring the rest of his men over to Cape Wrath, along with any noble captives."

"As you command, my lord. House Estermont has blood ties to both kings, as it happens. Good hostages."

"Good ransoms," said Homeless Harry, happily.

"It is time we sent for Prince Aegon as well," Lord Jon announced. "He will be safer here behind the walls of Griffin's Roost than back at camp."

"I'll send a rider," said Franklyn Flowers, "but the lad won't much like the idea of staying safe, I tell you that. He wants to be in the thick o' things."

So did we all at his age, Lord Jon thought, remembering.

"Has the time come to raise his banner?" asked Pease.

"Not yet. Let King's Landing think this is no more than an exile lord coming home with some hired swords to reclaim his birthright. An old familiar story, that. I will even write King Tommen, stating as much and asking for a pardon and the restoration of my lands and titles. That will give them something to chew over for a while. And whilst they dither, we will send out word secretly to likely friends in the stormlands and the Reach. And Dorne." That was the crucial step. Lesser lords might join their cause for fear of harm or hope of gain, but only the Prince of Dorne had the power to defy House Lannister and its allies. "Above all else, we must have Doran Martell."

"Small chance of that," said Strickland. "The Dornishman is scared of his own shadow. Not what you call daring."

No more than you. "Prince Doran is a cautious man, that's true. He will never join us unless he is convinced that we will win. So to persuade him we must show our strength."

"If Peake and Rivers are successful, we will control the better part of Cape Wrath," argued Strickland. "Four castles in as many days, that's a splendid start, but we are still only at half strength. We need to wait for the rest of my men. We are missing horses as well, and the elephants. Wait, I say. Gather our power, win some small lords to our cause, let Lysono Maar dispatch his spies to learn what we can of our foes."

Connington gave the plump captain-general a cool look. *This man is no Blackheart, no Bittersteel, no Maelys. He would wait until all seven hells were frozen if he could rather than risk another bout of blisters.* "We did not cross half the world to wait. Our best chance is to strike hard and fast, before King's Landing knows who we are. I mean to take Storm's End. A nigh-impregnable stronghold, and Stannis Baratheon's last foothold in the south. Once taken, it will give us a secure fastness to which we may retreat at need, and winning it will prove our strength."

The captains of the Golden Company exchanged glances. "If Storm's End is still held by men loyal to Stannis, we will be taking it from him, not the Lannisters," objected Brendel Byrne. "Why not make common cause with him against the Lannisters?"

"Stannis is Robert's brother, of that same ilk that brought down House Targaryen," Jon Connington reminded him. "Moreover, he is a thousand leagues away, with whatever meagre strength he still commands. The whole realm lies between us. It would take half a year just to reach him, and he has little and less to offer us."

"If Storm's End is so impregnable, how do you mean to take it?" asked Malo.

"By guile."

Homeless Harry Strickland disagreed. "We should wait."

"We shall." Jon Connington stood. "Ten days. No longer. It will take that long to prepare. On the morning of the eleventh day, we ride for Storm's End."

The prince arrived to join them four days later, riding at the head of a column of a hundred horse, with three elephants lumbering in his rear. Lady Lemore was with him, garbed once more in the white robes of a septa. Before them went Ser Rolly Duckfield, a snow-white cloak streaming from his shoulders.

A solid man, and true, Connington thought as he watched Duck dismount, *but not worthy of the Kingsguard.* He had tried his best to dissuade the prince from giving Duckfield that cloak, pointing out that the honor might best be held in reserve for warriors of greater renown whose fealty would add luster to their cause, and the younger sons of great lords whose support they would need in the coming struggle, but the boy would not be moved. "Duck will die for me if need be," he had said, "and that's all I require in my Kingsguard. The Kingslayer was a warrior of great renown, and the son of a great lord as well."

At least I convinced him to leave the other six slots open, else Duck might have six ducklings trailing after him, each more blindingly adequate than the last. "Escort His Grace to my solar," he commanded. "At once."

Prince Aegon Targaryen was not near as biddable as the boy Young Griff had been, however. The better part of an hour had passed before he finally turned up in the solar, with Duck at his side. "Lord Connington," he said, "I like your castle."

"Your father's lands are beautiful," he said. *His silvery hair was blowing in the wind, and his eyes were a deep purple, darker than this boy's.* "As do I, Your Grace. Please, be seated. Ser Rolly, we'll have no further need of you for now."

"No, I want Duck to stay." The prince sat. "We've been talking with Strickland and Flowers. They told us about this attack on Storm's End that you're planning."

Jon Connington did not let his fury show. "And did Homeless Harry try to persuade you to delay it?"

"He did, actually," the prince said, "but I won't. Harry's an old maid, isn't he? You have the right of it, my lord. I want the attack to go ahead . . . with one change. I mean to lead it."

THE SACRIFICE

On the village green, the queen's men built their pyre.

Or should it be the village white? The snow was knee deep everywhere but where the men had shoveled it away, to hack holes into the frozen ground with axe and spade and pick. The wind was swirling from the west, driving still more snow across the frozen surface of the lakes.

"You do not want to watch this," Aly Mormont said.

"No, but I will." Asha Greyjoy was the kraken's daughter, not some pampered maiden who could not bear to look at ugliness.

It had been a dark, cold, hungry day, like the day before and the day before that. They had spent most of it out on the ice, shivering beside a pair of holes they'd cut in the smaller of the frozen lakes, with fishing lines clutched in mitten-clumsy hands. Not long ago, they could count on hooking one or two fish apiece, and wolfswood men more practiced at ice-fishing were pulling up four or five. Today all that Asha had come back with was a chill that went bone deep. Aly had fared no better. It had been three days since either of them had caught a fish.

The She-Bear tried again. "*I* do not need to watch this."

It is not you the queen's men want to burn. "Then go. You have my word, I will not run. Where would I go? To Winterfell?" Asha laughed. "Only three days' ride, they tell me."

Six queen's men were wrestling two enormous pinewood poles into holes six other queen's men had dug out. Asha did not have to ask their purpose. She knew. *Stakes.* Nightfall would be on them soon, and the red god must be fed. *An offering of blood and fire,* the queen's men called it, *that the Lord of Light may turn his fiery eye upon us and melt these thrice-cursed snows.*

"Even in this place of fear and darkness, the Lord of Light protects us," Ser Godry Farring told the men who gathered to watch as the stakes were hammered down into the holes.

"What has your southron god to do with *snow*?" demanded Artos Flint. His black beard was crusted with ice. "This is the wroth of the old gods come upon us. It is them we should appease."

"Aye," said Big Bucket Wull. "Red Rahloo means nothing here. You will only make the old gods angry. They are watching from their island."

The crofter's village stood between two lakes, the larger dotted with small wooded islands that punched up through the ice like the frozen fists of some drowned giant. From one such island rose a weirwood gnarled and ancient, its bole and branches white as the surrounding snows. Eight days ago Asha had walked out with Aly Mormont to have a closer look at its slitted red eyes and bloody mouth. *It is only sap,* she'd told herself, *the red sap that flows inside these weirwoods.* But her eyes were unconvinced; seeing was believing, and what they saw was frozen blood.

"You northmen brought these snows upon us," insisted Corliss Penny. "You and your demon trees. R'hllor will save us."

"R'hllor will doom us," said Artos Flint.

A pox on both your gods, thought Asha Greyjoy.

Ser Godry the Giantslayer surveyed the stakes, shoving one to make certain it was firmly placed. "Good. Good. They will serve. Ser Clayton, bring forth the sacrifice."

Ser Clayton Suggs was Godry's strong right hand. *Or should it be his withered arm?* Asha did not like Ser Clayton. Where Farring seemed fierce in his devotion to his red god, Suggs was simply cruel. She had seen him at the nightfires, watching, his lips parted and his eyes avid. *It is not the god he loves, it is the flames,* she concluded. When she asked Ser Justin if Suggs had always been that way, he grimaced. "On

Dragonstone he would gamble with the torturers and lend them a hand in the questioning of prisoners, especially if the prisoner were a young woman."

Asha was not surprised. Suggs would take a special delight in burning her, she did not doubt. *Unless the storms let up.*

They had been three days from Winterfell for nineteen days. *One hundred leagues from Deepwood Motte to Winterfell. Three hundred miles as the raven flies.* But none of them were ravens, and the storm was unrelenting. Each morning Asha awoke hoping she might see the sun, only to face another day of snow. The storm had buried every hut and hovel beneath a mound of dirty snow, and the drifts would soon be deep enough to engulf the longhall too.

And there was no food, beyond their failing horses, fish taken from the lakes (fewer every day), and whatever meagre sustenance their foragers could find in these cold, dead woods. With the king's knights and lords claiming the lion's share of the horsemeat, little and less remained for the common men. Small wonder then that they had started eating their own dead.

Asha had been as horrified as the rest when the She-Bear told her that four Peasebury men had been found butchering one of the late Lord Fell's, carving chunks of flesh from his thighs and buttocks as one of his forearms turned upon a spit, but she could not pretend to be surprised. The four were not the first to taste human flesh during this grim march, she would wager—only the first to be discovered.

Peasebury's four would pay for their feast with their lives, by the king's decree . . . and by burning end the storm, the queen's men claimed. Asha Greyjoy put no faith in their red god, yet she prayed they had the right of that. If not, there would be other pyres, and Ser Clayton Suggs might get his heart's desire.

The four flesh-eaters were naked when Ser Clayton drove them out, their wrists lashed behind their backs with leathern cords. The youngest of them wept as he stumbled through the snow. Two others walked like men already dead, eyes fixed upon the ground. Asha was surprised to see how ordinary they appeared. *Not monsters,* she realized, *only men.*

The oldest of the four had been their serjeant. He alone remained defiant, spitting venom at the queen's men as they prodded him along with their spears. "Fuck you all, and fuck your red god too," he said. "You hear me, Farring? *Giantslayer?* I laughed when your fucking cousin died, Godry. We should have eaten him too, he smelled so good when they roasted him. I bet the boy was nice and tender. Juicy." A blow from a spear butt drove the man to his knees but did not silence him. When he rose he spat out a mouthful of blood and broken teeth and went right on. "The cock's the choicest part, all crisped up on the spit. A fat little sausage." Even as they wrapped the chains around him, he raved on. "Corliss Penny, come over here. What sort of name is Penny? Is that how much your mother charged? And you, Suggs, you bleeding bastard, you—"

Ser Clayton never said a word. One quick slash opened the serjeant's throat, sending a wash of blood down his chest.

The weeping man wept harder, his body shaking with each sob. He was so thin that Asha could count every rib. "No," he begged, "please, he was dead, he was dead and we was hungry, *please . . .*"

"The serjeant was the clever one," Asha said to Aly Mormont. "He goaded Suggs into killing him." She wondered if the same trick might work twice, should her own turn come.

The four victims were chained up back-to-back, two to a stake. There they hung, three live men and one dead one, as the Lord of Light's devout stacked split logs and broken branches under their feet, then doused the piles with lamp oil. They had to be swift about it. The snow was falling heavily, as ever, and the wood would soon be soaked through.

"Where is the king?" asked Ser Corliss Penny.

Four days ago, one of the king's own squires had succumbed to cold and hunger, a boy named Bryen Farring who'd been kin to Ser Godry. Stannis Baratheon stood grim-faced by the funeral pyre as the lad's body was consigned to the flames. Afterward the king had retreated to his watchtower. He had not emerged since . . . though from time to time His Grace was glimpsed upon the tower roof, outlined against the beacon fire that burned there night and day. *Talking to the red god,* some said. *Calling out for Lady Melisandre,* insisted others. Either way, it seemed to Asha Greyjoy, the king was lost and crying out for help.

"Canty, go find the king and tell him all is ready," Ser Godry said to the nearest man-at-arms.

"The king is here." The voice was Richard Horpe's.

Over his armor of plate and mail Ser Richard wore his quilted doublet, blazoned with three death's-head moths on a field of ash and bone. King Stannis walked beside him. Behind them, struggling to keep pace, Arnolf Karstark came hobbling, leaning on his black-thorn cane. Lord Arnolf had found them eight days past. The northman had brought a son, three grandsons, four hundred spears, two score archers, a dozen mounted lances, a maester, and a cage of ravens . . . but only enough provisions to sustain his own.

Karstark was no lord in truth, Asha had been given to understand, only castellan of Karhold for as long as the true lord remained a captive of the Lannisters. Gaunt and bent and crooked, with a left shoulder half a foot higher than his right, he had a scrawny neck, squinty grey eyes, and yellow teeth. A few white hairs were all that separated him from baldness; his forked beard was equal parts white and grey, but always ragged. Asha thought there was something sour about his smiles. Yet if the talk was true, it was Karstark who would hold Winterfell should they take it. Somewhere in the distant past House Karstark had sprouted from House Stark, and Lord Arnolf had been the first of Eddard Stark's bannermen to declare for Stannis.

So far as Asha knew, the gods of the Karstarks were the old gods of the north, gods they shared with the Wulls, the Norreys, the Flints, and the other hill clans. She wondered if Lord Arnolf had come to view the burning at the king's behest, that he might witness the power of the red god for himself.

At the sight of Stannis, two of the men bound to the stakes began to plead for mercy. The king listened in silence, his jaw clenched. Then he said to Godry Farring, "You may begin."

The Giantslayer raised his arms. "*Lord of Light, hear us.*"

"*Lord of Light, defend us,*" the queen's men chanted, "*for the night is dark and full of terrors.*"

Ser Godry raised his head toward the darkening sky. "*We thank *you for the sun that warms us and pray that you will return it to us, Oh lord, that it might light our path to your enemies.*" Snowflakes melted on his face. "*We thank you for the stars that watch over us by night, and pray that you will rip away this veil that hides them, so we might glory in their sight once more.*"

"*Lord of Light, protect us,*" the queen's men prayed, "*and keep this savage dark at bay.*"

Ser Corliss Penny stepped forward, clutching the torch with both hands. He swung it about his head in a circle, fanning the flames. One of the captives began to whimper.

"*R'hllor,*" Ser Godry sang, "*we give you now four evil men. With glad hearts and true, we give them to your cleansing fires, that the darkness in their souls might be burned away. Let their vile flesh be seared and blackened, that their spirits might rise free and pure to ascend into the light. Accept their blood, Oh lord, and melt the icy chains that bind your servants. Hear their pain, and grant strength to our swords that we might shed the blood of your enemies. Accept this sacrifice, and show us the way to Winterfell, that we might vanquish the unbelievers.*"

"*Lord of Light, accept this sacrifice,*" a hundred voices echoed. Ser Corliss lit the first pyre with the torch, then thrust it into the wood at the base of the second. A few wisps of smoke began to rise. The captives began to cough. The first flames appeared, shy as maidens, darting and dancing from log to leg. In moments both the stakes were engulfed in fire.

"*He was dead,*" the weeping boy screamed, as the flames licked up his legs. "We found him dead . . . please . . . we was *hungry* . . ." The fires reached his balls. As the hair around his cock began to burn, his pleading dissolved into one long wordless shriek.

Asha Greyjoy could taste the bile in the back of her throat. On the Iron Islands, she had seen priests of her own people slit the throats of thralls and give their bodies to the sea to honor the Drowned God. Brutal as that was, this was worse.

Close your eyes, she told herself. *Close your ears. Turn away. You do not need to see this.* The queen's men were singing some paean of praise for red R'hllor, but she could not hear the words above the shrieks. The heat of the flames beat against her face, but even so she shivered. The air grew thick with smoke and the stink of burnt flesh, and one of the bodies still twitched against the red-hot chains that bound him to the stake.

After a time the screaming stopped.

Wordless, King Stannis walked away, back to the solitude of his watchtower. *Back to his beacon fire,* Asha knew, *to search the flames for answers.* Arnolf Karstark made to hobble after him, but Ser Richard Horpe took him by the arm and turned him toward the longhall. The watchers began to drift away, each to his own fire and whatever meagre supper he might find.

Clayton Suggs sidled up beside her. "Did the iron cunt enjoy the show?" His breath stank of ale and onions. *He has pig eyes,* Asha thought. That was fitting; his shield and surcoat showed a pig with wings. Suggs pressed his face so close to hers that she could count the blackheads on his nose and said, "The crowd will be even bigger when it's you squirming on a stake."

He was not wrong. The wolves did not love her; she was ironborn and must answer for the crimes of her people, for Moat Cailin and Deepwood Motte and Torrhen's Square, for centuries of reaving along the stony shore, for all Theon did at Winterfell.

"Unhand me, ser." Every time Suggs spoke to her, it left her yearning for her axes. Asha was as good a finger dancer as any man on the isles and had ten fingers to prove it. *If only I could dance with this one.* Some men had faces that cried out for a beard. Ser Clayton's face cried out for an axe between the eyes. But she was axeless here, so the best that she could do was try to wrench away. That just made Ser Clayton grasp her all the tighter, gloved fingers digging into her arm like iron claws.

"My lady asked you to let her go," said Aly Mormont. "You would do well to listen, ser. Lady Asha is not for burning."

"She will be," Suggs insisted. "We have harbored this demon worshiper amongst us too long." He released his grip on Asha's arm all the same. One did not provoke the She-Bear needlessly.

That was the moment Justin Massey chose to appear. "The king has other plans for his prize captive," he said, with his easy smile. His cheeks were red from the cold.

"The king? Or you?" Suggs snorted his contempt. "Scheme all you like, Massey. She'll still be for the fire, her and her king's blood. There's power in king's blood, the red woman used to say. Power to please our lord."

"Let R'hllor be content with the four we just sent him."

"Four baseborn churls. A beggar's offering. Scum like that will never stop the snow. She might."

The She-Bear spoke. "And if you burn her and the snows still fall, what then? Who will you burn next? Me?"

Asha could hold her tongue no longer. "Why not Ser Clayton? Perhaps R'hllor would like one of his own. A faithful man who will sing his praises as the flames lick at his cock."

Ser Justin laughed. Suggs was less amused. "Enjoy your giggle, Massey. If the snow keeps falling, we will see who is laughing then." He glanced at the dead men on their stakes, smiled, and went off to join Ser Godry and the other queen's men.

"My champion," Asha said to Justin Massey. He deserved that much, whatever his motives. "Thank you for the rescue, ser."

"It will not win you friends amongst the queen's men," said the She-Bear. "Have you lost your faith in red R'hllor?"

"I have lost faith in more than that," Massey said, his breath a pale mist in the air, "but I still believe in supper. Will you join me, my ladies?"

Aly Mormont shook her head. "I have no appetite."

"Nor I. But you had best choke down some horsemeat all the same, or you may soon wish you had. We had eight hundred horses when we marched from Deepwood Motte. Last night the count was sixty-four."

That did not shock her. Almost all of their big destriers had failed, including Massey's own. Most of their palfreys were gone as well. Even the garrons of the northmen were faltering for want of fodder. But what did they need horses for? Stannis was no longer marching anywhere. The sun and moon and stars had been gone so long that Asha was starting to wonder whether she had dreamed them. "I will eat."

Aly shook her head. "Not me."

"Let me look after Lady Asha, then," Ser Justin told her. "You have my word, I shall not permit her to escape."

The She-Bear gave her grudging assent, deaf to the japery in his tone. They parted there, Aly to her tent, she and Justin Massey to the longhall. It was not far, but the drifts were deep, the wind was gusty, and Asha's feet were blocks of ice. Her ankle stabbed at her with every step.

Small and mean as it was, the longhall was the largest building in the village, so the lords and captains had taken it for themselves, whilst Stannis settled into the stone watchtower by the lakeshore. A pair of guardsmen flanked its door, leaning on tall spears. One lifted the greased door flap for Massey, and Ser Justin escorted Asha through to the blessed warmth within.

Benches and trestle tables ran along either side of the hall, with room for fifty men . . . though twice that number had squeezed themselves inside. A fire trench had been dug down the middle of the earthen floor, with a row of smokeholes in the roof above. The wolves had taken to sitting on one side of the trench, the knights and southron lords upon the other.

The southerners looked a sorry lot, Asha thought—gaunt and hollow-cheeked, some pale and sick, others with red and wind-scoured faces. By contrast the northmen seemed hale and healthy, big ruddy men with beards as thick as bushes, clad in fur and iron. They might be cold and hungry too, but the marching had gone easier for them, with their garrons and their bear-paws.

Asha peeled off her fur mittens, wincing as she flexed her fingers. Pain shot up her legs as her half-frozen feet began to thaw in the warmth. The crofters had left behind a good supply of peat when they fled, so the air was hazy with smoke and the rich, earthy smell of burning turf. She hung her cloak on a peg inside the door after shaking off the snow that clung to it.

Ser Justin found them places on the bench and fetched supper for the both of them—ale and chunks of horsemeat, charred black outside and red within. Asha took a sip of ale and fell upon the horse flesh. The portion was smaller than the last she'd tasted, but her belly still rumbled at the smell of it. "My thanks, ser," she said, as blood and grease ran down her chin.

"Justin. I insist." Massey cut his own meat into chunks and stabbed one with his dagger.

Down the table, Will Foxglove was telling the men around him that Stannis would resume his march on Winterfell three days hence. He'd had it from the lips of one of the grooms who tended the king's horses. "His Grace has seen victory in his fires," Foxglove said, "a victory that will be sung of for a thousand years in lord's castle and peasant's hut alike."

Justin Massey looked up from his horsemeat. "The cold count last night reached eighty." He pulled a piece of gristle from his teeth and flicked it to the nearest dog. "If we march, we will die by the hundreds."

"We will die by the thousands if we stay here," said Ser Humfrey Clifton. "Press on or die, I say."

"Press on *and* die, I answer. And if we reach Winterfell, what then? How do we take it? Half our men are so weak they can scarce put one foot before another. Will you set them to scaling walls? Building siege towers?"

"We should remain here until the weather breaks," said Ser Ormund Wylde, a cadaverous old knight whose nature gave the lie to his name. Asha had heard rumors that some of the men-at-arms were wagering on which of the great knights and lords would be the next to die. Ser Ormund had emerged as a clear favorite. *And how much coin was placed on me, I wonder?* Asha thought. *Perhaps there is still time to put down a wager.* "Here at least we have some shelter," Wylde was insisting, "and there are fish in the lakes."

"Too few fish and too many fishermen," Lord Peasebury said gloomily. He had good reason for gloom; it was his men Ser Godry had just burned, and there were some in this very hall who had been heard to say that Peasebury himself surely knew what they were doing and might even have shared in their feasts.

"He's not wrong," grumbled Ned Woods, one of the scouts from Deepwood. Noseless Ned, he was called; frostbite had claimed the tip of his nose two winters past. Woods knew the wolfwood as well as any man alive. Even the king's proudest lords had learned to listen when he spoke. "I know them lakes. You been on them like maggots on a corpse, hundreds o' you. Cut so many holes in the ice it's a bloody wonder more haven't fallen through. Out by the island, there's places look like a cheese the rats been at." He shook his head. "Lakes are done. You fished them out."

"All the more reason to march," insisted Humfrey Clifton. "If death is our fate, let us die with swords in hand."

It was the same argument as last night and the night before. *Press on and die, stay here and die, fall back and die.*

"Feel free to perish as you wish, Humfrey," said Justin Massey. "Myself, I would sooner live to see another spring."

"Some might call that craven," Lord Peasebury replied.

"Better a craven than a cannibal."

Peasebury's face twisted in sudden fury. "You—"

"Death is part of war, Justin." Ser Richard Horpe stood inside the door, his dark hair damp with melting snow. "Those who march with us will have a share in all the plunder we take from Bolton and his bastard, and a greater share of glory undying. Those too weak to march must fend for themselves. But you have my word, we shall send food once we have taken Winterfell."

"*You will not take Winterfell!*"

"Aye, we will," came a cackle from the high table, where Arnolf Karstark sat with his son Arthor and three grandsons. Lord Arnolf shoved himself up, a vulture rising from its prey. One spotted hand clutched at his son's shoulder for support. "We'll take it for the Ned and for his daughter. Aye, and for the Young Wolf too, him who was so cruelly slaughtered. Me and mine will show the way, if need be. I've said as much to His Good Grace the king. *March,* I said, and before the moon can turn, we'll all be bathing in the blood of Freys and Boltons."

Men began to stamp their feet, to pound their fists against the tabletop. Almost all were northmen, Asha noted. Across the fire trench, the southron lords sat silent on the benches.

Justin Massey waited until the uproar had died away. Then he said, "Your courage is admirable, Lord Karstark, but courage will not breach the walls of Winterfell. How do you mean to take the castle, pray? With snowballs?"

One of Lord Arnolf's grandsons gave answer. "We'll cut down trees for rams to break the gates."

"And die."

Another grandson made himself heard. "We'll make ladders, scale the walls."

"And die."

Up spoke Arthor Karstark, Lord Arnolf's younger son. "We'll raise siege towers."

"And die, and die, and die." Ser Justin rolled his eyes. "Gods be good, are all you Karstarks mad?"

"*Gods?*" said Richard Horpe. "You forget yourself, Justin. We have but one god here. Speak not of demons in this company. Only the Lord of Light can save us now. Wouldn't you agree?" He put his hand upon the hilt of his sword, as if for emphasis, but his eyes never left the face of Justin Massey.

Beneath that gaze, Ser Justin wilted. "The Lord of Light, aye. My faith runs as deep as your own, Richard, you know that."

"It is your courage I question, Justin, not your faith. You have preached defeat every step of the way since we rode forth from Deepwood Motte. It makes me wonder whose side you are on."

A flush crept up Massey's neck. "I will not stay here to be insulted." He wrenched his damp cloak down from the wall so hard that Asha heard it tear, then stalked past Horpe and through the door. A blast of cold air blew through the hall, raising ashes from the fire trench and fanning its flames a little brighter.

Broken quick as that, thought Asha. *My champion is made of suet.* Even so, Ser Justin was one of the few who might object should the queen's men try to burn her. So she rose to her feet, donned her own cloak, and followed him out into the blizzard.

She was lost before she had gone ten yards. Asha could see the beacon fire burning atop the watchtower, a faint orange glow floating in the air. Elsewise the village was gone. She was alone in a white world of snow and silence, plowing through snowdrifts as high as her thighs. "*Justin?*" she called. There was no answer. Somewhere to her left she heard a horse whicker. *The poor thing sounds frightened. Perhaps he knows that he's to be tomorrow's supper.* Asha pulled her cloak about her tightly.

She blundered back onto the village green unknowing. The pinewood stakes still stood, charred and scorched but not burned through. The chains about the dead had cooled by now, she saw, but still held the corpses fast in their iron embrace. A raven was perched atop one, pulling at the tatters of burned flesh that clung to its blackened skull. The blowing snow had covered the ashes at the base of the pyre and crept up the dead man's leg as far as his ankle. *The old gods mean to bury him,* Asha thought. *This was no work of theirs.*

"Take a good long gander, cunt," the deep voice of Clayton Suggs said, behind her. "You'll look just as pretty once you're roasted. Tell me, can squids scream?"

God of my fathers, if you can hear me in your watery halls beneath the waves, grant me just one small throwing axe. The Drowned God did not answer. He seldom did. That was the trouble with gods. "Have you seen Ser Justin?"

"That prancing fool? What do you want with him, cunt? If it's a fuck you need, I'm more a man than Massey."

Cunt again? It was odd how men like Suggs used that word to demean women when it was the only part of a woman they valued. And Suggs was worse than Middle Liddle. *When he says the word, he means it.* "Your king gelds men for rape," she reminded him.

Ser Clayton chuckled. "The king's half-blind from staring into fires. But have no fear, cunt, I'll not rape you. I'd need to kill you after, and I'd sooner see you burn."

There's that horse again. "Do you hear that?"

"Hear what?"

"A horse. No, horses. More than one." She turned her head, listening. The snow did queer things to sound. It was hard to know which direction it had come from.

"Is this some squid game? I don't hear—" Suggs scowled. "Bloody hell. Riders." He fumbled at his sword belt, his hands clumsy in their fur-and-leather gloves, and finally succeeded in ripping his longsword from its scabbard.

By then the riders were upon them.

They emerged from the storm like a troop of wraiths, big men on small horses, made even bigger by the bulky furs they wore. Swords rode on their hips, singing their soft steel song as they rattled in their scabbards. Asha saw a battle-axe strapped to one man's saddle, a warhammer on another's back. Shields they bore as well, but so obscured by snow and ice that the arms upon them could not be read. For all her layers of wool and fur and boiled leather, Asha felt naked standing there. *A horn,* she thought, *I need a horn to rouse the camp.*

"Run, you stupid cunt," Ser Clayton shouted. "Run warn the king. Lord Bolton is upon us." A brute he might have been, but Suggs did not want for courage. Sword in hand, he strode through the snow, putting himself between the riders and the king's tower, its beacon glimmering behind him like the orange eye of some strange god. "Who goes there? Halt! *Halt!*"

The lead rider reined up before him. Behind were others, perhaps as many as a score. Asha had no time to count them. Hundreds more might be out there in the storm, coming hard upon their heels. Roose Bolton's entire host might be descending on them, hidden by darkness and swirling snow. These, though . . .

They are too many to be scouts and too few to make a vanguard. And two were all in black. *Night's Watch,* she realized suddenly. "Who are you?" she called.

"Friends," a half-familiar voice replied. "We looked for you at Winterfell, but found only Crowfood Umber beating drums and blowing horns. It took some time to find you." The rider vaulted from his saddle, pulled back his hood, and bowed. So thick was his beard, and so crusted with ice, that for a moment Asha did not know him. Then it came. "*Tris?*" she said.

"My lady." Tristifer Botley took a knee. "The Maid is here as well. Roggon, Grimtongue, Fingers, Rook . . . six of us, all those fit enough to ride. Cromm died of his wounds."

"What is this?" Ser Clayton Suggs demanded. "You're one of hers? How did you get loose of Deepwood's dungeons?"

Tris rose and brushed the snow from his knees. "Sybelle Glover was offered a handsome ransom for our freedom and chose to accept it in the name of the king."

"What ransom? Who would pay good coin for sea scum?"

"I did, ser." The speaker came forward on his garron. He was very tall, very thin, so long-legged that it was a wonder his feet did not drag along the ground. "I had need of a strong escort to see me safely to the king, and Lady Sybelle had need of fewer mouths to feed." A scarf concealed the tall man's features, but atop his head was perched the queerest hat Asha had seen since the last time she had sailed to Tyrosh, a brimless tower of some soft fabric, like three cylinders stacked one atop the other. "I was given to understand that I might find King Stannis here. It is most urgent that I speak with him at once."

"And who in seven stinking hells are you?"

The tall man slid gracefully from his garron, removed his peculiar hat, and bowed. "I have the honor to be Tycho Nestoris, a humble servant of the Iron Bank of Braavos."

Of all the strange things that might have come riding out of the night, the last one Asha Greyjoy would ever have expected was a Braavosi banker. It was too absurd. She had to laugh. "King Stannis has taken the watchtower for his seat. Ser Clayton will be pleased to show you to him, I'm sure."

"That would be most kind. Time is of the essence." The banker studied her with shrewd dark eyes. "You are the Lady Asha of House Greyjoy, unless I am mistaken."

"I am Asha of House Greyjoy, aye. Opinions differ on whether I'm a lady."

The Braavosi smiled. "We've brought a gift for you." He beckoned to the men behind him. "We had expected to find the king at Winterfell. This same blizzard has engulfed the castle, alas. Beneath its walls we found Mors Umber with a troop of raw green boys, waiting for the king's coming. He gave us this."

A girl and an old man, thought Asha, as the two were dumped rudely in the snow before her. The girl was shivering violently, even in her furs. If she had not been so frightened, she might even have been pretty, though the tip of her nose was black with frostbite. The old man . . . no one would ever think him comely. She had seen scarecrows with more flesh. His face was a skull with skin, his hair bone-white and filthy. And he *stank.* Just the sight of him filled Asha with revulsion.

He raised his eyes. "Sister. See. This time I knew you."

Asha's heart skipped a beat. "*Theon?*"

His lips skinned back in what might have been a grin. Half his teeth were gone, and half of those still left him were broken and splintered. "Theon," he repeated. "My name is Theon. You have to know your *name*."

VICTARION

The sea was black and the moon was silver as the Iron Fleet swept down on the prey.

They sighted her in the narrows between the Isle of Cedars and the rugged hills of the Astapori hinterlands, just as the black priest Moqorro had said they would. "Ghiscari," Longwater Pyke shouted down from the crow's nest. Victarion Greyjoy watched her sail grow larger from the forecastle. Soon he could make out her oars rising and falling, and the long white wake behind her shining in the moonlight, like a scar across the sea.

Not a true warship, Victarion realized. *A trading galley, and a big one.* She would make a fine prize. He signaled to his captains to give chase. They would board this ship and take her.

The captain of the galley had realized his peril by then. He changed course for the west, making for the Isle of Cedars, perhaps hoping to shelter in some hidden cove or run his pursuers onto the jagged rocks along the island's northeast coast. His galley was heavy laden, though, and the ironborn had the wind. *Grief* and *Iron Victory* cut across the quarry's course, whilst swift *Sparrowhawk* and agile *Fingerdancer* swept behind her. Even then the Ghiscari captain did not strike his banners. By the time *Lamentation* came alongside the prey, raking her larboard side and splintering her oars, both ships were so close to the haunted ruins of Ghozai that they could hear the monkeys chattering as the first dawn light washed over the city's broken pyramids.

Their prize was named *Ghiscari Dawn,* the galley's captain said when he was delivered to Victarion in chains. She was out of New Ghis and returning there by way of Yunkai after trading at Meereen. The man spoke no decent tongue but only a guttural Ghiscari, full of growls and hisses, as ugly a language as Victarion Greyjoy had ever heard. Moqorro translated the captain's words into the Common Tongue of Westeros. The war for Meereen was won, the captain claimed; the dragon queen was dead, and a Ghiscari by the name of Hizdak ruled the city now.

Victarion had his tongue torn out for lying. Daenerys Targaryen was *not* dead, Moqorro assured him; his red god R'hllor had shown him the queen's face in his sacred fires. The captain could not abide lies, so he had the Ghiscari captain bound hand and foot and thrown overboard, a sacrifice to the Drowned God. "Your red god will have his due," he promised Moqorro, "but the seas are ruled by the Drowned God."

"There are no gods but R'hllor and the Other, whose name may not be said." The sorcerer priest was garbed in somber black, but for a hint of golden thread at collar, cuffs, and hem. There was no red cloth aboard the *Iron Victory,* but it was not meet that Moqorro go about in the salt-stained rags he had been wearing when the Vole fished him from the sea, so Victarion had commanded Tom Tidewood to sew new robes for him from whatever was at hand, and had even donated some of his own tunics to the purpose. Of black and gold those were, for the arms of House Greyjoy showed a golden kraken on a black field, and the banners and sails of their ships displayed the same. The crimson-and-scarlet robes of the red priests were alien to the ironborn, but Victarion had hoped his men might accept Moqorro more easily once clad in Greyjoy colors.

He hoped in vain. Clad in black from head to heel, with a mask of red-and-orange flames tattooed across his face, the priest appeared more sinister than ever. The crew shunned him when he walked the deck, and men would spit if his shadow chanced to fall upon them. Even the Vole, who had fished the red priest from the sea, had urged Victarion to give him to the Drowned God.

But Moqorro knew these strange shores in ways the ironborn did not, and secrets of the dragonkind as well. *The Crow's Eye keeps wizards, why shouldn't I?* His black sorcerer was more puissant than all of Euron's three, even if you threw them in a pot and boiled them down to one. The Damphair might disapprove, but Aeron and his pieties were far away.

So Victarion closed his burned hand into a mighty fist, and said, "*Ghiscari Dawn* is no fit name for a ship of the Iron Fleet. For you, wizard, I shall rename her *Red God's Wroth.*"

His wizard bowed his head. "As the captain says." And the ships of the Iron Fleet numbered four-and-fifty once again.

The next day a sudden squall descended on them. Moqorro had predicted that as well. When the rains moved on, three ships were found to have vanished. Victarion had no way to know whether they had foundered, run aground, or been blown off course. "They know where we are going," he told his crew. "If they are still afloat, we will meet again." The iron captain had no time to wait for laggards. Not with his bride encircled by her enemies. *The most beautiful woman in the world has urgent need of my axe.*

Besides, Moqorro assured him that the three ships were not lost. Each night, the sorcerer priest would kindle a fire on the forecastle of the *Iron Victory* and stalk around the flames, chanting prayers. The firelight made his black skin shine like polished onyx, and sometimes Victarion could swear that the flames tattooed on his face were dancing too, twisting and bending, melting into one another, their colors changing with every turn of the priest's head.

"The black priest is calling demons down on us," one oarsman was heard to say.

When that was reported to Victarion, he had the man scourged until his back was blood from shoulders to buttocks. So when Moqorro said, "Your lost lambs will return to the flock off the isle called Yaros," the captain said, "Pray that they do, priest. Or you may be the next to taste the whip."

The sea was blue and green and the sun blazing down from an empty blue sky when the Iron Fleet took its second prize, in the waters north and west of Astapor.

This time it was a Myrish cog named *Dove*, on her way to Yunkai by way of New Ghis with a cargo of carpets, sweet green wines, and Myrish lace. Her captain owned a Myrish eye that made far-off things look close—two glass lenses in a series of brass tubes, cunningly wrought so that each section slid into the next, until the eye was no longer than a dirk. Victarion claimed that treasure for himself. The cog he renamed *Shrike*. Her crew would be kept for ransom, the captain decreed. They were neither slaves nor slavers, but free Myrmen and seasoned sailors. Such men were worth good coin. Sailing out of Myr, the *Dove* brought them no fresh news of Meereen or Daenerys, only stale reports of Dothraki horsemen along the Rhoyne, the Golden Company upon the march, and others things Victarion already knew.

"What do you see?" the captain asked his black priest that night, as Moqorro stood before his nightfire. "What awaits us on the morrow? More rain?" It smelled like rain to him.

"Grey skies and strong winds," Moqorro said. "No rain. Behind come the tigers. Ahead awaits your dragon."

Your dragon. Victarion liked the sound of that. "Tell me something that I do not know, priest."

"The captain commands, and I obey," said Moqorro. The crew had taken to calling him the Black Flame, a name fastened on him by Steffar Stammerer, who could not say "Moqorro." By any name, the priest had powers. "The coastline here runs west to east," he told Victarion. "Where it turns north, you will come on two more hares. Swift ones, with many legs."

And so it came to pass. This time the prey proved to be a pair of galleys, long and sleek and fast. Ralf the Limper was the first to sight them, but they soon outdistanced *Woe* and *Forlorn Hope*, so Victarion sent *Iron Wing*, *Sparrowhawk*, and *Kraken's Kiss* to run them down. He had no swifter ships than those three. The pursuit lasted the best part of the day, but in the end both galleys were boarded and taken, after brief but brutal fights. They had been running empty, Victarion learned, making for New Ghis to load supplies and weapons for the Ghiscari legions encamped before Meereen ... and to bring fresh legionaries to the war, to replace all the men who'd died. "Men slain in battle?" asked Victarion. The crews of the galleys denied it; the deaths were from a bloody flux. The pale mare, they called it. And like the captain of the *Ghiscari Dawn,* the captains of the galleys repeated the lie that Daenerys Targaryen was dead.

"Give her a kiss for me in whatever hell you find her," Victarion said. He called for his axe and took their heads off there and then. Afterward he put their crews to death as well, saving only the slaves chained to the oars. He broke their chains himself and told them they were now free men and would have the privilege of rowing for the Iron Fleet, an honor that every boy in the Iron Islands dreamed of growing up. "The dragon queen frees slaves and so do I," he proclaimed.

The galleys he renamed *Ghost* and *Shade.* "For I mean them to return and haunt these Yunkishmen," he told the dusky woman that night after he had taken his pleasure of her. They were close now, and growing closer every day. "We will fall upon them like a thunderbolt," he said, as he squeezed the woman's breast. He wondered if this was how his brother Aeron felt when the Drowned God spoke to him. He could almost hear the god's voice welling up from the depths of the sea. *You shall serve me well, my captain,* the waves seemed to say. *It was for this I made you.*

But he would feed the red god too, Moqorro's fire god. The arm the priest had healed was hideous to look upon, pork crackling from elbow to fingertips. Sometimes when Victarion closed his hand the skin would split and smoke, yet the arm was stronger than it had ever been. "Two gods are with me now," he told the dusky woman. "No foe can stand before two gods." Then he rolled her on her back and took her once again.

When the cliffs of Yaros appeared off their larboard bows, he found his three lost ships waiting for him, just as Moqorro had promised. Victarion gave the priest a golden torque as a reward.

Now he had a choice to make: should he risk the straits, or take the Iron Fleet around the island? The memory of Fair Isle still rankled in the iron captain's memory. Stannis Baratheon had descended on the Iron Fleet from both north and south whilst they were trapped in the channel between the island and the mainland, dealing Victarion his most crushing defeat. But sailing around Yaros would cost him precious days. With Yunkai so near, shipping in the straits was like to be heavy, but he did not expect to encounter Yunkish warships until they were closer to Meereen.

What would the Crow's Eye do? He brooded on that for a time, then signaled to his captains. "We sail the straits."

Three more prizes were taken before Yaros dwindled off their sterns. A fat galleas fell to the Vole and *Grief,* and a trading galley to Manfryd Merlyn of *Kite.* Their holds were packed with trade goods, wines and silks and spices, rare woods and rarer scents, but the ships themselves were the true prize. Later that same day, a fishing ketch was taken by *Seven Skulls* and *Thrall's Bane.* She was a small, slow, dingy thing, hardly worth the effort of boarding. Victarion was displeased to hear that it had taken two of his own ships to bring the fishermen to heel. Yet it was from their lips that he heard of the black dragon's return. "The silver queen is gone," the ketch's master told him. "She flew away upon her dragon, beyond the Dothraki sea."

"Where is this Dothraki sea?" he demanded. "I will sail the Iron Fleet across it and find the queen wherever she may be."

The fisherman laughed aloud. "That would be a sight worth seeing. The Dothraki sea is made of grass, fool."

He should not have said that. Victarion took him around the throat with his burned hand and lifted him bodily into the air. Slamming him back against the mast, he squeezed till the Yunkishman's face turned as black as the fingers digging into his flesh. The man kicked and writhed for a while, trying fruitlessly to pry loose the captain's grip. "No man calls Victarion Greyjoy a fool and lives to boast of it." When he opened his hand, the man's limp body flopped to the deck. Longwater Pyke and Tom Tidewood chucked it over the rail, another offering to the Drowned God.

"Your Drowned God is a demon," the black priest Moqorro said afterward. "He is no more than a thrall of the Other, the dark god whose name must not be spoken."

"Take care, priest," Victarion warned him. "There are godly men aboard this ship who would tear out your tongue for speaking such blasphemies. Your red god will have his due, I swear it. My word is iron. Ask any of my men."

The black priest bowed his head. "There is no need. The Lord of

Light has shown me your worth, lord Captain. Every night in my fires I glimpse the glory that awaits you."

Those words pleased Victarion Greyjoy mightily, as he told the dusky woman that night. "My brother Balon was a great man," he said, "but I shall do what he could not. The Iron Islands shall be free again, and the Old Way will return. Even Dagon could not do that." Almost a hundred years had passed since Dagon Greyjoy sat the Seastone Chair, but the ironborn still told tales of his raids and battles. In Dagon's day a weak king sat the Iron Throne, his rheumy eyes fixed across the narrow sea where bastards and exiles plotted rebellion. So forth from Pyke Lord Dagon sailed, to make the Sunset Sea his own. "He bearded the lion in his den and tied the direwolf's tail in knots, but even Dagon could not defeat the dragons. But I shall make the dragon queen mine own. She will share my bed and bear me many mighty sons."

That night the ships of the Iron Fleet numbered sixty.

Strange sails grew more common north of Yaros. They were very near to Yunkai, and the coast between the Yellow City and Meereen would be teeming with merchantmen and supply ships coming and going, so Victarion took the Iron Fleet out into the deeper waters, beyond the sight of land. Even there they would encounter other vessels. "Let none escape to give warning to our foes," the iron captain commanded. None did.

The sea was green and the sky was grey the morning *Grief* and *Warrior Wench* and Victarion's own *Iron Victory* captured the slaver galley from Yunkai in the waters due north of the Yellow City. In her holds were twenty perfumed boys and four score girls destined for the pleasure houses of Lys. Her crew never thought to find peril so close to their home waters, and the ironborn had little trouble taking her. She was named the *Willing Maiden*.

Victarion put the slavers to the sword, then sent his men below to unchain the rowers. "You row for me now. Row hard, and you shall prosper." The girls he divided amongst his captains. "The Lyseni would have made whores of you," he told them, "but we have saved you. Now you need only serve one man instead of many. Those who please their captains may be taken as salt wives, an honorable station." The perfumed boys he wrapped in chains and threw into the sea. They were unnatural creatures, and the ship smelled better once cleansed of their presence.

For himself, Victarion claimed the seven choicest girls. One had red-gold hair and freckles on her teats. One shaved herself all over. One was brown-haired and brown-eyed, shy as a mouse. One had the biggest breasts he had ever seen. The fifth was a little thing, with straight black hair and golden skin. Her eyes were the color of amber. The sixth was white as milk, with golden rings through her nipples and her nether lips, the seventh black as a squid's ink. The slavers of Yunkai had trained them in the way of the seven sighs, but that was not why Victarion wanted them. His dusky woman was enough to satisfy his appetites until he could reach Meereen and claim his queen. No man had need of candles when the sun awaited him.

The galley he renamed the *Slaver's Scream*. With her, the ships of the Iron Fleet numbered one-and-sixty. "Every ship we capture makes us stronger," Victarion told his ironborn, "but from here it will grow harder. On the morrow or the day after, we are like to meet with warships. We are entering the home waters of Meereen, where the fleets of our foes await us. We will meet with ships from all three Slaver Cities, ships from Tolos and Elyria and New Ghis, even ships from Qarth." He took care not to mention the green galleys of Old Volantis that surely must be sailing up through the Gulf of Grief even as he spoke. "These slavers are feeble things. You have seen how they run before us, heard how they squeal when we put them to the sword. Every man of you is worth twenty of them, for only we are made of iron. Remember this when first we next spy some slaver's sails. Give no quarter and expect none. What need have we of quarter? We are the ironborn, and two gods look over us. We will seize their ships, smash their hopes, and turn their bay to blood."

A great cry went up at his words. The captain answered with a nod, grim-faced, then called for the seven girls he had claimed to be brought on deck, the loveliest of all those found aboard the *Willing Maiden*. He kissed them each upon the cheeks and told them of the honor that awaited them, though they did not understand his words. Then he had them put aboard the fishing ketch that they had captured, cut her loose, and had her set afire.

"With this gift of innocence and beauty, we honor both the gods," he proclaimed, as the warships of the Iron Fleet rowed past the burning ketch. "Let these girls be reborn in light, undefiled by mortal lust, or let them descend to the Drowned God's watery halls, to feast and dance and laugh until the seas dry up."

Near the end, before the smoking ketch was swallowed by the sea, the cries of the seven sweetlings changed to joyous song, it seemed to Victarion Greyjoy. A great wind came up then, a wind that filled their sails and swept them north and east and north again, toward Meereen and its pyramids of many-colored bricks. *On wings of song I fly to you, Daenerys,* the iron captain thought.

That night, for the first time, he brought forth the dragon horn that the Crow's Eye had found amongst the smoking wastes of great Valyria. A twisted thing it was, six feet long from end to end, gleaming black and banded with red gold and dark Valyrian steel. *Euron's hellhorn.* Victarion ran his hand along it. The horn was as warm and smooth as the dusky woman's thighs, and so shiny that he could see a twisted likeness of his own features in its depths. Strange sorcerous writings had been cut into the bands that girded it. "Valyrian glyphs," Moqorro called them.

That much Victarion had known. "What do they say?"

"Much and more." The black priest pointed to one golden band. "Here the horn is named. '*I am Dragonbinder,*' it says. Have you ever heard it sound?"

"Once." One of his brother's mongrels had sounded the hellhorn at the kingsmoot on Old Wyk. A monster of a man he had been, huge and shaven-headed, with rings of gold and jet and jade around arms thick with muscle, and a great hawk tattooed across his chest. "The sound it made . . . it burned, somehow. As if my bones were on fire, searing my flesh from within. Those writings glowed red-hot, then white-hot and painful to look upon. It seemed as if the sound would never end. It was like some long scream. A thousand screams, all melted into one."

"And the man who blew the horn, what of him?"

"He died. There were blisters on his lips, after. His bird was bleeding too." The captain thumped his chest. "The hawk, just here. Every feather dripping blood. I heard the man was all burned up inside, but that might just have been some tale."

"A true tale." Moqorro turned the hellhorn, examining the queer letters that crawled across a second of the golden bands. "Here it says, '*No mortal man shall sound me and live.*'"

Bitterly Victarion brooded on the treachery of brothers. *Euron's gifts are always poisoned.* "The Crow's Eye swore this horn would bind dragons to my will. But how will that serve me if the price is death?"

"Your brother did not sound the horn himself. Nor must you." Moqorro pointed to the band of steel. "Here. '*Blood for fire, fire for blood.*' Who blows the hellhorn matters not. The dragons will come to the horn's master. You must *claim* the horn. With blood."

THE UGLY LITTLE GIRL

Eleven servants of the Many-Faced God gathered that night
beneath the temple, more than she had ever seen together at
one time. Only the lordling and the fat fellow arrived by the
front door; the rest came by secret ways, through tunnels and hidden
passages. They wore their robes of black and white, but as they took
their seats each man pulled his cowl down to show the face he had
chosen to wear that day. Their tall chairs were carved of ebony and
weirwood, like the doors of the temple above. The ebon chairs
had weirwood faces on their backs, the weirwood chairs faces of
carved ebony.

One of the other acolytes stood across the room with a flagon of
dark red wine. She had the water. Whenever one of the servants
wished to drink, he would raise his eyes or crook a finger, and one
or both of them would come and fill his cup. But mostly they stood,
waiting on looks that never came. *I am carved of stone,* she reminded
herself. *I am a statue, like the Sealords that stand along the Canal of
the Heroes.* The water was heavy, but her arms were strong.

The priests used the language of Braavos, though once for several
minutes three spoke heatedly in High Valyrian. The girl understood the
words, mostly, but they spoke in soft voices, and she could not always
hear. "I know this man," she did hear a priest with the face of a plague
victim say. "I know this man," the fat fellow echoed, as she was pouring

for him. But the handsome man said, "I will give this man the gift, I know him not." Later the squinter said the same thing, of someone else.

After three hours of wine and words, the priests took their leave . . . all but the kindly man, the waif, and the one whose face bore the marks of plague. His cheeks were covered with weeping sores, and his hair had fallen out. Blood dripped from one nostril and crusted at the corners of both eyes. "Our brother would have words with you, child," the kindly man told her. "Sit, if you wish." She seated herself in a weirwood chair with a face of ebony. Bloody sores held no terror for her. She had been too long in the House of Black and White to be afraid of a false face.

"Who are you?" plague face asked when they were alone.

"No one."

"Not so. You are Arya of House Stark, who bites her lip and cannot tell a lie."

"I was. I'm not now."

"Why are you here, liar?"

"To serve. To learn. To change my face."

"First change your heart. The gift of the Many-Faced God is not a child's plaything. You would kill for your own purposes, for your own pleasures. Do you deny it?"

She bit her lip. "I—"

He slapped her.

The blow left her cheek stinging, but she knew that she had earned it. "Thank you." Enough slaps, and she might stop chewing on her lip. *Arya* did that, not the night wolf. "I do deny it."

"You lie. I can see the truth in your eyes. You have the eyes of a wolf and a taste for blood."

Ser Gregor, she could not help but think. *Dunsen, Raff the Sweetling. Ser Ilyn, Ser Meryn, Queen Cersei.* If she spoke, she would need to lie, and he would know. She kept silent.

"You were a cat, they tell me. Prowling through the alleys smelling of fish, selling cockles and mussels for coin. A small life, well suited for a small creature such as you. Ask, and it can be restored to you. Push your barrow, cry your cockles, be content. Your heart is too soft to be one of us."

He means to send me away. "I have no heart. I only have a hole. I've killed lots of people. I could kill you if I wanted."

"Would that taste sweet to you?"

She did not know the right answer. "Maybe."

"Then you do not belong here. Death holds no sweetness in this house. We are not warriors, nor soldiers, nor swaggering bravos puffed up with pride. We do not kill to serve some lord, to fatten our purses, to stroke our vanity. We never give the gift to please ourselves. Nor do we choose the ones we kill. We are but servants of the God of Many Faces."

"*Valar dohaeris.*" *All men must serve.*

"You know the words, but you are too proud to serve. A servant must be humble and obedient."

"I obey. I can be humbler than anyone."

That made him chuckle. "You will be the very goddess of humility, I am sure. But can you pay the price?"

"What price?"

"The price is you. The price is all you have and all you ever hope to have. We took your eyes and gave them back. Next we will take your ears, and you will walk in silence. You will give us your legs and crawl. You will be no one's daughter, no one's wife, no one's mother. Your name will be a lie, and the very face you wear will not be your own."

She almost bit her lip again, but this time she caught herself and stopped. *My face is a dark pool, hiding everything, showing nothing.* She thought of all the names that she had worn: Arry, Weasel, Squab, Cat of the Canals. She thought of that stupid girl from Winterfell called Arya Horseface. Names did not matter. "I can pay the price. Give me a face."

"Faces must be earned."

"Tell me how."

"Give a certain man a certain gift. Can you do that?"

"What man?"

"No one that you know."

"I don't know a lot of people."

"He is one of them. A stranger. No one you love, no one you hate, no one you have ever known. Will you kill him?"

"Yes."

"Then on the morrow, you shall be Cat of the Canals again. Wear that face, watch, obey. And we will see if you are truly worthy to serve Him of Many Faces."

So the next day she returned to Brusco and his daughters in the house on the canal. Brusco's eyes widened when he saw her, and Brea gave a little gasp. "*Valar morghulis,*" Cat said, by way of greeting. "*Valar dohaeris,*" Brusco replied.

After that it was as if she had never been away.

She got her first look at the man she must kill later that morning as she wheeled her barrow through the cobbled streets that fronted on the Purple Harbor. He was an old man, well past fifty. *He has lived too long,* she tried to tell herself. *Why should he have so many years when my father had so few?* But Cat of the Canals had no father, so she kept that thought to herself.

"*Cockles and mussels and clams,*" Cat cried as he went past, "*oysters and prawns and fat green mussels.*" She even smiled at him. Sometimes a smile was all you needed to make them stop and buy. The old man did not smile back. He scowled at her and went on past, sloshing through a puddle. The splash wet her feet.

He has no courtesy, she thought, watching him go. *His face is hard and mean.* The old man's nose was pinched and sharp, his lips thin, his eyes small and close-set. His hair had gone to grey, but the little pointed beard at the end of his chin was still black. Cat thought it must be dyed and wondered why he had not dyed his hair as well. One of his shoulders was higher than the other, giving him a crooked cast.

"He is an evil man," she announced that evening when she returned to the House of Black and White. "His lips are cruel, his eyes are mean, and he has a villain's beard."

The kindly man chuckled. "He is a man like any other, with light in him and darkness. It is not for you to judge him."

That gave her pause. "Have the gods judged him?"

"Some gods, mayhaps. What are gods for if not to sit in judgment over men? The Many-Faced God does not weigh men's souls, however. He gives his gift to the best of men as he gives it to the worst. Elsewise the good would live forever."

The old man's hands were the worst thing about him, Cat decided the next day, as she watched him from behind her barrow. His fingers were long and bony, always moving, scratching at his beard, tugging at an ear, drumming on a table, twitching, twitching, twitching. *He has hands like two white spiders.* The more she watched his hands, the more she came to hate them.

"He moves his hands too much," she told them at the temple. "He must be full of fear. The gift will bring him peace."

"The gift brings all men peace."

"When I kill him he will look in my eyes and thank me."

"If he does, you will have failed. It would be best if he takes no note of you at all."

The old man was some sort of merchant, Cat concluded after watching him for a few days. His trade had to do with the sea, though she never saw him set foot upon a ship. He spent his days sitting in a soup shop near the Purple Harbor, a cup of onion broth cooling at his elbow as he shuffled papers and sealing wax and spoke in sharp tones to a parade of captains, shipowners, and other merchants, none of whom seemed to like him very much.

Yet they brought him money: leather purses plump with gold and silver and the square iron coins of Braavos. The old man would count it out carefully, sorting the coins and stacking them up neatly, like with like. He never looked at the coins. Instead he bit them, always on the left side of his mouth, where he still had all his teeth. From time to time he'd spin one on the table and listen to the sound it made when it came clattering to a stop.

And when all the coins had been counted and tasted, the old man would scrawl upon a parchment, stamp it with his seal, and give it to the captain. Else he'd shake his head and shove the coins back across the table. Whenever he did that, the other man would get red-faced and angry, or pale and scared-looking.

Cat did not understand. "They pay him gold and silver, but he only gives them writing. Are they stupid?"

"A few, mayhaps. Most are simply cautious. Some think to cozen him. He is not a man easily cozened, however."

"But what is he *selling* them?"

"He is writing each a binder. If their ships are lost in a storm or taken by pirates, he promises to pay them for the value of the vessel and all its contents."

"Is it some kind of wager?"

"Of a sort. A wager every captain hopes to lose."

"Yes, but if they win . . ."

". . . they lose their ships, oftimes their very lives. The seas are dangerous, and never more so than in autumn. No doubt many a captain sinking in a storm has taken some small solace in his binder back in Braavos, knowing that his widow and children will not want." A sad smile touched his lips. "It is one thing to write such a binder, though, and another to make good on it."

Cat understood. *One of them must hate him. One of them came to the House of Black and White and prayed for the god to take him.* She wondered who it had been, but the kindly man would not tell her. "It is not for you to pry into such matters," he said. "Who are you?"

"No one."

"No one asks no questions." He took her hands. "If you cannot do this thing, you need only say so. There is no shame in that. Some are made to serve the Many-Faced God and some are not. Say the word, and I shall lift this task from you."

"I will do it. I said I would. I will."

How, though? That was harder.

He had guards. Two of them, a tall thin man and a short thick one. They went with him everywhere, from when he left his house in the morning till he returned at night. They made certain no one got close to the old man without his leave. Once a drunk almost staggered into him as he was coming home from the soup shop, but the tall one stepped between them and gave the man a sharp shove that knocked him to the ground. At the soup shop, the short one always tasted the onion broth first. The old man waited until the broth had cooled before he took a sip, long enough to be sure his guardsman had suffered no ill effects.

"He's afraid," she realized, "or else he knows that someone wants to kill him."

"He does not know," said the kindly man, "but he suspects."

"The guards go with him even when he slips out to make water," she said, "but he doesn't go when they do. The tall one is the quicker. I'll wait till he is making water, walk into the soup shop, and stab the old man through the eye."

"And the other guard?"

"He's slow and stupid. I can kill him too."

"Are you some butcher of the battlefield, hacking down every man who stands in your way?"

"No."

"I would hope not. You are a servant of the Many-Faced God, and we who serve Him of Many Faces give his gift only to those who have been marked and chosen."

She understood. *Kill him. Kill only him.*

It took her three more days of watching before she found the way, and another day of practicing with her finger knife. Red Roggo had taught her how to use it, but she had not slit a purse since back before they took away her eyes. She wanted to make certain that she still knew how. *Smooth and quick, that's the way, no fumbling,* she told herself, and she slipped the little blade out of her sleeve, again and again and again. When she was satisfied that she still remembered how to do it, she sharpened the steel on a whetstone until its edge glimmered silver-blue in the candlelight. The other part was trickier, but the waif was there to help her. "I will give the man the gift on the morrow," she announced as she was breaking her fast.

"Him of Many Faces will be pleased." The kindly man rose. "Cat of the Canals is known to many. If she is seen to have done this deed, it might bring down trouble on Brusco and his daughters. It is time you had another face."

The girl did not smile, but inside she was pleased. She had lost Cat once, and mourned her. She did not want to lose her again. "What will I look like?"

"Ugly. Women will look away when they see you. Children will stare and point. Strong men will pity you, and some may shed a tear. No one who sees you will soon forget you. Come."

The kindly man took the iron lantern off its hook and led her past the still black pool and the rows of dark and silent gods, to the steps at the rear of the temple. The waif fell in behind them as they were making their descent. No one spoke. The soft scuff of slippered feet on the steps was the only sound. Eighteen steps brought them to the vaults, where five arched passageways spread out like the fingers of a man's hand. Down here the steps grew narrower and steeper, but the girl had run up and down them a thousand times and they held no terrors for her. Twenty-two more steps and they were at the subcellar. The tunnels here were cramped and crooked, black wormholes twisting through the heart of the great rock. One passage was closed off by a heavy iron door. The priest hung the lantern from a hook, slipped a hand inside his robe, and produced an ornate key.

Gooseprickles rose along her arms. *The sanctum.* They were going lower still, down to the third level, to the secret chambers where only the priests were permitted.

The key clicked three times, very softly, as the kindly man turned it in a lock. The door swung open on oiled iron hinges, making not a sound. Beyond were still more steps, hewn out of solid rock. The priest took down the lantern once again and led the way. The girl followed the light, counting the steps as she went down. *Four five six seven.* She found herself wishing that she had brought her stick. *Ten eleven twelve.* She knew how many steps there were between the temple and the cellar, between the cellar and the subcellar, she had even counted the steps on the cramped winding stair that spiraled up into the garret and the rungs on the steep wooden ladder that ascended to the rooftop door and the windy perch outside.

This stair was unknown to her, however, and that made it perilous. *One-and-twenty two-and-twenty three-and-twenty.* With every step the air seemed to grow a little colder. When her count reached thirty she knew that they were under even the canals. *Three-and-thirty four-and-thirty.* How deep were they going to go?

She had reached fifty-four when the steps finally ended at another iron door. This one was unlocked. The kindly man pushed it open and stepped through. She followed, with the waif on her heels. Their footsteps echoed through the darkness. The kindly man lifted his lantern and flicked its shutters wide open. Light washed over the walls around them.

A thousand faces were gazing down on her.

They hung upon the walls, before her and behind her, high and low, everywhere she looked, everywhere she turned. She saw old faces and young faces, pale faces and dark faces, smooth faces and wrinkled faces, freckled faces and scarred faces, handsome faces and homely faces, men and women, boys and girls, even babes, smiling faces, frowning faces, faces full of greed and rage and lust, bald faces and faces bristling with hair. *Masks,* she told herself, *it's only masks,* but even as she thought the thought, she knew it wasn't so. They were skins.

"Do they frighten you, child?" asked the kindly man. "It is not too late for you to leave us. Is this truly what you want?"

Arya bit her lip. She did not know what she wanted. *If I leave, where will I go?* She had washed and stripped a hundred corpses, dead things did not frighten her. *They carry them down here and slice their faces off, so what?* She was the night wolf, no scraps of skin could frighten her. *Leather hoods, that's all they are, they cannot hurt me.* "Do it," she blurted out.

He led her across the chamber, past a row of tunnels leading off into side passages. The light of his lantern illuminated each in turn. One tunnel was walled with human bones, its roof supported by columns of skulls. Another opened on winding steps that descended farther still. *How many cellars are there?* she wondered. *Do they just go down forever?*

"Sit," the priest commanded. She sat. "Now close your eyes, child." She closed her eyes. "This will hurt," he warned her, "but pain is the price of power. Do not move."

Still as stone, she thought. She sat unmoving. The cut was quick, the blade sharp. By rights the metal should have been cold against her flesh, but it felt warm instead. She could feel the blood washing down her face, a rippling red curtain falling across her brow and cheeks and chin, and she understood why the priest had made her close her eyes. When it reached her lips the taste was salt and copper. She licked at it and shivered.

"Bring me the face," said the kindly man. The waif made no answer, but she could hear her slippers whispering over the stone floor. To the girl he said, "Drink this," and pressed a cup into her hand. She drank it down at once. It was very tart, like biting into a lemon. A thousand years ago, she had known a girl who loved lemon cakes. *No, that was not me, that was only Arya.*

"Mummers change their faces with artifice," the kindly man was saying, "and sorcerers use glamors, weaving light and shadow and desire to make illusions that trick the eye. These arts you shall learn, but what we do here goes deeper. Wise men can see through artifice, and glamors dissolve before sharp eyes, but the face you are about to don will be as true and solid as that face you were born with. Keep your eyes closed." She felt his fingers brushing back her hair. "Stay still. This will feel queer. You may be dizzy, but you must not move."

Then came a tug and a soft rustling as the new face was pulled down over the old. The leather scraped across her brow, dry and stiff, but as her blood soaked into it, it softened and turned supple. Her cheeks grew warm, flushed. She could feel her heart fluttering beneath her breast, and for one long moment she could not catch her breath. Hands closed around her throat, hard as stone, choking her. Her own hands shot up to claw at the arms of her attacker, but there was no one there. A terrible sense of fear filled her, and she heard a noise, a hideous *crunch*ing noise, accompanied by blinding pain. A face floated in front of her, fat, bearded, brutal, his mouth twisted with rage. She heard the priest say, "Breathe, child. Breathe out the fear. Shake off the shadows. He is dead. She is dead. Her pain is gone. *Breathe.*"

The girl took a deep shuddering breath, and realized it was true. No one was choking her, no one was hitting her. Even so, her hand was shaking as she raised it to her face. Flakes of dried blood crumbled at the touch of her fingertips, black in the lantern light. She felt her cheeks, touched her eyes, traced the line of her jaw. "My face is still the same."

"Is it? Are you certain?"

Was she certain? She had not felt any change, but maybe it was not something you could feel. She swept a hand down across her face from top to bottom, as she had once seen Jaqen H'ghar do, back at Harrenhal. When he did it, his whole face had rippled and changed. When she did it, nothing happened. "It feels the same."

"To you," said the priest. "It does not look the same."

"To other eyes, your nose and jaw are broken," said the waif. "One side of your face is caved in where your cheekbone shattered, and half your teeth are missing."

She probed around inside her mouth with her tongue, but found no holes or broken teeth. *Sorcery,* she thought. *I have a new face. An ugly, broken face.*

"You may have bad dreams for a time," warned the kindly man. "Her father beat her so often and so brutally that she was never truly free of pain or fear until she came to us."

"Did you kill him?"

"She asked the gift for herself, not for her father."

You should have killed him.

He must have read her thoughts. "Death came for him in the end, as it comes for all men. As it must come for a certain man upon the morrow." He lifted up the lamp. "We are done here."

For now. As they made their way back to the steps, the empty eyeholes of the skins upon the walls seemed to follow her. For a moment she could almost see their lips moving, whispering dark sweet secrets to one another in words too faint to hear.

Sleep did not come easily that night. Tangled in her blankets, she twisted this way and that in the cold dark room, but whichever way she turned, she saw the faces. *They have no eyes, but they can see me.* She saw her father's face upon the wall. Beside him hung her lady mother, and below them her three brothers all in a row. *No. That was some other girl. I am no one, and my only brothers wear robes of black and white.* Yet there was the black singer, there the stableboy she'd killed with Needle, there the pimply squire from the crossroads inn, and over there the guard whose throat she'd slashed to get them out of Harrenhal. The Tickler hung on the wall as well, the black holes that were his eyes swimming with malice. The sight of him brought back the feel of the dagger in her hand as she had plunged it into his back, again and again and again.

When at last day came to Braavos, it came grey and dark and overcast. The girl had hoped for fog, but the gods ignored her prayers as gods so often did. The air was clear and cold, and the wind had a nasty bite to it. *A good day for a death,* she thought. Unbidden, her prayer came to her lips. *Ser Gregor, Dunsen, Raff the Sweetling. Ser Ilyn, Ser Meryn, Queen Cersei.* She mouthed the names silently. In the House of Black and White, you never knew who might be listening.

The vaults were full of old clothing, garments claimed from those who came to the House of Black and White to drink peace from the temple pool. Everything from beggar's rags to rich silks and velvets could be found there. *An ugly girl should dress in ugly clothing,* she decided, so she chose a stained brown cloak fraying at the hem, a musty green tunic smelling of fish, and a pair of heavy boots. Last of all she palmed her finger knife.

There was no haste, so she decided to take the long way round to the Purple Harbor. Across the bridge she went, to the Isle of the Gods. Cat of the Canals had sold cockles and mussels amongst the temples here, whenever Brusco's daughter Talea had her moon blood flowing and took to her bed. She half-expected to see Talea selling there today, perhaps outside the Warren where all the forgotten godlings had their forlorn little shrines, but that was silly. The day was too cold, and Talea never liked to wake this early. The statue outside the shrine of the Weeping Lady of Lys was crying silver tears as the ugly girl walked by. In the Gardens of Gelenei stood a gilded tree a hundred feet high with leaves of hammered silver. Torchlight glimmered behind windows of leaded glass in the Lord of Harmony's wooden hall, showing half a hundred kinds of butterflies in all their bright colors.

One time, the girl remembered, the Sailor's Wife had walked her rounds with her and told her tales of the city's stranger gods. "That is the house of the Great Shepherd. Three-headed Trios has that tower with three turrets. The first head devours the dying, and the reborn emerge from the third. I don't know what the middle head's supposed to do. Those are the Stones of the Silent God, and there the entrance to the Patternmaker's Maze. Only those who learn to walk it properly will ever find their way to wisdom, the priests of the Pattern say. Beyond it, by the canal, that's the temple of Aquan the Red Bull. Every thirteenth day, his priests slit the throat of a pure white calf, and offer bowls of blood to beggars."

Today was not the thirteenth day, it seemed; the Red Bull's steps were empty. The brother gods Semosh and Selloso dreamed in twin temples on opposite sides of the Black Canal, linked by a carved stone bridge. The girl crossed there and made her way down to the docks, then through the Ragman's Harbor and past the half-sunken spires and domes of the Drowned Town.

A group of Lysene sailors were staggering from the Happy Port as she went by, but the girl did not see any of the whores. The Ship was closed up and forlorn, its troupe of mummers no doubt still abed. But farther on, on the wharf beside an Ibbenese whaler, she spied Cat's old friend Tagganaro tossing a ball back and forth with Casso, King of Seals, whilst his latest cutpurse worked the crowd of onlookers. When she stopped to watch and listen for a moment, Tagganaro glanced at her without recognition, but Casso barked and clapped his flippers. *He knows me,* the girl thought, *or else he smells the fish.* She hurried on her way.

By the time she reached the Purple Harbor, the old man was ensconced inside the soup shop at his usual table, counting a purse of coins as he haggled with a ship's captain. The tall thin guard was hovering over him. The short thick one was seated near the door, where he would have a good view of anyone who entered. That made no matter. She did not intend to enter. Instead she perched atop a wooden piling twenty yards away as the blustery wind tugged at her cloak with ghostly fingers.

Even on a cold grey day like this, the harbor was a busy place. She saw sailors on the prowl for whores, and whores on the prowl for sailors. A pair of bravos passed in rumpled finery, leaning on each other as they staggered drunkenly past the docks, their blades rattling at their sides. A red priest swept past, his scarlet and crimson robes snapping in the wind.

It was almost noon before she saw the man she wanted, a prosperous shipowner she had seen doing business with the old man three times before. Big and bald and burly, he wore a heavy cloak of plush brown velvet trimmed with fur and a brown leather belt ornamented with silver moons and stars. Some mishap had left one leg stiff. He walked slowly, leaning on a cane.

He would do as well as any and better than most, the ugly girl decided. She hopped off the piling and fell in after him. A dozen strides put her right behind him, her finger knife poised. His purse was on his right side, at his belt, but his cloak was in her way. Her blade flashed out, smooth and quick, one deep slash through the velvet and he never felt a thing. Red Roggo would have smiled to see it. She slipped her hand through the gap, slit the purse open with the finger knife, filled her fist with gold . . .

The big man turned. "What—"

The movement tangled her arm in the folds of his cloak as she was pulling out her hand. Coins rained around their feet. "*Thief!*" The big man raised his stick to strike at her. She kicked his bad leg out from under him, danced away, and bolted as he fell, darting past a mother with a child. More coins fell from between her fingers to bounce along the ground. Shouts of "*thief, thief*" rang out behind her. A potbellied innkeep passing by made a clumsy grab for her arm, but she spun around him, flashed past a laughing whore, raced headlong for the nearest alley.

Cat of the Canals had known these alleys, and the ugly girl remembered. She darted left, vaulted a low wall, leapt across a small canal, and slipped through an unlocked door into some dusty storeroom. All sounds of pursuit had faded by then, but it was best to be sure. She hunkered down behind some crates and waited, arms wrapped around her knees. She waited for the best part of an hour, then decided it was safe to go, climbed straight up the side of the building, and made her way across the rooftops almost as far as the Canal of Heroes. By now the shipowner would have gathered up coins and cane and limped on to the soup shop. He might be drinking a bowl of hot broth and complaining to the old man about the ugly girl who had tried to rob his purse.

The kindly man was waiting for her at the House of Black and White, seated on the edge of the temple pool. The ugly girl sat next to him and put a coin on the lip of the pool between them. It was gold, with a dragon on one face and a king on the other.

"The golden dragon of Westeros," said the kindly man. "And how did you come by this? We are no thieves."

"It wasn't stealing. I took one of his, but I left him one of ours."

The kindly man understood. "And with that coin and the others in his purse, he paid a certain man. Soon after that man's heart gave out. Is that the way of it? Very sad." The priest picked up the coin and tossed it into the pool. "You have much and more to learn, but it may be you are not hopeless."

That night they gave her back the face of Arya Stark.

They brought a robe for her as well, the soft thick robe of an acolyte, black upon one side and white upon the other. "Wear this when you are here," the priest said, "but know that you shall have little need of it for the present. On the morrow you will go to Izembaro to begin your first apprenticeship. Take what clothes you will from the vaults below. The city watch is looking for a certain ugly girl, known to frequent the Purple Harbor, so best you have a new face as well." He cupped her chin, turned her head this way and that, nodded. "A pretty one this time, I think. As pretty as your own. Who are you, child?"

"No one," she replied.

CERSEI

On the last night of her imprisonment, the queen could not sleep. Each time she closed her eyes, her head filled with forebodings and fantasies of the morrow. *I will have guards,* she told herself. *They will keep the crowds away. No one will be allowed to touch me.* The High Sparrow had promised her that much.

Even so, she was afraid. On the day Myrcella sailed for Dorne, the day of the bread riots, gold cloaks had been posted all along the route of the procession, but the mob had broken through their lines to tear the old fat High Septon into pieces and rape Lollys Stokeworth half a hundred times. And if that pale soft stupid creature could incite the animals when fully clothed, how much more lust would a queen inspire?

Cersei paced her cell, restless as the caged lions that had lived in the bowels of Casterly Rock when she was a girl, a legacy of her grandfather's time. She and Jaime used to dare each other to climb into their cage, and once she worked up enough courage to slip her hand between two bars and touch one of the great tawny beasts. She was always bolder than her brother. The lion had turned his head to stare at her with huge golden eyes. Then he licked her fingers. His tongue was as rough as a rasp, but even so she would not pull her hand back, not until Jaime took her by the shoulders and yanked her away from the cage.

"Your turn," she told him afterward. "Pull his mane, I dare you." *He never did. I should have had the sword, not him.*

Barefoot and shivering she paced, a thin blanket draped about her shoulders. She was anxious for the day to come. By evening it would all be done. *A little walk and I'll be home, I'll be back with Tommen, in my own chambers inside Maegor's Holdfast.* Her uncle said it was the only way to save herself. Was it, though? She could not trust her uncle, no more than she trusted this High Septon. *I could still refuse. I could still insist upon my innocence and hazard all upon a trial.*

But she dare not let the Faith sit in judgment on her, as that Margaery Tyrell meant to do. That might serve the little rose well enough, but Cersei had few friends amongst the septas and sparrows around this new High Septon. Her only hope was trial by battle, and for that she must needs have a champion.

If Jaime had not lost his hand . . .

That road led nowhere, though. Jaime's sword hand was gone, and so was he, vanished with the woman Brienne somewhere in the riverlands. The queen had to find another defender or today's ordeal would be the least of her travails. Her enemies were accusing her of treason. She had to reach Tommen, no matter the costs. *He loves me. He will not refuse his own mother. Joff was stubborn and unpredictable, but Tommen is a good little boy, a good little king. He will do as he is told.* If she stayed here, she was doomed, and the only way she would return to the Red Keep was by walking. The High Sparrow had been adamant, and Ser Kevan refused to lift a finger against him.

"No harm will come to me today," Cersei said when the day's first light brushed her window. "Only my pride will suffer." The words rang hollow in her ears. *Jaime may yet come.* She pictured him riding through the morning mists, his golden armor bright in the light of the rising sun. *Jaime, if you ever loved me . . .*

When her gaolers came for her, Septa Unella, Septa Moelle, and Septa Scolera led the procession. With them were four novices and two of the silent sisters. The sight of the silent sisters in their grey robes filled the queen with sudden terrors. *Why are they here? Am I to die?* The silent sisters attended to the dead. "The High Septon promised that no harm would come to me."

"Nor will it." Septa Unella beckoned to the novices. They brought lye soap, a basin of warm water, a pair of shears, and a long straight-razor. The sight of the steel sent a shiver through her. *They mean to shave me. A little more humiliation, a raisin for my porridge.* She would not give them the pleasure of hearing her beg. *I am Cersei of House Lannister, a lion of the Rock, the rightful queen of these Seven Kingdoms, trueborn daughter of Tywin Lannister. And hair grows back.* "Get on with it," she said.

The elder of the two silent sisters took up the shears. A practiced barber, no doubt; her order often cleaned the corpses of the noble slain before returning them to their kin, and trimming beards and cutting hair was part of that. The woman bared the queen's head first. Cersei sat as still as a stone statue as the shears clicked. Drifts of golden hair fell to the floor. She had not been allowed to tend it properly penned up in this cell, but even unwashed and tangled it shone where the sun touched it. *My crown,* the queen thought. *They took the other crown away from me, and now they are stealing this one as well.* When her locks and curls were piled up around her feet, one of the novices soaped her head and the silent sister scraped away the stubble with a razor.

Cersei hoped that would be the end of it, but no. "Remove your shift, Your Grace," Septa Unella commanded.

"Here?" the queen asked. "Why?"

"You must be shorn."

Shorn, she thought, *like a sheep.* She yanked the shift over her head and tossed it to the floor. "Do what you will."

Then it was the soap again, the warm water, and the razor. The hair beneath her arms went next, then her legs, and last of all the fine golden down that covered her mound. When the silent sister crept between her legs with the razor, Cersei found herself remembering all the times that Jaime had knelt where she was kneeling now, planting kisses on the inside of her thighs, making her wet. His kisses were always warm. The razor was ice-cold.

When the deed was done she was as naked and vulnerable as a woman could be. *Not even a hair to hide behind.* A little laugh burst from her lips, bleak and bitter.

"Does Your Grace find this amusing?" said Septa Scolera.

"No, septa," said Cersei. *But one day I will have your tongue ripped out with hot pincers, and that will be hilarious.*

One of the novices had brought a robe for her, a soft white septa's robe to cover her as she made her way down the tower steps and through the sept, so any worshipers they met along the way might be spared the sight of naked flesh. *Seven save us all, what hypocrites they are.* "Will I be permitted a pair of sandals?" she asked. "The streets are filthy."

"Not so filthy as your sins," said Septa Moelle. "His High Holiness has commanded that you present yourself as the gods made you. Did you have sandals on your feet when you came forth from your lady mother's womb?"

"No, septa," the queen was forced to say.

"Then you have your answer."

A bell began to toll. The queen's long imprisonment was at an end. Cersei pulled the robe tighter, grateful for its warmth, and said, "Let us go." Her son awaited her across the city. The sooner she set out, the sooner she would see him.

The rough stone of the steps scraped her soles as Cersei Lannister made her descent. She had come to Baelor's Sept a queen, riding in a litter. She was leaving bald and barefoot. *But I am leaving. That is all that matters.*

The tower bells were singing, summoning the city to bear witness to her shame. The Great Sept of Baelor was crowded with faithful come for the dawn service, the sound of their prayers echoing off the dome overhead, but when the queen's procession made its appearance a sudden silence fell and a thousand eyes turned to follow her as she made her way down the aisle, past the place where her lord father had lain in state after his murder. Cersei swept by them, looking neither right nor left. Her bare feet slapped against the cold marble floor. She could feel the eyes. Behind their altars, the Seven seemed to watch as well.

In the Hall of Lamps, a dozen Warrior's Sons awaited her coming. Rainbow cloaks hung down their backs, and the crystals that crested their greathelms glittered in the lamplight. Their armor was silver plate polished to a mirror sheen, but underneath, she knew, every man of them wore a hair shirt. Their kite shields all bore the same device: a crystal sword shining in the darkness, the ancient badge of those the smallfolk called Swords.

Their captain knelt before her. "Perhaps Your Grace will recall me. I am Ser Theodan the True, and His High Holiness has given me command of your escort. My brothers and I will see you safely through the city."

Cersei's gaze swept across the faces of the men behind him. And there he was: Lancel, her cousin, Ser Kevan's son, who had once professed to love her, before he decided that he loved the gods more. *My blood and my betrayer.* She would not forget him. "You may rise, Ser Theodan. I am ready."

The knight stood, turned, raised a hand. Two of his men stepped to the towering doors and pushed them open, and Cersei walked through them into the open air, blinking at the sunlight like a mole roused from its burrow.

A gusty wind was blowing, and it set the bottom of her robe snapping and flapping at her legs. The morning air was thick with the old familiar stinks of King's Landing. She breathed in the scents of sour wine, bread baking, rotting fish and nightsoil, smoke and sweat and horse piss. No flower had ever smelled so sweet. Huddled in her robe, Cersei paused atop the marble steps as the Warrior's Sons formed up around her.

It came to her suddenly that she had stood in this very spot before, on the day Lord Eddard Stark had lost his head. *That was not supposed to happen. Joff was supposed to spare his life and send him to the Wall.* Stark's eldest son would have followed him as Lord of Winterfell, but Sansa would have stayed at court, a hostage. Varys and Littlefinger had worked out the terms, and Ned Stark had swallowed his precious honor and confessed his treason to save his daughter's empty little head. *I would have made Sansa a good marriage. A Lannister marriage. Not Joff, of course, but Lancel might have suited, or one of his younger brothers.* Petyr Baelish had offered to wed the girl himself, she recalled, but of course that was impossible; he was much too lowborn. *If Joff had only done as he was told,*

Winterfell would never have gone to war, and Father would have dealt with Robert's brothers.

Instead Joff had commanded that Stark's head be struck off, and Lord Slynt and Ser Ilyn Payne had hastened to obey. *It was just there,* the queen recalled, gazing at the spot. Janos Slynt had lifted Ned Stark's head by the hair as his life's blood flowed down the steps, and after that there was no turning back.

The memories seemed so distant. Joffrey was dead, and all Stark's sons as well. Even her father had perished. And here she stood on the steps of the Great Sept again, only this time it was her the mob was staring at, not Eddard Stark.

The wide marble plaza below was as crowded as it had been on the day that Stark had died. Everywhere she looked the queen saw eyes. The mob seemed to be equal parts men and women. Some had children on their shoulders. Beggars and thieves, taverners and tradesfolk, tanners and stableboys and mummers, the poorer sort of whore, all the scum had come out to see a queen brought low. And mingled in with them were the Poor Fellows, filthy, unshaven creatures armed with spears and axes and clad in bits of dinted plate, rusted mail, and cracked leather, under roughspun surcoats bleached white and blazoned with the seven-pointed star of the Faith. The High Sparrow's ragged army.

Part of her still yearned for Jaime to appear and rescue her from this humiliation, but her twin was nowhere to be seen. Nor was her uncle present. That did not surprise her. Ser Kevan had made his views plain during his last visit; her shame must not be allowed to tarnish the honor of Casterly Rock. No lions would walk with her today. This ordeal was hers and hers alone.

Septa Unella stood to her right, Septa Moelle to her left, Septa Scolera behind her. If the queen should bolt or balk, the three hags would drag her back inside, and this time they would see to it that she never left her cell.

Cersei raised her head. Beyond the plaza, beyond the sea of hungry eyes and gaping mouths and dirty faces, across the city, Aegon's High Hill rose in the distance, the towers and battlements of the Red Keep blushing pink in the light of the rising sun. *It is not so far.* Once she reached its gates, the worst of her travails would be over. She would have her son again. She would have her champion. Her uncle had promised her. *Tommen is waiting for me. My little king. I can do this. I must.*

Septa Unella stepped forward. "A sinner comes before you," she declared. "She is Cersei of House Lannister, queen dowager, mother to His Grace King Tommen, widow of His Grace King Robert, and she has committed grievous falsehoods and fornications."

Septa Moelle moved up on the queen's right. "This sinner has confessed her sins and begged for absolution and forgiveness. His High Holiness has commanded her to demonstrate her repentance by putting aside all pride and artifice and presenting herself as the gods made her before the good people of the city."

Septa Scolera finished. "So now this sinner comes before you with a humble heart, shorn of secrets and concealments, naked before the eyes of gods and men, to make her walk of atonement."

Cersei had been a year old when her grandfather died. The first thing her father had done on his ascension was to expel his own father's grasping, lowborn mistress from Casterly Rock. The silks and velvets Lord Tytos had lavished on her and the jewelry she had taken for herself had been stripped from her, and she had been sent forth naked to walk through the streets of Lannisport, so the west could see her for what she was.

Though she had been too young to witness the spectacle herself, Cersei had heard the stories growing up from the mouths of washerwomen and guardsmen who had been there. They spoke of how the woman had wept and begged, of the desperate way she clung to her garments when she was commanded to disrobe, of her futile efforts to cover her breasts and her sex with her hands as she hobbled barefoot and naked through the streets to exile. "Vain and proud she was, before," she remembered one guard saying, "so haughty you'd think she'd forgot she come from dirt. Once we got her clothes off her, though, she was just another whore."

If Ser Kevan and the High Sparrow thought that it would be the same with her, they were very much mistaken. Lord Tywin's blood was in her. *I am a lioness. I will not cringe for them.*

The queen shrugged off her robe.

She bared herself in one smooth, unhurried motion, as if she were back in her own chambers disrobing for her bath with no one but her bedmaids looking on. When the cold wind touched her skin, she shivered violently. It took all her strength of will not to try and hide herself with her hands, as her grandfather's whore had done. Her fingers tightened into fists, her nails digging into her palms. They were looking at her, all the hungry eyes. But what were they seeing? *I am beautiful,* she reminded himself. How many times had Jaime told her that? Even Robert had given her that much, when he came to her bed in his cups to pay her drunken homage with his cock.

They looked at Ned Stark the same way, though.

She had to move. Naked, shorn, barefoot, Cersei made a slow descent down the broad marble steps. Gooseprickles rose on her arms and legs. She held her chin high, as a queen should, and her escort fanned out ahead of her. The Poor Fellows shoved men aside to open a way through the crowd whilst the Swords fell in on either side of her. Septa Unella, Septa Scolera, and Septa Moelle followed. Behind them came the novice girls in white.

"*Whore!*" someone cried out. A woman's voice. Women were always the cruelest where other women were concerned.

Cersei ignored her. *There will be more, and worse. These creatures have no sweeter joy in life than jeering at their betters.* She could not silence them, so she must pretend she did not hear them. She would not see them either. She would keep her eyes on Aegon's High Hill across the city, on the towers of the Red Keep shimmering in the light. That was where she would find her salvation, if her uncle had kept his part of their bargain.

He wanted this. Him and the High Sparrow. And the little rose as well, I do not doubt. I have sinned and must atone, must parade my shame before the eyes of every beggar in the city. They think that this will break my pride, that it will make an end to me, but they are wrong.

Septa Unella and Septa Moelle kept pace with her, with Septa Scolera scurrying behind, ringing a bell. "*Shame,*" the old hag called, "*shame upon the sinner, shame, shame.*" Somewhere off to the right, another voice sang counterpoint to hers, some baker's boy shouting,

"Meat pies, three pence, hot meat pies here." The marble underfoot was cold and slick, and Cersei had to step carefully for fear of slipping. Their path took them past the statue of Baelor the Blessed, standing tall and serene upon his plinth, his face a study in benevolence. To look at him, you would never guess what a fool he'd been. The Targaryen dynasty had produced kings both bad and good, but none as beloved as Baelor, that pious gentle septon-king who loved the smallfolk and the gods in equal parts, yet imprisoned his own sisters. It was a wonder that his statue did not crumble at the sight of her bare breasts. Tyrion used to say that King Baelor was terrified of his own cock. Once, she recalled, he had expelled all the whores from King's Landing. He prayed for them as they were driven from the city gates, the histories said, but would not look at them.

"Harlot," a voice screamed. Another woman. Something flew out of the crowd. Some rotted vegetable. Brown and oozing, it sailed above her head to splash at the foot of one of the Poor Fellows. *I am not afraid. I am a lioness.* She walked on. "Hot pies," the baker's boy was crying. "Getcha hot pies here." Septa Scolera rang her bell, singing, "*Shame, shame, shame upon the sinner, shame, shame.*" The Poor Fellows went before them, forcing men aside with their shields, walling off a narrow path. Cersei followed where they led, her head held stiffly, her eyes on the far distance. Every step brought the Red Keep nearer. Every step brought her closer to her son and her salvation.

It seemed to take a hundred years to cross the plaza, but finally marble gave way to cobblestones beneath her feet, shops and stables and houses closed in all around them, and they began the descent of Visenya's Hill.

The going was slower here. The street was steep and narrow, the crowds jammed together tightly. The Poor Fellows shoved at those who blocked the way, trying to move them aside, but there was nowhere to go, and those in the back of the crowd were shoving back. Cersei tried to keep her head up, only to step in something slick and wet that made her slip. She might have fallen, but Septa Unella caught her arm and kept her on her feet. "Your Grace should watch where she sets her feet."

Cersei wrenched herself free. "Yes, septa," she said in a meek voice, though she was angry enough to spit. The queen walked on, clad only in gooseprickles and pride. She looked for the Red Keep, but it was hidden now, walled off from her gaze by the tall timbered buildings to either side. "*Shame, shame,*" sang Septa Scolera, her bell clanging. Cersei tried to walk faster, but soon came up against the backs of the Stars in front of her and had to slow her steps again. A man just ahead was selling skewers of roast meat from a cart, and the procession halted as the Poor Fellows moved him out of the way. The meat looked suspiciously like rat to Cersei's eyes, but the smell of it filled the air, and half the men around them were gnawing away with sticks in hand by the time the street was clear enough for her to resume her trek. "Want some, Your Grace?" one man called out. He was a big, burly brute with pig eyes, a massive gut, and an unkempt black beard that reminded her of Robert. When she looked away in disgust, he flung the skewer at her. It struck her on the leg and tumbled to the street, and the half-cooked meat left a smear of grease and blood down her thigh.

The shouting seemed louder here than on the plaza, perhaps because the mob was so much closer. "Whore" and "sinner" were most common, but "brotherfucker" and "cunt" and "traitor" were flung at her as well, and now and again she heard someone shout out for Stannis or Margaery. The cobbles underfoot were filthy, and there was so little space that the queen could not even walk around the puddles. *No one has ever died of wet feet,* she told herself. She wanted to believe the puddles were just rainwater, though horse piss was just as likely.

More refuse showered down from windows and balconies: half-rotted fruit, pails of beer, eggs that exploded into sulfurous stink when they cracked open on the ground. Then someone flung a dead cat over the Poor Fellows and Warrior's Sons alike. The carcass hit the cobbles so hard that it burst open, spattering her lower legs with entrails and maggots.

Cersei walked on. *I am blind and deaf, and they are worms,* she told herself. "*Shame, shame,*" the septas sang. "Chestnuts, hot roast chestnuts," a peddler cried. "Queen Cunt," a drunkard pronounced solemnly from a balcony above, lifting his cup to her in a mocking toast. "All hail the royal teats!" *Words are wind,* Cersei thought. *Words cannot harm me.*

Halfway down Visenya's Hill the queen fell for the first time, when her foot slipped in something that might have been nightsoil. When Septa Unella pulled her up, her knee was scraped and bloody. A ragged laugh rippled through the crowd, and some man shouted out an offer to kiss it and make it better. Cersei looked behind her. She could still see the great dome and seven crystal towers of the Great Sept of Baelor atop the hill. *Have I really come such a little way?* Worse, a hundred times worse, she had lost sight of the Red Keep. "Where . . . where . . . ?"

"Your Grace." The captain of her escort stepped up beside her. Cersei had forgotten his name. "You must continue. The crowd is growing unruly."

Yes, she thought. *Unruly.* "I am not afraid—"

"You should be." He yanked at her arm, pulling her along beside him. She staggered down the hill—downward, ever downward—wincing with every step, letting him support her. *It should be Jaime beside me.* He would draw his golden sword and slash a path right through the mob, carving the eyes out of the head of every man who dared to look at her.

The paving stones were cracked and uneven, slippery underfoot, and rough against her soft feet. Her heel came down on something sharp, a stone or piece of broken crockery. Cersei cried out in pain. "I asked for sandals," she spat at Septa Unella. "You could have given me sandals, you could have done that much." The knight wrenched at her arm again, as if she were some common serving wench. *Has he forgotten who I am?* She was the queen of Westeros; he had no right to lay rough hands on her.

Near the bottom of the hill, the slope gentled and the street began to widen. Cersei could see the Red Keep again, shining crimson in the morning sun atop Aegon's High Hill. *I must keep walking.* She wrenched free of Ser Theodan's grasp. "You do not need to drag me, ser." She limped on, leaving a trail of bloody footprints on the stones behind her.

She walked through mud and dung, bleeding, goosefleshed, hobbling. All around her was a babble of sound. "My wife has sweeter teats than those," a man shouted. A teamster cursed as the Poor Fellows ordered his wagon out of the way. "*Shame, shame, shame on the sinner,*" chanted the septas. "Look at this one," a whore called from a brothel window, lifting her skirts to the men below, "it's not had half as many cocks up it as hers." Bells were ringing, ringing, ringing. "That can't be the queen," a boy said, "she's saggy as my mum." *This is my penance,* Cersei told herself. *I have sinned most grievously, this is my atonement. It will be over soon, it will be behind me, then I can forget.*

The queen began to see familiar faces. A bald man with bushy side-whiskers frowned down from a window with her father's frown, and for an instant looked so much like Lord Tywin that she stumbled. A young girl sat beneath a fountain, drenched in spray, and stared at her with Melara Hetherspoon's accusing eyes. She saw Ned Stark, and beside him little Sansa with her auburn hair and a shaggy grey dog that might have been her wolf. Every child squirming through the crowd became her brother Tyrion, jeering at her as he had jeered when Joffrey died. And there was Joff as well, her son, her firstborn, her beautiful bright boy with his golden curls and his sweet smile, he had such lovely lips, he . . .

That was when she fell the second time.

She was shaking like a leaf when they pulled her to her feet. "Please," she said. "Mother have mercy. I confessed."

"You did," said Septa Moelle. "This is your atonement."

"It is not much farther," said Septa Unella. "See?" She pointed. "Up the hill, that's all."

Up the hill. That's all. It was true. They were at the foot of Aegon's High Hill, the castle above them.

"Whore," someone screamed.

"Brotherfucker," another voice added. "Abomination."

"Want a suck on this, Your Grace?" A man in a butcher's apron pulled his cock out of his breeches, grinning. It did not matter. She was almost home.

Cersei began to climb.

If anything, the jeers and shouts were cruder here. Her walk had not taken her through Flea Bottom, so its denizens had packed onto the lower slopes of Aegon's High Hill to see the show. The faces leering out at her from behind the shields and spears of the Poor Fellows seemed twisted, monstrous, hideous. Pigs and naked children were everywhere underfoot, crippled beggars and cutpurses swarmed like roaches through the press. She saw men whose teeth had been filed into points, hags with goiters as big as their heads, a whore with a huge striped snake draped about breasts and shoulders, a man whose cheeks and brow were covered with open sores that wept grey pus. They grinned and licked their lips and hooted at her as she went limping past, her breasts heaving with the effort of the climb. Some shouted obscene proposals, others insults. *Words are wind,* she thought, *words cannot hurt me. I am beautiful, the most beautiful woman in all Westeros, Jaime says so, Jaime would never lie to me. Even Robert, Robert never loved me, but he saw that I was beautiful, he wanted me.*

She did not feel beautiful, though. She felt old, used, filthy, ugly. There were stretch marks on her belly from the children she had borne, and her breasts were not as firm as they had been when she was younger. Without a gown to hold them up, they sagged against her chest. *I should not have done this. I was their queen, but now they've seen, they've seen, they've seen. I should never have let them see.* Gowned and crowned, she was a queen. Naked, bloody, limping, she was only a woman, not so very different from their wives, more like their mothers than their pretty little maiden daughters. *What have I done?*

There was something in her eyes, stinging, blurring her sight. She could not cry, she would not cry, the worms must never see her weep. Cersei rubbed her eyes with the heels of her hands. A gust of cold wind made her shiver violently.

And suddenly the hag was there, standing in the crowd with her pendulous teats and her warty greenish skin, leering with the rest, with malice shining from her crusty yellow eyes. "*Queen you shall be,*" she hissed, "*until there comes another, younger and more beautiful, to cast you down and take all you hold most dear.*"

And then there was no stopping the tears. They burned down the queen's cheeks like acid. Cersei gave a sharp cry, covered her nipples with one arm, slid her other hand down to hide her slit, and began to run, shoving her way past the line of Poor Fellows, crouching as she scrambled crab-legged up the hill. Partway up she stumbled and fell, rose, then fell again ten yards farther on. The next thing she knew she was crawling, scrambling uphill on all fours like a dog as the good folks of King's Landing made way for her, laughing and jeering and applauding her.

Then all at once the crowd parted and seemed to dissolve, and there were the castle gates before her, and a line of spearmen in gilded halfhelms and crimson cloaks. Cersei heard the gruff, familiar sound of her uncle growling orders and glimpsed a flash of white to either side as Ser Boros Blount and Ser Meryn Trant strode toward her in their pale plate and snowy cloaks. "My son," she cried. "Where is my son? Where is Tommen?"

"Not here. No son should have to bear witness to his mother's shame." Ser Kevan's voice was harsh. "Cover her up."

Then Jocelyn was bending over her, wrapping her in a soft clean blanket of green wool to cover her nakedness. A shadow fell across them both, blotting out the sun. The queen felt cold steel slide beneath her, a pair of great armored arms lifting her off the ground, lifting her up into the air as easily as she had lifted Joffrey when he was still a babe. *A giant,* thought Cersei, dizzy, as he carried her with great strides toward the gatehouse. She had heard that giants could still be found in the godless wild beyond the Wall. *That is just a tale. Am I dreaming?*

No. Her savior was real. Eight feet tall or maybe taller, with legs as thick around as trees, he had a chest worthy of a plow horse and shoulders that would not disgrace an ox. His armor was plate steel, enameled white and bright as a maiden's hopes, and worn over gilded mail. A greathelm hid his face. From its crest streamed seven silken plumes in the rainbow colors of the Faith. A pair of golden seven-pointed stars clasped his billowing cloak at the shoulders.

A white cloak.

Ser Kevan had kept his part of the bargain. Tommen, her precious little boy, had named her champion to the Kingsguard.

Cersei never saw where Qyburn came from, but suddenly he was there beside them, scrambling to keep up with her champion's long strides. "Your Grace," he said, "it is so good to have you back. May I have the honor of presenting our newest member of the Kingsguard? This is Ser Robert Strong."

"Ser Robert," Cersei whispered, as they entered the gates.

"If it please Your Grace, Ser Robert has taken a holy vow of silence," Qyburn said. "He has sworn that he will not speak until all of His Grace's enemies are dead and evil has been driven from the realm."

Yes, thought Cersei Lannister. *Oh, yes.*

TYRION

The pile of parchments was formidably high. Tyrion looked at it and sighed. "I had understood you were a band of brothers. Is this the love a brother bears a brother? Where is the trust? The friendship, the fond regard, the deep affection that only men who have fought and bled together can ever know?"

"All in time," said Brown Ben Plumm.

"After you sign," said Inkpots, sharpening a quill.

Kasporio the Cunning touched his sword hilt. "If you would like to start the bleeding now, I will happ'ly oblige you."

"How kind of you to offer," said Tyrion. "I think not."

Inkpots placed the parchments before Tyrion and handed him the quill. "Here is your ink. From Old Volantis, this. 'Twill last as long as proper maester's black. All you need do is sign and pass the notes to me. I'll do the rest."

Tyrion gave him a crooked grin. "Might I read them first?"

"If you like. They are all the same, by and large. Except for the ones at the bottom, but we'll get to those in due course."

Oh, I am sure we will. For most men, there was no cost to joining a company, but he was not most men. He dipped the quill into the inkpot, leaned over the first parchment, paused, looked up. "Would you prefer me to sign *Yollo* or *Hugor Hill*?"

Brown Ben crinkled up his eyes. "Would you prefer to be returned to Yezzan's heirs or just beheaded?"

The dwarf laughed and signed the parchment, *Tyrion of House Lannister.* As he passed it left to Inkpots, he riffled through the pile underneath. "There are . . . what, fifty? Sixty? I'd thought there were five hundred Second Sons."

"Five hundred thirteen at present," Inkpots said. "When you sign our book, we will be five hundred fourteen."

"So only one in ten receives a note? That hardly seems fair. I thought you were all share-and-share-alike in the free companies." He signed another sheet.

Brown Ben chuckled. "Oh, all share. But not alike. The Second Sons are not unlike a family . . ."

". . . and every family has its drooling cousins." Tyrion signed another note. The parchment crinkled crisply as he slid it toward the paymaster. "There are cells down in the bowels of Casterly Rock where my lord father kept the worst of ours." He dipped his quill in the inkpot. *Tyrion of House Lannister,* he scratched out, promising to pay the bearer of the note one hundred golden dragons. *Every stroke of the quill leaves me a little poorer . . . or would, if I were not a beggar to begin with.* One day he might rue these signatures. *But not this day.* He blew on the wet ink, slid the parchment to the paymaster, and signed the one beneath. And again. And again. And again. "This wounds me deeply, I will have you know," he told them between signatures. "In Westeros, the word of a Lannister is considered good as gold."

Inkpots shrugged. "This is not Westeros. On this side of the narrow sea, we put our promises on paper." As each sheet was passed to him, he scattered fine sand across the signature to drink up excess ink, shook it off, and set the note aside. "Debts written on the wind tend to be . . . forgotten, shall we say?"

"Not by us." Tyrion signed another sheet. And another. He had found a rhythm now. "A Lannister always pays his debts."

Plumm chuckled. "Aye, but a sellsword's word is worthless."

Well, yours is, thought Tyrion, *and thank the gods for that.* "True, but I will not be a sellsword until I've signed your book."

"Soon enough," said Brown Ben. "After the notes."

"I am dancing as fast as I can." He wanted to laugh, but that would have ruined the game. Plumm was enjoying this, and Tyrion had no intention of spoiling his fun. *Let him go on thinking that he's bent me over and fucked me up the arse, and I'll go on buying steel swords with parchment dragons.* If ever he went back to Westeros to claim his birthright, he would have all the gold of Casterly Rock to make good on his promises. If not, well, he'd be dead, and his new brothers could wipe their arses with these parchments. Perhaps some might turn up in King's Landing with their scraps in hand, hoping to convince his sweet sister to make good on them. *And would that I could be a roach in the rushes to witness that.*

The writing on the parchments changed about halfway down the pile. The hundred-dragon notes were all for serjeants. Below them the amounts suddenly grew larger. Now Tyrion was promising to pay the bearer one thousand golden dragons. He shook his head, laughed, signed. And again. And again. "So," he said as he was scrawling, "what will be my duties with the company?"

"You are too ugly to be Bokkoko's butt boy," said Kasporio, "but you might do as arrow fodder."

"Better than you know," said Tyrion, refusing to rise to the bait. "A small man with a big shield will drive the archers mad. A wiser man than you once told me that."

"You will work with Inkpots," said Brown Ben Plumm.

"You will work *for* Inkpots," said Inkpots. "Keeping books, counting coin, writing contracts and letters."

"Gladly," said Tyrion. "I love books."

"What else would you do?" sneered Kasporio. "Look at you. You are not fit to fight."

"I once had charge of all the drains in Casterly Rock," Tyrion said mildly. "Some of them had been stopped up for years, but I soon had them draining merrily away." He dipped the quill in the ink again. Another dozen notes, and he would be done. "Perhaps I could supervise your camp followers. We can't have the men stopped up, now can we?"

That jape did not please Brown Ben. "Stay away from the whores," he warned. "Most o' them are poxy, and they talk. You're not the first escaped slave to join the company, but that don't mean we need to shout your presence. I won't have you parading about where you might be seen. Stay inside as much as you can, and shit into your bucket. Too many eyes at the latrines. And never go beyond our camp without my leave. We can dress you up in squire's steel, pretend you're Jorah's butt boy, but there's some will see right through that. Once Meereen is taken and we're away to Westeros, you can prance about all you like in gold and crimson. Till then, though . . ."

". . . I shall live beneath a rock and never make a sound. You have my word on that." *Tyrion of House Lannister*, he signed once more, with a flourish. That was the last parchment. Three notes remained, different from the rest. Two were written on fine vellum and made out by name. For Kasporio the Cunning, ten thousand dragons. The same for Inkpots, whose true name appeared to be Tybero Istarion. "*Tybero?*" said Tyrion. "That sounds almost Lannister. Are you some long-lost cousin?"

"Perhaps. I always pay my debts as well. It is expected of a paymaster. Sign."

He signed.

Brown Ben's note was the last. That one had been inscribed upon a sheepskin scroll. *One hundred thousand golden dragons, fifty hides of fertile land, a castle, and a lordship. Well and well. This Plumm does not come cheaply.* Tyrion plucked at his scar and wondered if he ought to make a show of indignation. When you bugger a man you expect a squeal or two. He could curse and swear and rant of robbery, refuse to sign for a time, then give in reluctantly, protesting all the while. But he was sick of mummery, so instead he grimaced, signed, and handed the scroll back to Brown Ben. "Your cock is as big as in the stories," he said. "Consider me well and truly fucked, Lord Plumm."

Brown Ben blew on his signature. "My pleasure, Imp. And now, we make you one o' us. Inkpots, fetch the book."

The book was leather-bound with iron hinges, and large enough to eat your supper off. Inside its heavy wooden boards were names and dates going back more than a century. "The Second Sons are amongst the oldest of the free companies," Inkpots said as he was turning pages. "This is the fourth book. The names of every man to serve with us are written here. When they joined, where they fought, how long they served, the manner of their deaths—all in the book. You will find famous names in here, some from your Seven Kingdoms. Aegor Rivers served a year with us, before he left to found the Golden Company. Bittersteel, you call him. The Bright Prince, Aerion Targaryen, he was a Second Son. And Rodrik Stark, the Wandering Wolf, him as well. No, not that ink. Here, use this." He unstoppered a new pot and set it down.

Tyrion cocked his head. "Red ink?"

"A tradition of the company," Inkpots explained. "There was a time when each new man wrote his name in his own blood, but as it happens, blood makes piss-poor ink."

"Lannisters love tradition. Lend me your knife."

Inkpots raised an eyebrow, shrugged, slipped his dagger from its sheath, and handed it across hiltfirst. *It still hurts, Halfmaester, thank you very much*, thought Tyrion, as he pricked the ball of his thumb. He squeezed a fat drop of blood into the inkpot, traded the dagger for a fresh quill, and scrawled, *Tyrion of House Lannister, Lord of Casterly Rock,* in a big bold hand, just below Jorah Mormont's far more modest signature.

And it's done. The dwarf rocked back on the camp stool. "Is that all that you require of me? Don't I need to swear an oath? Kill a baby? Suck the captain's cock?"

"Suck whatever you like." Inkpots turned the book around and dusted the page with a bit of fine sand. "For most of us, the signature suffices, but I would hate to disappoint a new brother-in-arms. Welcome to the Second Sons, Lord Tyrion."

Lord Tyrion. The dwarf liked the sound of that. The Second Sons might not enjoy the shining reputation of the Golden Company, but they had won some famous victories over the centuries. "Have other lords served with the company?"

"Landless lords," said Brown Ben. "Like you, Imp."

Tyrion hopped down from the stool. "My previous brother was entirely unsatisfactory. I hope for more from my new ones. Now how do I go about securing arms and armor?"

"Will you want a pig to ride as well?" asked Kasporio.

"Why, I did not know your wife was in the company," said Tyrion. "That's kind of you to offer her, but I would prefer a horse."

The bravo reddened, but Inkpots laughed aloud and Brown Ben went so far as to chuckle. "Inkpots, show him to the wagons. He can have his pick from the company steel. The girl too. Put a helm on her, a bit o' mail, might be some will take her for a boy."

"Lord Tyrion, with me." Inkpots held the tent flap to let him waddle through. "I will have Snatch take you to the wagons. Get your woman and meet him by the cook tent."

"She is not my woman. Perhaps you should get her. All she does of late is sleep and glare at me."

"You need to beat her harder and fuck her more often," the paymaster offered helpfully. "Bring her, leave her, do what you will. Snatch will not care. Come find me when you have your armor, and I will start you on the ledgers."

"As you wish."

Tyrion found Penny asleep in a corner of their tent, curled up on a thin straw pallet beneath a heap of soiled bedclothes. When he touched her with the toe of his boot, she rolled over, blinked at him, and yawned. "Hugor? What is it?"

"Talking again, are we?" It was better than her usual sullen silence. *All over an abandoned dog and pig. I saved the two of us from slavery, you would think some gratitude might be in order.* "If you sleep any longer, you're like to miss the war."

"I'm sad." She yawned again. "And tired. So tired."

Tired or sick? Tyrion knelt beside her pallet. "You look pale." He felt her brow. *Is it hot in here, or does she have a touch of fever?* He dared not ask that question aloud. Even hard men like the Second Sons were terrified of mounting the pale mare. If they thought Penny was sick, they would drive her off without a moment's hesitation. *They might even return us to Yezzan's heirs, notes or no notes.* "I have signed their book. The old way, in blood. I am now a Second Son."

Penny sat up, rubbing the sleep from her eyes. "What about me? Can I sign too?"

"I think not. Some free companies have been known to take women, but . . . well, they are not Second Daughters, after all."

"*We*," she said. "If you're one of them, you should say *we*, not *they*. Has anyone seen Pretty Pig? Inkpots said he'd ask after her. Or Crunch, has there been word of Crunch?"

Only if you trust Kasporio. Plumm's not-so-cunning second-in-command claimed that three Yunkish slave-catchers were prowling through the camps, asking after a pair of escaped dwarfs. One of them was carrying a tall spear with a dog's head impaled upon its point, the way that Kaspo told it. Such tidings were not like to get Penny out of bed, however. "No word as yet," he lied. "Come. We need to find some armor for you."

She gave him a wary look. "Armor? Why?"

"Something my old master-at-arms told me. 'Never go to battle naked, lad,' he said. I take him at his word. Besides, now that I'm a sellsword, I really ought to have a sword to sell." She still showed no signs of moving. Tyrion seized her by the wrist, pulled her to her feet, and threw a fistful of clothing into her face. "Dress. Wear the cloak with the hood and keep your head down. We're supposed to be a pair of likely lads, just in case the slave-catchers are watching."

Snatch was waiting by the cook tent chewing sourleaf when the two dwarfs turned up, cloaked and hooded. "I hear the two o' you are going to fight for us," the serjeant said. "That should have them pissing in Meereen. Either o' you ever killed a man?"

"I have," said Tyrion. "I swat them down like flies."

"What with?"

"An axe, a dagger, a choice remark. Though I'm deadliest with my crossbow."

Snatch scratched at his stubble with the point of his hook. "Nasty thing, a crossbow. How many men you kill with that?"

"Nine." His father counted for at least that many, surely. Lord of Casterly Rock, Warden of the West, Shield of Lannisport, Hand of the King, husband, brother, father, father, father.

"Nine." Snatch snorted and spat out a mouthful of red slime. Aiming for Tyrion's feet, perhaps, but it landed on his knee. Plainly that was what he thought of "nine." The serjeant's fingers were stained a mottled red from the juice of the sourleaf he chewed. He put two of them into his mouth and whistled. "*Kem!* Get over here, you fucking pisspot." Kem came running. "Take Lord and Lady Imp to the wagons, have Hammer fix them up with some company steel."

"Hammer might be passed-out drunk," Kem cautioned.

"Piss in his face. That'll wake him up." Snatch turned back to Tyrion and Penny. "We never had no bloody dwarfs before, but boys we never lacked for. Sons o' this whore or that one, little fools run off from home to have adventures, butt boys, squires, and the like. Some o' their shit might be small enough to fit imps. It's the shit they were wearing when they died, like as not, but I know that won't bother fuckers fierce as you two. Nine, was it?" He shook his head and walked away.

The Second Sons kept their company armor in six big wayns drawn up near the center of their camp. Kem led the way, swinging his spear as if it were a staff. "How does a King's Landing lad end up with a free company?" Tyrion asked him.

The lad gave him a wary squint. "Who told you I was from King's Landing?"

"No one." *Every word out of your mouth reeks of Flea Bottom.* "Your wits gave you away. There's no one clever as a Kingslander, they say."

That seemed to startle him. "Who says that?"

"Everyone." *Me.*

"Since when?"

Since I just made it up. "For ages," he lied. "My father was wont to say it. Did you know Lord Tywin, Kem?"

"The Hand. Once I saw him riding up the hill. His men had red cloaks and little lions on their helms. I liked those helms." His mouth tightened. "I never liked the Hand, though. He sacked the city. And then he smashed us on the Blackwater."

"You were there?"

"With Stannis. Lord Tywin come up with Renly's ghost and took us in the flank. I dropped my spear and ran, but at the ships this bloody knight said, 'Where's your spear, boy? We got no room for cravens,' and they buggered off and left me, and thousands more besides. Later I heard how your father was sending them as fought with Stannis to the Wall, so I made my way across the narrow sea and joined up with the Second Sons."

"Do you miss King's Landing?"

"Some. I miss this boy, he . . . he was a friend of mine. And my brother, Kennet, but he died on the bridge of ships."

"Too many good men died that day." Tyrion's scar was itching fiercely. He picked at it with a fingernail.

"I miss the food too," Kem said wistfully.

"Your mother's cooking?"

"Rats wouldn't eat my mother's cooking. There was this pot shop, though. No one ever made a bowl o' brown like them. So thick you could stand your spoon up in the bowl, with chunks of this and that. You ever have yourself a bowl o' brown, Halfman?"

"A time or two. Singer's stew, I call it."

"Why's that?"

"It tastes so good it makes me want to sing."

Kem liked that. "Singer's stew. I'll ask for that next time I get back to Flea Bottom. What do you miss, Halfman?"

Jaime, thought Tyrion. *Shae. Tysha. My wife, I miss my wife, the wife I hardly knew.* "Wine, whores, and wealth," he answered. "Especially the wealth. Wealth will buy you wine and whores." *It will also buy you swords, and the Kems to wield them.*

"Is it true the chamber pots in Casterly Rock are made of solid gold?" Kem asked him.

"You should not believe everything you hear. Especially where House Lannister is concerned."

"They say all Lannisters are twisty snakes."

"Snakes?" Tyrion laughed. "That sound you hear is my lord father, slithering in his grave. We are *lions*, or so we like to say. But it makes no matter, Kem. Step on a snake or a lion's tail, you'll end up just as dead."

By then they had reached the armory, such as it was. The smith, this fabled Hammer, proved to be a freakish-looking hulk with a left arm that appeared twice as thick as his right. "He's drunk more than not," Kem said. "Brown Ben lets it go, but one day we'll get us a real armorer." Hammer's apprentice was a wiry red-haired youth called

Nail. *Of course. What else?* mused Tyrion. Hammer was sleeping off
a drunk when they reached the forge, just as Kem had prophesied,
but Nail had no objection to the two dwarfs clambering through the
wagons. "Crap iron, most of it," he warned them, "but you're welcome
to anything you can use."

Under roofs of bent wood and stiffened leather, the wagon beds
were heaped high with old weaponry and armor. Tyrion took one
look and sighed, remembering the gleaming racks of swords and
spears and halberds in the armory of the Lannisters below Casterly
Rock. "This may take a while," he declared.

"There's sound steel here if you can find it," a deep voice growled.
"None of it is pretty, but it will stop a sword."

A big knight stepped down from the back of a wagon, clad head
to heel in company steel. His left greave did not match his right, his
gorget was spotted with rust, his vambraces rich and ornate, inlaid
with niello flowers. On his right hand was a gauntlet of lobstered
steel, on his left a fingerless mitt of rusted mail. The nipples on his
muscled breastplate had a pair of iron rings through them. His
greathelm sported a ram's horns, one of which was broken.

When he took it off, he revealed the battered face of Jorah
Mormont.

*He looks every inch a sellsword and not at all like the half-broken
thing we took from Yezzan's cage,* Tyrion reflected. His bruises had
mostly faded by now, and the swelling in his face had largely subsided,
so Mormont looked almost human once again . . . though only vaguely
like himself. The demon's mask the slavers had burned into his
right cheek to mark him for a dangerous and disobedient slave would
never leave him. Ser Jorah had never been what one might call a
comely man. The brand had transformed his face into something
frightening.

Tyrion grinned. "As long as I look prettier than you, I will be
happy." He turned to Penny. "You take that wagon. I'll start with this
one."

"It will go faster if we look together." She plucked up a rusted iron
halfhelm, giggled, and stuck it on her head. "Do I look fearsome?"

You look like a mummer girl with a pot on her head. "That's a halfhelm. You want a greathelm." He found one, and swapped it for the halfhelm.

"It's too big." Penny's voice echoed hollowly inside the steel. "I can't see out." She took the helm off and flung it aside. "What's wrong with the halfhelm?"

"It's open-faced." Tyrion pinched her nose. "I am fond of looking at your nose. I would rather that you kept it."

Her eyes got big. "You like my nose?"

Oh, Seven save me. Tyrion turned away and began rooting amongst some piles of old armor toward the back of the wagon.

"Are there any other parts of me you like?" Penny asked.

Perhaps she meant that to sound playful. It sounded sad instead. "I am fond of all of your parts," Tyrion said, in hopes of ending any further discussion of the subject, "and even fonder of mine own."

"Why should we need armor? We're only mummers. We just *pretend* to fight."

"You pretend very well," said Tyrion, examining a shirt of heavy iron mail so full of holes that it almost looked moth-eaten. *What sort of moths eat chainmail?* "Pretending to be dead is one way to survive a battle. Good armor is another." *Though there is precious little of that here, I fear.* At the Green Fork, he had fought in mismatched scraps of plate from Lord Lefford's wagons, with a spiked bucket helm that made it look as if someone had upended a slops pail over his head. This company steel was worse. Not just old and ill fitting, but dinted, cracked, and brittle. *Is that dried blood, or only rust?* He sniffed at it but still could not be sure.

"Here's a crossbow." Penny showed it to him.

Tyrion glanced at it. "I cannot use a stirrup winch. My legs are not long enough. A crank would serve me better." Though, if truth be told, he did not want a crossbow. They took too long to reload. Even if he lurked by the latrine ditch waiting for some enemy to take a squat, the chances of his losing more than one quarrel would not be good.

Instead he picked up a morningstar, gave it a swing, put it down again. *Too heavy.* He passed over a warhammer (too long), a studded mace (also too heavy), and half a dozen longswords before he found a dirk he liked, a nasty piece of steel with a triangular blade. "This might serve," he said. The blade had a bit of rust on it, but that would only make it nastier. He found a wood-and-leather sheath that fit and slipped the dirk inside.

"A little sword for a little man?" joked Penny.

"It's a dirk and made for a big man." Tyrion showed her an old longsword. "This is a sword. Try it."

Penny took it, swung it, frowned. "Too heavy."

"Steel weighs more than wood. Chop through a man's neck with that thing, though, and his head is not like to turn into a melon." He took the sword back from her and inspected it more closely. "Cheap steel. And notched. Here, see? I take back what I said. You need a better blade to hack off heads."

"I don't *want* to hack off heads."

"Nor should you. Keep your cuts below the knee. Calf, hamstring, ankle . . . even giants fall if you slice their feet off. Once they're down, they're no bigger than you."

Penny looked as though she was about to cry. "Last night I dreamed my brother was alive again. We were jousting before some great lord, riding Crunch and Pretty Pig, and men were throwing roses at us. We were so happy . . ."

Tyrion slapped her.

It was a soft blow, all in all, a little flick of the wrist, with hardly any force behind it. It did not even leave a mark upon her cheek. But her eyes filled with tears all the same.

"If you want to dream, go back to sleep," he told her. "When you wake up, we'll still be escaped slaves in the middle of a siege. Crunch is dead. The pig as well, most like. Now find some armor and put it on, and never mind where it pinches. The mummer show is over. Fight or hide or shit yourself, as you like, but whatever you decide to do, you'll do it clad in steel."

Penny touched the cheek he'd slapped. "We should never have run. We're not sellswords. We're not any kind of swords. It wasn't so bad with Yezzan. It wasn't. Nurse was cruel sometimes but Yezzan never was. We were his favorites, his . . . his . . ."

"*Slaves*. The word you want is *slaves*."

"Slaves," she said, flushing. "We were his *special* slaves, though. Just like Sweets. His treasures."

His pets, thought Tyrion. *And he loved us so much that he sent us to the pit, to be devoured by lions.*

She was not all wrong. Yezzan's slaves ate better than many peasants back in the Seven Kingdoms and were less like to starve to death come winter. Slaves were chattels, aye. They could be bought and sold, whipped and branded, used for the carnal pleasure of their owners, bred to make more slaves. In that sense they were no more than dogs or horses. But most lords treated their dogs and horses well enough. Proud men might shout that they would sooner die free than live as slaves, but pride was cheap. When the steel struck the flint, such men were rare as dragon's teeth; elsewise the world would not have been so full of slaves. *There has never been a slave who did not choose to be a slave*, the dwarf reflected. *Their choice may be between bondage and death, but the choice is always there.*

Tyrion Lannister did not except himself. His tongue had earned him some stripes on the back in the beginning, but soon enough he had learned the tricks of pleasing Nurse and the noble Yezzan. Jorah Mormont had fought longer and harder, but he would have come to the same place in the end.

And Penny, well . . .

Penny had been searching for a new master since the day her brother Groat had lost his head. *She wants someone to take care of her, someone to tell her what to do.*

It would have been too cruel to say so, however. Instead Tyrion said, "Yezzan's special slaves did not escape the pale mare. They're dead, the lot of them. Sweets was the first to go." Their mammoth master had died on the day of their escape, Brown Ben Plumm had told him. Neither he nor Kasporio nor any of the other sellswords knew the fate of the denizens of Yezzan's grotesquerie . . . but if Pretty Penny needed lies to stop her mooning, lie to her he would. "If you want to be a slave again, I will find you a kind master when this war is done, and sell you for enough gold to get me home," Tyrion promised her. "I'll find you some nice Yunkishman to give you another pretty golden collar, with little bells on it that will tinkle everywhere you go. First, though, you will need to survive what's coming. No one buys dead mummers."

"Or dead dwarfs," said Jorah Mormont. "We are all like to be feeding worms by the time this battle is done. The Yunkai'i have lost this war, though it may take them some time to know it. Meereen has an army of Unsullied infantry, the finest in the world. And Meereen has dragons. Three of them, once the queen returns. She will. She must. Our side consists of two score Yunkish lordlings, each with his own half-trained monkey men. Slaves on stilts, slaves in chains . . . they may have troops of blind men and palsied children too, I would not put it past them."

"Oh, I know," said Tyrion. "The Second Sons are on the losing side. They need to turn their cloaks again and do it now." He grinned. "Leave that to me."

THE KINGBREAKER

A pale shadow and a dark, the two conspirators came together in the quiet of the armory on the Great Pyramid's second level, amongst racks of spears, sheaves of quarrels, and walls hung with trophies from forgotten battles.

"Tonight," said Skahaz mo Kandaq. The brass face of a blood bat peered out from beneath the hood of his patchwork cloak. "All my men will be in place. The word is *Groleo*."

"Groleo." *That is fitting, I suppose.* "Yes. What was done to him . . . you were at court?"

"One guardsman amongst forty. All waiting for the empty tabard on the throne to speak the command so we might cut down Bloodbeard and the rest. Do you think the Yunkai'i would ever have dared present *Daenerys* with the head of her hostage?"

No, thought Selmy. "Hizdahr seemed distraught."

"Sham. His own kin of Loraq were returned unharmed. You saw. The Yunkai'i played us a mummer's farce, with noble Hizdahr as chief mummer. The issue was never Yurkhaz zo Yunzak. The other slavers would gladly have trampled that old fool themselves. This was to give Hizdahr a pretext to kill the dragons."

Ser Barristan chewed on that. "Would he dare?"

"He dared to kill his queen. Why not her pets? If we do not act, Hizdahr will hesitate for a time, to give proof of his reluctance and allow the Wise Masters the chance to rid him of the Stormcrow and the bloodrider. *Then* he will act. They want the dragons dead before the Volantene fleet arrives."

Aye, they would. It all fit. That did not mean Barristan Selmy liked it any better. "That will not happen." His queen was the Mother of Dragons; he would not allow her children to come to harm. "The hour of the wolf. The blackest part of night, when all the world's asleep." He had first heard those words from Tywin Lannister outside the walls of Duskendale. *He gave me a day to bring out Aerys. Unless I returned with the king by dawn of the following day, he would take the town with steel and fire, he told me. It was the hour of the wolf when I went in and the hour of the wolf when we emerged.* "Grey Worm and the Unsullied will close and bar the gates at first light."

"Better to attack at first light," Skahaz said. "Burst from the gates and swarm across the siege lines, smash the Yunkai'i as they come stumbling from their beds."

"No." The two of them had argued this before. "There is a peace, signed and sealed by Her Grace the queen. We will not be the first to break it. Once we have taken Hizdahr, we will form a council to rule in his place and demand that the Yunkai'i return our hostages and withdraw their armies. Should they refuse, then and only then will we inform them that the peace is broken, and go forth to give them battle. Your way is dishonorable."

"Your way is stupid," the Shavepate said. "The hour is ripe. Our freedmen are ready. Hungry."

That much was true, Selmy knew. Symon Stripeback of the Free Brothers and Mollono Yos Dob of the Stalwart Shields were both eager for battle, intent on proving themselves and washing out all the wrongs they had suffered in a tide of Yunkish blood. Only Marselen of the Mother's Men shared Ser Barristan's doubts. "We discussed this. You agreed it would be my way."

"I agreed," the Shavepate grumbled, "but that was before Groleo. The head. The slavers have no honor."

"We do," said Ser Barristan.

The Shavepate muttered something in Ghiscari, then said, "As you wish. Though we will rue your old man's honor before this game is done, I think. What of Hizdahr's guards?"

"His Grace keeps two men by him when he sleeps. One on the door of his bedchamber, a second within, in an adjoining alcove. Tonight it will be Khrazz and Steelskin."

"Khrazz," the Shavepate grumbled. "That I do not like."

"It need not come to blood," Ser Barristan told him. "I mean to talk to Hizdahr. If he understands we do not intend to kill him, he may command his guards to yield."

"And if not? Hizdahr must not escape us."

"He will not escape." Selmy did not fear Khrazz, much less Steelskin. They were only pit fighters. Hizdahr's fearsome collection of former fighting slaves made indifferent guards at best. Speed and strength and ferocity they had, and some skill at arms as well, but blood games were poor training for protecting kings. In the pits their foes were announced with horns and drums, and after the battle was done and won the victors could have their wounds bound up and quaff some milk of the poppy for the pain, knowing that the threat was past and they were free to drink and feast and whore until the next fight. But the battle was never truly done for a knight of the Kingsguard. Threats came from everywhere and nowhere, at any time of day or night. No trumpets announced the foe: vassals, servants, friends, brothers, sons, even wives, any of them might have knives concealed beneath their cloaks and murder hidden in their hearts. For every hour of fighting, a Kingsguard knight spent ten thousand hours watching, waiting, standing silent in the shadows. King Hizdahr's pit fighters were already growing bored and restive with their new duties, and bored men were lax, slow to react.

"I shall deal with Khrazz," said Ser Barristan. "Just make certain I do not need to deal with any Brazen Beasts as well."

"Have no fear. We will have Marghaz in chains before he can make mischief. I told you, the Brazen Beasts are mine."

"You say you have men amongst the Yunkishmen?"

"Sneaks and spies. Reznak has more."

Reznak cannot be trusted. He smells too sweet and feels too foul. "Someone needs to free our hostages. Unless we get our people back, the Yunkai'i will use them against us."

Skahaz snorted through the noseholes of his mask. "Easy to speak of rescue. Harder to do. Let the slavers threaten."

"And if they do more than threaten?"

"Would you miss them so much, old man? A eunuch, a savage, and a sellsword?"

Hero, Jhogo, and Daario. "Jhogo is the queen's bloodrider, blood of her blood. They came out of the Red Waste together. Hero is Grey Worm's second-in-command. And Daario . . ." *She loves Daario.* He had seen it in her eyes when she looked at him, heard it in her voice when she spoke of him. ". . . Daario is vain and rash, but he is dear to Her Grace. He must be rescued, before his Stormcrows decide to take matters into their own hands. It can be done. I once brought the queen's father safely out of Duskendale, where he was being held captive by a rebel lord, but . . ."

". . . you could never hope to pass unnoticed amongst the Yunkai'i. Every man of them knows your face by now."

I could hide my face, like you, thought Selmy, but he knew the Shavepate was right. Duskendale had been a lifetime ago. He was too old for such heroics. "Then we must needs find some other way. Some other rescuer. Someone known to the Yunkishmen, whose presence in their camp might go unnoticed . . ."

"Daario calls you Ser Grandfather," Skahaz reminded him. "I will not say what he calls me. If you and I were the hostages, would he risk his skin for us?"

Not likely, he thought, but he said, "He might."

"Daario might piss on us if we were burning. Elsewise do not look to him for help. Let the Stormcrows choose another captain, one who knows his place. If the queen does not return, the world will be one sellsword short. Who will grieve?"

"And when she does return?"

"She will weep and tear her hair and curse the Yunkai'i. Not us. No blood on our hands. You can comfort her. Tell her some tale of the old days, she likes those. Poor Daario, her brave captain . . . she will never forget him, no . . . but better for all of us if he is dead, yes? Better for Daenerys too."

Better for Daenerys, and for Westeros. Daenerys Targaryen loved her captain, but that was the girl in her, not the queen. *Prince Rhaegar loved his Lady Lyanna, and thousands died for it. Daemon Blackfyre loved the first Daenerys, and rose in rebellion when denied her. Bittersteel and Bloodraven both loved Shiera Seastar, and the Seven Kingdoms bled. The Prince of Dragonflies loved Jenny of Oldstones so much he cast aside a crown, and Westeros paid the bride price in corpses.* All three of the sons of the fifth Aegon had wed for love, in defiance of their father's wishes. And because that unlikely monarch had himself followed his heart when he chose his queen, he allowed his sons to have their way, making bitter enemies where he might have had fast friends. Treason and turmoil followed, as night follows day, ending at Summerhall in sorcery, fire, and grief.

Her love for Daario is poison. A slower poison than the locusts, but in the end as deadly. "There is still Jhogo," Ser Barristan said. "Him, and Hero. Both precious to Her Grace."

"We have hostages as well," Skahaz Shavepate reminded him. "If the slavers kill one of ours, we kill one of theirs."

For a moment Ser Barristan did not know whom he meant. Then it came to him. "The queen's cupbearers?"

"*Hostages,*" insisted Skahaz mo Kandaq. "Grazdar and Qezza are the blood of the Green Grace. Mezzara is of Merreq, Kezmya is Pahl, Azzak Ghazeen. Bhakaz is Loraq, Hizdahr's own kin. All are sons and daughters of the pyramids. Zhak, Quazzar, Uhlez, Hazkar, Dhazak, Yherizan, all children of Great Masters."

"Innocent girls and sweet-faced boys." Ser Barristan had come to know them all during the time they served the queen, Grazhar with his dreams of glory, shy Mezzara, lazy Miklaz, vain, pretty Kezmya, Qezza with her big soft eyes and angel's voice, Dhazzar the dancer, and the rest. "Children."

"Children of the Harpy. Only blood can pay for blood."

"So said the Yunkishman who brought us Groleo's head."

"He was not wrong."

"I will not permit it."

"What use are hostages if they may not be touched?"

"Mayhaps we might offer three of the children for Daario, Hero, and Jhogo," Ser Barristan allowed. "Her Grace—"

"—is not here. It is for you and me to do what must be done. You know that I am right."

"Prince Rhaegar had two children," Ser Barristan told him. "Rhaenys was a little girl, Aegon a babe in arms. When Tywin Lannister took King's Landing, his men killed both of them. He served the bloody bodies up in crimson cloaks, a gift for the new king." *And what did Robert say when he saw them? Did he smile?* Barristan Selmy had been badly wounded on the Trident, so he had been spared the sight of Lord Tywin's gift, but oft he wondered. *If I had seen him smile over the red ruins of Rhaegar's children, no army on this earth could have stopped me from killing him.* "I will not suffer the murder of children. Accept that, or I'll have no part of this."

Skahaz chuckled. "You are a stubborn old man. Your sweet-faced boys will only grow up to be Sons of the Harpy. Kill them now or kill them then."

"You kill men for the wrongs they have done, not the wrongs that they may do someday."

The Shavepate took an axe down off the wall, inspected it, and grunted. "So be it. No harm to Hizdahr or our hostages. Will that content you, Ser Grandfather?"

Nothing about this will content me. "It will serve. The hour of the wolf. Remember."

"I am not like to forget, ser." Though the bat's brass mouth did not move, Ser Barristan could sense the grin beneath the mask. "Long has Kandaq waited for this night."

That is what I fear. If King Hizdahr was innocent, what they did this day would be treason. But how could he be innocent? Selmy had heard him urging Daenerys to taste the poisoned locusts, shouting at his men to slay the dragon. *If we do not act, Hizdahr will kill the dragons and open the gates to the queen's enemies. We have no choice in this.* Yet no matter how he turned and twisted this, the old knight could find no honor in it.

The rest of that long day raced past as swiftly as a snail.

Elsewhere, he knew, King Hizdahr was consulting with Reznak mo Reznak, Marghaz zo Loraq, Galazza Galare, and his other Meereenese advisors, deciding how best to respond to Yunkai's demands . . . but

Barristan Selmy was no longer a part of such councils. Nor did he have a king to guard. Instead he made the rounds of the pyramid from top to bottom, to ascertain that the sentries were all at their posts. That took most of the morning. He spent that afternoon with his orphans, even took up sword and shield himself to provide a sterner test for a few of the older lads.

Some of them had been training for the fighting pits when Daenerys Targaryen took Meereen and freed them from their chains. Those had had a good acquaintance with sword and spear and battle-axe even before Ser Barristan got hold of them. A few might well be ready. *The boy from the Basilisk Isles, for a start. Tumco Lho.* Black as maester's ink he was, but fast and strong, the best natural swordsman Selmy had seen since Jaime Lannister. *Larraq as well. The Lash.* Ser Barristan did not approve of his fighting style, but there was no doubting his skills. Larraq had years of work ahead of him before he mastered proper knightly weapons, sword and lance and mace, but he was deadly with his whip and trident. The old knight had warned him that the whip would be useless against an armored foe . . . until he saw how Larraq used it, snapping it around the legs of his opponents to yank them off their feet. *No knight as yet, but a fierce fighter.*

Larraq and Tumco were his best. After them the Lhazarene, the one the other boys called Red Lamb, though as yet that one was all ferocity and no technique. Perhaps the brothers too, three lowborn Ghiscari enslaved to pay their father's debts.

That made six. *Six out of twenty-seven.* Selmy might have hoped for more, but six was a good beginning. The other boys were younger for the most part, and more familiar with looms and plows and chamber pots than swords and shields, but they worked hard and learned quickly. A few years as squires, and he might have six more knights to give his queen. As for those who would never be ready, well, not every boy was meant to be a knight. *The realm needs candle-makers and innkeeps and armorers as well.* That was as true in Meereen as it was in Westeros.

As he watched them at their drills, Ser Barristan pondered raising Tumco and Larraq to knighthood then and there, and mayhaps the Red Lamb too. It required a knight to make a knight, and if something should go awry tonight, dawn might find him dead or in a dungeon. Who would dub his squires then? On the other hand, a young knight's repute derived at least in part from the honor of the man who conferred knighthood on him. It would do his lads no good at all if it was known that they were given their spurs by a traitor, and might well land them in the dungeon next to him. *They deserve better,* Ser Barristan decided. *Better a long life as a squire than a short one as a soiled knight.*

As the afternoon melted into evening, he bid his charges to lay down their swords and shields and gather round. He spoke to them about what it meant to be a knight. "It is chivalry that makes a true knight, not a sword," he said. "Without honor, a knight is no more than a common killer. It is better to die with honor than to live without it." The boys looked at him strangely, he thought, but one day they would understand.

Afterward, back at the apex of the pyramid, Ser Barristan found Missandei amongst piles of scrolls and books, reading. "Stay here tonight, child," he told her. "Whatever happens, whatever you see or hear, do not leave the queen's chambers."

"This one hears," the girl said. "If she may ask—"

"Best not." Ser Barristan stepped out alone onto the terrace gardens. *I am not made for this,* he reflected as he looked out over the sprawling city. The pyramids were waking, one by one, lanterns and torches flickering to life as shadows gathered in the streets below. *Plots, ploys, whispers, lies, secrets within secrets, and somehow I have become part of them.*

Perhaps by now he should have grown used to such things. The Red Keep had its secrets too. *Even Rhaegar.* The Prince of Dragonstone had never trusted him as he had trusted Arthur Dayne. Harrenhal was proof of that. *The year of the false spring.*

The memory was still bitter. Old Lord Whent had announced the tourney shortly after a visit from his brother, Ser Oswell Whent of the Kingsguard. With Varys whispering in his ear, King Aerys became convinced that his son was conspiring to depose him, that Whent's tourney was but a ploy to give Rhaegar a pretext for meeting with as many great lords as could be brought together. Aerys had not set foot outside the Red Keep since Duskendale, yet suddenly he announced that he would accompany Prince Rhaegar to Harrenhal, and everything had gone awry from there.

If I had been a better knight . . . if I had unhorsed the prince in that last tilt, as I unhorsed so many others, it would have been for me to choose the queen of love and beauty . . .

Rhaegar had chosen Lyanna Stark of Winterfell. Barristan Selmy would have made a different choice. Not the queen, who was not present. Nor Elia of Dorne, though she was good and gentle; had she been chosen, much war and woe might have been avoided. His choice would have been a young maiden not long at court, one of Elia's companions . . . though compared to Ashara Dayne, the Dornish princess was a kitchen drab.

Even after all these years, Ser Barristan could still recall Ashara's smile, the sound of her laughter. He had only to close his eyes to see her, with her long dark hair tumbling about her shoulders and those haunting purple eyes. *Daenerys has the same eyes.* Sometimes when the queen looked at him, he felt as if he were looking at Ashara's daughter . . .

But Ashara's daughter had been stillborn, and his fair lady had thrown herself from a tower soon after, mad with grief for the child she had lost, and perhaps for the man who had dishonored her at Harrenhal as well. She died never knowing that Ser Barristan had loved her. *How could she?* He was a knight of the Kingsguard, sworn to celibacy. No good could have come from telling her his feelings. *No good came from silence either. If I had unhorsed Rhaegar and crowned Ashara queen of love and beauty, might she have looked to me instead of Stark?*

He would never know. But of all his failures, none haunted Barristan Selmy so much as that.

The sky was overcast, the air hot, muggy, oppressive, yet there was something in it that made his spine tingle. *Rain,* he thought. *A storm is coming. If not tonight, upon the morrow.* Ser Barristan wondered if he would live to see it. *If Hizdahr has his own Spider, I am as good as dead.* Should it come to that, he meant to die as he had lived, with his longsword in his hand.

When the last light had faded in the west, behind the sails of the prowling ships on Slaver's Bay, Ser Barristan went back inside, summoned a pair of serving men, and told them to heat some water for a bath. Sparring with his squires in the afternoon heat had left him feeling soiled and sweaty.

The water, when it came, was only lukewarm, but Selmy lingered in the bath until it had grown cold and scrubbed his skin till it was raw. Clean as he had ever been, he rose, dried himself, and clad himself in whites. Stockings, smallclothes, silken tunic, padded jerkin, all fresh-washed and bleached. Over that he donned the armor that the queen had given him as a token of her esteem. The mail was gilded, finely wrought, the links as supple as good leather, the plate enameled, hard as ice and bright as new-fallen snow. His dagger went on one hip, his longsword on the other, hung from a white leather belt with golden buckles. Last of all he took down his long white cloak and fastened it about his shoulders.

The helm he left upon its hook. The narrow eye slit limited his vision, and he needed to be able to see for what was to come. The halls of the pyramid were dark at night, and foes could come at you from either side. Besides, though the ornate dragon's wings that adorned the helm were splendid to look upon, they could too easily catch a sword or axe. He would leave them for his next tourney if the Seven should grant him one.

Armed and armored, the old knight waited, sitting in the gloom of his small chamber adjoining the queen's apartments. The faces of all the kings that he had served and failed floated before him in the darkness, and the faces of the brothers who had served beside him in the Kingsguard as well. He wondered how many of them would have done what he was about to do. *Some, surely. But not all. Some would not have hesitated to strike down the Shavepate as a traitor.* Outside the pyramid, it began to rain. Ser Barristan sat along in the dark, listening. *It sounds like tears,* he thought. *It sounds like dead kings, weeping.*

Then it was time to go.

The Great Pyramid of Meereen had been built as an echo to the Great Pyramid of Ghis whose collossal ruins Lomas Longstrider had once visited. Like its ancient predecessor, whose red marble halls were now the haunt of bats and spiders, the Meereenese pyramid boasted three-and-thirty levels, that number being somehow sacred to the gods of Ghis. Ser Barristan began the long descent alone, his white cloak rippling behind him as he started down. He took the servants' steps, not the grand stairways of veined marble, but the narrower, steeper, straighter stairs hidden within the thick brick walls.

Twelve levels down he found the Shavepate waiting, his coarse features still hidden by the mask he had worn that morning, the blood bat. Six Brazen Beasts were with him. All were masked as insects, identical to one another.

Locusts, Selmy realized. "Groleo," he said.

"Groleo," one of the locusts replied.

"I have more locusts if you need them," said Skahaz.

"Six should serve. What of the men on the doors?"

"Mine. You will have no trouble."

Ser Barristan clasped the Shavepate by the arm. "Shed no blood unless you must. Come the morrow we will convene a council and tell the city what we've done and why."

"As you say. Good fortune to you, old man."

They went their separate ways. The Brazen Beasts fell in behind Ser Barristan as he continued his descent.

The king's apartments were buried in the very heart of the pyramid, on the sixteenth and seventeenth levels. When Selmy reached those floors, he found the doors to the interior of the pyramid chained shut, with a pair of Brazen Beasts posted as guards. Beneath the hoods of their patchwork cloaks, one was a rat, the other a bull.

"Groleo," Ser Barristan said.

"Groleo," the bull returned. "Third hall to the right." The rat unlocked the chain. Ser Barristan and his escort stepped through into a narrow, torchlit servants' corridor of red and black brick. Their footsteps echoed on the floors as they strode past two halls and took the third one to the right.

Outside the carved hardwood doors to the king's chambers stood Steelskin, a younger pit fighter, not yet regarded as of the first rank. His cheeks and brow were scarred with intricate tattoos in green and black, ancient Valyrian sorcerer's signs that supposedly made his flesh and skin as hard as steel. Similar markings covered his chest and arms, though whether they would actually stop a sword or axe remained to be seen.

Even without them, Steelskin looked formidable—a lean and wiry youth who overtopped Ser Barristan by half a foot. "Who goes there?" he called out, swinging his longaxe sideways to bar their way. When he saw Ser Barristan, with the brass locusts behind him, he lowered it again. "Old Ser."

"If it please the king, I must needs have words with him."

"The hour is late."

"The hour is late, but the need is urgent."

"I can ask." Steelskin slammed the butt of his longaxe against the door to the king's apartments. A slidehole opened. A child's eye appeared. A child's voice called through the door. Steelskin replied. Ser Barristan heard the sound of a heavy bar being drawn back. The door swung open.

"Only you," said Steelskin. "The beasts wait here."

"As you wish." Ser Barristan nodded to the locusts. One returned his nod. Alone, Selmy slipped through the door.

Dark and windowless, surrounded on all sides by brick walls eight feet thick, the chambers that the king had made his own were large and luxurious within. Great beams of black oak supported the high ceilings. The floors were covered with silk carpets out of Qarth. On the walls were priceless tapestries, ancient and much faded, depicting the glory of the Old Empire of Ghis. The largest of them showed the last survivors of a defeated Valyrian army passing beneath the yoke and being chained. The archway leading to the royal bedchamber was guarded by a pair of sandalwood lovers, shaped and smoothed and oiled. Ser Barristan found them distasteful, though no doubt they were meant to be arousing. *The sooner we are gone from this place, the better.*

An iron brazier gave the only light. Beside it stood two of the queen's cupbearers, Draqaz and Qezza. "Miklaz has gone to wake the king," said Qezza. "May we bring you wine, ser?"

"No. I thank you."

"You may sit," said Draqaz, indicating a bench.

"I prefer to stand." He could hear voices drifting through the archway from the bedchamber. One of them was the king's.

It was still a good few moments before King Hizdahr zo Loraq, Fourteenth of That Noble Name, emerged yawning, knotting the sash that closed his robe. The robe was green satin, richly worked with pearls and silver thread. Under it the king was quite naked. That was good. Naked men felt vulnerable and were less inclined to acts of suicidal heroism.

The woman Ser Barristan glimpsed peering through the archway from behind a gauzy curtain was naked as well, her breasts and hips only partially concealed by the blowing silk.

"Ser Barristan." Hizdahr yawned again. "What hour is it? Is there news of my sweet queen?"

"None, Your Grace."

Hizdahr sighed. " 'Your *Magnificence,*' please. Though at his hour, 'Your Sleepiness' would be more apt." The king crossed to the sideboard to pour himself a cup of wine, but only a trickle remained in the bottom of the flagon. A flicker of annoyance crossed his face. "Miklaz, wine. At once."

"Yes, Your Worship."

"Take Draqaz with you. One flagon of Arbor gold, and one of that sweet red. None of our yellow piss, thank you. And the next time I find my flagon dry, I may have to take a switch to those pretty pink cheeks of yours." The boy went running off, and the king turned back to Selmy. "I dreamed you found Daenerys."

"Dreams can lie, Your Grace."

" 'Your Radiance' would serve. What brings you to me at this hour, ser? Some trouble in the city?"

"The city is tranquil."

"Is it so?" Hizdahr looked confused. "Why have you come?"

"To ask a question. Magnificence, are you the Harpy?"

Hizdahr's wine cup slipped through his fingers, bounced off the carpet, rolled. "You come to my bedchamber in the black of night and ask me that? Are you mad?" It was only then that the king seemed to notice that Ser Barristan was wearing his plate and mail. "What . . . why . . . how dare you . . ."

"Was the poison your work, Magnificence?"

King Hizdahr backed away a step. "The locusts? That . . . that was the Dornishman. Quentyn, the so-called prince. Ask Reznak if you doubt me."

"Have you proof of that? Has Reznak?"

"No, else I would have had them seized. Perhaps I should do so in any case. Marghaz will wring a confession out of them, I do not doubt. They're all poisoners, these Dornish. Reznak says they worship snakes."

"They eat snakes," said Ser Barristan. "It was your pit, your box, your seats. Sweet wine and soft cushions, figs and melons and honeyed locusts. You provided all. You urged Her Grace to try the locusts but never tasted one yourself."

"I . . . hot spices do not agree with me. She was my wife. My queen. Why would I want to poison her?"

Was, he says. He believes her dead. "Only you can answer that, Magnificence. It might be that you wished to put another woman in her place." Ser Barristan nodded at the girl peering timidly from the bedchamber. "That one, perhaps?"

The king looked around wildly. "*Her?* She's nothing. A bedslave." He raised his hands. "I misspoke. Not a slave. A free woman. Trained in pleasure. Even a king has needs, she . . . she is none of your concern, ser. I would never harm Daenerys. Never."

"You urged the queen to try the locusts. I heard you."

"I thought she might enjoy them." Hizdahr retreated another step. "Hot and sweet at once."

"Hot and sweet and poisoned. With mine own ears I heard you commanding the men in the pit to kill Drogon. Shouting at them."

Hizdahr licked his lips. "The beast devoured Barsena's flesh. Dragons prey on men. It was killing, burning . . ."

". . . burning men who meant harm to your queen. Harpy's Sons, as like as not. Your friends."

"Not my friends."

"You say that, yet when you told them to stop killing they obeyed. Why would they do that if you were not one of them?"

Hizdahr shook his head. This time he did not answer.

"Tell me true," Ser Barristan said, "did you ever love her, even a little? Or was it just the crown you lusted for?"

"Lust? You dare speak to me of *lust*?" The king's mouth twisted in anger. "I lusted for the crown, aye . . . but not half so much as she lusted for her sellsword. Perhaps it was her precious captain who tried to poison her, for putting him aside. And if I had eaten of his locusts too, well, so much the better."

"Daario is a killer but not a poisoner." Ser Barristan moved closer to the king. "Are you the Harpy?" This time he put his hand on the hilt of his longsword. "Tell me true, and I promise you shall have a swift, clean death."

"You presume too much, ser," said Hizdahr. "I am done with these questions, and with you. You are dismissed from my service. Leave Meereen at once and I will let you live."

"If you are not the Harpy, give me his name." Ser Barristan pulled his sword from the scabbard. Its sharp edge caught the light from the brazier, became a line of orange fire.

Hizdahr broke. "Khrazz!" he shrieked, stumbling backwards toward his bedchamber. "Khrazz! *Khrazz!*"

Ser Barristan heard a door open, somewhere to his left. He turned in time to see Khrazz emerge from behind a tapestry. He moved slowly, still groggy from sleep, but his weapon of choice was in his hand: a Dothraki *arakh,* long and curved. A slasher's sword, made to deliver deep, slicing cuts from horseback. *A murderous blade against half-naked foes, in the pit or on the battlefield.* But here at close quarters, the *arakh*'s length would tell against it, and Barristan Selmy was clad in plate and mail.

"I am here for Hizdahr," the knight said. "Throw down your steel and stand aside, and no harm need come to you."

Khrazz laughed. "Old man. I will eat your heart." The two men were of a height, but Khrazz was two stone heavier and forty years younger, with pale skin, dead eyes, and a crest of bristly red-black hair that ran from his brow to the base of his neck.

"Then come," said Barristan the Bold.

Khrazz came.

For the first time all day, Selmy felt certain. *This is what I was made for,* he thought. *The dance, the sweet steel song, a sword in my hand and a foe before me.*

The pit fighter was fast, blazing fast, as quick as any man Ser Barristan had ever fought. In those big hands, the *arakh* became a whistling blur, a steel storm that seemed to come at the old knight from three directions at once. Most of the cuts were aimed at his head. Khrazz was no fool. Without a helm, Selmy was most vulnerable above the neck.

He blocked the blows calmly, his longsword meeting each slash and turning it aside. The blades rang and rang again. Ser Barristan retreated. On the edge of his vision, he saw the cupbearers watching with eyes as big and white as chicken eggs. Khrazz cursed and turned a high cut into a low one, slipping past the old knight's blade for once, only to have his blow scrape uselessly off a white steel greave. Selmy's answering slash found the pit fighter's left shoulder, parting the fine linen to bite the flesh beneath. His yellow tunic began to turn pink, then red.

"Only cowards dress in iron," Khrazz declared, circling. No one wore armor in the fighting pits. It was blood the crowds came for: death, dismemberment, and shrieks of agony, the music of the scarlet sands.

Ser Barristan turned with him. "This coward is about to kill you, ser." The man was no knight, but his courage had earned him that much courtesy. Khrazz did not know how to fight a man in armor. Ser Barristan could see it in his eyes: doubt, confusion, the beginnings of fear. The pit fighter came on again, screaming this time, as if sound could slay his foe where steel could not. The *arakh* slashed low, high, low again.

Selmy blocked the cuts at his head and let his armor stop the rest, whilst his own blade opened the pit fighter's cheek from ear to mouth, then traced a raw red gash across his chest. Blood welled from Khrazz's wounds. That only seemed to make him wilder. He seized the brazier with his off hand and flipped it, scattering embers and hot coals at Selmy's feet. Ser Barristan leapt over them. Khrazz slashed at his arm and caught him, but the *arakh* could only chip the hard enamel before it met the steel below.

"In the pit that would have taken your arm off, old man."

"We are not in the pit."

"*Take off that armor!*"

"It is not too late to throw down your steel. Yield."

"Die," spat Khrazz . . . but as he lifted his *arakh*, its tip grazed one of the wall hangings and hung. That was all the chance Ser Barristan required. He slashed open the pit fighter's belly, parried the *arakh* as it wrenched free, then finished Khrazz with a quick thrust to the heart as the pit fighter's entrails came sliding out like a nest of greasy eels.

Blood and viscera stained the king's silk carpets. Selmy took a step back. The longsword in his hand was red for half its length. Here and there the carpets had begun to smolder where some of the scattered coals had fallen. He could hear poor Qezza sobbing. "Don't be afraid," the old knight said. "I mean you no harm, child. I want only the king."

He wiped his sword clean on a curtain and stalked into the bedchamber, where he found Hizdahr zo Loraq, Fourteenth of His Noble Name, hiding behind a tapestry and whimpering. "Spare me," he begged. "I do not want to die."

"Few do. Yet all men die, regardless." Ser Barristan sheathed his sword and pulled Hizdahr to his feet. "Come. I will escort you to a cell." By now, the Brazen Beasts should have disarmed Steelskin. "You will be kept a prisoner until the queen returns. If nothing can be proved against you, you will not come to harm. You have my word as a knight." He took the king's arm and led him from the bedchamber, feeling strangely light-headed, almost drunk. *I was a Kingsguard. What am I now?*

Miklaz and Draqaz had returned with Hizdahr's wine. They stood in the open door, cradling the flagons against their chests and staring wide-eyed at the corpse of Khrazz. Qezza was still crying, but Jezhene had appeared to comfort her. She hugged the younger girl, stroking her hair. Some of the other cupbearers stood behind them, watching. "Your Worship," Miklaz said, "the noble Reznak mo Reznak says to t-tell you, come at once."

The boy addressed the king as if Ser Barristan were not there, as if there were no dead man sprawled upon the carpet, his life's blood slowly staining the silk red. *Skahaz was supposed to take Reznak into custody until we could be certain of his loyalty. Had something gone awry?* "Come where?" Ser Barristan asked the boy. "Where does the seneschal want His Grace to go?"

"Outside." Miklaz seemed to see him for the first time. "Outside, ser. To the t-terrace. To see."

"To see what?"

"D-d-dragons. The dragons have been loosed, ser."

Seven save us all, the old knight thought.

THE DRAGONTAMER

The night crept past on slow black feet. The hour of the bat gave way to the hour of the eel, the hour of the eel to the hour of ghosts. The prince lay abed, staring at his ceiling, dreaming without sleeping, remembering, imagining, twisting beneath his linen coverlet, his mind feverish with thoughts of fire and blood.

Finally, despairing of rest, Quentyn Martell made his way to his solar, where he poured himself a cup of wine and drank it in the dark. The taste was sweet solace on his tongue, so he lit a candle and poured himself another. *Wine will help me sleep*, he told himself, but he knew that was a lie.

He stared at the candle for a long time, then put down his cup and held his palm above the flame. It took every bit of will he had to lower it until the fire touched his flesh, and when it did he snatched his hand back with a cry of pain.

"Quentyn, are you mad?"

No, just scared. I do not want to burn. "Gerris?"

"I heard you moving about."

"I could not sleep."

"Are burns a cure for that? Some warm milk and a lullaby might serve you well. Or better still, I could take you to the Temple of the Graces and find a girl for you."

"A whore, you mean."

"They call them Graces. They come in different colors. The red ones are the only ones who fuck." Gerris seated himself across the table. "The septas back home should take up the custom, if you ask me. Have you noticed that old septas always look like prunes? That's what a life of chastity will do to you."

Quentyn glanced out at the terrace, where night's shadows lay thick amongst the trees. He could hear the soft sound of falling water. "Is that rain? Your whores will be gone."

"Not all of them. There are little snuggeries in the pleasure gardens, and they wait there every night until a man chooses them. Those who are not chosen must remain until the sun comes up, feeling lonely and neglected. We could console them."

"They could console me, is what you mean."

"That too."

"That is not the sort of consolation I require."

"I disagree. Daenerys Targaryen is not the only woman in the world. Do you want to die a man-maid?"

Quentyn did not want to die at all. *I want to go back to Yronwood and kiss both of your sisters, marry Gwyneth Yronwood, watch her flower into beauty, have a child by her. I want to ride in tourneys, hawk and hunt, visit with my mother in Norvos, read some of those books my father sends me. I want Cletus and Will and Maester Kedry to be alive again.* "Do you think Daenerys would be pleased to hear that I had bedded some whore?"

"She might be. Men may be fond of maidens, but women like a man who knows what he's about in the bedchamber. It's another sort of swordplay. Takes training to be good at it."

The gibe stung. Quentyn had never felt so much a boy as when he'd stood before Daenerys Targaryen, pleading for her hand. The thought of bedding her terrified him almost as much as her dragons had. What if he could not please her? "Daenerys has a paramour," he said defensively. "My father did not send me here to amuse the queen in the bedchamber. You know why we have come."

"You cannot marry her. She has a husband."

"She does not love Hizdahr zo Loraq."

"What has love to do with marriage? A prince should know better. Your father married for love, it's said. How much joy has he had of that?"

Little and less. Doran Martell and his Norvoshi wife had spent half their marriage apart and the other half arguing. It was the only rash thing his father had ever done, to hear some tell it, the only time he had followed his heart instead of his head, and he had lived to rue it. "Not all risks lead to ruin," he insisted. "This is my duty. My destiny." *You are supposed to be my friend, Gerris. Why must you mock my hopes? I have doubts enough without your throwing oil on the fire of my fear.* "This will be my grand adventure."

"Men die on grand adventures."

He was not wrong. That was in the stories too. The hero sets out with his friends and companions, faces dangers, comes home triumphant. Only some of his companions don't return at all. *The hero never dies, though. I must be the hero.* "All I need is courage. Would you have Dorne remember me as a failure?"

"Dorne is not like to remember any of us for long."

Quentyn sucked at the burned spot on his palm. "Dorne remembers Aegon and his sisters. Dragons are not so easily forgotten. They will remember Daenerys as well."

"Not if she's died."

"She lives." *She must.* "She is lost, but I can find her." *And when I do, she will look at me the way she looks at her sellsword. Once I have proven myself worthy of her.*

"From dragonback?"

"I have been riding horses since I was six years old."

"And you've been thrown a time or three."

"That never stopped me from getting back into the saddle."

"You've never been thrown off a thousand feet above the ground," Gerris pointed out. "And horses seldom turn their riders into charred bones and ashes."

I know the dangers. "I'll hear no more of this. You have my leave to go. Find a ship and run home, Gerris." The prince rose, blew the candle out, and crept back to his bed and its sweat-soaked linen sheets. *I should have kissed one of the Drinkwater twins, or maybe both of them.*

I should have kissed them whilst I could. I should have gone to Norvos to see my mother and the place that gave her birth, so she would know that I had not forgotten her. He could hear the rain falling outside, drumming against the bricks.

By the time the hour of the wolf crept upon them, the rain was falling steadily, slashing down in a hard, cold torrent that would soon turn the brick streets of Meereen into rivers. The three Dornishmen broke their fast in the predawn chill—a simple meal of fruit and bread and cheese, washed down with goat milk. When Gerris made to pour himself a cup of wine, Quentyn stopped him. "No wine. There will be time enough for drink afterward."

"One hopes," said Gerris.

The big man looked out toward the terrace. "I knew it would rain," he said in a gloomy tone. "My bones were aching last night. They always ache before it rains. The dragons won't like this. Fire and water don't mix, and that's a fact. You get a good cookfire lit, blazing away nice, then it starts to piss down rain and next thing your wood is sodden and your flames are dead."

Gerris chuckled. "Dragons are not made of wood, Arch."

"Some are. That old King Aegon, the randy one, he built wooden dragons to conquer us. That ended bad, though."

So may this, the prince thought. The follies and failures of Aegon the Unworthy did not concern him, but he was full of doubts and misgivings. The labored banter of his friends was only making his head ache. *They do not understand. They may be Dornish, but I am Dorne. Years from now, when I am dead, this will be the song they sing of me.* He rose abruptly. "It's time."

His friends got to their feet. Ser Archibald drained the last of his goat's milk and wiped the milk mustache from his upper lip with the back of a big hand. "I'll get our mummer's garb."

He returned with the bundle that they had collected from the Tattered Prince at their second meeting. Within were three long hooded cloaks made from myriad small squares of cloth sewn together, three cudgels, three shortswords, three masks of polished brass. A bull, a lion, and an ape.

Everything required to be a Brazen Beast.

"They may ask for a word," the Tattered Prince had warned them when he handed over the bundle. "It's *dog*."

"You are certain of that?" Gerris had asked him.

"Certain enough to wager a life upon it."

The prince did not mistake his meaning. "My life."

"That would be the one."

"How did you learn their word?"

"We chanced upon some Brazen Beasts and Meris asked them prettily. But a prince should know better than to pose such questions, Dornish. In Pentos, we have a saying. Never ask the baker what went into the pie. Just eat."

Just eat. There was wisdom in that, Quentyn supposed.

"I'll be the bull," Arch announced.

Quentyn handed him the bull mask. "The lion for me."

"Which makes a monkey out of me." Gerris pressed the ape mask to his face. "How do they breathe in these things?"

"Just put it on." The prince was in no mood for japes.

The bundle contained a whip as well—a nasty piece of old leather with a handle of brass and bone, stout enough to peel the hide off an ox. "What's that for?" Arch asked.

"Daenerys used a whip to cow the black beast." Quentyn coiled the whip and hung it from his belt. "Arch, bring your hammer as well. We may have need of it."

It was no easy thing to enter the Great Pyramid of Meereen by night. The doors were closed and barred each day at sunset and remained closed until first light. Guards were posted at every entrance, and more guards patrolled the lowest terrace, where they could look down on the street. Formerly those guards had been Unsullied. Now they were Brazen Beasts. And that would make all the difference, Quentyn hoped.

The watch changed when the sun came up, but dawn was still half an hour off as the three Dornishmen made their way down the servants' steps. The walls around them were made of bricks of half a hundred colors, but the shadows turned them all to grey until touched by the light of the torch that Gerris carried. They encountered no one on the long descent. The only sound was the scuff of their boots on the worn bricks beneath their feet.

The pyramid's main gates fronted on Meereen's central plaza, but the Dornishmen made their way to a side entrance opening on an alley. These were the gates that slaves had used in former days as they went about their masters' business, where smallfolk and tradesmen came and went and made their deliveries.

The doors were solid bronze, closed with a heavy iron bar. Before them stood two Brazen Beasts, armed with cudgels, spears, and short swords. Torchlight glimmered off the polished brass of their masks—a rat and a fox. Quentyn gestured for the big man to stay back in the shadows. He and Gerris strode forward together.

"You come early," the fox said.

Quentyn shrugged. "We can leave again, if you like. You're welcome to stand our watch." He sounded not at all Ghiscari, he knew; but half the Brazen Beasts were freed slaves, with all manner of native tongues, so his accent went unremarked.

"Bugger that," the rat remarked.

"Give us the day's word," said the fox.

"Dog," said the Dornishman.

The two Brazen Beasts exchanged a look. For three long heartbeats Quentyn was afraid that something had gone amiss, that somehow Pretty Meris and the Tattered Prince had gotten the word wrong. Then the fox grunted. "Dog, then," he said. "The door is yours." As they moved off, the prince began to breathe again.

They did not have long. The real relief would doubtless turn up shortly. "Arch," he called, and the big man appeared, the torchlight shining off his bull's mask. "The bar. Hurry."

The iron bar was thick and heavy, but well oiled. Ser Archibald had no trouble lifting it. As he was standing it on end, Quentyn pulled the doors open and Gerris stepped through, waving the torch. "Bring it in now. Be quick about it."

The butcher's wagon was outside, waiting in the alley. The driver gave the mule a lick and rumbled through, iron-rimmed wheels *clack*ing loudly over bricks. The quartered carcass of an ox filled the wagon bed, along with two dead sheep. Half a dozen men entered afoot. Five wore the cloaks and masks of Brazen Beasts, but Pretty Meris had not troubled to disguise herself. "Where is your lord?" he asked Meris.

"I have no *lord*," she answered. "If you mean your fellow prince, he is near, with fifty men. Bring your dragon out, and he will see you safe away, as promised. Caggo commands here."

Ser Archibald was giving the butcher's wagon the sour eye. "Will that cart be big enough to hold a dragon?" he asked.

"Should. It's held two oxen." The Corpsekiller was garbed as a Brazen Beast, his seamed, scarred face hidden behind a cobra mask, but the familiar black *arakh* slung at his hip gave him away. "We were told these beasts are smaller than the queen's monster."

"The pit has slowed their growth." Quentyn's readings had suggested that the same thing had occurred in the Seven Kingdoms. None of the dragons bred and raised in the Dragonpit of King's Landing had ever approached the size of Vhagar or Meraxes, much less that of the Black Dread, King Aegon's monster. "Have you brought sufficient chains?"

"How many dragons do you have?" said Pretty Meris. "We have chains enough for ten, concealed beneath the meat."

"Very good." Quentyn felt light-headed. None of this seemed quite real. One moment it felt like a game, the next like some nightmare, like a bad dream where he found himself opening a dark door, knowing that horror and death waited on the other side, yet somehow powerless to stop himself. His palms were slick with sweat. He wiped them on his legs and said, "There will be more guards outside the pit."

"We know," said Gerris.

"We need to be ready for them."

"We are," said Arch.

There was a cramp in Quentyn's belly. He felt a sudden need to move his bowels, but knew he dare not beg off now. "This way, then." He had seldom felt more like a boy. Yet they followed; Gerris and the big man, Meris and Caggo and the other Windblown. Two of the sellswords had produced crossbows from some hiding place within the wagon.

Beyond the stables, the ground level of the Great Pyramid became a labyrinth, but Quentyn Martell had been through here with the queen, and he remembered the way. Under three huge brick arches they went, then down a steep stone ramp into the depths, through the dungeons and torture chambers and past a pair of deep stone cisterns. Their footsteps echoed hollowly off the walls, the butcher's cart rumbling behind them. The big man snatched a torch down from a wall sconce to lead the way.

At last a pair of heavy iron doors rose before them, rust-eaten and forbidding, closed with a length of chain whose every link was as thick around as a man's arm. The size and thickness of those doors was enough to make Quentyn Martell question the wisdom of this course. Even worse, both doors were plainly dinted by something inside trying to get out. The thick iron was cracked and splitting in three places, and the upper corner of the left-hand door looked partly melted.

Four Brazen Beasts stood guarding the door. Three held long spears; the fourth, the serjeant, was armed with short sword and dagger. His mask was wrought in the shape of a basilisk's head. The other three were masked as insects.

Locusts, Quentyn realized. "Dog," he said.

The serjeant stiffened.

That was all it took for Quentyn Martell to realize that something had gone awry. "Take them," he croaked, even as the basilisk's hand darted for his shortsword.

He was quick, that serjeant. The big man was quicker. He flung the torch at the nearest locust, reached back, and unslung his warhammer. The basilisk's blade had scarce slipped from its leather sheath when the hammer's spike slammed into his temple, crunching through the thin brass of his mask and the flesh and bone beneath. The serjeant staggered sideways half a step before his knees folded under him and he sank down to the floor, his whole body shaking grotesquely.

Quentyn stared transfixed, his belly roiling. His own blade was still in its sheath. He had not so much as reached for it. His eyes were locked on the serjeant dying before him, jerking. The fallen torch was on the floor, guttering, making every shadow leap and twist in a monstrous mockery of the dead man's shaking. The prince never saw the locust's spear coming toward him until Gerris slammed into him, knocking him aside. The spearpoint grazed the cheek of the lion's head he wore. Even then the blow was so violent it almost tore the mask off. *It would have gone right through my throat,* the prince thought, dazed.

Gerris cursed as the locusts closed around him. Quentyn heard the sound of running feet. Then the sellswords came rushing from the shadows. One of the guards glanced at them just long enough for Gerris to get inside his spear. He drove the point of his sword under the brass mask and up through the wearer's throat, even as the second locust sprouted a crossbow bolt from his chest.

The last locust dropped his spear. "Yield. I yield."

"No. You die." Caggo took the man's head off with one swipe of his *arakh*, the Valyrian steel shearing through flesh and bone and gristle as if they were so much suet. "Too much noise," he complained. "Any man with ears will have heard."

"Dog," Quentyn said. "The day's word was supposed to be dog. Why wouldn't they let us pass? We were told . . ."

"You were told your scheme was madness, have you forgotten?" said Pretty Meris. "Do what you came to do."

The dragons, Prince Quentyn thought. *Yes. We came for the dragons.* He felt as though he might be sick. *What am I doing here? Father, why? Four men dead in as many heartbeats, and for what?* "Fire and blood," he whispered, "blood and fire." The blood was pooling at his feet, soaking into the brick floor. The fire was beyond those doors. "The chains . . . we have no key . . ."

Arch said, "I have the key." He swung his warhammer hard and fast. Sparks flew when the hammmerhead struck the lock. And then again, again, again. On his fifth swing the lock shattered, and the chains fell away in a rattling clatter so loud Quentyn was certain half the pyramid must have heard them. "Bring the cart." The dragons would be more docile once fed. *Let them gorge themselves on charred mutton.*

Archibald Yronwood grasped the iron doors and pulled them apart. Their rusted hinges let out a pair of screams, for all those who might have slept through the breaking of the lock. A wash of sudden heat assaulted them, heavy with the odors of ash, brimstone, and burnt meat.

It was black beyond the doors, a sullen stygian darkness that seemed alive and threatening, hungry. Quentyn could sense that there was something in that darkness, coiled and waiting. *Warrior, grant me courage,* he prayed. He did not want to do this, but he saw no other way. *Why else would Daenerys have shown me the dragons? She wants me to prove myself to her.* Gerris handed him a torch. He stepped through the doors.

The green one is Rhaegal, the white Viserion, he reminded himself. *Use their names, command them, speak to them calmly but sternly. Master them, as Daenerys mastered Drogon in the pit.* The girl had been alone, clad in wisps of silk, but fearless. *I must not be afraid. She did it, so can I.* The main thing was to show no fear. *Animals can smell fear, and dragons . . .* What did he know of dragons? *What does any man know of dragons? They have been gone from the world for more than a century.*

The lip of the pit was just ahead. Quentyn edged forward slowly, moving the torch from side to side. Walls and floor and ceiling drank the light. *Scorched,* he realized. *Bricks burned black, crumbling into ash.* The air grew warmer with every step he took. He began to sweat.

Two eyes rose up before him.

Bronze, they were, brighter than polished shields, glowing with their own heat, burning behind a veil of smoke rising from the dragon's nostrils. The light of Quentyn's torch washed over scales of dark green, the green of moss in the deep woods at dusk, just before the last light fades. Then the dragon opened its mouth, and light and heat washed over them. Behind a fence of sharp black teeth he glimpsed the furnace glow, the shimmer of a sleeping fire a hundred times brighter than his torch. The dragon's head was larger than a horse's, and the neck stretched on and on, uncoiling like some great green serpent as the head rose, until those two glowing bronze eyes were staring down at him.

Green, the prince thought, *his scales are green.* "Rhaegal," he said. His voice caught in his throat, and what came out was a broken croak. *Frog,* he thought, *I am turning into Frog again.* "The food," he croaked, remembering. "Bring the food."

The big man heard him. Arch wrestled one of the sheep off the wagon by two legs, then spun and flung it into the pit.

Rhaegal took it in the air. His head snapped round, and from between his jaws a lance of flame erupted, a swirling storm of orange-and-yellow fire shot through with veins of green. The sheep was burning before it began to fall. Before the smoking carcass could strike the bricks, the dragon's teeth closed round it. A nimbus of flames still flickered about the body. The air stank of burning wool and brimstone. *Dragonstink.*

"I thought there were two," the big man said.

Viserion. Yes. Where is Viserion? The prince lowered his torch to throw some light into the gloom below. He could see the green dragon ripping at the smoking carcass of the sheep, his long tail lashing from side to side as he ate. A thick iron collar was visible about his neck, with three feet of broken chain dangling from it. Shattered links were strewn across the floor of the pit amongst the blackened bones—twists of metal, partly melted. *Rhaegal was chained to the wall and floor the last time I was here,* the prince recalled, *but Viserion hung from the ceiling.* Quentyn stepped back, lifted the torch, craned his head back.

For a moment he saw only the blackened arches of the bricks above, scorched by dragonflame. A trickle of ash caught his eye, betraying movement. Something pale, half-hidden, stirring. *He's made himself a cave,* the prince realized. *A burrow in the brick.* The foundations of the Great Pyramid of Meereen were massive and thick to support the weight of the huge structure overhead; even the interior walls were three times thicker than any castle's curtain walls. But Viserion had dug himself a hole in them with flame and claw, a hole big enough to sleep in.

And we've just woken him. He could see what looked like some huge white serpent uncoiling inside the wall, up where it curved to become the ceiling. More ash went drifting downward, and a bit of crumbling brick fell away. The serpent resolved itself into a neck and tail, and then the dragon's long horned head appeared, his eyes glowing in the dark like golden coals. His wings rattled, stretching.

All of Quentyn's plans had fled his head. He could hear Caggo Corpsekiller shouting to his sellswords. *The chains, he is sending for the chains,* the Dornish prince thought. The plan had been to feed the beasts and chain them in their torpor, just as the queen had done. One dragon, or preferably both.

"More meat," Quentyn said. *Once the beasts were fed they will become sluggish.* He had seen it work with snakes in Dorne, but here, with these monsters . . . "Bring . . . bring . . ."

Viserion launched himself from the ceiling, pale leather wings unfolding, spreading wide. The broken chain dangling from his neck swung wildly. His flame lit the pit, pale gold shot through with red and orange, and the stale air exploded in a cloud of hot ash and sulfur as the white wings beat and beat again.

A hand seized Quentyn by the shoulder. The torch spun from his grip to bounce across the floor, then tumbled into the pit, still burning. He found himself face-to-face with a brass ape. *Gerris.* "Quent, this will not work. They are too wild, they . . ."

The dragon came down between the Dornishmen and the door with a roar that would have sent a hundred lions running. His head moved side to side as he inspected the intruders—Dornishmen, Windblown, Caggo. Last and longest the beast stared at Pretty Meris, sniffing. *The woman,* Quentyn realized. *He knows that she is female. He is looking for Daenerys. He wants his mother and does not understand why she's not here.*

Quentyn wrenched free of Gerris's grip. "Viserion," he called. *The white one is Viserion.* For half a heartbeat he was afraid he'd gotten it wrong. "Viserion," he called again, fumbling for the whip hanging from his belt. *She cowed the black one with a whip. I need to do the same.*

The dragon knew his name. His head turned, and his gaze lingered on the Dornish prince for three long heartbeats. Pale fires burned behind the shining black daggers of his teeth. His eyes were lakes of molten gold, and smoke rose from his nostrils.

"Down," Quentyn said. Then he coughed, and coughed again.

The air was thick with smoke and the sulfur stench was choking. Viserion lost interest. The dragon turned back toward the Windblown and lurched toward the door. Perhaps he could smell the blood of the dead guards or the meat in the butcher's wagon. Or perhaps he had only now seen that the way was open.

Quentyn heard the sellswords shouting. Caggo was calling for the chains, and Pretty Meris was screaming at someone to step aside. The dragon moved awkwardly on the ground, like a man scrabbling on his knees and elbows, but quicker than the Dornish prince would have believed. When the Windblown were too late to get out of his way, Viserion let loose with another roar. Quentyn heard the rattle of chains, the deep *thrum* of a crossbow.

"No," he screamed, "no, don't, *don't*," but it was too late. *The fool* was all that he had time to think as the quarrel caromed off Viserion's neck to vanish in the gloom. A line of fire gleamed in its wake—dragon's blood, glowing gold and red.

The crossbowman was fumbling for another quarrel as the dragon's teeth closed around his neck. The man wore the mask of a Brazen Beast, the fearsome likeness of a tiger. As he dropped his weapon to try and pry apart Viserion's jaws, flame gouted from the tiger's mouth. The man's eyes burst with soft popping sounds, and the brass around them began to run. The dragon tore off a hunk of flesh, most of the sellsword's neck, then gulped it down as the burning corpse collapsed to the floor.

The other Windblown were pulling back. This was more than even Pretty Meris had the stomach for. Viserion's horned head moved back and forth between them and his prey, but after a moment he forgot the sellswords and bent his neck to tear another mouthful from the dead man. A lower leg this time.

Quentyn let his whip uncoil. "Viserion," he called, louder this time. He could do this, he would do this, his father had sent him to the far ends of the earth for this, he would not fail him. "*VISERION!*" He snapped the whip in the air with a *crack* that echoed off the blackened walls.

The pale head rose. The great gold eyes narrowed. Wisps of smoke spiraled upward from the dragon's nostrils.

"Down," the prince commanded. *You must not let him smell your fear.* "Down, down, *down*." He brought the whip around and laid a lash across the dragon's face. Viserion *hiss*ed.

And then a hot wind buffeted him and he heard the sound of leathern wings and the air was full of ash and cinders and a monstrous

Giantsbane had roared to hear it. "Afraid of being carried off, is she? I hope you never said how big me member is, Jon Snow, that'd frighten any woman. I always wanted me one with a mustache." Then he laughed and laughed.

He would not be laughing now.

Jon had wasted enough time here. "I'm sorry to have troubled Your Grace. The Night's Watch will attend to this matter."

The queen's nostrils flared. "You still mean to ride to Hardhome. I see it on your face. *Let them die,* I said, yet you will persist in this mad folly. Do not deny it."

"I must do as I think best. With respect, Your Grace, the Wall is mine, and so is this decision."

"It is," Selyse allowed, "and you will answer for it when the king returns. And for other decisions you have made, I fear. But I see that you are deaf to sense. Do what you must."

Up spoke Ser Malegorn. "Lord Snow, who will lead this ranging?"

"Are you offering yourself, ser?"

"Do I look so foolish?"

Patchface jumped up. "I will lead it!" His bells rang merrily. "We will march into the sea and out again. Under the waves we will ride seahorses, and mermaids will blow seashells to announce our coming, oh, oh, oh."

They all laughed. Even Queen Selyse allowed herself a thin smile. Jon was less amused. "I will not ask my men to do what I would not do myself. I mean to lead the ranging."

"How bold of you," said the queen. "We approve. Afterward some bard will make a stirring song about you, no doubt, and we shall have a more prudent lord commander." She took a sip of wine. "Let us speak of other matters. Axell, bring in the wildling king, if you would be so good."

"At once, Your Grace." Ser Axell went through a door and returned a moment later with Gerrick Kingsblood. "Gerrick of House Redbeard," he announced, "King of the Wildlings."

Gerrick Kingsblood was a tall man, long of leg and broad of shoulder. The queen had dressed him in some of the king's old clothes, it appeared. Scrubbed and groomed, clad in green velvets and an ermine half-cape, with his long red hair freshly washed and his fiery beard shaped and trimmed, the wildling looked every inch a southron lord. *He could walk into the throne room at King's Landing, and no one would blink an eye*, Jon thought.

"Gerrick is the true and rightful king of the wildlings," the queen said, "descended in an unbroken male line from their great king Raymun Redbeard, whereas the usurper Mance Rayder was born of some common woman and fathered by one of your black brothers."

No, Jon might have said, *Gerrick is descended from a younger brother of Raymun Redbeard*. To the free folk that counted about as much as being descended from Raymun Redbeard's horse. *They know nothing, Ygritte. And worse, they will not learn.*

"Gerrick has graciously agreed to give the hand of his eldest daughter to my beloved Axell, to be united by the Lord of Light in holy wedlock," Queen Selyse said. "His other girls shall wed at the same time—the second daughter with Ser Brus Buckler and the youngest with Ser Malegorn of Redpool."

"Sers." Jon inclined his head to the knights in question. "May you find happiness with your betrothed."

"Under the sea, men marry fishes." Patchface did a little dance step, jingling his bells. "They do, they do, they do."

Queen Selyse sniffed again. "Four marriages can be made as simply as three. It is past time that this woman Val was settled, Lord Snow. I have decided that she shall wed my good and leal knight, Ser Patrek of King's Mountain."

"Has Val been told, Your Grace?" asked Jon. "Amongst the free folk, when a man desires a woman, he steals her, and thus proves his strength, his cunning, and his courage. The suitor risks a savage beating if he is caught by the woman's kin, and worse than that if she herself finds him unworthy."

"A savage custom," Axell Florent said.

Ser Patrek only chuckled. "No man has ever had cause to question my courage. No woman ever will."

Queen Selyse pursed her lips. "Lord Snow, as Lady Val is a stranger to our ways, please send her to me, that I might instruct her in the duties of a noble lady toward her lord husband."

That will go splendidly, I know. Jon wondered if the queen would be so eager to see Val married to one of her own knights if she knew Val's feelings about Princess Shireen. "As you wish," he said, "though if I might speak freely—"

"No, I think not. You may take your leave of us."

Jon Snow bent his knee, bowed his head, withdrew.

He took the steps two at a time, nodding to the queen's guards as he descended. Her Grace had posted men on every landing to keep her safe from murderous wildlings. Halfway down, a voice called out from above him. "Jon Snow."

Jon turned. "Lady Melisandre."

"We must speak."

"Must we?" *I think not.* "My lady, I have duties."

"It is those duties I would speak of." She made her way down, the hem of her scarlet skirts swishing over the steps. It almost seemed as if she floated. "Where is your direwolf?"

"Asleep in my chambers. Her Grace does not allow Ghost in her presence. She claims he scares the princess. And so long as Borroq and his boar are about, I dare not let him loose." The skinchanger was to accompany Soren Shieldbreaker to Stonedoor once the wayns carrying the Sealskinner's clan to Greenguard returned. Until such time, Borroq had taken up residence in one of the ancient tombs beside the castle lichyard. The company of men long dead seemed to suit him better than that of the living, and his boar seemed happy rooting amongst the graves, well away from other animals. "That thing is the size of a bull, with tusks as long as swords. Ghost would go after him if he were loose, and one or both of them would not survive the meeting."

"Borroq is the least of your concerns. This ranging . . ."

"A word from you might have swayed the queen."

"Selyse has the right of this, Lord Snow. *Let them die.* You cannot save them. Your ships are lost—"

"Six remain. More than half the fleet."

"Your ships are lost. *All* of them. Not a man shall return. I have seen that in my fires."

"Your fires have been known to lie."

"I have made mistakes, I have admitted as much, but—"

"A grey girl on a dying horse. Daggers in the dark. A promised prince, born in smoke and salt. It seems to me that you make nothing *but* mistakes, my lady. Where is Stannis? What of Rattleshirt and his spearwives? *Where is my sister?*"

"All your questions shall be answered. Look to the skies, Lord Snow. And when you have your answers, send to me. Winter is almost upon us now. I am your only hope."

"A fool's hope." Jon turned and left her.

Leathers was prowling the yard outside. "Toregg has returned," he reported when Jon emerged. "His father's settled his people at Oakenshield and will be back this afternoon with eighty fighting men. What did the bearded queen have to say?"

"Her Grace can provide no help."

"Too busy plucking out her chin hairs, is she?" Leathers spat. "Makes no matter. Tormund's men and ours will be enough."

Enough to get us there, perhaps. It was the journey back that concerned Jon Snow. Coming home, they would be slowed by thousands of free folk, many sick and starved. *A river of humanity moving slower than a river of ice.* That would leave them vulnerable. *Dead things in the woods. Dead things in the water.* "How many men are enough?" he asked Leathers. "A hundred? Two hundred? Five hundred? A thousand?" *Should I take more men, or fewer?* A smaller ranging would reach Hardhome sooner ... but what good were swords without food? Mother Mole and her people were already at the point of eating their own dead. To feed them, he would need to bring carts and wagons, and draft animals to haul them—horses, oxen, dogs. Instead of flying through the wood, they would be condemned to crawl. "There is still much to decide. Spread the word. I want all the leading men in the Shieldhall when the evening watch begins. Tormund should be back by then. Where can I find Toregg?"

"With the little monster, like as not. He's taken a liking to one o' them milkmaids, I hear."

He has taken a liking to Val. Her sister was a queen, why not her? Tormund had once thought to make himself the King-Beyond-the-Wall, before Mance had bested him. Toregg the Tall might well be dreaming the same dream. *Better him than Gerrick Kingsblood.* "Let them be," said Jon. "I can speak with Toregg later." He glanced up past the King's Tower. The Wall was a dull white, the sky above it whiter. *A snow sky.* "Just pray we do not get another storm."

Outside the armory, Mully and the Flea stood shivering at guard. "Shouldn't you be inside, out of this wind?" Jon asked.

"That'd be sweet, m'lord," said Fulk the Flea, "but your wolf's in no mood for company today."

Mully agreed. "He tried to take a bite o' me, he did."

"*Ghost?*" Jon was shocked.

"Unless your lordship has some other white wolf, aye. I never seen him like this, m'lord. All wild-like, I mean."

He was not wrong, as Jon discovered for himself when he slipped inside the doors. The big white direwolf would not lie still. He paced from one end of the armory to the other, past the cold forge and back again. "Easy, Ghost," Jon called. "Down. Sit, Ghost. *Down.*" Yet when he made to touch him, the wolf bristled and bared his teeth. *It's that bloody boar. Even in here, Ghost can smell his stink.*

Mormont's raven seemed agitated too. "*Snow*," the bird kept screaming. "*Snow, snow, snow.*" Jon shooed him off, had Satin start a fire, then sent him out after Bowen Marsh and Othell Yarwyck. "Bring a flagon of mulled wine as well."

"Three cups, m'lord?"

"Six. Mully and the Flea look in need of something warm. So will you."

When Satin left, Jon seated himself and had another look at the maps of the lands north of the Wall. The fastest way to Hardhome was along the coast . . . from Eastwatch. The woods were thinner near the sea, the terrain mostly flatlands, rolling hills, and salt marshes. And when the autumn storms came howling, the coast got sleet and hail and freezing rain rather than snow. *The giants are at Eastwatch, and Leathers says that some will help.* From Castle Black the way was more difficult, right through the heart of the haunted forest. *If the snow is this deep at the Wall, how much worse up there?*

Marsh entered snuffling, Yarwyck dour. "Another storm," the First Builder announced. "How are we to work in this? I need more builders."

"Use the free folk," Jon said.

Yarwyck shook his head. "More trouble than they're worth, that lot. Sloppy, careless, lazy . . . some good woodworkers here and there, I'll not deny it, but hardly a mason amongst them, and nary a smith. Strong backs, might be, but they won't do as they are told. And us with all these ruins to turn back into forts. Can't be done, my lord. I tell you true. It can't be done."

"It will be done," said Jon, "or they will live in ruins."

A lord needed men about him he could rely upon for honest counsel. Marsh and Yarwyck were no lickspittles, and that was to the good . . . but they were seldom any *help* either. More and more, he found he knew what they would say before he asked them.

Especially when it concerned the free folk, where their disapproval went bone deep. When Jon settled Stonedoor on Soren Shieldbreaker, Yarwyck complained that it was too isolated. How could they know what mischief Soren might get up to, off in those hills? When he conferred Oakenshield on Tormund Giantsbane and Queensgate on Morna White Mask, Marsh pointed out that Castle Black would now have foes on either side who could easily cut them off from the rest of the Wall. As for Borroq, Othell Yarwyck claimed the woods north of Stonedoor were full of wild boars. Who was to say the skinchanger would not make his own pig army?

Hoarfrost Hill and Rimegate still lacked garrisons, so Jon had asked their views on which of the remaining wildling chiefs and war lords might be best suited to hold them. "We have Brogg, Gavin the Trader, the Great Walrus . . . Howd Wanderer walks alone, Tormund says, but there's still Harle the Huntsman, Harle the Handsome, Blind Doss . . . Ygon Oldfather commands a following, but most are his own sons and grandsons. He has eighteen wives, half of them stolen on raids. Which of these . . ."

"None," Bowen Marsh had said. "I know all these men by their deeds. We should be fitting them for nooses, not giving them our castles."

"Aye," Othell Yarwyck had agreed. "Bad and worse and worst makes a beggar's choice. My lord had as well present us with a pack of wolves and ask which we'd like to tear our throats out."

It was the same again with Hardhome. Satin poured whilst Jon told them of his audience with the queen. Marsh listened attentively, ignoring the mulled wine, whilst Yarwyck drank one cup and then another. But no sooner had Jon finished than the Lord Steward said, "Her Grace is wise. Let them die."

Jon sat back. "Is that the only counsel you can offer, my lord? Tormund is bringing eighty men. How many should we send? Shall we call upon the giants? The spearwives at Long Barrow? If we have women with us, it may put Mother Mole's people at ease."

"Send women, then. Send giants. Send suckling babes. Is that what my lord wishes to hear?" Bowen Marsh rubbed at the scar he had won at the Bridge of Skulls. "Send them all. The more we lose, the fewer mouths we'll have to feed."

Yarwyck was no more helpful. "If the wildlings at Hardhome need saving, let the wildlings here go save them. Tormund knows the way to Hardhome. To hear him talk, he can save them all himself with his huge member."

This was pointless, Jon thought. *Pointless, fruitless, hopeless.* "Thank you for your counsel, my lords."

Satin helped them back into their cloaks. As they walked through the armory, Ghost sniffed at them, his tail upraised and bristling. *My brothers.* The Night's Watch needed leaders with the wisdom of Maester Aemon, the learning of Samwell Tarly, the courage of Qhorin Halfhand, the stubborn strength of the Old Bear, the compassion of Donal Noye. What it had instead was them.

The snow was falling heavily outside. "Wind's from the south," Yarwyck observed. "It's blowing the snow right up against the Wall. See?"

He was right. The switchback stair was buried almost to the first landing, Jon saw, and the wooden doors of the ice cells and storerooms had vanished behind a wall of white. "How many men do we have in ice cells?" he asked Bowen Marsh.

"Four living men. Two dead ones."

The corpses. Jon had almost forgotten them. He had hoped to learn something from the bodies they'd brought back from the weirwood grove, but the dead men had stubbornly remained dead. "We need to dig those cells out."

"Ten stewards and ten spades should do it," said Marsh.

"Use Wun Wun too."

"As you command."

Ten stewards and one giant made short work of the drifts, but even when the doors were clear again, Jon was not satisfied. "Those cells will be buried again by morning. We'd best move the prisoners before they smother."

"Karstark too, m'lord?" asked Fulk the Flea. "Can't we just leave that one shivering till spring?"

"Would that we could." Cregan Karstark had taken to howling in the night of late, and throwing frozen feces at whoever came to feed him. That had not made him beloved of his guards. "Take him to the Lord Commander's Tower. The undervault should hold him." Though partly collapsed, the Old Bear's former seat would be warmer than the ice cells. Its subcellars were largely intact.

Cregan kicked at the guards when they came through the door, twisted and shoved when they grabbed him, even tried to bite them. But the cold had weakened him, and Jon's men were bigger, younger, and stronger. They hauled him out, still struggling, and dragged him through thigh-high snow to his new home.

"What would the lord commander like us to do with his corpses?" asked Marsh when the living men had been moved.

"Leave them." If the storm entombed them, well and good. He would need to burn them eventually, no doubt, but for the nonce they were bound with iron chains inside their cells. That, and being dead, should suffice to hold them harmless.

Tormund Giantsbane timed his arrival perfectly, thundering up with his warriors when all the shoveling was done. Only fifty seemed to have turned up, not the eighty Toregg promised Leathers, but Tormund was not called Tall-Talker for naught. The wildling arrived red-faced, shouting for a horn of ale and something hot to eat. He had ice in his beard and more crusting his mustache.

Someone had already told the Thunderfist about Gerrick Kingsblood and his new style. "King o' the Wildlings?" Tormund roared. "Har! King o' My Hairy Butt Crack, more like."

"He has a regal look to him," Jon said.

"He has a little red cock to go with all that red hair, that's what he has. Raymund Redbeard and his sons died at Long Lake, thanks to your bloody Starks and the Drunken Giant. Not the little brother. Ever wonder why they called him the Red Raven?" Tormund's mouth split in a gap-toothed grin. "First to fly the battle, he was. 'Twas a song about it, after. The singer had to find a rhyme for *craven*, so . . ." He wiped his nose. "If your queen's knights want those girls o' his, they're welcome to them."

"*Girls*," squawked Mormont's raven. "*Girls, girls.*"

That set Tormund to laughing all over again. "Now there's a bird with sense. How much do you want for him, Snow? I gave you a son, the least you could do is give me the bloody bird."

"I would," said Jon, "but like as not you'd eat him."

Tormund roared at that as well. "*Eat*," the raven said darkly, flapping its black wings. "*Corn? Corn? Corn?*"

"We need to talk about the ranging," said Jon. "I want us to be of one mind at the Shieldhall, we must—" He broke off when Mully poked his nose inside the door, grim-faced, to announce that Clydas had brought a letter.

"Tell him to leave it with you. I will read it later."

"As you say, m'lord, only . . . Clydas don't look his proper self . . . he's more white than pink, if you get my meaning . . . and he's shaking."

"Dark wings, dark words," muttered Tormund. "Isn't that what you kneelers say?"

"We say, *Bleed a cold but feast a fever* too," Jon told him. "We say, *Never drink with Dornishmen when the moon is full.* We say a lot of things."

Mully added his two groats. "My old grandmother always used to say, *Summer friends will melt away like summer snows, but winter friends are friends forever.*"

"I think that's sufficient wisdom for the moment," said Jon Snow. "Show Clydas in if you would be so good."

Mully had not been wrong; the old steward *was* trembling, his face as pale as the snows outside. "I am being foolish, Lord Commander, but . . . this letter frightens me. See here?"

Bastard, was the only word written outside the scroll. No *Lord*

Snow or *Jon Snow* or *Lord Commander*. Simply *Bastard*. And the letter was sealed with a smear of hard pink wax. "You were right to come at once," Jon said. *You were right to be afraid.* He cracked the seal, flattened the parchment, and read.

> *Your false king is dead, bastard. He and all his host were smashed in seven days of battle. I have his magic sword. Tell his red whore.*

> *Your false king's friends are dead. Their heads upon the walls of Winterfell. Come see them, bastard. Your false king lied, and so did you. You told the world you burned the King-Beyond-the-Wall. Instead you sent him to Winterfell to steal my bride from me.*

> *I will have my bride back. If you want Mance Rayder back, come and get him. I have him in a cage for all the north to see, proof of your lies. The cage is cold, but I have made him a warm cloak from the skins of the six whores who came with him to Winterfell.*

> *I want my bride back. I want the false king's queen. I want his daughter and his red witch. I want his wildling princess. I want his little prince, the wildling babe. And I want my Reek. Send them to me, bastard, and I will not trouble you or your black crows. Keep them from me, and I will cut out your bastard's heart and eat it.*

It was signed,

> *Ramsay Bolton,*
> *Trueborn Lord of Winterfell.*

"Snow?" said Tormund Giantsbane. "You look like your father's bloody head just rolled out o' that paper."

Jon Snow did not answer at once. "Mully, help Clydas back to his chambers. The night is dark, and the paths will be slippery with snow. Satin, go with them." He handed Tormund Giantsbane the letter. "Here, see for yourself."

The wildling gave the letter a dubious look and handed it right back. "Feels nasty . . . but Tormund Thunderfist had better things to do than learn to make papers talk at him. They never have any good to say, now do they?"

"Not often," Jon Snow admitted. *Dark wings, dark words.* Perhaps there was more truth to those wise old sayings than he'd known. "It was sent by Ramsay Snow. I'll read you what he wrote."

When he was done, Tormund whistled. "Har. That's buggered, and no mistake. What was that about Mance? Has him in a cage, does he? How, when hundreds saw your red witch burn the man?"

That was Rattleshirt, Jon almost said. *That was sorcery. A glamor, she called it.* "Melisandre . . . *look to the skies,* she said." He set the letter down. "A raven in a storm. She saw this coming." *When you have your answers, send to me.*

"Might be all a skin o' lies." Tormund scratched under his beard. "If I had me a nice goose quill and a pot o' maester's ink, I could write down that me member was long and thick as me arm, wouldn't make it so."

"He has Lightbringer. He talks of heads upon the walls of Winterfell. He knows about the spearwives and their number." *He knows about Mance Rayder.* "No. There is truth in there."

"I won't say you're wrong. What do you mean to do, crow?"

Jon flexed the fingers of his sword hand. *The Night's Watch takes no part.* He closed his fist and opened it again. *What you propose is nothing less than treason.* He thought of Robb, with snowflakes melting in his hair. *Kill the boy and let the man be born.* He thought of Bran, clambering up a tower wall, agile as a monkey. Of Rickon's breathless laughter. Of Sansa, brushing out Lady's coat and singing to herself. *You know nothing, Jon Snow.* He thought of Arya, her hair as tangled as a bird's nest. *I made him a warm cloak from the skins of the six whores who came with him to Winterfell . . . I want my bride back . . . I want my bride back . . . I want my bride back . . .*

"I think we had best change the plan," Jon Snow said.

They talked for the best part of two hours.

Horse and Rory had replaced Fulk and Mully at the armory door with the change of watch. "With me," Jon told them, when the time came. Ghost would have followed as well, but as the wolf came padding after them, Jon grabbed him by the scruff of his neck and wrestled him back inside. Borroq might be amongst those gathering at the Shieldhall. The last thing he needed just now was his wolf savaging the skinchanger's boar.

The Shieldhall was one of the older parts of Castle Black, a long drafty feast hall of dark stone, its oaken rafters black with the smoke of centuries. Back when the Night's Watch had been much larger, its walls had been hung with rows of brightly colored wooden shields. Then as now, when a knight took the black, tradition decreed that he set aside his former arms and take up the plain black shield of the brotherhood. The shields thus discarded would hang in the Shieldhall.

Hundreds of knights meant hundreds of shields. Hawks and eagles, dragons and griffins, suns and stags, wolves and wyverns, manticores, bulls, trees and flowers, harps, spears, crabs and krakens, red lions and golden lions and chequy lions, owls, lambs, maids and mermen, stallions, stars, buckets and buckles, flayed men and hanged men and burning men, axes, longswords, turtles, unicorns, bears, quills, spiders and snakes and scorpions, and a hundred other heraldic charges had adorned the Shieldhall walls, blazoned in more colors than any rainbow ever dreamed of.

But when a knight died, his shield was taken down, that it might go with him to his pyre or his tomb, and over the years and centuries fewer and fewer knights had taken the black. A day came when it no longer made sense for the knights of Castle Black to dine apart. The Shieldhall was abandoned. In the last hundred years, it had been used only infrequently. As a dining hall, it left much to be desired—it was dark, dirty, drafty, and hard to heat in winter, its cellars infested with rats, its massive wooden rafters worm-eaten and festooned with cobwebs.

But it was large and long enough to seat two hundred, and half again that many if they crowded close. When Jon and Tormund entered, a sound went through the hall, like wasps stirring in a nest. The wildlings outnumbered the crows by five to one, judging by how little black he saw. Fewer than a dozen shields remained, sad grey things with faded paint and long cracks in the wood. But fresh torches burned in the iron sconces along the walls, and Jon had ordered benches and tables brought in. Men with comfortable seats were more inclined to listen, Maester Aemon had once told him; standing men were more inclined to shout.

At the top of the hall a sagging platform stood. Jon mounted it, with Tormund Giantsbane at his side, and raised his hands for quiet. The wasps only buzzed the louder. Then Tormund put his warhorn to his lips and blew a blast. The sound filled the hall, echoing off the rafters overhead. Silence fell.

"I summoned you to make plans for the relief of Hardhome," Jon Snow began. "Thousands of the free folk are gathered there, trapped and starving, and we have had reports of dead things in the wood." To his left he saw Marsh and Yarwyck. Othell was surrounded by his builders, whilst Bowen had Wick Whittlestick, Left Hand Lew, and Alf of Runnymudd beside him. To his right, Soren Shieldbreaker sat with his arms crossed against his chest. Farther back, Jon saw Gavin the Trader and Harle the Handsome whispering together. Ygon Oldfather sat amongst his wives, Howd Wanderer alone. Borroq leaned against a wall in a dark corner. Mercifully, his boar was nowhere in evidence. "The ships I sent to take off Mother Mole and her people have been wracked by storms. We must send what help we can by land or let them die." Two of Queen Selyse's knights had come as well, Jon saw. Ser Narbert and Ser Benethon stood near the door at the foot of the hall. But the rest of the queen's men were conspicuous in their absence. "I had hoped to lead the ranging myself and bring back as many of the free folk as could survive the journey." A flash of red in the back of the hall caught Jon's eye. Lady Melisandre had arrived. "But now I find I cannot go to Hardhome. The ranging will be led by Tormund Giantsbane, known to you all. I have promised him as many men as he requires."

"*And where will you be, crow?*" Borroq thundered. "Hiding here in Castle Black with your white dog?"

"No. I ride south." Then Jon read them the letter Ramsay Snow had written.

The Shieldhall went mad.

Every man began to shout at once. They leapt to their feet, shaking fists. *So much for the calming power of comfortable benches.* Swords were brandished, axes smashed against shields. Jon Snow looked to Tormund. The Giantsbane sounded his horn once more, twice as long and twice as loud as the first time.

"The Night's Watch takes no part in the wars of the Seven Kingdoms," Jon reminded them when some semblance of quiet had returned. "It is not for us to oppose the Bastard of Bolton, to avenge Stannis Baratheon, to defend his widow and his daughter. This *creature* who makes cloaks from the skins of women has sworn to cut my heart out, and I mean to make him answer for those words . . . but I will not ask my brothers to forswear their vows.

"The Night's Watch will make for Hardhome. I ride to Winterfell alone, unless . . ." Jon paused. ". . . is there any man here who will come stand with me?"

The roar was all he could have hoped for, the tumult so loud that the two old shields tumbled from the walls. Soren Shieldbreaker was on his feet, the Wanderer as well. Toregg the Tall, Brogg, Harle the Huntsman and Harle the Handsome both, Ygon Oldfather, Blind Doss, even the Great Walrus. *I have my swords*, thought Jon Snow, *and we are coming for you, Bastard.*

Yarwyck and Marsh were slipping out, he saw, and all their men behind them. It made no matter. He did not need them now. He did not *want* them. *No man can ever say I made my brothers break their vows. If this is oathbreaking, the crime is mine and mine alone.* Then Tormund was pounding him on the back, all gap-toothed grin from ear to ear. "Well spoken, crow. Now bring out the mead! Make them yours and get them drunk, that's how it's done. We'll make a wildling o' you yet, boy. Har!"

"I will send for ale," Jon said, distracted. Melisandre was gone, he realized, and so were the queen's knights. *I should have gone to Selyse first. She has the right to know her lord is dead.* "You must excuse me. I'll leave you to get them drunk."

"Har! A task I'm well suited for, crow. On your way!"

Horse and Rory fell in beside Jon as he left the Shieldhall. *I should talk with Melisandre after I see the queen*, he thought. *If she could see a raven in a storm, she can find Ramsay Snow for me.* Then he heard the shouting . . . and a roar so loud it seemed to shake the Wall. "That come from Hardin's Tower, m'lord," Horse reported. He might have said more, but the scream cut him off.

Val, was Jon's first thought. But that was no woman's scream. *That is a man in mortal agony.* He broke into a run. Horse and Rory raced after him. "Is it wights?" asked Rory. Jon wondered. Could his corpses have escaped their chains?

The screaming had stopped by the time they came to Hardin's Tower, but Wun Weg Wun Dar Wun was still roaring. The giant was dangling a bloody corpse by one leg, the same way Arya used to dangle her doll when she was small, swinging it like a morningstar when menaced by vegetables. *Arya never tore her dolls to pieces, though.* The dead man's sword arm was yards away, the snow beneath it turning red.

"Let him go," Jon shouted. "Wun Wun, *let him go.*"

Wun Wun did not hear or did not understand. The giant was bleeding himself, with sword cuts on his belly and his arm. He swung the dead knight against the grey stone of the tower, again and again and again, until the man's head was red and pulpy as a summer melon. The knight's cloak flapped in the cold air. Of white wool it had been, bordered in cloth-of-silver and patterned with blue stars. Blood and bone were flying everywhere.

Men poured from the surrounding keeps and towers. Northmen, free folk, queen's men . . . "Form a line," Jon Snow commanded them. "Keep them back. Everyone, but especially the queen's men." The dead man was Ser Patrek of King's Mountain; his head was largely gone, but his heraldry was as distinctive as his face. Jon did not want to risk Ser Malegorn or Ser Brus or any of the queen's other knights trying to avenge him.

Wun Weg Wun Dar Wun howled again and gave Ser Patrek's other arm a twist and pull. It tore loose from his shoulder with a spray of bright red blood. *Like a child pulling petals off a daisy*, thought Jon.

"Leathers, talk to him, calm him. The Old Tongue, he understands the Old Tongue. *Keep back*, the rest of you. Put away your steel, we're scaring him." Couldn't they see the giant had been cut? Jon had to put an end to this or more men would die. They had no idea of Wun Wun's strength. *A horn, I need a horn.* He saw the glint of steel, turned toward it. "*No blades!*" he screamed. "Wick, put that knife . . ."

. . . *away,* he meant to say. When Wick Whittlestick slashed at his throat, the word turned into a grunt. Jon twisted from the knife, just enough so it barely grazed his skin. *He cut me.* When he put his hand to the side of his neck, blood welled between his fingers. "*Why?*"

"For the Watch." Wick slashed at him again. This time Jon caught his wrist and bent his arm back until he dropped the dagger. The gangling steward backed away, his hands upraised as if to say, *Not me, it was not me.* Men were screaming. Jon reached for Longclaw, but his fingers had grown stiff and clumsy. Somehow he could not seem to get the sword free of its scabbard.

Then Bowen Marsh stood there before him, tears running down his cheeks. "For the Watch." He punched Jon in the belly. When he pulled his hand away, the dagger stayed where he had buried it.

Jon fell to his knees. He found the dagger's hilt and wrenched it free. In the cold night air the wound was smoking. "Ghost," he whispered. Pain washed over him. *Stick them with the pointy end.* When the third dagger took him between the shoulder blades, he gave a grunt and fell face-first into the snow. He never felt the fourth knife. Only the cold . . .

THE QUEEN'S HAND

The Dornish prince was three days dying.

He took his last shuddering breath in the bleak black dawn, as cold rain hissed from a dark sky to turn the brick streets of the old city into rivers. The rain had drowned the worst of the fires, but wisps of smoke still rose from the smoldering ruin that had been the pyramid of Hazkar, and the great black pyramid of Yherizan where Rhaegal had made his lair hulked in the gloom like a fat woman bedecked with glowing orange jewels.

Perhaps the gods are not deaf after all, Ser Barristan Selmy reflected as he watched those distant embers. *If not for the rain, the fires might have consumed all of Meereen by now.*

He saw no sign of dragons, but he had not expected to. The dragons did not like the rain. A thin red slash marked the eastern horizon where the sun might soon appear. It reminded Selmy of the first blood welling from a wound. Often, even with a deep cut, the blood came before the pain.

He stood beside the parapets of the highest step of the Great Pyramid, searching the sky as he did every morning, knowing that the dawn must come and hoping that his queen would come with it. *She will not have abandoned us, she would never leave her people,* he was telling himself, when he heard the prince's death rattle coming from the queen's apartments.

Ser Barristan went inside. Rainwater ran down the back of his white cloak, and his boots left wet tracks on the floors and carpets. At his command, Quentyn Martell had been laid out in the queen's own bed. He had been a knight, and a prince of Dorne besides. It seemed only kind to let him die in the bed he had crossed half a world to reach. The bedding was ruined—sheets, covers, pillows, mattress, all reeked of blood and smoke, but Ser Barristan thought Daenerys would forgive him.

Missandei sat at the bedside. She had been with the prince night and day, tending to such needs as he could express, giving him water and milk of the poppy when he was strong enough to drink, listening to the few tortured words he gasped out from time to time, reading to him when he fell quiet, sleeping in her chair beside him. Ser Barristan had asked some of the queen's cupbearers to help, but the sight of the burned man was too much for even the boldest of them. And the Blue Graces had never come, though he'd sent for them four times. Perhaps the last of them had been carried off by the pale mare by now.

The tiny Naathi scribe looked up at his approach. "Honored ser. The prince is beyond pain now. His Dornish gods have taken him home. See? He smiles."

How can you tell? He has no lips. It would have been kinder if the dragons had devoured him. That at least would have been quick. This . . . *Fire is a hideous way to die. Small wonder half the hells are made of flame.* "Cover him."

Missandei pulled the coverlet over the prince's face. "What will be done with him, ser? He is so very far from home."

"I'll see that he's returned to Dorne." *But how? As ashes?* That would require more fire, and Ser Barristan could not stomach that. *We'll need to strip the flesh from his bones. Beetles, not boiling.* The silent sisters would have seen to it at home, but this was Slaver's Bay. The nearest silent sister was ten thousand leagues away. "You should go sleep now, child. In your own bed."

"If this one may be so bold, ser, you should do the same. You do not sleep the whole night through."

Not for many years, child. Not since the Trident. Grand Maester

Pycelle had once told him that old men do not need as much sleep as the young, but it was more than that. He had reached that age when he was loath to close his eyes, for fear that he might never open them again. Other men might wish to die in bed asleep, but that was no death for a knight of the Kingsguard.

"The nights are too long," he told Missandei, "and there is much and more to do, always. Here, as in the Seven Kingdoms. But you have done enough for now, child. Go and rest." *And if the gods are good, you will not dream of dragons.*

After the girl was gone, the old knight peeled back the coverlet for one last look at Quentyn Martell's face, or what remained of it. So much of the prince's flesh had sloughed away that he could see the skull beneath. His eyes were pools of pus. *He should have stayed in Dorne. He should have stayed a frog. Not all men are meant to dance with dragons.* As he covered the boy once more, he found himself wondering whether there would be anyone to cover his queen, or whether her own corpse would lie unmourned amongst the tall grasses of the Dothraki sea, staring blindly at the sky until her flesh fell from her bones.

"No," he said aloud. "Daenerys is not dead. She was riding that dragon. I saw it with mine own two eyes." He had said the same a hundred times before . . . but every day that passed made it harder to believe. *Her hair was afire. I saw that too. She was burning . . . and if I did not see her fall, hundreds swear they did.*

Day had crept upon the city. Though the rain still fell, a vague light suffused the eastern sky. And with the sun arrived the Shavepate. Skahaz was clad in his familiar garb of pleated black skirt, greaves, and muscled breastplate. The brazen mask beneath his arm was new—a wolf's head with lolling tongue. "So," he said, by way of greeting, "the fool is dead, is he?"

"Prince Quentyn died just before first light." Selmy was not surprised that Skahaz knew. Word traveled quickly within the pyramid. "Is the council assembled?"

"They await the Hand's pleasure below."

I am no Hand, a part of him wanted to cry out. *I am only a simple knight, the queen's protector. I never wanted this.* But with the queen gone and the king in chains, someone had to rule, and Ser Barristan did not trust the Shavepate. "Has there been any word from the Green Grace?"

"She is not yet returned to the city." Skahaz had opposed sending the priestess. Nor had Galazza Galare herself embraced the task. She would go, she allowed, for the sake of peace, but Hizdahr zo Loraq was better suited to treat with the Wise Masters. But Ser Barristan did not yield easily, and finally the Green Grace had bowed her head and sworn to do her best.

"How stands the city?" Selmy asked the Shavepate now.

"All the gates are closed and barred, as you commanded. We are hunting down any sellswords or Yunkai'i left inside the city and expelling or arresting those we catch. Most seem to have gone to ground. Inside the pyramids, beyond a doubt. The Unsullied man the walls and towers, ready for any assault. There are two hundred high-born gathered in the square, standing in the rain in their *tokars* and howling for audience. They want Hizdahr free and me dead, and they want you to slay these dragons. Someone told them knights were good at that. Men are still pulling corpses from the pyramid of Hazkar. The Great Masters of Yherizan and Uhlez have abandoned their own pyramids to the dragons."

Ser Barristan had known all that. "And the butcher's tally?" he asked, dreading the answer.

"Nine-and-twenty."

"*Nine-and-twenty?*" That was far worse than he could ever have imagined. The Sons of the Harpy had resumed their shadow war two days ago. Three murders the first night, nine the second. But to go from nine to nine-and-twenty in a single night . . .

"The count will pass thirty before midday. Why do you look so grey, old man? What did you expect? The Harpy wants Hizdahr free, so he has sent his sons back into the streets with knives in hand. The dead are all freedmen and shavepates, as before. One was mine, a Brazen Beast. The sign of the Harpy was left beside the bodies, chalked on the pavement or scratched into a wall. There were messages as well. '*Dragons must die,*' they wrote, and '*Harghaz the Hero.*' '*Death to Daenerys*' was seen as well, before the rain washed out the words."

"The blood tax . . ."

"Twenty-nine hundred pieces of gold from each pyramid, aye," Skahaz grumbled. "It will be collected . . . but the loss of a few coins will never stay the Harpy's hand. Only blood can do that."

"So you say." *The hostages again. He would kill them every one if I allowed it.* "I heard you the first hundred times. No."

"Queen's Hand," Skahaz grumbled with disgust. "An old woman's hand, I am thinking, wrinkled and feeble. I pray Daenerys returns to us soon." He pulled his brazen wolf's mask down over his face. "Your council will be growing restless."

"They are the queen's council, not mine." Selmy exchanged his damp cloak for a dry one and buckled on his sword belt, then accompanied the Shavepate down the steps.

The pillared hall was empty of petitioners this morning. Though he had assumed the title of Hand, Ser Barristan would not presume to hold court in the queen's absence, nor would he permit Skahaz mo Kandaq to do such. Hizdahr's grotesque dragon thrones had been removed at Ser Barristan's command, but he had not brought back the simple pillowed bench the queen had favored. Instead a large round table had been set up in the center of the hall, with tall chairs all around it where men might sit and talk as peers.

They rose when Ser Barristan came down the marble steps, Skahaz Shavepate at his side. Marselen of the Mother's Men was present, with Symon Stripeback, commander of the Free Brothers. The Stalwart Shields had chosen a new commander, a black-skinned Summer Islander called Tal Toraq, their old captain, Mollono Yos Dob, having been carried off by the pale mare. Grey Worm was there for the Unsullied, attended by three eunuch serjeants in spiked bronze caps. The Stormcrows were represented by two seasoned sellswords, an archer named Jokin and the scarred and sour axeman known simply as the Widower. The two of them had assumed joint command of the company in the absence of Daario Naharis. Most of the queen's *khalasar* had gone with Aggo and Rakharo to search for her on the Dothraki sea, but the squinty, bowlegged *jaqqa rhan* Rommo was there to speak for the riders who remained.

And across the table from Ser Barristan sat four of King Hizdahr's erstwhile guardsmen, the pit fighters Goghor the Giant, Belaquo Bonebreaker, Camarron of the Count, and the Spotted Cat. Selmy had insisted on their presence, over the objections of Skahaz Shavepate. They had helped Daenerys Targaryen take this city once, and that should not be forgotten. Blood-soaked brutes and killers they might be, but in their own way they had been loyal . . . to King Hizdahr, yes, but to the queen as well.

Last to come, Strong Belwas lumbered into the hall.

The eunuch had looked death in the face, so near he might have kissed her on the lips. It had marked him. He looked to have lost two stone of weight, and the dark brown skin that had once stretched tight across a massive chest and belly, crossed by a hundred faded scars, now hung on him in loose folds, sagging and wobbling, like a robe cut three sizes too large. His step had slowed as well, and seemed a bit uncertain.

Even so, the sight of him gladdened the old knight's heart. He had once crossed the world with Strong Belwas, and he knew he could rely on him, should all this come to swords. "Belwas. We are pleased that you could join us."

"Whitebeard." Belwas smiled. "Where is liver and onions? Strong Belwas is not so strong as before, he must eat, get big again. They made Strong Belwas sick. Someone must die."

Someone will. Many someones, like as not. "Sit, my friend." When Belwas sat and crossed his arms, Ser Barristan went on. "Quentyn Martell died this morning, just before the dawn."

The Widower laughed. "The dragonrider."

"Fool, I call him," said Symon Stripeback.

No, just a boy. Ser Barristan had not forgotten the follies of his own youth. "Speak no ill of the dead. The prince paid a ghastly price for what he did."

"And the other Dornish?" asked Tal Taraq.

"Prisoners, for the nonce." Neither of the Dornishmen had offered any resistance. Archibald Yronwood had been cradling his prince's scorched and smoking body when the Brazen Beasts had found him, as his burned hands could testify. He had used them to beat out the flames that had engulfed Quentyn Martell. Gerris

Drinkwater was standing over them with sword in hand, but he had dropped the blade the moment the locusts had appeared. "They share a cell."

"Let them share a gibbet," said Symon Stripeback. "They unleashed two dragons on the city."

"Open the pits and give them swords," urged the Spotted Cat. "I will kill them both as all Meereen shouts out my name."

"The fighting pits will remain closed," said Selmy. "Blood and noise would only serve to call the dragons."

"All three, perhaps," suggested Marselen. "The black beast came once, why not again? This time with our queen."

Or without her. Should Drogon return to Meereen without Daenerys mounted on his back, the city would erupt in blood and flame, of that Ser Barristan had no doubt. The very men sitting at this table would soon be at dagger points with one another. A young girl she might be, but Daenerys Targaryen was the only thing that held them all together.

"Her Grace will return when she returns," said Ser Barristan. "We have herded a thousand sheep into the Daznak's Pit, filled the Pit of Ghrazz with bullocks, and the Golden Pit with beasts that Hizdahr zo Loraq had gathered for his games." Thus far both dragons seemed to have a taste for mutton, returning to Daznak's whenever they grew hungry. If either one was hunting man, inside or outside the city, Ser Barristan had yet to hear of it. The only Meereenese the dragons had slain since Harghaz the Hero had been the slavers foolish enough to object when Rhaegal attempted to make his lair atop the pyramid of Hazkar. "We have more pressing matters to discuss. I have sent the Green Grace to the Yunkishmen to make arrangements for the release of our hostages. I expect her back by midday with their answer."

"With words," said the Widower. "The Stormcrows know the Yunkai'i. Their tongues are worms that wriggle this way or that. The Green Grace will come back with worm words, not the captain."

"If it pleases the Queen's Hand to recall, the Wise Masters hold our Hero too," said Grey Worm. "Also the horselord Jhogo, the queen's own bloodrider."

"Blood of her blood," agreed the Dothraki Rommo. "He must be freed. The honor of the *khalasar* demands it."

"He shall be freed," said Ser Barristan, "but first we must needs wait and see if the Green Grace can accomplish—"

Skahaz Shavepate slammed his fist upon the table. "The Green Grace will accomplish *nothing*. She may be conspiring with the Yunkai'i even as we sit here. *Arrangements,* did you say? *Make arrangements?* What sort of *arrangements?*"

"Ransom," said Ser Barristan. "Each man's weight in gold."

"The Wise Masters do not need our gold, ser," said Marselen. "They are richer than your Westerosi lords, every one."

"Their sellswords will want the gold, though. What are the hostages to them? If the Yunkishmen refuse, it will drive a blade between them and their hirelings." *Or so I hope.* It had been Missandei who suggested the ploy to him. He would never have thought of such a thing himself. In King's Landing, bribes had been Littlefinger's domain, whilst Lord Varys had the task of fostering division amongst the crown's enemies. His own duties had been more straightforward. *Eleven years of age, yet Missandei is as clever as half the men at this table and wiser than all of them.* "I have instructed the Green Grace to present the offer only when all of the Yunkish commanders have assembled to hear it."

"They will refuse, even so," insisted Symon Stripeback. "They will say they want the dragons dead, the king restored."

"I pray that you are wrong." *And fear that you are right.*

"Your gods are far away, Ser Grandfather," said the Widower. "I do not think they hear your prayers. And when the Yunkai'i send back the old woman to spit in your eye, what then?"

"*Fire and blood,*" said Barristan Selmy, softly, softly.

For a long moment no one spoke. Then Strong Belwas slapped his belly and said, "Better than liver and onions," and Skahaz Shavepate stared through the eyes of his wolf's head mask and said, "You would break King Hizdahr's peace, old man?"

"I would shatter it." Once, long ago, a prince had named him Barristan the Bold. A part of that boy was in him still. "We have built a beacon atop the pyramid where once the Harpy stood. Dry wood soaked with oil, covered to keep the rain off. Should the hour come, and I pray that it does not, we will light that beacon. The flames will be your signal to pour out of our gates and attack. Every man of you will have a part to play, so every man must be in readiness at all times, day or night. We will destroy our foes or be destroyed ourselves." He raised a hand to signal to his waiting squires. "I have had some maps prepared to show the dispositions of our foes, their camps and siege lines and trebuchets. If we can break the slavers, their sellswords will abandon them. I know you will have concerns and questions. Voice them here. By the time we leave this table, all of us must be of a single mind, with a single purpose."

"Best send down for some food and drink, then," suggested Symon Stripeback. "This will take a while."

It took the rest of the morning and most of the afternoon. The captains and commanders argued over the maps like fishwives over a bucket of crabs. Weak points and strong points, how to best employ their small company of archers, whether the elephants should be used to break the Yunkish lines or held in reserve, who should have the honor of leading the first advance, whether their horse cavalry was best deployed on the flanks or in the vanguard.

Ser Barristan let each man speak his mind. Tal Toraq thought that they should march on Yunkai once they had broken through the lines; the Yellow City would be almost undefended, so the Yunkai'i would have no choice but to lift the siege and follow. The Spotted Cat proposed to challenge the enemy to send forth a champion to face him in single combat. Strong Belwas liked that notion but insisted he should fight, not the Cat. Camarron of the Count put forth a scheme to seize the ships tied up along the riverfront and use the Skahazadhan to bring three hundred pit fighters around the Yunkish rear. Every man there agreed that the Unsullied were their best troops, but none agreed on how they should be deployed. The Widower wanted to use the eunuchs as an iron fist to smash through the heart of the Yunkish defenses. Marselen felt they would be better placed at either end of the main battle line, where they could beat back any attempt by the foe to turn their flanks. Symon Stripeback wanted them split into three and divided amongst the three companies of freedmen. His Free Brothers were brave and eager for the fight, he claimed, but without the Unsullied to stiffen them he feared his unblooded troops might not have the discipline to face battle-seasoned sellswords by themselves. Grey Worm said only that the Unsullied would obey, whatever might be asked of them.

And when all that had been discussed, debated, and decided, Symon Stripeback raised one final point. "As a slave in Yunkai I helped my master bargain with the free companies and saw to the payment of their wages. I know sellswords, and I know that the Yunkai'i cannot pay them near enough to face dragonflame. So I ask you . . . if the peace should fail and this battle should be joined, will the dragons come? Will they join the fight?"

They will come, Ser Barristan might have said. *The noise will bring them, the shouts and screams, the scent of blood. That will draw them to the battlefield, just as the roar from Daznak's Pit drew Drogon to the scarlet sands. But when they come, will they know one side from the other?* Somehow he did not think so. So he said only, "The dragons will do what the dragons will do. If they do come, it may be that just the shadow of their wings will be enough to dishearten the slavers and send them fleeing." Then he thanked them and dismissed them all.

Grey Worm lingered after the others had left. "These ones will be ready when the beacon fire is lit. But the Hand must surely know that when we attack, the Yunkai'i will kill the hostages."

"I will do all I can to prevent that, my friend. I have a . . . notion. But pray excuse me. It is past time the Dornishmen heard that their prince is dead."

Grey Worm inclined his head. "This one obeys."

Ser Barristan took two of his new-made knights with him down into the dungeons. Grief and guilt had been known to drive good men into madness, and Archibald Yronwood and Gerris Drinkwater had both played roles in their friend's demise. But when they reached the cell, he told Tum and the Red Lamb to wait outside whilst he went in to tell the Dornish that the prince's agony was over.

Ser Archibald, the big bald one, had nothing to say. He sat on the edge of his pallet, staring down at his bandaged hands in their linen wrappings. Ser Gerris punched a wall. "I told him it was folly. I begged him to go home. Your bitch of a queen had no use for him, any man could see that. He crossed the world to offer her his love and fealty, and she laughed in his face."

"She never laughed," said Selmy. "If you knew her, you would know that."

"She spurned him. He offered her his heart, and she threw it back at him and went off to fuck her sellsword."

"You had best guard that tongue, ser." Ser Barristan did not like this Gerris Drinkwater, nor would he allow him to vilify Daenerys. "Prince Quentyn's death was his own doing, and yours."

"*Ours?* How are we at fault, ser? Quentyn was our friend, yes. A bit of a fool, you might say, but all dreamers are fools. But first and last he was our prince. We owed him our obedience."

Barristan Selmy could not dispute the truth of that. He had spent the best part of his own life obeying the commands of drunkards and madmen. "He came too late."

"He offered her his heart," Ser Gerris said again.

"She needed swords, not hearts."

"He would have given her the spears of Dorne as well."

"Would that he had." No one had wanted Daenerys to look with favor on the Dornish prince more than Barristan Selmy. "He came too late, though, and this folly . . . buying sellswords, loosing two dragons on the city . . . that was madness and worse than madness. That was treason."

"What he did he did for love of Queen Daenerys," Gerris Drinkwater insisted. "To prove himself worthy of her hand."

The old knight had heard enough. "What Prince Quentyn did he did for Dorne. Do you take me for some doting grandfather? I have spent my life around kings and queens and princes. Sunspear means to take up arms against the Iron Throne. No, do not trouble to deny it. Doran Martell is not a man to call his spears without hope of victory. Duty brought Prince Quentyn here. Duty, honor, thirst for glory . . . never love. Quentyn was here for dragons, not Daenerys."

"You did not know him, ser. He—"

"He's dead, Drink." Yronwood rose to his feet. "Words won't fetch him back. Cletus and Will are dead too. So shut your bloody mouth before I stick my fist in it." The big knight turned to Selmy. "What do you mean to do with us?"

"Skahaz Shavepate wants you hanged. You slew four of his men. Four of the *queen*'s men. Two were freedmen who had followed Her Grace since Astapor."

Yronwood did not seem surprised. "The beast men, aye. I only killed the one, the basilisk head. The sellswords did the others. Don't matter, though, I know that."

"We were protecting Quentyn," said Drinkwater. "We—"

"Be *quiet*, Drink. He knows." To Ser Barristan the big knight said, "No need to come and talk if you meant to hang us. So it's not that, is it?"

"No." *This one may not be as slow-witted as he seems.* "I have more use for you alive than dead. Serve me, and afterward I will arrange a ship to take you back to Dorne and give you Prince Quentyn's bones to return to his lord father."

Ser Archibald grimaced. "Why is it always ships? Someone needs to take Quent home, though. What do you ask of us, ser?"

"Your swords."

"You have thousands of swords."

"The queen's freedmen are as yet unblooded. The sellswords I do not trust. Unsullied are brave soldiers ... but not warriors. Not *knights*." He paused. "What happened when you tried to take the dragons? Tell me."

The Dornishmen exchanged a look. Then Drinkwater said, "Quentyn told the Tattered Prince he could control them. It was in his blood, he said. He had Targaryen blood."

"Blood of the dragon."

"Yes. The sellswords were supposed to help us get the dragons chained up so we could get them to the docks."

"Rags arranged for a ship," said Yronwood. "A big one, in case we got both dragons. And Quent was going to ride one." He looked at his bandaged hands. "The moment we got in, though, you could see none of it was going to work. The dragons were too wild. The chains . . . there were bits of broken chain everywhere, *big* chains, links the size of your head mixed in with all these cracked and splintered bones. And Quent, Seven save him, he looked like he was going to shit his smallclothes. Caggo and Meris weren't blind, they saw it too. Then one of the crossbowmen let fly. Maybe they meant to kill the dragons all along and were only using us to get to them. You never know with Tatters. Any way you hack it off, it weren't clever. The quarrel just made the dragons angry, and they hadn't been in such a good mood to start with. Then . . . then things got bad."

"And the Windblown blew away," said Ser Gerris. "Quent was screaming, covered in flames, and they were gone. Caggo, Pretty Meris, all but the dead one."

"Ah, what did you expect, Drink? A cat will kill a mouse, a pig will wallow in shit, and a sellsword will run off when he's needed most. Can't be blamed. Just the nature of the beast."

"He's not wrong," Ser Barristan said. "What did Prince Quentyn promise the Tattered Prince in return for all this help?"

He got no answer. Ser Gerris looked at Ser Archibald. Ser Archibald looked at his hands, the floor, the door.

"Pentos," said Ser Barristan. "He promised him Pentos. Say it. No words of yours can help or harm Prince Quentyn now."

"Aye," said Ser Archibald unhappily. "It was Pentos. They made marks on a paper, the two of them."

There is a chance here. "We still have Windblown in the dungeons. Those feigned deserters."

"I remember," said Yronwood. "Hungerford, Straw, that lot. Some of them weren't so bad for sellswords. Others, well, might be they could stand a bit of dying. What of them?"

"I mean to send them back to the Tattered Prince. And you with them. You will be two amongst thousands. Your presence in the Yunkish camps should pass unnoticed. I want you to deliver a message to the Tattered Prince. Tell him that I sent you, that I speak with the queen's voice. Tell him that we'll pay his price if he delivers us our hostages, unharmed and whole."

Ser Archibald grimaced. "Rags and Tatters is more like to give the two of us to Pretty Meris. He won't do it."

"Why not? The task is simple enough." *Compared to stealing dragons.* "I once brought the queen's father out of Duskendale."

"That was Westeros," said Gerris Drinkwater.

"This is Meereen."

"Arch cannot even hold a sword with those hands."

"He ought not need to. You will have the sellswords with you, unless I mistake my man."

Gerris Drinkwater pushed back his mop of sun-streaked hair. "Might we have some time to discuss this amongst ourselves?"

"No," said Selmy.

"I'll do it," offered Ser Archibald, "just so long as there's no bloody boats involved. Drink will do it too." He grinned. "He don't know it yet, but he will."

And that was done.

The simple part, at least, thought Barristan Selmy, as he made the long climb back to the summit of the pyramid. The hard part he'd left in Dornish hands. His grandfather would have been aghast. The Dornishmen were knights, at least in name, though only Yronwood impressed him as having the true steel. Drinkwater had a pretty face, a glib tongue, and a fine head of hair.

By the time the old knight returned to the queen's rooms atop the pyramid, Prince Quentyn's corpse had been removed. Six of the young cupbearers were playing some child's game as he entered, sitting in a circle on the floor as they took turns spinning a dagger. When it wobbled to a stop they cut a lock of hair off whichever of them the blade was pointing at. Ser Barristan had played a similar game with his cousins when he was just a boy at Harvest Hall . . . though in Westeros, as he recalled, kissing had been involved as well. "Bhakaz," he called. "A cup of wine, if you would be so good. Grazhar, Azzak, the door is yours. I am expecting the Green Grace. Show her in at once when she arrives. Elsewise, I do not wish to be disturbed."

Azzak scrambled to his feet. "As you command, Lord Hand."

Ser Barristan went out onto the terrace. The rain had stopped, though a wall of slate-grey clouds hid the setting sun as it made its descent into Slaver's Bay. A few wisps of smoke still rose from the blackened stones of Hazdar, twisted like ribbons by the wind. Far off to the east, beyond the city walls, he saw pale wings moving above a distant line of hills. *Viserion.* Hunting, mayhaps, or flying just to fly. He wondered where Rhaegal was. Thus far the green dragon had shown himself to be more dangerous than the white.

When Bhakaz brought his wine, the old knight took one long swallow and sent the boy for water. A few cups of wine might be just the thing to help him sleep, but he would need his wits about him when Galazza Galare returned from treating with the foe. So he drank his wine well watered, as the world grew dark around him. He was very tired, and full of doubts. The Dornishmen, Hizdahr, Reznak, the attack . . . was he doing the right things? Was he doing what Daenerys would have wanted? *I was not made for this.* Other Kingsguard had served as Hand before him. Not many, but a few. He had read of them in the White Book. Now he found himself wondering whether they had felt as lost and confused as he did.

"Lord Hand." Grazhar stood in the door, a taper in his hand. "The Green Grace has come. You asked to be told."

"Show her in. And light some candles."

Galazza Galare was attended by four Pink Graces. An aura of wisdom and dignity seemed to surround her that Ser Barristan could not help but admire. *This is a strong woman, and she has been a faithful friend to Daenerys.* "Lord Hand," she said, her face hidden behind shimmering green veils. "May I sit? These bones are old and weary."

"Grazhar, a chair for the Green Grace." The Pink Graces arrayed themselves behind her, with eyes lowered and hands clasped before them. "May I offer you refreshment?" asked Ser Barristan.

"That would be most welcome, Ser Barristan. My throat is dry from talking. A juice, perhaps?"

"As you wish." He beckoned to Kezmya and had her fetch the priestess a goblet of lemon juice, sweetened with honey. To drink it, the priestess had to remove her veil, and Selmy was reminded of just how old she was. *Twenty years my elder, or more.* "If the queen were here, I know she would join me in thanking you for all that you have done for us."

"Her Magnificence has always been most gracious." Galazza Galare finished her drink and fastened up her veil again. "Have there been any further tidings of our sweet queen?"

"None as yet."

"I shall pray for her. And what of King Hizdahr, if I may be so bold? Might I be permitted to see His Radiance?"

"Soon, I hope. He is unharmed, I promise you."

"I am pleased to hear that. The Wise Masters of Yunkai asked after him. You will not be surprised to hear that they wish the noble Hizdahr to be restored at once to his rightful place."

"He shall be, if it can be proved that he did not try to kill our queen. Until such time, Meereen will be ruled by a council of the loyal and just. There is a place for you on that council. I know that you have much to teach us all, Your Benevolence. We need your wisdom."

"I fear you flatter me with empty courtesies, Lord Hand," the Green Grace said. "If you truly think me wise, heed me now. Release the noble Hizdahr and restore him to his throne."

"Only the queen can do that."

Beneath her veils, the Green Grace sighed. "The peace that we worked so hard to forge flutters like a leaf in an autumn wind. These are dire days. Death stalks our streets, riding the pale mare from thrice-cursed Astapor. Dragons haunt the skies, feasting on the flesh of children. Hundreds are taking ship, sailing for Yunkai, for Tolos, for Qarth, for any refuge that will have them. The pyramid of Hazkar has collapsed into a smoking ruin, and many of that ancient line lie dead beneath its blackened stones. The pyramids of Uhlez and Yherizan have become the lairs of monsters, their masters homeless beggars. My people have lost all hope and turned against the gods themselves, giving over their nights to drunkenness and fornication."

"And murder. The Sons of the Harpy slew thirty in the night."

"I grieve to hear this. All the more reason to free the noble Hizdahr zo Loraq, who stopped such killings once."

And how did he accomplish that, unless he is himself the Harpy?

"Her Grace gave her hand to Hizdahr zo Loraq, made him her king and consort, restored the mortal art as he beseeched her. In return he gave her poisoned locusts."

"In return he gave her peace. Do not cast it away, ser, I beg you. Peace is the pearl beyond price. Hizdahr is of Loraq. Never would he soil his hands with poison. He is innocent."

"How can you be certain?" *Unless you know the poisoner.*

"The gods of Ghis have told me."

"My gods are the Seven, and the Seven have been silent on this matter. Your Wisdom, did you present my offer?"

"To all the lords and captains of Yunkai, as you commanded me . . . yet I fear you will not like their answer."

"They refused?"

"They did. No amount of gold will buy your people back, I was told. Only the blood of dragons may set them free again."

It was the answer Ser Barristan had expected, if not the one that he had hoped for. His mouth tightened.

"I know these were not the words you wished to hear," said Galazza Galare. "Yet for myself, I understand. These dragons are fell beasts. Yunkai fears them . . . and with good cause, you cannot deny. Our histories speak of the dragonlords of dread Valyria and the devastation that they wrought upon the peoples of Old Ghis. Even your own young queen, fair Daenerys who called herself the Mother of Dragons . . . we saw her burning, that day in the pit . . . even she was not safe from the dragon's wroth."

"Her Grace is not . . . she . . ."

". . . is dead. May the gods grant her sweet sleep." Tears glistened behind her veils. "Let her dragons die as well."

Selmy was groping for an answer when he heard the sound of heavy footsteps. The door burst inward, and Skahaz mo Kandaq stormed in with four Brazen Beasts behind him. When Grazhar tried to block his path, he slammed the boy aside.

Ser Barristan was on his feet at once. "What is it?"

"The trebuchets," the Shavepate growled. "All six."

Galazza Galare rose. "Thus does Yunkai make reply to your offers, ser. I warned you that you would not like their answer."

They choose war, then. So be it. Ser Barristan felt oddly relieved.

War he understood. "If they think they will break Meereen by throwing stones—"

"Not stones." The old woman's voice was full of grief, of fear. "Corpses."

DAENERYS

The hill was a stony island in a sea of green.

It took Dany half the morning to climb down. By the time she reached the bottom she was winded. Her muscles ached, and she felt as if she had the beginnings of a fever. The rocks had scraped her hands raw. *They are better than they were, though*, she decided as she picked at a broken blister. Her skin was pink and tender, and a pale milky fluid was leaking from her cracked palms, but her burns were healing.

The hill loomed larger down here. Dany had taken to calling it Dragonstone, after the ancient citadel where she'd been born. She had no memories of that Dragonstone, but she would not soon forget this one. Scrub grass and thorny bushes covered its lower slopes; higher up a jagged tangle of bare rock thrust steep and sudden into the sky. There, amidst broken boulders, razor-sharp ridges, and needle spires, Drogon made his lair inside a shallow cave. He had dwelt there for some time, Dany had realized when she first saw the hill. The air smelled of ash, every rock and tree in sight was scorched and blackened, the ground strewn with burned and broken bones, yet it had been home to him.

Dany knew the lure of home.

Two days ago, climbing on a spire of rock, she had spied water to the south, a slender thread that glittered briefly as the sun was going down. *A stream*, Dany decided. Small, but it would lead her to a larger stream, and that stream would flow into some little river, and all the rivers in this part of the world were vassals of the Skahazadhan. Once she found the Skahazadhan she need only follow it downstream to Slaver's Bay.

She would sooner have returned to Meereen on dragon's wings, to be sure. But that was a desire Drogon did not seem to share.

The dragonlords of old Valyria had controlled their mounts with binding spells and sorcerous horns. Daenerys made do with a word and a whip. Mounted on the dragon's back, she oft felt as if she were learning to ride all over again. When she whipped her silver mare on her right flank the mare went left, for a horse's first instinct is to flee from danger. When she laid the whip across Drogon's right side he veered right, for a dragon's first instinct is always to attack. Sometimes it did not seem to matter where she struck him, though; sometimes he went where he would and took her with him. Neither whip nor words could turn Drogon if he did not wish to be turned. The whip annoyed him more than it hurt him, she had come to see; his scales had grown harder than horn.

And no matter how far the dragon flew each day, come nightfall some instinct drew him home to Dragonstone. *His home, not mine.* Her home was back in Meereen, with her husband and her lover. That was where she belonged, surely.

Keep walking. If I look back I am lost.

Memories walked with her. Clouds seen from above. Horses small as ants thundering through the grass. A silver moon, almost close enough to touch. Rivers running bright and blue below, glimmering in the sun. *Will I ever see such sights again?* On Drogon's back she felt *whole*. Up in the sky the woes of this world could not touch her. How could she abandon that?

It was time, though. A girl might spend her life at play, but she was a woman grown, a queen, a wife, a mother to thousands. Her children had need of her. Drogon had bent before the whip, and so must she. She had to don her crown again and return to her ebon bench and the arms of her noble husband.

Hizdahr, of the tepid kisses.

The sun was hot this morning, the sky blue and cloudless. That was good. Dany's clothes were hardly more than rags, and offered little in the way of warmth. One of her sandals had slipped off during her wild flight from Meereen and she had left the other up by Drogon's cave, preferring to go barefoot rather than half-shod. Her *tokar* and veils she had abandoned in the pit, and her linen undertunic had never been made to withstand the hot days and cold nights of the Dothraki sea. Sweat and grass and dirt had stained it, and Dany had torn a strip off the hem to make a bandage for her shin. *I must look a ragged thing, and starved*, she thought, *but if the days stay warm, I will not freeze.*

Hers had been a lonely sojourn, and for most of it she had been hurt and hungry . . . yet despite it all she had been strangely happy here. *A few aches, an empty belly, chills by night . . . what does it matter when you can fly? I would do it all again.*

Jhiqui and Irri would be waiting atop her pyramid back in Meereen, she told herself. Her sweet scribe Missandei as well, and all her little pages. They would bring her food, and she could bathe in the pool beneath the persimmon tree. It would be good to feel clean again. Dany did not need a glass to know that she was filthy.

She was hungry too. One morning she had found some wild onions growing halfway down the south slope, and later that same day a leafy reddish vegetable that might have been some queer sort of cabbage. Whatever it was, it had not made her sick. Aside from that, and one fish that she had caught in the spring-fed pool outside of Drogon's cave, she had survived as best she could on the dragon's leavings, on burned bones and chunks of smoking meat, half-charred and half-raw. She needed more, she knew. One day she kicked at a cracked sheep's skull with the side of a bare foot and sent it bouncing over the edge of the hill. And as she watched it tumble down the steep slope toward the sea of grass, she realized she must follow.

Dany set off through the tall grass at a brisk pace. The earth felt warm between her toes. The grass was as tall as she was. *It never seemed so high when I was mounted on my silver, riding beside my sun-and-stars at the head of his khalasar.* As she walked, she tapped her thigh with the pitmaster's whip. That, and the rags on her back, were all she had taken from Meereen.

Though she walked through a green kingdom, it was not the deep rich green of summer. Even here autumn made its presence felt, and winter would not be far behind. The grass was paler than she remembered, a wan and sickly green on the verge of going yellow. After that would come brown. The grass was dying.

Daenerys Targaryen was no stranger to the Dothraki sea, the great ocean of grass that stretched from the forest of Qohor to the Mother of Mountains and the Womb of the World. She had seen it first when she was still a girl, newly wed to Khal Drogo and on her way to Vaes Dothrak to be presented to the crones of the *dosh khaleen*. The sight of all that grass stretching out before her had taken her breath away. *The sky was blue, the grass was green, and I was full of hope.* Ser Jorah had been with her then, her gruff old bear. She'd had Irri and Jhiqui and Doreah to care for her, her sun-and-stars to hold her in the night, his child growing inside her. *Rhaego. I was going to name him Rhaego, and the* dosh khaleen *said he would be the Stallion Who Mounts the World.* Not since those half-remembered days in Braavos when she lived in the house with the red door had she been as happy.

But in the Red Waste, all her joy had turned to ashes. Her sun-and-stars had fallen from his horse, the *maegi* Mirri Maz Duur had murdered Rhaego in her womb, and Dany had smothered the empty shell of Khal Drogo with her own two hands. Afterward Drogo's great *khalasar* had shattered. Ko Pono named himself Khal Pono and took many riders with him, and many slaves as well. Ko Jhaqo named himself Khal Jhaqo and rode off with even more. Mago, his bloodrider, raped and murdered Eroeh, a girl Daenerys had once saved from him. Only the birth of her dragons amidst the fire and smoke of Khal Drogo's funeral pyre had spared Dany herself from being dragged back to Vaes Dothrak to live out the remainder of her days amongst the crones of the *dosh khaleen*.

The fire burned away my hair, but elsewise it did not touch me. It had been the same in Daznak's Pit. That much she could recall, though much of what followed was a haze. *So many people, screaming and shoving.* She remembered rearing horses, a food cart spilling melons as it overturned. From below a spear came flying, followed by a flight of crossbow bolts. One passed so close that Dany felt it brush her cheek. Others skittered off Drogon's scales, lodged between them, or tore through the membrane of his wings. She remembered the dragon twisting beneath her, shuddering at the impacts, as she tried desperately to cling to his scaled back. The wounds were smoking. Dany saw one of the bolts burst into sudden flame. Another fell away, shaken loose by the beating of his wings. Below, she saw men whirling, wreathed in flame, hands up in the air as if caught in the throes of some mad dance. A woman in a green *tokar* reached for a weeping child, pulling him down into her arms to shield him from the flames. Dany saw the color vividly, but not the woman's face. People were stepping on her as they lay tangled on the bricks. Some were on fire.

Then all of that had faded, the sounds dwindling, the people shrinking, the spears and arrows falling back beneath them as Drogon clawed his way into the sky. Up and up and up he'd borne her, high above the pyramids and pits, his wings outstretched to catch the warm air rising from the city's sunbaked bricks. *If I fall and die, it will still have been worth it*, she had thought.

North they flew, beyond the river, Drogon gliding on torn and tattered wings through clouds that whipped by like the banners of some ghostly army. Dany glimpsed the shores of Slaver's Bay and the old Valyrian road that ran beside it through sand and desolation until it vanished in the west. *The road home.* Then there was nothing beneath them but grass rippling in the wind.

Was that first flight a thousand years ago? Sometimes it seemed as if it must be.

The sun grew hotter as it rose, and before long her head was pounding. Dany's hair was growing out again, but slowly. "I need a hat," she said aloud. Up on Dragonstone she had tried to make one for herself, weaving stalks of grass together as she had seen Dothraki women do during her time with Drogo, but either she was using the wrong sort of grass or she simply lacked the necessary skill. Her hats all fell to pieces in her hands. *Try again*, she told herself. *You will do better the next time. You are the blood of the dragon, you can make a hat.* She tried and tried, but her last attempt had been no more successful than her first.

It was afternoon by the time Dany found the stream she had glimpsed atop the hill. It was a rill, a rivulet, a trickle, no wider than her arm . . . and her arm had grown thinner every day she spent on Dragonstone. Dany scooped up a handful of water and splashed it on her face. When she cupped her hands, her knuckles squished in the mud at the bottom of the stream. She might have wished for colder, clearer water . . . but no, if she were going to pin her hopes on wishes, she would wish for rescue.

She still clung to the hope that someone would come after her. Ser Barristan might come seeking her; he was the first of her Queensguard, sworn to defend her life with his own. And her bloodriders were no strangers to the Dothraki sea, and their lives were bound to her own. Her husband, the noble Hizdahr zo Loraq, might dispatch searchers. And Daario . . . Dany pictured him riding toward her through the tall grass, smiling, his golden tooth gleaming with the last light of the setting sun.

Only Daario had been given to the Yunkai'i, a hostage to ensure no harm came to the Yunkish captains. *Daario and Hero, Jhogo and Groleo, and three of Hizdahr's kin.* By now, surely, all of her hostages would have been released. But . . .

She wondered if her captain's blades still hung upon the wall beside her bed, waiting for Daario to return and claim them. *"I will leave my girls with you,"* he had said. *"Keep them safe for me, beloved."* And she wondered how much the Yunkai'i knew about what her captain meant to her. She had asked Ser Barristan that question the afternoon the hostages went forth. "They will have heard the talk," he had replied. "Naharis may even have boasted of Your Grace's . . . of your great . . . regard . . . for him. If you will forgive my saying so, modesty is not one of the captain's virtues. He takes great pride in his . . . his swordsmanship."

He boasts of bedding me, you mean. But Daario would not have been so foolish as to make such a boast amongst her enemies. *It makes no matter. By now the Yunkai'i will be marching home.* That was why she had done all that she had done. For peace.

She turned back the way she'd come, to where Dragonstone rose above the grasslands like a clenched fist. *It looks so close. I've been walking for hours, yet it still looks as if I could reach out and touch it.* It was not too late to go back. There were fish in the spring-fed pool by Drogon's cave. She had caught one her first day there, she might catch more. And there would be scraps, charred bones with bits of flesh still on them, the remnants of Drogon's kills.

No, Dany told herself. *If I look back I am lost.* She might live for years amongst the sunbaked rocks of Dragonstone, riding Drogon by day and gnawing at his leavings every evenfall as the great grass sea turned from gold to orange, but that was not the life she had been born to. So once again she turned her back upon the distant hill and closed her ears to the song of flight and freedom that the wind sang as it played amongst the hill's stony ridges. The stream was trickling south by southeast, as near as she could tell. She followed it. *Take me to the river, that is all I ask of you. Take me to the river, and I will do the rest.*

The hours passed slowly. The stream bent this way and that, and Dany followed, beating time upon her leg with the whip, trying not to think about how far she had to go, or the pounding in her head, or her empty belly. *Take one step. Take the next. Another step. Another.* What else could she do?

It was quiet on her sea. When the wind blew the grass would sigh as the stalks brushed against each other, whispering in a tongue that only gods could understand. Now and again the little stream would gurgle where it flowed around a stone. Mud squished between her toes. Insects buzzed around her, lazy dragonflies and glistening green wasps and stinging midges almost too small to see. She swatted at them absently when they landed on her arms. Once she came upon a rat drinking from the stream, but it fled when she appeared, scurrying between the stalks to vanish in the high grass. Sometimes she heard birds singing. The sound made her belly rumble, but she had no nets to snare them with, and so far she had not come on any nests. *Once I dreamed of flying,* she thought, *and now I've flown, and dream of stealing eggs.* That made her laugh. "Men are mad and gods are madder," she told the grass, and the grass murmured its agreement.

Thrice that day she caught sight of Drogon. Once he was so far off that he might have been an eagle, slipping in and out of distant clouds, but Dany knew the look of him by now, even when he was no more than a speck. The second time he passed before the sun, his black wings spread, and the world darkened. The last time he flew right above her, so close she could hear the sound of his wings. For half a heartbeat Dany thought that he was hunting her, but he flew on without taking any notice of her and vanished somewhere in the east. *Just as well*, she thought.

Evening took her almost unawares. As the sun was gilding the distant spires of Dragonstone, Dany stumbled onto a low stone wall, overgrown and broken. Perhaps it had been part of a temple, or the hall of the village lord. More ruins lay beyond it—an old well, and some circles in the grass that marked the sites where hovels had once stood. They had been built of mud and straw, she judged, but long years of wind and rain had worn them away to nothing. Dany found eight before the sun went down, but there might have been more farther out, hidden in the grass.

The stone wall had endured better than the rest. Though it was nowhere more than three feet high, the angle where it met another, lower wall still offered some shelter from the elements, and night was coming on fast. Dany wedged herself into that corner, making a nest of sorts by tearing up handfuls of the grass that grew around the ruins. She was very tired, and fresh blisters had appeared on both her feet, including a matched set upon her pinky toes. *It must be from the way I walk*, she thought, giggling.

As the world darkened, Dany settled in and closed her eyes, but sleep refused to come. The night was cold, the ground hard, her belly empty. She found herself thinking of Meereen, of Daario, her love, and Hizdahr, her husband, of Irri and Jhiqui and sweet Missandei, Ser Barristan and Reznak and Skahaz Shavepate. *Do they fear me dead? I flew off on a dragon's back. Will they think he ate me?* She wondered if Hizdahr was still king. His crown had come from her, could he hold it in her absence? *He wanted Drogon dead. I heard him.* "Kill it," he screamed, "kill the beast," *and the look upon his face was lustful.* And Strong Belwas had been on his knees, heaving and shuddering. *Poison. It had to be poison. The honeyed locusts. Hizdahr urged them on me, but Belwas ate them all.* She had made Hizdahr her king, taken him into her bed, opened the fighting pits for him, he had no reason to want her dead. Yet who else could it have been? Reznak, her perfumed seneschal? The Yunkai'i? The Sons of the Harpy?

Off in the distance, a wolf howled. The sound made her feel sad and lonely, but no less hungry. As the moon rose above the grasslands, Dany slipped at last into a restless sleep.

She dreamed. All her cares fell away from her, and all her pains as well, and she seemed to float upward into the sky. She was flying once again, spinning, laughing, dancing, as the stars wheeled around her and whispered secrets in her ear. "To go north, you must journey south. To reach the west, you must go east. To go forward, you must go back. To touch the light you must pass beneath the shadow."

"Quaithe?" Dany called. "Where are you, Quaithe?"

Then she saw. *Her mask is made of starlight.*

"Remember who you are, Daenerys," the stars whispered in a woman's voice. "The dragons know. Do you?"

The next morning she woke stiff and sore and aching, with ants crawling on her arms and legs and face. When she realized what they were, she kicked aside the stalks of dry brown grass that had served as her bed and blanket and struggled to her feet. She had bites all over her, little red bumps, itchy and inflamed. *Where did all the ants come from?* Dany brushed them from her arms and legs and belly. She ran a hand across her stubbly scalp where her hair had burned away, and felt more ants on her head, and one crawling down the back of her neck. She knocked them off and crushed them under her bare feet. There were so many . . .

It turned out that their anthill was on the other side of her wall. She wondered how the ants had managed to climb over it and find her. To them these tumbledown stones must loom as huge as the Wall of Westeros. *The biggest wall in all the world*, her brother Viserys used to say, as proud as if he'd built it himself.

Viserys told her tales of knights so poor that they had to sleep beneath the ancient hedges that grew along the byways of the Seven Kingdoms. Dany would have given much and more for a nice thick hedge. *Preferably one without an anthill.*

The sun was only just coming up. A few bright stars lingered in the cobalt sky. *Perhaps one of them is Khal Drogo, sitting on his fiery stallion in the night lands and smiling down on me.* Dragonstone was still visible above the grasslands. *It looks so close. I must be leagues away by now, but it looks as if I could be back in an hour.* She wanted to lie back down, close her eyes, and give herself up to sleep. *No. I must keep going. The stream. Just follow the stream.*

Dany took a moment to make certain of her directions. It would not do to walk the wrong way and lose her stream. "My friend," she said aloud. "If I stay close to my friend I won't get lost." She would have slept beside the water if she dared, but there were animals who came down to the stream to drink at night. She had seen their tracks. Dany would make a poor meal for a wolf or lion, but even a poor meal was better than none.

Once she was certain which way was south, she counted off her paces. The stream appeared at eight. Dany cupped her hands to drink. The water made her belly cramp, but cramps were easier to bear than thirst. She had no other drink but the morning dew that glistened on the tall grass, and no food at all unless she cared to eat the grass. *I could try eating ants.* The little yellow ones were too small to provide much in the way of nourishment, but there were red ants in the grass, and those were bigger. "I am lost at sea," she said as she limped along beside her meandering rivulet, "so perhaps I'll find some crabs, or a nice fat fish." Her whip slapped softly against her thigh, *wap wap wap*. One step at a time, and the stream would see her home.

Just past midday she came upon a bush growing by the stream, its twisted limbs covered with hard green berries. Dany squinted at them suspiciously, then plucked one from a branch and nibbled at it. Its flesh was tart and chewy, with a bitter aftertaste that seemed familiar to her. "In the *khalasar*, they used berries like these to flavor roasts," she decided. Saying it aloud made her more certain of it. Her belly rumbled, and Dany found herself picking berries with both hands and tossing them into her mouth.

An hour later, her stomach began to cramp so badly that she could not go on. She spent the rest of that day retching up green slime. *If I stay here, I will die. I may be dying now.* Would the horse god of the

Dothraki part the grass and claim her for his starry *khalasar*, so she might ride the nightlands with Khal Drogo? In Westeros the dead of House Targaryen were given to the flames, but who would light her pyre here? *My flesh will feed the wolves and carrion crows*, she thought sadly, *and worms will burrow through my womb*. Her eyes went back to Dragonstone. It looked smaller. She could see smoke rising from its wind-carved summit, miles away. *Drogon has returned from hunting*.

Sunset found her squatting in the grass, groaning. Every stool was looser than the one before, and smelled fouler. By the time the moon came up she was shitting brown water. The more she drank, the more she shat, but the more she shat, the thirstier she grew, and her thirst sent her crawling to the stream to suck up more water. When she closed her eyes at last, Dany did not know whether she would be strong enough to open them again.

She dreamt of her dead brother.

Viserys looked just as he had the last time she'd seen him. His mouth was twisted in anguish, his hair was burnt, and his face was black and smoking where the molten gold had run down across his brow and cheeks and into his eyes.

"You are dead," Dany said.

Murdered. Though his lips never moved, somehow she could hear his voice, whispering in her ear. *You never mourned me, sister. It is hard to die unmourned*.

"I loved you once."

Once, he said, so bitterly it made her shudder. *You were supposed to be my wife, to bear me children with silver hair and purple eyes, to keep the blood of the dragon pure. I took care of you. I taught you who you were. I fed you. I sold our mother's crown to keep you fed*.

"You hurt me. You frightened me."

Only when you woke the dragon. I loved you.

"You sold me. You betrayed me."

No. You were the betrayer. You turned against me, against your own blood. They cheated me. Your horsey husband and his stinking savages. They were cheats and liars. They promised me a golden crown and gave me this. He touched the molten gold that was creeping down his face, and smoke rose from his finger.

"You could have had your crown," Dany told him. "My sun-and-stars would have won it for you if only you had waited."

I waited long enough. I waited my whole life. I was their king, their rightful king. They laughed at me.

"You should have stayed in Pentos with Magister Illyrio. Khal Drogo had to present me to the *dosh khaleen*, but you did not have to ride with us. That was your choice. Your mistake."

Do you want to wake the dragon, you stupid little whore? Drogo's khalasar was mine. I bought them from him, a hundred thousand screamers. I paid for them with your maidenhead.

"You never understood. Dothraki do not buy and sell. They give gifts and receive them. If you had waited . . ."

I did wait. For my crown, for my throne, for you. All those years, and all I ever got was a pot of molten gold. Why did they give the dragon's eggs to you? They should have been mine. If I'd had a dragon, I would have taught the world the meaning of our words. Viserys began to laugh, until his jaw fell away from his face, smoking, and blood and molten gold ran from his mouth.

When she woke, gasping, her thighs were slick with blood.

For a moment she did not realize what it was. The world had just begun to lighten, and the tall grass rustled softly in the wind. *No, please, let me sleep some more. I'm so tired.* She tried to burrow back beneath the pile of grass she had torn up when she went to sleep. Some of the stalks felt wet. Had it rained again? She sat up, afraid that she had soiled herself as she slept. When she brought her fingers to her face, she could smell the blood on them. *Am I dying?* Then she saw the pale crescent moon, floating high above the grass, and it came to her that this was no more than her moon blood.

If she had not been so sick and scared, that might have come as a relief. Instead she began to shiver violently. She rubbed her fingers through the dirt, and grabbed a handful of grass to wipe between her legs. *The dragon does not weep.* She was bleeding, but it was only woman's blood. *The moon is still a crescent, though. How can that be?* She tried to remember the last time she had bled. The last full moon? The one before? The one before that? *No, it cannot have been so long as that.* "I am the blood of the dragon," she told the grass, aloud.

Once, the grass whispered back, *until you chained your dragons in the dark.*

"Drogon killed a little girl. Her name was . . . her name . . ." Dany could not recall the child's name. That made her so sad that she would have cried if all her tears had not been burned away. "I will never have a little girl. I was the Mother of Dragons."

Aye, the grass said, *but you turned against your children.*

Her belly was empty, her feet sore and blistered, and it seemed to her that the cramping had grown worse. Her guts were full of writhing snakes biting at her bowels. She scooped up a handful of mud and water in trembling hands. By midday the water would be tepid, but in the chill of dawn it was almost cool and helped her keep her eyes open. As she splashed her face, she saw fresh blood on her thighs. The ragged hem of her undertunic was stained with it. The sight of so much red frightened her. *Moon blood, it's only my moon blood*, but she did not remember ever having such a heavy flow. *Could it be the water?* If it was the water, she was doomed. She had to drink or die of thirst.

"Walk," Dany commanded herself. "Follow the stream and it will take you to the Skahazadhan. That's where Daario will find you." But it took all her strength just to get back to her feet, and when she did all she could do was stand there, fevered and bleeding. She raised her eyes to the empty blue sky, squinting at the sun. *Half the morning gone already*, she realized, dismayed. She made herself take a step, and then another, and then she was walking once again, following the little stream.

The day grew warmer, and the sun beat down upon her head and the burnt remnants of her hair. Water splashed against the soles of her feet. She was walking in the stream. How long had she been doing that? The soft brown mud felt good between her toes and helped to soothe her blisters. *In the stream or out of it, I must keep walking. Water flows downhill. The stream will take me to the river, and the river will take me home.*

Except it wouldn't, not truly.

Meereen was not her home, and never would be. It was a city of strange men with strange gods and stranger hair, of slavers wrapped in fringed *tokar*s, where grace was earned through whoring, butchery was art, and dog was a delicacy. Meereen would always be the Harpy's city, and Daenerys could not be a harpy.

Never, said the grass, in the gruff tones of Jorah Mormont. *You were warned, Your Grace. Let this city be, I said. Your war is in Westeros, I told you.*

The voice was no more than a whisper, yet somehow Dany felt that he was walking just behind her. *My bear*, she thought, *my old sweet bear, who loved me and betrayed me.* She had missed him so. She wanted to see his ugly face, to wrap her arms around him and press herself against his chest, but she knew that if she turned around Ser Jorah would be gone. "I am dreaming," she said. "A waking dream, a walking dream. I am alone and lost."

Lost, because you lingered, in a place that you were never meant to be, murmured Ser Jorah, as softly as the wind. *Alone, because you sent me from your side.*

"You betrayed me. You informed on me, for gold."

For home. Home was all I ever wanted.

"And me. You wanted me." Dany had seen it in his eyes.

I did, the grass whispered, sadly.

"You kissed me. I never said you could, but you did. You sold me to my enemies, but you meant it when you kissed me."

I gave you good counsel. Save your spears and swords for the Seven Kingdoms, I told you. Leave Meereen to the Meereenese and go west, I said. You would not listen.

"I had to take Meereen or see my children starve along the march." Dany could still see the trail of corpses she had left behind her crossing the Red Waste. It was not a sight she wished to see again. "I had to take Meereen to feed my people."

You took Meereen, he told her, *yet still you lingered.*

"To be a queen."

You are a queen, her bear said. *In Westeros.*

"It is such a long way," she complained. "I was tired, Jorah. I was weary of war. I wanted to rest, to laugh, to plant trees and see them grow. I am only a young girl."

No. You are the blood of the dragon. The whispering was growing fainter, as if Ser Jorah were falling farther behind. *Dragons plant no trees. Remember that. Remember who you are, what you were made to be. Remember your words.*

"Fire and Blood," Daenerys told the swaying grass.

A stone turned under her foot. She stumbled to one knee and cried out in pain, hoping against hope that her bear would gather her up and help her to her feet. When she turned her head to look for him, all she saw was trickling brown water . . . and the grass, still moving slightly. *The wind,* she told herself, *the wind shakes the stalks and makes them sway.* Only no wind was blowing. The sun was overhead, the world still and hot. Midges swarmed in the air, and a dragonfly floated over the stream, darting here and there. And the grass was moving when it had no cause to move.

She fumbled in the water, found a stone the size of her fist, pulled it from the mud. It was a poor weapon but better than an empty hand. From the corner of her eye Dany saw the grass move again, off to her right. The grass swayed and bowed low, as if before a king, but no king appeared to her. The world was green and empty. The world was green and silent. The world was yellow, dying. *I should get up,* she told herself. *I have to walk. I have to follow the stream.*

Through the grass came a soft silvery tinkling.

Bells, Dany thought, smiling, remembering Khal Drogo, her sun-and-stars, and the bells he braided into his hair. *When the sun rises in the west and sets in the east, when the seas go dry and mountains blow in the wind like leaves, when my womb quickens again and I bear a living child, Khal Drogo will return to me.*

But none of those things had happened. *Bells,* Dany thought again. Her bloodriders had found her. "Aggo," she whispered. "Jhogo. Rakharo." Might Daario have come with them?

The green sea opened. A rider appeared. His braid was black and shiny, his skin as dark as burnished copper, his eyes the shape of bitter almonds. Bells sang in his hair. He wore a medallion belt and painted vest, with an *arakh* on one hip and a whip on the other. A hunting bow and a quiver of arrows were slung from his saddle.

One rider, and alone. A scout. He was one who rode before the *khalasar* to find the game and the good green grass, and sniff out foes wherever they might hide. If he found her there, he would kill her, rape her, or enslave her. At best, he would send her back to the crones of the *dosh khaleen*, where good *khaleesi* were supposed to go when their khals had died.

He did not see her, though. The grass concealed her, and he was looking elsewhere. Dany followed his eyes, and there the shadow flew, with wings spread wide. The dragon was a mile off, and yet the scout stood frozen until his stallion began to whicker in fear. Then he woke as if from a dream, wheeled his mount about, and raced off through the tall grass at a gallop.

Dany watched him go. When the sound of his hooves had faded away to silence, she began to shout. She called until her voice was hoarse . . . and Drogon came, snorting plumes of smoke. The grass bowed down before him. Dany leapt onto his back. She stank of blood and sweat and fear, but none of that mattered. "To go forward I must go back," she said. Her bare legs tightened around the dragon's neck. She kicked him, and Drogon threw himself into the sky. Her whip was gone, so she used her hands and feet and turned him north by east, the way the scout had gone. Drogon went willingly enough; perhaps he smelled the rider's fear.

In a dozen heartbeats they were past the Dothraki, as he galloped far below. To the right and left, Dany glimpsed places where the grass was burned and ashen. *Drogon has come this way before*, she realized. Like a chain of grey islands, the marks of his hunting dotted the green grass sea.

A vast herd of horses appeared below them. There were riders too, a score or more, but they turned and fled at the first sight of the dragon. The horses broke and ran when the shadow fell upon them, racing through the grass until their sides were white with foam, tearing the ground with their hooves . . . but as swift as they were, they could not fly. Soon one horse began to lag behind the others. The dragon descended on him, roaring, and all at once the poor beast was aflame, yet somehow he kept on running, screaming with every step, until Drogon landed on him and broke his back. Dany clutched the dragon's neck with all her strength to keep from sliding off.

The carcass was too heavy for him to bear back to his lair, so

Drogon consumed his kill there, tearing at the charred flesh as the grasses burned around them, the air thick with drifting smoke and the smell of burnt horsehair. Dany, starved, slid off his back and ate with him, ripping chunks of smoking meat from the dead horse with bare, burned hands. *In Meereen I was a queen in silk, nibbling on stuffed dates and honeyed lamb*, she remembered. *What would my noble husband think if he could see me now?* Hizdahr would be horrified, no doubt. But Daario . . .

Daario would laugh, carve off a hunk of horsemeat with his *arakh*, and squat down to eat beside her.

As the western sky turned the color of a blood bruise, she heard the sound of approaching horses. Dany rose, wiped her hands on her ragged undertunic, and went to stand beside her dragon.

That was how Khal Jhaqo found her, when half a hundred mounted warriors emerged from the drifting smoke.

EPILOGUE

"I am no traitor," the Knight of Griffin's Roost declared. "I am King Tommen's man, and yours."

A steady *drip-drip-drip* punctuated his words, as snowmelt ran off his cloak to puddle on the floor. The snow had been falling on King's Landing most of the night; outside the drifts were ankle deep. Ser Kevan Lannister pulled his cloak about himself more closely. "So you say, ser. Words are wind."

"Then let me prove the truth of them with my sword." The light of the torches made a fiery blaze of Ronnet Connington's long red hair and beard. "Send me against my uncle, and I will bring you back his head, and the head of this false dragon too."

Lannister spearmen in crimson cloaks and lion-crested halfhelms stood along the west wall of the throne room. Tyrell guards in green cloaks faced them from the opposite wall. The chill in the throne room was palpable. Though neither Queen Cersei nor Queen Margaery was amongst them, their presence could be felt poisoning the air, like ghosts at a feast.

Behind the table where the five members of the king's small council were seated, the Iron Throne crouched like some great black beast, its barbs and claws and blades half-shrouded in shadow. Kevan Lannister could feel it at his back, an itch between the shoulder blades. It was easy to imagine old King Aerys perched up there, bleeding from some fresh cut, glowering down. But today the throne was empty. He had seen no reason for Tommen to join them. Kinder to let the boy remain with his mother. The Seven only knew how long mother and son might have together before Cersei's trial . . . and possibly her execution.

Mace Tyrell was speaking. "We shall deal with your uncle and his feigned boy in due time." The new King's Hand was seated on an oaken throne carved in the shape of a hand, an absurd vanity his lordship had produced the day Ser Kevan agreed to grant him the office he coveted. "You will bide here until we are ready to march. Then you shall have the chance to prove your loyalty."

Ser Kevan took no issue with that. "Escort Ser Ronnet back to his chambers," he said. *And see that he remains there* went unspoken. However loud his protestations, the Knight of Griffin's Roost remained suspect. Supposedly the sellswords who had landed in the south were being led by one of his own blood.

As the echoes of Connington's footsteps faded away, Grand Maester Pycelle gave a ponderous shake of his head. "His uncle once stood just where the boy was standing now and told King Aerys how he would deliver him the head of Robert Baratheon."

That is how it is when a man grows as old as Pycelle. Everything you see or hear reminds you of something you saw or heard when you were young. "How many men-at-arms accompanied Ser Ronnet to the city?" Ser Kevan asked.

"Twenty," said Lord Randyll Tarly, "and most of them Gregor Clegane's old lot. Your nephew Jaime gave them to Connington. To rid himself of them, I'd wager. They had not been in Maidenpool a day before one killed a man and another was accused of rape. I had to hang the one and geld the other. If it were up to me, I would send them all to the Night's Watch, and Connington with them. The Wall is where such scum belong."

"A dog takes after its master," declared Mace Tyrell. "Black cloaks would suit them, I agree. I will not suffer such men in the city watch." A hundred of his own Highgarden men had been added to the gold cloaks, yet plainly his lordship meant to resist any balancing infusion of westermen.

The more I give him, the more he wants. Kevan Lannister was beginning to understand why Cersei had grown so resentful of the Tyrells. But this was not the moment to provoke an open quarrel. Randyll Tarly and Mace Tyrell had both brought armies to King's Landing, whilst the best part of the strength of House Lannister remained in the riverlands, fast melting away. "The Mountain's men were always fighters," he said in a conciliatory tone, "and we may have need of every sword against these sellswords. If this truly is the Golden Company, as Qyburn's whisperers insist—"

"Call them what you will," said Randyll Tarly. "They are still no more than adventurers."

"Perhaps," Ser Kevan said. "But the longer we ignore these adventurers, the stronger they grow. We have had a map prepared, a map of the incursions. Grand Maester?"

The map was beautiful, painted by a master's hand on a sheet of the finest vellum, so large it covered the table. "Here." Pycelle pointed with a spotted hand. Where the sleeve of his robe rode up, a flap of pale flesh could be seen dangling beneath his forearm. "Here and here. All along the coast, and on the islands. Tarth, the Stepstones, even Estermont. And now we have reports that Connington is moving on Storm's End."

"If it is Jon Connington," said Randyll Tarly.

"Storm's End." Lord Mace Tyrell grunted the words. "He cannot take Storm's End. Not if he were Aegon the Conqueror. And if he does, what of it? Stannis holds it now. Let the castle pass from one pretender to another, why should that trouble us? I shall recapture it after my daughter's innocence is proved."

How can you recapture it when you have never captured it to begin with? "I understand, my lord, but—"

Tyrell did not let him finish. "These charges against my daughter are filthy lies. I ask again, *why* must we play out this mummer's farce? Have King Tommen declare my daughter innocent, ser, and put an end to the foolishness here and now."

Do that, and the whispers will follow Margaery the rest of her life. "No man doubts your daughter's innocence, my lord," Ser Kevan lied, "but His High Holiness insists upon a trial."

Lord Randyll snorted. "What have we become, when kings and high lords must dance to the twittering of sparrows?"

"We have foes on every hand, Lord Tarly," Ser Kevan reminded him. "Stannis in the north, ironmen in the west, sellswords in the south. Defy the High Septon, and we will have blood running in the gutters of King's Landing as well. If we are seen to be going against the gods, it will only drive the pious into the arms of one or the other of these would-be usurpers."

Mace Tyrell remained unmoved. "Once Paxter Redwyne sweeps the ironmen from the seas, my sons will retake the Shields. The snows will do for Stannis, or Bolton will. As for Connington . . ."

"If it is him," Lord Randyll said.

". . . as for Connington," Tyrell repeated, "what victories has he ever won that we should fear him? He could have ended Robert's Rebellion at Stoney Sept. He failed. Just as the Golden Company has always failed. Some may rush to join them, aye. The realm is well rid of such fools."

Ser Kevan wished that he could share his certainty. He had known Jon Connington, slightly—a proud youth, the most headstrong of the gaggle of young lordlings who had gathered around Prince Rhaegar Targaryen, competing for his royal favor. *Arrogant, but able and energetic.* That, and his skill at arms, was why Mad King Aerys had named him Hand. Old Lord Merryweather's inaction had allowed the rebellion to take root and spread, and Aerys wanted someone young and vigorous to match Robert's own youth and vigor. "Too soon," Lord Tywin Lannister had declared when word of the king's choice had reached Casterly Rock. "Connington is too young, too bold, too eager for glory."

The Battle of the Bells had proved the truth of that. Ser Kevan had expected that afterward Aerys would have no choice but to summon Tywin once more . . . but the Mad King had turned to the Lords Chelsted and Rossart instead, and paid for it with life and crown. *That was all so long ago, though. If this is indeed Jon Connington, he will be a different man. Older, harder, more seasoned . . . more dangerous.* "Connington may have more than the Golden Company. It is said he has a Targaryen pretender."

"A feigned boy is what he has," said Randyll Tarly.

"That may be. Or not." Kevan Lannister had been here, in this very hall when Tywin had laid the bodies of Prince Rhaegar's children at the foot of the Iron Throne, wrapped up in crimson cloaks. *The girl had been recognizably the Princess Rhaenys, but the boy . . . a faceless horror of bone and brain and gore, a few hanks of fair hair. None of us looked long. Tywin said that it was Prince Aegon, and we took him at his word.* "We have these tales coming from the east as well. A second Targaryen, and one whose blood no man can question. Daenerys Stormborn."

"As mad as her father," declared Lord Mace Tyrell.

That would be the same father that Highgarden and House Tyrell supported to the bitter end and well beyond. "Mad she may be," Ser Kevan said, "but with so much smoke drifting west, surely there must be some fire burning in the east."

Grand Maester Pycelle bobbed his head. "Dragons. These same stories have reached Oldtown. Too many to discount. A silver-haired queen with three dragons."

"At the far end of the world," said Mace Tyrell. "Queen of Slaver's Bay, aye. She is welcome to it."

"On that we can agree," Ser Kevan said, "but the girl is of the blood of Aegon the Conqueror, and I do not think she will be content to remain in Meereen forever. If she should reach these shores and join her strength to Lord Connington and this prince of his, feigned or no . . . we must destroy Connington and his pretender *now*, before Daenerys Stormborn can come west."

Mace Tyrell crossed his arms. "I mean to do just that, ser. *After* the trials."

"Sellswords fight for coin," declared Grand Maester Pycelle. "With enough gold, we might persuade the Golden Company to hand over Lord Connington and the pretender."

"Aye, if we had gold," Ser Harys Swyft said. "Alas, my lords, our vaults contain only rats and roaches. I have written again to the Myrish bankers. If they will agree to make good the crown's debt to the Braavosi and extend us a new loan, mayhaps we will not have to raise the taxes. Elsewise—"

"The magisters of Pentos have been known to lend money as well," said Ser Kevan. "Try them." The Pentoshi were even less like to be of help than the Myrish money changers, but the effort must be made. Unless a new source of coin could be found, or the Iron Bank persuaded to relent, he would have no choice but to pay the crown's debts with Lannister gold. He dare not resort to new taxes, not with the Seven Kingdoms crawling with rebellion. Half the lords in the realm could not tell taxation from tyranny, and would bolt to the nearest usurper in a heartbeat if it would save them a clipped copper. "If that fails, you may well need to go to Braavos, to treat with the Iron Bank yourself."

Ser Harys quailed. "Must I?"

"You *are* the master of coin," Lord Randyll said sharply.

"I am." The puff of white hair at the end of Swyft's chin quivered in outrage. "Must I remind my lord, this trouble is not of my doing? And not all of us have had the opportunity to refill our coffers with the plunder of Maidenpool and Dragonstone."

"I resent your implication, Swyft," Mace Tyrell said, bristling. "No wealth was found on Dragonstone, I promise you. My son's men have searched every inch of that damp and dreary island and turned up not so much as a single gemstone or speck of gold. Nor any sign of this fabled hoard of dragon eggs."

Kevan Lannister had seen Dragonstone with his own eyes. He doubted very much that Loras Tyrell had searched every inch of that ancient stronghold. The Valyrians had raised it, after all, and all their works stank of sorcery. And Ser Loras was young, prone to all the rash judgments of youth, and had been grievously wounded storming the castle besides. But it would not do to remind Tyrell that his favorite son was fallible. "If there was wealth on Dragonstone, Stannis would have found it," he declared. "Let us move along, my lords. We have two queens to try for high treason, you may recall. My niece has elected trial by battle, she informs me. Ser Robert Strong will champion her."

"The silent giant." Lord Randyll grimaced.

"Tell me, ser, where did this man come from?" demanded Mace Tyrell. "Why have we never heard his name before? He does not speak, he will not show his face, he is never seen without his armor. Do we know for a certainty that he is even a knight?"

We do not even know if he's alive. Meryn Trant claimed that Strong took neither food nor drink, and Boros Blount went so far as to say he had never seen the man use the privy. *Why should he? Dead men do not shit.* Kevan Lannister had a strong suspicion of just who this Ser Robert really was beneath that gleaming white armor. A suspicion that Mace Tyrell and Randyll Tarly no doubt shared. Whatever the face hidden behind Strong's helm, it must remain hidden for now. The silent giant was his niece's only hope. *And pray that he is as formidable as he appears.*

But Mace Tyrell could not seem to see beyond the threat to his own daughter. "His Grace named Ser Robert to the Kingsguard," Ser Kevan reminded him, "and Qyburn vouches for the man as well. Be that as it may, we need Ser Robert to prevail, my lords. If my niece is proved guilty of these treasons, the legitimacy of her children will be called into question. If Tommen ceases to be a king, Margaery will cease to be a queen." He let Tyrell chew on that a moment. "Whatever Cersei may have done, she is still a daughter of the Rock, of mine own blood. I will not let her die a traitor's death, but I have made sure to draw her fangs. All her guards have been dismissed and replaced with my own men. In place of her former ladies-in-waiting, she will henceforth be attended by a septa and three novices selected by the High Septon. She is to have no further voice in the governance of the realm, nor in Tommen's education. I mean to return her to Casterly Rock after the trial and see that she remains there. Let that suffice."

The rest he left unsaid. Cersei was soiled goods now, her power at an end. Every baker's boy and beggar in the city had seen her in her shame and every tart and tanner from Flea Bottom to Pisswater Bend had gazed upon her nakedness, their eager eyes crawling over her breasts and belly and woman's parts. No queen could expect to rule again after that. In gold and silk and emeralds Cersei had been a queen, the next thing to a goddess; naked, she was only human, an aging woman with stretch marks on her belly and teats that had begun to sag . . . as the shrews in the crowds had been glad to point out to their husbands and lovers. *Better to live shamed than die proud,* Ser

Kevan told himself. "My niece will make no further mischief," he promised Mace Tyrell. "You have my word on that, my lord."

Tyrell gave a grudging nod. "As you say. My Margaery prefers to be tried by the Faith, so the whole realm can bear witness to her innocence."

If your daughter is as innocent as you'd have us believe, why must you have your army present when she faces her accusers? Ser Kevan might have asked. "Soon, I hope," he said instead, before turning to Grand Maester Pycelle. "Is there aught else?"

The Grand Maester consulted his papers. "We should address the Rosby inheritance. Six claims have been put forth—"

"We can settle Rosby at some later date. What else?"

"Preparations should be made for Princess Myrcella."

"This is what comes of dealing with the Dornish," Mace Tyrell said. "Surely a better match can be found for the girl?"

Such as your own son Willas, perhaps? Her disfigured by one Dornishman, him crippled by another? "No doubt," Ser Kevan said, "but we have enemies enough without offending Dorne. If Doran Martell were to join his strength to Connington's in support of this feigned dragon, things could go very ill for all of us."

"Mayhaps we can persuade our Dornish friends to deal with Lord Connington," Ser Harys Swyft said with an irritating titter. "That would save a deal of blood and trouble."

"It would," Ser Kevan said wearily. *Time to put an end to this.* "Thank you, my lords. Let us convene again five days hence. After Cersei's trial."

"As you say. May the Warrior lend strength to Ser Robert's arms." The words were grudging, the dip of the chin Mace Tyrell gave the Lord Regent the most cursory of bows. But it was something, and for that much Ser Kevan Lannister was grateful.

Randyll Tarly left the hall with his liege lord, their green-cloaked spearmen right behind them. *Tarly is the real danger,* Ser Kevan reflected as he watched their departure. *A narrow man, but iron-willed and shrewd, and as good a soldier as the Reach could boast. But how do I win him to our side?*

"Lord Tyrell loves me not," Grand Maester Pycelle said in gloomy tones when the Hand had departed. "This matter of the moon tea . . . I would never have spoken of such, but the Queen Dowager commanded me! If it please the Lord Regent, I would sleep more soundly if you could lend me some of your guards."

"Lord Tyrell might take that amiss."

Ser Harys Swyft tugged at his chin beard. "I am in need of guards myself. These are perilous times."

Aye, thought Kevan Lannister, *and Pycelle is not the only council member our Hand would like to replace.* Mace Tyrell had his own candidate for lord treasurer: his uncle, Lord Seneschal of Highgarden, whom men called Garth the Gross. *The last thing I need is another Tyrell on the small council.* He was already outnumbered. Ser Harys was his wife's father, and Pycelle could be counted upon as well. But Tarly was sworn to Highgarden, as was Paxter Redwyne, lord admiral and master of ships, presently sailing his fleet around Dorne to deal with Euron Greyjoy's ironmen. Once Redwyne returned to King's Landing, the council would stand at three and three, Lannister and Tyrell.

The seventh voice would be the Dornishwoman now escorting Myrcella home. *The Lady Nym. But no lady, if even half of what Qyburn reports is true.* A bastard daughter of the Red Viper, near as notorious as her father and intent on claiming the council seat that Prince Oberyn himself had occupied so briefly. Ser Kevan had not yet seen fit to inform Mace Tyrell of her coming. The Hand, he knew, would not be pleased. *The man we need is Littlefinger. Petyr Baelish had a gift for conjuring dragons from the air.*

"Hire the Mountain's men," Ser Kevan suggested. "Red Ronnet will have no further use for them." He did not think that Mace Tyrell would be so clumsy as to try to murder either Pycelle or Swyft, but if guards made them feel safer, let them have guards.

The three men walked together from the throne room. Outside the snow was swirling round the outer ward, a caged beast howling to be free. "Have you ever felt such cold?" asked Ser Harys.

"The time to speak of the cold," said Grand Maester Pycelle, "is not when we are standing out in it." He made his slow way across the outer ward, back to his chambers.

The others lingered for a moment on the throne room steps. "I put no faith in these Myrish bankers," Ser Kevan told his good-father. "You had best prepare to go to Braavos."

Ser Harys did not look happy at the prospect. "If I must. But I say again, this trouble is not of my doing."

"No. It was Cersei who decided that the Iron Bank would wait for their due. Should I send her to Braavos?"

Ser Harys blinked. "Her Grace . . . that . . . that . . ."

Ser Kevan rescued him. "That was a jape. A bad one. Go and find a warm fire. I mean to do the same." He yanked his gloves on and set off across the yard, leaning hard into the wind as his cloak snapped and swirled behind him.

The dry moat surrounding Maegor's Holdfast was three feet deep in snow, the iron spikes that lined it glistening with frost. The only way in or out of Maegor's was across the drawbridge that spanned that moat. A knight of the Kingsguard was always posted at its far end. Tonight the duty had fallen to Ser Meryn Trant. With Balon Swann hunting the rogue knight Darkstar down in Dorne, Loras Tyrell gravely wounded on Dragonstone, and Jaime vanished in the riverlands, only four of the White Swords remained in King's Landing, and Ser Kevan had thrown Osmund Kettleblack (and his brother Osfryd) into the dungeon within hours of Cersei's confessing that she had taken both men as lovers. That left only Trant, the feeble Boros Blount, and Qyburn's mute monster Robert Strong to protect the young king and royal family.

I will need to find some new swords for the Kingsguard. Tommen should have seven good knights about him. In the past the Kingsguard had served for life, but that had not stopped Joffrey from dismissing Ser Barristan Selmy to make a place for his dog, Sandor Clegane. Kevan could make use of that precedent. *I could put Lancel in a white cloak,* he reflected. *There is more honor in that than he will ever find in the Warrior's Sons.*

Kevan Lannister hung his snow-sodden cloak inside his solar, pulled off his boots, and commanded his serving man to fetch some fresh wood for his fire. "A cup of mulled wine would go down well," he said as he settled by the hearth. "See to it."

The fire soon thawed him, and the wine warmed his insides nicely. It also made him sleepy, so he dare not drink another cup. His day was far from done. He had reports to read, letters to write. *And supper with Cersei and the king.* His niece had been subdued and submissive since her walk of atonement, thank the gods. The novices who attended her reported that she spent a third of her waking hours with her son, another third in prayer, and the rest in her tub. She was bathing four or five times a day, scrubbing herself with horsehair brushes and strong lye soap, as if she meant to scrape her skin off.

She will never wash the stain away, no matter how hard she scrubs. Ser Kevan remembered the girl she once had been, so full of life and mischief. And when she'd flowered, ahhhh ... had there ever been a maid so sweet to look upon? *If Aerys had agreed to marry her to Rhaegar, how many deaths might have been avoided?* Cersei could have given the prince the sons he wanted, lions with purple eyes and silver manes ... and with such a wife, Rhaegar might never have looked twice at Lyanna Stark. The northern girl had a wild beauty, as he recalled, though however bright a torch might burn it could never match the rising sun.

But it did no good to brood on lost battles and roads not taken. That was a vice of old done men. Rhaegar had wed Elia of Dorne, Lyanna Stark had died, Robert Baratheon had taken Cersei to bride, and here they were. And tonight his own road would take him to his niece's chambers and face-to-face with Cersei.

I have no reason to feel guilty, Ser Kevan told himself. *Tywin would understand that, surely. It was his daughter who brought shame down on our name, not I. What I did I did for the good of House Lannister.*

It was not as if his brother had never done the same. In their father's final years, after their mother's passing, their sire had taken the comely daughter of a candlemaker as mistress. It was not unknown for a widowed lord to keep a common girl as bedwarmer ... but Lord Tytos soon began seating the woman beside him in the hall, showering her with gifts and honors, even asking her views on matters of state. Within a year she was dismissing servants, ordering about his household knights, even speaking for his lordship when he was indisposed. She grew so influential that it was said about Lannisport that any man who wished for his petition to be heard should kneel before her and speak loudly to her lap . . . for Tytos Lannister's ear was between his lady's legs. She had even taken to wearing their mother's jewels.

Until the day their lord father's heart had burst in his chest as he was ascending a steep flight of steps to her bed, that is. All the self-seekers who had named themselves her friends and cultivated her favor had abandoned her quickly enough when Tywin had her stripped naked and paraded through Lannisport to the docks, like a common whore. Though no man laid a hand on her, that walk spelled the end of her power. Surely Tywin would never have dreamed that same fate awaited his own golden daughter.

"It had to be," Ser Kevan muttered over the last of his wine. His High Holiness had to be appeased. Tommen needed the Faith behind him in the battles to come. And Cersei . . . the golden child had grown into a vain, foolish, greedy woman. Left to rule, she would have ruined Tommen as she had Joffrey.

Outside the wind was rising, clawing at the shutters of his chamber. Ser Kevan pushed himself to his feet. Time to face the lioness in her den. *We have pulled her claws. Jaime, though . . .* But no, he would not brood on that.

He donned an old, well-worn doublet, in case his niece had a mind to throw another cup of wine in his face, but he left his sword belt hanging on the back of his chair. Only the knights of the Kingsguard were permitted swords in Tommen's presence.

Ser Boros Blount was in attendance on the boy king and his mother when Ser Kevan entered the royal chambers. Blount wore enameled scale, white cloak, and halfhelm. He did not look well. Of late Boros had grown notably heavier about the face and belly, and his color was not good. And he was leaning against the wall behind him, as if standing had become too great an effort for him.

The meal was served by three novices, well-scrubbed girls of good birth between the ages of twelve and sixteen. In their soft white woolens, each seemed more innocent and unworldly than the last, yet the High Septon had insisted that no girl spend more than seven days in the queen's service, lest Cersei corrupt her. They tended the queen's wardrobe, drew her bath, poured her wine, changed her bedclothes of a morning. One shared the queen's bed every night, to ascertain she had no other company; the other two slept in an adjoining chamber with the septa who looked over them.

A tall stork of a girl with a pockmarked face escorted him into the royal presence. Cersei rose when he entered and kissed him lightly on the cheek. "Dear uncle. It is so good of you to sup with us." The queen was dressed as modestly as any matron, in a dark brown gown that buttoned up to her throat and a hooded green mantle that covered her shaved head. *Before her walk she would have flaunted her baldness beneath a golden crown.* "Come, sit," she said. "Will you have wine?"

"A cup." He sat, still wary.

A freckled novice filled their cups with hot spiced wine. "Tommen tells me that Lord Tyrell intends to rebuild the Tower of the Hand," Cersei said.

Ser Kevan nodded. "The new tower will be twice as tall as the one you burned, he says."

Cersei gave a throaty laugh. "Long lances, tall towers . . . is Lord Tyrell hinting at something?"

That made him smile. *It is good that she still remembers how to laugh.* When he asked if she had all that she required, the queen said, "I am well served. The girls are sweet, and the good septas make certain that I say my prayers. But once my innocence is proved, it would please me if Taena Merryweather might attend me once again. She could bring her son to court. Tommen needs other boys about him, friends of noble birth."

It was a modest request. Ser Kevan saw no reason why it should not be granted. He could foster the Merryweather boy himself, whilst Lady Taena accompanied Cersei back to Casterly Rock. "I will send for her after the trial," he promised.

Supper began with beef-and-barley soup, followed by a brace of quail and a roast pike near three feet long, with turnips, mushrooms, and plenty of hot bread and butter. Ser Boros tasted every dish that was set before the king. A humiliating duty for a knight of the Kingsguard, but perhaps all Blount was capable of these days . . . and wise, after the way Tommen's brother had died.

The king seemed happier than Kevan Lannister had seen him in a long time. From soup to sweet Tommen burbled about the exploits of his kittens, whilst feeding them morsels of pike off his own royal plate. "The bad cat was outside my window last night," he informed Kevan at one point, "but Ser Pounce hissed at him and he ran off across the roofs."

"The bad cat?" Ser Kevan said, amused. *He is a sweet boy.*

"An old black tomcat with a torn ear," Cersei told him. "A filthy thing, and foul-tempered. He clawed Joff's hand once." She made a face. "The cats keep the rats down, I know, but that one . . . he's been known to attack ravens in the rookery."

"I will ask the ratters to set a trap for him." Ser Kevan could not remember ever seeing his niece so quiet, so subdued, so demure. All for the good, he supposed. But it made him sad as well. *Her fire is quenched, she who used to burn so bright.* "You have not asked about your brother," he said, as they were waiting for the cream cakes. Cream cakes were the king's favorite.

Cersei lifted her chin, her green eyes shining in the candlelight. "Jaime? Have you had word?"

"None. Cersei, you may need to prepare yourself for—"

"If he were dead, I would know it. We came into this world together, Uncle. He would not go without me." She took a drink of wine. "Tyrion can leave whenever he wishes. You have had no word of him either, I suppose."

"No one has tried to sell us a dwarf's head of late, no."

She nodded. "Uncle, may I ask you a question?"

"Whatever you wish."

"Your wife . . . do you mean to bring her to court?"

"No." Dorna was a gentle soul, never comfortable but at home with friends and kin around her. She had done well by their children, dreamed of having grandchildren, prayed seven times a day, loved needlework and flowers. In King's Landing she would be as happy as one of Tommen's kittens in a pit of vipers. "My lady wife mislikes travel. Lannisport is her place."

"It is a wise woman who knows her place."

He did not like the sound of that. "Say what you mean."

"I thought I did." Cersei held out her cup. The freckled girl filled it once again. The cream cakes appeared then, and the conversation took a lighter turn. Only after Tommen and his kittens were escorted off to the royal bedchamber by Ser Boros did their talk turn to the queen's trial.

"Osney's brothers will not stand by idly and watch him die," Cersei warned him.

"I did not expect that they would. I've had the both of them arrested."

That seemed to take her aback. "For what crime?"

"Fornication with a queen. His High Holiness says that you confessed to bedding both of them—had you forgotten?"

Her face reddened. "No. What will you do with them?"

"The Wall, if they admit their guilt. If they deny it, they can face Ser Robert. Such men should never have been raised so high."

Cersei lowered her head. "I . . . I misjudged them."

"You misjudged a good many men, it seems."

He might have said more, but the dark-haired novice with the round cheeks returned to say, "My lord, my lady, I am sorry to intrude, but there is a boy below. Grand Maester Pycelle begs the favor of the Lord Regent's presence at once."

Dark wings, dark words, Ser Kevan thought. *Could Storm's End have fallen? Or might this be word from Bolton in the north?*

"It might be news of Jaime," the queen said.

There was only one way to know. Ser Kevan rose. "Pray excuse me." Before he took his leave, he dropped to one knee and kissed his niece upon the hand. If her silent giant failed her, it might be the last kiss she would ever know.

The messenger was a boy of eight or nine, so bundled up in fur he seemed a bear cub. Trant had kept him waiting out on the draw-bridge rather than admit him into Maegor's. "Go find a fire, lad," Ser Kevan told him, pressing a penny into his hand. "I know the way to the rookery well enough."

The snow had finally stopped falling. Behind a veil of ragged clouds, a full moon floated fat and white as a snowball. The stars shone cold and distant. As Ser Kevan made his way across the inner ward, the castle seemed an alien place, where every keep and tower had grown icy teeth, and all familiar paths had vanished beneath a white blanket. Once an icicle long as a spear fell to shatter by his feet. *Autumn in King's Landing*, he brooded. *What must it be like up on the Wall?*

The door was opened by a serving girl, a skinny thing in a fur-lined robe much too big for her. Ser Kevan stamped the snow off his boots, removed his cloak, tossed it to her. "The Grand Maester is expecting me," he announced. The girl nodded, solemn and silent, and pointed to the steps.

Pycelle's chambers were beneath the rookery, a spacious suite of rooms cluttered with racks of herbs and salves and potions and shelves jammed full of books and scrolls. Ser Kevan had always found them uncomfortably hot. Not tonight. Once past the chamber door, the chill was palpable. Black ash and dying embers were all that remained of the hearthfire. A few flickering candles cast pools of dim light here and there.

The rest was shrouded in shadow . . . except beneath the open window, where a spray of ice crystals glittered in the moonlight, swirling in the wind. On the window seat a raven loitered, pale, huge, its feathers ruffled. It was the largest raven that Kevan Lannister had ever seen. Larger than any hunting hawk at Casterly Rock, larger than the largest owl. Blowing snow danced around it, and the moon painted it silver.

Not silver. White. The bird is white.

The white ravens of the Citadel did not carry messages, as their dark cousins did. When they went forth from Oldtown, it was for one purpose only: to herald a change of seasons.

"Winter," said Ser Kevan. The word made a white mist in the air. He turned away from the window.

Then something slammed him in the chest between the ribs, hard as a giant's fist. It drove the breath from him and sent him lurching backwards. The white raven took to the air, its pale wings slapping him about the head. Ser Kevan half-sat and half-fell onto the window seat. *What . . . who . . .* A quarrel was sunk almost to the fletching in his chest. *No. No, that was how my brother died.* Blood was seeping out around the shaft. "Pycelle," he muttered, confused. "Help me . . . I . . ."

Then he saw. Grand Maester Pycelle was seated at his table, his head pillowed on the great leather-bound tome before him. *Sleeping*, Kevan thought . . . until he blinked and saw the deep red gash in the old man's spotted skull and the blood pooled beneath his head, staining the pages of his book. All around his candle were bits of bone and brain, islands in a lake of melted wax.

He wanted guards, Ser Kevan thought. *I should have sent him guards.* Could Cersei have been right all along? Was this his nephew's work? "Tyrion?" he called. "Where . . . ?"

"Far away," a half-familiar voice replied.

He stood in a pool of shadow by a bookcase, plump, pale-faced, round-shouldered, clutching a crossbow in soft powdered hands. Silk slippers swaddled his feet.

"Varys?"

The eunuch set the crossbow down. "Ser Kevan. Forgive me if you can. I bear you no ill will. This was not done from malice. It was for the realm. For the children."

I have children. I have a wife. Oh, Dorna. Pain washed over him. He closed his eyes, opened them again. "There are . . . there are hundreds of Lannister guardsmen in this castle."

"But none in this room, thankfully. This pains me, my lord. You do not deserve to die alone on such a cold dark night. There are many like you, good men in service to bad causes . . . but you were threatening to undo all the queen's good work, to reconcile Highgarden and Casterly Rock, bind the Faith to your little king, unite the Seven Kingdoms under Tommen's rule. So . . ."

A gust of wind blew up. Ser Kevan shivered violently.

"Are you cold, my lord?" asked Varys. "Do forgive me. The Grand Maester befouled himself in dying, and the stink was so abominable that I thought I might choke."

Ser Kevan tried to rise, but the strength had left him. He could not feel his legs.

"I thought the crossbow fitting. You shared so much with Lord Tywin, why not that? Your niece will think the Tyrells had you murdered, mayhaps with the connivance of the Imp. The Tyrells will suspect her. Someone somewhere will find a way to blame the

Dornishmen. Doubt, division, and mistrust will eat the very ground beneath your boy king, whilst Aegon raises his banner above Storm's End and the lords of the realm gather round him."

"Aegon?" For a moment he did not understand. Then he remembered. A babe swaddled in a crimson cloak, the cloth stained with his blood and brains. "Dead. He's dead."

"No." The eunuch's voice seemed deeper. "He is here. Aegon has been shaped for rule since before he could walk. He has been trained in arms, as befits a knight to be, but that was not the end of his education. He reads and writes, he speaks several tongues, he has studied history and law and poetry. A septa has instructed him in the mysteries of the Faith since he was old enough to understand them. He has lived with fisherfolk, worked with his hands, swum in rivers and mended nets and learned to wash his own clothes at need. He can fish and cook and bind up a wound, he knows what it is like to be hungry, to be hunted, to be afraid. Tommen has been taught that kingship is his right. Aegon knows that kingship is his duty, that a king must put his people first, and live and rule for them."

Kevan Lannister tried to cry out ... to his guards, his wife, his brother ... but the words would not come. Blood dribbled from his mouth. He shuddered violently.

"I am sorry." Varys wrung his hands. "You are suffering, I know, yet here I stand going on like some silly old woman. Time to make an end to it." The eunuch pursed his lips and gave a little whistle.

Ser Kevan was cold as ice, and every labored breath sent a fresh stab of pain through him. He glimpsed movement, heard the soft scuffling sound of slippered feet on stone. A child emerged from a pool of darkness, a pale boy in a ragged robe, no more than nine or ten. Another rose up behind the Grand Maester's chair. The girl who had opened the door for him was there as well. They were all around him, half a dozen of them, white-faced children with dark eyes, boys and girls together.

And in their hands, the daggers.

APPENDIX

THE KINGS AND THEIR COURTS

THE BOY KING

TOMMEN BARATHEON, the First of His Name, King of the Andals, the Rhoynar, and the First Men, Lord of the Seven Kingdoms, a boy of eight years,

—his wife, QUEEN MARGAERY of House Tyrell, thrice wed, twice widowed, accused of high treason, held captive in the Great Sept of Baelor,
—her lady companions and cousins, MEGGA, ALLA, and ELINOR TYRELL, accused of fornications,
—Elinor's betrothed, ALYN AMBROSE, squire,
—his mother, CERSEI of House Lannister, Queen Dowager, Lady of Casterly Rock, accused of high treason, captive in the Great Sept of Baelor,
—his siblings:
—his elder brother, {KING JOFFREY I BARATHEON}, poisoned during his wedding feast,
—his elder sister, PRINCESS MYRCELLA BARATHEON, a girl of nine, a ward of Prince Doran Martell at Sunspear, betrothed to his son Trystane,
—his kittens, SER POUNCE, LADY WHISKERS, BOOTS,
—his uncles:
—SER JAIME LANNISTER, called THE KINGSLAYER, twin to Queen Cersei, Lord Commander of the Kingsguard,
—TYRION LANNISTER, called THE IMP, a dwarf, accused and condemned for regicide and kinslaying,

—his other kin:
  —his grandfather, {TYWIN LANNISTER}, Lord of Casterly Rock, Warden of the West, and Hand of the King, murdered in the privy by his son Tyrion,
—his great-uncle, SER KEVAN LANNISTER, Lord Regent and Protector of the Realm, m. Dorna Swyft,
  —their children:
  —SER LANCEL LANNISTER, a knight of the Holy Order of the Warrior's Sons,
  —{WILLEM}, twin to Martyn, murdered at Riverrun,
  —MARTYN, twin to Willem, a squire,
  —JANEI, a girl of three,
—his great-aunt, GENNA LANNISTER, m. Ser Emmon Frey,
  —their children:
  —{SER CLEOS FREY}, killed by outlaws,
    —his son, SER TYWIN FREY, called TY,
    —his son, WILLEM FREY, a squire,
  —SER LYONEL FREY, Lady Genna's second son,
  —{TION FREY}, a squire, murdered at Riverrun,
  —WALDER FREY, called RED WALDER, a page at Casterly Rock,
—his great-uncle, {SER TYGETT LANNISTER}, m. Darlessa Marbrand
  —their children:
  —TYREK LANNISTER, a squire, vanished during the food riots in King's Landing,
    —LADY ERMESANDE HAYFORD, Tyrek's child wife,
—his great uncle, GERION LANNISTER, lost at sea,
  —JOY HILL, his bastard daughter,

—King Tommen's small council:
—SER KEVAN LANNISTER, Lord Regent,
—LORD MACE TYRELL, Hand of the King,
—GRAND MAESTER PYCELLE, counselor and healer,
—SER JAIME LANNISTER, Lord Commander of the Kingsguard,

—LORD PAXTER REDWYNE, grand admiral and master of ships,
—QYBURN, a disgraced maester and reputed necromancer, master of whisperers,

—Queen Cersei's former small council,
—{LORD GYLES ROSBY}, lord treasurer and master of coin, dead of a cough,
—LORD ORTON MERRYWEATHER, justiciar and master of laws, fled to Longtable upon Queen Cersei's arrest,
—AURANE WATERS, the Bastard of Driftmark, grand admiral and master of ships, fled to sea with the royal fleet upon Queen Cersei's arrest,

—King Tommen's Kingsguard:
—SER JAIME LANNISTER, Lord Commander,
—SER MERYN TRANT,
—SER BOROS BLOUNT, removed and thence restored,
—SER BALON SWANN, in Dorne with Princess Myrcella,
—SER OSMUND KETTLEBLACK,
—SER LORAS TYRELL, the Knight of Flowers,
—{SER ARYS OAKHEART}, dead in Dorne,

—Tommen's court at King's Landing:
—MOON BOY, the royal jester and fool,
—PATE, a lad of eight, King Tommen's whipping boy,
—ORMOND OF OLDTOWN, the royal harper and bard,
—SER OSFRYD KETTLEBLACK, brother to Ser Osmund and Ser Osney, a captain in the City Watch,
—NOHO DIMITTIS, envoy from the Iron Bank of Braavos,
—{SER GREGOR CLEGANE}, called THE MOUNTAIN THAT RIDES, dead of a poisoned wound,
—RENNIFER LONGWATERS, chief undergaoler of the Red Keep's dungeons,

—Queen Margaery's alleged lovers:
  —WAT, a singer styling himself THE BLUE BARD, a captive driven mad by torment,
  —{HAMISH THE HARPER}, an aged singer, died a captive,
  —SER MARK MULLENDORE, who lost a monkey and half an arm in the Battle of the Blackwater,
  —SER TALLAD called THE TALL, SER LAMBERT TURNBERRY, SER BAYARD NORCROSS, SER HUGH CLIFTON,
  —JALABHAR XHO, Prince of the Red Flower Vale, an exile from the Summer Isles,
  —SER HORAS REDWYNE, found innocent and freed,
  —SER HOBBER REDWYNE, found innocent and freed,

—Queen Cersei's chief accuser,
  —SER OSNEY KETTLEBLACK, brother to Ser Osmund and Ser Osfryd, held captive by the Faith,

—the people of the Faith:
  —THE HIGH SEPTON, Father of the Faithful, Voice of the Seven on Earth, an old man and frail,
    —SEPTA UNELLA, SEPTA MOELLE, SEPTA SCOLERA, the queen's gaolers,
    —SEPTON TORBERT, SEPTON RAYNARD, SEPTON LUCEON, SEPTON OLLIDOR, of the Most Devout,
    —SEPTA AGLANTINE, SEPTA HELICENT, serving the Seven at the Great Sept of Baelor,
    —SER THEODAN WELLS, called THEODAN THE TRUE, pious commander of the Warrior's Sons,
      —the "sparrows," the humblest of men, fierce in their piety,

—people of King's Landing:
  —CHATAYA, proprietor of an expensive brothel,
    —ALAYAYA, her daughter,
    —DANCY, MAREI, two of Chataya's girls,
  —TOBHO MOTT, a master armorer,

—lords of the crownlands, sworn to the Iron Throne:
  —RENFRED RYKKER, Lord of Duskendale,
    —SER RUFUS LEEK, a one-legged knight in his service,
    castellan of the Dun Fort at Duskendale,
  —{TANDA STOKEWORTH}, Lady of Stokeworth, died of
  a broken hip,
    —her eldest daughter, {FALYSE}, died screaming in the
    black cells,
      —{SER BALMAN BYRCH}, Lady Falyse's husband,
      killed in a joust,
    —her younger daughter, LOLLYS, weak of wit, Lady of
    Stokeworth,
      —her newborn son, TYRION TANNER, of the
      hundred fathers,
      —her husband, SER BRONN OF THE BLACKWATER,
      sellsword turned knight,
    —MAESTER FRENKEN, in service at Stokeworth,

King Tommen's banner shows the crowned stag of Baratheon, black
on gold, and the lion of Lannister, gold on crimson, combatant.

THE KING AT THE WALL

STANNIS BARATHEON, the First of His Name, second son of Lord Steffon Baratheon and Lady Cassana of House Estermont, Lord of Dragonstone, styling himself King of Westeros,

- —with King Stannis at Castle Black:
    - —LADY MELISANDRE OF ASSHAI, called THE RED WOMAN, a priestess of R'hllor, the Lord of Light,
    - —his knights and sworn swords:
        - —SER RICHARD HORPE, his second-in-command,
        - —SER GODRY FARRING, called GIANTSLAYER,
        - —SER JUSTIN MASSEY,
        - —LORD ROBIN PEASEBURY,
        - —LORD HARWOOD FELL,
        - —SER CLAYTON SUGGS, SER CORLISS PENNY, queen's men and fervent followers of the Lord of Light,
        - —SER WILLAM FOXGLOVE, SER HUMFREY CLIFTON, SER ORMUND WYLDE, SER HARYS COBB, knights
    - —his squires, DEVAN SEAWORTH and BRYEN FARRING
    - —his captive, MANCE RAYDER, King-Beyond-the-Wall,
        - —Rayder's infant son, "the wildling prince,"
            - —the boy's wet nurse, GILLY, a wildling girl,
                - —Gilly's infant son, "the abomination," fathered by her father {CRASTER},

—at Eastwatch-by-the-Sea:
  —QUEEN SELYSE of House Florent, his wife,
      —PRINCESS SHIREEN, their daughter, a girl of eleven,
        —PATCHFACE, Shireen's tattooed fool,
      —her uncle, SER AXELL FLORENT, foremost of the
      queen's men, styling himself the Queen's Hand,
      —her knights and sworn swords, SER NARBERT
      GRANDISON, SER BENETHON SCALES, SER
      PATREK OF KING'S MOUNTAIN, SER DORDEN
      THE DOUR, SER MALEGORN OF REDPOOL, SER
      LAMBERT WHITEWATER, SER PERKIN FOLLARD,
      SER BRUS BUCKLER
  —SER DAVOS SEAWORTH, Lord of the Rainwood, Admiral
  of the Narrow Sea, and Hand of the King, called THE
  ONION KNIGHT,
  —SALLADHAR SAAN of Lys, a pirate and sellsail, master
  of the *Valyrian* and a fleet of galleys,
  —TYCHO NESTORIS, emissary from the Iron Bank of
  Braavos.

Stannis has taken for his banner the fiery heart of the Lord of Light—a
red heart surrounded by orange flames upon a yellow field. Within
the heart is the crowned stag of House Baratheon, in black.

KING OF THE ISLES AND THE NORTH

The Greyjoys of Pyke claim descent from the Grey King of the Age of Heroes. Legend says the Grey King ruled the sea itself and took a mermaid to wife. Aegon the Dragon ended the line of the last King of the Iron Islands, but allowed the ironborn to revive their ancient custom and choose who should have primacy among them. They chose Lord Vickon Greyjoy of Pyke. The Greyjoy sigil is a golden kraken upon a black field. Their words are *We Do Not Sow*.

EURON GREYJOY, the Third of His Name Since the Grey King, King of the Iron Islands and the North, King of Salt and Rock, Son of the Sea Wind, and Lord Reaper of Pyke, captain of the *Silence*, called CROW'S EYE,

—his elder brother, {BALON}, King of the Iron Islands and the North, the Ninth of His Name Since the Grey King, killed in a fall,

—LADY ALANNYS, of House Harlaw, Balon's widow,

—their children:

—{RODRIK}, slain during Balon's first rebellion,

—{MARON}, slain during Balon's first rebellion,

—ASHA, captain of the *Black Wind* and conqueror of Deepwood Motte, m. Erik Ironmaker,

—THEON, called by northmen THEON TURN-CLOAK, a captive at the Dreadfort,

—his younger brother, VICTARION, Lord Captain of the Iron Fleet, master of the *Iron Victory*,

—his youngest brother, AERON, called DAMPHAIR, a priest of the Drowned God,

—his captains and sworn swords:

—TORWOLD BROWNTOOTH, PINCHFACE JON MYRE, RODRIK FREEBORN, THE RED OARSMAN, LEFT-HAND LUCAS CODD, QUELLON HUMBLE, HARREN HALF-HOARE, KEMMETT PYKE THE BASTARD, QARL THE THRALL, STONEHAND, RALF THE SHEPHERD, RALF OF LORDSPORT

—his crewmen:

—{CRAGORN}, who blew the hellhorn and died,

—his lords bannermen:

—ERIK IRONMAKER, called ERIK ANVIL-BREAKER and ERIK THE JUST, Lord Steward of the Iron Islands, castellan of Pyke, an old man once renowned, m. Asha Greyjoy,

—lords of Pyke:

  —GERMUND BOTLEY, Lord of Lordsport,

  —WALDON WYNCH, Lord of Iron Holt,

—lords of Old Wyk:

  —DUNSTAN DRUMM, The Drumm, Lord of Old Wyk,

  —NORNE GOODBROTHER, of Shatterstone,

  —THE STONEHOUSE,

—lords of Great Wyk:

  —GOROLD GOODBROTHER, Lord of the Hammer horn,

  —TRISTON FARWYND, Lord of Sealskin Point,

  —THE SPARR,

  —MELDRED MERLYN, Lord of Pebbleton,

—lords of Orkmont:

  —ALYN ORKWOOD, called ORKWOOD OF ORKMONT,

  —LORD BALON TAWNEY,

—lords of Saltcliffe:

  —LORD DONNOR SALTCLIFFE,

—LORD SUNDERLY
—lords of Harlaw:
—RODRIK HARLAW, called THE READER, Lord of Harlaw, Lord of Ten Towers, Harlaw of Harlaw,
—SIGFRYD HARLAW, called SIGFRYD SILVERHAIR, his great uncle, master of Harlaw Hall,
—HOTHO HARLAW, called HOTHO HUMPBACK, of the Tower of Glimmering, a cousin,
—BOREMUND HARLAW, called BOREMUND THE BLUE, master of Harridan Hill, a cousin,
—lords of the lesser isles and rocks:
—GYLBERT FARWYND, Lord of the Lonely Light,

—the ironborn conquerors:
—on the Shield Islands
—ANDRIK THE UNSMILING, Lord of Southshield,
—NUTE THE BARBER, Lord of Oakenshield,
—MARON VOLMARK, Lord of Greenshield,
—SER HARRAS HARLAW, Lord of Greyshield, the Knight of Grey Gardens,
—at Moat Cailin
—RALF KENNING, castellan and commander,
—ADRACK HUMBLE, short half an arm,
—DAGON CODD, who yields to no man,
—at Torrhen's Square
—DAGMER, called CLEFTJAW, captain of *Foamdrinker*,
—at Deepwood Motte
—ASHA GREYJOY, the kraken's daughter, captain of the *Black Wind*,
—her lover, QARL THE MAID, a swordsman,
—her former lover, TRISTIFER BOTLEY, heir to Lordsport, dispossessed of his lands,
—her crewmen, ROGGON RUSTBEARD, GRIMTONGUE, ROLFE THE DWARF, LORREN LONGAXE, ROOK, FINGERS, SIX-TOED HARL, DROOPEYE DALE, EARL HARLAW, CROMM,

HAGEN THE HORN and his beautiful red-haired
daughter,
—her cousin, QUENTON GREYJOY,
—her cousin, DAGON GREYJOY, called DAGON THE
DRUNKARD.

OTHER HOUSES GREAT AND SMALL

HOUSE ARRYN

The Arryns are descended from the Kings of Mountain and Vale. Their sigil is a white moon-and-falcon upon a sky blue field. House Arryn has taken no part in the War of the Five Kings.

ROBERT ARRYN, Lord of the Eyrie, Defender of the Vale, a sickly boy of eight years, called SWEETROBIN,
—his mother, {LADY LYSA of House Tully}, widow of Lord Jon Arryn, pushed from the Moon Door to her death,
—his guardian, PETYR BAELISH, called LITTLEFINGER, Lord of Harrenhal, Lord Paramount of the Trident, and Lord Protector of the Vale,
——ALAYNE STONE, Lord Petyr's natural daughter, a maid of three-and-ten, actually Sansa Stark,
——SER LOTHOR BRUNE, a sellsword in Lord Petyr's service, captain of guards at the Eyrie,
——OSWELL, a grizzled man-at-arms in Lord Petyr's service, sometimes called KETTLEBLACK,
——SER SHADRICK OF THE SHADY GLEN, called THE MAD MOUSE, a hedge knight in Lord Petyr's service,
——SER BYRON THE BEAUTIFUL, SER MORGARTH THE MERRY, hedge knights in Lord Petyr's service,
—his household and retainers:
——MAESTER COLEMON, counselor, healer, and tutor,
——MORD, a brutal gaoler with teeth of gold,
——GRETCHEL, MADDY, and MELA, servingwomen,
—his bannermen, the Lords of Mountain and Vale:

—YOHN ROYCE, called BRONZE YOHN, Lord of Runestone,
  —his son, SER ANDAR, heir to Runestone,
—LORD NESTOR ROYCE, High Steward of the Vale and castellan of the Gates of the Moon,
  —his son and heir, SER ALBAR,
  —his daughter, MYRANDA, called RANDA, a widow, but scarce used,
  —MYA STONE, bastard daughter of King Robert,
—LYONEL CORBRAY, Lord of Heart's Home,
  —SER LYN CORBRAY, his brother, who wields the famed blade Lady Forlorn,
  —SER LUCAS CORBRAY, his younger brother,
—TRISTON SUNDERLAND, Lord of the Three Sisters,
  —GODRIC BORRELL, Lord of Sweetsister,
  —ROLLAND LONGTHORPE, Lord of Longsister,
  —ALESANDOR TORRENT, Lord of Littlesister,
—ANYA WAYNWOOD, Lady of Ironoaks Castle,
  —SER MORTON, her eldest son and heir,
  —SER DONNEL, the Knight of the Bloody Gate,
  —WALLACE, her youngest son,
  —HARROLD HARDYNG, her ward, a squire oft called HARRY THE HEIR,
—SER SYMOND TEMPLETON, the Knight of Ninestars,
—JON LYNDERLY, Lord of the Snakewood,
—EDMUND WAXLEY, the Knight of Wickenden,
—GEROLD GRAFTON, the Lord of Gulltown,
—{EON HUNTER}, Lord of Longbow Hall, recently deceased,
  —SER GILWOOD, Lord Eon's eldest son and heir, now called YOUNG LORD HUNTER,
  —SER EUSTACE, Lord Eon's second son,
  —SER HARLAN, Lord Eon's youngest son,
  —Young Lord Hunter's household:
    —MAESTER WILLAMEN, counselor, healer, tutor,
—HORTON REDFORT, Lord of Redfort, thrice wed,

—SER JASPER, SER CREIGHTON, SER JON, his sons,
—SER MYCHEL, his youngest son, a new-made knight,
m. Ysilla Royce of Runestone,
—BENEDAR BELMORE, Lord of Strongsong,

—clan chiefs from the Mountains of the Moon,
—SHAGGA SON OF DOLF, OF THE STONE CROWS, pres-
ently leading a band in the kingswood,
—TIMETT SON OF TIMETT, OF THE BURNED MEN,
—CHELLA DAUGHTER OF CHEYK, OF THE BLACK
EARS,
—CRAWN SON OF CALOR, OF THE MOON
BROTHERS.

The Arryn words are *As High as Honor.*

HOUSE BARATHEON

The youngest of the Great Houses, House Baratheon was born during the Wars of Conquest when Orys Baratheon, rumored to be a bastard brother of Aegon the Conqueror, defeated and slew Argilac the Arrogant, the last Storm King. Aegon rewarded him with Argilac's castle, lands, and daughter. Orys took the girl to bride and adopted the banner, honors, and words of her line.

In the 283rd year after Aegon's Conquest, Robert of House Baratheon, Lord of Storm's End, overthrew the Mad King, Aenys II Targaryen, to win the Iron Throne. His claim to the crown derived from his grandmother, a daughter of King Aegon V Targaryen, though Robert preferred to say his warhammer was his claim.

> {ROBERT BARATHEON}, the First of His Name, King of the Andals, the Rhoynar, and the First Men, Lord of the Seven Kingdoms and Protector of the Realm, killed by a boar,
> —his wife, QUEEN CERSEI of House Lannister,
> —their children:
>> —{KING JOFFREY BARATHEON}, the First of His Name, murdered at his wedding feast,
>> —PRINCESS MYRCELLA, a ward in Sunspear, betrothed to Prince Trystane Martell,
>> —KING TOMMEN BARATHEON, the First of His Name,
> —his brothers:
>> —STANNIS BARATHEON, rebel Lord of Dragonstone

and pretender to the Iron Throne,
—his daughter, SHIREEN, a girl of eleven,
—{RENLY BARATHEON}, rebel Lord of Storm's End and
pretender to the Iron Throne, murdered at Storm's End
in the midst of his army,
—his bastard children:
—MYA STONE, a maid of nineteen, in the service of Lord
Nestor Royce, of the Gates of the Moon,
—GENDRY, an outlaw in the riverlands, ignorant of his
heritage,
—EDRIC STORM, his acknowledged bastard son by Lady
Delena of House Florent, hiding in Lys,
—SER ANDREW ESTERMONT, his cousin and
guardian,
—his guards and protectors:
—SER GERALD GOWER, LEWYS called THE
FISHWIFE, SER TRISTON OF TALLY HILL,
OMER BLACKBERRY,
—{BARRA}, his bastard daughter by a whore of King's
Landing, killed by the command of his widow,
—his other kin:
—his great-uncle, SER ELDON ESTERMONT, Lord of
Greenstone,
—his cousin, SER AEMON ESTERMONT, Eldon's son,
—his cousin, SER ALYN ESTERMONT, Aemon's
son,
—his cousin, SER LOMAS ESTERMONT, Eldon's son,
—his cousin, SER ANDREW ESTERMONT, Lomas's
son,

—bannermen sworn to Storm's End, the storm lords:
—DAVOS SEAWORTH, Lord of the Rainwood, Admiral of
the Narrow Sea, and Hand of the King,
—his wife, MARYA, a carpenter's daughter,
—their sons, {DALE, ALLARD, MATTHOS, MARIC},
killed in the Battle of the Blackwater,

—their son DEVAN, squire to King Stannis,

—their sons, STANNIS and STEFFON,

—SER GILBERT FARRING, castellan of Storm's End,

  —his son, BRYEN, squire to King Stannis,

  —his cousin, SER GODRY FARRING, called GIANT-SLAYER,

—ELWOOD MEADOWS, Lord of Grassfield Keep, seneschal at Storm's End,

—SELWYN TARTH, called THE EVENSTAR, Lord of Tarth,

  —his daughter, BRIENNE, THE MAID OF TARTH, also called BRIENNE THE BEAUTY,

    —her squire, PODRICK PAYNE, a boy of ten,

—SER RONNET CONNINGTON, called RED RONNET, the Knight of Griffin's Roost,

  —his younger siblings, RAYMUND and ALYNNE,

  —his bastard son, RONALD STORM,

  —his cousin, JON CONNINGTON, once Lord of Storm's End and Hand of the King, exiled by Aerys II Targaryen, believed dead of drink,

—LESTER MORRIGEN, Lord of Crows Nest,

  —his brother and heir, SER RICHARD MORRIGEN,

  —his brother, {SER GUYARD MORRIGEN, called GUYARD THE GREEN}, slain in the Battle of the Blackwater,

—ARSTAN SELMY, Lord of Harvest Hall,

  —his great-uncle, SER BARRISTAN SELMY,

—CASPER WYLDE, Lord of the Rain House,

  —his uncle, SER ORMUND WYLDE, an aged knight,

—HARWOOD FELL, Lord of Felwood,

—HUGH GRANDISON, called GREYBEARD, Lord of Grandview,

—SEBASTION ERROL, Lord of Haystack Hall,

—CLIFFORD SWANN, Lord of Stonehelm

—BERIC DONDARRION, Lord of Blackwater, called THE LIGHTNING LORD, an outlaw in the riverlands, oft slain and now thought dead,

—{BRYCE CARON}, Lord of Nightsong, slain by Ser Philip
   Foote on the Blackwater,
     —his slayer, SER PHILIP FOOTE, a one-eyed knight, Lord
      of Nightsong,
     —his baseborn half-brother, SER ROLLAND STORM,
      called THE BASTARD OF NIGHTSONG, pretender
      Lord of Nightsong,
—ROBIN PEASEBURY, Lord of Poddingfield,
—MARY MERTYNS, Lady of Mistwood,
—RALPH BUCKLER, Lord of Bronzegate,
   —his cousin, SER BRUS BUCKLER.

The Baratheon sigil is a crowned stag, black, on a golden field. Their
words are *Ours Is the Fury.*

HOUSE FREY

The Freys are bannermen to House Tully, but have not always been diligent in their duty. At the outset of the War of the Five Kings, Robb Stark won Lord Walder's allegiance by pledging to marry one of his daughters or granddaughters. When he wed Lady Jeyne Westerling instead, the Freys conspired with Roose Bolton and murdered the Young Wolf and his followers at what became known as the Red Wedding.

WALDER FREY, Lord of the Crossing,
—by his first wife, {LADY PERRA, of House Royce}:
  —{SER STEVRON FREY}, died after the Battle of Oxcross,
  —SER EMMON FREY, his second son,
  —SER AENYS FREY, leading the Frey forces in the north,
    —Aenys's son, AEGON BLOODBORN, an outlaw,
    —Aenys's son, RHAEGAR, an envoy to White Harbor,
  —PERRIANE, his eldest daughter, m. Ser Leslyn Haigh,
—by his second wife, {LADY CYRENNA, of House Swann}:
  —SER JARED FREY, an envoy to White Harbor,
  —SEPTON LUCEON, his fifth son,
—by his third wife, {LADY AMAREI of House Crakehall}:
  —SER HOSTEEN FREY, a knight of great repute,
  —LYENTHE, his second daughter, m. Lord Lucias Vypren,
  —SYMOND FREY, his seventh son, a counter of coins,
    an envoy to White Harbor,
  —SER DANWELL FREY, his eighth son,

—{MERRETT FREY}, his ninth son, hanged at Oldstones,
  —Merrett's daughter, WALDA, called FAT WALDA, m.
    Roose Bolton, Lord of the Dreadfort,
  —Merrett's son, WALDER, called LITTLE WALDER,
    eight, a squire in service to Ramsay Bolton,
—{SER GEREMY FREY}, his tenth son, drowned,
—SER RAYMUND FREY, his eleventh son,
—by his fourth wife, {LADY ALYSSA, of House Blackwood}:
  —LOTHAR FREY, his twelfth son, called LAME LOTHAR,
  —SER JAMMOS FREY, his thirteenth son,
    —Jammos's son, WALDER, called BIG WALDER,
      eight, a squire in service to Ramsey Bolton,
  —SER WHALEN FREY, his fourteenth son,
  —MORYA, his third daughter, m. Ser Flement Brax,
  —TYTA, his fourth daughter, called TYTA THE MAID,
—by his fifth wife, {LADY SARYA of House Whent}:
  —no progeny,
—by his sixth wife, {LADY BETHANY of House Rosby}:
  —SER PERWYN FREY, his Walder's fifteenth son,
  —{SER BENFREY FREY}, his Walder's sixteenth son, died
    of a wound received at the Red Wedding,
  —MAESTER WILLAMEN, his seventeenth son, in service
    at Longbow Hall,
  —OLYVAR FREY, his eighteenth son, once a squire to
    Robb Stark,
  —ROSLIN, his fifth daughter, m. Lord Edmure Tully at
    the Red Wedding, pregnant with his child,

—by his seventh wife, {LADY ANNARA of House Farring}:
  —ARWYN, his sixth daughter, a maid of fourteen,
  —WENDEL, his nineteenth son, a page at Seagard,
  —COLMAR, his twentieth son, eleven and promised to
    the Faith,
  —WALTYR, called TYR, his twenty-first son, ten,
  —ELMAR, his twenty-second and lastborn son, a boy of

nine briefly betrothed to Arya Stark,

—SHIREI, his seventh daughter and youngest child, a girl of seven,

—his eighth wife, LADY JOYEUSE of House Erenford,
—presently with child,

—Lord Walder's natural children, by sundry mothers,

—WALDER RIVERS, called BASTARD WALDER,

—MAESTER MELWYS, in service at Rosby,

—JEYNE RIVERS, MARTYN RIVERS, RYGER RIVERS, RONEL RIVERS, MELLARA RIVERS, others

HOUSE LANNISTER

The Lannisters of Casterly Rock remain the principal support of King Tommen's claim to the Iron Throne. They boast of descent from Lann the Clever, the legendary trickster of the Age of Heroes. The gold of Casterly Rock and the Golden Tooth has made them the wealthiest of the Great Houses. The Lannister sigil is a golden lion upon a crimson field. Their words are *Hear Me Roar!*

> {TYWIN LANNISTER}, Lord of Casterly Rock, Shield of Lannisport, Warden of the West, and Hand of the King, murdered by his dwarf son in his privy,
> —Lord Tywin's children:
> > —CERSEI, twin to Jaime, widow of King Robert I Baratheon, a prisoner at the Great Sept of Baelor,
> > —SER JAIME, twin to Cersei, called THE KINGSLAYER, Lord Commander of the Kingsguard,
> > > —his squires, JOSMYN PECKLEDON, GARRETT PAEGE, LEW PIPER,
> > > —SER ILYN PAYNE, a tongueless knight, lately the King's Justice and headsman,
> > > —SER RONNET CONNINGTON, called RED RONNET, the Knight of Griffin's Roost, sent to Maidenpool with a prisoner,
> > > —SER ADDAM MARBRAND, SER FLEMENT BRAX, SER ALYN STACKSPEAR, SER STEFFON SWYFT, SER HUMFREY SWYFT, SER LYLE CRAKEHALL called STRONGBOAR, SER JON BETTLEY called

BEARDLESS JON, knights serving with Ser Jaime's host at Riverrun,

—TYRION, called THE IMP, dwarf and kinslayer, a fugitive in exile across the narrow sea,

—the household at Casterly Rock:
—MAESTER CREYLEN, healer, tutor, and counselor,
—VYLARR, captain of guards,
—SER BENEDICT BROOM, master-at-arms,
—WHITESMILE WAT, a singer,

—Lord Tywin's siblings and their offspring:
—SER KEVAN LANNISTER, m. Dorna of House Swyft,
—LADY GENNA, m. Ser Emmon Frey, now Lord of Riverrun,
   —Genna's eldest son, {SER CLEOS FREY}, m. Jeyne of House Darry, killed by outlaws,
    —Cleos's eldest son, SER TYWIN FREY, called TY, now heir to Riverrun,
    —Cleos's second son, WILLEM FREY, a squire,
   —Genna's younger sons, SER LYONEL FREY, {TION FREY}, WALDER FREY called RED WALDER,
—{SER TYGETT LANNISTER}, died of a pox,
   —TYREK, Tygett's son, missing and feared dead,
    —LADY ERMESANDE HAYFORD, Tyrek's child wife,
—{GERION LANNISTER}, lost at sea,
   —JOY HILL, Gerion's bastard daughter, eleven,

—Lord Tywin's other close kin:
—{SER STAFFORD LANNISTER}, a cousin and brother to Lord Tywin's wife, slain in battle at Oxcross,
   —CERENNA and MYRIELLE, Stafford's daughters,
   —SER DAVEN LANNISTER, Stafford's son,
—SER DAMION LANNISTER, a cousin, m. Lady Shiera Crakehall,

—their son, SER LUCION,
—their daughter, LANNA, m. Lord Antario Jast,
—LADY MARGOT, a cousin, m. Lord Titus Peake,

—bannermen and sworn swords, Lords of the West:
—DAMON MARBRAND, Lord of Ashemark,
—ROLAND CRAKEHALL, Lord of Crakehall,
—SEBASTON FARMAN, Lord of Fair Isle,
—TYTOS BRAX, Lord of Hornvale,
—QUENTEN BANEFORT, Lord of Banefort,
—SER HARYS SWYFT, goodfather to Ser Kevan Lannister,
—REGENARD ESTREN, Lord of Wyndhall,
—GAWEN WESTERLING, Lord of the Crag,
—LORD SELMOND STACKSPEAR,
—TERRENCE KENNING, Lord of Kayce,
—LORD ANTARIO JAST,
—LORD ROBIN MORELAND,
—LADY ALYSANNE LEFFORD,
—LEWYS LYDDEN, Lord of the Deep Den,
—LORD PHILIP PLUMM,
—LORD GARRISON PRESTER,
—SER LORENT LORCH, a landed knight,
—SER GARTH GREENFIELD, a landed knight,
—SER LYMOND VIKARY, a landed knight,
—SER RAYNARD RUTTIGER, a landed knight
—SER MANFRYD YEW, a landed knight,
—SER TYBOLT HETHERSPOON, a landed knight.

HOUSE MARTELL

Dorne was the last of the Seven Kingdoms to swear fealty to the Iron Throne. Blood, custom, geography, and history all helped to set the Dornishmen apart from the other kingdoms. At the outbreak of the War of the Five Kings, Dorne took no part but when Myrcella Baratheon was betrothed to Prince Trystane, Sunspear declared its support for King Joffrey. The Martell banner is a red sun pierced by a golden spear. Their words are *Unbowed, Unbent, Unbroken*.

DORAN NYMEROS MARTELL, Lord of Sunspear, Prince of Dorne,
—his wife, MELLARIO, of the Free City of Norvos,
—their children:
  —PRINCESS ARIANNE, heir to Sunspear,
  —PRINCE QUENTYN, a new-made knight, fostered at Yronwood,
  —PRINCE TRYSTANE, betrothed to Myrcella Baratheon,
    —SER GASCOYNE OF THE GREENBLOOD, his sworn shield,
—his siblings:
  —{PRINCESS ELIA}, raped and murdered during the Sack of King's Landing,
    —her daughter {RHAENYS TARGARYEN}, murdered during the Sack of King's Landing,
    —her son, {AEGON TARGARYEN}, a babe at the breast, murdered during the Sack of King's Landing,

—{PRINCE OBERYN, called THE RED VIPER}, slain by Ser Gregor Clegane during a trial by combat,
  —his paramour, ELLARIA SAND, natural daughter of Lord Harmen Uller,
  —his bastard daughters, THE SAND SNAKES:
    —OBARA, his daughter by an Oldtown whore,
    —NYMERIA, called LADY NYM, his daughter by a noblewoman of Old Volantis,
    —TYENE, his daughter by a septa,
    —SARELLA, his daughter by a trader captain from the Summer Isles,
    —ELIA, his daughter by Ellaria Sand,
    —OBELLA, his daughter by Ellaria Sand,
    —DOREA, his daughter by Ellaria Sand,
    —LOREZA, his daughter by Ellaria Sand,

—Prince Doran's court
  —at the Water Gardens:
    —AREO HOTAH, of Norvos, captain of guards,
    —MAESTER CALEOTTE, counselor, healer, and tutor,
  —at Sunspear:
    —MAESTER MYLES, counselor, healer, and tutor,
    —RICASSO, seneschal, old and blind,
    —SER MANFREY MARTELL, castellan at Sunspear
    —LADY ALYSE LADYBRIGHT, lord treasurer,

—his ward, PRINCESS MYRCELLA BARATHEON, betrothed to Prince Trystane,
  —her sworn shield, {SER ARYS OAKHEART}, slain by Areo Hotah,
  —her bedmaid and companion, ROSAMUND LANNISTER, a distant cousin,

—his bannermen, the Lords of Dorne:
  —ANDERS YRONWOOD, Lord of Yronwood, Warden of the Stone Way, the Bloodroyal,

—YNYS, his eldest daughter, m. Ryon Allyrion,
—SER CLETUS, his son and heir,
—GWYNETH, his youngest daughter, a girl of twelve,
—HARMEN ULLER, Lord of Hellholt,
—DELONNE ALLYRION, Lady of Godsgrace,
—RYON ALLYRION, her son and heir,
—DAGOS MANWOODY, Lord of Kingsgrave,
—LARRA BLACKMONT, Lady of Blackmont,
—NYMELLA TOLAND, Lady of Ghost Hill,
—QUENTYN QORGYLE, Lord of Sandstone,
—SER DEZIEL DALT, the Knight of Lemonwood,
—FRANKLYN FOWLER, Lord of Skyreach, called THE
   OLD HAWK, the Warden of the Prince's Pass,
—SER SYMON SANTAGAR, the Knight of Spottswood,
—EDRIC DAYNE, Lord of Starfall, a squire,
—TREBOR JORDAYNE, Lord of the Tor,
—TREMOND GARGALEN, Lord of Salt Shore,
—DAERON VAITH, Lord of the Red Dunes.

HOUSE STARK

The Starks trace their descent from Brandon the Builder and the Kings of Winter. For thousands of years, they ruled from Winterfell as Kings in the North, until Torrhen Stark, the King Who Knelt, chose to swear fealty to Aegon the Dragon rather than give battle. When Lord Eddard Stark of Winterfell was executed by King Joffrey, the northmen foreswore their loyalty to the Iron Throne and proclaimed Lord Eddard's son Robb as King in the North. During the War of the Five Kings, he won every battle, but was betrayed and murdered by the Freys and Boltons at the Twins during his uncle's wedding.

> {ROBB STARK}, King in the North, King of the Trident, Lord of Winterfell, called THE YOUNG WOLF, murdered at the Red Wedding,
> —{GREY WIND}, his direwolf, killed at the Red Wedding,
> —his trueborn siblings:
>> —SANSA, his sister, m. Tyrion of House Lannister,
>>> —{LADY}, her direwolf, killed at Castle Darry,
>> —ARYA, a girl of eleven, missing and thought dead,
>>> —NYMERIA, her direwolf, prowling the riverlands,
>> —BRANDON, called BRAN, a crippled boy of nine, heir to Winterfell, believed dead,
>>> —SUMMER, his direwolf,
>> —RICKON, a boy of four, believed dead,
>>> —SHAGGYDOG, his direwolf, black and savage,
>>> —OSHA, a wildling woman once captive at Winterfell,
> —his bastard half-brother, JON SNOW, of the Night's Watch,

—GHOST, Jon's direwolf, white and silent,
—his other kin:
—his uncle, BENJEN STARK, First Ranger of the Night's Watch, lost beyond the Wall, presumed dead,
—his aunt, {LYSA ARRYN}, Lady of the Eyrie,
    —her son, ROBERT ARRYN, Lord of the Eyrie and Defender of the Vale, a sickly boy,
—his uncle, EDMURE TULLY, Lord of Riverrun, taken captive at the Red Wedding,
    —LADY ROSLIN, of House Frey, Edmure's bride, great with child,
—his great-uncle, SER BRYNDEN TULLY, called THE BLACKFISH, lately castellan of Riverrun, now a hunted man,

—bannermen of Winterfell, the Lords of the North:
—JON UMBER, called THE GREATJON, Lord of the Last Hearth, a captive at the Twins,
    —{JON, called THE SMALLJON}, the Greatjon's eldest son and heir, slain at the Red Wedding,
—MORS called CROWFOOD, uncle to the Greatjon, castellan at the Last Hearth,
—HOTHER called WHORESBANE, uncle to the Greatjon, likewise castellan at the Last Hearth,
—{CLEY CERWYN}, Lord of Cerwyn, killed at Winterfell,
—JONELLE, his sister, a maid of two-and-thirty,
—ROOSE BOLTON, Lord of the Dreadfort,
    —{DOMERIC}, his heir, died of a bad belly,
    —WALTON called STEELSHANKS, his captain,
    —RAMSAY BOLTON, his natural son, called THE BASTARD OF BOLTON, Lord of the Hornwood,
        —WALDER FREY and WALDER FREY, called BIG WALDER and LITTLE WALDER, Ramsay's squires,
        —BEN BONES, kennelmaster at the Dreadfort,
        —{REEK}, a man-at-arms infamous for his stench,

slain while posing as Ramsay,
—the Bastard's Boys, Ramsay's men-at-arms:
—YELLOW DICK, DAMON DANCE-FOR-ME, LUTON, SOUR ALYN, SKINNER, GRUNT,
—{RICKARD KARSTARK}, Lord of Karhold, beheaded by the Young Wolf for murdering prisoners,
—{EDDARD}, his son, slain in the Whispering Wood,
—{TORRHEN}, his son, slain in the Whispering Wood,
—HARRION, his son, a captive at Maidenpool,
—ALYS, his daughter, a maid of fifteen,
—his uncle ARNOLF, castellan of Karhold,
—CREGAN, Arnolf's elder son,
—ARTHOR, Arnolf's younger son,
—WYMAN MANDERLY, Lord of White Harbor, vastly fat,
—SER WYLIS MANDERLY, his eldest son and heir, very fat, a captive at Harrenhal,
—Wylis's wife, LEONA of House Woolfield,
—WYNAFRYD, their eldest daughter,
—WYLLA, their younger daughter,
—{SER WENDEL MANDERLY}, his second son, slain at the Red Wedding,
—SER MARLON MANDERLY, his cousin, commander of the garrison at White Harbor,
—MAESTER THEOMORE, counselor, tutor, healer,
—WEX, a boy of twelve, once squire to Theon Greyjoy, mute,
—SER BARTIMUS, an old knight, one-legged, one-eyed, and oft drunk, castellan of the Wolf's Den,
—GARTH, a gaoler and headsman,
—his axe, LADY LU,
—THERRY, a young turnkey,
—MAEGE MORMONT, Lady of Bear Island, the She-Bear,
—{DACEY}, her eldest daughter, slain at the Red Wedding,

—ALYSANE, her daughter, the young She-Bear

—LYRA, JORELLE, LYANNA, her younger daughters,

—{JEOR MORMONT}, her brother, Lord Commander of the Night's Watch, slain by his own men,

  —SER JORAH MORMONT, his son, an exile,

—HOWLAND REED, Lord of Greywater Watch, a crannogman,

—his wife, JYANA, of the crannogmen,

—their children:

  —MEERA, a young huntress,

  —JOJEN, a boy blessed with green sight,

—GALBART GLOVER, Master of Deepwood Motte, unwed,

—ROBETT GLOVER, his brother and heir,

  —Robert's wife, SYBELLE of House Locke,

—BENJICOT BRANCH, NOSELESS NED WOODS, men of the wolfswood sworn to Deepwood Motte,

—{SER HELMAN TALLHART}, Master of Torrhen's Square, slain at Duskendale,

  —{BENFRED}, his son and heir, slain by ironmen on the Stony Shore,

  —EDDARA, his daughter, captive at Torrhen's Square,

  —{LEOBALD}, his brother, killed at Winterfell,

    —Leobald's wife, BERENA of House Hornwood, captive at Torrhen's Square,

    —their sons, BRANDON and BEREN, likewise captives at Torrhen's Square,

—RODRIK RYSWELL, Lord of the Rills,

  —BARBREY DUSTIN, his daughter, Lady of Barrowton, widow of Lord Willam Dustin,

    —HARWOOD STOUT, her liege man, a petty lord at Barrowton,

  —{BETHANY BOLTON}, his daughter, second wife of Lord Roose Bolton, died of a fever,

—ROGER RYSWELL, RICKARD RYSWELL, ROOSE
RYSWELL, his quarrelsome cousins and bannermen,
—LYESSA FLINT, Lady of Widow's Watch,
—ONDREW LOCKE, Lord of Oldcastle, an old man,

—the chiefs of the mountain clans:
  —HUGO WULL, called BIG BUCKET, or THE WULL,
  —BRANDON NORREY, called THE NORREY,
    —BRANDON NORREY, the Younger, his son,
  —TORREN LIDDLE, called THE LIDDLE,
    —DUNCAN LIDDLE, his eldest son, called BIG
    LIDDLE, a man of the Night's Watch,
    —MORGAN LIDDLE, his second son, called
    MIDDLE LIDDLE,
    —RICKARD LIDDLE, his third son, called LITTLE
    LIDDLE,
  —TORGHEN FLINT, of the First Flints, called THE
  FLINT, or OLD FLINT,
    —BLACK DONNEL FLINT, his son and heir,
    —ARTOS FLINT, his second son, half-brother to
    Black Donnel.

The Stark arms show a grey direwolf racing across an ice-white field.
The Stark words are *Winter Is Coming*.

HOUSE TULLY

Lord Edmyn Tully of Riverrun was one of the first of the river lords to swear fealty to Aegon the Conqueror. King Aegon rewarded him by raising House Tully to dominion over all the lands of the Trident. The Tully sigil is a leaping trout, silver, on a field of rippling blue and red. The Tully words are *Family, Duty, Honor*.

EDMURE TULLY, Lord of Riverrun, taken captive at his wedding and held prisoner by the Freys,
—his bride, LADY ROSLIN of House Frey, now with child,
—his sister, {LADY CATELYN STARK}, widow of Lord Eddard Stark of Winterfell, slain at the Red Wedding,
—his sister, {LADY LYSA ARRYN}, widow of Lord Jon Arryn of the Vale, pushed to her death from the Eyrie,
—his uncle, SER BRYNDEN TULLY, called THE BLACKFISH, lately castellan of Riverrun, now an outlaw
—his household at Riverrun:
   —MAESTER VYMAN, counselor, healer, and tutor,
   —SER DESMOND GRELL, master-at-arms,
   —SER ROBIN RYGER, captain of the guard,
     —LONG LEW, ELWOOD, DELP, guardsmen,
   —UTHERYDES WAYN, steward of Riverrun,

—his bannermen, the Lords of the Trident:
   —TYTOS BLACKWOOD, Lord of Raventree Hall,
     —BRYNDEN, his eldest son and heir,
     —{LUCAS}, his second son, slain at the Red Wedding,

—HOSTER, his third son, a bookish boy,

—EDMUND and ALYN, his younger sons,

—BETHANY, his daughter, a girl of eight,

—{ROBERT}, his youngest son, died of loose bowels,

—JONOS BRACKEN, Lord of the Stone Hedge,

    —BARBARA, JAYNE, CATELYN, BESS, ALYSANNE, his five daughters,

    —HILDY, a camp follower,

—JASON MALLISTER, Lord of Seagard, a prisoner in his own castle,

    —PATREK, his son, imprisoned with his father,

    —SER DENYS MALLISTER, Lord Jason's uncle, a man of the Night's Watch,

—CLEMENT PIPER, Lord of Pinkmaiden Castle,

    —his son and heir, SER MARQ PIPER, taken captive at the Red Wedding,

—KARYL VANCE, Lord of Wayfarer's Rest,

—NORBERT VANCE, the blind Lord of Atranta,

—THEOMAR SMALLWOOD, Lord of Acorn Hall,

—WILLIAM MOOTON, Lord of Maidenpool,

    —ELEANOR, his daughter and heir, thirteen, m. Dickon Tarly of Horn Hill,

—SHELLA WHENT, dispossessed Lady of Harrenhal,

—SER HALMON PAEGE,

—LORD LYMOND GOODBROOK.

HOUSE TYRELL

The Tyrells rose to power as stewards to the Kings of the Reach, though they claim descent from Garth Greenhand, gardener king of the First Men. When the last king of House Gardener was slain on the Field of Fire, his steward, Harlen Tyrell, surrendered Highgarden to Aegon the Conqueror. Aegon granted him the castle and dominion over the Reach. Mace Tyrell declared his support for Renly Baratheon at the onset of the War of the Five Kings, and gave him the hand of his daughter Margaery. Upon Renly's death, Highgarden made alliance with House Lannister, and Margaery was betrothed to King Joffrey.

MACE TYRELL, Lord of Highgarden, Warden of the South, Defender of the Marches, and High Marshal of the Reach,
—his wife, LADY ALERIE, of House Hightower of Oldtown,
—their children:
——WILLAS, their eldest son, heir to Highgarden,
——SER GARLAN, called THE GALLANT, their second son, newly raised to Lord of Brightwater,
———Garlan's wife, LADY LEONETTE of House Fossoway,
——SER LORAS, the Knight of Flowers, their youngest son, a Sworn Brother of the Kingsguard, wounded on Dragonstone
——MARGAERY, their daughter, twice wed and twice widowed,
———Margaery's companions and ladies-in-waiting:
———her cousins, MEGGA, ALLA, and ELINOR TYRELL,
————Elinor's betrothed, ALYN AMBROSE, squire,

—LADY ALYSANNE BULWER, LADY ALYCE GRACEFORD, LADY TAENA MERRYWEATHER, MEREDYTH CRANE called MERRY, SEPTA NYSTERICA, her companions,
—his widowed mother, LADY OLENNA of House Redwyne, called THE QUEEN OF THORNS,
—his sisters:
   —LADY MINA, m. Paxter Redwyne, Lord of the Arbor,
      —her son, SER HORAS REDWYNE, called HORROR,
      —her son, SER HOBBER REDWYNE, called SLOBBER,
      —her daughter, DESMERA REDWYNE, sixteen,
   —LADY JANNA, wed to Ser Jon Fossoway,
—his uncles:
   —his uncle, GARTH TYRELL, called THE GROSS, Lord Seneschal of Highgarden,
      —Garth's bastard sons, GARSE and GARRETT FLOWERS,
   —his uncle, SER MORYN TYRELL, Lord Commander of the City Watch of Oldtown,
   —his uncle, MAESTER GORMON, serving at the Citadel,

—Mace's household at Highgarden:
   —MAESTER LOMYS, counselor, healer, and tutor,
   —IGON VYRWEL, captain of the guard,
   —SER VORTIMER CRANE, master-at-arms,
   —BUTTERBUMPS, fool and jester, hugely fat,

—his bannermen, the Lords of the Reach:
   —RANDYLL TARLY, Lord of Horn Hill, commanding King Tommen's army on the Trident,
   —PAXTER REDWYNE, Lord of the Arbor,
      —SER HORAS and SER HOBBER, his twin sons,
      —Lord Paxter's healer, MAESTER BALLABAR,
   —ARWYN OAKHEART, Lady of Old Oak,
   —MATHIS ROWAN, Lord of Goldengrove

—LEYTON HIGHTOWER, Voice of Oldtown, Lord of
  the Port,
—HUMFREY HEWETT, Lord of Oakenshield,
  —FALIA FLOWERS, his bastard daughter,
—OSBERT SERRY, Lord of Southshield,
—GUTHOR GRIMM, Lord of Greyshield,
—MORIBALD CHESTER, Lord of Greenshield,
—ORTON MERRYWEATHER, Lord of Longtable,
  —LADY TAENA, his wife, a woman of Myr,
    —RUSSELL, her son, a boy of six,
—LORD ARTHUR AMBROSE,
—LORENT CASWELL, Lord of Bitterbridge,

—his knights and sworn swords:
  —SER JON FOSSOWAY, of the green-apple Fossoways,
  —SER TANTON FOSSOWAY, of the red-apple Fossoways.

The Tyrell sigil is a golden rose on a grass-green field. Their words
are *Growing Strong*.

THE SWORN BROTHERS OF
THE NIGHT'S WATCH

JON SNOW, the Bastard of Winterfell, nine-hundred-and-ninety-eighth Lord Commander of the Night's Watch,
—GHOST, his white direwolf,
—his steward, EDDISON TOLLETT, called DOLOROUS EDD,

—at Castle Black
  —MAESTER AEMON (TARGARYEN), healer and counselor, a blind man, one hundred and two years old,
    —Aemon's steward, CLYDAS,
    —Aemon's steward, SAMWELL TARLY, fat and bookish,
  —BOWEN MARSH, Lord Steward,
    —THREE-FINGER HOBB, steward and chief cook,
    —{DONAL NOYE}, one-armed armorer and smith, slain at the gate by Mag the Mighty
    —OWEN called THE OAF, TIM TANGLETONGUE, MULLY, CUGEN, DONNEL HILL called SWEET DONNEL, LEFT HAND LEW, JEREN, TY, DANNEL, WICK WHITTLESTICK, stewards,
  —OTHELL YARWYCK, First Builder,
    —SPARE BOOT, HALDER, ALBETT, KEGS, ALF OF RUNNYMUDD, builders,
  —SEPTON CELLADOR, a drunken devout,

—BLACK JACK BULWER, First Ranger,
  —DYWEN, KEDGE WHITEYE, BEDWYCK called GIANT, MATTHAR, GARTH GREYFEATHER, ULMER OF THE KINGSWOOD, ELRON, GARRETT GREENSPEAR, FULK THE FLEA, PYPAR called PYP, GRENN called AUROCHS, BERNARR called BLACK BERNARR, TIM STONE, RORY, BEARDED BEN, TOM BARLEYCORN, GOADY BIG LIDDLE, LUKE OF LONGTOWN, HAIRY HAL, rangers
—LEATHERS, a wildling turned crow,
—SER ALLISER THORNE, former master-at-arms,
—LORD JANOS SLYNT, former commander of the City Watch of King's Landing, briefly Lord of Harrenhal,
—IRON EMMETT, formerly of Eastwatch, master-at-arms,
  —HARETH called HORSE, the twins ARRON and EMRICK, SATIN, HOP-ROBIN, recruits in training,

—at the Shadow Tower
  —SER DENYS MALLISTER, commander,
    —his steward and squire, WALLACE MASSEY,
    —MAESTER MULLIN, healer and counselor,
    —{QHORIN HALFHAND, SQUIRE DALBRIDGE, EGGEN}, rangers, slain beyond the Wall,
    —STONESNAKE, a ranger, lost afoot in Skirling Pass,

—at Eastwatch-by-the-Sea
  —COTTER PYKE, a bastard of the Iron Islands, commander,
    —MAESTER HARMUNE, healer and counselor,
    —OLD TATTERSALT, captain of the *Blackbird*,
    —SER GLENDON HEWETT, master-at-arms,
    —SER MAYNARD HOLT, captain of the *Talon*,
    —RUSS BARLEYCORN, captain of the *Storm Crow*.

the WILDLINGS, or THE FREE FOLK

MANCE RAYDER, King-Beyond-the-Wall, a captive at Castle Black,
—his wife, {DALLA}, died in childbirth,
—their newborn son, born in battle, as yet unnamed,
—VAL, Dalla's younger sister, "the wildling princess," a captive at Castle Black,
—{JARL}, Val's lover, killed in a fall,
—his captains, chiefs, and raiders:
—THE LORD OF BONES, mocked as RATTLESHIRT, a raider and leader of a war band, captive at Castle Black,
—{YGRITTE}, a young spearwife, Jon Snow's lover, killed during the attack on Castle Black,
—RYK, called LONGSPEAR, a member of his band,
—RAGWYLE, LENYL, members of his band,
—TORMUND, Mead-King of Ruddy Hall, called GIANTSBANE, TALL-TALKER, HORN-BLOWER, and BREAKER OF ICE, also THUNDERFIST, HUSBAND TO BEARS, SPEAKER TO GODS, and FATHER OF HOSTS,
—Tormund's sons, TOREGG THE TALL, TORWYRD THE TAME, DORMUND, and DRYN, his daughter MUNDA,
—THE WEEPER, called THE WEEPING MAN, a notorious raider and leader of a war band,

—{HARMA, called DOGSHEAD}, slain beneath the Wall,
  —HALLECK, her brother,
—{STYR}, Magnar of Thenn, slain attacking Castle Black,
  —SIGORN, Styr's son, new Magnar of Thenn,
—VARAMYR called SIXSKINS, a skinchanger and warg,
  called LUMP as a boy,
  —ONE EYE, SLY, STALKER, his wolves,
  —his brother, {BUMP}, killed by a dog,
  —his foster father, {HAGGON}, a warg and hunter,
—THISTLE, a spearwife, hard and homely,
—{BRIAR, GRISELLA}, skinchangers, long dead,
—BORROQ, called THE BOAR, a skinchanger, much
  feared,
—GERRICK KINGSBLOOD, of the blood of Raymun
  Redbeard,
  —his three daughters,
—SOREN SHIELDBREAKER, a famed warrior,
—MORNA WHITE MASK, the warrior witch, a raider,
—YGON OLDFATHER, a clan chief with eighteen wives,
—THE GREAT WALRUS, leader on the Frozen Shore,
—MOTHER MOLE, a woods witch, given to prophecy,
—BROGG, GAVIN THE TRADER, HARLE THE
  HUNTSMAN, HARLE THE HANDSOME, HOWD
  WANDERER, BLIND DOSS, KYLEG OF THE
  WOODEN EAR, DEVYN SEALSKINNER, chiefs and
  leaders amongst the free folk,
—{ORELL, called ORELL THE EAGLE}, a skinchanger
  slain by Jon Snow in the Skirling Pass,
—{MAG MAR TUN DOH WEG, called MAG THE
  MIGHTY}, a giant, slain by Donal Noye at the gate of
  Castle Black,
—WUN WEG WUN DAR WUN, called WUN WUN, a
  giant,
—ROWAN, HOLLY, SQUIRREL, WILLOW WITCH-EYE,
  FRENYA, MYRTLE, spearwives, captive at the Wall.

BEYOND THE WALL

—in the Haunted Forest
—BRANDON STARK, called BRAN, Prince of Winterfell
and heir to the North, a crippled boy of nine,
  —his companions and protectors:
    —MEERA REED, a maid of sixteen, daughter of Lord
    Howland Reed of Greywater Watch,
    —JOJEN REED, her brother, thirteen, cursed with
    greensight,
    —HODOR, a simple lad, seven feet tall,
  —his guide, COLDHANDS, clad in black, once perhaps
  a man of the Night's Watch, now a mystery,

—at Craster's Keep
  —the betrayers, once men of the Night's Watch:
    —DIRK, who murdered Craster,
    —OLLO LOPHAND, who slew the Old Bear, Jeor
    Mormont,
    —GARTH OF GREENAWAY, MAWNEY, GRUBBS,
    ALAN OF ROSBY, former rangers
    —CLUBFOOT KARL, ORPHAN OSS, MUTTERING
    BILL, former stewards,

—in the caverns beneath a hollow hill
  —THE THREE-EYED CROW, also called THE LAST
  GREENSEER, sorcerer and dreamwalker, once a man
  of the Night's Watch named BRYNDEN, now more

tree than man,
—the children of the forest, those who sing the song of
earth, last of their dying race:
—LEAF, ASH, SCALES, BLACK KNIFE,
SNOWYLOCKS, COALS.

ESSOS
BEYOND THE NARROW SEA

IN BRAAVOS

FERREGO ANTARYON, Sealord of Braavos, sickly and failing,
—QARRO VOLENTIN, First Sword of Braavos, his protector,
—BELLEGERE OTHERYS called THE BLACK PEARL, a courtesan descended from the pirate queen of the same name,
—THE VEILED LADY, THE MERLING QUEEN, THE MOONSHADOW, THE DAUGHTER OF THE DUSK, THE NIGHTINGALE, THE POETESS, famous courtesans,
—THE KINDLY MAN and THE WAIF, servants of the Many-Faced God at the House of Black and White,
    —UMMA, the temple cook,
    —THE HANDSOME MAN, THE FAT FELLOW, THE LORDLING, THE STERN FACE, THE SQUINTER, and THE STARVED MAN, secret servants of Him of Many Faces,
—ARYA of House Stark, a novice in service at the House of Black and White, also known as ARRY, NAN, WEASEL, SQUAB, SALTY, and CAT OF THE CANALS,
—BRUSCO, a fishmonger,
    —his daughters, TALEA and BREA,
—MERALYN, called MERRY, proprietor of the Happy Port, a brothel near the Ragman's Harbor,
    —THE SAILOR'S WIFE, a whore at the Happy Port,
        —LANNA, her daughter, a young whore,

—RED ROGGO, GYLORO DOTHARE, GYLENO DOTHARE, a scribbler called QUILL, COSSOMO THE CONJURER, patrons of the Happy Port,
—TAGGANARO, a dockside cutpurse and thief,
    —CASSO, KING OF THE SEALS, his trained seal,
—S'VRONE, a dockside whore of a murderous bent,
—THE DRUNKEN DAUGHTER, a whore of uncertain temper.

IN OLD VOLANTIS

the reigning triarchs:
—MALAQUO MAEGYR, Triarch of Volantis, a tiger,
—DONIPHOS PAENYMION, Triarch of Volantis, an elephant,
—NYESSOS VHASSAR, Triarch of Volantis, an elephant,

people of Volantis:
—BENERRO, High Priest of R'hllor, the Lord of Light,
  —his right hand, MOQORRO, a priest of R'hllor,
—THE WIDOW OF THE WATERFRONT, a wealthy freed-woman of the city, also called VOGARRO'S WHORE,
  —her fierce protectors, THE WIDOW'S SONS,
—PENNY, a dwarf girl and mummer,
  —her pig, PRETTY PIG,
  —her dog, CRUNCH,
—{GROAT}, brother to Penny, a dwarf mummer, murdered and beheaded,
—ALIOS QHAEDAR, a candidate for triarch,
—PARQUELLO VAELAROS, a candidate for triarch,
—BELICHO STAEGONE, a candidate for triarch,
—GRAZDAN MO ERAZ, an envoy from Yunkai.

ON SLAVER'S BAY

—in Yunkai, the Yellow City:
—YURKHAZ ZO YUNZAK, Supreme Commander of the Armies and Allies of Yunkai, a slaver and aged noble of impeccable birth,
—YEZZAN ZO QAGGAZ, mocked as the YELLOW WHALE, monstrously obese, sickly, hugely rich,
  —NURSE, his slave overseer,
  —SWEETS, a hermaphrodite slave, his treasure,
  —SCAR, a serjeant and slave soldier,
  —MORGO, a slave soldier,
—MORGHAZ ZO ZHERZYN, a nobleman oft in his cups, mocked as THE DRUNKEN CONQUEROR,
—GORZHAK ZO ERAZ, a nobleman and slaver, mocked as PUDDING FACE,
—FAEZHAR ZO FAEZ, a nobleman and slaver, known as THE RABBIT,
—GHAZDOR ZO AHLAQ, a nobleman and slaver, mocked as LORD WOBBLECHEEKS,
—PAEZHAR ZO MYRAQ, a nobleman of small stature, mocked as THE LITTLE PIGEON,
—CHEZDHAR ZO RHAEZN, MAEZON ZO RHAEZN, GRAZDHAN ZO RHAEZN, noblemen and brothers, mocked as THE CLANKER LORDS,
—THE CHARIOTEER, THE BEASTMASTER, THE PERFUMED HERO, noblemen and slavers,

—in Astapor, the Red City:
  —CLEON THE GREAT, called THE BUTCHER KING,
  —CLEON II, his successor, king for eight days,
  —KING CUTTHROAT, a barber, slit the throat of Cleon II
  to steal his crown,
  —QUEEN WHORE, concubine to King Cleon II, claimed
  the throne after his murder.

THE QUEEN ACROSS THE WATER

DAENERYS TARGARYEN, the First of Her Name, Queen of Meereen, Queen of the Andals and the Rhoynar and the First Men, Lord of the Seven Kingdoms, Protector of the Realm, *Khaleesi* of the Great Grass Sea, called DAENERYS STORMBORN, the UNBURNT, MOTHER OF DRAGONS,
—her dragons, DROGON, VISERION, RHAEGAL,
—her brother, {RHAEGAR}, Prince of Dragonstone, slain by Robert Baratheon on the Trident,
    —Rhaegar's daughter, {RHAENYS}, murdered during the Sack of King's Landing,
    —Rhaegar's son, {AEGON}, a babe in arms, murdered during the Sack of King's Landing,
—her brother {VISERYS}, the Third of His Name, called THE BEGGAR KING, crowned with molten gold,
—her lord husband, {DROGO}, a *khal* of the Dothraki, died of a wound gone bad,
    —her stillborn son by Drogo, {RHAEGO}, slain in the womb by the *maegi* Mirri Maz Duur,

—her protectors:
—SER BARRISTAN SELMY, called BARRISTAN THE BOLD, Lord Commander of the Queensguard,
    —his lads, squires training for knighthood:
        —TUMCO LHO, of the Basilisk Isles,
        —LARRAQ, called THE LASH, of Meereen,

—THE RED LAMB, a Lhazarene freedman,
—the BOYS, three Ghiscari brothers,
—STRONG BELWAS, eunuch and former fighting slave,
—her Dothraki bloodriders:
  —JHOGO, the whip, blood of her blood,
  —AGGO, the bow, blood of her blood,
  —RAKHARO, the *arakh*, blood of her blood,

—her captains and commanders:
  —DAARIO NAHARIS, a flamboyant Tyroshi sellsword, captain of the Stormcrows, a free company,
  —BEN PLUMM, called BROWN BEN, a mongrel sellsword, captain of the Second Sons, a free company.
  —GREY WORM, a eunuch, commander of the Unsullied, a company of eunuch infantry,
    —HERO, an Unsullied captain, second-in-command,
    —STALWART SHIELD, an Unsullied spearman,
  —MOLLONO YOS DOB, commander of the Stalwart Shields, a company of freedmen,
  —SYMON STRIPEBACK, commander of FREE BROTHERS, a company of freedmen,
  —MARSELEN, commander of the MOTHER'S MEN, a company of freedman, a eunuch, brother to Missandei,
  —GROLEO of Pentos, formerly captain of the great cog *Saduleon*, now an admiral without a fleet,
  —ROMMO, a *jaqqa rhan* of the Dothraki,

—her Meereenese court:
  —REZNAK MO REZNAK, her seneschal, bald and unctuous,
  —SKAHAZ MO KANDAQ, called THE SHAVEPATE, shaven-headed commander of the Brazen Beasts, her city watch,

—her handmaids and servants:
   —IRRI and JHIQUI, young women of the Dothraki,
   —MISSANDEI, a Naathi scribe and translator,
   —GRAZDAR, QEZZA, MEZZARA, KEZMYA, AZZAK,
     BHAKAZ, MIKLAZ, DHAZZAR, DRAQAZ, JHEZANE,
     children of the pyramids of Meereens, her cupbearers
     and pages,

—people of Meereen, highborn and common:
—GALAZZA GALARE, the Green Grace, high priestess at
   the Temple of the Graces,
   —GRAZDAM ZO GALARE, her cousin, a nobleman,
—HIZDAHR ZO LORAQ, a wealthy Meereenese nobleman,
   of ancient lineage,
   —MARGHAZ ZO LORAQ, his cousin,
—RYLONA RHEE, freedwoman and harpist,
—{HAZZEA}, a farmer's daughter, four years of age,
—GOGHOR THE GIANT, KHRAZZ, BELAQUO
   BONEBREAKER, CAMARRON OF THE COUNT,
   FEARLESS ITHOKE, THE SPOTTED CAT, BARSENA
   BLACKHAIR, STEELSKIN, pit fighters and freed slaves,

—her uncertain allies, false friends, and known enemies:
   —SER JORAH MORMONT, formerly Lord of Bear Island,
   —{MIRRI MAZ DUUR}, godswife and *maegi*, a servant
     of the Great Shepherd of Lhazar,
   —XARO XHOAN DAXOS, a merchant prince of Qarth,
   —QUAITHE, a masked shadowbinder from Asshai,
   —ILLYRIO MOPATIS, a magister of the Free City of
     Pentos, who brokered her marriage to Khal Drogo,
   —CLEON THE GREAT, butcher king of Astapor,

—the Queen's Suitors
   —on Slaver's Bay:
   —DAARIO NAHARIS, late of Tyrosh, a sellsword and captain
     of the Stormcrows,

—HIZDAHR ZO LORAQ, a wealthy Meereenese nobleman,
—SKAHAZ MO KANDAQ, called THE SHAVEPATE, a lesser
    nobleman of Meereen,
—CLEON THE GREAT, Butcher King of Astapor,

—in Volantis:
—PRINCE QUENTYN MARTELL, eldest son of Doran
    Martell, Lord of Sunspear and Prince of Dorne,
    —his sworn shields and companions:
        —{SER CLETUS YRONWOOD}, heir to Yronwood,
            slain by corsairs,
        —SER ARCHIBALD YRONWOOD, cousin to Cletus,
            called THE BIG MAN,
        —SER GERRIS DRINKWATER,
        —{SER WILLAM WELLS}, slain by corsairs
        —{MAESTER KEDRY}, slain by corsairs,

—on the Rhoyne:
—YOUNG GRIFF, a blue-haired lad of eighteen years,
    —his foster father, GRIFF, a sellsword late of the Golden
        Company,
    —his companion, teachers, and protectors:
        —SER ROLLY DUCKFIELD, called DUCK, a knight,
        —SEPTA LEMORE, a woman of the Faith,
        —HALDON, called THE HALFMAESTER, his tutor,
        —YANDRY, master and captain of the *Shy Maid*,
            —YSILLA, his wife,

—at sea:
—VICTARION GREYJOY, Lord Captain of the Iron Fleet,
    called THE IRON CAPTAIN,
    —his bedwarmer, a dusky woman without a tongue, a
        gift from Euron Crow's Eye,
    —his healer, MAESTER KERWIN, late of Greenshield, a
        gift from Euron Crow's Eye,
    —his crew on the *Iron Victory*:

—WULFE ONE-EAR, RAGNOR PYKE, LONGWATER PYKE, TOM TIDEWOOD, BURTON HUMBLE, QUELLON HUMBLE, STEFFAR STAMMERER

—his captains:

—RODRIK SPARR, called THE VOLE, captain of *Grief*,

—RED RALF STONEHOUSE, captain of *Red Jester*,

—MANFRYD MERLYN, captain of *Kite*,

—RALF THE LIMPER, captain of *Lord Quellon*,

—TOM CODD, called BLOODLESS TOM, captain of the *Lamentation*,

—DAEGON SHEPHERD, called THE BLACK SHEPHERD, captain of the *Dagger*.

The Targaryens are the blood of the dragon, descended from the high lords of the ancient Freehold of Valyria, their heritage marked by lilac, indigo, and violet eyes and hair of silver-gold. To preserve their blood and keep it pure, House Targaryen has oft wed brother to sister, cousin to cousin, uncle to niece. The founder of the dynasty, Aegon the Conqueror, took both his sisters to wife and fathered sons on each. The Targaryen banner is a three-headed dragon, red on black, the three heads representing Aegon and his sisters. The Targaryen words are *Fire and Blood*.

THE SELLSWORDS
MEN AND WOMEN OF
THE FREE COMPANIES

THE GOLDEN COMPANY, ten thousand strong, of uncertain loyalty:
—HOMELESS HARRY STRICKLAND, captain-general,
  —WATKYN, his squire and cupbearer,
—{SER MYLES TOYNE, called BLACKHEART}, four years dead, the previous captain-general,
—BLACK BALAQ, a white-haired Summer Islander, commander of the company archers,
—LYSONO MAAR, a sellsword late of the Free City of Lys, company spymaster,
—GORYS EDORYEN, a sellsword late of the Free City of Volantis, company paymaster,
—SER FRANKLYN FLOWERS, the Bastard of Cider Hall, a sellsword from the Reach,
—SER MARQ MANDRAKE, an exile escaped from slavery, scarred by pox,
—SER LASWELL PEAKE, an exile lord,
  —his brothers, TORMAN and PYKEWOOD,
—SER TRISTAN RIVERS, bastard, outlaw, exile,
—CASPOR HILL, HUMFREY STONE, MALO JAYN, DICK COLE, WILL COLE, LORIMAS MUDD, JON LOTHSTON, LYMOND PEASE, SER BRENDEL BYRNE, DUNCAN STRONG, DENYS STRONG, CHAINS, YOUNG JOHN MUDD, serjeants of the company,

—{SER AEGOR RIVERS, called BITTERSTEEL}, a bastard son of King Aegon IV Targaryen, founder of the company,
—{MAELYS I BLACKFYRE, called MAELYS THE MONSTROUS}, captain-general of the company, pretender to the Iron Throne of Westeros, member of the Band of Nine, slain during the War of the Ninepenny Kings,

THE WINDBLOWN, two thousand horse and foot, sworn to Yunkai,
—THE TATTERED PRINCE, a former nobleman of the Free City of Pentos, captain and founder,
    —CAGGO, called CORPSEKILLER, his right hand,
    —DENZO D'HAN, the warrior bard, his left hand,
    —HUGH HUNGERFORD, serjeant, former company paymaster, fined three fingers for stealing,
    —SER ORSON STONE, SER LUCIFER LONG, WILL OF THE WOODS, DICK STRAW, GINJER JACK, Westerosi sellswords,
    —PRETTY MERIS, the company torturer,
    —BOOKS, a Volantene swordsman and notorious reader,
    —BEANS, a crossbowman, late of Myr,
    —OLD BILL BONE, a weathered Summer Islander,
    —MYRIO MYRAKIS, a sellsword late of Pentos,

THE COMPANY OF THE CAT, three thousand strong, sworn to Yunkai,
—BLOODBEARD, captain and commander,

THE LONG LANCES, eight hundred horse-riders, sworn to Yunkai,
—GYLO RHEGAN, captain and commander,

THE SECOND SONS, five hundred horse-riders, sworn to Queen Daenerys,
—BROWN BEN PLUMM, captain and commander,
—KASPORIO, called KASPORIO THE CUNNING, a bravo,

second-in-command,
—TYBERO ISTARION, called INKPOTS, company paymaster,
—HAMMER, a drunken blacksmith and armorer,
  —his apprentice, called NAIL,
—SNATCH, a serjeant, one-handed,
—KEM, a young sellsword, from Flea Bottom,
—BOKKOKO, an axeman of formidable repute,
—UHLAN, a serjeant of the company,

THE STORMCROWS, five hundred horse-riders, sworn to Queen Daenerys,
—DAAERIO NAHARIS, captain and commander,
  —THE WIDOWER, his second-in-command,
  —JOKIN, commander of the company archers.

ACKNOWLEDGMENTS

The last one was a bitch. This one was three bitches and a bastard. Once again, my thanks to my long-suffering editors and publishers: to Jane Johnson and Joy Chamberlain at Voyager, and Scott Shannon, Nita Taublib, and Anne Groell from Bantam. Their understanding, good humor, and sage advice helped through the tough bits, and I will never cease to be grateful for their patience.

Thanks as well to my equally patient and endlessly supportive agents, Chris Lotts, Vince Gerardis, the fabulous Kay McCauley, and the late Ralph Vicinanza. Ralph, I wish you were here to share this day.

And thanks to Stephen Boucher, the wandering Aussie who helps keep my computer greased and humming whenever he drops by Santa Fe for a breakfast burrito (Xmas) and a side of jalapeño bacon.

Back here on the home front, thanks are also due to my dear friends Melinda Snodgrass and Daniel Abraham for their encouragement and support, to my webmaster Pati Nagle for maintaining my corner of the Internet, and to the amazing Raya Golden for the meals, the art, the unfailing good cheer that helped to brighten even the darkest days around Terrapin Station. Even if she did try to steal my cat.

As long as it has taken me to dance this dance, it would surely have taken twice as long without the assistance of my faithful (and acerbic) minion and sometime traveling companion Ty Franck, who tends to my computer when Stephen's not around, keeps the ravening virtual mobs from my virtual doorstep, runs my errands, does my filing, makes the coffee, walks the walk, and charges ten thousand dollars to change a light bulb—all while writing his own kick-ass books on Wednesdays.

Last, but far from my least, all my love and gratitude to my wife, Parris, who has danced every step of this beside me. Love ya, Phipps.

George R. R. Martin
May 13, 2011

SEASON 5

AVAILABLE NOW

SEASON 1-5